I0733529

LIGHT
DARK

ALEATHA ROMIG

NEW YORK TIMES BESTSELLING AUTHOR

A Romantic Thriller Novel

CONTENTS

PART TWO
AWAY FROM THE DARK

COPYRIGHT AND LICENSE INFORMATION

LIGHT DARK

Copyright @ 2024 Romig Works, LLC
2024 Edition
ISBN: 978-1-956414-87-5
Editing: Lisa Aurello
Cover Art: RBA Designs/ Romantic Book Affairs
Formatting: Romig Works LLC

All rights reserved. No part of this book may be reproduced or transmitted in any form or by any means, electronic or mechanical, including photocopying, recording, or by any informational storage and retrieval system, without the written permission from the copyright owner.

This is a work of fiction. Names, characters, places, and incidents either are the product of the author's imagination or are used fictitiously, and any resemblance to any actual persons, living or dead, events, or locales is entirely coincidental.

2024 Edition License

PRAISE FOR ALEATHA ROMIG

"Another awesome, twisty read from the master of suspense, Aleatha Romig! From the first page, I was captivated by this story, my heart racing as I tried to fit all the pieces together. When it all clicked, my mind was blown."

—A.L. JACKSON, NEW YORK TIMES BESTSELLING
AUTHOR

"Aleatha has always been a favourite of mine and this new genre was heartstoppingly good. I highly recommend!"

—PEPPER WINTERS, NEW YORK TIMES
BESTSELLING AUTHOR

"A riveting psychological suspense that deeply draws you into its tangled web. Thriller readers shouldn't miss this chilling tale of deception."

—VILMA'S BOOK BLOG

"Eerie, chilling and brimming with suspense - an all-around, fantastic read!"

—KENDALL RYAN, NEW YORK TIMES BESTSELLING
AUTHOR

PART ONE
INTO THE LIGHT

God gave us memory so that we may have roses in December.
—J. M. Barrie

PROLOGUE

An impenetrable fog cloaked the woman's thoughts, seeping into her being, binding and erasing everything she'd ever known. Before was gone. The only thing that mattered, with increasing urgency, was the present.

Desperately she tried to see past the darkness.

Nothing but black.

She winced with every turn, razor-sharp metal slicing her hands as she fought to escape the mangled cage. With only the howling wind as her guide, she searched for freedom, persisting until her bloodied fingers slid upon the vehicle's slick exterior.

As she lifted her face to the wind, sleet pelted her cheeks and frigid air contracted her lungs. Each breath was more painful than the last. Her heart raced and adrenaline surged while a low hiss and an overpowering stench of gasoline assaulted her senses. With a final shove, she freed herself from the wreckage, falling onto the wet, hard ground.

Still unable to see, she created visions in her mind. The offending odor of fuel wafting through the icy air became a monster's putrid breath, that of a dragon from a fairy tale capable of exhaling fire. Her imagination sounded an alarm that was both a nightmare and a beacon.

I need to get away.

As her other senses heightened, she moved to her hands and knees and began to crawl.

Right, left, then right again.

Without warning the dragon's fiery breath bellowed and heat rolled in waves around her, thawing the frozen air and knocking her flat. Thanking God that she'd awakened and gotten out of the vehicle in time, she hoarsely screamed to the darkness.

The darkness didn't reply.

She righted herself again and—inch by inch, foot by foot—crawled away from the dragon's heat, her confidence and speed building with each yard.

Then, suddenly, her head collided with an unseen force that struck her left cheek. Before she could process what had happened, a deep, commanding voice shattered her isolation.

"Don't!"

The single word echoed around her as pain, surpassing anything she'd ever felt, struck her lower leg. Crumbling, she collapsed to the icy ground.

"No! Stop!" she begged, unsure of what was happening.

With no sympathy for her pleas, the assault continued. Air left her lungs as her midsection sustained blow after blow. Turning into herself, she shielded her face and pulled her good leg to her chest.

"Stop!" the voice demanded.

Paralyzed by fear, she lay still, tears freezing upon her cheeks and her chest heaving with great, ragged breaths. Footsteps shuffled nearby before a new excruciating pain shot through her. She cried out as strong, masculine arms lifted her from the ground.

The clouding fog returned, settling upon her like a heavy blanket and lessening her pain with each of the man's steps. The scent of leather and musk replaced the odor of gasoline as the simplest question came to her mind.

Who am I?

Unable to find the answer, the woman settled her cheek against the man's chest. Her unseeing eyes closed, and she surrendered to the fog and the dark.

CHAPTER

ONE

S^{ara}

IN A PLACE WITHOUT LIGHT, I began to heal. Wrapped in protective nothingness, cold and pain no longer existed, concerns and deadlines were things of the past. I welcomed the dark, relishing its armor as it buffered me from the outside world. Slowly small recollections returned, flickers that made my body tense until I physically trembled. I recalled intense agony and an explosion of heat, yet my cocoon of blackness smothered the impending fire, keeping its flames at bay.

My mind sent signals that my body didn't obey. Helpless, my hands, feet, and even the lids of my eyes sat heavy and immobile. Occasionally actual voices penetrated my cocoon and infiltrated my darkness. With repetition they became familiar. They wanted me and, finally, I wanted them.

"Sara, can you hear me?" the strong, deep voice called from beyond the darkness.

"Keep talking, Brother. We aren't sure what a person hears while unconscious."

"Sara . . ." Warmth enveloped my hand as it was lifted from my side. "I'm here. It's Jacob. I'm not leaving you. You aren't leaving me." His voice cracked with emotion. "Come back."

Sara . . . Sara . . . the name echoed in my mind.

Brother? Is he talking to me? Am I Sara? Who is Jacob?

The obvious emotion in each syllable of his request impelled me to answer him, to ease his distress, but I couldn't. My mind and my body were still at odds.

The cocoon's layers that had been my refuge now swallowed my will. No longer did they protect—they strangled and suffocated, muting my ability to speak. The warmth of Jacob's hand and even the sound of his voice slipped away as I once again surrendered to the nothingness.

SMIDGENS OF LIFE scratched and tore at my darkened world. Slowly sounds returned, not only to register, but to linger—particularly one steady voice that called out over and over, repeating the name Sara.

The name ricocheted through my consciousness, and I searched for more, for more names, for faces. There were none. My only memory, the smallest semblance of recognition, was of piercing blue eyes. I couldn't remember the entirety of the face, but blue eyes filled the voids when the voices stilled and my world quieted to the steady rhythm of mechanical beeps. I longed for the familiarity of that gaze.

WITH TIME I GREW STRONGER, until finally I was fully cognizant of the world beyond me. As if a switch had been flipped, my battered body was suddenly present. I was no longer floating in nothingness—now there was a bed below me and a blanket upon my chest. The beeps that had been the backdrop of my unconsciousness became clearer. A clean, sterile scent permeated the stagnant air painfully filling my lungs. Exhaling slowly, I opened my eyes.

Adrenaline flooded my system, accelerating my heartbeat and sense of panic.

I can't see.

Lifting my too-heavy arm and reaching for my eyes, I heard a voice. The voice that had stayed with me through the darkness splintered the stillness with a welcome sound.

"Sara? Are you finally awake?"

A spark of recollection flickered in my dark world. Jacob. I'd heard the name repeatedly in my unconscious state. Instead of reaching for my eyes, I reached toward the hoarse voice, toward his face. At the first contact, I flinched; even the tips of my fingers were tender. Trying again, I connected with his scruffy cheek and traced his strong, defined jaw. With each caress I tried to imagine what I couldn't see, but my mind's canvas remained blank.

"I'm here. Thank The Light, Sara. I knew you'd come back. I knew you didn't want to leave me."

"I-I . . ." Squeaks like fingernails on a chalkboard came forth as I tried to form words. "C-can't." Beads of perspiration dotted my skin. I closed my cracked lips and wished away the dryness of my mouth.

"No, Sara," he reprimanded. "Don't talk. Your neck was hurt, damaging your vocal cords. Just listen."

I wanted to tell him that I couldn't see, but he was right about my neck. My throat ached. Sucking my lower lip between my teeth, I snagged its crusted surface. When I touched my neck, the skin was tender.

"Here." A cool, damp cloth touched my lips.

Instinctively I sucked the moisture from the rag.

"I need to confirm that you're allowed to drink. We'll find out soon."

He took the rag away, but I wanted more. "P-please, more."

A touch to my lips muted more of my request.

"Sara . . ." His words slowed. "I said no talking. Don't make me repeat myself." He lowered his voice to a whisper and brought his lips close to my ear. "Obeying isn't optional. Remember that."

Goose bumps materialized on my skin at his rebuke.

"They'll be in here soon to question you. Don't embarrass me."

Embarrass him? My pulse quickened as I struggled to understand. What the hell was he saying? This wasn't right.

"They've told me," he continued, "that after all that happened, your injuries could've been worse."

Wordlessly I asked the question I couldn't speak. Lifting my hand, I found a soft material covering my eyes.

Whatever it was, I wanted it gone; however, before I could remove the covering, Jacob stopped my hand.

"Your eyes were also injured in the accident. You hit your head. They say a nerve or something was damaged—there was an explosion." He moved my hand away from the material. "Don't touch the bandages. They need to stay in place and allow your eyes to rest."

An involuntary shudder raced through me as I recalled an explosion . . . and heat . . . and pain. Understanding that the bandages served a purpose, I nodded my unspoken comprehension. Simultaneously a groan escaped my lips and pain stampeded through my body. The simple bob of my head had caused my temples to throb, drowning out Jacob's words, leaving only a sickening internal buzz that echoed and twisted my empty stomach.

I pursed my lips and slowly exhaled in an attempt to calm the bubbling nausea. As it began to subside, the bed beneath me unexpectedly moved. I was being raised to a sitting position. Trying to hide the pain the movement inflicted, I pressed my lips together and willed my tears to stay behind the bandages.

The bed stopped, leaving me sitting up. I had so many questions. If only my throat weren't hurt and I could speak.

Jacob's gentle touch erased a renegade tear from my cheek. "I'm going to take you home, Sara. We'll get through this, together." His mellowed tone, as well as his vow, broke through my inner turmoil, endearing this man I couldn't recall to me. As I took in his promise, warm lips brushed my forehead.

A cloud of leather and musk enveloped me—his scent. I again searched for recognition but found none. Any memories I'd had of Jacob or of my past were gone. He obviously knew me—not only knew me, but expected me to know him, to trust him. To obey him.

I'm not a dog.

One moment he'd reprimand me like a child and the next offer kindness and support. His tone when he'd reminded me to be silent scared me, yet the fleeting kiss upon my forehead left me wanting. The pendulum swing was too much and too new. Releasing the breath I'd held, I smiled toward his warmth.

Then I heard his footsteps walk away, and my panic returned.

From farther away he said, "Sara, I'll be right back. They need to know you're finally awake. Do not speak to anyone." With a sigh he added, "We don't want you hurting your vocal cords."

They? Who needs to know? Doctors and nurses?

I was obviously in a hospital bed. Once I heard the click of the closing door, I sat and listened to the room around me. Confident that I was indeed alone, I reached again for the soft bandage securely covering my eyes. Following it with my fingers, I found that the softness went all the way around my head and that under the material were hard domes covering both eyes.

My eyes could already be healed. How could someone else know if I could see? As the instinct to remove the bandages grew stronger, the word obey sounded in my head and I lowered my hands. Jacob had said my vocal cords and eyes had been injured in an accident. As I shifted, the pain told me he was right about the accident. I was probably more injured than he'd said. I took a mental inventory: my side hurt the worst, but my left leg came second. Reaching below the blanket, I found the edge of something hard, a cast.

I sighed and allowed my head to sink into the pillow. Each

discovery was too much. Nothing seemed familiar. Nothing seemed right.

My cracked lips as well as the stale, dry taste in my mouth reminded me of the damp washcloth Jacob had offered me earlier. Fumbling for what I couldn't see, I reached beyond the bed rails. When I did, I realized there was something attached to my right arm. An IV? Beyond that I found only air. My shoulders slumped, and I tucked my suddenly cold hands under the warm blanket and rubbed my still-sore fingertips.

Beneath the blanket I reached for the fourth finger of my left hand and found a ring. As I slowly turned it, the smooth surface remained the same. I was wearing a wedding band. I was married. How could I be married and not remember? Was I married to Jacob?

Questions continued to come fast and furious, each one without an answer, each one more unsettling than the one before.

While I searched for memories, the sound of the opening door brought me back to the present. Footsteps shuffled about the room while multiple people spoke at once. Though none of them spoke directly to me, I seemed to be the topic of conversation. Struggling to understand the ongoing discussions, I listened for Jacob's deep voice. Finally the roar faded to a low murmur and then to silence as anticipation filled the room.

"Sara," Jacob said, breaking the tension.

With a sense of relief, I inclined my face ever so slightly toward his familiar voice. His warm breath grazed my skin.

"The Commission," he continued, "confirmed that you can't speak, not yet, but they have questions. Right now they need to know that you're hearing and understanding. So"—he picked up my hand—"I want you to respond by squeezing my hand."

I tried to keep up, but I had no point of reference. Who or what was the Commission? Why did it have a say in my care? Unable to voice my concerns, I waited as Jacob's fingers intertwined with mine.

"When a question is asked," Jacob directed, "squeeze my hand once for yes and twice for no. Do you understand?"

I squeezed my answer, ignoring my tender fingertips.

"Brother Timothy is here to ask you some questions."

Brother? Is he my brother? Do I have a brother?

I'd expected to see my doctor, or rather expected that he or she would see me. My mind spun. Brother Timothy was perhaps a part of the Commission. As Jacob's grip tightened, I sensed that he was genuinely worried about what was about to happen. This must be the situation he'd been thinking of when he warned me not to embarrass him. I wanted to comply, but I also wished he'd given me more prompting, more background. Then again, I hadn't spoken. There was no way he could know that I didn't remember anything.

"First," Jacob began, "the Commission wants confirmation that you remember me, your husband. You do remember me, don't you?"

I hesitated, wanting to squeeze his hand only once, to give him something for his dedication and support. After all, I recalled him in recent memories—he'd been by my bedside while I slept in the darkness. But I couldn't lie. Unless . . . unless he was the man with the blue eyes. I latched on to that glimmer of hope. If he was my blue-eyed vision, then I did remember him.

"Sara, stay with us. Tell everyone that you remember me." His plea swelled with emotion, not only in his voice, but flowing in waves from his hand to mine.

In this unknown world, he'd been my one constant. Apprehensively I squeezed. The room seemed to hold its collective breath as I deliberated the second squeeze. Finally I relaxed my grip.

Jacob sighed, leaned closer, and brushed my hair away from my forehead. This still felt wrong. Nevertheless I needed time to make sense of everything. During that time, I didn't want to fight the darkness alone. I took strength from his warm breath and adoration.

An unfamiliar voice spoke from near the end of my bed. "Sister Sara, I hope you recognize the seriousness of this situation."

Why did they all talk strangely? I couldn't understand why he called me sister, but by the way the small hairs on the back of my neck stood at attention, I recognized that whatever was happening was serious.

"Sara," Jacob reminded me. "Brother Timothy needs you to respond."

I squeezed Jacob's hand once to indicate I understood.

"She understands," Jacob said.

"If you could speak," Brother Timothy continued, "I'd ask you for a full account of the incident. I'd ask you to describe in detail your role and the aftermath. Since you're unable to talk, we'll begin with questions. Once I have your answers, I'll take what I find informative back to the rest of the Commission. We'll decide what should be passed on to Father Gabriel. Of course, the final decree regarding this transgression lies solely with him. The two of you will abide by Father Gabriel's decision."

My tired mind spun. What decree? Who is Father Gabriel? And by "the two of you," does he mean Jacob and me? What have we done?

The throbbing returned to my temples as Jacob's fingers unlaced from mine and both of his hands encased my one. I tried, again, to recall the accident, but incomplete memories of dragon-sharp teeth and fiery breath created an unfinished mosaic.

Before my mind was able to fill in the blanks or I could respond, Jacob verbally agreed to everything that Brother Timothy had just said.

"Sara, do you remember why you took Jacob's truck the day of the incident?"

I had no recollection of having taken a truck. If Jacob and I were married, wouldn't it be my truck too? I lowered my chin to my chest and squeezed Jacob's hand twice.

"She said yes, Brother. She remembers."

My face snapped toward Jacob's voice, sending pain surging through my head. I hadn't indicated yes—I'd squeezed twice, which meant no.

Brother Timothy continued, "Did you have your husband's permission to drive his truck?"

"I told you that she—"

Brother Timothy interrupted Jacob's reply. "We're here to get answers from Sister Sara. If you're not willing to wait for your wife's responses, we can have Lilith hold her hand. Sister Sara, yes or no?"

I now understood why Jacob had completely covered my hand with both of his. He was going to answer the questions the way he chose, regardless of how I replied. I squeezed twice—no—and waited.

"She said yes, she had my permission. Which I believe is the same answer I gave the Commission."

Brother Timothy went on with his questions, asking if I remembered where I'd been going, if I knew that what I'd done had been beyond my approved scope.

My approved scope?

My heart thundered in my chest with each question and each answer that Jacob gave on my behalf. In a short time, I learned details about the accident that I couldn't recall. Apparently I had been driving Jacob's truck to pick up supplies he needed. Since I'd been following my husband's instructions, I hadn't realized that driving alone outside the community was forbidden.

"Do you remember who was responsible for your incident?"

The room waited for my answer. It didn't matter that I didn't know who was responsible or recall anything relating to the accident; I wouldn't be the one to answer. As the silence grew, I fidgeted against the mattress. My leg and ribs ached and even swallowing hurt. I squeezed Jacob's hand twice.

"Yes, Brother, she remembers."

As the voices murmured among themselves at this response, a chill passed through me, then the temperature of the room seemed to rise. I wanted to scream. Perspiration beaded on my chest and dripped uncomfortably between my breasts. Jacob's grip tightened and I flinched as someone touched my neck.

Brother Timothy raised his voice above the din. "Sister Sara, your current physical suffering is a sign of the correction you deserve for your actions. God taught us, saying, 'I will punish the world for its evil and the wicked for their iniquity.' God doesn't punish the righteous. Therefore your suffering is evidence of your evil intent."

"Brother," Jacob replied, my hand still in his. "She just respectfully indicated that her intent wasn't evil. She did what I demanded. Her intent was to obey her husband. With the icy roads I should have considered her lack of driving experience before sending her to complete my errand."

"When Sara is able to speak, you'll both be brought before the Commission. It'll be up to Father Gabriel to determine if correction is complete."

"As her husband, I take responsibility for her actions. I guarantee that my wife didn't willfully disobey the laws of The Light. If she had, I'd see to her correction myself."

I fell back to my pillow, unable to comprehend the discussion around me. Why is this happening? Why are they discussing me, without me?

Mute as I was, with my eyes covered and my hand encased in Jacob's, no one but my husband noticed my lack of participation. I remained still as he continued to relay my nonexistent responses, leaving me a bystander to my own story and unable to affect its outcome.

Maybe this wasn't real, maybe it was a bad dream and the scene would soon fade. My stomach twisted as their exchange continued and they discussed my insubordination and correction. Each time Brother Timothy condemned, Jacob reminded him that my transgressions were alleged, not proven. It was as if suddenly I were on trial in my hospital room instead of in a court of law.

It wasn't until I heard the word banishment that their conversation again registered. Whatever had been said had apparently been the parting word. Murmurs floated above the sound of various sets of feet exiting, then finally there was silence. When the door clicked closed I released my breath.

Turning toward my husband, I waited for an explanation. Nothing. I was about to pull my hand away when I felt a tug on my right arm and a woman spoke.

"Brother Jacob, Dr. Newton would like to examine Sister Sara now."

So many brothers and sisters. So unfamiliar.

"Are you giving her more medicine?" Jacob asked.

"After the doctor comes. He'd like her to be awake."

"Tell him he'll need to wait until morning. She's had enough commotion for her first day.

Bring her medicine, something to drink, and let her sleep."

I pressed my lips together in protest. Not that anyone noticed. They were doing it again. Discussing me while I was right there. Why does no one else find this wrong?

"I'm sorry," the woman, who I assumed was a nurse, said. "The Commission hasn't approved her intake of fluids. Refusal of nutrients is an approved decree."

Jacob's grip tensed. "I'm quite aware of the Commission's approved decrees."

"I'm sorry, Brother. I didn't mean to . . ."

"It's been over a week. She needs more than what she's getting from that needle."

"I believe they'll discuss it in the morning since Brother Timothy was able to see and talk to her. They should have a revised decision by tomorrow. I can't go against . . ."

Jacob sighed and his grip remained tight. "I understand," he conceded. "Then bring me ice chips. If we hurry before they melt, they'll be solids and not liquids. That won't violate the Commission's authority."

"Brother?"

"Bring me ice."

CHAPTER

TWO

S tella

IT WAS past three in the afternoon when I finished chasing leads—ones that seemed to go nowhere—and dragged my tired self back to the TV station. I plugged in my dead cell phone and collapsed at my desk. As I laid my head on my arm, I realized, only slightly ashamed, that I was wearing the same blouse and slacks I'd worn the day before. When I'd been out in the field, it hadn't occurred to me, but here, I was suddenly self-conscious.

I must've bumped my mouse, because a light brighter than the Michigan summer sun filled my cubicle, and my monitor roared to life. The number flashing at the top of my screen mocked my exhaustion, alerting me to the hundreds of e-mails all in desperate need of immediate response. That's what happened when I spent my entire day out of the office. Sighing, I scooted my chair closer and began to scroll.

Rarely did true leads pop up in my inbox. Most of them came on the street or from reliable sources. Many times they came from people who preferred to remain anonymous. It wasn't until the really damning evidence was discovered that names and sources were needed. Even then, thanks to the First Amendment, most sources could remain undisclosed.

Today I'd spent hours with the border patrol. It was a stimulating way to spend a day, watching cars pass from the United States to Canada and vice versa for hours on end. The US Border Patrol wasn't keen on allowing reporters or investigative journalists open access, but thankfully, I had a friend who had a friend, which was the way most of this worked.

Unfortunately, today it hadn't done me much good.

As I finished reading the second page of e-mails, my cell phone rang, its melody alerting me to my caller.

"Hello, Bernard."

"Stella, where are you?"

"About thirty feet away," I replied with a tired laugh.

"In my office."

The phone went silent.

I lifted my brow and stared at the screen. Dylan, the man I'd left early this morning in his warm bed, was right; Barney, as Dylan called him, was a pompous ass. The civilized world used salutations: hello and good-bye. Shrugging away my annoyance, I pulled myself to my feet and walked to my boss's office. Before I reached his door, he stood, walked toward me, and motioned to the chairs facing his desk. As I sat, he closed the door.

"I didn't realize you were back," he said, as he sat behind his desk. "How are you?"

I eyed him suspiciously. In the nearly a year I'd worked for him, I'd replied to every one of his requests for discussion. I'd dragged myself to this office, to coffee shops, bars, restaurants, and a million other places at all hours of the day and night. Never once had he stood as I approached. Never once had he greeted me with more than a shrug before beginning his rant. This new, unfamiliar adherence to etiquette frightened me more than his normal pompous behavior.

"What did you learn?"

I shook my head. "Nothing. I spent half the day at the border. Around eleven I followed up on some leads at the shipyard. I talked to some people, but honestly, nothing stuck out."

His eyes fell to his desk. Despite nearing retirement, Bernard was still a handsome man—tall, tan, fit. The only suggestions of his age were his salt-and-pepper hair and the fine lines around his eyes. Currently his hair was slicked back, his face was made up for the cameras, and he was dressed in a nice suit. Though the news wouldn't be starting for another hour or so, judging by his attire, he'd been filming one of his stories. That meant he would be needed back on the set to introduce the story during the five and six o'clock news. As I waited for him to look back up, it hit me. I'd never known him to look away. It was one of his things, one of his one-upmanship tendencies.

Is he going to move me off this story, or fire me?

I sat forward on the edge of the seat, my nerves electrified, waking my body with a surge of adrenaline. "I'll keep looking. You don't need to worry. If there's as big of a drug operation out there as they say, someone's going to talk. I've got feelers all over. Don't take me off this. I'll get the story."

His dark eyes peered upward, but I couldn't read his expression.

"No one's moving you off the story. This isn't about the drugs."

"But you just asked—"

"I don't do touchy-feely shit, but it's no secret how much we all cared about Mindy . . ."

My stomach sank. "Oh, God, h-have they, have they found her?"

"The medical examiner called for you, over an hour ago. She said she tried your cell. I tried your cell—"

"The damn battery died. I plugged it in at my desk as soon as I got here."

"She's not sure if it's Mindy. She only said it's a female meeting Mindy's description."

"Where did they find her?" I asked, afraid of the answer. "Was this body found in the river too?"

Bernard shook his head. "No. This one was found in an abandoned building in Highland Heights."

"Highland Heights?" I sucked my lower lip between my teeth and fought the bubbling nausea. "Mindy wouldn't go to Highland Heights." It was one of the worst parts of Detroit, riddled with gangs, crime, drugs, and poverty.

"I know," he said. "It doesn't make sense." He leaned forward. "Listen, I'm due on the set in a few. If you wait, Foster can go with you. You shouldn't go to the morgue alone. I know how hard it was last time."

"No, thanks, Bernard. I can handle it. I need to do it for Mindy and for Mr. and Mrs. Rosemont. I promised them I would."

"Are you sure you can drive? It's almost rush hour and . . ."

I lifted my hand. "Please, just let me go. I've already wasted time. The sooner I go, the sooner we'll know."

"Call me and let me know what you learn. Don't worry about coming back here tonight. There's nothing that can't wait, but call me."

Nodding, I stood and rushed to my cubicle. Turning off my computer, I grabbed my partially charged cell phone and purse and headed out, all the while avoiding my coworkers' eyes. I hoped it looked as if I were heading out to chase another lead, not to possibly identify the body of my missing best friend.

Skipping the elevator, I hurried down the back steps to the garage and got in my car. As I drove toward the Office of the Wayne County Medical Examiner, my mind filled with memories of Mindy. It was almost the end of July, and she'd been missing for nearly two weeks. I did what I'd done a thousand times since the morning she hadn't shown up for work—I remembered.

My mind flashed back to our freshman year of college nearly ten years before. She'd been sitting across the aisle from me in a journalism seminar. As I thought back, I believed that one reason I'd noticed her was that we looked alike: blonde hair and similar build. I remembered her chewing on the cap of her pen, reading our assignment, and I'd thought I had her beat. I'd already read it. That was still my approach to everything, always sizing up my competition.

Little had I known, Mindy had already read our assignment. She was rereading, because that was who she was. It turned out we were made to be best friends. Fate paired us for our first group project and sheer determination kept us together. During the next five years we were roommates, classmates in college and a master's program, friends, enemies, and everything in between.

Though we'd do anything for each other—and had, many times —it was our competitive spirit that continually pushed us through the long hours of classes and studying, and on to our internships. Together we celebrated success and mourned loss. No matter what life threw at us—asshole professors, scumbag boyfriends, dreaded hangovers—we knew that the one constant was each other. Of course, that closeness never stopped our siblinglike rivalry, the one that drove us to be the best. We vied for the top GPA, and through it all, neither one of us backed down.

After graduate school we went our separate ways to follow our dreams. It wasn't until Mindy landed her job at the WCJB TV station that we found our way back together. At the time I was working for a big law firm in downtown Detroit as an investigator. I'd had an internship in a crime lab as an undergraduate student and one with Homeland Security during graduate school. Those experiences had taught me how to delve into people's personal business and spot inconsistencies. At our firm a client's innocence or lack thereof was never at issue—finding the evidence to substantiate their innocence was my job. In only a short time, I became one of the people on whom the partners depended to find answers.

Then, when Mindy introduced me to the people at WCJB, our friendship opened the door to my current position working for

Bernard Cooper, the lead investigative journalist at WCJB. Not only did Bernard work for the top TV station in Detroit, but he also was well known in the industry. His stories were often picked up for national broadcasts. The mere mention of his name inspired fear and respect. Because of him politicians unexpectedly withdrew from elections and corporations faced millions of dollars in fines. Corruption on any level was his to expose. Whether it was a scandal involving mob bosses, gangs, or the dangers of contaminated lemons at a local restaurant chain, no story was above or beneath him. Stories were everywhere—we just had to find them.

Since Mindy's parents lived in California, they'd authorized me to make visual confirmation should her body be found. Of course, they'd come here after her disappearance, but there was no sense summoning them each time a body matching Mindy's description surfaced.

My reminiscing ended as I entered the county government building and took a deep breath. I'd been here only a week before, asked to identify a bloated body that, thankfully, hadn't turned out to be Mindy. However, memories of the stench-filled examination room and the unnatural color of the body's stretched skin brought back a rush of nausea. Swallowing the rising bile, I steadied my steps and willed my investigative mask of indifference in place.

As I descended through the winding catacombs on my way to the ME's office, my mind spun with possibilities. While the number of homicides in Detroit had decreased since the early 1990s, so had the population. Detroit still had the dubious distinction of one of the highest violent crime rates in the nation. The city where I lived and my best friend had disappeared was dangerous, and I was about to witness another of its casualties. I'd encountered death in the course of my job—often. But that was different. That was work. This was personal.

As I rounded the final corner, I stopped and my eyes locked on the compassionate but piercing stare of Dylan Richards.

"Why are you here?" I asked.

His confident swagger disappeared as he moved silently toward me. Each step measured the time I stood rooted to the tile.

"I didn't want you to do this alone," he said, reaching for my hands. His warmth enveloped my fingers, making me suddenly aware of the coolness of my own body.

"How did you know to come here? Do you know that this is her?" My anxiety rose with each question, as did the pitch of my voice. "Have you seen her?"

He shook his head. "I haven't seen her, and I don't know. I was at the police station and heard the buzz. I tried to reach you, but your phone went to voice mail. I sent you a couple of texts. When you didn't answer, I took a chance and called Barney. He told me that he'd just told you about this." Dylan squeezed my hand again. "Like I said, I didn't want you to do this alone."

THREE

S ara

THE MOMENT THE NURSE LEFT, Jacob wordlessly released my hand, scooted his chair across the floor, and began pacing, his footsteps sounding from near the foot of my bed. I didn't need to see him to know his mood—his irritation was evident in each stomp. I waited for him to say something about what had just happened. I wanted him to explain who Brother Timothy and Father Gabriel were and what power they possessed. I wanted to know how these men had the right to withhold water from me or anyone else. I wanted to understand the allegations that Brother Timothy mentioned. I needed answers.

Though it seemed as if Jacob had defended me and my behavior, he'd also lied and answered each question without regard for my response. I wanted to understand why he'd done that. With each strike of his hard-soled shoes that drummed a staccato beat across the tile floor, I sensed his unease as mine grew.

The rhythm of Jacob's pacing monopolized my thoughts, playing in a loop with a four-four count: four strides to cross the width of the room, the fourth step containing a scuff—his turn—then four strides back again.

My mind swirled with theories. Maybe we'd argued before the accident. Maybe he hadn't sent me out on the icy roads. Each thought increased my anxiety, causing it to rise degree by degree until it neared the boiling point. I imagined the man who continued to pace. The vision I created had blue eyes and a scruffy jaw. I wasn't sure if that image was my memory returning or an imagined portrait based on the feel of his hands and face.

Suddenly my heart stilled as a loud knock echoed throughout the room. Pressing my lips together, I cringed at the thought of someone from the Commission returning.

"I have the ice chips," the nurse said, with the opening of the door. "Would you like me to feed Sara?"

Internally I groaned. Again I wasn't being addressed, only spoken about. After all, I was Sara. Maybe someone can ask me?

Before I had time to dwell on my lack of autonomy, Jacob replied, "No, give me the cup. I'll take care of it."

"It's my assignment—"

"Sister, if we hurry before the ice melts, it won't violate the Commission's authority. But if the Commission decides that ice is a fluid, it'll be my responsibility, not yours. I asked for ice and you brought it to me, not Sara."

"Thank you," she replied. "I won't mention it."

"But if it's mentioned," he said with authority, "you gave the ice to me."

"Yes, Brother. Do you need anything else?"

"Sara's medication. Dr. Newton said her body heals best while she sleeps."

"I'll get it, but first I'll give you some time with your ice. The sleep medication works very fast."

Seconds later the door clicked shut and, judging by the silence, I believed the nurse had left. Suddenly everything I'd wanted to say and learn dissolved under my growing need for the moisture of the ice chips. Unconsciously my tongue darted to my chapped, cracked lips as I waited for the cool wetness Jacob controlled.

Finally I heard Jacob scoot the chair beside my bed closer. In my mind I'd created images of my tiny world. In those images the cushion of the chair where Jacob sat was covered in plastic or vinyl. I didn't know the color but had determined the material by the hiss it made as he lowered his weight.

Jacob brushed my cheek, wiping away a tear that I hadn't realized I'd shed. I turned away from his touch. This wasn't right. I couldn't put my finger on my reasoning, but deep down I didn't believe I was someone who cried or allowed others to control my every move. Jacob pulled my chin back toward him. I waited for his words of support and encouragement. They didn't come. Instead he simply demanded, "Open your mouth."

The bristling of my spine told me to fight, but if I did, I wouldn't get the moisture my body craved. After only a moment's hesitation, I did as he instructed. My reward for obeying came in the form of a tiny sliver of ice. It wasn't much, but the cold moisture felt like rain on the dry cracked earth. Closing my lips, I savored the clean, fresh goodness sliding down my throat.

"Again."

I did as he said, wanting more: more ice, more water, more of his deep voice. I was tired of the silence, and judging by Jacob's earlier pacing, he had things he wanted to say. I waited, but other than the sound of his directives, the stillness lingered. Over and over, I opened my mouth, and each time he fed me chips of ice. Soon we fell into a rhythm, and even his directives disappeared. Each time, I'd swallow and then immediately open my lips, unashamedly greedy for the next piece of heavenly coolness. As my throat numbed, I wondered if I'd ever enjoyed frozen water as much as I did at this moment. My new obsession with devouring the entire cup superseded my wish to hear him speak. My concerns temporarily disappeared into a calming fog as his fingers brushed my lips and I contentedly took what he gave.

Suddenly the door opened and our forged connection shattered. I quickly closed my mouth as Jacob's chair moved. In those few seconds, my heart skipped a beat, and I feared the sound of Brother Timothy's voice. Instead I heard Jacob speak to the nurse, calling her by name, Sister Raquel.

As they discussed my medications and she tugged on my IV, I tried to recall all the things I'd wanted to say. I wanted to tell Jacob that I didn't remember the accident, the Commission, The Light, or even him. I wanted answers, to know more about us, who we were, and why we'd come to be somewhere that felt so wrong.

My questions were on the tip of my tongue, yet I couldn't ask them. It wasn't only because he'd told me not to talk; it was as if their urgency was fading. It took all my might to hold on to them. Fatigue hit me like a freight train, causing Jacob's and Sister Raquel's words to slur and my limbs to grow increasingly heavy. In no time at all, my tiny, unfamiliar world floated away.

As I woke slowly from a deep sleep, my mind lingered in that space where the world was both a dream and a reality. It wasn't until I tried to open my eyes and found only darkness that everything came rushing back. Everything . . . that word normally encompassed so much. But now, to me, it meant only recalling what had happened the day before.

My name is Sara. My husband's name is Jacob. According to him, our last name is Adams. I've been in an accident and am in a hospital.

No matter how I tried, I couldn't remember anything before the previous day. Have I blocked it all out? Why? And why do my recent memories seem wrong, like they belong to someone else?

I lay still and a smile graced my lips as I recalled the previous night's ice chips. I couldn't recall Jacob, yet his protectiveness filled me with an unfamiliar sense of warmth. Then the sound of the door brushing over the tile brought me back to the present.

"Brother Jacob?" a female voice whispered.

I waited, wondering if it was a nurse who was speaking. A few seconds later, when the woman repeated Jacob's name, the chair moved against the floor and my bed creaked. Jacob must have been sleeping with his head on the mattress.

"Sister Lilith, why are you here?"

Lilith? The name sounded familiar to me.

"The Assembly will convene soon. I was sent to stay with Sara."

"Why?"

"You've been summoned."

"Summoned now? Surely they understand I need to stay here."

Summoned? That sounded so ominous.

"I'm sure they'll discuss it with you. Each one of us has a job that must be completed. If one person doesn't fulfill their assignment, it affects the entire community. Not only has Sara's job gone undone for the last week, but so has yours. I'm sure you can guess whose job the Commission views as the most crucial. It was one thing while she lay unconscious, but now she's—"

"Now she's injured, unable to speak or get up. Dr. Newton hasn't been in since she woke. Instead her energy was used up on your husband's visit."

Husband? That was why her name sounded familiar—Brother Timothy had mentioned Lilith when he was here . . . had it been the day before? She must've been in that crowd of people.

Jacob continued, "I understand the importance of my job, but I've been in touch with Brother Micah. No delivery or pickup has gone undone . . ."

His determination increased with each sentence as he continued his defense. Sister Lilith spoke firmly but Jacob held his own. I rolled my shoulders and straightened my neck. With the volume of their conversation, there was no way I would've stayed asleep, not without medication. The last thing I gleaned from their conversation was something Jacob said about me eating. I pressed my lips together and waited for her response.

"Father Gabriel"—Sister Lilith's voice softened—"knows what's best. We must trust him, even when we don't understand his ways. Only he knows the plans and what's best for the community. If Sister Sara purposely chose to disobey—"

Jacob interrupted, "She didn't. I've testified. You were here yesterday. You heard Sara's responses to Timothy's questions."

"Brother Timothy and we heard your responses," she replied. "We've yet to hear hers. They're expecting you at Assembly. I'm not privy to know the thoughts of the Commission, but I'd assume that after Assembly your petition for Sara's nutrients will be heard. I'm confident that without your presence, it won't. Truly, as with all things, the decision is yours."

Jacob was part of this, part of some assembly. What does that mean? And how can she threaten me but say that the decision is his?

For the first time since the room cleared the night before, Jacob gathered my hand in his.

"Sara, can you hear me?"

I squeezed his hand once.

"You won't be alone. Sister Lilith is here. I'll contact Dr. Newton and tell him not to examine you until I return. Do you understand?"

I squeezed his hand.

"I'm also going to call Brother Luke. I believe he'll allow Sister Elizabeth to come and sit with you. Above all, you must rest your vocal cords." His tone turned more empathic. "No matter what anyone says, it's important that you don't speak. It doesn't matter who it is. As your husband, I forbid speaking. Is that clear?"

Though his demand seemed archaic, there was something more in Jacob's voice than a dictatorial directive. Strategically hidden between the words was a warning, one I planned to heed. He wasn't so much restricting my speech as he was talking about whom I could trust.

Could this be the reason for my accident? Were these people dangerous? My questions continued as I squeezed his hand.

"I'll be back as soon as I can, and then we'll learn what Dr. Newton has to say."

I had the distinct feeling that there was no love lost between Sister Lilith and my husband. I didn't know why, but I didn't care much for her either. Yet, for some reason, I felt differently about the Elizabeth he'd mentioned. There was something about her name that felt warm.

With a cursory squeeze of my hand, Jacob was gone.

As Sister Lilith moved across the room, the click of her shoes was different from Jacob's or even Sister Raquel's. After hearing her take a few more steps, I decided she was wearing high heels. Resting quietly against the pillow, I hoped again that this was just some long nightmare; however, it wasn't. With each passing moment it became more obvious why I'd blocked my memories of this life. It was simply too bizarre.

Sister Lilith's footsteps stopped as someone new entered the room.

"Good morning, Sister Sara."

I recognized Raquel's voice, and my cheeks rose. Finally I was being addressed directly.

While Sister Raquel moved the bedsheets, she spoke with Sister Lilith. The more I listened, the more I liked Raquel. She was respectful of whatever power Brother Timothy's wife held, yet at the same time she was efficient with her job, explaining her duties and what we'd be doing for the next thirty or so minutes. According to the conversations I'd overheard, I'd been unconscious for nearly a week. With my second day of consciousness, I wanted to move—but mostly I was thrilled to learn I'd be able to shower. Politely, Sister Raquel asked Sister Lilith to step into the hall. The awkward silence that followed had me picturing some sort of standoff. I don't know if that really happened, but thankfully, the door finally opened and closed and Raquel sighed.

Every part of my body ached from my injuries, inactivity, and lack of nutrients. Sister Raquel's voice reassured me as she talked me through each task. Before I could leave the bed, there were tubes to be removed. I had no idea what they were giving me through the IV. Jacob said it fed me, but I suspected it was delivering medication too. Once I was unattached, Sister Raquel urged me to the edge of the bed. Even sitting on my own took effort.

"Don't put any weight on your bad leg. Eventually you'll have a walking cast. This isn't it. We'll use a wheelchair to get you around for now."

She directed me to move from the bed to the chair and then rolled me to what I assumed was a bathroom. Without strength or sight, I was totally at her mercy. Throughout her instructions, she asked if I was all right or comfortable. Remembering Jacob's warning, I only moved my head. The first time I did, I expected the throbbing from the day before, but it didn't return.

Maybe I was healing.

Now if only my memories would come back.

Sister Raquel removed something that felt like tape from my side, explaining that I had at least one broken rib. Then she fashioned some kind of covering for my cast that fastened tightly on my upper thigh. As she secured the material, I envisioned plastic wrap surrounding my leg. To prevent my leg from bearing weight, she directed my hand to a handle above my head. I guessed it was suspended from the ceiling. Holding tight, I was supposed to navigate on my one good leg; however, my underused muscles rebelled, cramping with each exhausting step.

I began to wonder if it was worth the effort until I sat on a plastic bench, she turned on the shower, and warm water rained upon my skin and hair. The clean scent of soap and shampoo filled my senses, washing away the musty remains of the hospital bed and tubes.

Without thinking about the consequences, I opened my lips, filling my mouth with the water that continued to rain.

"Not too much, Sara; it wouldn't be good for you," Sister Raquel whispered, reminding me of the Commission's decree.

After I rinsed off, she helped me out of the shower and dried my skin. She wrapped me in a soft robe as droplets of water continued to fall from my hair, and she said, "Your hair is quite pretty."

I contemplated her comment and realized I couldn't picture my own hair. By the way it clung to my back, I knew it was long, but no matter how hard I tried, I couldn't envision the color.

Would I even know my own reflection? I was lost in thoughts of other things I'd forgotten when Raquel helped me into the wheelchair, handed me a toothbrush, and directed my hand toward a cup of water. Unsure what to do with the water, I hesitated, not knowing if it was a test, or if she wanted me to drink.

"If you're all right in here, I'm going to leave you alone for a moment while you brush your teeth. I need to go back in your room and change your sheets. When I come back, I'll bring a fresh nightgown."

I nodded. The little bit of water I'd consumed in the shower had merely whetted my thirst. I wanted more. As soon as I sensed that Raquel was gone, I drained the cup and hastily refilled it. At the rush of the running water, a cold chill tingled down my spine. I remembered Sister Lilith and felt sure that if she heard, she wouldn't hesitate to reprimand me for my blatant disregard of the Commission's decree. Nevertheless my thirst prevailed as I drank another cup of water before brushing my teeth.

Sister Raquel returned and whispered, "Elizabeth just arrived. I'm pretty sure Sister Lilith is ready to go, but she won't leave until she sees you again."

My tired muscles tensed and the water in my stomach churned at the mere mention of her name.

"Don't worry," Raquel continued, "They're both still in the hallway. We're the only ones in here. Before I take you back out, I want to get you dressed and comb your hair, and I need to replace the bandages on your eyes. It's not good for them to stay wet."

I sucked my lip between my freshly brushed teeth to keep from speaking. She was going to remove the bandage around my head. What if I can see? What if my eyes aren't damaged? Then again, what if they are?

Raquel slipped a fresh nightgown over my head. Taking in the soft material, I felt long sleeves and buttons that ran down its entire front.

Whether from exhaustion or from being disconnected from the medicine, my fingers shook badly as I tried to fasten the buttons. The water I'd managed to drink sloshed violently in my otherwise empty stomach.

"Are you all right?" Sister Raquel asked as she reached out to stop me from falling forward.

I shook my head, perspiration coating my freshly washed skin.

"I was going to change your bandage and braid your hair, but let's get you back to bed." Concern laced each word. "I don't want to be the one explaining to Father Gabriel why you collapsed in the bathroom."

Father Gabriel? Wouldn't she tell Jacob?

I heard the opening of the door and footsteps as Raquel wheeled me toward the bed. Though the footsteps sounded similar, they were different, letting me know that more than one person had entered my room. When my chair stopped, another set of hands helped me stand. I turned my covered eyes in that person's direction.

"Sara, I've missed you," the person said. It wasn't Sister Lilith, which meant it must be Sister Elizabeth. "I'm so glad Brother Jacob called so I could come to see you." From the location of her voice, she was taller than me, and by the way she held my hand and referred to me without the awkward title Sister, I got the feeling we were friends.

"I'll inform the Commission that she's doing better."

Our reunion stilled at the sound of Sister Lilith's voice coming from near the door. The way she referred to me made the hair on the back of my neck stand on end.

"Thank you, Sister Lilith, for staying until I could arrive." Though it was polite, ice rolled from Elizabeth's response. It seemed we all felt the same about Sister Lilith.

Sister Lilith didn't respond, but I heard the door open and, eventually, the click-clack of her heels disappeared into the distance.

My nausea calmed a bit as I exhaled and settled on the clean sheets. Elizabeth adjusted my cast, putting pillows under my leg, while Raquel, on my right, reconnected my IV. The way they chatted felt familiar and safe. For the first time since I'd awoken from my accident, the atmosphere didn't feel wrong.

Was Elizabeth my friend or, perhaps, a sister? Do I have family, other than a husband? Do I have children? Are Jacob and I parents? How old are we? My hand flew to my lips to stop me from speaking. I had so many questions.

As I rested against the pillow, their soft voices filled the once-frightening room with a feeling of friendship. My earlier bout of nausea had passed but the perspiration left me chilled. As if reading my thoughts, Elizabeth pulled the blankets over my shivering body. I managed a tired smile as the warmth enveloped me. Though I wanted to hear everything they said, in no time at all, their voices drifted away and sleep stole my first real chance for answers.

FOUR

S ara

A HEATED CONVERSATION infiltrated my dream, harsh words seeping unwontedly into the blissful scene before me. I tuned out the voices and inhaled the sweet scent of lavender. Step by step, I traveled across a purple-dotted meadow as tall grass brushed my bare legs. As I paused under the sun's rays, my toes sank into the soft, cool ground and my skin radiated warmth. On the horizon, pink and purple clouds swirled together like paint upon a canvas. The brilliant sky was like a pair of blue eyes, shining with happiness.

The voice's clatter wafted in ripples, small at first and only a word or two. But then it crashed like waves upon a beach destined to bear a hurricane's wrath, each burst larger and louder than the one before.

I scanned the horizon in search of peace. The colorful clouds turned dark and ominous, bubbling and swirling above, changing the crystal-clear hues to varying shades of gray. I stood in awe of the building storm, while the wind howled and long hair whipped violently about my face.

The louder the wind roared, the more acutely aware I became of my impending doom. Panic swelled as strands of blonde tingled with electricity. Scanning in all directions, I sought shelter from the storm and then the harsh voices awoke me.

"I'll need confirmation," an unfamiliar voice boomed.

"You have it, from me," Jacob growled. "Have you forgotten that I'm a member of the Assembly?"

"The Assembly is under the Commission. The decree came from the Commission."

"Then call them. Ask! I stood before them and talked for nearly an hour. Father Gabriel himself gave the approval. I want food in here before she wakes. She hasn't eaten anything in nearly a week. I'm not waiting any longer."

"Calm down. You're going to wake her."

"I'm past calm. Tell me what she can eat."

"If—"

"Not if," Jacob interjected. "What can her body tolerate?"

"When I receive word that the decree has been lifted, we'll need to start her with a bland diet: Jell-O, soup, rice. She could have some bread, but not too much."

"Then go. Have it prepared. I told you the decree's been removed. If you don't believe me, call them."

"I can't question the Commission. It's up to them to notify me." The unfamiliar voice gasped, then pleaded, "No, don't call . . ."

"This has gone on long enough," Jacob said. His voice remained fierce but sounded more in control. "Hello, Brother Daniel. I'm with Dr. Newton. Apparently he hasn't received the message regarding my wife . . . Yes, he's here . . . I told him . . . Yes, let me hand him the phone."

Jacob was arguing with my doctor? What kind of doctor was

this? Surely there had to be more doctors in this hospital, people not under the control of the Commission.

"Hello, Brother Daniel?" Dr. Newton's greeting came out more like a question. "Yes, I realize he is . . . Yes, I understand that the Assembly is a governing party and as a member his word is true. I wanted to be . . . Right away. Good-bye." There was a pause, then Dr. Newton continued, "Brother Jacob, I'll have Sister Deborah bring in food."

Jacob exhaled.

The doctor's tone became commanding as he moved closer to my bed. "You should wake her and take her to the bathroom. She's no longer catheterized and can't get out of the bed alone. That cast isn't for walking." There was a tug on my IV. "She'll have one that she can walk on once I receive approval. I'll return after she's eaten. It's past time for my exam."

"Thank you." Though the thunder was gone from Jacob's voice, the storm was still present.

"You should understand my insistence. I'm not losing her to starvation, not after all she's been through."

"I do, but you know that we all have rules. My oath is to help people, but I too have a family. Following decrees isn't optional. We all know that."

"Yes, we do," Jacob said defiantly. "That won't happen this time. I won't allow it."

The doctor's words brought my reality back with a vengeance. I was at the mercy of these people, people I couldn't see or remember. People with frightening tones, rules, and decrees. I clenched my teeth and searched my memories for anything. Anything to confirm that I belonged here, or anything to confirm that I didn't.

Jacob approached, brushing my hair away from my forehead, and spoke. "I'm sure you're awake. I don't think even you could sleep through that."

Even me? What does he mean?

I nodded. As his large hand lingered on my hair, I remembered part of my dream and wondered if my hair was blonde.

"Sara, the nurse will bring you some food. Dr. Newton wants me to help you get up before she comes."

I reached up to my eyes. Though I felt the dampness of my hair, the bandages were dry.

"Sister Raquel replaced your bandages." His fingers raked my hair. "But she couldn't brush or braid your hair with you asleep."

A lump formed in my chest. She'd changed my bandages and I'd missed it.

"I'm going to lift you from the bed."

The blankets moved and cool air permeated my warm haven, but before the chill registered, Jacob's arms cradled my back and legs. I winced as he lifted me. Pain emanated from my side. Sucking in a breath, I braced for him to set me in the wheelchair, but he didn't. Instead he held me close and stepped effortlessly away from the bed. Reaching toward him, my hands spanned the breadth of his shoulders and came to rest upon his chest. Laying my cheek against his soft shirt, I inhaled the scent of leather and musk. With each step his scruffy chin brushed the top of my head. For only a second, something triggered a memory, but just as quickly it was gone.

We had apparently crossed the room, since Jacob said, "We're in the bathroom. Raquel said you did well this morning, though I'm not sure how much of this you can do on your own."

I reached up and pointed, hoping he'd see the handle that I'd used earlier. He must have, because he gently placed my good foot on the floor and directed my hand to the handle. At the thought of what I needed to do, blood rushed to my cheeks. I quickly lowered my chin, not wanting Jacob to sense my embarrassment. After all, he didn't know that to me he was a stranger. To him we were married. He'd no doubt seen me naked many times.

His large hands framed my cheeks and lifted my face toward his. Though I couldn't see him, we were very close. His warm breath tickled my nose, and his words were soft and reassuring. "I'd leave you alone for privacy, but the way you're shaking, I'm afraid you might fall."

I blindly lifted my face toward the handle. The apparatuses that held it in place clinked with my movements. I hadn't realized how badly my hands and legs were trembling.

"Let me help you," he offered as he released my face.

My trembling eased at his tone. It was as if he was asking instead of telling. Nodding my approval, I released the handle and placed my hands on his chest. Slowly he moved his hands to the hem of my nightgown. As he moved my gown slowly upward, his pulse beneath my hands quickened. Once the nightgown was above my waist, I felt his body stiffen.

I lowered my chin, unsure of what my expression revealed. There were too many thoughts trying to take root. Bewilderment and uncertainty swirled with embarrassment, yet they all seemed just beyond my reach. Taking a deep breath, I concentrated on the task at hand. Jacob and I worked together in silence. He spoke only to alert me of our movements, which I appreciated. Each one, no matter how gentle he tried to make it, aggravated my tender side. With his alert, I'd bite my lower lip and hold my breath. It didn't stop the pain, but at least I avoided wincing. By the time he placed me back in my bed, the telltale copper taste let me know that I'd punctured the inside of my lower lip.

Heavy silence loomed around us as we waited for my food. By the sound of Jacob's footsteps and occasional sighs I sensed that he too was fighting a whirlwind of thoughts, though I doubted we were thinking the same things. With each passing moment, I contemplated my options. I wanted food, but I wanted more than that. I needed more than that. I needed to understand what had happened with my accident as well as what was happening now.

The questions weren't only in my mind. They filled the room, swirling around us, taunting me. Like the faceless shadows in my dreams, they mocked me with the knowledge they refused to share.

As time passed, I felt increasingly trapped—claustrophobic—as if I needed air.

What do I normally do for an outlet?

The answer washed over me with a cleansing release.

I run.

A strange sense of relief filled me as I closed my eyes and imagined paths and trails. It was so real. I not only saw the sun's long beams dancing through the tall trees, I felt the warmth as I passed through the shafts of light and my feet pounded the ground. I pushed my body, exercising its limits. No longer suffocating in an unknown world, I was moderating my breathing, keeping my pulse steady as I gained the strength to continue. I never doubted my ability to keep going. The motion came naturally. Peering beyond the woods, I spotted the open meadow where a cool morning mist had settled near the ground. Inhaling the fresh air, I smiled at the dew glistening like diamonds in the early light.

I audibly gasped at the intense memory. My body tensed. I wasn't there, I was here. However, what I'd imagined couldn't have been a dream. The terrain was familiar, more so than anything around me. I tensed as Jacob once again touched my hair.

"Sara, are you all right? What happened?"

I nodded with newfound strength. I was all right. I would be. I had a memory, a real memory. Since I couldn't tell him what had happened, I smiled and moved my head from side to side. I wanted to say that nothing was wrong. For the first time since I'd awakened in this unfamiliar world, something seemed right.

I concentrated on the images I'd created. Just like physically running, the thoughts relaxed me, easing the blanket of doubt and worry.

"I should look for your brush. Do you think you can brush your hair?" Jacob asked. "It's unlike you for it to be like this." With each sentence his fingers smoothed and caressed my long unruly tresses. Before I noticed he'd left, he was back. Placing a handle in my hand, he said, "You're much better at this than I."

Careful not to snag the bandages, I pulled the bristles through my hair. As I did, the floral scent of shampoo reminded me of the lavender flowers in my dream. I imagined the long blonde hair blowing in the wind and wondered if that was what I was brushing.

The length seemed right. It was the color that eluded me. Once silkiness replaced the tangles, I began to braid. The rote motion came without effort and resulted in a loose braid, beginning on my left and lying upon my right shoulder. As my fingers neared the end, Jacob placed a hair tie in my hand.

It was silly, only a braid, but my chest no longer ached. It was the first thing I'd done on my own. My hands remembered what to do just as my mind recalled running. It was only a start, but I clung to it.

When the door opened, my hunger woke with a vengeance.

"Place it over here," Jacob directed.

Where's "here"?

Tension returned to my shoulders as I pressed my lips together, suppressing the comments I instinctively knew wouldn't be welcomed. This macho-man routine was getting old. After the door opened and closed, wheels moved against the floor. With this new sound, I envisioned a table, one that could move in front of me and over my bed. I reached out.

"No, Sara. You didn't forget about blessing the food, did you?"

I had. It hadn't occurred to me. Consuming it was my only thought.

I bowed my head as Jacob's deep voice filled the room. He thanked Father Gabriel and the Commission for my food. Really? He asked God to use its nutrients to help me heal. OK. When he paused, I began to move, but then he spoke again: "Let this food be a reminder that privileges given can be taken away. Thank you for correcting my wife and reminding me of my role. We won't fail you again, for we trust you and Father Gabriel in all things. Amen."

I didn't move. My hunger suddenly waned.

What does all of that mean? What correction? Is Jacob agreeing with Brother Timothy that my suffering is because I sinned?

"Sara," he said, lifting my chin. "You need to eat."

He was right. I needed to eat, get strong, and get away. This wasn't right. Everything about this wasn't right. In my heart I knew I didn't belong here. I reached again for the tray. This time, wordlessly, Jacob captured my hands and placed them upon my lap. Apparently, just as with the ice chips the night before, Jacob planned to feed me.

"Open."

At that first command, my teeth clenched. I understood why he'd helped me last night, I'd been weak, but now I was relatively certain I could lift a spoon and find my mouth. Nevertheless, with just one word, he'd made it clear: food was coming, but only through him. Unable to argue, I could still refuse.

Though I entertained the thought, when the spoon touched my lip, I did as he'd said and opened my mouth. Bite by bite, my anger faded as my stomach filled. The soup—more like broth—was my favorite. I may have even hummed after the first bite. Each time it hit my tongue I savored the warmth and flavor. Even with Jacob's careful feeding, the salty chicken broth occasionally dribbled down my chin. The first time it happened, Jacob laughed. It wasn't loud, barely a scoff, but it made me smile. I couldn't remember my husband's laugh. Since I'd awakened, I'd mostly heard his anger and commands. Surely there was more to our marriage than that. It wasn't until the soup and Jell-O were finished that he placed a small roll into my hands.

"Here's a little bread. You can probably handle this on your own."

I nodded, rolling the bread between my hands, assessing the size. Lifting it to my nose, I inhaled the scent. When I placed it between my teeth, the hard outer crust gave way to a soft warm center. Each bite melted in my mouth as I sparingly nibbled. I didn't want it to end, but as it did, I realized that it was the chewing I enjoyed as much as the roll. Deprivation formed the strangest needs. All too soon the roll was gone, and a straw appeared at my lips.

"Dr. Newton said to go easy on liquids, but here's some water."

I pursed my lips and sucked. The cool water reminded me that my throat felt better, even better than it had the day before. At the sound of his name, I remembered the doctor's promise to return. Just as the thought occurred, I heard the door open.

"Doctor," Jacob said, perhaps to inform me of who'd entered.

"I assume you're ready for me?"

I nodded, forgetting that rarely did anyone speak to me.

"Yes," Jacob replied. "Sara's finished her meal. Assuming her body handles it, I want her to have a larger portion for dinner."

Dinner? I guess I just ate lunch?

I had no way to judge time. Hearing that the day was only half-over filled my mind with a mixture of thoughts. While the promise of more food excited me, the idea of spending more time in this dark, unfamiliar life made me uneasy. Silently I longed for the familiarity of my dreams.

"We'll need to assess . . ."

Jacob reached for my hand. "She's lost entirely too much weight. I'm not sure of the amount, but she's skin and bones."

"Sister Sara," Dr. Newton began. "I need to complete your examination. Then we'll discuss your injuries. Do you understand?"

I nodded, feeling Jacob's reassuring squeeze. With the slightest shift, his callused fingers caressed my knuckles, and I wondered what Jacob did for a living. From his hand I guessed that he worked hard physically, and when he'd carried me to the bathroom, I'd sensed how much bigger he was than I.

What did my accident do to his work? What about me? What do I do?

As my bed reclined for my examination, I realized the man holding my hand had argued for me, supported and assisted me, yet I didn't know him.

Do I love him? Does he love me?

No matter how hard I searched the recesses of my mind, the answers mocked me, willfully staying beyond my reach.

CHAPTER

FIVE

J acob

I WANTED to see her eyes. Over thirty years of studying people, reading them, and somehow I'd forgotten that eyes were key. Without them I had only secondary and insignificant clues.

I understood why she wasn't allowed to see, at least not yet. Just because the psychology made sense didn't mean I approved. Taking a wife had been my duty, responsibility, and obligation to The Light. I'd seen and agreed with the process in the past—but that had been in theory and from a distance. This was up close and personal.

I'd known that eventually my time would come. I'd hoped it wouldn't, that I could avoid it, but refusing a wife when she was presented wasn't an option. Taking on this responsibility cemented my bond to The Light and solidified my standing in the community.

My compliance and cooperation assured Father Gabriel, the Commission, and the Assembly of my faithfulness.

My gaze darted to Sara's face. Her hand had just clamped into a tight ball within my grasp. Though I couldn't see her eyes, her lower lip blanched from the tight hold of her teeth. Damn, she'd bite clean through it if she didn't stop putting it in that vise grip. I'd seen the drops of blood earlier today when I'd returned her to her bed. At least this time, I wasn't the cause of her lip-biting. This reaction was caused by the movement of the bed as Dr. Newton reclined it. I guessed it was the damn broken rib or ribs. Why Raquel hadn't rewrapped it after Sara's shower, I didn't know. I would say something, but then she'd probably be corrected. They might even decide to replace her as Sara's main caregiver. I didn't want that.

What I wanted was for that horrible dark bruise, those shades of purple and green, to go away. Seeing it when I'd lifted her nightgown had been like experiencing the kick all over again. The reverberations had sent shock waves through both of us. Maybe I didn't want to see her eyes. The pain she felt, when the bed reclined or when I lifted her, seeped from her pores and filled the room with its stench.

Doesn't Dr. Newton realize what he's doing?

I glanced up, but he wasn't looking at me.

He was looking at her.

My teeth rattled as I clamped them tight and assessed his expression. He was the community's sole physician, and I expected to see compassion and the desire to heal in his face. Instead images of Dr. Mengele popped into my thoughts.

What kind of doctor participates in the things Dr. Newton does without reservation?

I might not have signed up for this mission, but, damn it, Sara was now my wife.

Who the hell am I kidding?

I was as responsible as Dr. Newton, if not more. Not for all the other women who'd come to the community in this same way, but for Sara. When the Commission explained what needed to be done, I didn't question. Orders were orders. I obeyed them as well as gave them. That's how I'd advanced as fast as I had within the community—I understood rules and procedures. The Light wasn't that different from the military. My training there served me well, and my experience in the army created the perfect history for a faithful follower.

Dr. Newton spoke, refocusing my attention. "I'm going to unbutton your gown to better see your injuries."

Though she nodded, I reapplied the pressure to my poor teeth. I'd be lucky if they weren't splinters of enamel by the time this was done. Dr. Newton started at the top button of her nightgown, near the neckline, and worked his way down. He'd managed to unfasten a few buttons when I let go of her hand and pushed his away. I'd seen under her gown and knew she wasn't wearing a bra.

Her breasts may have been smaller than I preferred, but they were pleasantly round and firm. Earlier, in the bathroom, probably due to the temperature, I'd noticed how her nipples hardened and how the pink around them darkened.

It didn't matter if they were small or large: they were mine. I also knew damn well that they hadn't been injured during her accident, and Newton knew that too. He'd examined her before. There was no reason for him to see her breasts again. Loosening my clenched jaw, I said, "Her injuries are lower. I'll help you." I wanted to say more, but Sara didn't need to listen to a pissing contest above her exposed body.

The good doctor's hands went up willingly in surrender, but the smirk on his face once again made my jaw go rigid. The arrogant ass. There was no way in hell he would ever examine her without me present. I wouldn't allow it. If I had to petition the Commission, I would. They wanted me to take having a wife seriously, and I was.

Taking a deep breath, I refastened the gown's top buttons and undid the ones starting at the bottom. Sara's exposed skin dotted with goose bumps as I laid the fabric of her nightgown aside. With the blankets down, she was now visible from her toes to past her navel. All the right parts were covered. No doubt in the dark, the world outside The Light, she'd worn less on a beach than what she wore now as panties. That didn't matter. When she'd been in the dark she hadn't been my wife. Now she was, and having Newton's eyes on her pissed me off.

I held my tongue and concentrated on her cast. The damn thing went halfway up her left thigh. Since only her tibia was broken, the cast could easily have stopped below her knee. It was one more piece of the psychological warfare, part of the plan to wear her down, take away her abilities, and make her dependent. The more physical limitations she endured, the easier it was to instill psychological limitations.

The Light had a job, a calling. Its original followers had been predominantly male. Father Gabriel's teachings originated from fundamentalist roots. Women were appreciated for the strength through which they fulfilled their duties—and because men had needs. According to Father Gabriel's teachings, those needs were best served by wives. While some women found their way to The Light of their own volition, others—like Sara—were acquired. The acquisition and indoctrination process was in a continual state of revision. Each case was gauged by its success or failure. Though the entire community participated in the acquisition, ultimately it was the participants in each acquisition who were responsible for the outcome. In our case that would be Sara and me. Because I was her husband, my role was infinitely important. The only road to my continued success within The Light was through her.

I took Sara's hand again in mine. We will not fail. The mantra repeated like a chant in the recesses of my mind. I'd witnessed failure, and I'd labored too long to allow that to be my end. Though Sara's hand trembled, I refused to let emotion cloud my objective. We would succeed.

"Squeeze your husband's hand when I touch a place that hurts."

The asshole went for the epicenter, directly above the broken ribs. As he did, Sara moaned and squeezed with all her might, before clamping her lips tightly together.

"There," I said, looking up to the doctor's raised brows.

"You broke at least one rib in your accident," he explained.

Her lip was back between her teeth as she nodded her understanding.

"There isn't much that can be done. We'll have to wait. They'll heal in time. Now what about here?" The doctor continued his exercise until he'd discussed her broken ribs, broken leg, and possible concussion. He explained that her cheek had hit the steering wheel of the truck. If she could have seen herself in a mirror, she'd have known that wasn't the case, but she seemed to take the doctor at his word. Touching her tender throat, he asked again if she had pain. Her squeeze was softer than before.

"Does that mean that it doesn't hurt there as much as before?" I asked.

She nodded.

"I believe you'll be able to talk within a day or two," Dr. Newton said. "Tomorrow or Friday we'll remove this cast and set a new one that'll allow you to walk. Your bone was broken, but luckily not severely. It didn't break the skin. That'll help with your recovery."

"What about food and drink?" I asked.

"How are you feeling now?" he asked her. "Did you handle the lunch OK?"

She nodded.

"Another day of bland and then we'll reevaluate."

"I want to take her home." I'd agreed to accept the Commission's and Father Gabriel's power, but I didn't like Newton's. I'd seen too many things over the past three years that I'd been at the Northern Light. In my opinion even the Commission didn't fully trust him—if they did, he'd be part of the Assembly.

"We'll need to watch how she adapts to the walking cast and alert the Commission. Where she goes from here is ultimately their decision."

By the way she flinched at his last statement, the process was working. She was beginning to understand how much the Commission ultimately controlled. Tomorrow at Assembly they'd ask, and I'd be honest. I'm sure they'd be quite proud of themselves—the recent refinements with the indoctrination process were proving effective. The old ways produced slower results. As a member of the Assembly, I normally would've been pleased too, but this time was different. I wasn't only an Assemblyman—I was her husband. The tighter Sara clung to my hand, the less content with the process I became.

Freeing my hand, I began closing the buttons of her nightgown. As I did, Sara raised her arm and pointed to her eyes. Father Gabriel's teachings instructed me to reprimand her, to remind her of a rule she'd never heard, that females answered questions—they didn't question. Instead I inwardly smirked at her ingenuity. The only rule she'd been told was not to speak, and while she obeyed, she'd found a way to communicate.

My wife was smart and resourceful. She'd learn quickly and we would succeed.

Newton's beady eyes widened and met mine.

I squared my shoulders and relayed her question. "When will you be able to remove the bandages from her eyes?"

His lips pursed. He'd probably report this to anyone who'd listen. Surely Lilith and Timothy were chomping at the bit for me to fail. The way I saw it, Sara had a simple question. It wasn't as if she demanded equality; she simply wanted to know when she might regain sight.

"Brother," Dr. Newton began, effectively removing her from the discussion. "As we've discussed, the concussion likely affected her optic nerve. Unfortunately that wasn't the only injury to her eyes. When your truck exploded, the intense light and heat damaged her retinas. Both injuries require rest and time. I don't foresee the bandages being removed anytime in the near future. It could easily be weeks."

"Thank you, Doctor. If there's nothing else, I believe my wife needs rest."

I supported The Light and Father Gabriel, but as I pulled the blankets over Sara's closed gown, I vowed to do what I could to make this easier on her. She was a person who'd lost the right to choose her future. It was now my responsibility, and I intended to do anything necessary for our survival. The stakes were too high.

"One last thing," Dr. Newton said. "I was informed that Sara's schedule will be set as of tomorrow."

"Her schedule?"

"Yes. She needs to be awake, dressed, and have breakfast eaten by the time you leave for Assembly."

My body tensed as I consciously loosened my grip on Sara's hand. Modulating my voice, I asked, "Who informed you of this?"

"Sister Lilith."

This time Sara's grasp shuddered. She was a quick study.

"Because . . ." I coaxed.

"I don't remember," Dr. Newton replied flippantly, his lips sliding into a sleazy grin. Shrugging, he added, "It was something about training."

Training?

I released Sara's hand and stepped toward the door, hoping that Newton would get the hint that I wanted him out. I wanted them all out. "Thank you, I'll be sure she's ready in the morning. As long as you believe she's healthy enough." Being the only physician, Dr. Newton could provide her with a valid reason to avoid Lilith's training, at least for a few more days.

"From what I could tell—with my limited examination—yes, your wife is healthy enough to begin training."

Asshole!

I shook my head. Clearly this was Newton's plan. If I wouldn't allow him full access to Sara, he'd throw her to the wolves.

Hell no. I'd fight it.

I opened the door and watched it shut behind the doctor, wishing it had a lock.

In four steps I crossed the room. This small space felt like a damn cage, but I refused to leave Sara's side. The soles of my boots created a rhythm as I paced back and forth, a habit I'd started as a teen. I processed thoughts better when I moved. I'd rather be moving in one direction, but living in this godforsaken region of Alaska, in a walled community, didn't offer many opportunities for running. It was better in the summer, but now, with the sunlight waning, it was freezing cold. I had to hand it to Father Gabriel, though. There was nothing like being isolated in the middle of nowhere to bring people together and help form a cohesive group.

The rush for Sara's training didn't make sense. Are they trying for another failure?

From the corner of my eye, I noticed the movement of her hand and my steps stilled.

Shit. She'd just wiped away a tear.

What the hell am I supposed to do?

CHAPTER

SIX

S tella

STANDING outside the door to the Wayne County Morgue, I gave Dylan a strained smile.

"Really?" I asked, shaking my head.

"Really. I haven't been in. If they knew for sure it was her, they wouldn't need you. After last time I thought it might help if you weren't alone."

I feigned a smile. I appreciated his help; however, having him here, holding my hand, set fire to my emotions, causing them to bubble to the top instead of remaining hidden behind a mask of indifference.

"Thank you, Dylan. But I need to walk in there as a journalist, not a friend. I'm not sure I can take seeing my friend laid out on a large stainless table."

He tilted his head. "But Stella Montgomery, sleuth investigator, can?"

"No, not really, but sleuth investigator"—I couldn't help but smile, releasing a bit of the tension at his description—"can keep it together until she's alone."

"How about you don't have to be alone?" Holding my hand and stepping back, Dylan looked deep into my eyes, and his gaze narrowed. I knew that look. His police wheels were spinning. "You know," he said curiously, "I raced down here as soon as Barney told me you'd left. WCJB is closer than the precinct. How did I get here before you?"

I shrugged. "My mind's a blur. I missed my exit and . . ." I let my voice fade to a whisper. "I found myself headed north."

"Tell me you didn't go to Highland Heights."

I straightened my neck and set my shoulders back defensively. "Don't. Don't play macho policeman. If that's Mindy in there, then they found her in that neighborhood in an abandoned house. If it's her, I needed to see it. I need to find out who did this. That's what I do."

"If, Stella. *If* is the imperative word. You're putting the cart before the horse." His mussed, dark-blond hair failed to hide his furrowed brow as he repeated his question, slower this time. "Did you go to Highland Heights alone, without telling anyone?"

I knew that telling someone where you're going—leaving a trail —was rule number one, but rules were meant to be broken. Sometimes moving on instinct didn't allow for time to check in. Not appreciating his interrogation, I shook off his grip. "I just drove around, all right? I didn't get out."

"Christ, are you trying to turn up missing too?"

I'd never, in all my adult life, answered to anyone. This relationship—or whatever it was—with Dylan was still in its infancy. We were still working on our boundaries, and he'd just crossed one of mine. With heat rising to my face and my jaw clenched, I replied, "I'm not having this conversation with you in the hallway outside of the morgue. Why are you here, anyway? To lecture me on safety? Because right now I'm safe, but whoever the hell is on that table isn't."

Dylan's gaze softened. "No, I didn't come here to lecture you. I came because last time you did this alone. I didn't want you to do that again. I know how upsetting it was for you. I hope to God this isn't Mindy, but if it is . . ."

I sighed. "I appreciate that, I do. I just don't need lectures right now." I let out another long breath. "Seeing dead bodies never gets easier, at least not to me."

"No, it doesn't. Each one, no matter what they did or what happened to them, was a person, someone's kid."

Or sister, or brother, or best friend.

Dylan once again grasped my hand. "Let's get this over with. They're ready for us."

I held back my tears, steeled my resolve, and nodded. Together we walked through the doors and entered the cold room, cold both in temperature and personality. The buzz of the lights combined with the offending odor threw my nerves into overdrive. Dylan's hand became a vise as I took in the surroundings. It was the same as it'd been a week earlier, with cement walls, tile floors, and tables and countertops made of a shiny, disinfected metal.

A young, thin woman entered from the other side of the room at the same time that we came in. I barely noticed her as I concentrated on the body, lying on a table near the far end of the room, a silhouette covered with a white sheet.

"Thank you for coming. I'll skip all the formalities and make this as quick as possible," the young technician said.

Biting my lip, I nodded.

"We only need for you to give us your impression. You don't need to look any longer than necessary."

I nodded again, fearful that if I spoke I'd taste the strange aroma hanging in the air.

"It's not too late," she continued. "If you'd like to go to another room, we can do this via closed-circuit cameras. You don't have to be in here."

Though bile bubbled in my throat, I released Dylan's hand and straightened my stance. "I assure you, if this is Mindy, I do need to be here. Please continue."

The young woman grabbed the edge of the sheet with her blue-gloved hands and slowly lowered it. Panic ran through me when I saw blonde hair, blonde like Mindy's, like mine. Next I saw eyes, their lids partially closed, hiding their color. Did this body have the same pale eyes that Mindy and I shared? The cheeks were bruised in various shades. And then the tech lowered the sheet past the nose and mouth and I knew. I knew.

"It's not her. It's not her." Relief crashed down as I leaned against Dylan's tall frame, grasping his bicep to keep myself from falling. The worry that had propelled me toward the body had evaporated, leaving me physically weak.

The body before us was now uncovered to just above her breasts, with her arms visible, giving us a full view of the plethora of injuries marking her skin. Whoever she was, she'd lived through hell and died there. The relief that washed through me left a sickening trail of remorse. I was thrilled that this wasn't Mindy, but, as Dylan had said, it was still a person, someone who might or might not have had a family. Someone who might or might not be missed.

How did she get to this table, to the house where she was found? What is her story?

And what about Mindy?

The theory that my friend's disappearance was voluntary was ridiculous. An intelligent, successful twenty-nine-year-old woman didn't decide one day to disappear. Even if she had, with GPS, traffic cameras, surveillance, it wouldn't be easy, not without help. Mindy had no reason to walk away from her life. She wouldn't have. She had every reason to stay.

Standing beside the table, I found myself back to more questions than answers, back to imagining scenarios that made my stomach turn. I'd researched the number of female disappearances nation-wide. The numbers were staggering and, looking at the woman before me, I knew that numbers were only a part of the story. Each report was a life.

What I saw in this woman's injuries took my imagination to dark places. Her bruises were an array of colors, indicating a pattern of abuse. Yellow and green peppered her exposed arms and cheekbone. I knew enough from my time in the crime lab to determine that she'd gotten those over a week ago. There was also a purple crescent under her left eye and a dark bluish-purple band surrounding her throat. Something besides hands had made the mark around her neck. The first finger and thumb were the strongest and usually left definitive marks. The customary differentiation of fingers was missing. This bruise on this body's throat was a consistent dark color, indicating that whatever had been around her neck, had been in place for a long time. She also had lacerations. There was a partially healed wound visible on her chest above the edge of the sheet.

Now that I knew this wasn't Mindy, my investigative side took over. I longed to remove the sheet and meet this woman, understand her, and learn her story. However, it was more than that. The vile taste in my mouth, the way the tiny hairs on my arms rose, told me that part of me feared that Mindy could be experiencing, at this very moment, the same terror that this woman had known.

I needed answers, for Mindy, for this woman, and for any other women who had disappeared from their lives to awaken in a nightmare.

"Miss Montgomery?"

The technician's voice pulled me back to the cold room.

"Yes?"

"If you need to sit down, you may go into one of our rooms for a few minutes before you leave. We realize this is difficult. I'm sorry we've brought you in here twice. I hope you know that we wouldn't do that if we didn't think there was a possibility . . ."

I straightened my shoulders. "No, I don't need to sit down, and I want you to call me. If there's even a chance that you have Mindy, call me again. I'll be here." I looked up toward Dylan, then back to the young lady. "Thank you. What about this woman?"

"We'll run some more tests to see if we can find any markers. Since the tips of her fingers have been burned, our only means of identification are DNA and dental records. Those are both long shots unless she matches a missing-persons list or a national registry."

My gaze dropped to the woman's hands. The way they lay next to her still body, I hadn't noticed anything about them, but now I saw that the skin on the tips of her fingers was ghostly white.

"Burned?" I asked. "With what?"

"We're not exactly sure. As you can see, it wasn't fire. We're assuming acid."

"When?" My voice came out softer than I liked.

Dylan reached for my wrist, pulling me gently toward the door. I didn't move. I steadied my feet and turned back to the technician. I couldn't help it. The questions came fast and furious.

What the hell happened to this woman? Do you think someone put her fingers in acid before she died?"

"I really can't—"

"Stella, let's go," Dylan said. "This isn't your story."

I turned to face him. "Whose story or case will it be? Who'll give a shit about her or what she suffered?"

"It's an open investigation," the technician volunteered. "The police are working on it."

"If someone were to use an acid strong enough to take away her fingerprints, wouldn't there be more damage to her skin?" I asked.

The young woman nodded. "If it were done all at once. However, if it's done over time, each application takes away a little more. Then it scars, making the final result more effective. Some terrorist groups willingly do this to lose their previous identities." She looked down. "I really shouldn't say any more."

"Stella, we need to go." Dylan placed his hand on my shoulder.

I nodded as I scanned the features of the woman on the table.

Briefly I wondered what she had looked like before she was hurt, killed, and left for rat food in an abandoned house. That was what some asshole had done. If drugged-out kids hadn't gone into the house to shoot up or hook up in the middle of a Detroit summer, this woman would've been consumed by rodents, greatly reducing any hope of identification.

Shaking my head, I looked back at the technician. That's when I saw it, a look in her eyes that seemed to plead for my help, asking me to use the resources at my discretion to do something.

I tested the waters. "Thank you for your help. What's your name? I apologize for not asking sooner."

"Tracy, Dr. Tracy Howell, assistant forensic pathologist."

I stood straighter. "Doctor. Again, I apologize. I just assumed you were a technician."

Dr. Howell smiled. "I'm used to it. It's all right. When people enter our labs, they aren't in the best place. I'm sorry, Miss Montgomery, that your friend is still missing. Thank you for stopping by." Her eyes shifted to Dylan, then back to me. I got the feeling that Dr. Howell didn't want to talk with others around.

"Call me Stella, please. Thank you again, Doctor."

As Dylan and I walked through the door to the hallway, I took one last look over my shoulder and saw Dr. Howell cover the blonde woman's head with the sheet. The vision of the woman settled into the back of my mind: her yellow hair combed away from her battered face; her eyes partially opened, irises hidden by the veiled lids; her fingers curved slightly, their distinguishing marks burned away.

And something else.

One of the earlobes, the one on the right, was split, as if an earring had been ripped from the ear. My feet stopped. We'd made it to the security gate but I'd suddenly forgotten how to move.

"What is it?" Dylan asked in a low voice.

I barely heard his question as I tried to make sense of the injury. Should I go back and confirm what I saw?

Mindy's ears weren't pierced. That was one of the things I'd specifically told the medical examiner.

Why did Dr. Howell call me down here if she knew it wasn't Mindy?

Perhaps there was a simple explanation. With all the injuries the woman had, her ear could have gone unnoticed.

"You're scaring me. Are you going into shock? What's the matter?"

I shook my head. "I was just thinking about Mindy."

Mindy and I used to joke about getting tattoos. Neither of us had actually wanted one, but we were curious. We'd wondered what the fascination was, why people continued to get them. The subject didn't come up every day, usually only when we'd had a little too much to drink. Regardless, it always ended the same way, with Mindy biting her lip and recounting her fear of needles, telling how she'd reacted when her mom took her to a store in the mall to have her ears pierced.

She'd begged and pleaded with her mother for weeks. All her friends had pierced ears and she'd wanted them too, until she was there, sitting on the stool, watching the clerk pick up the silver gun. She'd usually start to laugh as she recalled how she'd been struck by an overwhelming wave of panic. How she'd screamed at the top of her lungs, completely out of control. She'd even fallen from the stool. Needless to say, she never had her ears pierced, and after we saw The Girl with the Dragon Tattoo, we never again even joked about getting a tattoo.

Dylan's warm hand rubbed a circle on the small of my back. "Why don't I take you home? I'm sure if you call Barney he'll understand. This is too hard on you. I don't like that they keep calling. I think they should call me. If I'm not sure, then I'll have you come down and confirm. That woman obviously wasn't Mindy."

I shook my head. "Thank you, but I want to be the one they call, and I can't go home. I still have work that needs to be done at the station. Besides, I don't think sitting in my apartment with only memories and a vivid imagination is a good idea."

Dylan took my hand and walked me through the building. By the time we made it to the parking lot, I'd tucked Mindy away, to a safe place. "Where's your car?"

Pointing to the left, he said, "It's right over there."

I turned and spotted his unmarked Charger.

"How about when you're done with work, you come back to my place, instead of going home to that empty apartment?" Dylan leaned closer. "You left in a hurry this morning and besides, I'd like to learn more about that vivid imagination of yours."

I blushed, liking how he'd twisted my comment. "I'd like that too, but I didn't go home yesterday, and I don't have any clean clothes. Oh, and then there's Fred. I need to check on him."

Dylan's eyes sparkled in the warm Detroit summer sunshine. "Fred's a fish. I think he'll make it. As for clothes, I have this amazing new technology. It's called a washing machine. I bought one because I'd heard they were all the rage. I can cook some dinner, you can experiment with the new technology?"

I tilted my head and sighed. "You're terrible. If I used that amazing new technology, what would I possibly wear? I mean, I need all my clothes clean."

"Oh! That's the fun part. That's where your vivid imagination comes in. If you need help"—he pulled me close, circling my waist— "I'm sure I can come up with a few ideas that don't require clothes."

I reached for his shoulders, stood up on my toes, and kissed his cheek. "Thank you for being here. I appreciate it. But I think I'll take a rain check. The same outfit at work for three days, even if it's clean, will get people talking, and seriously, you don't know Fred. He mopes if I'm not there. It's really sad to see his little blue betta fins all drooped. Bye."

As I walked away, my phone buzzed, and I opened the text message:

Dylan: FRESH SALMON?

He definitely wasn't playing fair. Cooking wasn't my thing.

I started my car and looked in my rearview mirror. Dylan hadn't pulled away. He hadn't even gotten into his car. Instead he was leaning against the Charger, his long, jean-covered legs crossed at the ankles, his black, short-sleeved shirt looking too damn good stretched over his chest. I backed my car out and drove toward him. His face lit up, glowing triumphantly from his sparkling eyes to his shiny white teeth.

I came to a stop and rolled down my window. "You're not playing fair! You know how I am about your cooking."

He laughed. "You know how I feel about yours. That's why I offered. I'll cook some salmon on the grill, with some asparagus, a few cold beers . . ." He pouted. "But if you'd rather hang out with Barney."

I shook my head. "Give me an hour and I'll call you. No promises."

He winked. "I'll be waiting."

I rolled up my window, cranked the air conditioning, and headed back to the station.

Even the thought of his cooking made my stomach rumble and growl, but no, I couldn't go back to his house tonight. It wasn't that Bernard needed me, though I needed to call him to tell him the body wasn't Mindy's. What I wanted to do had nothing to do with work or with the drug distribution happening at the port. What I wanted was to call Dr. Tracy Howell and find out why she'd called me down to the morgue twice, and what she was really trying to tell me.

I reached for my phone to call Bernard and saw my wrinkled slacks. I definitely needed to go home. Turning my car toward my apartment, I decided to call Bernard and do more research from home.

CHAPTER
SEVEN

S ara

AFTER I HEARD Jacob walk Dr. Newton to the door, I expected him to explain what the doctor meant about my training.

Will I be left alone with Sister Lilith? Will Raquel or Elizabeth be there? For some reason, I suspected that this was a women-only thing. Do I remember that or do I just suspect it?

Instead of talking to me, however, Jacob resumed his pacing. Back and forth, four steps. Though he was still taking big strides, his shoes didn't pound the floor with the force and intensity they had last night.

One, two, three, four—turn, one, two, three, four—turn . . .

I lay back and searched for my memories, hoping for something, a clue, a crumb . . . anything. I couldn't understand how I'd willingly come to this place, a place where shadows of perversion lingered outside my reach. I also wondered why I'd want to do training and if I'd done it before. Does everyone do it? If I did, why am I doing it again? I tried to clear my mind, to think about nothing, in the hope that something would come. Nothing did.

It didn't make sense. Everyone here knew me. Everyone knew my past . . . except me. I wasn't ready to face the reality that the problem must be me.

Time passed as tears slid silently from beneath the bandages and down my cheeks. Even that felt wrong. I wasn't a crier. Then again, maybe I was.

I didn't try to stop the tears. They were my wordless appeal to my husband, my unspoken request for support. I needed more than him fighting for me while others were present. I needed him to help me when we were alone, to explain why this all felt wrong. Mindlessly I wiped away the tears that I'd vowed to let rain free. The longer they fell, the more I understood: my tears didn't matter. Nothing mattered.

"Sara."

Lost in my own thoughts, I startled at Jacob's voice beside me. I hadn't heard his pacing cease. I didn't move or turn in his direction. It was too late. I didn't care anymore. If showing weakness was what it took to get his attention, then I didn't want him or his support.

Instead what I wanted was to get away . . . away to a place where I wasn't powerless, where I had a voice, where I belonged. I didn't know where that was. All I knew with increasing certainty was that it wasn't here. Here, I was trapped.

My dampened face fell toward my chest as my tears morphed into sobs, each one deeper than the one before. The cries didn't come from my throat but from my soul, consuming me. Each sob thrust deep into my heart, splitting it open, crying out for my stolen sense of self.

Under this onslaught, my heart was unable to beat at its normal rhythm, instead thudding in my chest, a dull repeating sound echoing in my ears. Without its steady rhythm I'd cease to exist. Then I realized . . . it had already happened. I no longer existed.

Whoever I really am is gone.

I gasped, but air wouldn't inflate my lungs. My heart, my lungs . . . internally I was disappearing.

The bed rail beside me lowered. Jacob lifted my hand, but I couldn't feel his touch. Even his words were gone. I heard only the sound of my cries. The bed shifted, but where our bodies connected there was no warmth. Mine no longer belonged to me. Jacob held someone else's hand, his leg pressed against someone else's thigh. The wails grew louder and louder.

Who was this desperate person?

Sara.

Jacob spoke to her, to Sara. He called her by name as he tried to calm her. His words were there, but I didn't listen. His tone was comforting, but I was beyond calming. It didn't matter, because he wasn't talking to me. He was talking to the woman on the edge of panic, the woman who willingly lived a life of subservience. A woman who could exist in this strange and terrible place.

That's not me! I didn't want any of this. I wasn't that person. There'd been a mistake, a terrible mistake. Sara and I were two different people, and somehow I had to make him understand. I didn't know who I was, but without a doubt, I wasn't Sara.

With a fleeting gasp, air finally came, finding its way to my lungs. The deep breath momentarily stilled the sobs, though the ringing in my ears continued. My inhalation brought the sharp pain back to my side. It was the hurt that Brother Timothy said was mine to bear for sins I'd committed.

Anger sparked a fire that had nearly died. I didn't commit any sins. Perhaps Sara had, I didn't know nor did I care. The only sin I recalled was allowing others to determine my future, to dominate my life and body. A cold chill went through me and a sour taste filled my mouth as I remembered Dr. Newton's recent examination. I hadn't been able to see their faces, but they had been there, both he and Jacob standing, touching and viewing my exposed body. It felt wrong, almost immoral. These people preached against sin, accused me of transgressions, yet expected me to submit to their violations.

Another jolt of pain in my side reinforced my newfound determination. Whoever I truly was, wasn't gone, not yet. I needed to fight. But I couldn't do it alone. Mentally I reached for Sara and she and I united. I wasn't her, but I needed her body to save me. I couldn't stay trapped any longer. I wouldn't.

"Sara, that's enough." Jacob's caring tone was gone. He grabbed my chin.

I pulled away from his grip.

My freedom was short-lived as Jacob recaptured my chin, his hold stronger than before.

"I'm your husband. You'll show me the respect—"

Shaking my head violently, I broke free. If I had been thinking clearly, I would have realized the futility of my protest, but I wasn't thinking clearly. I was done living someone else's life.

"Don't touch me!" I screamed, blindly pushing against his unmoving chest with a new jolt of strength. Speaking came so effortlessly that I didn't think about his warning or the consequences. The words spewed forth, louder and louder. "Stop! I'm not Sara! I'm not your wife! I don't know you!" Each statement lifted the weight of helplessness from my chest. "I don't belong here! You've all made a mis—"

My right cheek stung with the force of his slap.

Stunned back into silence, I covered my cheek and turned away. The hurt faded as I waited for Jacob's next move. My earlier misjudgment was suddenly clear. No matter who I was, in my current condition, I was at his mercy—their mercy. With my lower lip tightly held between my teeth, new tears flowed, burning my eyes and leaving a trail of shame. For the first time, I welcomed the bandages that covered my eyes. I'd use them to my advantage, hide behind them and block out the world around me. I'd try to block him out.

But I couldn't. I felt his strong hold, pinching my chin, pulling my face back to his. The lunch I'd eaten earlier solidified in my stomach.

"You. Are. Sara. Adams." Jacob spoke each word staccato, as if saying them slowly made them true. He continued to hold my face painfully close to his as he took a deep breath. His exhalation skirted across my dampened cheeks. "Your speaking restrictions will resume, but first, since you apparently are capable of talking, repeat after me"—What the hell?—"'My name is Sara Adams,'" he continued.

The stone my lunch had become in my stomach moved to my throat. I didn't speak, keeping my lip securely between my teeth. His grasp on my chin moved behind my head, forcing my tender neck forward.

His tone morphed into a menacing whisper as he spoke through clenched jaws. "'My. Name. Is. Sara. Adams.' Don't make me repeat your instructions."

My teeth released their captive and my breathing stuttered. "M-my name is Sara Adams."

Though his hand remained, the pressure eased.

"'I am the wife of Jacob Adams.'"

I swallowed my tears, tasting the salty liquid. I'd say his words; that didn't mean I believed them. "I am the wife of Jacob Adams."

He released my neck, and he moved to brush away my tears. Though his intent may have been gentle, I flinched at the contact.

"Sara, do not pull away from me. I don't want to punish you. Hurting you has never been my goal."

I stilled, holding my breath and concentrating on remaining motionless as he wiped my tears.

"Our roles are clear. As your husband, I'm the head of our household. With that title comes responsibility. You're my responsibility. Your behavior reflects on me. How do you think it looks when a man can't control his own wife? When we said our vows, you promised to honor and obey."

Though I didn't mean to respond, involuntarily my head moved ever so slightly from side to side. Had he not been holding my cheek, he might not have noticed, but he was and he did. With increased volume, Jacob said, "Sara? You've already disobeyed me by speaking. Explain why you're shaking your head."

"It's nothing," I said, my voice barely a whisper.

"Nothing?"

"I didn't mean to shake my head," I lied. I didn't remember vows, and if I'd said them, I couldn't imagine having said those. Do people really still say *obey*?

"But you did. You meant to shake your head, and now you're lying. You realize that lying is a sin, don't you?"

Oh my God! I nodded, not wanting to have this conversation. Suddenly I didn't want any conversation. I wanted to go back to not talking, to both of us not talking.

"No, Sara." He was again speaking slowly and calmly. "Right now we're talking. You may respond verbally." When I hesitated, he added, "You will respond verbally."

Is he serious?

"I'm very tired. I think maybe that when I hit my head in the accident it affected my memory. Things are fuzzy." I lowered my chin again. "Please, let me go back to sleep." I needed to use the restroom, but I wasn't about to ask for his help. Maybe Raquel or Elizabeth would return, or the nurse who'd brought my lunch. Deborah.

"Not yet. You didn't answer my question."

"Your question?" I couldn't remember his question.

"Lying. You remember what lying is, don't you?"

"Yes, I know lying is a sin."

"What happens to sinners?"

"They go to hell?"

"Was that a question?" He took my hand. "If it was, yes, when sinners die they go to hell. I'm talking about before that. I'm talking about what happens when sinners are still alive. As my wife, it's my responsibility to keep you from sin. How do I do that, Sara?"

The dryness of my mouth made speaking difficult. I truly didn't know what he wanted, but at this point I'd say whatever it was to make him go away. "Jacob, I'm sorry. I won't sin."

"That's a big promise. One that isn't your burden to bear. It's mine. It's my job to see that you live a virtuous life. It's my job to correct you when you fail. That's why I slapped you. It was punishment, punishment for disobeying, correction for your outburst." He again caressed my cheek. "It's up to you, Sara. It always has been. If you obey my rules and those of Father Gabriel, there's no need for correction. The rules keep you from sin. You don't want to be a sinner, do you?"

I shook my head, not understanding why his words affected me. "No, I don't."

Jacob lifted the end of my braid and his tone lightened. "We have a lot to discuss, and you said you're tired, but first." He paused. "It's nearly three in the afternoon. Do you need to use the restroom again?"

Damn. I hated that I needed him or anyone for such basic things. I nodded.

"Sara? We're speaking, so speak."

"Yes, I do."

The bed shifted as Jacob released my hand and stood. His footsteps moved to the right side of my bed. By the tugging, I figured that he was fumbling with my IV.

"I've watched them hook and unhook this many times," he said. "But I'm not sure how they did it." Things clanked. "This pole is on wheels. I think I can carry you and move it at the same time."

I considered offering to hold on to it, but I didn't know how the speech restriction worked. Would he tell me when it had been reinstated? Instead of talking, I waited until he pulled back the blankets. The cool air reminded me of Dr. Newton and his exam, and I shuddered.

"Jacob?"

"Yes?"

"May I tell you something?"

He smoothed my hair away from my forehead. The repetitive motion was beginning to remind me of someone petting a dog or a cat. "You've always been able to be honest with me."

Always? How long has that been? I raked my lower lip between my teeth.

"Why are you doing that? Were you not planning on being honest?"

"No, I was. It's that it's about Dr. Newton, and I don't know if I should say anything."

"You asked to speak. There must be something you want to say."

I contemplated my words. Finally I replied, "I don't remember him. That's all. Should I?" My pulse raced. I didn't remember Dr. Newton or anyone else, but that wasn't what I'd wanted to say. I'd wanted to say that Dr. Newton gave me the creeps, that I didn't like him, or Brother Timothy, or Sister Lilith, but could I? Could I be that honest?

His arms moved behind my back and under my legs. "I'm going to lift you."

I started to nod, but changed my mind and replied, "I'm ready."

As he lifted, I inhaled, clenching my teeth. By the time I exhaled through the pain from my rib, Jacob was speaking, his chest vibrating with his deep voice. I'd missed some of what he'd said.

". . . for years. I'm not sure why you wouldn't remember him. What other things don't you remember?"

He lowered me to the floor, and directed my hand to the handle. I'd learned before that the handle slid across the room, supporting me from the shower, to the sink, to the toilet.

"May I have some privacy?"

"No."

What the hell? My shoulders tensed as I searched for an appropriate response. Oh, I had a response—I just didn't think my husband would appreciate it. The words on the tip of my tongue were probably a sin too.

"Sara, you're not strong enough to move on your own. I told you that it's never been my goal to hurt you and that I'm responsible for you. Do you remember me saying that?"

"Yes."

"Very good. See, your memory's improving." Asshole, you said that a few minutes ago.

"I'm sure you'll remember more with time. For now you need my help. I wouldn't want you to fall, or be injured. Now let me help you."

I released the handle and held his shoulders as he lifted my gown and lowered my panties. My good leg stiffened and heat flooded my cheeks. If he noticed, he didn't say anything.

"Go ahead," he continued, "hold on to my neck and you can sit."

This is so embarrassing. I did as he said. With my left leg straight in the cast, I wasn't comfortable, but I was where I needed to be. Modestly I pulled my nightgown over my knees.

"You do remember that we're married, right?" The small amount of amusement in his voice brought a shy grin to my lips. Maybe this is progress.

I nodded. It was a lie, but right now my whole life was a lie. I needed to get stronger before I could fight it.

"I'll step back to the room, but I'm leaving the door open. When you need me, you may speak."

I may? So much for progress. I waited until his footsteps moved away. When I was confident he was gone, I shook my head. I wasn't sure why I did. Maybe I was rattling my brain in an effort to get everything to fall into place, to try to understand how I'd come to live this life.

The recent events went through my mind. The smile at his amusement disappeared with the thumping of my temples. He'd slapped me. My husband had actually slapped me. He'd claimed it was justifiable. He'd called it correction.

My temples entered a full throb, beating in time with my heart. I lifted my fingertips to my right cheek. It was tender, but not as tender as my left, and that had been hurt in the accident . . . how long ago?

I was glad I'd distracted Jacob from his question about what I didn't remember. I was afraid to answer honestly. After all, when I told him the truth, it earned me correction. As I thought about it, I supposed it could've been the way I said it, or more accurately, screamed it. Regardless, I didn't know if I wanted to risk it again. I believed that deep down I was a fighter; however, I wasn't stupid. I'd play this role until I figured it out.

After I finished, I called out, and Jacob helped me to the sink. When I turned the knob on the sink, my throat clenched. I'd had a drink with my lunch, but I wanted another. As I blindly fumbled around the sink, Jacob directed my hands to the dispenser of soap. Though that wasn't what I sought, I washed my hands. Once I was done, I searched again.

"What are you doing?" he asked.

Why do his questions make me uncomfortable? "I'm searching for the cup. There was one earlier when I brushed my teeth. I thought since I was here, I'd get a drink."

Handing me a towel, he replied, "If you want a drink, you need to ask."

"Well, that won't do me much good if I'm not allowed to speak." My pulse quickened as the atmosphere of the room changed. I immediately knew that I shouldn't have replied and braced myself for more correction.

Instead Jacob said, "Hold on to my neck, I'm going to take you back to bed."

I did as he said and reached for the pole attached to my IV.

"If your speech is restricted, you won't ask. You'll wait until I offer. That goes for anything, not only a drink."

As he carried me back to bed with the pole following close behind, I contemplated his answer. Why would I need to ask for everything? I don't remember my age, but I'm an adult.

Settling back onto my bed, I took a deep breath and did as he'd said. "May I have a drink?"

He didn't respond as I heard him maneuver the IV pole back to the other side of my bed and felt him straighten my blankets. Just as I debated asking again, a straw touched my lips. I sucked, wanting to reach out and hold the cup, but cautious that I'd be corrected. Unsure when I'd have another opportunity, I continued drinking as long as he offered. It wasn't until air filled the straw that he took it away.

"Thank you."

"We do have more to discuss, but you haven't officially been cleared to speak."

I nodded, waiting for more.

"For right now, you may speak only to me and only when we're alone. Is that understood?"

"Yes."

"Sara, it doesn't matter what anyone else says. No one has the authority to override my rules. No one except Father Gabriel. Remember that."

I nodded.

"This is of the utmost importance." He lifted my hand and inter-twined our fingers. "Who is your husband?"

"You."

"And who makes your rules?"

Heaviness filled my chest. Though I didn't like the answer I was about to utter, I'd learned my lesson—or Sara's lesson—and didn't hesitate. "You do."

"What will happen if you disobey me?" His warm hand tensed as he waited for my answer.

"You'll correct me." I hated the words the second they left my mouth, but by the way his lips brushed my forehead, it was the right answer, or at least the one he wanted. "May I please rest?"

I didn't want to talk anymore.

He petted my hair. "I'll put the bed back a little so you can sleep."

As it began to recline, he said, "Sara, I want what's best for you. The responsibility that Father Gabriel and God bestowed upon me as your husband is great. A component of that responsibility is your correction. It's only one part of the overall picture, but it's a part I've always taken seriously. We don't want another incident like the one that got you in this bed. To help you, I won't hesitate to reinforce your obedience. Remember that."

The bed stopped, and my thoughts drifted to the ache in my cheek. Obviously he wouldn't hesitate.

"As long as you behave appropriately," he continued, "you have nothing to fear. Father Gabriel often says that this arrangement is a blessing for wives. As a wife you don't question. By doing as you're told, you're relieved of the responsibility of decisions. Correction is at my discretion, and once it is delivered, the transgression is over. For example, today's outburst, your disobedience with speaking— you've been punished and it's done. Once the correction is complete, you no longer need to feel guilty. It's as if it never happened. It's a blessing. Don't you agree?"

Though I was sleepy, his explanation ricocheted around my brain. I didn't agree. I wasn't a child or a pet. Nevertheless I saw the appeal of putting things behind us and moving on. Then I remembered what Brother Timothy had said, that only Father Gabriel could decide if my punishment was complete. The anticipation of what was yet to come was unnerving. Instead of answering I asked, "Are corrections always corporal?"

"See what I mean? Isn't it better to not worry about that and move on?"

I was fading into sleepiness. I wasn't sure if the answer I was about to utter was mine or Sara's, but either way, it felt like the easiest way to end this discussion and allow me to rest.

"Yes, thank you."

"You're welcome. Now get some sleep."

I nodded against the pillow. I didn't want to think about the people with the strange familial titles or about governing bodies that held unknown power. As much as I hated myself for condoning any part of Jacob's correction, I was thankful that my outburst was behind us. For my sanity I needed to fall asleep thinking about the man who'd defended and helped me, not the husband I couldn't remember who claimed to be my disciplinarian.

Is that what Sara did? Is that how she survived?

CHAPTER
EIGHT

S ara

I CAN DO THIS . . .

To survive I needed to convince myself that I could reclaim my life. No matter how hard I wished, my current situation wasn't a dream or even a nightmare—if it were, I could wake and it would be over. So far three days and nights had passed and I was still here, in Sara's life.

During the last night, I had awakened to the sound of Jacob's steady breathing. Knowing he was asleep, I lay awake thinking about everything. I thought about the things that people took for granted and vowed to myself that in the future, I'd value the mundane knowledge that most people never questioned. I would, because I now knew what it was like to have it outside my reach. Simple, basic facts were gone. I couldn't recall my own reflection, the color of my eyes or hair, or the shape of my face. My birthday and even my age were mysteries. I didn't know if I had family, other than Jacob, though I assumed that if we had children he would've mentioned them, especially during some part of his responsibility discussion.

Sadly, I didn't know me.

Yet there were some aspects of this life that had felt clear. Like Raquel and Elizabeth. With them everything seemed right, as if I were safe. The opposite was true about the strange people with titles that seemed unfamiliar. Merely the mention of their names and the brother and sister references caused my chest to tighten and pulse to quicken. Though I couldn't recall my past, the anxiety those people and their power instilled in me was palpably real.

Jacob remained unclear. As I had listened to his breathing, knowing that he was once again sleeping with his head upon my bed, I'd found myself conflicted by his dichotomy. His presence, even in sleep, gave me a sense of protection from the outside world. With him near, I didn't fear the Commission, Dr. Newton, or even the apparently all-powerful Father Gabriel. Jacob was my husband and my protector. And yet a sense of uncertainty also nagged at my soul. Yes, he kept me safe from everything outside our bubble—it was inside our bubble that concerned me.

Due to my injuries my options were limited, but they did exist. Jacob had made that clear. I could obey his and Father Gabriel's rules or disobey them—it was up to me. In my darkened world, I decided to do my best to obey. I definitely had issues with what I was obeying, with how my husband believed he had the right to exercise complete domination at his discretion. I didn't understand how I'd gotten to this point or why I'd agreed to this in the past. However, the large gaps—really, gaping caverns—in my memory gave me hope. I must've had a reason. Apparently at one time I'd willingly chosen him and this life. I must have seen more to my husband. Maybe if I learned to think like Sara, I could figure out how to survive.

Following Dr. Newton's examination, I'd admittedly been over-whelmed. I had been rendered powerless to communicate, my emotions too jumbled to articulate. At that time, my body began to surrender, but as I drifted toward nothingness, my mind fought back. During my outburst I'd learned something about myself. I'd learned that I was a survivor, not a quitter, and I wouldn't quit fighting.

My verbal tirade had come from the depths of panic. If I wanted to win my fight—if I wanted not only to survive, but to recover and remember—I needed to battle smarter.

My first goal was to get stronger. And as I did, I needed to understand my battlefield. Lashing out in the darkness wasn't, and wouldn't be, successful. I needed to size up my opponents, distinguish my allies from my enemies, and learn the rules of my new war.

Jacob believed I already knew his and Father Gabriel's rules, and he expected me to follow them. I'd obey as long as those rules helped me heal and gain strength. Plus, admittedly, I didn't want to fight alone. I needed allies in this strange world. It seemed clear that my battle would be better fought with Jacob than against him.

I'd heard his determination when he answered Brother Timothy and Sister Lilith's questions, and when he argued with Dr. Newton. I'd also felt his slap—his correction.

Jacob stood strong for what he believed, and he believed that I was his wife, Sara. He was willing to fight for that. I was going to fight to discover myself. If I truly was Sara, then we were striving for the same thing.

Since my eyes were covered and my speaking was restricted, my battle plan was to concentrate on surveillance. I'd spend my days as a sponge, absorbing everything around me. In many ways sight blinded people to the truth, and in my current condition I wasn't preoccupied by appearances or visual distractions. The bandages allowed me to go beyond the surface and hear the true intentions of those around me.

"Sara," Jacob said, pulling me from my thoughts and back to the present.

He held a straw to my lips. As I sipped, the water moistened my throat, helping me wash down the oatmeal he'd been feeding me. I'd obediently accepted each spoonful but I hadn't liked it. It was warm and slightly sweet, but it was also thick, too thick to drink and yet not thick enough to chew. Thankfully, it hadn't been my only food. I'd also had a banana and toast and had even been allowed to hold them and feed myself. As I continued sipping the water, he spoke.

"I'm going to need to leave soon for Assembly. I wanted to talk to Sister Lilith, to remind her that you're still not cleared to speak. I'll talk with Raquel, and she can relay my message. I don't want her trying to . . . well, even if she tells you that you're cleared to speak, remember that I said no."

I had no intention of speaking with Sister Lilith, though I was becoming increasingly curious about what she planned to say. Since Jacob and I were still alone, I whispered, "I promise, I won't speak." I got the feeling that this training made him as uncomfortable as it did me. If we were fighting on the same side, I wanted to reassure him that my compliance wasn't in question. "I've given everything you've told me a lot of thought. You can trust me to do as you've said." I reached to find his hand. Once I found it, I added, "I hope you already do . . . trust me, I mean. After all, we're married. You trusted me enough to ask me to be your wife, didn't you?" I was fishing for more about our past.

He cleared his throat. "Um, yes."

I didn't know what his answer meant, but I tried for more. "May I continue?"

"Sara, we have rules, not just my rules—the community's rules, The Light's rules. I'm sure reminding you of some of those will be part of Sister Lilith's plan."

"OK."

"Tell me you remember them. After all, we've lived and abided by The Light for a while now."

How long is a while? I pressed my lips together and lowered my chin. "I'm sorry, I don't. I want to." I did. I wanted to understand the world around me.

"That's why it's better to listen when Sister Lilith is here. Be cautious of what you agree to or disagree with. She and Brother Timothy have been very suspicious of what preceded your accident. I don't want her interpreting your lack of memory as guilt."

A sheen of perspiration coated my freshly washed skin. "B-but," I stuttered, "I really don't remember. Please." I squeezed his hand. "You answered their questions before. What you said, that's all I know. Tell me what happened."

"I will, but not yet."

"Why?"

Jacob sighed. "One strictly enforced rule was put into place by Father Gabriel to teach patience. That's one of the reasons so many of us follow him. He has answers, reasons behind each decree. He didn't create the rules for The Light arbitrarily; each one has meaning and purpose. As I said, this rule teaches that patience is a virtue. God's word instructs men to marry virtuous women. Therefore all women of The Light, such as yourself, are forbidden from questioning men, including your husband. This teaches you, and all the women, patience. Answers will be revealed in God's time, not yours."

I tried to understand. "You're saying that I can't ask you what happened? I'm supposed to wait until you tell me?"

"Yes," he said with a laugh. Kissing the top of my head, he added, "You do realize that was a question, yes?"

The corners of my lips moved upward. "No, I mean, now I do." I let go of his hand as my smile faded. "Does that mean you're going to . . . correct me?"

He reached for my hand. "I wish we had more time to discuss this right now." His thumb slowly moved in a circle, caressing my knuckles. "We originally learned all of this together. That was easier than explaining it now. It feels like I'm introducing you to a whole new way of life when in truth we chose this path together. Do you remember yesterday when I told you that I'd accepted responsibility for you?"

I nodded, trying unsuccessfully to stop my slight trembling.

"Part of that responsibility," he continued, "includes recognizing that not all violations are equal." He leaned closer and his body warmed my side. When he lifted my hand to his lips, my shaking stilled. Instead of correction, he was delivering gentle kisses to the tops of my knuckles. "Sara, whether you recall the particulars or not, we have a good marriage. You're not abused; you're disciplined. Correction is never done in anger. Father Gabriel teaches that men must lead. It's our job, how we were created. Taking responsibility for you is required, but you and I love one another and I accepted that challenge willingly. I do what I need to do to help you and make your life easier. Correction defines your boundaries, giving you the freedom to feel safe. Since the delivery of the correction, as well as the mode, is up to me, I can also decide when there are exceptions, times when correction isn't necessary. Part of my responsibility is to decipher intent." He lifted my chin. "I don't think that a moment ago you intended to question again, did you?"

I shook my head. "No, I didn't."

"I believe you. Your honesty is part of this equation. Sara, we've always been honest with one another. Don't let this problem with your memory change that."

I still didn't like the premise, but his explanation and absolution eased a bit of my apprehension. "Thank you for explaining. I'm sorry that I don't remember all of the rules. I'll try." I wanted to remember. I also liked this Jacob, the one who explained things. I wanted him on my side.

"I know you will. I'll be back as soon as I can. Sara." His tone changed when he said my name, clearly meaning that whatever he was about to say was beyond question. "No more talking, and be cognizant of your nonverbal responses to Sister Lilith's questions."

I nodded.

"Very good," Jacob said, petting my hair as he stood. The bed shifted and the warmth of his body against mine vanished. The tangible void sent a chill through me, reminding me that soon I'd be left alone—alone with Sister Lilith.

"Brother Jacob?"

Warmth returned as I grinned toward the sound of Raquel's now familiar voice from the doorway. It wasn't the first time she'd entered my room today. She'd been in earlier to help with my shower. Well, not really with my shower. Jacob had done that. She'd helped by putting whatever she used over my cast to keep it dry. Jacob was the one who'd washed my body. I'd expected to remember his touch, but I hadn't. It didn't feel wrong—it felt foreign, but then again, so did everything else.

Just now, when he'd kissed my hand, the sensation was different, unexpected—soft and affectionate. I liked that side of my husband. That was the side that made me feel safe and loved. I blushed at the memory of his using that word, saying that we loved one another. Even if I didn't remember, I was loved.

Lost in my thoughts, I'd forgotten my plan to be a sponge and missed part of Raquel and Jacob's conversation.

". . . I want that made perfectly clear." I didn't need to hear Jacob's entire speech. I knew what he was emphasizing.

"I will," Raquel replied. "I'd be happy to stay with Sara, to make this easier for her on her first day. Sister Lilith can't deny my presence, if you authorize it."

My heart leaped. I wanted it, but she wasn't asking me. Actually, she wasn't asking Jacob either—she was offering. Sucking my lower lip between my teeth, I made a mental note to think about semantics later and waited for his response. There was definitely a trick to being a . . . what did he call it? . . . a woman of The Light.

"Thank you." He sighed with relief. "By the smile on my wife's face, if she'd stop biting that lip, I think she'd be happy to have you." He tugged my lip free. "Remember my rules."

I nodded, grinning over his answer.

"I'll be back as soon as I can." His lips brushed the top of my head, then the door opened and he was gone.

"Sara," Raquel said once we were alone. "Are you nervous about this? You've done it before; we all have. It's pretty standard for one of the Commission wives to do a review after an incident. Father Gabriel believes that it helps all of us stay focused on his teachings. After something as traumatic as your accident, evil thoughts could try to confuse your mind. If you didn't go through a review, others in the community could question your commitment, and that could lead to dissent. The Light practices a single mind-set of enlightenment, all working as one, doing God's work, and fulfilling Father Gabriel's teaching." She giggled lightheartedly. "Oh, listen to me going on. I know you know all of that. Feel free to reach out and push me if I talk too much."

I wanted to tell her I didn't know, or at least I didn't remember. Either way, I appreciated her talking. I was also relieved to learn that this wasn't specifically about me. It was common protocol.

Hoping she was watching, I mouthed, Thank you.

"Oh, you say that now," she answered, as if I'd spoken. "After a few hours of listening to her read Father Gabriel's word and preaching at you, you won't be thanking me." She pulled the blankets back and moved the wheelchair close. "Brother Jacob must have brought you some more nightgowns. I meant to say something earlier. That's a great color on you."

Really? What color is it?

I reached over to my braid.

"You're good at that. Or did Brother Jacob do it?"

I shook my head with an amused grin.

"I wasn't sure, but it's pretty. I'm better at helping other people braid than doing it myself. I guess that's why this is my calling, helping others. If I had to braid my own hair, well, it'd look awful. That's why I usually wear mine in a bun, or a messy bun, or sometimes..."

Sister Raquel filled every moment after Jacob's departure with talk and the entire time, though I never said a word, I was part of the conversation. Soon I was back in bed and completely relaxed. I laughed at some of her stories and also practiced my sponging, learning things by listening to her friendly voice. I also learned more about my training. She joked that I'd undoubtedly already heard all the lessons and sermons that Sister Lilith would recite, and if I promised not to snore, I could probably catch a catnap under my bandages and still be able to answer all her questions.

When Sister Raquel mentioned her husband, Benjamin, her voice filled with adoration. I got the sense that their relationship was similar to what Jacob had described, one where she put her full trust in Benjamin and he assumed full responsibility for her. Her obvious contentment with her marriage gave me hope for my own. The only time she sounded sad was at the mention of children, sharing that she and Benjamin didn't have any. Even then, she quickly said that she believed God would provide them in His time. She confessed in a whisper that she needed to work on her patience.

I realized that if she and Benjamin were trying to have children, Father Gabriel must not preach against sex. For some reason that made me smile. I couldn't remember having been with Jacob in that way, but he said we had a good marriage and loved one another. The idea of being intimate didn't scare me as much as the thought of his correction. As a matter of fact, as my thoughts lingered on his washing and drying me, parts of my body woke from their sleep. I pondered who my husband was in the bedroom. Is he the protector with a reassuring tone or the disciplinarian who demands obedience?

I wouldn't be finding out as long as my leg and rib were in their current conditions, but with the way my insides tingled, I suspected that whoever he was, I liked him.

Raquel's conversation reassured me. Instead of facing Sister Lilith alone, I would have her by my side. Therefore when the door opened and Sister Lilith's high-heeled shoes entered, I was confident that I was ready to begin.

"Sister Sara," she began, "It's Sister Lilith. I'm happy to see you're ready to start this review of your training."

I nodded.

Raquel sat beside me on the bed where Jacob had been as she spoke. "I'm sorry if you weren't notified, Sister Lilith. Brother Jacob asked me to stay, at least for today. You see, Sara can't get to and from her bed to the bathroom by herself. Brother Jacob didn't want to burden you with the task." Though I'd zoned out through part of Jacob and Raquel's conversation, I didn't think Jacob had gone into that much detail.

"Well, yes," Sister Lilith replied. "We could always call for you . . ."

"Sister, I would go"—Sister Raquel's shoulder rubbed mine as it shrugged with her casual reply—"but I'm confident that Benjamin would punish me if I disobeyed Brother Jacob. And I wouldn't want Brother Timothy to learn that you suggested my disobedience."

"Of course not," she responded quickly. "Sister Raquel, we'll make do with all three of us today. I wasn't suggesting disobedience. We'll just forget that we even discussed it."

Oh, that is definitely a conversation I'm glad I sponged. I liked Raquel. "Sister Raquel?" Sister Lilith asked. "Before we begin, do you know Dr. Newton's plans for Sister Sara's cast? I believe I heard she'll be receiving a walking cast soon." From the sound of the chair over the tile, I could tell she'd brought it from beside my bed toward the foot.

"I don't. He'll be here later. I'll let him know you're curious."

"Thank you. I'm just thinking it'll make our future review sessions easier for Sister Sara."

"Yes, I understand."

"Now, Sister Sara, since you're unable to respond, once I've read Father Gabriel's declaration of faith for The Light, I'll ask you basic yes-and-no questions. Your answers will help me determine where we'll go from there. Do you understand?"

I nodded.

Pages fluttered. "We the members of The Light believe in Father Gabriel and the enlightenment . . ."

CHAPTER

NINE

J acob

Father Gabriel began each morning at Assembly with prayer. Only the members of the Assembly and the Commission were worthy to meet daily with our leader, though that privilege didn't always mean meeting in person.

Our campus in Alaska was one of three campuses of The Light. Ours, the Northern Light, was the largest and the most productive, but Father Gabriel's leadership was needed at all campuses. Because of this he often traveled. Though all the communities lived modestly, The Light possessed the latest technology. With protected webinars and teleconferencing, and because of different time zones, it didn't matter where Father Gabriel was on any given day. He was always able to attend the morning Assembly of each campus.

Whether he was with us, or somewhere else, his aura of authority filled the room.

There were four commissioners at each campus, making up Father Gabriel's circle of twelve disciples. These were Father Gabriel's inner sanctum, the men he most trusted. Under the Commissioners there were twelve Assemblymen at each campus. The Assemblymen shared the Commissioners' burdens and were fully accountable to them. These sixteen men and their wives were the chosen of each campus. The system Father Gabriel put into place worked well to govern The Light and was especially efficient when he was away and as the campuses continued to grow.

At last census the Northern Light had over 450 followers who all lived, worshipped, and worked for Father Gabriel and The Light. The Western Light had nearly three hundred, and the Eastern Light, the first campus, had over one hundred. The Eastern Light purposely remained small due to its urban location. It had neither the space nor the isolation of the Northern and Western Light communities. The Eastern Light served primarily as the point of entry for many of the followers. Once they were tested and found acceptable, they were assigned to one of the larger campuses. Assignment was usually based on the follower's abilities as well as the needs of each campus.

As Father Gabriel's voice transcended the miles and his prayer wished blessings on our souls, my thoughts returned to Sara, to Sister Lilith's intentions, and Sara's healing.

This is wrong. My body and mind should be focused on Father Gabriel.

Internal conflict was one reason I'd resisted the assignment of a wife. Another reason was my desire to succeed. Throughout my life, no matter the endeavor—from the military to The Light—my goal had always been success. With the addition of a wife, everything changed. For the first time, success wasn't contingent only upon me, but also upon Sara.

Before the Commission assigned a follower a wife, especially one in need of indoctrination, the husband-to-be received training. As a member of the Assembly, I'd been involved with many trainings. I knew the strict protocol and what was expected.

Since my assignment to the Assembly nearly a year ago, I'd listened to followers who claimed to be having difficulty with the indoctrination protocol. From my lofty position, I'd piously remind those followers that they were but a part of Father Gabriel's body of believers, as were their new wives, and all parts of the body must work together. I'd said, "We've been taught that if something causes us to lose our way, we must remove it. It's written that if your eye causes you to stumble, gouge it out. It's better to enter the kingdom of Light with only one eye than to be cast out." Then I'd ask, "Is your new wife causing you to lose your way, to forget Father Gabriel's teachings, or will you be able to control her and help her become a productive member of the body?"

Though everyone claimed they'd succeed, there were failures. Insubordinate members of the body were banished and removed— the ultimate penalty, paid with the ultimate price. My head knew the answers. Hell, I'd said the answers. I also knew the consequences.

However, now, for the first time in my memory, I felt conflicted. I was supposed to train and rule Sara, yet in a very short time, even without her eyes and with a limited ability to speak, she'd developed a power over me. When she'd asked me about my asking her to marry me, I was taken aback, and when her hands trembled at the mere thought of my correction, my stomach turned. Kissing her hand was a reflex. I didn't consider the penalties. I knew the prescribed timetable. At this point my affection was to be limited and nonsexual. The touching of her hair and even platonic kisses to her head were acceptable, but not affection or comfort, not yet.

As Father Gabriel concluded the opening prayer, guilt tugged at my conscience, and I contemplated confessing my affectionate behavior. The only thing stopping me was concern regarding punishment. I didn't worry about myself; I never had. I was a firm believer that if I did wrong, I deserved correction. I'd never expected less of myself than I did of my subordinates. Everyone was accountable.

Now was different. Though I hadn't planned on it, nor wanted it, now I cared. I cared about someone other than myself. I knew what Sara had endured and what was still to come.

"...blessed by me, Father Gabriel, The Light of our God. Amen."

"Amen," came resoundingly from all sixteen men around the large conference table. I scanned the eyes around me.

Do they also have these conflicting thoughts or is it just me?

As soon as my gaze was met by Brother Timothy's, I knew that I wouldn't confess my show of affection. I couldn't risk it, not as long as Sara was vulnerable. With Brother Timothy's eyes on me, I refused to show or admit to weakness.

I'd never understood the animosity that glowed in his eyes. When I'd first arrived at the Northern Light nearly three years before, he and Sister Lilith were the only unwelcoming followers. With time I'd learned to ignore them. Their enmity didn't affect my goal. Even after being appointed to the Assembly, I was able to ignore them.

Suddenly the thought crossed my mind: the Commission had assigned Sara to me.

Was I assigned Sara to fail? Does Brother Timothy dislike me so much as to capitalize on this unfamiliar assignment? Will Sara undo my success?

I forced myself to concentrate on the words spoken around me. The Assemblymen had begun reading their daily reports. We each had a specific topic, and since each topic was approached daily, the reports were often quick. It was a good way to keep the Assembly, the Commission, and Father Gabriel current on the overall status of the community.

My primary job for The Light was as one of the pilots. I transported Father Gabriel from campus to campus and flew supplies to the Northern Light. My military training had been significant in preparing me for The Light. Most importantly, I'd flown a C-12A in and out of Iraq, and also, I thrived under the regimented life. Taking and giving orders, as well as following and implementing rules, were my forte.

As an Assemblyman I was to oversee and settle disputes. Father Gabriel required cohesive living on all his campuses. Everyone's behavior was continually monitored. Any disobedience was brought to me. If I believed the behavior warranted correction, I took the offense to the Commission. If the Commission forwarded it to Father Gabriel, the usual course of action was public correction. Banishment was the ultimate punishment. Simply the knowledge that such punishments were possible served as a powerful deterrent.

Brother Raphael, the longest-standing Commissioner, conducted the morning meetings. At the Northern Light he was second in reverence only to Father Gabriel. His deep voice reverberated through the conference room. "Brother Jacob, please share your report."

I stood and addressed the Commission and Assembly. After my report was complete, he asked Brother Luke about some new followers. Luke and his wife Elizabeth were responsible for all new followers at the Northern Light.

Luke went on, talking about a husband and wife who'd come to The Light, how they were progressing well with their training and would soon be granted an apartment. Brother Raphael went on to ask the Assemblyman in charge of housing how soon an apartment would be ready. As they discussed the possible housing and job assignments for this new couple, the temperature of the room seemed to rise and my palms moistened. Though I knew Sara was the next topic of conversation, I tried to think of anything else. The way Brother Raphael had retained his Boston accent through all the years. The way Luke's back straightened with pride as he spoke about the new followers' success.

My eyes met Brother Timothy's and his cold glare interrupted my thoughts. Purposely I moved my gaze to Brother Daniel's face and took in its approving shine. As my overseer, Brother Daniel had repeatedly put his trust in me and my abilities.

Damn, I have to do this. I won't fail him or add fuel to Brother Timothy's dislike.

"Brother Jacob," Brother Raphael said. "I could ask Brother Luke, but let's skip ahead. Your new wife is awake. Please tell us how things are progressing at the clinic, and if you believe we have any problems or glitches with her progress."

I stood again and inhaled, my usual confidence waning. If I didn't say something about my unease, I feared it'd be noticed. I needed to tackle the subject head on. "I apologize for my less-than-stellar presentation. I've spent the last ten nights sleeping in a chair, my head on the end of Sara's bed." I shrugged my shoulders. "It's less than conducive to a good night's sleep. If my demeanor seems off, I plead matrimonial insomnia."

Benjamin laughed, breaking my mounting tension and coming to my rescue. "No, Brother Jacob, in another month we can rib you about matrimonial insomnia; now you're just exhausted. At least in a month you'll have a smile." Laughter came from all around the table before Benjamin continued, "Raquel told me about your wife. It sounds as though she's coming along."

I nodded, eternally grateful for the change in formality. "Being in this position is considerably different from training someone for it. Currently Sister Lilith"—I turned toward my nemesis—"thank you, Brother Timothy, currently Sister Lilith is beginning Sara's training."

"Why?" Brother Raphael spoke sharply.

"I was told—"

Brother Timothy interrupted. "You see, Sara seemed to be doing well, very well, and she isn't coming to us as a mere follower. She'll be filling the role of a wife of an Assemblyman, part of the chosen. Her success is paramount and, after what has happened in the past . . . we believed it was better to jump ahead and begin Sara's training. Father Gabriel teaches that an idle mind is the devil's playground. Keeping Sara occupied, engaged, and learning is—"

"Brother Jacob?" The entire room stopped—moving, breathing,

everything—at the rare sound of Father Gabriel's voice. He was often more of an observer of our meetings than a participant.

"Yes, Father Gabriel." I turned respectfully toward the screen.

"I want to hear the particulars, not about what others are doing. Sara was given to you. You've been absent from us since her arrival and accident over a week ago until yesterday. Yesterday you pleaded the case for her nutrients. I see what's happening. I want to hear it from you."

He sees what's happening? What does that mean?

My pulse quickened. "Father, what particulars?"

"Taking on a wife is a big responsibility. The Lord chose the church as his bride, and now your bride has arrived. It's your responsibility to acclimate her. Tell us, how is it progressing?"

"I believe it's progressing well. So far she doesn't seem to have memories of her life in the dark. She's nervous and scared, which is normal. The loss of sight, as well as her injuries, are keeping her dependent. I'm doing what I've told others to do, teaching her the rules, her role as my wife, and the restrictions she can expect, all the while convincing her this was, and has been, her life." I took a breath. "Speaking of restrictions, I know her sight must be restricted until some of her injuries heal. However, I'd like to have the cast on her leg changed to one that would allow her to wa—"

"It's not time!" Brother Timothy interjected.

"Brother Timothy." Father Gabriel's voice transcended the miles. "It wasn't time for Sister Lilith to begin training either. Let Brother Jacob continue. And let me make myself clear: I don't want history to repeat itself. The Eastern Light usually weeds out failures. Sara is at the Northern Light. We must all work toward her success."

"Yes, Father," Brother Timothy replied.

"Brother Jacob, tell us if there have been any problems."

"Only one." I swallowed. "Though Sara was forbidden to speak, yesterday she did."

Murmurs came from around the table.

"What was your response?" Father Gabriel asked.

"I corrected her. I take my responsibility seriously. The Commission is ultimately responsible, but it's my duty to teach, correct, and bring her into The Light."

The room waited as Father Gabriel sat quietly, his fingers steepled before him, thinking and watching. His customary shirt and tie, without a suit coat, were a stark contrast to the cherry-paneled wall behind him.

"Yes," Father Gabriel finally said. "Brother Timothy was right—most new followers don't come into The Light as chosen. Sister Sara has already achieved a status most women never will. While this is unusual, thankfully, Brother Jacob, you have a better understanding of the acclimation protocol than the average follower. I'm pleased to learn that you're compliant and capable of handling situations as they occur. I'm certain you're aware of the consequences not only to Sara but to you should this indoctrination fail?"

"Yes, Father, I am," I answered, steadfast.

"Brother Luke," Father Gabriel continued. "Sister Sara's continued treatment is under your supervision. You and Dr. Newton decide when it's time for her cast to be changed. However, I have a few more questions for Brother Jacob."

"Yes, Father?"

"Tell us how your wife responded when she learned of your control over her necessities: eating, using the restroom, sleeping, drinking, and hygiene."

"She hasn't fought my control. She's acquiesced."

"And when you corrected her? What did you do? How did she respond?"

I looked toward Brother Daniel. His expression instructed me to answer honestly. The lump in my throat grew, but I continued. "When she spoke, without permission, I utilized corporal punishment. I slapped her. It was a swift carriage of correction."

"Acceptable," Father Gabriel replied. "Go on."

"I then required her to repeat her name and that we were wed." Before anyone could speak, I added, "And she did. That was yesterday. This morning I discussed it with her further. Though she seems confused, I believe she's a quick learner and is adapting."

I wasn't completely forthcoming—I didn't tell them about her trembling or my affection—but I'd answered truthfully.

"Brother Jacob?" Brother Timothy's voice dominated the room.

"Yes?"

"We know what happened during the incident. Tell the Commission what happened yesterday during Dr. Newton's examination."

I stood taller and clenched my teeth. Timothy's question meant one thing: Newton had talked to him.

"Was there a problem?" Luke asked.

"I take the responsibility you've entrusted to me very seriously," I began. "That goes for all my responsibilities, from my quest to follow The Light to my assignment on the Assembly. One day Sara will be mine in all ways. I've helped her with things that by The Light's decree aren't to be shared by those not bound by marriage. Father, you speak of modesty for our women. Therefore I demanded to be present during Dr. Newton's examination, and only allowed him access to Sara's injuries." I took a deep breath and turned back to Brother Daniel. I wouldn't mention her questioning her eyes unless it was brought up.

"Brother Timothy?" Brother Daniel asked. "Is there something I missed? Are you aware of anything else that happened during Sister Sara's examination that wasn't acceptable?"

I held my breath as Timothy glared in my direction.

"Dr. Newton doesn't believe he was allowed full access to his patient."

"Brother Timothy?"

We all turned toward Father Gabriel's voice.

"Yes, Father?" Timothy responded.

"Perhaps you've forgotten what it's like to have a new wife. I believe Brother Jacob's protectiveness is supported by my doctrine. Do you see a problem with that? If so, please, Brother, enlighten us."

I bit my tongue, wanting to interject, but happy with Father Gabriel's input.

"No, not at all." Brother Timothy sat taller. "However, I'm concerned that we won't be able to get a good assessment of Sister Sara until Dr. Newton and my wife are able to spend significant time with her."

"Fine. Brother Jacob." Father Gabriel changed the subject. "Have you continued Sister Sara's speech restriction? Since she's spoken, she obviously knows she can do so without damage to her vocal cords?"

"Yes, Father. I'm only allowing her to speak with me."

"And?"

"And she's obeyed. I realize that speaking now is sooner than the protocol recommends. For that reason, Father, I request your permission to allow her to only speak to me, for the next few days. As we all know, this early stage of indoctrination is extremely formative. If you agree, I'd continue to allow Sister Lilith's training and Sister Raquel's assistance. Of course Dr. Newton can treat her, with me present, but I request that for now she only be questioned in a yes-no format by anyone other than me." This was a rare opportunity to bypass the Commission, and I presented my case. "She's still confused, as is standard. Even if she's allowed to get the walking cast, with her other injuries she won't be able to move without pain. I understand this important stage. I've seen what can happen. For Sara, myself, and our future family, I ask that I be allowed to be the one who walks my wife into The Light."

My request was brazen and unusual, but then again, Brother Timothy was right, most women were given to followers who needed the guidance of the Assembly. As a member of the Assembly, I was exercising my right, or so I hoped.

"Brother, after Assembly, I'll meet with the Commission. Brother Daniel will contact you later with my answer. Shall we carry on?"

"Thank you, Father," I said, resuming my seat and avoiding Brother Timothy's glare.

"Now," Brother Raphael said. "It's time for our report regarding the powerhouse. With the colder-than-normal November temperatures, tell us about the turbines. Is there any fear of them freezing?"

TWO AND A HALF hours after I'd left Sara, I returned to the clinic. Though parts of it resembled a hospital, only Dr. Newton had a medical degree. The others who staffed the clinic were there on assignment based on their attributes. Most of the support staff's skills were acquired here at the Northern Light, unless they came willingly with prior knowledge. Either way, the dedication and commitment of the followers made them excellent learners. As I approached Sara's room, one of the only single rooms—the primary one used for acclimation of acquired followers—I listened.

Hearing only silence, I assumed Lilith had left. Though I considered looking for Raquel to learn more about the training, I chose instead to open the door. I was right: Sara was alone. With the head of her bed reclined, I saw only the back of her head, her golden braid loose from lying against the pillow. I waited for her to turn, wondering if she was awake or asleep, and then I heard the sniffles and saw her shoulders shudder. She was awake—and was crying.

Clenching my teeth, sure that this was Lilith's doing, I moved cautiously to the side of her bed and continued my assignment.

"Sara?"

At the sound of my voice, her shoulders sagged. Slowly she turned in my direction. Her cheeks were damp and blotchy. The bandages, with their solid domed patch over each eye, allowed her tears to escape. When she didn't speak, I moved closer. Raising the head of her bed and lowering the side rail, I sat beside her. Fear and sadness not only showed on her wet cheeks but settled around her like a cloud.

Screw the timetable and the rules. She won't make it through this in this shape.

With my leg against her wounded body, I grabbed a tissue and began to dry her cheeks.

Where the hell is Raquel, and most importantly, what did Lilith do?

My chest ached at Sara's labored breathing. Surely she had things to say, but she was obeying my last command and remaining silent. When her breathing finally settled, I said, "No one else is here, you may speak. What is it? Why are you crying?"

TEN

S tella

DETROIT IN JULY might as well be Miami. The humidity and heat were as intense without the benefit of the Atlantic Ocean. The Detroit River was definitely not as spectacular. Stepping into the cool air conditioning of Jumbo's, I eyed a table near the back, next to a pool table. Thankfully, it was still too early for the players to be out. Come ten o'clock, this place would be rocking.

Though I'd been thinking about that cold beer Dylan had mentioned before I left him in the parking lot, I ordered lemonade and sat down to wait for Dr. Howell.

I kept remembering the pierced ear of the woman on the table—well, more accurately, the injured ear. Maybe it wasn't a piercing injury. Maybe I'd read too much into the expression I thought I saw when Tracy Howell looked at me.

When I looked up, I smiled, seeing the doctor walking toward me. She'd looked young at the morgue, but now, with a maxi-skirt, T-shirt, and flip-flops, and her long, dark hair flowing loosely down her back, she looked more like a high school student than a forensic pathologist.

Dr. Howell didn't return my smile as she settled in the seat across from me. Glancing from side to side, she did little to hide her nerves. "Stella," she began. "Once again, I apologize for calling you in today. The blonde hair and the body type, both similar to Mindy's . . . I just had to be sure."

"Doctor, how many unidentified bodies—female bodies—do you see?"

She shrugged. "Too many."

I tilted my head. "I've been called down twice in two weeks, for blonde females. Is that par for the course?"

Dr. Howell's let her eyes fall to the table, suddenly interested in a sticky substance left by patrons before us. "I'd be happy to talk about Mindy Rosemont."

"That's the thing, I think we are. I think you're trying to tell me something." With my hair secured in a low ponytail, my exposed brow rose questioningly. "Is there any chance that I'm on to something?"

She sighed and leaned forward. "I can't be quoted."

"You won't be. I'm not sure if this will become a story. I don't even know if this will help me find Mindy or at least find out what happened to her, but please, tell me what you know. If I'm totally off base then we can get a beer, rack some balls, and call it a night."

Dr. Howell looked at me contemplatively. For a moment I expected her to stand and walk to the cue box, but then she sat back and sighed. "Let's start by you calling me Tracy. I'm not sure what I know. I've only been with the Wayne County ME for about five months, but from what I've seen, something is going on. We see a lot of gang and gun violence, and historically, the profile of our unclaimed bodies tends to be young males. Ethnicity varies. It used to be more Blacks and Latinos, but not anymore. White males are dying as fast as everyone else. Those deaths are sad, but they make sense. There are multiple causes: fights, shootings, knives, and of course drugs. With drug deaths we see women too, many of those are prostitutes. The thing that's different about the more recent female bodies is that many don't have illegal drugs in their systems. Some, like the one today, are beaten up, but not all. As you've heard, we have a backlog on rape kits. But the ones that have been completed often don't show sexual activity. Many of them have varying degrees of that burned-off fingerprint thing."

"Are they all blondes?"

"No, their hair color doesn't seem to matter. They range in age from about eighteen to about thirty." She slapped the table and firmed her shoulders. "Do you see the problem?"

My eyes widened. "Besides the obvious issue of women dying all around us?"

"I'm talking about the lack of consistency. I've taken my concerns to my bosses and been told that it is what it is. We report our findings to the National Center for Health Statistics and they compile statistical data. If there's an unusual occurrence in their findings, they'll notify the police and Wayne County. But I don't think there will be a statistically significant occurrence. The victims vary just enough. While men go missing, it's the women that I'm the most concerned about. The ones I've seen, or learned about while going back in the records, also vary in ethnicity."

I sipped my lemonade and thought about all she'd just said. "You knew that the woman today wasn't Mindy, didn't you?"

"I want you to find your friend. I just thought . . ."

I reached out and covered her hand. "I can't promise anything. I won't even take any of this to Bernard until I have more, but I'll look around, ask some questions, do some research. If there's any chance that this information will help me find Mindy, I'll do it."

Tracy nodded. "I can't go on the record, but if there's any way I can help, if you need information, I can . . ." She reached into her purse and took out a flash drive. Handing it to me, she said, "Here. Just know that I'll deny that what's on there came from me."

I rolled the drive between my fingers. "What's on this?"

"Something that you don't want to view on a full stomach. I started going back through the records and looking into deaths of women in this specific age group who didn't fit the typical profile. It's really the only two matching criteria, age and sex. I only went back ten years. That drive contains names and pictures as well as victims who will forever be nameless. The examination results are there too, if an autopsy was done."

"Isn't there always an autopsy with suspicious deaths?"

She shrugged. "Not all the deaths were suspicious. In some cases the cause was obvious. I've been putting the data together and looking for a connection. I feel like it's there, but I just don't know what it is. I was hoping that maybe you could take a look. Maybe you'll see a pattern that I don't."

"I'll do it."

"I recognized the man with you today. I know he's a detective with the homicide and narcotics unit of DPD."

I nodded.

"I've seen him in the lab before. What I haven't seen before is Detective Richards holding someone's hand, supporting them. He's usually a hard-ass."

I sat up straight. "Detective Richards and I are dating."

"It's none of my business, but don't you see that as a conflict of interest?"

"You're right, it's not any of your business."

Tracy persisted. "Well, what I mean is that you're an investigative journalist and he works for the people who try to keep all of this shit covered up."

I sucked my lower lip between my teeth and contemplated my response. "Tracy, you work for Wayne County. Do you believe they handle cases differently than the Detroit Police Department?"

"Unfortunately, no. I don't blame you for thinking what I said was a dis on your boyfriend. It really wasn't. It's this whole city. No city wants to be known for its crime. The mayor, the chamber of commerce, they're constantly harping about revitalization. They're bidding on businesses, improved infrastructure, human capital, and social programs. They don't want to acknowledge that we have a real problem, a new real problem."

"New? You said you have data going back ten years."

"I do," Tracy admitted. "But ten years is new, new for all the revitalization that's been happening."

She was right. It was. If we had some pattern of random women being kidnapped and killed, no company would want to invest in Detroit. "So you're saying that it's the system, or systems. No one in authority wants to admit this is happening."

"Yes. And I'd rather you don't say anything to Detective Richards. If you do, please don't say it was me that started you on this quest for answers."

"Don't worry. Dylan and I keep work out of our private lives. Professional courtesy," I added.

"Thank you, Stella. If I'm wasting your time, I'm sorry. I just feel like we have something significant occurring, and everyone is turning a blind eye."

Hours later I turned away from the computer screen, wishing I could unsee what I'd seen. The information that Tracy had compiled was compelling and sickening. The women in Dr. Howell's files didn't seem to have one common denominator other than being dead. Even the injuries they'd sustained varied: some showed signs of only recent trauma, others patterns of ongoing abuse.

I rubbed my throbbing temples and forced myself to walk away from my computer. It was nearly midnight, and all I'd managed to do was scan the collection of pictures, autopsy results, and police reports. Just enough to turn my stomach. My goal had been to get an overview of what Tracy was trying to tell me. As a woman, I'd hoped that the crazy things on television or in books were fiction, only fiction. As an investigative journalist, I knew they weren't. Yet before tonight I'd never seen information compiled so succinctly about crimes against women taking place in my own city.

In an effort to clear my head, I wandered through my apartment and checked my phone. Dylan never texted me back after I let him know that I wouldn't be coming over. It didn't bother me. This relationship was relatively new. While I appreciated his having met me at the morgue, I needed space. I'd been on my own for too long to suddenly jump into anything serious. Staying at his house was nice—more than nice. But I wasn't ready to leave a change of clothes or a toothbrush.

It would take more than hot, steamy sex and salmon on the grill to prompt me to move Fred's fishbowl. Joint custody of a fish was more domesticated than I wanted to do right now. Besides, I had my own washing machine.

I needed to go to bed. It'd been a long day. Yet at the same time, I couldn't stop thinking about the last profile I'd read on Dr. Howell's memory drive. The picture the victim's parents had given to the police showed two daughters: two beautiful twenty-year-old coeds with their entire lives before them, smiling for the camera. Unfortunately, no one had realized how short a time their entire lives would be.

The victim named in the profile was twenty-year-old Elisa Ortiz. Even postmortem, her attractiveness was obvious. She was tall, five feet nine inches, and fit, 135 pounds, with vibrant red hair and striking green eyes. The image was permanently etched behind my lids.

I poured myself a glass of wine and contemplated her unusual case.

In some ways Elisa Ortiz could be considered a lucky one. She'd been identified. As I thought about the Rosemonts and Mindy, I knew in my heart that closure was important.

Collapsing on the couch, I sipped my wine. The thing nagging at me about the Elisa case was that she wasn't the only Ortiz daughter to have gone missing seven years ago. Elisa had an identical twin sister, Emma. Making the investigative leap, I pulled up the National Missing and Unidentified Persons System and learned that, even now, Emma Ortiz was considered missing.

According to the information in Dr. Howell's report, the two sisters had been close and lived together in a small apartment near the campus of Wayne State University. There was no evidence of risky or suspicious behavior in either of their background checks. According to testimonials, the two sisters were inseparable college students with good GPAs. Interviews with Wayne State professors and students unanimously produced stories of friendly, yet quiet, young women. No one recalled seeing either woman with a young man, much less partying. By all accounts the two spent most of their time at school, at the library, in the gym, or in their apartment. Their parents confirmed these descriptions and added that their daughters were never in trouble, never had serious boyfriends, and were actively involved in their church in their hometown.

Apparently the only thing Elisa and Emma Ortiz did, besides study, was work out. They did it often. That was their activity the night they went missing. The gym willingly surrendered a surveillance video showing both women arriving, working out, and leaving. The video also confirmed that neither woman made it to their car, even though it was parked right outside the gym. The case had stumped the DPD and was still considered open.

Taking another sip of wine, I thought about how the circumstances of this case defied Dylan's belief that there was safety in numbers. These two sisters had gone to the gym together. One theory was that they were taken at the same time. There was also speculation they'd left willingly.

Neither theory could be verified. Food in their refrigerator and a load of laundry in their dryer seemed to refute the theory of a planned exodus. Even their toothbrushes and bank cards were still in their apartment.

The gym, which had long since closed its doors for good, had time-lapse video of the parking lot. The older surveillance system consisted of a rotation of cameras: thirty seconds per camera with four cameras. The feed featuring the sisters and their car stopped recording as the women exited the gym's door. In the minute and a half it took to get back to that angle, they were gone. Nothing suspicious was found on any of the other feeds. There were no witnesses to their disappearance. It was as if the two women had literally vanished into thin air.

I shook my head and took another drink of wine.

Elisa Ortiz's body was found four days later, abandoned naked near the state fair grounds. According to the ME's report, her time of death was over thirty-six hours before her discovery. The examination revealed facial cranial injuries believed to have been caused by blunt force trauma: bruising around her left eye and cheek, as well as zygomatic and nasal fractures. Bruising was also evident around her neck, and on her arms, legs, and torso.

While working at the crime lab, I learned that the location of facial injuries was a surprisingly accurate indication of the mode of trauma. Muggings and domestic abuse—intimate partner violence —were most often associated with injuries like Elisa Ortiz's. Injuries to the upper third of the face usually indicated damage inflicted by another person. Those injuries, though typically not life-threatening, were often accompanied by tissue trauma and nerve damage, which could vary from paralysis of the facial muscles to damage to the optic nerve. In some cases the nerve damage led to temporary or permanent loss of feeling and/or sight.

In most cases, the more severe the trauma, the closer the victim and assailant were thought to have been. Crimes of passion could yield horrendous trauma. However, since there wasn't evidence that either Elisa or Emma were involved in an intimate relationship, and Elisa's examination showed no evidence of sexual assault, police theorized that her injuries were from a mugging or a random act of violence.

The second most common cause of facial injuries in both men and women was automobile accidents. Those injuries differed from perpetrator-inflicted injuries in their location—car accidents most often inflicted damage to the lower half of the face. When the victim's face collided with the steering wheel or dashboard, the typical injuries were fractured mandibles—broken jaws.

Elisa Ortiz's most severe injuries were to her torso. The post-mortem photographs showed a large hematoma with midsection distention. The autopsy had discovered severe internal hemorrhaging caused by a ruptured spleen and lacerated liver. The cause of death had been ruled cardiac arrest due to internal bleeding.

I topped off my glass of wine and ran a new Internet search. My stomach twisted. Perhaps it was due to the alcohol on an empty stomach, but I chose to blame the information on my screen. From what I gleaned, the human body was constructed to protect its fragile organs, so for the kind of trauma that Elisa had experienced, extreme blunt force trauma was needed. When these organs were injured and left untreated, a slow and painful death occurred. Some injuries, like a ruptured aorta, result in death rather quickly, but Elisa hadn't been that fortunate. Her time of death had been estimated at ten to fifteen hours post-trauma.

Draining my glass, I backed up Tracy's memory drive on my laptop and turned off my computer.

Why had someone done this to this woman, and what the hell happened to Emma?

CHAPTER

ELEVEN

S^{ara}

I DIDN'T NEED to hear Jacob's voice to know he was the one who entered my room. I knew his footsteps against the tile and the unique way he opened the door. If those clues weren't enough, after he entered, the faint scent of leather and musk, the manly aroma I'd learned to associate with him, broke through the antiseptic odor.

If I weren't so hysterical, I'd have found my ability to perceive without sight fascinating, but I was, for a lack of a better word, hysterical. I couldn't think or reason. I didn't know what he'd do or say or what I could possibly do in return. Somehow I'd done something terrible. I just couldn't remember.

Sister Lilith had spoken only a little about marriage. In that short time, she'd reinforced everything Jacob had said. Apparently it was the way we all lived in The Light. However, instead of going into detail regarding my role as a wife in The Light, she emphasized that I was the wife of an Assemblyman, and that because of that my behavior, meaning the incident, reflected poorly not only on Jacob but also on all the Assembly wives. She said that the other eleven women were appalled by my behavior, and the entire community was waiting for Father Gabriel's decree. Banishment was still an option. If that was chosen, it would include Jacob. She said that though Jacob had the right to and responsibility for my correction, when my behavior represented so many, for the cohesiveness of the community, the members of The Light needed to witness Father Gabriel's decree. Consequences were coming, not only from Jacob, but also from Father Gabriel. If God hadn't chosen to punish me with my injuries, the other correction would've already been delivered.

None of that was said in front of Raquel.

During most of the training I'd been lulled into a false sense of security, sitting beside Raquel and listening intently as she discussed Father Gabriel's teachings and the beliefs shared in The Light. I didn't remember the things she discussed and many seemed foreign, yet occasionally something seemed familiar.

I didn't nap, as Raquel had joked that I might. I paid attention and answered all Sister Lilith's questions with a nod or shake of my head. I didn't understand my motivation other than a new desire not to further embarrass Jacob.

When Raquel was called away to help with another patient, she asked Sister Lilith if she was about done. Sister Lilith said yes, but she wasn't. Like a snake in the grass, she was waiting.

In my current state, Sister Lilith's berating hit me hard. I didn't know how to respond. I didn't have enough information. Technically I wasn't supposed to say anything, but I didn't know how to react. What upset me was Sister Lilith's promise that correction was coming—correction for blatant insubordination. Then, as she was about to leave, she whispered her promise to return in the morning for more time alone.

I couldn't put my finger on it, but in the three days since I'd awoken, it seemed as though my true self had slipped further away.

Each day, while I questioned my own identity, the answer became more clear. I was Sara Adams. Though I still wanted to understand the oddities of this strange world, more and more of me wanted to be the Sara Jacob expected me to be.

Maybe I was going crazy. I didn't care anymore about the color of my hair or features of my face. I wanted to know my state of mind. How had I become someone who could be reduced to tears twice in two days? Not just tears, not salty drops of water gently gliding down my cheeks. No, I was crying ugly sobs that ached in my chest as my eyes and nose leaked profusely, covering not only my face but my pillow too.

"Sara?"

I was so lost in Sister Lilith's words, I'd almost forgotten that Jacob was there. As the bed moved upward, I slowly turned his way. It wasn't bravery that gave me the strength to face him, even though, according to Lilith, I should be turning toward his wrath. It was a combination of shame and duty. I'd failed him, and as his wife, I needed to learn my fate.

My temples ached as I tried to reason. Could I speak and ask him what had happened?

No. I couldn't ask questions. I needed to wait for answers.

Oh, God! The wait was worse than knowing my fate.

Silently Jacob lifted my chin as the bed rail lowered. Sitting with his leg touching my arm, he gently wiped my face, cleaning away the evidence of my second meltdown in two days. I'd expected punishment, yet in mere moments his silent support gave me strength. Taking a ragged breath, I shuddered, trying to process his conflicting reactions.

Instead of discipline, his large hands delivered tenderness. Instead of a cold wrath, his body against mine provided warmth. Strong and reserved, his voice flowed with compassion. "No one else is here; you may speak. What is it? Why are you crying?"

I gasped for air to replace the sobs. With a firm grip on my chin, he continued to wipe away new tears as I evaluated his actions against Sister Lilith's words. They didn't match.

Though I understood that I was completely at his mercy, something spoke to my heart. From the internal chaos I heard a voice. Speaking softly, it whispered, Believe in yourself. You are stronger than this. Always stay true.

"Sara, don't make me repeat myself. You're upset. Part of my responsibility is helping you. I can't help you if you don't tell me what happened. Does this have to do with Sister Lilith?"

Stay true . . . I nodded.

"Let me hear you," he reprimanded. "The Commission knows you're speaking. I've asked for your speech to be restricted to only me for a while. I'll soon learn if my petition was granted." He paused. When I didn't respond, he repeated himself, the second time firmer than the one before. "Sara, speak now."

You are strong . . . "I'm so confused."

Jacob framed my cheeks and held my face close to his, allowing our noses to touch. He asked, "What happened? Why are you confused?"

"I don't understand what's happening. I don't remember what happened or what I did, but she said it was bad . . ." My voice faded.

Tilting my head forward, Jacob kissed my hair. "Listen to me."

Nodding, I tried to gauge his response, but his voice was soft and gentle.

"It's not Sister Lilith's place to say that to you. You're my responsibility. We'll get through this together."

"But because of the Assembly." My phrases were interrupted by feeble attempts to breathe. "I've jeopardized your position, and she said I shamed all the Assembly wives."

"She told you that?"

"Yes, and that we could be banished . . . I'm not even sure what that means, but all your hard work for the Assembly and Father Gabriel . . ." I gulped the oxygen that wouldn't stay in my lungs. "Gone."

"When she spoke, did you verbally respond to her?"

My head began moving from side to side as soon as his question began. "No. I haven't spoken to anyone, anyone but you."

"And she said all of this, in front of Raquel?"

"No, Raquel had to leave. Sister Lilith said it when we were alone."

The hands that still held my face tensed, yet his voice remained composed and reassuring. "Of course she did. She didn't know you were able to repeat it to me. Don't worry. I was just with the Assembly, Commission, and Father Gabriel. I can honestly say I don't think banishment is going to happen."

I covered his hand with mine. "You're upset. I feel it."

He kissed my hair again. "I am upset, but not at you. Do you remember Sister Raquel's husband?"

"I don't remember anyone, but she talked about him. His name is Benjamin."

"Brother Benjamin. All men deserve a title," he corrected. "And yes, if you don't remember him, you probably don't remember that he's also on the Assembly. Does Raquel seem ashamed of you?"

"No. No she doesn't, but why? Why would Sister Lilith say that?"

He released my cheeks, and his finger came to my lips. "No questions."

I lowered my face again and exhaled. "Jacob, I'm no good at this. I really can't remember why I was in your truck, or why I had an accident. I can't remember anything before three days ago. Except I feel like I'm not very good at following rules. I don't understand why you married me, why I'm here, in The Light . . . I'm not an Assemblyman's wife. You should just let them banish me before you end up losing all you've accomplished. I'm not who you think I am." The sobs were gone, but an occasional tear continued to flow.

Jacob lifted my hands and kissed the knuckles. A faint smile crossed my lips as I remembered him doing the same thing earlier this morning. Wrapping both of my hands within his grasp, he began, "Sara Adams, you're my wife." He wasn't saying it as he had when he wanted me to repeat after him. This time his tone made it more of a plea. "I married you and you married me. I'd do it again in a heartbeat. I'm honored to be on the Assembly, and I'm also honored to be your husband." He leaned down until our foreheads touched. "This road won't be easy, but never doubt where you belong or with whom. I don't know what I'd do without you, and I pray I never find out.

"We pledged our devotion to The Light and Father Gabriel, but before that, we pledged our love to one another. If I have to start from the beginning and recount our entire lives again to help you remember, I'll do it. I'd do whatever I needed to do to help you remember us. Sara, I'd marry you again." My chest ached with his declaration. "Sara, would you marry me?"

I couldn't speak as his words soaked deeper and deeper into my heart. My tears were dry. There probably weren't any left. However, the lump within my throat continued to grow, making my reply impossible. The man holding my hands and affirming his love overwhelmed me. Despite my shortcomings, he was declaring his devotion to me and our marriage. Finding myself lost in his grasp and surrounded by his masculine scent, I wondered if I deserved his steadfast love. I didn't know.

And then I remembered the voice: believe in yourself. I would believe, and even if I hadn't deserved Jacob's love in the past, I would in the future. Because for the first time, a part of me wanted it.

"Sara?"

I lifted my unseeing eyes, leaving only a whisper between our lips. "Yes, Jacob, I believe I'd marry you again."

With our hands still connected, our lips came together. His were firm and demanding, yet soft and accommodating. His kiss gave and took in equal portions, causing a firestorm to erupt deep within. My chest no longer cried from shame; instead my body screamed with desire. Without thinking, I willingly surrendered to the man with the fervent kiss. His kiss awakened me, my body, and my yearning. I had no doubt that this man filled my days and nights with earth-quaking passion. With only a kiss, I no longer wondered who my husband was in the bedroom; I knew. He was a man who conquered unapologetically and bestowed unsparingly.

When our lips parted, Jacob asked with a smile to his voice, "Are you better?"

"I am, thank you." Calm warmth settled over me as I thought about what he'd said when he found me crying. He'd said that part of his responsibility was helping me. I still couldn't wrap my head around all of it, but my life was becoming clearer. I was his. Yes, he'd correct me, but he'd also make things right and help me feel better. "Jacob?"

"Yes?"

"I don't remember anything from our past, and I won't lie to you and say I do. I get the feeling that isn't who we are. I don't think we lie to one another, do we?"

"Honesty is best."

"And there's something else," I said.

"Go on."

"I don't like the idea of being corrected, but I love how protective you are. I remember you saying I can't ask, so I won't, but I hope that you'll be patient with me." I allowed my grin to grow. "Because I'm anxious to be your wife again, in every way. Your kiss . . ." The blood rushed to my cheeks. "Well, since we're married, I hope I can say this. Your kiss makes me want more, makes me want to remember. I'm sorry for whatever happened. Thank you for standing by me."

"I'll always stand by you. I'll also be patient, but I will correct you, even while I'm being patient. I told you, correction isn't done out of anger, but for you. As a matter of fact, you just said something . . ."

I held my breath.

He went on, "You said you can't ask. That's not accurate. You may ask . . . actually, for many things you're required to ask. I told you that you can't question. There's a difference."

"I'm not sure I understand."

"You may ask for my patience, for things you need or desire. Remember, we spoke about you asking for a drink of water."

I remembered that.

"What you may not do is question. When I told you that I'd tell you what happened before the accident, but not now, you asked why. That's questioning my statement, my word. Those truths, the reasons behind decrees, decisions, and yes, even corrections, do not need to be explained to you. As a woman you must accept them, as faith that your husband or any man of The Light has the right answers. I promise, I'll never make a decision that will cause either of us harm."

"But you'll . . ." I purposely stopped, pressing my lips together, as my heart rate quickened.

"But I'll what?"

"I don't think I'm allowed to finish the sentence."

"But I'll . . . correct you?" he asked, properly completing my sentence.

I nodded.

"You're right. Normally you wouldn't be allowed to finish that sentence, or begin it, for that matter; however, to help you remember or at least understand, there'll need to be a few exceptions, and the answer is yes. Yes, I'll correct you when needed. Correction isn't harm. It may include pain, but it's not harm. Harm means physical or psychological damage. Why would I do that to my wife, the woman I've vowed to love and protect?"

I didn't know. There seemed to be a lot of things that I didn't know. Shrugging, I replied, "Thank you." I reached up to his face. With healing fingertips, I roamed the features of the man I longed to remember. "For loving me and protecting me. Thank you for the patience and exceptions. I know they're at your discretion, but knowing that you'll grant them makes me happy. I really am trying to understand. I want to be the wife you married, the one you want."

"I know you do. You always have."

Our lips reunited. Though only brief, the taste of his kiss combined with our connection rekindled the flicker of desire.

"Mrs. Adams," he said breathily, "you have a lot of healing to do before you can be my wife again in every way, to use your words, not mine. While we wait for that to happen, I hope you know, I want that too. I won't rush you, but just know I want it."

I sensed that Jacob had a way of getting what he wanted. As he stood, my cheeks filled with a healthy blush. The truth was I wanted it too.

"Hello?" Since I hadn't heard the door, I surmised that Jacob was talking on his phone. He continued, "Yes, that's great news. Thank you . . . Oh? What? . . . No, I haven't heard from him, but as long as I'm present, I have no issues . . . When? . . . Yes, we'll both be ready . . . Thank you, Brother Daniel."

After a few moments, he turned toward me. "Sara, it's about time to eat lunch, and Brother Daniel just informed me that you'll be receiving your walking cast this afternoon."

"OK." It wasn't as if I had any say in my treatment, but why would someone else be telling Jacob about my care? Shouldn't it be Dr. Newton making those decisions?

The covers moved from my legs, causing me to shiver at the cool air.

"It really will be good for you to start walking and rebuild your muscles again." His arms moved beneath me, and he said, "I'm going to lift you."

I nodded and prepared for my side to hurt.

"Why do you do that?" Jacob asked as he carried me toward the bathroom.

"Do what?"

"Bite your lip. It's not new. But now, without your eyes, I guess I've been watching your lips. The other day I thought you might put a hole through it."

I started to giggle, but sucked my lip between my teeth as he lowered my one good leg to the ground. Once I was standing, I released my lip and said, "I don't think about it, but maybe I do it to ease the pain from my ribs."

He smoothed my hair, tucking some behind my ear. "I don't want your ribs to hurt. I didn't want any of this."

Of course not. Who'd want their wife in an automobile accident?

"I know. It'll take time, but it'll heal."

He lifted my gown. "Even with your bruises, you're beautiful." He unexpectedly brushed his fingers over the side of one of my breasts, sending goose bumps up and down my skin and bringing a gasp from my lips. "I hope that healing doesn't take too much time."

Reaching for his shoulders, I stood perfectly still. Only the sound of breathing echoed throughout the bathroom. Reverently he lowered my panties. After what seemed like an eternity, he lifted one of my hands to the handle. "You'd better sit, and I'd better leave you alone."

I nodded, wondering if my desire was as obvious to his eyes as his was to my ears.

Once I was done, and as he carried me back to my bed, I asked, "Would it be asking or questioning to ask what you meant on the phone about you being present? I'm hoping it's about Sister Lilith." I added the last part hoping to take away from my question.

Jacob's chest expanded and contracted with a big breath. "That would be questioning. I know Lilith upset you. She won't be back today."

"She said she'd be back tomorrow, and we'd be alone again."

Jacob placed me on the bed. "Yes, she will and you will, but I'll make sure she doesn't discuss anything with you that she shouldn't. If I return tomorrow to a wife as upset as you were today, I'll have a talk with the Commission, and I guarantee that she'll be in worse shape." He tucked the blanket back around my cast and legs. "She may be a Commissioner's wife, but she's still a woman, and the Commission approved my petition. You may speak to me, but only to me."

"Thank you," I replied, nodding.

"Thank you?" Jacob asked. "You're all right with that?"

"Yes, although I'd love to talk to Raquel, if I can only speak to you, I can't talk to Sister Lilith, and she can only ask me yes-and-no questions. I really don't want to say more to her than that, and then there's Dr. Newton . . ."

"What about Dr. Newton?"

I exhaled and hoped that my honesty wouldn't get me in trouble. "I understand that he's a man and deserves respect, but I get a weird feeling from him." I sat very still, waiting for my correction.

Jacob brushed my cheek. "Sara, never be afraid to be honest with me. I need to know these things to protect you." He scoffed. "Perhaps God's time is now."

I didn't know what he meant, so I waited.

"Your question, about what I said on the phone about being present. It wasn't about Lilith. It was about Dr. Newton. I've forbidden him from being alone with you for any medical procedure. I must be present."

I smiled and reached for his hand. "It's always been like this, hasn't it? You protecting me?"

He touched my lips. "I am protecting you, but stop questioning. I can only be patient for so long."

His amused tone made me smile. As I settled quietly against the pillows waiting for my lunch, I decided that though this life still didn't feel right, it no longer felt wrong.

CHAPTER

TWELVE

S ara

I LIFTED my face toward the swish of the opening door. Even after almost two weeks, my body reacted to sounds as if I could see, but I couldn't, not yet. I hadn't even tried. My bandages were always changed in the bathroom with the door shut and the lights off. Raquel reassured me that the room could double as a darkroom if I ever wanted to develop film. I didn't, but it was good to know.

Dr. Newton explained that healing took time. He was especially concerned about the damage done by the flash of the explosion and warned that premature exposure to light could cause irreparable damage. Though I was curious, after he said that, I knew I'd wait.

"Hi, Sara."

Recognizing familiar voices was getting to be one of my specialties. Excited and somewhat wobbly, I stood. "Elizabeth! I didn't know you were coming to see me today."

She rushed my way and steadied my shoulders. "Should you be doing that? Standing, all by yourself?"

I grinned. "I can do more than that. I can walk. Watch," I said, taking one step and then another. "Jacob walked me around and around this room. I know every square inch. As long as no one moves the furniture on me, I'm pretty good. I'm not very fast, but I'm good."

"Well, look at you go! You'll be back to running before you know it."

I stopped and turned toward her voice. "Running?"

"Don't look so scared. You know what I mean."

"No, I mean, yes." My heart fluttered. "Oh, I remembered running. I did. It's something I used to do."

"You remembered it, like right now?"

Reaching through the air, I found my way to the chair and sat. As I ran my hands over the vinyl cushion, I smiled. I had been right about the material. "No, it wasn't right now. It was one of the first days after I woke. I don't remember exactly. It was before I was supposed to talk, and I was feeling stressed out. I didn't know where I was or even who I was. I felt like I was going to explode, but I couldn't. I didn't have a valve to release the pressure. Do you know what I mean?" I paused for her to respond. When she didn't, I giggled. "Hey, I'm not seeing head shakes, so I'd appreciate some verbal clues to know you're still there."

Elizabeth laughed. "Oh, sorry. I'm definitely here. So how did that make you remember running?"

I shrugged. "I don't know. I was thinking about ways to calm down, to release some stress, and it just came to me. I remembered running through a woods. There were tall trees and a meadow." I pressed my lips together, trying to recall. "I don't know. There was sunlight streaming down in beams through the leaves." I shrugged again. "That's about it."

"Wow, not a lot of sunlight this time of year. Must have been summer. So, did you remember anything else, anything before your accident?"

I shook my head.

"That's not fair; you didn't give me a verbal clue."

"No, I guess it isn't. But I'd take seeing over being able to shake my head any day."

"Hopefully, you'll be able to do both soon."

I sighed. "I hope so."

"So, any other memories?"

"Not really. The good news is that things are becoming more familiar." I smiled as big as I could. "And more comfortable. Like I recognized your voice and smiling doesn't hurt my face. My side still hurts, but the headaches aren't as frequent."

"That's wonderful, and you're walking!" Her tone became more serious. "If you do remember anything else, be sure to tell Brother Jacob. I'm sure he was happy you had one memory."

I found a string on my robe and tugged.

"Sara?"

I didn't respond.

"You did tell him about remembering running, didn't you?"

"No, um, I guess I'd forgotten about it, until you mentioned it. Besides, I'm sure he has other things to think about than a few random memories."

Elizabeth moved closer and touched my knee. Judging from the direction from which her voice came, she was bending or kneeling down on the floor. "A few random? You only said running."

"Yes, only running and the woods and sunshine. It's not that big of a deal."

"Are you taking your medicine?"

"Of course, I don't have much choice. I don't even know what I'm taking. Each morning either Jacob or Raquel hands me a cup with pills and I swallow them. I wanted to ask." I leaned back and sighed. "But I can't."

"No, you can't. You also can't keep secrets from Brother Jacob. If I didn't tell Luke something . . . well, let's just say I'd remember to tell him the next time."

My muscles tightened. "I wasn't hiding this from Jacob. I just forgot."

"Then tell him that. Since you weren't able to speak when you had the memory, he should go easy on you." She patted my knee. "Hey, enough about that. Have you been listening to the recordings?"

I nodded, still thinking about Jacob. Would he really be upset over something so trivial? Things were going well. I was doing better with not questioning, yet asking. It wasn't easy. I wasn't sure if at one time I had been naturally inquisitive or if it was because I was trying to remember so much. Either way, questioning came too easily. Usually, once I'd start to question, I'd catch myself.

I was petrified when he'd first told me I could speak to anyone who came to see me, but he'd reassured me it was safe. He'd allow only certain people to visit. Nevertheless I knew one of those people would be Sister Lilith. However, ever since the day she'd upset me, she never came alone. Sister Ruth, Brother Daniel's wife, came with her. I didn't know if that was Jacob's doing or not, but I liked Sister Ruth, and the extra company. She didn't say much. But she was a hugger and always smelled like vanilla. By the way she swallowed my shoulders in her embrace, I believed she was a bigger woman. I might not remember this life, and I'd figured out that women could be freer with their speech with one another than with men, but I knew asking about someone's weight or size wasn't appropriate. I didn't want to offend her. With her present, Sister Lilith never mentioned the accident or my impending punishment. She talked about my position as an Assembly wife and about the importance of my remembering Father Gabriel's teachings, and we studied.

At first I studied out of curiosity. I wanted to understand our world better. As time passed I found myself desiring to learn more.

"Sara?"

"Sorry. Yes, I've been listening to them, a lot. It's the only noise I have when I'm all alone. I like listening to Father Gabriel's voice. He's so knowledgeable. And listening to him and doing my training with Sister Lilith, well, it all makes sense. I guess."

"You guess?"

"I just wonder why I can't remember any of it. I mean, it's very interesting and some of it's pretty deep. It seems like something I shouldn't forget."

"You shouldn't!" Elizabeth said lightheartedly. "That's why you're listening and working with Sister Lilith, so you won't."

"Oh, Elizabeth, please tell me something, something about anything outside of this room. I'm going stir-crazy in here. Now that I can walk, I can't wait to get home."

"Well, this time of year, there isn't a lot outside, but the northern lights sure have been gorgeous."

"Northern lights?"

"You know, the colorful bands of light in the sky, the aurora borealis."

"Um, yes. I think so."

"Sara, they're beautiful. It's the best part of the dark season . . ."

I tried to picture what Elizabeth described as she went on about the colors. Apparently the lights are usually a brilliant yellow-green, but lately they'd been red, blue, and even purple. The excitement in her voice made them sound even more beautiful. Though I imagined their radiance, I longed for the time when I'd be able to truly see them.

If they're that visible, why don't I remember them?

"I thought you needed to be north to see those?" I asked when she paused.

"You do, silly. I don't think many people are farther north than us—"

The door opened and Elizabeth stood. My pulse quickened as she reached for my arm. Her hand trembled as she silently helped me stand. I was about to ask who was here, when he spoke.

"Sister Sara, Sister Elizabeth."

I gasped and grabbed Elizabeth's arm for support. For a moment I feared falling as my knees weakened. I knew the voice; I'd been listening to it for hours a day. Father Gabriel was in my room. As I tried to reason, I realized I was wearing only a nightgown and robe, mere feet from our leader. Bashfully I pulled the lapels closer together.

What am I supposed to do? Do I kneel or curtsy? I don't know.

"Father," Elizabeth replied.

"Sister Elizabeth, it's nice to see you helping your sister."

"Yes, Father."

"And Sister Sara, you're standing. Our God is good to help you heal." He reached for my hand and held it as he said, "I heard you were feeling better, and I wanted to see for myself."

"F-Father Gabriel, thank you."

"It's all right, Sister, you may sit. You're suddenly pale. Perhaps you're not well."

I felt back for the chair and replied, "Father, I'm just surprised."

"You knew me. You remembered my voice."

Oh! When Jacob gave me permission to talk to anyone who visited my room, I was certain he hadn't anticipated Father Gabriel. Yet I'd already spoken and I couldn't refuse Father Gabriel, could I?

"I've been listening to your sermons. I've been hearing your voice throughout my days."

"That's very good news. However, I'd hoped your memory was returning."

I lowered my chin and moved my head from side to side. "No, I'm sorry. I'm trying."

"That's what I've heard, Sister. That's all we can ask. I came today to personally invite you back to service. I know you've been working with Sisters Lilith and Ruth, but I miss seeing you seated with the Assembly wives. I think it's time that your seat is filled."

"Yes, Father."

"Very good. I'll see you tonight."

"Tonight?"

Someone else had entered my room with Father Gabriel, though whoever it was hadn't spoken, and I didn't know his identity. But by his sharp intake of breath, I knew it was a man.

Oh, shit. Did I just question Father Gabriel?

"Tonight," I repeated more confidently, "will be wonderful, with my husband's permission."

The drumming of my heart echoed in my ears as I tried to decipher whether I'd saved myself, or made it worse.

Do I need my husband's permission, or does Father Gabriel's invitation supersede Jacob's orders?

"Very good, Sister. It seems as though Brother Jacob was correct, you're relearning the ways of The Light well. Sister Elizabeth, you may assist Sister Sara during this evening's service."

"Yes, Father," Elizabeth replied, "with my husband's permission, I'd be happy to."

When she reached down and squeezed my hand, I exhaled. I'd said that right.

"We'll leave you ladies to your devotions. Tonight."

"Thank you, Father," Elizabeth and I said in unison.

Neither of us spoke for a few moments after the shutting of the door. The silence continued to grow as my trepidation waned and shock grew. Finally I squeezed Elizabeth's hand one more time and whispered, "Holy shit!"

"Sara!" Elizabeth exclaimed with a giggle. "Don't let Brother Jacob or any other man hear you speak that way."

"But Father Gabriel was here! Oh, I need to tell Jacob." I stood and took a step toward my bed. "Elizabeth, I need clothes. Do I have clothes here? I can't go to service in a nightgown and robe." Falling back to the edge of the bed, I doubled forward and held my head. "Oh my gosh! Will I be punished for wearing this when he visited?"

"That's up to Brother Jacob, but you didn't have much choice. It wasn't like he announced he was coming." She was speaking from across the room, near my closet. "You have a skirt and sweater here, but I don't think you should change without . . ."

"I know, without Jacob's knowledge." My voice sounded defeated, even to me. "Be honest, please. Will Jacob be upset? Did I really question Father Gabriel?"

"I can't presume to answer for Brother Jacob, but you recovered beautifully." She sat beside me and gently elbowed my good side. "Father Gabriel even smiled at your response."

He smiled? Is that good?

"Who was the other person, and why didn't he announce himself? That's rude. It's obvious I can't see."

Elizabeth reached for my knee and lowered her voice. "Sara, I want to help you. I'm trying, but you need to be mindful. If we weren't friends, I could share this with Luke, and he'd tell Brother Jacob. The other person was Brother Timothy, and you should remember that a man doesn't owe us his words. He grants them. Your saying that he was rude makes you prideful. And the language you used makes you vulgar."

A tear escaped my bandages and slid down my cheek. "That's what I don't understand. I'm not good at this. I'm really not."

Elizabeth's arms wrapped around my shoulders and pulled me toward her. "You are. You were, and you'll get better again. I won't say anything, but you should."

"What?" I pulled away and sat straight.

"Our husbands can't be with us all the time. If we're honest about our transgressions when they're away, it shows them that we are trustworthy."

Prideful and vulgar?

More tears joined the stream. "No, I'm supposed to be at service tonight. I don't want Jacob upset with me. I need him. If I tell him, he'll be angry."

"He won't be upset. However, if he thinks your behavior warrants punishment, he'll handle it. Besides, other than walking you to your seat, he can't be with you at service."

"He can't?" I asked.

"No, he sits with the Assemblymen. As wives of the Assembly, we sit together just behind the Commission wives."

"So that's why Father Gabriel told you to assist me? You'll be with me?"

"With Luke's permission I will. So will Raquel. I believe Brother Benjamin will also approve."

I reached out and patted her leg. The material of her jeans made me think. "You're wearing jeans?"

"I am." She giggled. "That's a subject change."

"I guess it is. Why do I have a skirt?"

"Well, you have jeans too, if that's what you're asking. I've seen you wear them. I'd guess that Brother Jacob thought a skirt would be easier with your cast." Oh, that makes sense. "And we all wear dresses or skirts to service, even in this cold weather," she added. "Most of us are more casual for evening prayer. There're some who feel the need to always be dressed up. I'm sure you've noticed the high heels. I mean, we wear most everything we did in the dark, within reason. All the fashions in our store are approved first by the Commission. Our bodies are our temples, and we don't share that with anyone but our husbands."

She stood and continued, "With as cold as it's been, whether we're at evening prayer or our jobs, most women of The Light wear jeans and warm boots. Truthfully, modesty is dictated by Father Gabriel, but the particulars are up to our husbands. You wore jeans and warm boots before. I don't know why that would change."

I nodded. Of course it is up to him. Everything seems to be up to my husband.

"Sara, it's still early in the afternoon. Service isn't until seven. I'll speak with Luke about assisting you, and he'll talk to Jacob."

Suddenly the memory of what Sister Lilith had said about the Assembly wives came back. "Elizabeth?"

"What?"

"Are you appalled by me?"

"What? No!"

"Do the other wives of the Assembly hate me?"

"Of course not. Father Gabriel doesn't preach hate." She wrapped her arms around me and hugged. "We're all sisters."

I smiled a sad smile. "Thank you."

"As long as Luke approves, I won't leave your side. Who knows? Maybe you'll recognize the voices."

I nodded.

Maybe?

~

As my afternoon progressed, my anxiety grew. Though I listened to Father Gabriel's recordings, I couldn't concentrate. The words prideful and vulgar kept repeating in my mind.

How is it that it was my friend who upset me—not Sister Lilith, not Jacob, but my friend?

Maybe it was because I cared what Elizabeth thought. I cared about her friendship.

Will she decide she doesn't want to be friends any longer if I can't remember the past, if I'm too different? What will happen if I do as she suggests and confess to Jacob? Don't we have enough happening, with going to service?

Remembering the running, I tried to pace the confines of my room. Though the cast made my left leg longer than my right, causing an uneven gait that aggravated my rib, I continued to move. Freedom was more important than the pain. After so long in my bed, I relished the ability to stand, walk, and sit of my own accord. Yet with each minute I waited for Jacob, my apprehension of the unknown grew. I knew this room and was familiar with it. I'd counted the steps from my bed to the wall, my bed to the bathroom, and my bed to . . . anywhere within these four walls. I knew what was expected of me here.

What will happen out there, at service? What will happen when Jacob returns?

I rolled my head and shoulders, trying to relieve the tight muscles. My mind wanted to run, yet my body could hardly handle the pacing. Obviously my strength wasn't up to par. After a few laps, I'd sit, rest, and then try it again. During my walks I stopped at the closet multiple times to see my clothes. Of course I couldn't see. I could touch and feel. Elizabeth could be right, I might have jeans at home, but I didn't here. Mostly everything I touched was soft and long—nightgowns, I assumed. I found the skirt and sweater she'd mentioned. Now I wondered about a bra. I hadn't worn one since I'd awakened. It was one more thing to add to my stress.

If saying shit is vulgar, what will happen if I go to service without a bra?

Perhaps it was from my exercise, or maybe an escape mechanism, but as the hours passed, tiredness overcame me, and I decided to nap. That was where I was, in a dream world, when Jacob finally returned. Though his entering woke me, I didn't move. Remembering my transgressions, I lay still listening to his footsteps.

Is he upset or am I nervous and paranoid?

Panic pricked at my skin as I tried to decipher his mood. Each slap of his shoes against the tile echoed throughout the room, reverberating off the walls and accelerating my already too-rapid pulse. Slowly I turned, summoning what little bit of courage existed within me, and said, "Jacob?"

His steps lightened as he came closer and brushed my forehead with his lips. I didn't understand why we hadn't shared another kiss like the one over a week before. Maybe he knew I still needed to heal and didn't want one thing to lead to another. Right now I didn't know what I wanted. It was probably absolution.

"How was your afternoon?" he asked.

Shit! What does that mean? Do I have to tell him everything, or does he already know?

I wanted to ask, but I knew better. All I could do was answer. Moving my legs to the side of the bed, I sat, smoothed my hair, and replied, "Eventful."

"Really? Do tell."

The slight humor to his tone gave me strength. "Elizabeth came to see me."

"She did? That was nice. Did you have a nice chat?"

"Jacob, while Elizabeth was here . . ." My words trailed away.

"Did something happen?"

My face paled, my stomach twisted, and a sheen of perspiration coated my skin. Fighting the nausea, I went on. "Yes, actually. Do you remember . . ." No, stupid, that's a question. I rephrased. "I remembered that you said I could speak to anyone who came to my room."

"Yes. Of course you may speak to Elizabeth."

"Jacob, Father Gabriel came here this afternoon."

"Go on."

Shit! Shit! He's too calm.

"Sara, tell me about Father Gabriel's visit."

"Well, at first I was shocked. I knew his voice the moment he spoke. I've been listening to his recordings." The sentences ran together. "He was very nice and said that he wants me at service tonight, that he missed seeing me sitting with the Assembly wives, and that he was glad I was feeling better. Oh! And he told Elizabeth that she could assist me tonight, because I guess you have to sit with the Assembly." I took a breath.

"Then I guess we'd better both get ready for service tonight."

I nodded, swallowing the bile that had made its way from my stomach.

"Is that all?" he asked.

"All . . . that he said? Yes, I think."

He sat beside me and reached for my hand. "Perhaps you should think harder."

Tears trickled from my bandaged eyes. "I've told you before that I'm not good at this."

"You are. You were. You just need to be reminded." He cleared his throat. "I won't ask again."

I took a deep breath. "I may have questioned Father Gabriel."

"You *may* have?" He asked, still too calm. "You don't know?"

I stood and moved away from him. Holding on to the back of the chair for support, I replied, "I'd forgotten what day of the week it was. I mean, every day is the same. When he said he wanted me at service, I forgot it was Wednesday. I was shocked he meant tonight."

"And what did you say?"

"I repeated *tonight*, and my tone may have sounded like a question, because Brother Timothy made a noise. As soon as he did, I realized what I'd done, and I said it again and told him that I'd be happy to be there. I added with your permission. I tried to make it seem like I didn't question"—my run-on sentence was interrupted only by muffled sobs—"but I did." I took a breath. "And after he left, I whispered a curse word to Elizabeth, which apparently makes me vulgar." I confessed the last part dejectedly.

"Oh! I didn't know about the swearing."

I nodded with a sigh.

"Is there anything else?"

"Yes," I might as well admit everything. "Brother Timothy never spoke while he was here. I didn't even know it was him with Father Gabriel until later when I asked Elizabeth. I said I thought it was rude of him to not announce his presence"—I shrugged—"since I can't see. And, well, she reminded me that as women we aren't owed men's words, and thinking I was owed them made me prideful."

Jacob lifted my chin. "If I'm keeping count, we now have questioning, vulgarity, and pridefulness. You did have an eventful afternoon."

I shrugged, completely thrown off by his calm tone. "Will we still be going to service?"

"Yes."

Maybe that is all there is. Maybe I just need to confess?

"May I get ready?"

"Do you really think I can let this behavior pass?"

My heartbeat came back to my ears, echoing louder than before as my body began to tremble. What was he going to do? "I'm very sorry. I am trying."

"Yes, Sara, you are. While the vulgarity and pridefulness are new, we've been working on the questioning for some time now."

"And I'm getting bet—"

His finger touched my lips.

"There is still room for improvement. Don't you agree?"

With his finger still in place, I nodded.

"I believe it's time for a lesson in consequences, a punishment to help you remember."

Though his hand hadn't moved, I leaned slightly away. "Please, I promise—" This time he covered my mouth completely.

"Sara, do not make this worse. This is the way it is. You knew that there would be correction when you confessed, didn't you?"

I nodded. Though I'd hoped otherwise, I'd known.

"If we were home, we'd do this in our bedroom, but since we're here, go to the bathroom and prepare."

He released his hold, but I didn't move. I couldn't. Fear paralyzed my trembling body.

"Sara?"

"I-I don't know what you want me to do."

"Go into the bathroom, remove your clothes, and wait for me."

"But what about service?" My inner monologue screamed, calling me by name: *Sara, stop asking questions!* "I'm sorry." As I took a step toward the bathroom, a sob bubbled from my chest. "I told you everything. I was honest." I couldn't have hidden the defeat from my voice if I'd wanted.

I did as he said, entered the bathroom, removed my clothes, and waited. When he didn't come, I found my robe and put it over my shoulders. I didn't put my arms in the sleeves, but I didn't like being naked and alone. I wasn't sure how long he made me wait, but each minute was worse than the one before. When the door finally opened, I was sitting on the closed toilet, with my head down.

"Take my hand," he commanded.

I reached out to him. As our hands connected, I stood and my robe fell from my shoulders. Silently he moved me to the sink and turned me to face it.

"Put your hands on the edge of the vanity and don't let go of the counter, until I give you permission. Do you understand?"

"Yes," I replied, my trembling hands moist. When I gripped the edge, they slid upon the smooth surface. I gripped tighter.

"Move your legs back and apart. Brace yourself."

I continued to obey, still unsure of what was about to happen. It was then that I heard the distinct sound of his belt as he unbuckled it and pulled it from each loop.

No! This can't be happening!

My knees went weak. I bit my lip and fell forward onto the counter, still gripping the edge. The first contact wasn't his belt, but his hand. He ran it over my behind, rubbing and warming my skin.

"Sara, your honesty has earned you leniency. However, it's my job to watch over you and correct you." He continued caressing. "I need you to remember your place, especially now that we'll be out among more followers. I want you to remember the rules. I'm doing this to help you. Do you understand?"

"Yes, Jacob."

I sucked my lip back between my teeth. Though I'd replied appropriately, it wasn't what I wanted to say. I wanted to scream, to tell him he was crazy, tell him that I'd remember next time. I would. He didn't need to do this. I also wanted to tell him to just get on with it. Stop making me wait. But then the caress ended, and I changed my mind. I didn't want him to get on with it. I wanted to beg for it not to happen.

The still air filled with a whistle and then a crack.

It was a split second before the pain registered. In those milliseconds, I knew that I'd never forget this. I also knew that I'd never had this done to me. If I had, I'd remember, because I sure as hell wasn't ever going to forget this.

"Sara, you need to count. Next time I won't remind you."

Next time? No freakin' way! I am stronger than this.

"One."

Whistle. Crack!

"Two." Tears fell from my cheeks to the vanity below.

CHAPTER

THIRTEEN

S tella

"HE WORKS in narcotics and homicide, right?"

I stared incredulously at Bernard, hoping that maybe I'd misheard his innuendo, or that the chatter of the other patrons and clinking of the dishes had affected my hearing. "Umm, yes, he does, and I work for you. Would you like me sharing my research with him?"

Bernard's lips formed a tight line before he replied, "No. You know I wouldn't. I want to break this story, not DPD." He leaned across the small coffee shop table in Midtown where we'd met. "But Stella, you have a hell of a great resource at your disposal. I mean, I knew you two were friends, but I didn't realize how friendly you were until he called me. The guy was very determined to learn your location." He sighed and leaned back. Picking up his coffee cup, he asked, "What if you'd been out on assignment instead of going to the

Wayne County Medical Examiner? Would he have expected me to tell him where you were then?" His brows rose. "I got the distinct impression that he doesn't often take no for an answer."

I shook my head. "Really? You're Bernard Cooper, since when do you worry about someone not taking no for an answer? I've never known you to even be fazed by the word. As a matter of fact, isn't that your calling card?"

"I don't take no for an answer, and yes, it is my calling card." His jaw clenched.

Unsure where this was going, I replied, "You lost me."

"I realize that this is overstepping my bounds, but, well, I have Mindy in the back of my brain, and I want to be sure you're all right. Does Detective Richards take no for an answer?"

Oh my God!

My neck stiffened. "I don't know if I should be flattered or offended. Let me tell you that yes, you've overstepped your bounds, but not just once. You've overstepped your bounds on two counts: First, Dylan and I do not talk work while we're together. We recognize the conflict of interest. So no, I won't ask him for information that could substantiate the rumors that something big is happening on the drug front. Second, my personal relationship is none of your business. While I appreciate your concern, I hope you know me well enough to know that I wouldn't be with a man who didn't take no for an answer. I'm not wired that way." I tilted my head to the side and took a drink of my coffee. When he didn't respond, I added, "After all, I love this job, and I'm damn good at it. But if I can tell my boss, the great Bernard Cooper, to mind his own damn business and take his suggestion to spy on my boyfriend and shove it up his ass, I think I can handle Dylan Richards. And since you've admitted to not taking no for an answer, should I be concerned about your wife?"

By the look on Bernard's face and the color of his neck and cheeks, I might have gone a little too far. Unfortunately, speaking my mind had never been something I was good at monitoring. In business I was usually pretty good at filtering, but not when it came to my personal life. My mouth would take on a mind of its own.

This was both business and personal. I should have filtered. I'd blame the fact that I hadn't on lack of sleep or worry over my friend. No matter the cause, I'd look for another job before I let Bernard Cooper or anyone else think that he or she could tell me what to do when it wasn't something I was comfortable doing.

The longer Bernard remained silent, the clearer my future became. Finally I nodded and threw my phone in my purse. As I began to scoot from the booth, Bernard said, "So you're walking away from this job you love because I'm concerned about you?"

I sat back down. "I assumed by your silence I was done."

His lips curled upward. "I like your fortitude. I really do. I don't know if Mindy would've reacted that determined. I just hope that you'll remember that inner strength as you keep doing your research and if and when you're called down to the ME's office, if it's not a false alarm." He lowered his voice. "I know I'm a hard-ass. It's who I am. At the same time, I like your determination. I have since I hired you. Keep it. Don't compromise it for anyone. In this business and many others it'll take you far." He grinned. "Hell, maybe I should fire you."

My eyes widened.

"Not because you're not good at your job, but because you're too good. If I keep you here, one day you'll probably have my job."

Wow, I wasn't expecting that.

"You've got a good gut," Bernard continued. "It's just that I've seen this kind of thing too many times." He lowered his eyes to the table, avoiding eye contact for the second time in recent memory. "Even with my own sister. It's not something I talk about, but it might be part of the reason I want to expose as many injustices as I can."

Who is this man?

"Remember," he went on. "You're stronger than you even know. Keep that gut instinct alive and stay true to yourself. Don't let Dylan

Richards or anyone else stop your dream." He took a deep breath. "I wish I'd said that to my sister, or that someone else would have. You've got a bright future. Your reaction tells me that you believe that. You know you're talented. That's not conceit. It's believing in yourself.

"After you called to tell me it wasn't Mindy, I thought about Detective Richards's call, his determination to find you, and about Mindy's disappearance and how it was affecting everyone, especially you.

"Years ago my boss sat me down and gave me some great advice. He said that when the shit hits the fan, it's not time to turn away. It means the source of the manure is close and that means one thing: something is growing. Though it may stink, it's going to be big. Remember that, especially in our business, it means we're close. So put on your shitkickers and plow through. Believe in yourself"—he smiled as he looked deep into my moist eyes—"even if it means telling off your boss.

"And in case you didn't get it from that story, my wife's the one person who can emphatically tell me no."

I was suddenly rethinking every negative thought I'd ever had about Bernard. Maybe he could be a pompous ass, but perhaps that was his veneer and possibly underneath there was a real person. At nearly twenty years my senior he'd seen more than I had. He'd also been in this business for two-thirds of my life. Taking his advice suddenly seemed like a good idea.

"Thank you. I'll stay true. It's who I am, who my parents raised me to be. That's why I won't stop my search for Mindy. That doesn't mean I'll let my work for you or WCJB slip."

"I know you won't."

I sat taller. "I also won't use my personal relationship with Dylan to get a story, any more than he'd use my research to break a case."

Bernard nodded once, his expression undecipherable. "Then get your believing, true ass out there. I have the next three weeks of stories ready, and Foster has a few follow-ups I can always air. But I want more. I want to find out what's happening with the border patrol and if there's any connection between the drugs and the increase in missing persons."

I'd begun to stand when he told me to get my ass out there, but with his words I sat again. "What did you just say?"

His dark eyes sparkled. "You do listen well. That's one of your best attributes. For your information, I don't sit in my office all day and play solitaire, letting you and Foster have all the fun. I got where I am by doing my own research. You and Foster are good, very good. That's why you're my lead investigators. That doesn't mean I've forgotten how to get in the trenches. I still know my way around this town and have my share of connections. Those you made at that fancy law firm, Preston and Butler, aren't the only ones who can help with this."

"You've been talking drugs for three weeks. Now, you're suddenly throwing missing persons into the equation. Do you think they're connected?"

He shrugged.

I leaned forward and lowered my voice. "Don't shit with me. If you want me to break the damn story why wouldn't you share this with me, one of your lead investigators?"

"You've got great questions, now figure out the answers." His gaze narrowed. "Think about it."

I didn't look away. "You didn't expect me to agree to ask Dylan for information or spy on him, did you?"

His shoulder rose and lowered.

"It was a test," I confirmed.

He lifted his coffee cup toward me. "Congratulations, Stella, you passed."

Instead of clinking cups, I glared.

"Calm down. I only recently got the tip, and in light of Mindy, I think it deserves investigation. I needed to be sure that if I put you on it, you'd keep your head in the game and not let your personal life get in the way."

I inhaled and pressed my lips together.

"I don't only mean Detective Richards, though I don't want him knowing what you're doing, or, more accurately, the DPD knowing. I'm also talking about Mindy. This case could reveal nothing or it may shed light on everything. The only way to know is to do what I said, get your ass out there. Go check out what's happening on the border today, talk to your contacts, and come back to the station this afternoon. I'll share what I have then."

"Thanks, Bernard. I'll keep my phone charged. If I don't hear from you, I'll see you this afternoon."

"Be there by three, unless you get something else."

I threw a five on the table and with a wink said, "You've already overstepped enough bounds. I'll get my own coffee."

CHAPTER

FOURTEEN

S^{ara}

THE CLANK of the belt buckle hitting the floor alerted me to the end of my sentence. My whimpers and Jacob's labored breaths were the only sounds bouncing off the bathroom walls and rumbling through my head. The last spoken word had come from my lips—five. Though it was gone, the memory of it continued to echo in the distance.

Five. Five. Five.

My heart clenched, forgetting its normal rhythm, and seized in my chest as my bare breasts lay flat against the cool, smooth vanity top. Uncertainty paralyzed me, making me immobile while the counter's edge dug deeper into my hips, and my toes throbbed from supporting my weight. Not only couldn't I move, more importantly, I hadn't received permission to do so. By some miracle my hands were still where Jacob had placed them, their grip a vise, keeping me suspended and saving me from falling. Though my hands had done what he instructed, I hadn't been the one to keep them there.

I'd left. Not literally. No, literally, I was captive in a life I detested from the depths of my soul. I completely understood why I didn't remember: I didn't want to. I'd left metaphorically, in an out-of-body experience. However, my reprieve had been short-lived, and now I was back. Though the punishment was done, the pain went on. Each lash of Jacob's belt burned like fire through my nervous system. Synapse after synapse sparked with impulses until my entire body was consumed by flames.

"Sara, you may let go of the counter."

It took a moment before my brain and hands worked together. I heard his voice, yet the vise wouldn't loosen. When it finally did, my arms dropped to my sides. With my cheek still against the counter, I waited.

"Stand up and give me your hand."

The belt hadn't struck only my behind, but also the tops of my thighs. Transferring my weight brought back the intensity of each strike. Biting my lip, I tasted the copper of my blood. Maybe I had bitten a hole through it, as Jacob had predicted. I stood straighter, still facing the sink, lowered my chin to my chest, and lifted my hand.

Taking my hand, Jacob guided it toward my wounds. The tips of my fingers detected the raised skin. My fingertips flinched back, as if the evidence of his correction were actual fire, trails of hot coals waiting to cause more destruction.

"Do you feel the welts?"

I nodded.

"Sara, this punishment was done to help you remember. Do you need more help remembering to speak when I ask you a question?"

"No, I remember." My voice choked hoarsely. It wasn't that I'd cried out; I hadn't. I'd remained silent throughout the correction, except for speaking the numbers I'd been required to say. "Yes, I feel them."

"Your skin isn't broken. I told you I'd never cause irreparable damage." Once again he guided my hand to the welts. "If you could see, I'd have you look at them. They're red, raised, and angry markings on your pale skin."

I swallowed the sobs that shook my shoulders as I envisioned each welt.

"As you may or may not remember, five is the standard number of strikes per infraction. How many infractions did you commit?"

My heart raced to the point of making me faint. I couldn't take ten more. I couldn't. Turning my body toward his, I lifted my face and pleaded. Panic spilled from my voice. "Three. Please don't . . . I . . . can't . . ."

He softly brushed my cheek. "Stop. I said your honesty earned you leniency. Five is all you'll get today."

I nodded as the relief of his clemency washed over me.

"Sara, I wanted you to touch the welts because they're your reminders not to question. Tonight when you walk or sit, each time you feel the pain, consider it a cue to think before you speak. Can you do that?"

"Yes."

He pulled a tissue from the box and wiped my cheeks. "It's up to you if more reminders will be necessary. I can't allow you to embarrass me in front of Father Gabriel or anyone else. Even your behavior in front of Elizabeth was unacceptable. I'll need to discuss it with Brother Luke. As I've said before, it's up to you. Only you can decide if today's correction will help you behave appropriately or if you'll need more assistance. Sara, will you need more reminders?"

I ran my fingers over the fiery raised skin again, suddenly intrigued by the sensations. "No, Jacob. I'm sorry I embarrassed you." I fought to catch my breath. "I'd like to avoid future reminders."

His lips brushed my forehead. "Very good. So would I."

The eerie calmness that had infiltrated his voice since he'd come back to my room this afternoon faded. As emotion returned to his tone, I found myself drawn to the man who had praised my answer.

"Now," Jacob continued, tucking a piece of my hair behind my ear. "That's done. Let's get us both ready for service."

"I . . . you . . . please, let me stay here."

"Nonsense. No one, not even the wife of an Assemblyman, can refuse a direct invitation from Father Gabriel; besides, I'm happy to have you at my side again as we enter the temple."

"But . . ."

"Sara, this is over. Remember what I said before? Correction works well, because the responsibility is transferred from you to me. You have your reminders to help you avoid future correction, but this infraction, as well as punishment, is done. It's history and now it's time to move on. We need to eat and change. We have service in an hour and a half, and as part of the Assembly, we must arrive in a timely manner."

As I contemplated the service with so many people I couldn't remember, the panic returned. Though I had five painful reasons reinforcing why I shouldn't, I leaned into Jacob's chest. The softness of his shirt brushed my cheek as his heartbeat drummed at my ear. Slowly his arms surrounded me, bringing warmth and security. I wrapped my arms around his trim waist, and for the first time that I could remember, really felt the firmness of his torso. My tears finally stopped, but I couldn't speak. Instead my naked body molded to his, silently saying what my lips couldn't admit.

I wasn't sure how to describe my whirlwind of emotions. I wasn't sure I could have if I'd been asked. The entire time I was bent over the vanity and the numbers came from my lips, I'd hated the man delivering the pain. It was an all-consuming hate, one that filled every cell of my body. In those minutes I'd understood why I'd blocked out the memories of my life: it was because they were too awful to remember. Red like the color Jacob described, as well as the blood that trickled from my lip, had filled my unseeing eyes. Hatred such as I couldn't recall had scratched like a wildcat to break free, to scream vulgarities and proclaim its presence.

And then it was over and now his voice was back.

FIFTEEN

Jacob

THOUGH MY TRAINING told me to walk away and let Sara deal with the consequences of her correction alone, my body refused to cooperate. I tried to resist, but when she melted into me, with her body trembling, my arms took on a mind of their own. As I embraced her petite form, she stole another piece of my heart, a piece that was never meant to be shared. I'd carried her and helped her, but never had I truly held her, not like this. When she was engulfed in my hold, our size difference became suddenly apparent. I was wearing boots and she was completely nude, and I towered over her by nearly a head. With her face pressed against my chest my resolve shattered as my internal battle raged.

Sara had been found guilty of forgetting a rule she'd never known, and as her husband, I was responsible for delivering the punishment. I understood the principle of the correction, but this wasn't theory: it was reality.

I had held the leather belt in my hand and sensed the vibration as it crashed down upon her fragile body. Each strike had marred not only her but also me. As she'd spoken the numbers I demanded, I'd reminded myself that this was for her success and survival; nevertheless that reasoning hadn't appeased my self-loathing. She should hate me, not only for this, but for everything, yet here she was clinging to my shirt and waist as if she were holding on for dear life, afraid that if she let go, she might fly away, like dust in the wind. That wouldn't happen. I wouldn't let it. I couldn't.

I hadn't chosen Sara as my wife; then again, I hadn't refused her. That wasn't even possible. If I had, all that I'd accomplished and learned would have been lost. For me to succeed, she needed to as well. As we stood silent, apart from her occasional ragged breaths, for minutes upon minutes, she wrapped in my arms, I resolved that though the stakes were high, I was all in. She hadn't asked for this nor did she know how she'd complicated my mission, but she was here, and if this was what I needed to do for both of us to succeed, I would.

Sara's trembling finally calmed, yet her shoulders continued to quake with each broken gasp. Looking to the mirror, I saw the long unfettered ringlets of gold that flowed around her face and over my arms. No longer was her hair secured in the braid she'd woven this morning. Now it cascaded down her back, swaying slightly with each breath. I worked to keep my eyes on her hair and not look lower, but my gaze was pulled to the horror and evidence of my punishment—the reminders—I'd left behind. Five distinctively long, angry welts crisscrossed her firm round bottom and extended below onto her toned upper thighs. With the bathroom lighting, the redness glowed in stark contrast to the paleness of her complexion.

My chest continued to dampen as her tears soaked my shirt. Rubbing her bare back gently up and down, I stayed conscious of her skin and mindful to keep my large hand from straying to where it'd been marked. I'd caused her enough pain. In the three weeks since her arrival and incident, she'd begun to heal. My chest ached with the knowledge that her beautiful skin was once again spoiled, and this time I was responsible.

Each time I started to move, she burrowed closer, settling herself not only under my skin, but deeper into my heart. My body reacted as any man's would to the closeness of a naked woman, but I knew it wasn't time. Sara needed comfort, not sex. If we came together now, she'd forever associate sex with punishment, and when the time came, that wasn't what I wanted nor did I want it to be sex. When the time was right, I wanted to make love to the woman in my arms.

My belt lay curled on the tile floor by our feet, like a snake ready to strike. Its vile venom had hurt Sara, soaking into her flesh and causing her agony. If it had been a real snake, I'd have ripped its head from its long coiled body. Its fangs would no longer strike, and she'd be able to sleep soundly knowing the danger was gone. But that wouldn't happen. To her the danger was me. She didn't understand the levels and powers at work in our lives. She could never know the true danger that lurked around each corner. The only way to keep her safe was to stay on course. Her only objective was to embrace Sara and become Sara. Her conformity to The Light was the only means of saving her.

"Sara," I said, lifting her chin and seeing the blotches of red on her cheeks and neck. "We need to get ready. Raquel went home to prepare for service, so I'm going to cover your cast and put you in a warm shower." The way her body tensed, I knew what she was thinking. "The warm water will sting at first, but with time it'll make your welts feel better. I also have some ointment that you've said helped in the past."

My words were a grave. With each statement about the past we'd never shared I dug deeper and deeper.

She nodded against my shirt, and then, as if remembering to speak, she said, "If you say so."

I kissed her hair. "I do. I also think we should change your bandages around your eyes. Dr. Newton said it's not good to allow them to stay damp."

"All right." Her shoulders sagged while her voice carried a faraway tone, like a sad melody that had lost its zeal. I wanted obedience, not a lifeless zombie. Somehow I had to discover the way to help her find that place of contentment, the place where she was safe and happy and in accordance with Father Gabriel's Light.

I directed her to sit on the closed toilet. As she did, I remembered finding her there before . . . before I'd broken her. When her sore bottom connected with the cool seat, her lower lip disappeared between her teeth. It took every ounce of control I had not to fall to my knees and beg for her forgiveness. I couldn't. According to The Light this was her doing, not mine.

"I'm going to wrap your cast first," I said once she was settled.

"Does everyone go to service?"

I didn't know if she was trying to get her mind on other things, but if so, I'd gladly help.

"Yes," I replied. "This is a big community. We all have jobs, but Sunday and Wednesday service are the only time that all jobs stop. Well, except for the powerhouse; that can't stop."

"Pow—" She stopped herself, then rephrased. "May I ask what that is?"

She is learning.

"It's what it sounds like. It's the place where hydropower turns turbines. They then work generators that supply power to our entire community."

"Like water?"

"Yes, though wind would work, it'd be more visible and less predictable. As long as the river flows, we have power."

"Will you tell me where we are, or is that something I need to wait to learn?"

I finished securing the plastic around her cast, reached for her hand, and helped her stand. Though it had to feel better to stand, she still grimaced with the movement. "Like I said before, we came here together, you and I. You knew where we were coming since before we arrived. You knew we were moving to the Northern Light, in Far North, Alaska."

As her head moved slowly from side to side her hair fell about her face. "I don't understand how it's all gone—my memory. It seems like I'd remember moving to Alaska or where we lived before."

"We don't have time to wash your hair," I said, changing the subject and removing the old hair tie dangling uselessly from a few strands of her hair. Once it was free, I raked my fingers down the length of blonde. "Besides, we washed it this morning and it still looks good. You'll need to redo your braid—it fell out."

"Do I have to keep it in a braid?"

The small fraction of emotion in her question made my cheeks rise. "Of course not. That's how you wore it most of the time in the past. That's why I mentioned it."

"Oh," she sighed. "Raquel mentioned a messy bun once. I think I'd like a messy bun for service." Her voice softened as she added, "If that's all right with you."

"As long as you remember how to secure it, it's fine. I can help with a lot, but you don't want me fixing your hair."

At the sound of my self-deprecating statement, she lifted her face toward mine, and her lips formed a stunning smile. In that grin she planted a glimmer of hope for our future. I felt the small seedling in my chest, its shell broken by roots that needed care, sunshine, and nutrients. I prayed a silent prayer to Father Gabriel that one day it would bloom.

"Here," I said as I handed her the hairbrush.

These weeks that she was required to spend without sight gave me the clear advantage. I could stare and study my wife without her being self-conscious. As she brushed her hair, I watched, admiring how truly beautiful she was, especially now that her cheeks were mostly clear. The earlier bruising and more recent red blotches were about gone, revealing her creamy soft skin. Though the purple of her throat had faded considerably, now merely a brown tint, it still needed to be covered. That was why Raquel had gotten Sara the turtleneck sweater.

Tonight would be Sara's first introduction to the followers. Everyone in the community understood the importance of making each follower feel welcomed. Newly acquired members were different. They didn't realize they were new. For that reason they were primarily surrounded by people who'd help with their acclimation. The entire Assembly and Commission, and their wives, were Sara's support group . . . well, with the exception of Brother Timothy and Sister Lilith. Since Brother Daniel was my overseer, he'd also become Sara's. That was why Sister Ruth had stepped in with her training. After Sara's breakdown, I'd gone to both of them privately and discussed my concern. I didn't ask for Sister Ruth's help, as that could have caused more problems with Lilith and Brother Timothy. However, I placed a bet on Sister Ruth's caring nature; my wager paid off.

As Lilith had explained to Sara, as an Assemblyman's wife, she held a special place of honor. For that, as well as other reasons, her transition into The Light was more difficult than that of a mere follower. Yet at the same time, the people in this inner circle of the chosen knew the way into The Light better than anyone, and would do their best to facilitate her success.

"There, that will work for my shower," she announced as she fastened the clip I'd recently handed her behind her head. I grinned at the blanched spot on her lip. She'd had it securely tucked between her teeth as she concentrated on her hair. With her announcement she'd released it, allowing the pink to return.

As the warm water assaulted her backside, her grip on my hand tightened. Insensitively I choked out the words I knew to say. "Will you remember not to question?"

"Yes, Jacob," she replied through gritted teeth.

It took a little time, but when her muscles relaxed, I knew she was finally more comfortable. Once she was out of the shower, I applied the ointment, explaining the whole time how it had helped her in the past. We turned off the light in the bathroom, and I replaced the bandages around her eyes. It wasn't until she was dressed and ready for service that she mentioned her punishment.

"I assume I'll be sitting at the service."

It was the first time I'd seen my wife, as my wife, in anything other than a nightgown. I couldn't help but stare at her splendor. She'd done as she'd asked to and secured her hair near the nape of her neck. Her turtleneck was black and ribbed, fitting snugly to her breasts, and disappeared at her small waist into the skirt that stopped about midcalf. The skirt was made of a blue-jean material. Over the turtleneck she wore a jacket that matched the skirt. The boot she wore on her right foot went almost to her knee and had a heel that nearly matched the height of the cast. With it on, she walked better than she had with slippers. Raquel had chosen her clothes, including the white bra and panties hidden beneath. Around Sara's neck I'd secured a necklace.

Dangling from the chain was a silver cross. It was an exact duplicate of the one worn by all the Assembly and Commission wives.

There was something about Sara's presence and confidence, despite her punishment, that mesmerized me. As I stared at her, the only thing I could think, the only thing that registered, was that she was mine. All mine. Though my mind recognized the errors of our ways, in this world she was mine. Father Gabriel and The Light had given her to me, uniting us as husband and wife.

I tried to concentrate on her statement.

"Yes," I replied as she walked confidently toward me and the table that held our dinner.

Somewhat nervously she reached for her new necklace and slid the silver cross from side to side. Taking a deep breath, she dropped her chin a bit and asked, "May I please stand to eat?"

"Why, Sara?"

Yes, I am an ass.

"Because my reminders are still sore, and if you'll allow me, I'd like to let them rest."

She was more perfect than I'd ever imagined. It wasn't that in reality I needed this submission, but damn, it was hot. "What's the purpose of the pain?" I asked.

"It's to remind me to think before I speak and to not question."

"If I allow you to stand, will you continue to remember?"

As her lip quivered, twisting the knife in my heart, she replied, "Yes, I'll remember."

"You may stand."

"Thank you."

So insanely hot!

I readjusted myself, lessening the physical pressure of my obvious attraction.

We'd practiced walking about the room, but leaving the clinic was different. She had to completely trust me and allow me to lead her through a dark world. With her coat and gloves secured, we made our way out of her room, down the quiet halls, and out into the cold night. As she breathed the frigid air, I asked, "Are you all right? It's been a few weeks since you were out of the clinic."

With her petite hand wrapped in mine, she replied, "I am, as long as you're with me."

The thing was, I knew without a doubt that she meant it. In this warped world, I was her anchor. It was the plan from the beginning, but the fact that it had worked both elated and sickened me.

She deserved a hell of a lot more than this.

Once we were in the temple, we were greeted by everyone. Though I'd given her only a brief synopsis on how to respond, she did so appropriately. To those she didn't know, she smiled and nodded, all the while holding tight to my hand. It wasn't until we met up with Brother Benjamin and Sister Raquel that we released our grip, and I placed her hand in Raquel's.

"Sara, I'll come and get you once service is over. Sister Raquel will take you to Sister Elizabeth. Sister Ruth is seated in front of your seat. They'll all be there for you and watch over you."

Raquel smiled in my direction as she squeezed Sara's hand.

"Thank you," Sara replied. "I'll be fine." She turned toward Raquel, understanding that she could speak to others who she knew. "Thank you too," she said.

Raquel nodded toward Brother Benjamin and me. "We'll be fine, I promise."

Murmurs filled the large room with the sound of normal preservice chatting as Benjamin and I made our way to the Assemblymen's seats. Once we were in our places, I glanced out to the congregation of followers. Sara and Raquel were making their way to the Assembly wives' seats, where Elizabeth was waiting. Though Sara tried to hide it, each time she sat or moved, her expression revealed her discomfort. After a while I watched as Sara's and Elizabeth's heads went together, and Elizabeth held Sara's hand. The two appeared to be speaking quietly between themselves. I wondered if Sara was confessing her punishment.

Just before service began, Brother Timothy leaned toward me. "I see Sister Sara made it here tonight."

"Yes, Brother, Father Gabriel invited her."

"Oh, I know. I just wasn't sure if she'd be able to walk, but it appears as though sitting is more her issue."

My body temperature rose. "Brother, she informed me of what occurred while you and Father Gabriel were in her room. I've taken care of my wife's impudence." I lifted my brow and settled my eyes on Lilith. "Perhaps you should follow suit."

Though I listened to Father Gabriel, my gaze never left my wife. Not being able to sit with her increased my anxiety. While I trusted Raquel and Elizabeth, they weren't me, and I was ultimately responsible. Nonetheless, as the evening progressed, my apprehension waned. If someone hadn't known the truth, they'd truly believe Sara Adams was back following her incident.

The word incident filled me with dread. Father Gabriel still hadn't pronounced his decree for Sara's perceived part. It was essential to the plan, the timetable, and the protocol, but that didn't mean

I liked it or was comfortable with my wife suffering more correction. After closing prayer Brother Daniel came to me.

"Brother Jacob, I'm very pleased with Sister Sara's presence here tonight. You should be proud."

A little of the tension left my shoulders. "Thank you, Brother. I am."

"Father Gabriel would like to speak to us for a few minutes."

"Now?" I asked nervously, looking out toward the moving people.

"Yes."

As he passed by, I reached for Benjamin's arm. "Brother, I need to speak with Father Gabriel. May I ask you—"

He didn't let me finish. "No need to ask. I'll get the ladies and escort them to the conservatory. We'll wait for you there."

Luke stepped closer. "Would you mind including Elizabeth? I'm part of this meeting we're about to have."

Benjamin nodded, unquestioning. "I've got your backs," he said with a grin as he walked toward our wives, still seated where they'd been.

Luke's elbow hit my ribs and he whispered, "You've got it bad."

"What?" My eyes opened wide. "Do you know something about this meeting?"

Laughter rumbled from his throat. "No, I don't know anything about the meeting. What I mean is that you've got it bad for your wife."

I shrugged. "Shouldn't I?"

"Eventually. Things are a little early. She could still . . ."

My heart stopped beating as I mentally finished his sentence. She could still be banished. Her probationary period wasn't complete. Truthfully, no one was ever completely without that threat. It didn't happen often to established members, but it could. Though I'd never been told, I had the feeling that had been the fate of the pilot I'd replaced.

Luke patted my shoulder. "Hey, forget I said that. Sara did great here tonight. I think you've got this covered."

I reached for his arm and stopped his steps before we neared Father Gabriel's office. "After this meeting I need to speak to you about something that happened earlier today."

The corner of Luke's mouth moved upward into a lopsided, knowing grin. "Elizabeth told me."

"Vulgarity? Prideful?" I asked, letting go of my grasp and repeating the words Sara had used earlier today.

He nodded. "New followers. It's my job. Elizabeth and I see and hear things like that often. It's not the end of the line for her, and besides, I watched Sara tonight. I believe you took care of it. Am I correct?"

"I did."

He patted my shoulder again. "Then we're good. It was dealt with, and according to The Light, it is as if it never happened."

I sighed with relief. "Wait a minute. Elizabeth told you? Were you planning on telling me?"

"I was. But Elizabeth said she encouraged Sara to tell you herself. We wanted to give her the chance. Again, we do this new-follower stuff all the time. Believe me when I say I only bring the bigger issues to the Assembly. We'd be there all day if I brought every detail. Of course I'll report this to your overseer, but I know Brother Daniel, and I bet he'll feel the same. The infraction happened. You took care of it. The issue has been resolved."

"Thanks."

"What about the memory she spoke of?" Luke asked.

"What memory?"

How much shit is going to be thrown at me tonight?

"Listen," Luke said, reaching for my arm. "You and Sara obviously had an eventful afternoon. As her husband, what you do is at your discretion. As the new-follower coordinator, can I offer some advice?"

I nodded.

"Sara mentioned to Elizabeth that she had a memory of recreational running. She said she had the memory one of the first days after the incident. It happened before she was allowed to speak, and she'd forgotten all about it, until Elizabeth mentioned running."

His words echoed with the beat of my erratic heart. Surely Luke could see the way my chest pulsed.

What other memories has she had?

Luke went on. "Sara also said that she hasn't had any other memories and has been taking her medication. Elizabeth encouraged her to tell you if any more memories returned." He rested his hand on my shoulder. "Here's my advice, you had a lot to deal with this afternoon. It doesn't matter how many times we tell Sara that none of this is new, it is. The memory was probably not her biggest concern when you returned. She not only had her transgressions with Elizabeth but her one with Father Gabriel. Sara doesn't understand the significance of recalling a memory. If she's punished for not relaying that particular bit of information to you, she'll learn to fear memories; more accurately, she'll fear telling you. It's your choice, but remember that's why Brother Daniel and I are here. We'll be happy to give advice, and we want you both to succeed. The Light isn't a singular journey. You're not in this alone."

I sighed. "It's more difficult on this side than sitting on the Assembly."

Luke nodded. "I was there once. Well, Elizabeth wasn't acquired, but she still had to be indoctrinated. We're here for you, and for Sara. Now, let's see what's happening in there." He inclined his head toward Father Gabriel's office.

I nodded. Taking a deep breath, Luke and I entered the office.

From behind his desk, Father Gabriel looked up. Brother Daniel was already there, seated at one of the chairs facing him. Beside Brother Daniel were two empty chairs.

"Brothers," Father Gabriel greeted us. "Have a seat. Before we meet with the Assembly and Commission in the morning, I want to discuss my decree regarding Sara's retribution for the incident."

SIXTEEN

S tella

DYLAN'S VOICE had that edge, the one that said he was serious. "No. I didn't call you to have you run to Highland Heights. I called to tell you to stay away."

"That doesn't make sense," I replied. Though I wasn't fazed by his tone, I was concerned about letting him know that I was already there. I'd been in Highland Heights most of the morning, not far off Woodward Avenue, sitting in my car parked in the lot of one of the few open businesses.

"What doesn't make sense is you wanting to come here. It's dangerous!" His voice was getting louder by the minute. "This is body number three in less than two weeks."

"Same house?" Sirens sounded from the phone and outside my open window. I quickly pushed the button to raise the window, hoping that Dylan would think the sounds were all occurring around him.

"No. I shouldn't even be telling you this. I need to get back to work."

My mind raced with questions as I turned from side to side, searching for the source of the sound. The sirens' roar grew louder and then softer, but they were nowhere to be seen.

How close is he?

"Where, Dylan? Is it near where the other two bodies were found? Is it a woman? A man? What's her age? Is she blonde?"

"Seriously?" he asked in disbelief. "Stay away from Highland Heights. The DPD will be covering the entire area today and tonight. If one patrolman, one detective, or hell, even a Highland Heights traffic cop tells me that he or she saw you or your car here, so help me . . ."

His sentence trailed away.

My shoulders stiffened as my brows rose. The temperature inside my car wasn't going up only due to the closed windows. "Finish your threat, Detective Richards. I'd like to know exactly what you planned to say before I tell you to stick it up your—"

"It wasn't a threat." He exhaled. "Listen to me and I'll make you a deal."

"What kind of deal?"

"You stay away from here today, and in the morning, I'll escort you to the crime scene."

The opportunity sounded too good to be true. My curiosity was piqued. "Why? What are you hiding from me?" My hand moved to my suddenly racing heart. "Oh my God, do you think it's Mindy?"

"No. I know it isn't. Stella . . ."

I sighed. "Thank God. Then why? Why would you be willing to do that?"

More voices, growing louder, came through the phone, mingling with the sirens. "Listen, I've got to go. Just shut up." He paused.

Though my lips came together, and my rebuttal was on the tip of my tongue, I stayed silent since his time was obviously short.

Dylan continued hurriedly, "I'm offering because I know you. You're not going to listen to me unless you know you'll get to see this. Call me a controlling ass, I don't care. I don't want something to happen to you because you're in the wrong place. Just let the DPD handle it today. Tomorrow early, after dawn and before all the idiots hit the street, I'll bring you to both houses. That way you'll get a look at the crime scenes, satisfy your curiosity, and I'll know you're safe." He lowered his volume. "I'm hanging up. Tell me we have a deal."

Shit!

"OK, we have a deal."

"Good-bye."

"Bye—" I didn't have a chance to say it before the phone went dead. I shook my head. Turning on my ignition, I cranked the air conditioning and smoothed back my hair. Inhaling the cooled air, I lifted my ponytail from my neck and redirected the air-conditioning vent. Though it was past Labor Day and autumn was approaching, it hadn't stopped the heat. I'd lived in the area long enough to know that it could, any day. Seventy degrees one day and thirty the next. Welcome to autumn in Michigan.

I contemplated Dylan's warning. I drove a gray Ford Fusion, an inconspicuous car, for a reason. There had to be hundreds of them in the Detroit metropolitan area. Besides, it was only ten thirty in the morning.

If I leave this parking lot now, even to leave Highland Heights, will Dylan or one of the other officers see me? If they do, will they know it is me? How am I supposed to wait almost twenty-four hours before I learn more?

Waiting wasn't my thing, but then again, neither was surveillance, and I did it. Waiting was a big part of my job. The investigators on television had it easy. They parked their car and then boom, their suspect would walk right in front of them. That wasn't the way it worked in real life. I'd been sitting in this parking lot since before the sun came up, around six this morning, and my legs were beginning to feel it.

I grinned. Maybe it wasn't the surveillance my legs were feeling. Maybe it was the aftereffects of last night's activities. Dylan had made me an offer I couldn't refuse. Oh, I could have, but I hadn't wanted to.

At first I'd decided to cancel our evening plans. I was getting nowhere fast on my research, and I needed to jump in with both feet. Over the last two-plus weeks, I'd made it through all Dr. Howell's cases more than once. I'd even deciphered Bernard's sketchy information regarding drugs and missing persons. There were a few unsolved cases as well as people who crossed the border with increased regularity. That wasn't in itself a crime, but some of their information was questionable. Could that connect them to the drugs?

None of it made sense. There were dots to be connected; I just couldn't make out the picture they formed. Plus I'd promised the Rosemonts, once again, that I wouldn't stop. It was one thing to say it on the phone or in an e-mail, but the week before I'd said it while holding their hands. They'd been back to Detroit for the second time since Mindy's disappearance. I didn't blame them. Even though I'd promised to do everything at this end, they felt helpless in California and needed to feel involved. I didn't hold much hope that a solution would materialize from the flyers they'd put all over the city, but then again, who was I to fault them? I wasn't making progress either.

With that search for answers at the forefront of my mind, I'd made the decision to go straight home from work and forgo Dylan's house. Imagine my surprise when thirty minutes after I arrived home, he showed up at my door. Though I wanted to be mad, as soon as my gaze met his I knew I couldn't. It wasn't only the way he stood outside my door, his long legs barely covered by torn jeans, biceps bulging from his sleeves, and that smug sexy grin that turned my insides to jelly. It was what I saw as I scanned lower. My stomach growled as I saw the six-pack of beer in one hand and a pizza in the other. However, what sealed his fate was the package of time-release fish feeder blocks on top of the pizza box. Even now I had a difficult time keeping a smile from sneaking across my weary face. Shaking my head at the memory, I knew Detective Dylan Richards was getting to me.

I still wasn't sure if I was the relationship type. This was the first time I'd ever been with anyone as long as I had been with Dylan. That didn't mean I was ready to become more serious. However, it was becoming increasingly clear that if I didn't want it to go that way, I'd need distance and a Teflon coating for my heart.

It didn't bother me that others warned me about his hard-ass ways. The Dylan Richards I knew wasn't a tough detective. The one who was getting under my skin was the one who drove across the city to support me at the morgue and brought me fish food. Granted, the fish food was time-released, which allowed me to leave Fred on his own for a few days, but still, when I combined that with his sexier-than-hell grin and the bedroom-blue eyes, my pulse pitter-pattered and my insides tightened. The mere thought of him not only beside me, but inside me, had my mind replaying scenes that were probably illegal in some states.

I sighed and tried to concentrate on the task at hand.

The building I'd staked out all morning appeared as empty as it had when I'd arrived. Bernard's contact had shared the address, saying three different vehicles from there crossed the Canadian border almost every day. The vehicles were driven by different people, but all the passport information included this Gerald Street address. The obvious problem was that the address wasn't a home. It was some big abandoned building.

Over the past four hours, with the help of my hot spot, an Internet search, and my imagination, I'd constructed a story of a bustling neighborhood. In 1907 Henry Ford had built an automobile plant not far from where I sat. In the next thirteen years the population of this area had grown to over forty thousand. Five years later Chrysler was founded here. This area had thrived.

Then, during my lifetime, the latter decades of the twentieth century, Highland Heights experienced the same problems as Detroit and many other cities. Declining population led to loss of tax base. That, along with loss of employment opportunities, created increasing crime. At its peak this city within a city had boasted over fifty thousand residents. Today there were barely ten thousand.

Unfortunately, the exodus had left an excess of unused and abandoned buildings. Though the cities of Highland Heights and Detroit tried to keep the buildings boarded up or demolished, as long as they stood, they were magnets for illicit use. That the woman I'd seen at the morgue, as well as two more people, had been found dead inside one of them wasn't hard to believe.

I knew my imagination was running wild. Spending all my spare time dissecting Tracy Howell's "compilation theory" was getting to me. Every death and disappearance didn't have to be related. Though this neighborhood was a melting pot for crimes, so were other areas of the city. High-risk behaviors made areas like this good spots for deaths from self-inflicted causes, such as drug use. Unfortunately, they also made good dumping grounds. There were too many reasons for death among Dr. Howell's cases to assume that all, or even a large number, of them were related.

The area needed more places like the building I was sitting behind: a health clinic. Dr. Howell was right. New businesses wouldn't be willing to set up shop here if it was publicized that just down the street dead bodies kept surfacing.

The building I watched used to be a school, and the one next to it had once been a fire station. As I sat, I imagined what they were like in their heydays. Instead of being desolate, the area would've been filled with people. At one time children had run along the streets and played in the attached lots. Instead of dirt and debris, there had been grass, trees, and playground equipment. As I scanned the area, I knew that Dylan's concern was warranted. Going purely by the number of abandoned buildings in this neighborhood, it wasn't safe. However, the way I saw it, it was daylight, and I'd left my trail of bread crumbs. Bernard and Foster knew exactly where I was.

With each minute of nothing, I considered calling Bernard. His earlier suggestion to use Dylan as an informant might have been a test, but it had pissed me off. Now I wondered whether, if I told him about Dylan's offer, he'd think the sharing of information went both ways.

Shrugging, I decided it could wait until after I received my tour tomorrow morning.

Therefore, instead of Bernard, I dialed Dr. Howell's cell phone. I was ready to leave a message when she finally answered on the fourth ring.

"Hi, Charlotte," she answered. "I'm surprised you're calling me at work."

Charlotte?

"OK," I replied, "I get it, you can't talk. Did you know another body's been found in Highland Heights?"

"Sure did." Tracy's upbeat tone combined with the morbid subject made me grin. She was obviously in the presence of someone she didn't want to include in our conversation.

"It was found in the same neighborhood as the woman from a week ago," I said softly, hoping my voice didn't transcend the phone and reach the unintended listener.

"Sounds about right. I'll call you after I get off work. I'm not sure if we can meet for a drink, but I'll let you know."

"Thanks, I'll be waiting for your call."

When the phone disconnected, I wondered who Charlotte was—I mean, besides me.

Unlike with my wasted morning, at least with that brief conversation I'd learned something. The ME's office had already received the call. Maybe I wouldn't have to wait until tomorrow for details. Maybe I'd get them this evening from Dr. Howell.

As I was about to give up on the abandoned building, a late-model black Suburban pulled up and around to the front. It stopped near the neighboring building, the one that looked like an old fire station. Though there were three large garage-type doors, the two men who got out of the SUV walked between the buildings.

I reached for my camera. While my phone took good pictures, my Nikon was capable of much more. With the two-hundred-millimeter-focal-length lens, the zooming abilities were superb. I pointed and snapped a rapid series of shots. The two men who walked between the buildings were white, average height, wearing dark jeans and white T-shirts. If I were to guess, I'd have put them roughly in their thirties. As I continued to take the photos, the word nondescript came to mind. The driver remained in the vehicle. Seeing him through the windshield, I couldn't get a great picture, but I saw that he was Black man and wearing a similar white T-shirt. From my angle, I couldn't make out much more.

Whatever the men did between the buildings didn't take long. In less than five minutes, they were out, and the Suburban pulled away, past me and toward Woodward. Ignoring Dylan's warning, I backed out of my space and pulled out of the parking lot, just in time to watch the Suburban turn right on Woodward. Justifying my decision —the SUV had turned in the direction in which I would need to go to get back to WCJB—I followed.

Since Woodward Avenue was a main thoroughfare, I wasn't concerned about the occupants of the SUV questioning my presence. That was, until we turned right onto Glendale Avenue. The hairs on the back of my neck tingled in warning. For a warm late-summer morning, the streets were very quiet. While I waited at a light at Second Avenue, the Suburban turned right. Once the stoplight changed, I followed. I turned just in time to see the black SUV pull into a parking lot behind a white brick building.

I continued to drive and circled the block.

Thankfully, wherever Dylan and the rest of the police were wasn't nearby. Approaching again from the front of the building, I slowed near the corner of Second and Glendale Avenues. During my circle I passed multiple buildings that weren't only abandoned, but charred remains of what had once been homes. As a matter of fact, I was currently across the street from one. An overgrowth of shrubbery near the intersection hid my location as I pulled to the side of the road.

Peering about, I didn't see a single person. Maybe it was the police presence somewhere in the vicinity, but for whatever reason, despite its being almost midday, the neighborhood was deadly still. I turned off the ignition, locked my car, and stepped onto the sidewalk. Weeds brushed my pant legs as I made my way through the debris littering the street and sidewalk.

Moving slowly around the overgrowth of bushes, I scanned the front of the building, the one where the SUV had parked. If I were to guess, it was or used to be an office building. Four stories tall, it had many windows in front, all covered interiorly by long white vertical blinds. This building's surroundings looked different from those of most buildings in the area. Unlike where I stood, there weren't any overgrown bushes or grass; even the sidewalk in front was clear of weeds and debris. A black chain-link fence surrounded the entire building, yet there didn't appear to be a lock of any kind on the front gate. Above the front entrance was a blue awning with white letters that simply read "The Light."

I snapped more pictures. Rotating from left to right I photographed the entire intersection. On the southwest corner, across Second Avenue from The Light, was a large limestone building surrounded by a rod iron fence. As I zoomed my camera, I made out the words Public Schools of Highland Heights etched in the stone. The trees and bushes as well as ground clutter indicated that, like many others, it was abandoned. Across from the old school was the skeleton of a house, decimated by fire, and on the corner where I stood was another building. The broken windows told me that it too was empty.

Getting back in my car, I watched the vertical blinds covering the windows on the front side of The Light. I didn't notice any movement. If the building held people, they were hidden. As I slowly drove toward the intersection, a group of three women walked from the back of The Light, coming from near the parking lot. From that distance I couldn't make out distinguishing characteristics, but I could tell that they were women.

What are they doing?

I watched as they crossed Second Avenue toward the old school and disappeared behind an overgrowth of trees. Reaching for my camera, I waited for more people. When no one else emerged, I laid my camera down and drove forward, crossing the intersection. Driving slowly, I peered in the direction in which they had gone. The iron gate on the far side of the trees was closed. Beyond it was a door, but it had a "Do Not Trespass" sign attached and a chain laced through the handle from the outside.

Where did the women go?

They couldn't have entered that door. If they had, someone would have needed to chain it again from the outside. Even with my active imagination that seemed improbable; besides, the lock looked rusty and old. Stopping my car, I grabbed my camera. Quickly I took pictures of the side of the school. Looking back to The Light building, I noticed more windows, also covered from within. I snapped a few more pictures. The Suburban was still parked in the lot behind the building, along with a half-dozen other cars, none of which were new.

The wail of sirens in the distance propelled me to leave. Soon I was headed north and then east, back to Woodward Avenue.

Within ten minutes I was out of Highland Heights and safely into the North End of Detroit. I couldn't recall for sure, but I didn't remember having seen any police cars. Honestly, other than the patrons of the health clinic where I'd spent most of my morning, the men in my pictures, and the three women, I hadn't seen anyone. Hopefully, no one would report my whereabouts to my overprotective boyfriend.

I shrugged. If they did, he'd need to deal. Then again, I didn't want to lose my morning tour.

~

"WAKE UP, SLEEPYHEAD."

Dylan's raspy voice invaded my dream. I couldn't remember what I'd been seeing behind my closed eyes, but whatever it had been, I was confident the man above me was better. As I inhaled his musky scent, my lips formed a smile, only for it to morph into a pout.

"What if I don't want to?"

"Then I guess your lovely tour of downtown Highland Heights will need to wait."

My eyes sprang open and I started to sit. A laugh rumbled deep in Dylan's throat as he leaned over me, stopping my upward motion. The vibrations of his chest electrified my bare nipples, making them hard and tight, while my insides fluttered.

"I don't think I've gotten that quick of a reaction from you this early in the morning, ever. Not even when I was offering something a hell of a lot better than two rat-infested boarded-up houses."

This time I laughed. "I think it's the lovely description that has me enthralled. Who could pass up a tour of rat-infested boarded-up houses in lovely downtown Highland Heights?" I asked, mocking his words. "Besides, that other offer of yours, well . . ." I shrugged. "I've had that before."

Dylan rolled away, laying his head on the pillow and covering his eyes with his hard bicep. "You're seriously messing with my self-confidence."

I lifted my head and moved toward him. My long hair teased his skin. After a quick kiss on his cheek, I said, "I doubt that. I've never known a more—"

His finger touched my lips and his eyes sparkled. "Stop right there. Let me imagine the rest of the sentence, and just maybe, I might recover."

My grin blossomed into a full-out smile. "I'm so glad. I'd hate to be responsible for any of your nonexistent self-esteem issues."

Dylan captured my shoulders and pulled me close, flattening my breasts against his chest and sending my hair cascading around my face. We were two people in a tunnel of blonde. "I think," he teased, "we should skip the tour and work on my nonexistent issues."

I pulled away. "As I recall, we worked on your issues last night."

"But I have more."

Turning slightly, I peeked at the blankets and playfully shook my head at the way they now tented. Kissing his lips, I reminded him, "You're the one who told me we had to do this early, before . . . what did you say? The idiots came out?"

"That was me, wasn't it?"

"It was, and I want my tour."

Dylan looked at the clock, which read half past five. "Sunrise is a little after seven. We don't want to arrive before sunrise and surprise the rats."

My whole body quivered. "Yuck. It'd be all right with me if you quit mentioning those."

He poked my side, making me laugh. "You can always change your mind."

"Nope," I squeaked from the tickling. "Stop! You offered me a tour. I want it."

"OK. I was thinking that if we drove separately to WCJB, you could leave your car and ride with me to Highland Heights. Then I'll take you back to the station." He sighed. "Heck, we'll probably get you to work before Barney."

I slapped his shoulder. "Bernard. What about you?"

"What about me?"

"Last time I checked you needed to go to work too."

Dylan threw back the covers, stood, and stretched. Suddenly my eyes found it difficult to make their way up his sculpted body. It wasn't that I didn't enjoy his handsome face, I did. I also liked his shoulders, abs, and everything lower. "Hey," he said with a laugh. "My eyes are up here."

"Umm . . ." I sighed. Slowly I moved my gaze up to his blue smirk and winked.

"You, Miss Montgomery, happen to be dating a detective. Once I'm in the car, I can log on, and we're good. I'm officially on duty."

"If you get an exciting call, do I get to come along?"

"And have it end up on WCJB's evening news? No way."

"You're no fun," I said, jutting my lower lip out as far as it would go.

Dylan reached for my hand. "We've got a little time. How about you join me in the shower, and I show you how much fun I can be?"

I shrugged as I stood. "I guess, but I think a police chase would be more exciting."

Dylan slapped my behind, and the crack echoed through his bedroom.

"Ouch!"

His eyes sparkled. "Don't forget, I have issues."

Tracing my finger teasingly down his chest, I stepped close and kissed his neck. "Detective Richards, we all know that."

An hour later we were in Dylan's unmarked Charger on our way to Highland Heights. I pulled the black case I'd thrown in the back-seat up to the front. I opened it, removed my Nikon, and began changing the lens. I wouldn't need the zooming power of yesterday. Well, unless there was a rat; then I'd be so far out of one of those houses, I would need the two-hundred-millimeter.

Dylan glanced my way. "Hey, what do you think you're doing?"

"It seems rather obvious, but if you're having problems, I'm changing the lens on my camera."

"No. You're not taking pictures. I'm taking you into a secured crime scene. I'm not losing my job."

"It's not like I'm going to take your picture," I replied. "Besides, it helps me remember everything. I can go home and study the pictures."

"No."

"They'll never end up on one of Bernard's broadcasts, I promise." I turned on the screen and scrolled through my pictures from yesterday.

Dylan looked in my direction and his knuckles blanched as his grip tightened on the steering wheel. "When did you take those?"

I looked up from the image of the white brick building with the blue awning.

Shit!

"Yesterday," I replied sheepishly.

"I thought we had a deal. I guess I should take you back to WCJB."

"We do have a deal," I pleaded. "The thing was, when you called, I was kind of already in Highland Heights. I left soon after our conversation."

"Jesus, Stella. Why?"

This time of the morning the traffic hadn't yet built. I watched the landmarks in New Center as we continued heading north on Woodward Avenue. If he wasn't turning around, I guessed I could answer him, at least partially. "I was staking out an abandoned building. It was an address from a source. I heard the sirens, but never saw the police cars. So, see, I wasn't really near you."

"Staking out an abandoned building doesn't exactly narrow down your location."

"Do you go to Highland Heights often?" I asked.

"The HHPD and DPD work together on some things. Usually Highland Heights takes care of its cases and we do ours. There's been some crossover lately."

"Why? What's changed?"

The morning sky was an array of reds and pinks as the sun brought light where dark had prevailed. Dylan turned right off Woodward, away from the sunrise, onto Cortland. This street was only two blocks south of Glendale, where I'd been yesterday. Dylan ran his fingers through his hair.

I started thinking about the body they'd found yesterday. This one was a man. No wonder Dylan had answered so fast that it wasn't Mindy. According to my talk with Tracy the night before, the guy was a typical gang member, one with the right tats and piercings. Even she didn't believe her compilation theory applied to him.

We had crossed Hamilton Avenue by the time Dylan finally spoke again.

"Do you recognize this area?"

"Not really. Why?"

"Because from the picture I saw, you weren't that fucking far from here yesterday." The way he emphasized the last word reminded me of Tracy saying how he was usually more of a hard-ass.

I reached out and covered his hand on the steering wheel, reminding him that I wasn't part of his work; I was his girlfriend. "Thank you for being concerned. I really wasn't here for Mindy or because of that other body. I was here for WCJB."

"What does Barney have you doing? The man's a lunatic sending you here. Why doesn't he send Foster? Or maybe he could man up and do it himself."

"You know I can't tell you what he has me doing."

The Charger stopped along the side of Cortland, in front of a house with plywood-covered windows and doors and bright-yellow police tape roped across the front porch.

Dylan put the car in park and turned my way. "Then show me the same courtesy. I'm bringing you here for one reason, so you won't come on your own. Fine, don't tell me what you're researching with that church. Just don't come back here alone, and don't ask me why DPD is working with HHPD."

Church?

There were so many questions I wanted to ask, but I didn't. He was right. If I wasn't willing to share, I shouldn't ask him to do it. I squeezed his hand, smiled my brightest smile, and nodded. "Agreed, Detective, now may I please have my tour?"

He took a deep breath and exhaled. Shaking his head, he said, "Yes, by all means. I believe we traded hot sex for this."

"Um, was the shower that forgettable?"

His grin showed me the return of the man I was falling for, not the hard-ass who liked to tell me where I could and could not go. "No," he said, "not forgettable, just quick. I hope that when we're done with this tour, you don't think it was a good trade."

CHAPTER

SEVENTEEN

S ara

As Jacob slipped my nightgown over my head, my mind swirled with the happenings of the evening. I hadn't known what to expect at service, and it'd been all right, some parts even nice. With both Elizabeth and Raquel helping me, I'd made it through. My two friends alternated directing me, whispering when it was time to stand or time to sit. I tried to hide what had happened between Jacob and me —my correction—but apparently each time I sat down, the truth was evident. The strange thing, the part I struggled to understand, was that neither of my friends thought it was wrong. Elizabeth even told me she was proud of me for being honest. I thought maybe Raquel would respond differently; after all, she was my friend and my nurse. She'd seen my injuries from the accident and should understand that I didn't need more. Instead she squeezed my hand, told me she understood, and reminded me that when I prayed, I should thank God for a husband who loved me enough to correct me. Though it didn't make sense, I followed her advice.

Another part of the evening that left me uneasy came after service. I'd made it until the end, and as my reward, I wanted to be alone with my husband. However, that wasn't what happened. Instead Brother Benjamin came to us and announced that Brothers Luke and Jacob would be delayed, and then he and Raquel took Elizabeth and me with them to another room. The entire time my heart thudded with questions. It was Elizabeth's squeeze of my hand that told me what her words couldn't. Not only didn't we have a choice, we couldn't ask why. It wasn't until later, when I overheard Brother Benjamin speaking with another man, that I even knew our husbands were meeting with Father Gabriel. When I heard that, my stomach twisted, sure that their meeting had something to do with me, with what I'd done.

If it had, after Jacob retrieved me, he never mentioned a word. After all, he'd said my infraction had occurred, had been corrected, and was now done—his responsibility. Maybe he was right. It wasn't that he seemed upset; it was that he'd hardly spoken. I wanted to ask, to learn if I'd done all right at service and what had happened in his meeting, but the evidence of my earlier correction kept my questions at bay.

Jacob had been right when he'd said that the welts would serve as reminders. Without them I might have blurted out the thousand questions I had running through my head or the one invitation I wanted to bestow. Instead, as he helped me into bed and kissed my forehead, I took a deep breath, bit my lip, and silently scooted all the way to the right.

"Sara, if you're trying to get away from me, the bed isn't that big."

"I'm not trying to get away from you. I'm making room for you."

"What?" he asked.

"You've spent every night since I woke sleeping in that chair. I'm sure you'd be more comfortable in the bed." I held my breath.

He brushed my cheek.

"You don't . . ."

I reached for his hand.

"Please, don't punish me. You said I could ask for things I need, just not question. I'm not questioning why you've slept in the chair. I'm asking you to please sleep in the bed."

He exhaled. "I don't want to hurt you."

Though the irony of his statement wasn't lost on me, I heard more than his words; I heard his compassion. His sincerity pulled at my heartstrings and made me smile. "I know it's up to you, but if I could choose, I'd want you here"—I brushed the space beside me—"with me." The strong, brave front I'd tried to project while outside this room evaporated. "I . . ." My breathing stuttered. "I missed you during service." The bed moved as he sat.

"Brother Benjamin . . ."

I nodded. Brother Benjamin had told me of Jacob's delay. That didn't mean I liked it.

I scooted closer to the far edge of the bed, near the rail. As Jacob lay back against my pillow, he wrapped his arm around my shoulder and drew me close. Judging by the texture of his shirt, he was still wearing the clothes he'd worn to service. That probably meant he was only pacifying me; nevertheless I curled my body toward him and rested my head on his chest. His subtle scent reminded me of our body wash, fresh and clean; however, as I buried my cheek in the cotton, his signature leather-and-musk cloud filled my senses.

Though I'd hoped to learn more about his meeting, with the events of the day and the warmth of his silent embrace, in no time at all, I began to drift off to sleep. I was nearly there when Jacob moved. Rolling me to my back, he hovered close and smoothed my long hair away from my face.

"Are you still awake?" he asked, his minty breath blowing over me.

"Yes."

"I'm sorry . . ."

His simple apology had my full attention. I wasn't sure I remembered hearing those words from him.

"... I meant to tell you how well you did at service."

I smiled. "Thank you. I was scared, but Raquel and Elizabeth were with me the entire time. And Brother Benjamin," I added, suddenly fearful of not acknowledging that a man had helped.

He continued to run his fingers through my hair. "I didn't want you to think that I'd been quiet because of anything you'd done. You were perfect."

It was difficult for me not to ask the questions running through my tired mind, but lying on my back helped me remember. "Thank you, Jacob. I want you to be proud. I'm sorry that I embarrassed you. I'm sure that's what Father Gabriel was speaking to you about."

His hand and breath stilled, as if he was considering his words carefully. "We're leaving the clinic tomorrow. However, instead of going to our apartment, we'll be staying at the pole barn for a while."

"I don't remember our apartment or the pole barn, but I'll go wherever you take me."

His lips brushed mine. The light touch ignited a spark that detonated flickers of yearning throughout my body. I lifted my lips to his, wanting more than the chaste endearment.

"Sara, I . . ." Jacob didn't complete his sentence; instead his hand slipped behind my head, pulling me toward him. His kiss, no longer apathetic, devoured. Zeal radiated from his lips, and soon his breaths were labored. Like magnets we were drawn toward one another, closer and closer. My body liquefied, becoming pliable to his touch, while conversely, his hardened, ready to claim what was already his.

As the heat of our passion washed over us, I forgot my punishment. My attention went elsewhere. A tug on my hair propelled my head to tilt, while the persistence of his minty tongue encouraged my lips to part. Whimpers and moans reverberated in my mouth and bubbled forth. They were wordless sounds declaring my body's approval.

The large, strong hands that had delivered pain now brought

pleasure. I reached for his broad shoulders, opening my arms and willfully surrendering to his kisses. With a palpable hunger, his mouth moved from my lips to my neck and down to my collarbone. His actions sent shivers to my toes and tremors to my insides. Each kiss moved lower until he reached the neckline of my nightgown. The bra I'd worn to service was gone. My breaths quickened as each button came undone, leaving me bare and exposed to his desires.

The sound of my heart echoed in my ears as he praised my beauty and whispered admiration for what was his. When he wasn't speaking, his lips moved lower as his five o'clock shadow tantalized my sensitive skin. It was as his skilled fingers joined the assault, kneading my breasts and twisting my hardened nipples, that primal sounds came from in my throat. It wasn't that I feared speaking. It was that words weren't forming. Wanting what he could give, I reached for his head, wove my fingers through his hair, and pulled him closer.

Suddenly he stopped and pulled away, leaving me open to the cool air.

Dazed and chilled, I reached for my nightgown. Embarrassed and hurt, I began to button it.

"Did I do something wrong?" The cool temperature of the room turned glacial as I realized my mistake. "Jacob, I'm sorry. I know not to question. It's just that . . ." The whirlwind of my emotions cycloned out of control. Though my nightgown wasn't completely buttoned, I rolled away, lost in my darkened world, as tears rained onto my pillow.

Reaching for my shoulder, Jacob turned me back toward him, wiped my tears, and kissed my nose. "You are so stubborn. You're going to be the death of us yet."

I didn't understand what had just happened.

How did we go from hot and steamy to frigid in record time?

My heart ached as the bed shifted and Jacob stood. Then seconds later it shifted again to his weight. This time when he pulled me to his chest, his shirt was soft. A T-shirt, I presumed. When I curled into him as I'd done before, my bare leg met his. The skin-to-skin contact brought a smile to my saddened lips. He'd gotten out of bed to remove his clothes, not to leave me. He was going to sleep with me.

He kissed the top of my head. "You didn't do anything wrong. We're in a hospital bed in the community clinic. It's not the most romantic place to make love to my wife."

I exhaled, thankful he'd explained his reasoning.

Gently rubbing my back, he continued, "Besides, like I said, I'm worried about your ribs. I weigh a lot more than you. I don't want to make them worse."

"I don't have to be on the bottom."

Oh, shit! I bit my lip. Did I really just say that?

The bed shook with the quake of his laughter. "Good night, Sara."

THE NEXT AFTERNOON I burrowed my gloved hands deep inside my thick coat and sat silently as Jacob drove us away from the clinic. Judging from the height of the vehicle as he'd helped me into my seat, we were in a truck. I wanted to ask if it belonged to him.

After all, didn't I wreck his truck?

Instead I listened as the heater blew ferociously within and the wind howled outside. I was stuck in a battle of temperatures, and judging by my chattering teeth, the outside was winning. I tried to remember the time of year. Elizabeth had mentioned the dark season. Based on the temperature, it had to be winter. Then again, I didn't know if it ever got warm in Far North, Alaska.

Whatever time of year it was, I couldn't seem to get warm. On one foot I wore the boot from last night. On the other my cast was covered by a sort of sock. Under my long skirt I wore warm leggings, but despite it all, my body still shivered. The farther we drove, the more I thought about my friends. I'd recently told Elizabeth how anxious I was to leave my room. Now in less than twenty-four hours

I'd done it twice, and this time we weren't returning, at least for a little while.

The new paradigm left me scared and lonely. As the reality of my circumstance settled in my consciousness, my desire to question slipped away. The acceptance of my life was a relief that allowed me to concentrate on what and who was around me. Outside the community I'd have Jacob, but I would also miss Raquel's constant presence and Elizabeth's visits. I even wondered about Sisters Lilith and Ruth. With Sister Ruth's presence, I'd come to enjoy my training. It was nice to have the women to talk to, people I could question, who could teach me the things I'd forgotten.

I tried to imagine a pole barn but had no frame of reference. I didn't even know what it was. The longer I thought about where we were going and how we were getting there, the more questions I had.

Can we live in a barn? Why do we want to?

It wasn't as if Jacob usually talked a lot, but ever since the previous night's service he had been quieter than normal. I believed it had something to do with his meeting, but what that something was I'd probably never know. If one day I learned, it would be in God's time. I reached for the door, to my right, and found a handle. My grip tightened as the tires bounced upon the uneven road.

"Are you all right?" Jacob asked, bringing my thoughts to the present.

Biting my lip, I nodded.

His gloved hand reached for my leg. "Sara," he said gently, "I can't help you if you're not honest with me. Don't try to hide your thoughts and feelings. I'll find out the truth."

"It's my ribs. The way the truck's bouncing . . . they hurt."

"There. Was that difficult? Is there more?" he asked.

When I covered his hand with mine, he turned his palm up and laced our fingers together. Taking a deep breath, I said, "I don't remember anything. I don't know where we're going other than what you've said. I don't even know what a pole barn is. Will"—I swallowed and rephrased—"I'm wondering if there'll be animals."

His laughter filled the truck, momentarily masking the wind and the squeak of the tires bouncing upon the uneven road. "I'm proud of you. You said all of that without questioning once." He squeezed my hand. "Very good. A pole barn is a type of building. No, there won't be any animals. One small section of the building has living quarters. Even without your sight, I believe you'll be able to navigate it well. There's a loft with a bedroom. The main level is one room with a kitchen and living area and a small separated bathroom. The rest is more of a hangar."

I turned in his direction and tried to imagine what he described. "The rest has an airplane." I tried to avoid any inflection that could make my words sound like a question.

"Airplanes, two." He sighed. "I keep forgetting that you don't remember. I'm a pilot. Father Gabriel needs me to get back to work. Now that you're doing better, I can. Last night he decided it would be better if you were with me out at the hangar, rather than leaving you in our apartment alone."

"I'll be alone while you're at Assembly and when you're working." My heartbeat quickened.

"You will, sometimes. Other times people will come to stay with you. All members of The Light pull their weight. We all work to fulfill Father Gabriel's dream. There's another pilot, Brother Micah, here at the Northern Light. For the last three weeks, since the accident, he's been handling everything alone. There's also another pilot who comes here who isn't a member of The Light, Xavier. He sometimes helps out by bringing supplies. Father Gabriel trusts him, so we do too."

I braced myself again as the terrain turned bumpier.

"We're almost there. Xavier is the reason the pole barn has living quarters. Sometimes when he brings supplies, he can't leave the same day. The Northern Light is located in a very remote part of the Far North region. This building is removed from the community so he has a place to stay."

"I know I can't say what I'm thinking without a question."

"If you ask, will it make you feel better?"

I shrugged. "I suppose. It depends on your answer, and if I have permission to ask."

The truck slowed to make another turn.

"Go ahead. You have my permission, but I can't promise I'll answer."

"You said you're a pilot and that sometimes Xavier needs to stay here overnight. Are you ever gone overnight?"

"I am."

I turned toward the window that I couldn't see and tried to quell the panic bubbling in my chest. I hated being so dependent on him, but I was.

"Father Gabriel won't ask me to do any overnight trips until you're fully recovered. And by the time I do, we'll be home in our apartment. You'll have the entire community. I'd never leave you alone out here for more than a few hours."

I nodded as the truck came to a stop. A mechanical sound—a garage door rising—came from outside, and then we slowly moved forward.

"Don't open your door," Jacob warned. "I'll help you out, but we need to wait for the door to close. This time of year, we need to be careful. The tall fences keep the polar bears out of the community, but out here you never know."

My face spun back toward him. "Oh my gosh, polar bears!"

He scoffed. "It's not like they're always outside our door. Technically we're only on the edge of the circumpolar north, but it's better to be safe. Don't you agree?"

"I do." I thought for a minute as the door descended. "But it's winter, they should be hibernating."

"We're not into meteorological winter yet, but I agree it feels like it; however, no, polar bears don't hibernate."

I sucked my lip between my teeth.

How could I forget I live with polar bears?

My door opened and Jacob reached for my chin. With his gloved hand he teased my lip free. "Don't worry. We're safe. Remember, I meant what I said. I promised to take care of you. I'd never do anything that caused you harm. That includes leaving you alone with polar bears."

I forced my cheeks to rise and reached for his hand. "Good."

"Now let's get inside the living quarters where it's warmer."

As I started to ease myself from the truck, Jacob said, "Hold on to my neck, I'll carry you."

"Oh, you don't have to do that. I can walk. It's actually easier with the boot on my other foot."

Undeterred, he wrapped me in his arms. "I've noticed that."

Shaking my head, I did as he said and reached for his neck. He effortlessly lifted me from my seat. After a few steps, I pulled his face toward mine and kissed his cheek.

"What was that for?"

"I was just thinking. Since I don't remember any of this, you carrying me like this, is like being carried over the threshold for the first time. It's like we're newlyweds."

"You did say you'd marry me again." His tone dropped. "But that was before—"

I interrupted him with another kiss, this time a light brush to his lips. "I still would," I assured him.

"Then by all means, Mrs. Adams, newlyweds we can be."

CHAPTER
EIGHTEEN

J acob

I POUNDED my palms against the steering wheel, trying with all my might to give the truck some of my frustration. At least when I struck it, the truck didn't cry or melt into my arms. I understood a truck, knew how it worked and how to fix it when it had problems. It was like our planes. Micah and I not only flew them, we knew how to fix them and service them—the mechanical part, not the technology. That shit was complicated. I grabbed a fistful of my hair and began my inner monologue.

Get yourself together, Jacob. You will do this.

I took one last glance at the door to the living quarters before I pushed the garage door button. I couldn't go back. If I did I wouldn't want to leave. Besides, I needed to be at Assembly in less than a half an hour.

Why does she want me with her? Why doesn't she hate me?

It wasn't that I wanted Sara to hate me, I didn't, but she should.

Backing out of the pole barn, I waited and watched the door fully close. Glancing at the clock on the dashboard, I saw it was almost half past eight on Friday morning and the sky was still dark. There had been a time in my life when that would've bothered me, or that it was still twilight at noon, or darkening by four, but right now I had too much happening to give it more than a fleeting thought.

Sara didn't even realize that this was her Commission-invoked retribution. I needed to inform her before she faced the Assembly, the Commission, or any of the wives—especially before she faced Father Gabriel.

As I drove toward the community, my mind drifted back to the meeting after Wednesday night's service. Father Gabriel had wasted no time on preliminaries, coming right to the point...

Brothers, have a seat. Before we meet with the Assembly and Commission in the morning, I want to discuss my decree regarding Sara's retribution for the incident."

As I sat, I had tried to still the worry that ricocheted through my thoughts like an old-fashioned pinball.

"In similar cases I've pronounced an array of decrees. Your wife, as well as followers who're unaware, believe that Sara was your wife in the dark. While Sara believes she's lived here, the followers believe she was recently brought here. They all believe she took your truck and in the act of fleeing, she had an accident."

My back stiffened.

"Brother?"

"Father, I haven't discussed it with Sara. I told her I'd tell her when the time was right. All she knows is what I was told to say to Brother Timothy, the day she awoke."

"Which doesn't match, does it?"

"No. In that scenario, I was told to say that she took my truck for supplies with my permission."

Have I been set up?

Father Gabriel nodded. "I also believe you said that she remembered, but she doesn't."

"Yes."

"As a member of the Assembly, your word is to be true. What you said wasn't."

Well, hell, unless I'd said she didn't have an accident. Unless I'd said it was all staged with the right amount of drugs in her system and that a psycho Assemblyman beat the shit out of her before my eyes. That he would've done more, but I stopped him . . . unless I'd said that even after I stopped the assault, Sara received more injuries after she was given to Dr. Newton . . . unless I'd told Brother Timothy what he already knew—that the entire incident was all a deception—then I would've lied.

"Yes, Father."

"My judgment therefore must rectify both transgressions and placate the followers."

"Yes, Father."

"I've sought the advice of my Commission. Now that Sara is better, acclimating to the community and staking her claim as an Assemblyman's wife, her punishment needs to be public."

My gaze flashed toward Luke's. Though he didn't look my way, I saw the shock he was trying to hide. Sure that my heart had stopped beating, I almost doubled over with the pain of his verdict. I was in charge of disputes. I knew the meaning of public correction. Everything in me wanted to question, protest, and offer myself in her stead, but I knew it wouldn't help her cause. His decision was already made. The entire room stilled as everyone awaited my response.

Swallowing my objections, I said, "I'll honor your decision."

Brother Daniel exhaled. "Very good. I knew you had it in you." His cheeks stretched with the breadth of his smile.

Confused, I looked back to Father Gabriel.

"Brother Jacob, you truly are a man of The Light. I believe that once this is complete we'll be able to trust you with even more."

"Thank you . . . ?"

If Sara had used the same inflection, I probably would have repri-

manded her. There was obviously a question mark hanging somewhere in the air.

Father Gabriel laughed. "Well, that wasn't as pronounced as your wife's question earlier today."

I shook my head. "I'm sorry. I'm still processing."

"Temporary banishment," he decreed.

Temporary?

I gripped the arms of the chair. My knuckles blanching from my hold. Fuck this! Banishment was death. No one could ever be permitted to leave The Light: not after they worked in the processing plant, not after they knew what we did here, especially not me. I knew about the other campuses.

"Brother, your self-control is impressive. Let me explain. Sara has been seen. She's developed relationships, not only with you, but also with Sisters Elizabeth and Raquel, as well as Sisters Lilith and Ruth. She's learning my teachings. Our goal is for her to desire our community and her husband. If I'm interpreting your clenched jaw, the heat in your brown eyes, and the grip you have on that chair, you've begun to feel protective of her?"

Consciously I released the chair's arms, relaxed my shoulders, and loosened my bite. Inhaling and exhaling, I admitted, "I have."

"Sexual attraction will come. I don't believe any man is impervious to it, not when he's been granted a virtuous wife, and she's been placed in his bed."

I nodded.

"Beginning tomorrow, Sara will be banished from the community."

I held my breath.

"For two weeks. During that time the two of you will live out at the hangar, in the living quarters. It's already been set up with supplies for your stay. The Northern Light needs you to return to your job. Micah hasn't complained, but we need you."

I gasped the air as it filled my lungs.

Two weeks. Thank The Light. Two weeks is doable.

"Of course, I'm more than willing."

"During the two weeks, she'll only see you, unless a member of the Commission or one of their wives receives permission to visit."

See?

"Father, she still isn't able to see anyone."

His lips pursed and his brow furrowed. With his elbows on his desk, Father Gabriel steepled his fingers. "After one week Dr. Newton will visit the pole barn and remove the bandages. Then, when she returns to the community, she'll be able to fully appreciate being back and begin a job."

"Do I understand that she'll be excluded from service during that time?"

"You both will."

I sat taller.

"Of course, we won't go into detail about this to anyone other than the Assembly and Commission, but the followers will draw their own conclusions. Once you return I'll personally welcome you both back. The correction will be done."

"As if it never occurred," Brother Daniel added. "However, Brother Jacob, you will continue to attend Assembly."

"And begin flights," Father Gabriel said.

"Sara will be left alone while I'm flying."

"Yes, it'll give her time to study my recordings and lament her transgression. Isolation is a powerful tool."

"Thank you for this correction. I'll work to bring Sara back to the community a fully active follower and the wife of an Assemblyman."

"We have no doubt you will," Brother Daniel said.

Father Gabriel stood. "Saturday, after Commission, you will fly me to the Western Light. I have some business to attend to."

I did the math in my head. If we left by eleven, by the time we flew there, he conducted his business, and I returned, it would be at least ten o'clock at night. In the Citation X, the flight alone would be three hours each way.

"I'll have the plane ready. Should I plan for overnight?"

I know the answer I want, but how isolated does he plan on making Sara?

"No. We won't leave Sara alone overnight, not until she's back to the community. This punishment is to help her want the community, not frighten her into hating us. I may stay there for a while. If that's the case, you and Brother Micah can pick up supplies and head back. I'll know more by Saturday."

I sighed. "Thank you."

Now as I drove through the final gate on Friday morning, I took a deep breath. In less than two weeks this would all be done: Sara and I would be part of the community. As a couple we'd be welcomed into The Light.

I smiled at the thought of how well she'd adapted to the pole barn. Yesterday, instead of lamenting her public correction, as Father Gabriel had said she would, she seemed to play house. I'd expected her to sit as she had in the clinic, but she hadn't. Of her own accord, Sara had used her hands and wandered around. Though I gave her a tour, with independent exploration she again found the bathroom and the kitchen, learned the location of each piece of furniture, and even went up and down the steps to the loft, careful to grip the banister. She also spent over an hour in the kitchen, opening drawers and cabinets, feeling the contents.

Each time she was sure of what she'd found, she'd announced it triumphantly. Father Gabriel had been wrong when he'd said the attraction would come. Sara was so damn cute with her discoveries, the attraction was there. She was also mastering the art of asking without questioning. Honestly, watching her curb her innate desire to question was sexy as hell.

The attraction was sometimes so there, it hurt.

After Sara mastered the contents of the kitchen, she asked to cook. Thankfully, the refrigerator was fully stocked with food that needed only to be warmed. After she had her sight, cooking would be her responsibility; however, since I was supposed to keep her safe, her wielding knives, maneuvering hot burners, and navigating the oven without sight was currently forbidden.

When I'd left the pole barn this morning, she was washing

dishes, which seemed safe enough. Nevertheless I had visions of her breaking a glass, trying to clean it up, and bleeding out on the kitchen floor. Now, that may seem like extreme thinking, but that's what this whole thing had done to me. It had caused extra stress and sleepless nights. It was all beginning to take its toll.

Though I was the only member who needed to drive to Assembly, thankfully, I wasn't the last to arrive. As I found my way to my seat, Benjamin stopped me. "How is Sara?"

I shrugged. "Ignorance is bliss. She's doing better than me."

He nodded. "Raquel's worried. She knows better than to ask, but she's heard rumors. The wives talk."

His comment set my skin on fire as I thought about the wives gossiping about Sara. It was ridiculous. They all knew the truth. They all knew she wasn't really guilty, not of anything other than having been acquired.

"It's none of my business," he continued, "but you need to tell her. If Lilith or even Ruth show up and she's unaware that she's being punished, it could be worse."

I nodded. "Well, since they need their husbands to drive them outside of the community, I guess I'm safe through the Commission meeting."

Benjamin took a deep breath. "I'm going to share something with you. It happened before you came to The Light, but"—his face saddened—"Raquel was acquired."

I leaned back. "Wow, I didn't know. She's done great. It's difficult to tell which females came which way to The Light, once they're fully indoctrinated."

"I just wanted you to know, I understand what you're going through."

"Were you on the Assembly?"

"No, you've got it rougher on that one. I was doing what I do now, working with Brother Raphael in the lab. While in the dark I was a pharmacist. I didn't have the chemistry and compound pharmacy experience—then," he added with a grin. "Anyway, I was working with Brother Raphael, and I have to say, he helped me get through it."

I looked around. "So, was Sister Rebecca, Brother Raphael's wife was . . . acquired?"

He nodded. "You'd be surprised."

"Do you? Did you?" I ran my hand through my hair. "Have you ever been sorry?"

"No!" he whispered definitively. "It's the way of The Light. Brother Raphael helped me come to terms with that. God made Raquel for me. I wouldn't have known that if it weren't for Father Gabriel. We've been together over five years."

"Do you love her?"

I knew the answer by the way his eyes shone. "More than my own life."

"Thanks," I said, genuinely appreciative.

"When you go back out there, talk to her. Trust me. You don't want Lilith being the one to tell her."

I nodded. "You're right. I don't."

"Brothers, it's time to begin," Brother Raphael's voice, with his Boston accent, thundered over the chatter from about the room. "Father Gabriel's ready to pray."

CHAPTER

NINETEEN

S ara

I RAN my fingers along the surface of the bed, making sure that the blankets were straight and the pillows were in place. I wasn't sure if I'd always done these domesticated-type things, but I supposed I had. Jacob hadn't been the one to tell me I needed to do them, or that they were my responsibility. It had been Sister Lilith, during her training. I didn't mind. To be honest, on my first full day of freedom from my hospital room since my accident, I enjoyed doing anything. Besides, this place wasn't that big, so there wasn't too much I could do.

Since Jacob had left for Assembly, I'd washed our breakfast dishes, straightened the living room, and made the bed. I didn't know if he'd notice, but doing it made me feel as if I'd accomplished something.

As I sat on the edge of the freshly made bed, my thoughts went to unmaking it . . . with my husband. So far all I could remember was actually sleeping with him, his arm around me and my head on his shoulder. The steady beat of his heart and the rhythm of his breaths gave me comfort. Though I couldn't wait to see him with my eyes, in my mind I'd created a picture. While he slept, I'd gently traced his face. I'd lightly run my finger over his brow and nose, and along his defined jaw. I'd caressed his shoulders and felt the definition of his muscles. His hardness had pushed against my hips, and I knew that the top of my head fit under his chin when we stood and he held me close. I had no way of knowing if the image I'd created was accurate, but in my heart I remembered the scruffy jaw I'd detected with my touch, and piercing blue eyes.

Smiling, I remembered inviting him to sleep with me at the clinic. Though I had been nervous, I was glad I'd done it. I'd had no way of knowing it would be our last night there; however, having spent the one night in his arms made our first night here more comfortable. My thoughts drifted to that night after service, the hunger in his touch and the way his lips had claimed my body. Just the memories made me tingle. Lying back on the bed, I held my side and sighed. If only he weren't so worried about my ribs.

Courtesy of the truck ride yesterday, the injury was more aggravated then it had been. I'd tried hiding it. Shaking my head, I wondered if it was possible to hide anything from him. According to Elizabeth it wasn't allowed. The way I saw it, I wasn't lying. I was withholding information for the benefit of both of us. By the way his breathing became labored and his body hardened that night at the clinic, I wasn't the only one who wanted to make love.

It seemed as if it didn't matter if I told Jacob what I was thinking or not; he knew. Somehow he always seemed to know, sometimes even before I did. Maybe it was because we'd been together so long.

If only I could remember how long.

The sound of the rising garage door pulled me from my carnal thoughts, and I covered my cheeks. With a giggle I hoped they weren't as flushed as they felt. If they were, he would know what I'd been thinking . . . I shook my head. I didn't want that conversation. Exhaling, I willed the pink away.

When I heard the garage door lowering, I stood and made my way toward the stairs. Wearing the boot on my right foot made walking with my cast much easier. As I approached the landing, I took a deep breath and visualized the stairs. Since I'd counted them multiple times, I knew there were fifteen steps. I might not have my sight, but I was trying to be as self-sufficient as possible. I made it only to the second step from the top when I heard his voice.

"Sara?"

"I'm coming down," I called, taking one step at a time, cautious not to go too fast.

Even before I reached the bottom step, I knew he was there. When we went to service, I'd realized why I associated him with the scent of leather; it was his coat. When he wasn't wearing it, just the right amount of aroma lingered around him. When he wore it, as now, the leather scent was overpowering. That, plus the sound of his boots walking and stopping on the wood floor, prompted me to stop on the fourteenth step. If I went one more, I was afraid I'd run into him.

"Sara." His voice came from very close.

Gripping the banister, I tilted my face toward his. Smiling and hoping my cheeks had returned to their normal color, I replied, "Yes?"

"Did you hear the garage door go up?"

"Yes."

"And what did you think that meant?"

"I assumed it meant you were here."

"So you knew I was home and yet you chose to not greet me?"

What the hell?

"Answer me," he demanded, his tone now too calm. "Why weren't you waiting for me at the door?"

The thoughts I'd entertained upstairs evaporated. I knew this tone. I not only recognized it, but with everything in me, I wanted to avoid it. My heartbeat quickened and my mouth dried like the Sahara. "I was on my—"

Interrupting, he rebuked, "On your way is not there, waiting as you're supposed to be. When I return, I expect to find you waiting for me, greeting your husband."

The bubble of apprehension that had waned and waxed in my chest since I awoke nearly three weeks earlier began to grow. "At the door . . . wh . . . I'm sorry . . . I didn't know . . . you didn't tell me to—"

He grasped my arm, the harsh movement a stark contrast to the eerie calmness of his voice. "Do tell, Sara, are you blaming me for your forgetfulness?"

What the hell is his problem?

"I'm sorry," I pleaded. "I'm not blaming . . . I didn't remember. If you told me . . . from now on, I'll do it."

"Must I remind you of everything?"

"I'm trying to remember; I am. I'll be there from now on, at the door, when you come home."

"Perhaps you need a reminder?"

My body sagged and my knees weakened. The bubble within me grew and popped, filling my nervous system with dread. "No. I don't need a reminder. I'll remember from now on. Please give me another chance." If it hadn't been for his iron grip on my forearm, I might have fallen to the step where I stood.

If I had, I wasn't sure if it would have been because of the sudden dizziness his tone induced, the bout of trembling, or that it would've enabled me to beg. It wasn't something I was proud of considering, but to avoid his belt, at that moment, I was willing.

"Sara, go to the door."

Inhaling more pleas, I nodded. When he released my arm, I stepped down and down again. Around the steps, past the closet, I found the door between the living quarters and the garage.

He was right behind me, his voice still eerily calm. "You may stand or kneel; the choice has always been yours."

I swallowed the vile bile bubbling from my stomach. In that

moment I couldn't for the life of me fathom that merely minutes ago I had been having pleasant thoughts about this man. I also couldn't imagine kneeling.

Who does that?

I brought my feet together, straightened my neck, and said, "I'll stand, thank you."

He reached for my chin and lowered it.

"This is where you are to be when I arrive, and if you choose to stand, your head will be bowed."

"Yes, Jacob."

I didn't move from where I had been told to be, as the rustling of his coat filled the silence.

"Reach out your hands. You may take my coat and hang it in the closet under the stairs."

It was heavier than I'd expected, causing me to wobble slightly when he laid it in my arms. Inside the closet I fumbled until I found a hanger. Once his coat was secure, I closed the door. When I turned he was right in front of me, grasping my shoulders. I sucked my bottom lip between my teeth and waited for the order I didn't want to hear.

Will he tell me to go to the bathroom like last time, or our bedroom?

"Sara, we have so much happening right now. I do not want, nor do I have time, to rehash basics. You must remember."

The tears teetered as I nodded within his grip. "I'm trying."

"Trying and doing are two different things. Remember that. If you can't, the next time I won't be as lenient."

My body sagged with the rush of relief that I wasn't going to be corrected. "Thank you, Jacob. I will be waiting next time."

He took my hand and led me to the couch. Handing me a tissue, he said, "I'm going to tell you exactly why we came out here, out of the community." His calmness was gone. The voice beckoning me was my husband's, that of the man I wanted to know.

"Thank you," I said cautiously, taking the tissue.

"They figured it out."

"I don't understand."

"They know that I answered for you, when Brother Timothy was in your room."

My trembling resumed. "What . . . I don't know what that means. He said I needed to go before the Commission."

"You don't. At least not right now. I've been before them, multiple times."

"You have? In my place?"

Devotion and sadness rang in his words. "You've been through enough. I tried."

"But you told them the truth."

His grip on my hands tightened. "I told them what I thought was best."

Everything inside me screamed to ask, to question. Instead I waited.

"Do you remember the way you reacted in the hospital, before I slapped you?"

Ashamed of the memory, I nodded and softly replied, "Yes."

"That's how you were before the accident. You were upset, grabbed my keys, and rushed out. I didn't know your intentions, but the Commission decided that you were trying to leave The Light."

I shook my head frantically. "No! I wouldn't do that. I wouldn't leave you, or The Light, or Father Gabriel." The shaking of my head slowed, and I tilted it to the side. "I don't think I would."

"I want to believe that. I want to believe that it was a misunderstanding."

My head ached as I desperately searched my memories. "I don't remember anything . . ."

His large palms framed my cheeks. "Sara, I've put everything on the line for you. We must be honest with one another."

I nodded.

"Would you rather leave and go back to the dark, than be here . . . with me?"

I pulled from his grip and stood. The sudden disconnection gave me the strength I needed to think. One minute I'd fantasized about him, the next I'd feared him. Each step that took me away from him shed light on my answer. Stopping on the other side of the sofa, I took a deep breath and began, "I'm being completely honest. I don't remember anything before waking in the hospital."

"Anything?"

My head moved slowly from side to side.

"And?" he asked.

"And all I know is what's happened since." I paused. "I know that you've been with me. Not just with me, but I've heard you fight for me. I heard what you said to Dr. Newton. I trust that you were protecting me with Brother Timothy, and now you just said that you've testified for me." I took a deep breath. "I know that you care for me, that you want me, and you love me enough to correct me." Sighing, I made my way back to him, sat, and palmed his cheeks. His stubbly jaw abraded my hands and reminded me of the way it tantalized my breasts. "Jacob, I'll continue to apologize for not remembering, but just because I don't remember, doesn't mean I don't want to. I have no idea what I was doing that day or why I took your truck, but I promise, now, I want to be here, with you."

"Sara, here isn't where we should be."

My hands dropped to my lap as I tried to comprehend his meaning.

Compared to the hospital, I like here.

"We've been temporarily banished," he explained.

Unable to think or reason, I stopped breathing. That was the word Brother Timothy had used. Banished. "What about your position? Are they taking it away? What about your job? Why did they do this? What will happen to us? What about our friends? Is there anything we can do?"

He reached for my hands and held them still.

"Stop. I can't even count the number of times you just questioned."

Though I knew from his tone that I wasn't truly in trouble, I lowered my chin, ashamed that I'd suddenly forgotten all my training.

He lifted my unseeing eyes to his. "This is it," he continued to explain. "This is our punishment. No one, other than the occasional Commissioner or his wife, will be allowed to see us or speak to us for the next two weeks. No friends, no service, only isolation."

My chest pounded, and then after a moment I squeezed his hands and asked, "May I still have you? May we have each other?"

"Do you still want me?" Jacob asked.

I nodded. "I don't know why I did what I did. I don't remember taking your truck, but please, believe me, I'm sorry, and I won't do it again." I leaned toward him and rested my cheek on his chest. "From what I've learned since I've awoken, I do. I do want you. I don't understand everything that you expect out of me, but I do want you."

His embrace surrounded me. "I can't tell you how good that is to hear."

I sat back, pulling away. "Wait." The alarm was louder than my words. "Do you still want me?"

He pulled me back to his chest and chuckled. "You have no idea how badly I want you, but Sara, you have at least one broken rib."

I let the tips of my lips move upward and shrugged. "I think I gave you an option. I'm a little scared to repeat it."

He brushed my cheek. "There are some things that, while said in the privacy of our home, or personal space like a clinic bed . . . are not only acceptable, but valued."

"Valued, not heeded?"

Jacob lifted my face toward his. The tips of our noses brushed one another as he shook his head. "So much questioning . . ."

Though he'd just reprimanded me, his breathing told me that correction was not uppermost on his mind. I tilted my lips toward his, and his gentle kiss lingered.

"Heal, my dear wife. We'll get through this, and when we do, we'll have forever ahead of us."

"As long as you're with me, they can banish us for as long as they want."

"We're in this together; however, even with our banishment, I have a job to do. Tomorrow I must fly."

My breathing hitched. "Please, tell me how long you'll be gone."

"I'm not sure. I'm transporting Father Gabriel. If you have an emergency, there's a phone in the kitchen."

"I don't know who to call or how."

S tella

DYLAN and I made a deal the other morning when he took me to the house on Cortland Street. We agreed to keep our work to ourselves unless we believed it held a connection to Mindy. The problem with that deal was that after going through Dr. Howell's files, I was convinced everything had to do with Mindy's disappearance. Even the woman at Starbucks was suspicious.

I mean who writes an S like that?

Dr. Howell's information didn't point to a conspiracy, more a compilation. Each case was a piece of a larger puzzle. Unfortunately, each piece didn't necessarily belong to the same puzzle. I found myself constantly second-guessing and wondering if I was trying to make the wrong pieces fit. After all, there was probably a good reason that members of The Light were going back and forth to Canada.

Back at WCJB I worked on my research. The Light made for a very broad Internet search. There were literal lights, lighting stores, lighting-supply chains. Though I didn't think he realized what he'd done, Dylan's comment about a church was responsible for narrowing my search. While there were hundreds of churches with Light in their names, there were only a few churches named The Light. It just so happened that one of them was located in Detroit, Highland Heights to be exact. According to the website, The Light was a beacon against darkness and a home of healing for the lost. It was a self-sustaining place of devotion founded on fundamentalist beliefs that offered enlightenment to its members and freedom from the constraints of the dark.

Gabriel Clark had begun The Light in Detroit over fifteen years ago. The relatively short biography of the founder spoke of Gabriel Clark's personal calling to The Light and his willingness to share his journey with those in need. His picture was the stereotypical promotional picture showing a smiling, handsome man in his late forties or early fifties. His slicked-back blond hair and expensive silk suit reminded me of a television evangelist. However, neither Gabriel Clark nor The Light offered sermons through social media. To hear Father Gabriel, as he was referred to on the site, a prospective member was required to attend a visitors' assembly at one of the church's campuses or informational hubs. The website mentioned that there were campuses throughout the country, but the locator page indicated only the one in Detroit. There were no local informational hubs.

Out of curiosity I clicked the form one was required to fill out to attend a visitors' assembly. It didn't give a time or date for an assembly; instead it was more of a questionnaire, pretty straightforward at first, but as I scrolled the questions became more personal and intrusive. It went from name, address, sex, age, marital status, number of children, and religious affiliation to essay-type questions. These had unlimited space for answers that were to include the personal background, triumphs and challenges, and even employment history of prospective members and spouses. Near the bottom was a statement I'd also seen on the website that discussed the applicant's willingness to participate as a full-time committed believer.

What does that even mean?

The more I read, the more the hairs on the back of my neck came to attention. At the very bottom the form said that upon receipt, a Visitor Specialist would contact the applicant.

My thoughts went to the women I'd seen crossing the street. It was difficult to say because of how far away I'd been, but I couldn't remember anything distinguishing about them. I couldn't even remember what they were wearing. I seemed to recall slacks or maybe jeans. They hadn't been wearing handmade dresses such as I'd associate with more conservative groups or cults.

That word cult sent shivers down my spine. I opened a new tab and typed it in the browser. The definition I found said it was a system of religious veneration and devotion directed toward a particular figure or object.

Is that what this church is? Or am I reading too much into it? What does "full-time committed believers" mean, and why are they crossing the Canadian border daily?

I checked the website again. There was nothing to indicate that The Light was an international church, and the site said only that there were multiple locations within the United States. That was when I noticed the Outreach tab and clicked. Preserve the Light was at the top of the screen, with pictures of jars of jams and jellies. The blurb said that the church's homegrown, homemade jams and jellies helped support its outreach. A testimonial from a member of The Light read as follows:

"I was lost in a world of darkness, using my body to support deadly habits, when I found The Light. Today, I only use my body to create

Preserve the Light, serve my husband, and follow Father Gabriel. I've never been as content and fulfilled. The Light and Father Gabriel saved me. Please purchase Preserve the Light so others may be saved." The testimonial was attributed to "Follower of The Light, Sister Abigail Miller."

Serve her husband? My skin crawled.

Well, at least this woman wasn't out selling her body anymore, and the location in Highland Heights made sense, if the ministry was about helping people who were dependent on drugs or alcohol. I wasn't sure why or if I believed there was a connection, but I wanted to learn more.

I started with Preserve the Light. Clicking on the Order Here box, I filled out my request. Ten dollars was a lot to pay for a jar of jelly, but I reasoned that it was for a ministry. After entering my shipping information, I selected strawberry. With the weather turning colder and the leaves changing, the fruit reminded me of summer.

The other agreement that Dylan and I had come to was that I'd stay out of Highland Heights. Maybe it wasn't so much of an agreement as it was him telling me to stay out. I didn't want to argue about it, but if my work took me back there, I couldn't say no . . . or more like I wouldn't say no. It was Bernard's informant who had led me to The Light, so I owed it to Bernard to be sure there wasn't a connection between The Light and the drug smuggling we were trying to uncover at the border. The idea that there was a connection between this church and missing or dead women came to mind. Just as quickly I dismissed it. That was ludicrous and likely a result of my vivid imagination. Besides, nothing about those women set off my radar. Then again, I was a ways away.

Two things were for sure. One, I was excited about my home-made jam. I hadn't had good strawberry jam since I was a little girl. Thinking about my grandmother's jam had my mouth watering. Two, I was going back to Highland Heights. I wanted to find out what was going on in that school building across the street from The

Light. If it was only a jam factory, then I'd be able to tell Bernard that the lead hadn't panned out.

That wasn't a conversation I'd relish. This investigation was taking longer than either of us had expected, and coming up with dead ends seemed to be my new specialty. Thank God, Foster was keeping Bernard busy with some new stories. Nevertheless my boss was definitely getting anxious. It wasn't until I'd gotten him, maybe not on board, but at least entertaining the compilation theory that he'd agreed to let me keep working this angle. In order to do that, I'd had to share some of the information I'd learned from Dr. Howell. I didn't tell him my source, but I gave him a taste of the incidence of women dying from suspicious causes over the last ten years in the Detroit area. When I did I watched his wheels turn. Even the slightest possibility of a connection between the dead and missing women and the drug smuggling made his brow and upper lip glisten with perspiration. Bernard foamed at the mouth like a rabid dog with the need to uncover this story.

When my phone rang, I glanced at the date on the screen and my heart clenched. It'd been six weeks to the day since I'd last spoken to Mindy. I tried to suppress the lump in my throat as I answered the phone.

"Hello, Stella Montgomery."

"It's Foster."

"Hi, I obviously didn't look at the number. What can I do for you? You're saving my ass keeping Bernard busy. Otherwise he'd be chewing it every chance he had."

Eddie Foster's laugh filled my ear. "Not a problem. We all have some stories that fall into place better than others. Have you found anything lately?"

"Jelly."

"What?"

"Never mind," I said, waving my free hand. "What do you need?"

"It's not so much what I need. I have a couple questions for you."

"OK, shoot."

Foster cleared his throat. "You know we keep an eye on our own, right?"

"You're making me nervous. What are your questions?" I bit my lip.

"What do you know about real estate in Bloomfield Hills?"

"I know that some of the partners at Preston and Butler live there, and it costs more than I'll ever have."

"OK, have you ever heard of Motorists of America?"

I shook my head toward the phone, as if he could see me. "No, Foster. Is this for a story?"

"No, not really. Like I said, we keep an eye on our own."

"Hey, I love you, but jump ahead. My mind's so rattled with this case, I'm missing the point."

"Motorists of America, MOA, was a retirement endeavor set up in the late sixties for employees of the big auto companies. It was a private option for members of UAW and Teamsters. It didn't replace their union dues or retirement; it was billed to supplement it." I had no idea where he was going. "That was fifty years ago. I'll spare you the history. Let's just say it was one of the many ventures that didn't deliver. The funny thing is that I remembered it was something Mindy had mentioned, and recently I was doing a search and it came up."

"Foster?" We'd already canvassed all of Mindy's research. MOA hadn't been there, so it must have been a while ago that she'd mentioned it.

"Give me a minute."

Securing my lip once more to stop from telling him I didn't care, I nodded.

"I can give you more detail, but obviously you want the Cliffs-Notes. MOA declared bankruptcy in the eighties. Operations stopped, but it wasn't dissolved."

My patience was wearing thin.

"After bankruptcy a company is unable to . . ."

"Foster, I really want to care. Are you saying this isn't a story and somehow has something to do with me?"

"Jesus, Stella, listen a minute. MOA has a list of assets a mile long, valued in the millions, hell, billions. I don't know. I just got started into all of this. The part that jumped out at me, the reason I even stumbled upon this, was because of a six-bedroom home in Bloomfield Hills."

"Are you and Kim house shopping?"

"Like we could afford to live there. No, I may have been running some searches on Dylan Richards and his name popped up on a utility bill, gas, for that six-bedroom. His name was only there one month, and then it was changed, but you know how slow utility companies are? Their records last forever."

What the hell?

I shook my head. "Let me save you any further trouble. It's not my Dylan Richards; you've got the wrong one. Next, explain to me why in the hell you're running a search on my boyfriend."

"I suppose that's possible, that it's not him. What's his father's name?"

I bit my lower lip. "Um, Mr. Richards? We haven't really made it to the parent part of this relationship. He doesn't talk about them. Now answer my other question."

"Bernard asked me to check him out."

"Holy shit!" I covered my mouth and looked around the office. Apparently my outburst had gone unheard, or people were used to them. Not drawing attention, I lowered my voice. "Don't. He's a cop. We've only just started discussing allowing Fred to visit. Seriously, he's a detective. I promise we're good. He's good." I ran my hands down the length of my ponytail and twisted the end.

"Fred?" Foster asked.

"Never mind. Actually, this pisses me off."

"Cool your jets. Bernard comes across all corncob-up-the-ass-ish, but listen, I've worked for him for a long time. He's got good instincts and, well, he said he'd feel better if everything checked out."

I straightened my neck and shook my shoulders. After pursing my lips, I asked, "And what else did you find?"

"Stuff I'm sure you know, criminal justice at Wayne State, straight to DPD where he spent five years as a patrolman before making detective and moving straight to narcotics and homicide. That's a bit unusual, but the flags aren't red, only amber. I mean, usually people start with less prestigious assignments. Your man went to the top. Personally, he's been dating this hot investigative journalist . . ."

If Eddie weren't happily married with two kids I might have been offended, but since he was I just laughed.

"Seriously," he went on, "commendations, few complaints. The only thing that struck me as odd was the one-point-four-million-dollar home owned by MOA with his name on the gas bill. I'm diving deeper into MOA. I just wanted to ask if he had that kind of money lying around. Did a rich uncle die?"

"Foster, you've got the wrong Dylan Richards. I've been to his house. It's a nice renovated two-story in Brush Park: backyard, fence, and plenty of shelf room for Fred." I giggled. "He's my fish. I hate leaving him. He gets depressed."

Foster scoffed. "Well, Fred should be glad he doesn't live at my house. I don't know what my kids do to their goldfish, but I bet we buy a new one at least once a week. Kim said that when she enters the pet shop, all the goldfish try to hide behind the little castle."

"OK, remind me not to let your kids babysit Fred."

"Listen, Stella, I'll look into this. You're probably right, and don't say anything to Bernard. He doesn't want anyone to know he's a nice guy. I'll talk to you later."

"Hey, wait." I had an idea. "Did Bernard ever have you check on anyone for Mindy?"

"Stella . . ."

"Come on. Did he?"

"You know she wasn't dating anyone when she disappeared."

I nodded. "I know, but before that. I mean we were tight, but I was super busy when I worked for Preston and Butler. I didn't know if . . . ? Or did he ever have you investigate her?"

"I wish I could tell you yes. If I had, I would have already given it to the police. Stella, we all want her back. I wouldn't hold anything like that without sharing it."

I shrugged. "It was worth a try. Thanks, Foster. Go find Bernard some more stories and stop worrying about Dylan."

"Yes, ma'am. Bye." The line went dead.

I took a deep breath. I wasn't sure Mindy's disappearance would ever get easier, not as long as I didn't know. The thought of identifying her came back. I scrolled through my contacts until I found Tracy Howell, and I hit "Call."

"Charlotte, so nice of you to call."

I snickered. "I only do it because I love my new name. It's like I have this whole dual personality thing happening." After the first time she'd called me that, I'd learned that Charlotte was her sister. She'd recently spoken to her and it was the first name that had popped into her head.

"I was going to call you."

"You were? Is it about Min—"

"No," she interrupted. "No, this was about something else. Could I call you back tonight? Will you be free?"

"I can be. Give me a time."

"How about six?"

"Sounds good, bye." It was funny how even a glimmer of hope could make my body tingle with anticipation. I couldn't wait to find out what she had to say. I looked at the corner of my screen. Damn, it was after one and I'd forgotten all about lunch. Grabbing my purse and phone, I logged off my computer and walked toward Bernard's office, but before I reached the door I made myself stop and take a deep breath. I didn't care if he was being nice. Having Dylan investigated was definitely a violation of my privacy. Another deep breath. I walked to his door.

"Bernard, I'm heading . . ." His office was empty. So I grabbed a Post-it from his desk and wrote him a note:

BERNARD, *Grabbing lunch and going to stake out a church for a couple hours. If you need me, call. Stella.*

ON THE CORNER diagonally across from The Light was a burned-out house, its driveway blocked by an overgrown tree with saplings all around. I pulled my car behind the foliage and sat. In another few weeks this wouldn't work, the leaves would be gone. As it was they were various shades of orange and red and doing a great job of hiding my gray car. Unfortunately, they also blocked my vision, seriously limiting my view of the church and totally blocking my view of the old school building. Before I'd parked, I'd driven around the old school twice. While there still wasn't any indication that it was being used, I did see an alcove that I hadn't noticed before. It faced toward Glendale Avenue, but what lay beyond was hidden inside. No matter how slow I drove, I couldn't see if there was an actual door. My curiosity was building. Since this wasn't the door I'd noticed with the chain and lock, and based on where I'd seen the women cross, it would be the only place they could have entered.

I looked for a worn path in the overgrown grass, but I didn't find one. There was a cracked sidewalk that would hide footprints. I was sure Bernard wouldn't appreciate my postponing this research until I could see tracks in the snow.

The streets weren't as empty as they'd been the last time I was here. I watched the occasional man or woman walk across the intersection, but no one went into or out of The Light. I knew Dylan would be mad if he knew I was there, but that didn't stop me. I'd driven to my apartment from WCJB and grabbed a bite to eat. There I'd developed a plan. I'd run. It didn't matter that I'd gone five miles this morning; a woman jogging along the streets would be less conspicuous than one walking, especially one with a thousand-dollar camera.

After one more look around, I eased myself from my car into the autumn air. The afternoon sun had raised the temperature considerably since my morning run, yet again I wore long tight running pants and a long-sleeved T. Putting my purse in the trunk of my car with my camera, I grabbed my keys and phone. With my phone in hand, I hit my camera app and stretched, all the while watching for anyone.

Taking a deep breath, I headed east.

While driving I'd noticed a small park about a half a block past The Light. I started running toward it. The dilapidated surface of the road required my attention as I evened my strides. The last thing I wanted was a twisted ankle during my reconnaissance mission. I slowed as I neared the gate that I presumed the women had entered. There was a rust-free chain holding it closed. I snapped a picture. I'd need to compare it to the pictures I'd taken last time, but I didn't remember the lock being there. Without getting through the fence, there was no way I could be sure there was a door in the alcove.

As I snapped the picture, I noticed the same SUV I'd seen before turn onto Second Avenue and head toward me. I moved to the side of the street, placed the phone to my ear, and continued to run. Keeping my head down, I watched as the SUV eased into the same parking lot as before. When I turned into the park, I stopped and watched through the colorful bushes. This time four men got out of the SUV. Damn, I want my Nikon.

Using my phone, I snapped pictures as they made their way out of the vehicle and around to a back entrance. Three of them were wearing blue jeans as before, but one was in a suit. I gasped. That was the man I'd seen earlier today on the website, Gabriel Clark.

What do they call him? Father Gabriel?

I was about to stop photographing when the men opened the

door and a stream of women came out. Each one appeared to bow her head as she passed the men. They were headed toward the school.

Shit! Fuck!

I wanted to run back in that direction, but could I? The men had seen me running, and they were still in the parking lot. I watched from a distance as one of the women opened the gate and the rest entered. Then, after the gate was secure, they all disappeared into the alcove.

I knew it!!!

CHAPTER

TWENTY-ONE

S ara

Father Gabriel's strong recorded voice echoed throughout the living quarters. I walked the length of the room and tried to concentrate on his lesson. While his teachings were instructional and some of his stories made me smile, listening while sitting on the sofa wasn't working for me. Despite my best efforts, my eyes kept closing, and I was pretty sure I'd even fallen asleep more than once. It wasn't that Father Gabriel's lessons were boring or that I wasn't curious to learn more about what we believed, it was that Jacob had needed to wake earlier than normal this morning, which meant I had too. Though Jacob still didn't think I was healed enough for all my wifely duties, despite my current lack of vision I was able to make him coffee and breakfast each morning.

He and Brother Micah left before five o'clock this morning to retrieve Father Gabriel from the Eastern Light. Jacob had taken him to the Western Light less than a week ago. I didn't know how Father Gabriel got from the Western to the Eastern Light, where those places were, or even how far apart they were from one another. Though I was curious, I didn't ask. I knew that if I talked about these things to Elizabeth or Raquel they'd tell me that if I needed to know, Jacob would tell me. They'd also tell me that I should be happy with whatever information my husband gave, and I was. After all, if he hadn't told me where he was going and when he'd be back, I wouldn't have known when to be ready to greet him.

During this first week of banishment, he'd done other things to help me. One was finding me a clock without a covering over the hands. With it I could tell time by myself, which was especially helpful while he was away. Every step toward more independence helped me feel stronger and more like the person I believed I had been before I lost my memories.

Although Jacob told me when to expect him, his arrival was contingent on Father Gabriel. Wherever the Eastern Light was, I figured it was far away, because even though he and Brother Micah left early, they weren't scheduled to return until after six in the evening. I suspected that their goal was to have Father Gabriel back to the Northern Light in time for tonight's service.

Even if Father Gabriel made it back in time, Jacob and I still weren't allowed to attend. Not only had we missed last Sunday's, we'd be missing one more week. We'd almost completed our first week of banishment.

During our time away I'd learned more about asking and questioning. When I asked how The Light had service with Father Gabriel gone, Jacob explained that Father Gabriel could conduct service from anywhere. His image was projected on a big screen in the temple, and with the technology he could even see all the followers. Since I couldn't remember any of what he described, I was becoming increasingly anxious to see it with my own eyes. I'd had contact only with Jacob since we'd arrived at the pole barn. Though Brother

Micah worked in the hangar, he never entered the living quarters. I hadn't even heard his voice; most of the time I knew he was there only because of the noises coming from the other end of the building. However, noises didn't necessarily indicate his presence; according to Jacob, other men came to load and unload supplies as well as help maintain the planes. He mentioned them as a reminder that I wasn't allowed to leave the living quarters. With our banishment, I was allowed to speak only to Jacob and the Commissioners or their wives.

I didn't care about the Commission; mostly I missed Raquel and Elizabeth. Since I'd woken from the accident, my world had seemed very small. The longer we were separated, the more I realized the important role my friends played.

The other day, after everyone left the hangar, Jacob took me out and gave me a tour. I couldn't see the planes, but I could experience them. First he took me inside the smaller plane. It had two seats for pilots, a large open area for cargo, and even multiple jump seats for extra or unexpected passengers. Because we were so far away from everything, with so many people, I understood why he needed to transport a lot of supplies; what I didn't understand was how or why he had unexpected passengers, but I didn't ask. Even though there were two pilots' seats, apparently the smaller plane could be flown solo. I figured it was the one Brother Micah used while Jacob was with me.

As soon as Jacob opened the cabin of the second jet, I knew it was different. If he flew in it often, the luxurious interior undoubtedly added to his signature scent. The furnishings in the passenger cabin were covered in the softest leather I recalled ever feeling. Walking up and down the aisle, I ran my fingers over the multiple chairs and the sleek interior. Unlike the smaller plane, this jet required two pilots. Jacob laughed when I sat in one of the cushy chairs and told him I was ready for him to take me someplace, now or later. Since the jet held ten people and usually flew only Brother Micah, Jacob, and Father Gabriel, I'd been serious. If Father Gabriel had been restricted to the smaller plane while I was in the clinic, I understood why he wanted Jacob back to work.

Even though I was essentially as trapped in the pole barn as I had been in the clinic, I wasn't in a hurry to leave. I knew this was punishment, and I shouldn't like it, but I kind of did. It gave me a chance to stop worrying about a past I couldn't remember and relearn my role as Jacob's wife. Things were continuing to improve since the first day when I'd forgotten to greet him at the door. Thankfully our banishment was the only punishment I'd endured since the previous week. My goal was to keep it that way. As long as I kept that eerie calmness out of Jacob's voice, I was even beginning to enjoy his company.

Sometimes the wind would howl, and I'd think about the polar bears. However, knowing how big the pole barn was eased some of my worry. The living quarters were only a tiny part compared to the building as a whole. After all, the hangar had to be large enough to hold two jets, as well as all sorts of other things, like cool carts that attached to the jets and moved them in and out of the hangar. There was also a whole shop area with tools and an office area with desks and computers. When I thanked Jacob for my tour, he said I'd been out there before. Of course, I didn't remember.

Just as I finished rewinding Father Gabriel's lesson, the sound of the rising garage door startled me. After that first day, I'd gotten very good at distinguishing that sound from other clatter. I hurried to the clock, wondering if I'd slept more than I'd realized, but it was only twenty minutes after three. Jacob wasn't due back for more than three hours.

My pulse raced as I stood in dark silence, waiting for a knock. With each moment my nerves stretched and my palms moistened. With my blood pumping in my ears, I wondered what to do. I hadn't gone through the door to the garage without Jacob and suddenly wondered if it even had a lock.

The knock never came; instead I held my breath as my fear materialized and the door opened. As soon as the click of high heels upon the wood floor registered, I recognized my guest.

She wasn't alone. When she entered I'd heard two distinct sets of footsteps. Figuring the other person was either Sister Ruth or Brother Timothy I sighed with relief, knowing that they were people with whom I could speak. I was also glad that I'd restarted the lesson. If they'd entered with the recording near the end, with the way my mind was wandering, I'm sure I would've failed their round of twenty questions.

"Sister Sara," Sister Lilith finally greeted me.

"Sister Lilith," I replied.

"We heard that Brother Jacob would be gone and decided this was a good opportunity to speak to you."

"Thank you, that's very kind of you."

"Hmmm," she hummed.

Her strange reply brought the fine hairs on my arms to attention. While the unique scent of her perfume, as well as her steps, let me know she was getting closer, the citrus reminded me that I didn't smell vanilla. Sister Ruth wasn't the person still near the door. I took a chance and turned in that direction.

"Brother Timothy, welcome."

"Sister," he said.

"I see you're adapting well without sight," Sister Lilith said. "I do hope that your eyes will be better soon."

"Thank you; I'm patient for God's time."

As silence filled with the click-clack of her high heels, I envisioned her taking a white glove and evaluating my housecleaning skills. If she was, I wasn't concerned. I'd dusted, pushed a dust mop back and forth, and even washed and put away my dishes from lunch.

"Sister, we have questions and feel it's time for your answers," Brother Timothy said.

This wasn't right. Jacob had said I didn't need to go before the Commission. I struggled with my next move. If it had been only

Lilith, I could've questioned her, but it wasn't. I knew from experience that I couldn't question Brother Timothy. Reaching for one of the four chairs at the table, I did my best to weigh each word. "Brother, Sister, if you'd like, we may sit, and I'll be happy to answer anything that Brother Jacob has given me permission to discuss."

Chairs moved, the screech of the legs over the floor indicating my guests' locations. Since the person on my right sat first, that was Brother Timothy. I waited until Sister Lilith was seated before I sat.

"Sara," Sister Lilith began. "While I'm pleased with your progress, I'm here on behalf of the Commission and Assembly wives."

I couldn't believe her. She'd lied about that before. Nevertheless I was careful about what I said. "Thank you for taking the time to come all the way out. I know that I'm only allowed to speak to the Commission and Commission wives. Your visit means a lot."

"This is more than a visit," Brother Timothy began. "This is officially part of your correction."

My stomach twisted.

"Sister, I'm going to get straight to the matter at hand. Do you remember when I came to your room, right after you awoke after your incident?"

I turned toward his voice. "Yes, Brother Timothy, I do."

"Do you remember me asking you questions about your incident?"

"Yes."

"Do you remember your answers?"

My pulse quickened. "Brother, I must obey my husband. I haven't received his permission to discuss this with you or anyone."

"Sara," Sister Lilith said. "Father Gabriel teaches that next to him, the Commission rules our community. Brother Timothy is one of Father Gabriel's chosen. Brother Jacob may be on the Assembly, but he does not supersede my husband."

"Sister, I've learned so much through your training. Thank you. I believe I learned that what you said is true for you. Since only Father

Gabriel has the power to supersede our husbands, I must obey Jacob." Though my heart was about to leap from my chest, I sat tall, confident in my response. Turing toward Brother Timothy I added, "I'm sorry, only with my husband's permission may I answer your questions."

"Sister," he asked, his volume lowered. "Did Brother Jacob inform you that you could only speak with the Commission and their wives, or did he not?"

Shit!

"Yes, Brother, he did."

"Are you aware that I'm on the Commission and that makes Sister Lilith a Commissioner's wife?"

"Yes."

"Does it not seem that Brother Jacob then indeed gave his permission?"

My head went from side to side, swinging the low ponytail I'd secured earlier this morning across my back. "I'm sorry. I don't believe that he meant—"

"Sister." Brother Timothy slapped the table. The reverberating sound caused me to jump as it echoed throughout the living quarters. "Do you presume to know what Brother Jacob meant? Are we to understand that you've been given the gift of discernment concerning all men or only your husband?"

"No, I don't presume . . ."

"Rest assured that this will be discussed with Brother Jacob."

My breaths came fast and shallow with the realization that I was not going to win. If I didn't answer, Brother Timothy and Sister Lilith would tell of my lack of cooperation, if I did, I was disobeying Jacob. I was damned if I did and damned if I didn't.

Lilith spoke. "Sara, obeying your husband is your duty; however, so is being truthful. You told us, through Brother Jacob, that you remembered why you were in his truck. You said that you were obeying Brother Jacob. Now we've been told you don't remember. Tell me, were you lying then . . . or now?"

"I'm not lying. I wasn't."

"So it was Brother Jacob then? An Assemblyman was the one who lied?"

"N-no, that's not—"

"Brother Jacob testified before the Commission saying that you're having difficulty with your memory. That was why my wife was helping you remember your training. Tell us, Sister, are you truly having problems with your memory, or are you selectively forgetting details to justify your behavior?"

"I am . . . I'm really having trouble." I couldn't think straight. They were twisting my words. I moved my slick palms to my lap and rubbed them over my skirt.

"So if you don't remember what happened before your incident, tell us, who lied in your hospital room, you or Brother Jacob?" Brother Timothy questioned.

Shit!

"Please, please," I begged. "If we could wait for Brother Jacob, when he's home we can answer everything together." Tears streamed from my bandages.

"Sister Sara, you do remember that this isn't your home, don't you?" Sister Lilith asked.

"Brother Jacob told me that we have an apartment. We're only here for our banishment."

"That's correct. You're here as punishment for your sins. When one among us transgresses, Father Gabriel teaches swift appropriate retribution for their disobedience. Do you remember that?" she asked.

"Yes, I mean, I know that now."

"So you didn't know that before, when you drove away in Brother Jacob's truck?"

Once again my head moved from side to side. "I don't remember what I was doing, but I do know about punishment."

"Yes, Sister, I believe you do, and not solely in theory." She leaned closer. "Tell us what Brother Jacob did last Wednesday after your lapse in judgment, after you had the audacity to question Father Gabriel."

I wanted to disappear. That was supposed to be over. Jacob said it was over, but the glares I couldn't see burned my skin, expecting my response. Balling my fists in my lap, I willed my tears to stay hidden; instead they slipped from my bandages onto my charred cheeks and interrupted my words. "He . . . punished . . . me."

"Did you deserve your husband's punishment?"

I nodded.

"Sister?" Brother Timothy said.

"Yes."

"Why?" Her interrogation continued.

"Because I questioned Father Gabriel."

"Will you do that again?"

"No."

"Why?"

"Because I don't want to embarrass my husband again."

"Is that the only reason?"

I took a ragged breath. "I don't want to be punished."

"What form of punishment did Brother Jacob choose to implement, to help you reach this decision?" Brother Timothy asked.

My heavy chest heaved as I fought with myself, not wanting this conversation. "He used his belt."

"After his correction was complete, did you remember it?"

"Yes."

How could I forget?

"How?"

"I don't understand"—I hiccupped a breath—"why we're having this . . ."

"Sister, what did Brother Jacob say about the evidence he left on your skin from his correction?"

"He said . . . it was my reminder."

"Sister," Brother Timothy's deep voice echoed. "Calm yourself."

Though I nodded, calming myself wouldn't happen as long as their interrogation continued.

"Do you believe his reminder was useful?" Sister Lilith asked.

"I won't forget."

"Very good. Now this correction that you and Brother Jacob are currently enduring," Brother Timothy said, joining the cross-examination. "What will help you remember—be your reminder—not to lie to a Commissioner again?"

My breaths stuttered, as panic infiltrated my reply. "I-I didn't lie."

"What will be your reminder, Sister?"

"I-I don't know . . . memories?"

"But you said you're having difficulty remembering." Sister Lilith's condescending tone twisted my already knotted stomach.

I shook my head. "Sister, I have difficulty remembering before my accident. I recall everything since."

"Isn't that convenient?" Brother Timothy asked.

"I'm sorry. I don't believe I should say anything else." I tried unsuccessfully to fill my lungs.

"Very well," Sister Lilith said, her chair moving.

Thank Father Gabriel, they are leaving.

"Sister, stand," she demanded.

My body stilled. "What?"

"Is the ability to hear another of your medical problems, or is it only obeying?" Brother Timothy asked.

I scooted back my chair and reached for the table. With shaky knees I stood. The movement of Brother Timothy's chair let me know that we were all standing.

"As we told you, we're here on behalf of the Commission. While Father Gabriel's decree has far-reaching implications, The Light believes that retribution of sin cleanses the soul. Playing house out here alone is hardly severe enough punishment for lying to my husband."

"Sister, I didn't lie. I was confused, and this punishment was Father Gabriel's ruling."

"Yes, and we're here today to deliver your reminder, to help you not commit this sin again."

"M-my reminder? What . . . why are you . . . ?"

"Rest assured," Brother Timothy said. "I'll discuss your continued questioning with your husband."

My body trembled as I contemplated Jacob's response. I tightened my grip on the table, and then a strange sound caught my attention.

"Hair," Brother Timothy explained in a tone that reminded me of Jacob's eerie calm, "is a woman's crowning glory. The reminder you'll receive today will help you to remember to be truthful. This reminder won't only be for you, but also for your husband. Each time he sees your short hair—"

What the hell is he saying?

"—he'll remember the shame you brought to him. Sister, the entire community will see your reminder and know of your punishment."

"My hair? What do you mean?"

"Sister, expect your husband to be informed of your continued disobedience."

The next few seconds occurred in a blur. The sounds I heard, the snip and clip, suddenly made sense. It was as though my darkened world moved in slow motion; nevertheless I couldn't catch it. As I reached for my hair, Sister Lilith lifted my ponytail and cut.

"No!" I screamed, my ponytail sagging in my grip. "Why?!"

Sister Lilith's hand connected with my cheek. "That is enough questioning. You're in the presence of a Commissioner. Apparently the reminders you've been given require reapplication."

Stumbling to the table, I found that my knees no longer held my weight. I fell into the chair I'd recently vacated, still gripping my detached ponytail.

Oh my God. What did they do? What will Jacob say? Will he punish me for this?

Though their voices were close, I couldn't distinguish them with any clarity. Their phrases faded into my internal mayhem.

"... when you think about this, remember that it was done for your own good. It seems as though Brother Jacob has more work ahead of him." What am I going to do? "Your willfulness needs continued correction." Why are they doing this? "Remember this reminder was your doing and, as always, avoiding future reminders is your choice." My hair! Jacob! "Prepare yourself for your husband's additional correction when he returns." Oh, please. This can't be happening. "As you yourself said, you are his responsibility; only he can truly correct your behavior."

Perhaps I was in shock, but I didn't respond. There was nothing I could say as their accusations and warnings swirled through the air and my mind. The meanings of their words, the shock at my loss, and the promise of impending punishment paralyzed me. The weight of it all held me captive until their footsteps disappeared behind the closing door and the garage door went up and down.

Finally freed, I moved and took a ragged breath.

When I did, my entire body revolted. Shock waves swept through me from my head to my toes. The knotting in my stomach painfully twisted, propelling the remnants of my long-ago-eaten lunch upward. With perspiration dotting my brow, I hurried toward the bathroom. Falling to my knees, I emptied the contents of my stomach into the toilet. Over and over I retched until nothing but heaves racked my body. My clammy and trembling body, as well as the reality of what had happened and would happen, pinned me to the floor.

As the fog lifted, I remembered my ponytail. Panic erupted when I realized that in my desperation I'd dropped it. "No . . . no . . ." I cried, making it shakily to my knees and desperately searching the darkness. The strands were scattered, like the shards of my heart. With painstaking determination I gathered the pieces together. Once

I had them in one place, I hugged them close. The uneven tips of my hair brushed my wet cheeks as I held my detached ponytail, pulled my knees to my chest, and cried.

Time lost its meaning.

Finally I made my way to my feet and the sink. After carefully placing my hair on the vanity, I cupped water in my hands, rinsed the awful taste from my mouth, and washed my tearstained cheeks. Slowly thoughts began to surface, reminding me of my choices. Brother Timothy had said it was my choice, and so had Jacob.

What if I chose to leave?

Obviously there wasn't a lock on the door. I could leave. Tears resumed as sobs resonated from deep within. Instead of fear, sorrow overwhelmed me as my thoughts went to my husband. I recalled how he'd helped me wash my hair and the way he'd run his fingers through its length. No matter how hard I tried, I couldn't make myself reach for the hair now dangling near my cheeks. My haircut of disgrace. Though my trembling had stopped, my rapid pulse remained.

Did I want to leave? If I did, where would I go? Would I take Jacob's truck again? Was this why I'd taken it last time? Had it been because of fear? Had the fear been of Jacob or others? Driving wasn't an option. I couldn't see, much less drive, but I could walk . . . to where, to whom? Wouldn't I have had the same questions before? Where had I been going then?

As I remembered the polar bears I heard the distinct sound of the garage door opening. With a heavy heart I knew . . . I knew with clarity that this time it was Jacob.

Clutching the remnants of my long hair, I debated my options. Go to the door, confess my questioning of Brother Timothy, and receive punishment, or stay in the bathroom, close the door, hide, and, of course, receive punishment. As I caressed the length of hair, I knew there weren't options. Jacob might have said I had choices, even Brother Timothy had said the choice was mine, but it wasn't.

Like everything since I'd awoken, my fate would be determined by Jacob.

For the first time since Sister Lilith had taken the scissors and cut my hair, I dared to touch what remained. Placing the neatly gathered strands back on the vanity, I raised my fingers to the ends that skirted my cheeks. My empty stomach knotted as I followed them toward the back of my head. They were even shorter there than in the front. The tears and trembling I'd finally stilled bubbled, clogging my throat with an erupting sob. My sorrow wasn't as much for what I was about to receive, as for what I'd lost.

Everything was happening in slow motion, even the closing of the garage door, but finally the sound stopped. With my chin to my chest, arms tightly wrapped around my midsection, and lip secured between my teeth, I willed my feet forward, through the kitchen, around the table where I'd been uncrowned of the glory Brother Timothy had determined I no longer deserved, and toward the door. Shame from my loss left a gaping hole as I stopped exactly where Jacob had told me to be. As the knob turned, my memories went to that afternoon when he'd reminded me where to greet him: even then he'd given me a choice.

No longer strong enough to face my husband, ashamed that once again he was about to suffer embarrassment at my hands, I chose the option that less than a week ago had seemed impossible. As the door opened, I sank to my knees.

TWENTY-TWO

J acob

With the doorknob still in my hand, I heard Sara's sobs echoing throughout the dimmed room.

What the hell happened?

"Sara?" I called, flipping the light switch. The relief of being back to the Northern Light and having Father Gabriel back in time for service was gone. My wife was on the floor, her body quaking with shuddering breaths.

Reaching for her shoulders, I lifted her from the ground and stifled a gasp. What I saw was unquestionably the cause of her anguish. Her beautiful hair was cut—not cut, butchered. The sight ignited a fire inside me, detonating rage such as I hadn't known in years, not since I was a young man in the heat of a war I willingly fought but never wanted. Clenching my jaw, I made the same vow I had then.

This will not beat . . . us.

It wasn't the same vow; this time one word was different.

Sara's body trembled as my grip upon her petite frame tightened. I pulled her close, unaware of my cool leather coat. Though its temperature undoubtedly added to her shaking, all I could think about was holding her, wrapping my arms around her, and sheltering her from whoever had done this.

Who did this?

"I-I'm sorry," she muttered.

Her apology tore my heart to shreds. "Shhh, you're all right."

"No, I'm not."

Her words came out muffled against my embrace. As I cradled her in my arms, her body sagged. "You're OK; I'm here now," I tried to soothe as I carried her to the sofa. When I sat her down, she reached out and clung to me, burying her face in the crook of my neck. Her tears dampened my skin.

"Sara, let me take off my coat. It'll be all right. I don't know what happened, but I promise, it'll be all right."

She gripped me tighter. "N-no, my hair . . . it'll never be all right."

I kissed the top of her head. I'd only partially seen what had happened, but now, in the brightness of the room, I clearly saw the tattered tips of her once-long hair. Caressing her back, I waited until she took a deep breath and her grip lessened. Easing my arms out of my coat, I let it fall to the sofa. Once again I pulled her close, and asked, "Tell me what happened. You didn't do this, did you?"

Her head moved from side to side against my chest.

"Who?" I asked again.

She didn't answer as hiccups sabotaged her quest for air. I lifted her chin. "Sara, tell me." My voice was harsher than I'd intended. "Tell me who did this to you."

"They said it was my fault, my reminder of what I did." With each word she tried unsuccessfully to lower her chin. Stubbornly, with the return of my fury, I refused to loosen my hold.

They?

I knew. I knew whom she meant, but I needed to hear it from her.

"They? Who they? And what did you do?"

Like liquid, her body freed itself from my grasp, flowing from my lap and pooling on the floor. As she clung to my legs, her sobs returned. At first her murmurings were unintelligible, but soon I understood.

". . . said I lied, o-or you lied. They wouldn't let me wait for you. I-I tried." Her head dropped lower. "I told them I couldn't discuss it . . . y-you hadn't given me permission. I'm sorry, I know what you're going to do. I-I know I was wrong. I didn't . . . I don't . . . understand why they did this . . . I questioned . . ." She shook her head with her forehead near the floor. "You never said I could . . . I tried . . . he said I presumed . . . I didn't . . . I wasn't . . . but she said I needed more correction . . ." Her volume fluctuated, as did the speed of her words, some coming fast and low while others came slow and loud. With each of her phrases the muscles of my neck tightened. "I'm so sorry . . ."

When I reached again for her shoulders, she wordlessly resisted, her body going limp in her effort to remain prone.

"Sara, stop apologizing." My heart broke, shattering at her desperation. "Please, let me hold you. You don't belong on the floor."

Her face snapped up toward mine. Blotches of red covered her cheeks, neck, and chest. "I do," she declared with conviction. "I don't deserve you. You deserve a wife who isn't a disgrace. I'm an embarrass—"

"Stop now." I waited as her words floated away, replaced with more tears. Again I demanded, "Sara, stand up." Her body obeyed. "I've asked you before. No more apologies. I want names. Don't make me remind you that I should be answered the first time."

With her arms wrapped around her midsection, her entire body shuddered. Even her long skirt fluttered with movement. Finally she replied, "Brother Timothy and Sister Lilith."

I gripped the arm of the sofa. Every cell in my body desired to drive to the community and confront the cowards who'd done this in my absence. I didn't understand their problem with me, but whatever it was, it was with me, not Sara. Yet I couldn't drive to the community, not now, not with my shattered wife standing before me, holding herself and shivering as if the she were outside in the Alaska cold instead of inside in a warmed building. Taking a deep breath, I willed my anger away. Sara needed something different.

As I stood, Sara took a step back. Her trepidation of me twisted the proverbial knife in my heart.

"Sara, do you think you can get away from me?"

Her breathing hitched as she shook her head. The severed ends of her hair swung about her face. "No."

"Do you want to?"

Her lip disappeared between her teeth before she whispered, "No, but I'm afraid."

Watching her stand in front of me, I wondered about Brother Timothy and Sister Lilith's intent. Was it to break her, to break us, to assure my failure? If that was their intention, they'd never win. Despite it all, Sara had the strength to answer me honestly.

"You're afraid of me, your husband?"

She shook her head. "No, not of you, of what you're going to do."

I ran my hands up and down her arms, barely touching, yet warming my palms on the sleeves of her sweater. "What is it that I'm going to do?"

Releasing her lip, she replied, "I know I was wrong. I deserve your correction."

My hands reached for hers. "Let me hear your transgressions, and then I'll make that decision."

"But Sister Lilith told me you would, that I deserved and needed . .."

The temperature of the room rose a degree with each mention of their names. Nevertheless I couldn't let Sara sense that anger. If correction was coming, it wasn't to be done out of anger, but out of responsibility. "Your correction isn't up to Sister Lilith or Brother Timothy; it's at my discretion. Do you want me to ask again for your transgressions?"

"No," she answered quickly. "I spoke to them without your permission, and after . . . my hair . . . I questioned . . . them both. Brother Timothy said I presumed discernment." She shook her head. "I didn't mean to, but he's a Commissioner, so I must have."

"Is there anything else?"

Her lip blanched as she concentrated. "I think I fell asleep during Father Gabriel's teaching. I didn't mean to," she added quickly. "It's that we woke early."

I couldn't stop the smile that crept across my face at her childlike honesty. I kissed the top of her head. "That would make four, unless you have more to add."

Her hand flinched in mine at the number four. I knew what she was thinking: four transgressions equaled twenty lashes. Releasing one hand, I led her toward the stairs. "Let's go upstairs."

She didn't fight or beg; instead her shoulders sagged and she willingly walked toward our room. As we reached the top step, Sara said, "Jacob . . ."

"Yes?"

"I understand why you're doing what you're doing. I'm not asking for leniency, but I want you to know how truly sorry I am."

The redness on her cheeks and neck had nearly faded.

"Sara, it's time to prepare."

Nodding, she sat on the bed and removed her boot. When she stood and her black-and-white-striped skirt fell to the floor, I marveled at her calm. It was as Father Gabriel taught: once she'd given her transgressions to me, they were no longer her concern. As she pulled her sweater over her head, my pretense disappeared.

My gaze roamed her beautiful body, covered only by her bra and panties. The last remaining evidence of her accident was her cast.

Other than that, her flawless skin glowed under our bedroom lights. I stepped closer, wanting to brush her arms as I had her sleeves, needing to touch her.

This time she didn't step away; instead her face inclined as my chest met hers.

"Though your answer won't change my decision, I want to know"—my arms ached to hold her, yet remained still as I completed my question—"do you believe you deserve correction?"

After only a moment's hesitation, she replied, "I love and trust you. If it's your wish, I accept it. If you choose otherwise, I'll accept that too."

My arms no longer obeyed. They wrapped around her and pulled her to me. With my lips against her hair, I said, "I had no intention of punishing you." She melted into me. Lifting the tips of her hair, I continued, "This wasn't supposed to happen. It wasn't Father Gabriel's decree. You've had enough reminding for one day. My dearest wife, I don't think you need any more. Do you?"

Moving her head from side to side against my chest, she said, "Thank you. I'm still very sorry."

As I lifted her chin, my body ached for her. "No more apologies. You were wronged; you didn't do anything wrong."

"But—"

I brushed my lips against hers to stop her rebuttal. However, instead of stilling her words, the connection served as a release. The desire I'd kept corralled for too long raged like a wildfire. Its flames consumed any remaining semblance of willpower. My grasp moved to the back of her neck. Only briefly did I think about the long blonde locks that were no longer there. They didn't matter. My only thought, my only need was to get closer to Sara, to feel her warmth beneath me, to take what God and Father Gabriel had given to me. To please her in the way I'd never done.

Moans filled our room as she pressed her body toward mine and began undoing the buttons of my shirt.

Though I ached at the confinement of my jeans, I wouldn't hurt her any more, not today, not after all she'd been through. "Sara, what about your ribs?"

Sliding my shirt over my shoulders, she reached for the hem of the thermal beneath. "Please, Jacob." Once she'd stripped my chest, her petite hands roamed my shoulders, arms, and torso, seeing what her eyes couldn't.

I unfastened her bra and gently pulled it away, freeing her small breasts. As I palmed one of them, her nipple beaded, and I decided their size was perfect. Holding her hips tightly against me, I bent down and sucked the hardened nipple. Her whimpers encouraged me as she wove her fingers through my hair.

It was as she reached for the buckle of my belt that I regained a small bit of control. Stopping her hands, I said, "Sara."

"Please let me unbuckle it. I want to associate your belt with more than pain."

Fuck!

I released her hands and watched as she unlatched it, pulled it from the loops, and dropped it to the floor. Her smile melted my heart while at the same time sending more blood to my already engorged erection. It wasn't until she released the button and zipper of my jeans that I sprung from the confines of my boxer shorts.

"Oh, Jacob," she purred as she grasped my width and ran her hand along my length. My heartbeat soared when she dropped to her knees.

"God, you're amazing," I remarked, "but I want you to stand." Reaching for her hands, I helped her up. As she stood, our lips collided and our tongues danced. "Trust me, I'd love that, but I need to be inside of you. It's been so long, I don't think I could hold back."

Her grin was the trigger to my explosion. I'd never make it in her sexy mouth. Taking her hand, I led her to the bed and removed my boots. In record time I littered the floor with my clothes.

"Now," I said with a smirk as I turned toward Sara.

Her chest rose and fell in anticipation as she scooted back against the pillows.

Magical sounds escaped her lips as I looped my fingers in the waistband of her panties and slowly lowered them down her legs and over her cast. Beginning at her exposed ankle, I tenderly kissed the insides of her legs, alternating between them, each touch of my lips higher than the one before. Though her skin was covered in goose bumps and her muscles tightened, she willingly opened herself, allowing me full access.

"Oh, oh," she panted, her hands clenching the sheets as my tongue lapped her essence.

With each taste, a war raged within me. My hardening erection demanded what my mouth was enjoying. Sara's bucking hips and sexy moans encouraged my every move, prompting my tongue to delve deeper. Though I suspected she wasn't a virgin, I'd also spent enough time around other men to know that I was large, larger than most, and I didn't want to hurt her. She'd be able to handle my girth better after she'd released. Lapping and sucking, I continued tormenting her body until her muscles tensed and she called out my name.

"Oh, God, Jacob, that . . . that . . ."

Slowly, I worked my way up her beautiful body until she was completely surrounded.

Reaching for my face, she pulled my lips to hers and dove inside.

While our tongues intertwined, I positioned myself, ready to claim my wife. "If I'm too heavy, we can do what you . . ."

"Please, take me," she breathlessly interrupted. "I need you inside of me."

It wasn't a request she needed to make twice. Back and forth, I moved as she shifted her hips. Once I was completely buried, I stilled and gazed down at my wife. She was so damn beautiful. In the light of our first time, I didn't see her hair. I saw the contented smile on the face of the woman who was completely mine. I'd already claimed her mind; her answer when I'd asked if she deserved to be corrected told me that. Now I also had her body.

"What's the matter?" she asked, her hands holding my shoulders.

"Nothing." I kissed her grin. "I'm just watching the most lovely woman in the world and thinking how damn lucky I am."

Her cheeks flushed, and I began to shift my hips. Our movements and rhythms occurred in sync. While one gave the other took, and then we'd switch, always giving more. My lips teased her nipples, kissed her lips, and moved everywhere in between.

Father Gabriel had given me this woman, my wife. Though I'd resisted, with our bodies united I couldn't ignore the overwhelming emotion she evoked. The passion of our fervent desire filled our room. When she once again detonated, her legs stiffened, sounds escaped her lips, and her body hugged mine from within. The spasms pushed me over the edge: one final thrust and with a guttural groan I collapsed, our bodies still connected.

With reckless disregard for the possibilities our futures held, I kissed my wife and whispered, "I love you."

Her demure grin returned. "I love you too. It's just . . ." She didn't finish her sentence.

"What?"

She shook her head. "I'm embarrassed."

Easing out, I lay on my side, pulled her close, and spooned with her, her back against my front. Holding her in my arms, I peppered the top of her head with kisses. "You can always tell me anything. Why are you embarrassed?"

She shrugged in my embrace. "Maybe I'm more ashamed."

"You've piqued my curiosity."

Her neck craned to brush her lips to mine. "I just can't believe I couldn't remember that. I mean, it was like, wow." Her hands came up to cover her face. "See, I'm blushing."

My chest vibrated with soft laughter. She may have been blushing, but while her confession stoked my ego, the proximity of her soft, naked body had me considering a second round. Part of me was on its way to recovery at that very second. It was the scent of her shampoo, the flowery aroma, that brought our most recent problem back to my mind. I rolled her to her back and kissed her nose. Playing with the ends of her hair, I smiled, hoping she could hear it in my voice. "It's cute."

She exhaled and pursed her lips.

"It is!" I exclaimed.

"No, it's not. I'm ugly. I know you like my hair." She burrowed her face into my chest. "Liked."

I brushed her cheek. "I like your hair. I love you, no matter what your hair looks like."

"But I'm ugly."

I caressed her arm, her warmth combining with mine. "Sara Adams, you could never be ugly. Even if you were bald, you're the most gorgeous woman in the world. And by the way, you're not allowed to argue with me. If I say you're beautiful, you're beautiful."

"I don't even remember what color it is."

I laughed. "It's the most beautiful color of corn silk and sunshine."

Her neck straightened. "So it is blonde?"

I drew her face to mine. With our noses touching, I nodded. "It is."

She cuddled closer. "Thank you."

Inhaling the combined scent of flowers and lovemaking, I sighed, "No, Sara, thank you." And then I remembered the time of night and how I'd found her. "Have you eaten? Are you hungry?"

She pulled away. "Oh, I'm sorry. I'm not, but I'll make you . . ."

I hugged her tight. "I'm not hungry. Like I've told you before, you're mine, all mine, and you're my responsibility. I wanted to be sure you're all right."

Her fingers splayed on my chest before she traced the edge of my jaw. "I wasn't, but now I am." Another kiss. I kissed her forehead.

"One more thing about tonight." I had to tell her this. I didn't want to wait.

"Yes?"

"When I got home, and again at the couch . . ." I took a deep breath and lifted her face to mine. "I know I gave you the option the other day, but Sara Adams, you're the wife of an Assemblyman. Don't kneel. You don't belong on the ground. I'm perfectly content with your words and the bowing of your head." It had killed me seeing her grovel. "Do you understand?"

"Yes." She paused. "I'm just wondering if there could ever be any exceptions. I mean, earlier, you didn't let me finish . . ."

Laughter bubbled from my throat. "I suppose there can always be exceptions. Get some sleep. It's been a long day."

"Good night, Jacob."

TWENTY-THREE

S ara

I NERVOUSLY WAITED for Jacob's return. He'd left earlier than normal this morning for Assembly. He hadn't mentioned Brother Timothy or Sister Lilith, and I couldn't ask, but the subject hung in the air like a thick cloud. When I washed my hair this morning, I'd gotten a better idea of how much was left. It was longer in the front, hanging just past my chin, and shorter in back. She'd cut it right at my ponytail tie.

Though I should've been listening to Father Gabriel's teachings, my mind was too much of a whirlwind to concentrate. Before Jacob left he told me that Brother Micah would be in the hangar today, as would others. Apparently they'd picked up supplies while at the Eastern Light, and they needed to be unloaded and driven back to the community. When I asked how they transported supplies, since the larger plane was mostly that soft luxurious cabin, he'd said that under the cabin was a large cargo area accessible from the outside.

Admittedly, it'd taken me a while, but I was getting the hang of asking, not questioning.

I'd recently heard a lesson about the sin of being prideful. It reminded me of Elizabeth's comment, and I decided it was one of my areas that needed work. Raquel had once said she needed to work on her patience. So it must be all right to have areas that needed improvement, as long as you recognized them. However, instead of working on it, this morning I was relishing in it. I wasn't prideful for myself; I was prideful for my husband, the important work he did for Father Gabriel and on the Assembly, and mostly his discernment. I'd been ready to accept his correction last night, conceding my transgressions and accepting his judgment. When he'd led me upstairs I knew what was coming, or I thought I did. I said more than one silent prayer that he'd show leniency. Despite the fact that the thought of twenty lashes seemed incomprehensible, once I confessed, there was a peace in knowing it was no longer in my hands. That didn't mean that I expected what happened. Never in a million years could I have foreseen his contrary reaction.

My face flushed as I thought about last night. It wasn't as if it had been our first time making love, but to me it had felt that way. How I could ever have forgotten Jacob's mastery in bed was beyond me. I'd been right when I predicted that he conquered unapologetically and bestowed unsparingly. Maybe it hadn't been a prediction, but a memory. Either way my body ached—in the best way—with my reminders of last night. Unlike other reminders that I wanted to avoid, the ones I currently experienced could recur every day and I wouldn't complain. I knew that making love didn't change our dynamic, but in a way it did. As I made his breakfast and prepared his coffee, I'd realized how much I wanted to please him. Especially if he still supported me with the way I looked. Maybe it wasn't prideful that I felt, but blessed.

While I debated, sounds echoed from the hangar. I knew Jacob had told me about Brother Micah and the others so that I wouldn't panic at every noise. Of course it also helped when he mentioned that Brother Timothy would be at Assembly and Sister Lilith couldn't drive out of the community alone. Though that made me feel better about me, I still worried about him. I doubted he would let their actions go without some kind of confrontation.

I bit my lip wondering if Jacob, an Assemblyman, could confront Brother Timothy, a Commissioner. And what would happen if he did?

As the garage door rose, I hurried to the clock. It was almost ten thirty. Assembly would be over. Hoping this was Jacob, I went to my spot near the door. Briefly I recalled my husband's words from the night before about kneeling. I wasn't sure how he did it, but despite my obvious transgressions and his supreme power over my life, he made me feel loved and worthy. I no longer had lingering feelings of resentment about waiting for him to enter. I was happy to do it.

The door opened and my breath hitched. Instead of only Jacob, there were multiple voices.

Lowering my chin, I waited.

"Sara," Jacob said, placing his co

t in my arms. "Dr. Newton is here with me. We have a surprise." He kissed my cheek.

I nodded. "Dr. Newton."

"Sister Sara."

Cautiously I walked toward the closet carrying Jacob's and Dr. Newton's coats. My mind was a blur of questions. Was this about my eyes? Jacob had changed the bandages this morning, but could the bandages be ready to be permanently removed?

As I began to juggle their coats, a hand touched my shoulder. I spun toward it, immediately recognizing the touch as well as a faint scent of honeysuckle. "I-I thought..."

Raquel hugged my shoulders. "Let me help you with those coats."

I nodded, the sound of Jacob's and Dr. Newton's voices reminding me that we were limited in what we could say.

She took one of the coats from my hand and we both reached for hangers. Quietly she whispered, "I don't know everything, but Brother Jacob got a special dispensation from the Commission and Father Gabriel. Since I work with Dr. Newton, they let me come." She squeezed my hand. "I've missed you."

The lump in my throat made it hard to speak. "I've missed you too," I whispered. I hadn't realized just how much until that moment.

"Sara," Jacob called, "it's time to do this."

"All right," I replied, allowing Raquel to lead me to one of the kitchen chairs.

"Sister Raquel," Dr. Newton said, "turn off the lights and close the drapes. We need to progress slowly."

Jacob reached for my hand, and his voice came as if he was kneeling near my chair. "Dear God and Father Gabriel, I pray that you've seen fit to heal my wife's sight."

"Amen," came from all.

I bit my lip, amazed given how fast my heart was beating that it stayed contained within my chest. Like Jacob's actions last night, this caught me off guard. I'd had no idea this was coming. If I had, I'd have spent my entire morning imagining what I hoped to see. Squeezing Jacob's hand, I confessed, "I'm scared."

"We'll survive no matter what happens today. You've done well for the last three weeks. If you don't have sight, we'll learn how to go on."

I nodded. He was right, as usual. That didn't mean I wanted to learn to cope. I wanted to see him, to gaze into the piercing blue eyes I remembered, to see their approval and admiration.

"Sister Raquel," Dr. Newton said, "hand me the scissors, so I may remove these bandages."

"No!" I blurted without thinking. Jacob unwound them. He didn't cut them.

"Sara?"

Suddenly trembling, I pulled toward Jacob. "I-I'm sorry. I'm sorry, Dr. Newton." I sat straight. "It's the scissors. I'm sorry. I do want the bandages off. I didn't mean . . ."

Raquel touched my knee. "It's all right. We understand. Let's get these bandages off, and then I'm going to help you with your hair."

She is?

I took a deep breath and nodded again. "I'm ready."

"Keep your eyes closed," Dr. Newton said.

I nodded. The snip and clip of the scissors echoed through the pole barn like nails on a chalkboard, yet I remained still. The tightening of my grip on Jacob's hand and my clenched teeth were the only indicators of my apprehension. While Dr. Newton cut the bandages from around my head, Raquel removed them. Though we changed them daily, my heart trepidatiously soared as I thought that they would not need to be replaced, but at the same time I feared it wouldn't matter.

"Sister Sara, tell me about your headaches."

"I haven't had any for a while. A little yesterday, but I think it was stress."

Jacob squeezed my hand reassuringly.

"That's a good sign regarding your optic nerve," Dr. Newton said. "My biggest concern has always been the flash from the explosion. However, it's been four weeks since your accident. If they're going to heal, they'll be healed by now."

I nodded.

"OK, Sister, this is it. Slowly open your eyes."

I took a deep breath and exhaled. Fluttering my lids, I gasped.

I saw light!

I squeezed Jacob's hand and blinked a few more times. The room was dim, very dim. I knew what I wanted to see. Turning my head, I took in the man who'd been by my side throughout my memory. With his forehead on my leg, his closed-eyed profile made him look as if he were praying.

Tears escaped as my smile grew.

I can see! I see my husband.

As I beheld the dark, wavy hair that covered his ears, my heart stilled. The jaw and chin I'd traced in the middle of the night were also covered with the same dark hair, only unlike the longer waves on his head, it was trimmed close to his face. I saw his closed eyes and high cheekbones. He was bent forward, silently waiting for my response. His light shirt—the color difficult to distinguish in the darkened room—stretched across the broad shoulders that I'd caressed. On his shirt were darker stripes that crisscrossed over the material. The darkness of my skirt contrasted with his skin. As I reached for his hair, my heart overflowed with emotion, as I saw what I could recall only feeling.

"Jacob, I can see." My voice was barely a whisper.

Dr. Newton and Raquel sighed. I wasn't ready to look at them. I needed to fully see the man kneeling at my feet. My cheeks rose as his handsome face turned my way. Moisture glistened in his eyes— his dark-brown eyes.

My elation evaporated. I squeezed my eyes shut, trying to hide my disappointment.

"Sara, what happened? Are you in pain?"

I willed myself to listen, to hear the man I loved.

He didn't have piercing blue eyes!

Shaking my head, I inhaled and exhaled. "No, I'm just emotional."

A lovely dark-haired woman with light-olive skin, probably in her late twenties, hugged me. Her white shiny smile drew me in. Her round cheeks had just the right amount of pink, and her blue eyes sparkled with compassion. "Of course you are. This is a miracle. Praise God. Praise Father Gabriel."

I nodded, noticing how her hair was secured at the nape of her neck in a low bun. Staring at her slender frame, I recalled how she'd helped me at the hospital, getting me in and out of bed. The turtle-neck sweater she wore under her scrubs accentuated her long neck. I reached for the necklace Jacob had placed around my neck, seeing the same cross on her. On her feet she had warm boots, and I wondered if she wore running shoes in the clinic. Her footsteps had always sounded different from Jacob's or Lilith's. I took her hands in mine. "Raquel, I didn't remember what you looked like. You're so pretty."

She smiled and lowered her chin. "Thank you, so are you."

Touching my hair, I said, "Not anymore."

She turned to Jacob, who was now standing. I craned my neck upward, seeing how tall he truly was.

I'd hoped that my sight would reveal the answers I'd been missing, allowing the pieces of the puzzle to fall into place, but it didn't. Instead of its shining light on my life, everything was suddenly more foreign. When Jacob nodded at Raquel, I started to ask what they were planning, but stopped myself.

"Honey," Raquel said, "when Brother Jacob told me what happened, I offered to help."

I shook my head. "I don't think anyone can help."

"It really is cute. It just needs to be evened up a bit."

Jacob squeezed my shoulder. "I told you it was going to be all right, and I said it was cute. Need I remind you that I'm always right?"

I could tell by his voice he was joking; nevertheless my cheeks flushed as I lowered my chin and said, "No, I believe you."

"Good, Dr. Newton and I'll go out to the hangar for a little bit and let you two ladies do the beauty parlor thing. Then I need to return Dr. Newton and Raquel to the community."

My pulse quickened at the idea of being alone, especially now that the Commission meeting was surely done. Before I could say anything, Dr. Newton spoke, and I turned his way.

With my eyes down, I noticed both of the men's shoes. Jacob wore boots, work boots with a hard sole. Those were the boots I'd heard pace my hospital room as well as walk the wooden floors of the living quarters. Dr. Newton wore shoes that too had a hard sole, and slacks as opposed to Jacob's jeans. Dr. Newton was older and shorter than Jacob and had gray in his thin hair. He was rather nondescript—neither handsome nor homely.

"Sister Sara, is anything blurry?" he asked.

"No."

Raquel opened the curtains. No wonder they did such a good job keeping the sun out, there wasn't any, not really. I looked to the clock, the one with the hands I could feel. It was nearly noon, yet it looked like dusk through the windows. "It's so dark," I commented.

"That's what happens in the dark season," Jacob replied, as he turned on lights. "It won't start getting lighter, well, until . . . February."

I shook my head.

Shouldn't some of this be familiar? February? What month is it?

"Sister, let me look closer at your eyes."

Dr. Newton shone a bright light directly into them. He then asked me to read a few things at various distances. Though I was thrilled everything was working, the strange sense of wrongness I'd had when I first awoke was back.

When Raquel and I were alone, I asked, "What month is it?"

"It's November, but December is coming fast." She squeezed my hand. "I'm so excited that you'll be home soon. There's so much happening with the holidays around the corner."

I stood.

"Where are you going?" she asked.

"To find a mirror."

"Oh, no." She giggled. I really have missed her. "Not yet. Let me work a little bit, then you can."

I scrunched my nose. "Is it that bad? Come on, be honest."

She squared her shoulders, and her petite frame stood tall. "You know I'm always honest, brutally, even, and I agree with Brother Jacob, it's cute. You'll probably start a whole new trend."

I sat back in the chair. "Oh, I'm sure. Can I be the one to cut Sister

Lilith's?" I quickly covered my lips with the tips of my fingers as my eyes opened wide.

Shit! I was so overwhelmed, I wasn't filtering.

Raquel came close and whispered, "Only if I'm the one who gets to hold her down."

We both stifled our laughter.

When she first brought out the scissors, I had to remind myself that this was my friend and we had Jacob's approval. Ignoring the sounds, I concentrated on my breathing. Soon Raquel had me forgetting about the scissors. She clipped and chatted, talked and snipped. Every now and then she stood back and assessed. The pieces of hair that fell to the ground were short, an inch here and half an inch there. Seeing them reminded me of my ponytail. I'd looked for it this morning, on the vanity where I'd left it, but it was gone. I was sure Jacob had thought he was helping me, and I didn't say anything, but I missed it.

While she worked, Raquel spoke about the other Assembly wives. There were twelve of us altogether. I couldn't keep up with all the names. One named Deborah was expecting a baby very soon. I was confident that I'd be able to spot her in the crowd. Another named Esther had recently had her second. Apparently she was very tired, especially with her time away from her job coming to an end. I learned that the Assembly wives didn't sit together only at service, but that twice a week, during prayer meetings, we met separately with the Commission wives for study. Even the word Commission made me bristle.

"Raquel, what do you know about what happened today, with Jacob I mean? How'd he get you here?"

She shrugged. "I really don't know. Benjamin was the one who told me I could come. I didn't know about what'd happened, umm . . . with your hair . . . until Brother Jacob told me during the drive here."

I bit my lip. "I'm afraid he'll get in trouble if he pursues this, and I'm also afraid they'll come back."

She was looking at me and shaking her head.

My hand went to my hair. "Is it worse?"

"No!" Her worried expression morphed to one of glee. "Not at all. It really is cute. I remember this style, longer in front than in back. It fits your face very well."

"Well, thank you for fixing it, but I want it to grow back."

"It will."

After a quick glance toward the door, I whispered, "You remember the dark?"

She nodded.

"What's it . . . is it . . . ?" I sagged my shoulders. "I don't remember. I wish I did. I wish I remembered anything."

"It may all come back. I know I work with Dr. Newton, but I don't know that much about memory things. I know what I've been taught."

I contemplated the dark. It seemed like such a scary place.

Why would I take Jacob's keys? Why would I want to leave people like Raquel?

"There!" she proclaimed. Removing the towel from my shoulders and looking to the floor, she said, "Oh, Sara, I'm sorry. We should have put towels on the ground. I've made a mess."

I stood and brushed the hair from my lap. "Don't worry about it. I'll get it cleaned up. First I want to see."

With a tight-lipped smile, Raquel looked as if she were about to burst. "I want you to, but I think we should wait—"

"Please, don't say for Jacob. I want to see my own reflection." I might have sounded like a three-year-old, but I wanted to see.

"I tell you what. Where's the broom? Let's get this cleaned, and if he's not back, you can slip into the bathroom."

I liked her. She didn't tell me I was willful or prideful. She'd even offered to hold Lilith down while I cut her hair. I wrapped her in my arms for a quick hug. "Thank you, Raquel. I'll miss you during the next week. I can't wait to get back to the community."

"Good. We all want you back."

As we were putting the broom and dustpan away, the door to the garage opened. Deciding to err on the side of caution, I forgot about the mirror and hurried toward the door.

Despite his unfamiliar eyes, his smile melted me. In the eyes I didn't remember I saw love and adoration that filled me with warmth like a flame to a candle.

Tenderly Jacob brushed my cheek and lifted the hair near my face. As he let it fall, his grin grew. "I like it. Turn around."

I did. When our eyes met again he reached for my hand.

"Have you seen it?"

"No, I was waiting for you."

Out of the corner of my eye, I caught Raquel's change in expression and had to consciously keep from rolling my eyes.

"Then let's go." Jacob tugged my hand. "Close your eyes," he commanded, as we neared the bathroom.

I did as he said, and he led me to the vanity. The warmth of his body behind me filled me with strength. With his hands on my hips, he told me to open my eyes. There in the mirror were two strangers. I opened my eyes wider, watching the woman in the mirror do the same. When I lifted my hair, so did she. Jacob's description of its color had been accurate, corn silk and sunshine—very blonde. Raquel was also right: the way the hair framed my cheeks worked with my oval face. I tilted my head from side to side. Though I hadn't seen it before, my hair was now all even with layers toward the back. Soon the anxiety left my eyes, mellowing them, leaving behind a baby-blue sheen of contentment. Directly behind and above me in the mirror was Jacob watching my every move.

When I finally shrugged, I lifted a corner of my mouth in a half smile. "I guess it's all right."

Raquel squealed from the doorway and clapped her hands. I hadn't realized she was standing there.

"Sara." In one word he reprimanded me. "All right?" he asked, repeating my words.

Lowering my chin, I raised my eyes and met his gaze in the reflection. "No, it's better than all right. It's cute."

His smile blossomed. "That's better."

While I retrieved everyone's coats, Jacob said, "Sara, you'll need your coat too."

My lips snapped shut, holding back the questions that threatened to come forth. Finally I said, "All right."

I hadn't noticed it before—because I hadn't been able to see— but the truck had a backseat. Raquel and I sat there while Jacob drove and Dr. Newton rode in front. For most of the ride, Jacob and Dr. Newton discussed things and people with names I didn't recognize. Getting to the community wasn't as easy as it had sounded. There were three different rows of fences with gates. The inside one was more of a wall. Codes were needed to open each gate. The whole setup seemed pretty elaborate for polar bears. With each new barrier I felt unfamiliarity and uneasiness.

No matter what, I was ready to be back inside the fences and walls; obviously it was much safer in there than out where we were. I stared at the unfamiliar buildings as we drove into the community.

When we arrived at the clinic, Raquel gave me a hug before getting out. "One week, I can't wait."

"Thank you for this," I said, pinching my hair with my gloved hands.

"You'll start a trend; I'm almost certain."

I knew that wouldn't happen, but it made me smile.

I wanted to move to the front, but instead I bit my lip and waited. It didn't take long until Jacob gave me permission. I understood how Raquel, or anyone, could have problems with patience. Waiting for permission to do things that seemed natural seemed, well, unnatural. Once my seat belt was fastened, I couldn't get enough of what was outside the windows. There were people of all ages and skin colors coming and going, some other vehicles, and many buildings. It truly was a community. Despite the cold, there wasn't a lot of snow.

"Does it help to see? Is it coming back?" Jacob asked.

"Yes, it helps to see, but no, it's not coming back."

He laid his hand on my leg, just as he'd done the first day he drove us out to the pole barn. I placed mine on top of his, seeing the difference in size for the first time. As our fingers intertwined, he replied, "That makes sense." Glancing my way and then back to the road, his brow furrowed. "I think I was hoping . . ."

"I'm sorry. So was I."

His hand squeezed mine. "But you can see. That's the most important thing."

"I disagree. If that's wrong, you can punish me, but my sight isn't the most important thing to me."

I saw the surprise in his expression. "You do? It's not?" With a hint of amusement in his tone, he continued, "Well, you've gone this far, please continue. What is the most important part, to you?"

Shit! I hadn't thought that offer through.

Forcing a smile and pretending I hadn't just volunteered for punishment, I replied, "The part where you didn't leave me alone in the pole barn. That's the most important thing to me. Thank you."

The corner of his mouth went up. "I hope you like Sister Ruth."

"Oh, I do!"

"Good, because she'll be with you whenever I need to fly. Tomorrow I have a short trip to Fairbanks for supplies."

Though the road was still rough, my ribs were much better than they'd been a week before. I sighed and leaned back against the seat.

"What is it?"

I pursed my lips before revealing a grin. "I don't think I'll be able to sleep through any more of Father Gabriel's lessons."

"Is that what you've been doing?" Though he'd made his tone serious, now that I could see the gleam in his brown eyes, I knew he was teasing.

"Not intentionally. I only remember doing it that one time, that I've already told you about."

"Sister Ruth will keep you honest."

"I'm already honest."

He lifted our gloved hands to his lips. "I liked seeing you with Raquel. It reminds me of how it was before . . ."

"Thank you for doing whatever you did to get permission for her to come out. I feel a lot better about everything than I did yesterday."

"That's my job."

I lifted his hand and brushed it against my cheek. "You're very good at it."

CHAPTER

TWENTY-FOUR

S tella

I GIGGLED as Dylan teased my neck, gently pulling back my long hair and kissing that spot that sent goose bumps up and down my arms and legs.

"You don't play fair," I said, through laughter and chills. "What if I had work to do at home?" The truth was that I wanted this break as much as he did.

"You work too much; besides, I never claimed to play fair."

I did work too much, not that it'd done me any good as of late. I'd spent the majority of my spare time in the last week home alone, devoted to my quest. Turning toward Dylan, I kissed his soft lips. "I'm glad you talked me out of work tonight, but you're a cop—aren't you supposed to be fair and be all about the rules?"

His kisses dipped lower. "I'll never be fair when it comes to you. If I have to play dirty to get you to spend time with me, I'll do it

250

every time, and as for rules, I never took you as much of a rule person."

I reached for his face and pulled his stunning blue gaze to mine. "You're right. I don't do the rule thing, not very well, at least. Tell me, though"—I grinned—"if you made rules, would breaking them be fun?"

His sexy bedroom expression morphed into a bright smile. "You're something else. In the mood of hot, popular women's fiction, sure, I'm willing, but in real life . . . hell, no. I'm not into that, and besides, I wouldn't try to change your sexier-than-shit rebellious ways. I can only think of one rule that might make me change my mind."

My shoulders slumped. This was a subject I was tired of debating. "I can't help where my job takes me."

He sat up with his stubbly jaw set and the muscles in his cheeks clenching. "I don't know how to emphasize this any other way. Do not go to Highland Heights. If I have to fucking go talk to Barney, I will."

I closed my eyes and shook my head.

This wasn't some pissing contest. It was my life and my decisions. Besides, Bernard didn't even know I'd been in Highland Heights the week before. I didn't want to get his hopes up. Not that I'd learned anything definitive. When I couldn't run back down Second Avenue, because of the men and the SUV, I'd gone around the block, looping around the old school. From an empty lot I had a view of the back of the old school building. In an area covered on both sides by the building, there was a greenhouse. It wasn't big; nonetheless there were about a half-dozen women in it, moving around. If I were to take everything at face value, I'd say that the greenhouse allowed The Light to grow the produce for its Preserve the Light preserves. Then I'd say that in that old school building, the women were making preserves. If I logically took it one more step, I'd say The Light's cars crossed the border daily to deliver jellies and jams.

What I'd spent the majority of last week deciding was if everything was truly that logical. Was I paranoid by nature, or was my gut telling me that it was a cover for something else?

Since my greenhouse discovery over a week before, I'd furthered my research. That didn't mean I'd advanced my knowledge on The Light. Information on the church was limited at best, yet I couldn't shake the feeling that things weren't as they appeared.

Maybe everything made too much sense?

Dylan stood, bringing me back to the present, and ran his hand through his dark-blond hair. "Tell me that you haven't been back to Highland Heights, not since I took you there. Come on, Stella. Please tell me that you're not that dumb."

The fine hairs on the back of my neck stood as I inhaled, sat, and pulled the sheet around my breasts. "Seriously, you're calling me dumb?"

"You know I don't think you're dumb, but if you go back there . . ."

"This conversation went from fun to shit faster than I ever imagined."

His chest expanded and contracted as his volume rose. "And the shit's going to hit the fan if I learn you've gone back there. Your safety isn't debatable."

What had Bernard said about shit hitting the fan? He said that when the shit hit the fan, it wasn't time to turn away. It meant the source of the manure was close and something was growing. Though it might stink, whatever it was, it was going to be big. He'd said that it was time to put on my shitkickers and plow through, to believe in myself . . .

Believe in myself.

I took a deep breath. "If this doesn't pertain to Mindy, we can't discuss it, remember?"

"A while back, you asked about DPD and HHPD working together. I'm not giving you particulars, but HHPD has been monitoring their residents. For the last . . . I don't know how many years . . . they've been working on this big initiative. They're watching populations, trying to get to know people and help. The thing is that women have been disappearing."

My eyes opened wide. "Shit! Do they have statistics? What...?"

"Stop it. Stop asking. Fuck! I shouldn't." He exhaled. "I'm not talking everyone, not women like Mindy, not professional, educated women. I'm talking about runaways, drug addicts, and prostitutes. Not all of them," he added, and took a deep breath, and paced the width of his room.

You really can't call it disappearing when it's a runaway. It's difficult because they're a transient population." He took another breath. "Some of them end up in the morgue, where you've been called. It's the others—they evaporate into thin air. Of course, it doesn't have to indicate foul play. One of the most viable theories is what's happening"—he pointed—"out the window."

I glanced at his bedroom window and into the darkness beyond the panes of glass. Now that we were officially in autumn, the early part of October, the days were getting shorter. It would get worse when the time changed. With standard time we'd fall back an hour. "I'm not seeing anything," I said, "except for your reflection, if you stand there."

He sighed. "It's Michigan. The leaves are changing and it's getting cold. You've lived around here long enough to know that winters can be brutal."

"Yes?"

"If you were homeless or a runaway, would you want to live here through the winter?"

"Hmm," I acknowledged, "I've never thought of it that way."

"Say that HHPD was in contact with a few of these women or even one of them, and the next time they stop to check on her, she's missing. Who's to say she didn't hitch a ride to a better climate?"

I nodded. "Why are you telling me this? I thought this was out of our range of sharing."

"Because I'm a cop—hell, I'm a detective—and Highland Heights scares the shit out of me. There's no reason for you to be there. Yes, it's high crime and there are bodies showing up . . ."

"Bodies? More? Have there been new ones?"

Dylan knelt on the bed and crawled toward me, his movements graceful and defined. Though I wasn't sure I'd ever tire of watching him without a shirt—all the working out, the CrossFit or whatever he and his police buddies did religiously, certainly yielded results—I suddenly had the sensation of being prey. Even so, I fought the urge to reach out and touch the definition in his bicep. Before he had the chance to say anything, I leaned forward and kissed his lips. "I get it. You're protective. I like it. I also have a job to do, not to mention a promise to keep." I was losing my battle of wills as his kisses returned me to the horizontal position. "Dylan, you didn't answer me."

"Shhh." He fanned my hair over the pillow and touched my lips. "I've said more than I should. Stop asking questions. I love your inquisitive nature, but it makes me nervous. Some people aren't as forgiving."

Though Dylan's actions were monopolizing my thoughts, my gut told me that there was something more in Highland Heights. I wasn't sure I could ever stop asking questions. And what people? Did Dylan know what was happening? And was that why he was trying to protect me?

It was then that I remembered Foster's call. "Dylan?"

He laughed. "See, you can't follow instructions worth shit."

I shrugged. "Fine, I won't ask you what I wanted to ask." I kissed his cheek. "By the way, it had nothing to do with Highland Heights, Mindy, or bodies. It's actually kind of funny, but never mind."

"Oh, no, now I'm curious."

I reached for the waistband of his shorts. Tugging at the elastic, with a grin I said, "I suppose it can wait."

His chest inflated before he blew out a deep breath. "Yeah, I think something else just came up."

Walking from Dylan's bathroom, I made my way to his dresser and opened the top drawer. I couldn't believe I'd caved and brought clothes over to his house. I hadn't brought many, but even I admitted it was nice, better than showing up to work in the same clothes as the day before. Admittedly, with the food tablets, Fred was doing better on his own than he used to do. I'd put an old clock radio near his bowl, and twice a day, for two hours at a time, he had the pleasure of listening to music. I realized that a little music didn't put me in the running for fish owner of the year, but the way I saw it, it was all about meeting his needs. He was a fish. He needed food and water, and a little interaction.

What was better than R&B?

Dressed for the day, I secured my hair in a low side braid that lay on my shoulder and made my way to the kitchen. Though I wanted to see the sexy guy with the jeans hanging low on his hips, it was the aroma of bacon that propelled me down the stairs.

Stopping in the doorway, I stared. Standing at the stove, still shirtless with his dark-blond hair all bedhead sexy, was Dylan. Not only was he handsomer than hell, he was making magic in a frying pan. Sneaking up behind him, I wrapped my arms around his waist, and whispered, "Aren't you afraid of bacon grease?"

He planted a kiss on my lips. "Don't you remember who you're talking to? I'm not afraid of anything."

I was about to remind him of his lecture regarding Highland Heights, when I was distracted by a row of bacon strips neatly arranged on a paper towel near the stove. I picked up a crispy piece, put it in my mouth, and bit off the end. Ambrosia exploded in my mouth. "How do you do that? When I fry bacon it's either black and sets off the fire alarm or is limp and gross."

Dylan's eyes twinkled. "Yeah, no one likes limp."

I slapped his shoulder. "Hey, have you seen my phone?"

"Yes, it's plugged in over there. It's been ready to self-destruct for the last hour. Why do you think I keep inviting you to my house? I'd rather avoid the fire alarm." He shrugged. "Though, I admit, it was nice to meet your neighbors when the firemen evacuated your floor."

I contemplated slapping him again, but opted for shaking my head as I turned in the direction he'd pointed. "It wasn't that bad," I contended. "If you would've opened the window like I said, we could've avoided the entire fireman thing."

"Sorry, I was busy putting out the flames."

There had not been flames! But instead of correcting him, I swiped the screen of my phone to three text messages.

The first one was from Bernard. It simply had my name with a question mark. The second was from Tracy.

Tracy Howell: CHARLOTTE, ARE YOU FREE? CAN YOU MEET ME FOR LUNCH?

TEXT ME, AND WE'LL SET A TIME.

I'd wondered what had happened to her. The last time we met, she'd told me she might have a new angle and when she knew more, she'd let me know. All that she'd said was that it might shed some light on a recurring injury. I hadn't heard from her since.

Sitting at Dylan's breakfast bar, I remembered what I'd wanted to ask him the night before; however, instead of jumping into real estate that I knew he couldn't afford, I asked, "Do you need any help?"

"No, we don't have time for fires."

"Very funny. Fine. Have I told you about my parents?"

"A little," he said with his attention more on the food. "Do you want an egg?"

"Sure." I looked down at the third message.

Dina Rosemont: STELLA, IT'S DINA. WE'VE BEEN GETTING A FEW CALLS FROM OUR FLYERS. I'VE CONTACTED DPD, BUT IF YOU HAVE A MINUTE, CAN YOU CALL ME? I'D LIKE TO DISCUSS YOUR THOUGHTS ABOUT THIS WOMAN WHO'S CALLED TWICE.

"Stella?"

I looked up. "I'm sorry. What?"

"How do you want it?"

I moved my head back and forth. "Want what?"

He inhaled and exhaled. "Sex. Do you want it on the table or the floor? Maybe the counter?" He held up the spatula. "I've been thinking about our conversation last night, and I'm ready if you want to break my rules."

"You're hilarious." My tone wasn't amused.

"Your egg . . . scrambled, fried?"

"Oh, I don't care. No matter how you make it, it'll be better than the breakfast bar I usually eat."

"What about your parents?" he asked. "I know they live in Chicago. You went to visit them a month or so ago."

I had. After spending time with the Rosemonts, I'd wanted to hug my mom and dad. "Where are yours?" I asked.

He turned, his face suddenly solemn. "Umm. I'm sorry. I guess I planned on telling you this . . ."

I put my phone down and walked toward him. "What is it? I'm sorry. Is it bad?"

He shook his head as his shoulders moved up and down. "My parents died in a robbery gone bad. Same old adage: wrong place, wrong time. I was a senior in high school and they were on a business trip." His glistening eyes drew me toward the blue. "That may be why I'm the way I am about you and Highland Heights. I don't think I could take another . . ." He turned toward the sizzling pan on the stove.

I rubbed his back, not knowing what to say.

After he'd flipped the egg, he turned back and kissed my cheek. "You're trying to distract me from my cooking, aren't you? You're secretly into firemen more than cops and didn't know how to break it to me."

I stepped behind him, wrapped my arms around his waist, and put my cheek against his shoulder. "I'm sorry. I shouldn't have just blurted that out. Do you have other family?"

"No siblings, I had grandparents. My mom's parents stepped in after . . . well, since I was already eighteen, it was more of a formality. They're both gone now: grandfather by cancer and grandmother, six months later, by a broken heart. See, there's nothing good in that story. I guess that's why I haven't said anything."

I feigned a smile. "So no rich uncle?"

He spun toward me. "Why would you even say that?"

I shook my head. "It's nothing. I just . . . in a couple of months it'll be our first Christmas together"—I shrugged—"unless you get rid of me before then because of my cooking."

He reached for a plate and plopped a fried egg in the center. "No need for two cooks in the kitchen. I've been doing this as long as I remember. Cooking was something I enjoyed doing with my mom, and after . . . it reminded me of her."

I swallowed my sorrow. "With everything . . . I guess more because of Mindy . . . I want to spend time with my parents at Christmas. I was wondering if you'd be willing to come with me to Chicago."

He walked our plates to the breakfast bar. "I usually work the holidays. That way the people who actually have families can have the time off. Besides, I look forward to that check: it's overtime— time and a half plus holiday pay."

"You've been with DPD long enough, you can get the time off, can't you? Please see if you can get it off. My folks will love you. My mom talks way too much, especially after a few glasses of wine, and my dad is great, a little quiet until you get to know him. We just can't tell him you're a Tigers fan. He's really into baseball, and the Cubs have always been his team." I tried lightening the mood. "However, I'm warning you right now, watch out for my little sister. She's recently gone through a divorce." I tightened my smile and moved my shoulders. "And I'll be honest: I don't think there's a male who's safe within fifty feet of her, but don't worry, I promise to run interference."

Dylan winked as he took a bite of his toast. "Wait, before you run interference, let me know, can she cook?"

"Yep, I taught her everything she knows."

"Hmm, so her ex was the one who filed, right?"

I shook my head. It was good to see his smile. My phone buzzed and I swiped the screen. Exhaling, I said, "That's number two from His Majesty, Bernard."

"Even a royal summons can't keep you from your breakfast."

Carefully I stacked the egg and bacon on one half of the toast and put the other half on top. "Look. I've got this! I'm an eat-on-the-run expert." Kissing his cheek, I said, "Please think about asking for the time off."

He slipped his fingers in the belt loops of my slacks and pulled me close. "Promise me, no Highland Heights."

All I could see was blue, the same eyes that only minutes ago had been sad. "I'll do my best."

"Don't forget," he said with another sexy wink, "I have my spatula, and I'm willing to use it."

"Maybe you could use one from my kitchen. It's less likely to be in the dishwasher."

He grinned as I picked up my egg-and-bacon sandwich and grabbed a napkin. On my way to WCJB, I planned to call Bernard. However, sitting in my car, instead of thinking about my boss, my thoughts went to Dylan. Maybe it was time to take the next step. I was ready to let Fred visit.

As I drove I decided that Foster obviously had the wrong Dylan Richards. The one I'd just left had no rich uncle, had no family to speak of, and was willing to work Christmas for the extra money. It didn't take an investigative journalist to know he couldn't afford a $1.4 million home in a rich neighborhood.

After finishing my breakfast sandwich, I checked the clock. Since Dina Rosemont lived near San Francisco and it was three hours earlier there, her call would need to wait. As I waited to access the interstate in a slow-moving line of traffic, I pecked a text message to Tracy.

Stella: LUNCH SOUNDS GREAT UNLESS I'M CALLED AWAY. TELL ME WHEN AND WHERE.

And then one to Bernard.

Stella: I'M ON MY WAY, ABOUT THIRTY MINUTES OUT.

My phone immediately buzzed.

Bernard: MEET ME AT THE COFFEE SHOP. USUAL TABLE.

Shit!

My stomach twisted. No doubt he was pissed about my lack of progress. My continual dead ends were beginning to wear on me, and I was a hell of a lot more patient than he. I'd gotten my job based on results. In the last seven weeks I'd produced exactly nothing. I knew Bernard had faith in me, but faith wouldn't keep me employed.

My lack of progress sure wasn't for lack of trying. Since the afternoon I'd run near The Light, I'd spent most of my free time doing research, and not only at work. I'd spent hours alone in my apartment surfing the Net. After continually coming up empty on The Light, three nights ago I'd found something. It wasn't about The Light, but it was interesting.

I was on one of those searches where I clicked site after site, following bread crumbs that kept me moving forward yet never seeming to reach a destination. I was about to call it a night when I poured one last glass of wine and stumbled across a blog post with an interesting thread of comments.

The original post was dated from over five years earlier, and buried deep in the Internet. It was written by a woman who claimed her daughter and son-in-law had been kidnapped by a cult. Though they'd disappeared, with the help of an investigator she'd located them. Once she did, she'd contacted the local police. Her daughter refused to speak to her, or anyone, but her son-in-law had sent a message saying that they were happy and willingly living within the community. Without probable cause, the local police refused to do any more. The woman took her concerns to the federal level, but without proof of wrongdoing, the authorities' hands were tied. Her post asked for help understanding cults and asked why a young woman who had always had a good relationship with her family would suddenly turn her back on them.

Maybe it was the wine, but the post made me sad, and, of course, reminded me of Mindy. Though this woman's situation was difficult, at least she knew her daughter was alive. The Rosemonts didn't have that luxury. The last sentence warned people to recognize that even in this day and age, cults still existed.

Hours passed, and I found myself enthralled by the comment thread. The ones immediately following HeartbrokenMother372's post were sympathetic to her plight. I continued reading, hoping that I'd learn if she'd ever gotten her daughter back. Unfortunately, I never saw anything else from HeartbrokenMother372, but the more I read, the more I wanted to know. With each comment I found myself questioning my belief and understanding of cults. There were more than a few posts that discounted their existence given modern technology, especially within the United States, stating the difficulty of being truly isolated in this day and age. I wondered if these people had ever heard of Waco.

With my bottle of wine about gone, I continued to read. Though none of the information I gleaned was referenced, I knew from experience that obscure sources often shed the most light. One man posted about his personal experience with living near what people in his community considered a cult. He called them a sect. He didn't give the location of his town, city, or state, but he mentioned something about skiing. He also said that in all the years he'd lived there, he'd never seen any of the women or children who lived in the sect and had seen only a few of the men. Nevertheless he estimated that hundreds of people lived in the encampment. He claimed that the general consensus was that as long as the people in the sect didn't bother the townspeople, the townspeople wouldn't bother them.

As I scrolled I found posts referencing a group of people with whom I was familiar. After all, I'd lived in Michigan for many years and recognized the term Amish. It wasn't uncommon in a rural area, especially south and east of where I lived now, down into Indiana,

Ohio, and Pennsylvania, to drive over a hill and meet up with a horse and buggy. To me the Amish were always good, moral people who simply shunned technology. Though I couldn't imagine not driving a car or having my cell phone with me at all times, I accepted them for who they were and had never considered them a cult, but the comments made me think.

The definition I'd seen earlier had said that a cult was a system of religious veneration and devotion directed toward a particular figure or object. I was relatively certain the Amish believed similarly to most Judeo-Christian groups.

Could that mean that cults didn't need to have nonconventional beliefs? Could they truly exist in the open, where most outsiders turned a blind eye?

The comment that I hadn't been able to shake was from a woman who claimed that for over a year she had been an unwilling member of a cult. The date on her post was from only one year earlier, and her online name was MistiLace92.

Everything else I'd read thus far had been from outsiders looking in. Even the original post was from a mother whose daughter had willingly gone to live with a group. This was different and made the hairs on the back of my neck stand at attention. I read the comment.

I DON'T KNOW what to do. I'm scared and need help. I just found this thread. I'm hoping someone will see this and know what to do. No one believes me, but I swear it's true.

I lost over a year of my life to a cult. I'm afraid if I name them, they'll hurt me. I just want people to know that this is real and it can happen to anyone.

During the year I was held captive, I watched people come willingly into this community. I wasn't one of them, though I thought I was. Let me explain. One day I woke up and I was someone else, someone everyone knew, a follower of this group and of a man. I couldn't remember anything prior to my waking. For some reason my mind played tricks on me. I was obviously the one with the issues. Everyone else knew me.

They told me I was married. I had no proof otherwise. My husband was abusive, yet I had no option but to be obedient. His behavior was accepted by everyone around me. It was the way the entire community lived. We all had jobs and requirements. I still don't know exactly what I did; I helped to package things. I worked on an assembly line, and all I saw were plain boxes going into bigger plain boxes. Ten hours a day I did that. I wasn't alone; everyone did something. The thing that's hard to explain was that we all did it willingly. We weren't paid, but we had food and shelter and friends. I accepted my life, until one day, when I was instructed to tell a new follower that she wasn't new, that she belonged with us that I began to see. My husband told me it was our leader's will and an honor to do his work. That was when my questions came back.

I wasn't the woman they said I was. They'd done the same thing to me.

I know that if they find me, they'll kill me. I just know it. Leaving wasn't an option. There were select chosen members who decided the fate of others. I didn't know them well, but if they considered me a threat, I'm sure I'd be eliminated—banished.

As soon as I got away, I told the police my story. They said I was crazy.

Before I disappeared, I had a drug problem. The police said that what I described was impossible. They said I'd hallucinated, and if I pursued my claims, they'd have me institutionalized.

Help! I want to tell my story. Someone please help me.

I WANTED TO COMMENT, in hopes MistiLace92 would respond. Unfortunately, the comment thread had been closed.

As soon as I got to WCJB the next day, I contacted a friend with an affinity for everything computers. It took him all of fifteen minutes to track down the IP address for MistiLace92's post. It originated from a public library in Columbia Falls, Montana. I called the Columbia Falls Police Department. It transferred me to three different people. Finally I was informed that there weren't records of a Misti or anyone else filing a report with such claims. I sent the comment and IP information to their e-mail address; minutes later I received a response claiming the IP address was incorrect. My friend swore it wasn't.

I asked if there could possibly be a cult nearby. They told me no. A search for Misti Lace came up empty for that area; however, I found a Misti Lacey on the national registry of missing persons. Unfortunately, Misti Lacey's only living relative, her mother, was now deceased. I'd hit another dead end.

I wasn't sure if my interest in MistiLace92 was connected to my interest in Mindy, but whatever the reason, for the previous few nights, her story had haunted my dreams.

As I drove toward the coffee shop I still wondered: if MistiLace92 was really Misti Lacey, why was she still on the registry of missing persons? Her post had been made over a year ago.

Shouldn't she be found?

CHAPTER
TWENTY-FIVE

S ara

As I lay on my side, wrapped in Jacob's embrace with his bare chest against my back, the skin-to-skin contact seemed right, yet I couldn't shake the unfamiliarity of his stare. With our legs slightly bent, I caressed his arms and wondered about the blue eyes from my dreams. Maybe that was all they had been, a dream. I sighed and nuzzled my cheek against the pillow.

"You've been quiet since we came back from the community. Do you have something you want to say?"

"I don't think so."

"Are you sure?"

Closing my eyes, in the dark of the bedroom, forced the tear teetering on my lid to fall to the pillow below. Shaking my head, I said, "No, Jacob. I'm not sure of anything."

We'd just made love and I was crying, not exactly what a

husband wanted from his wife. There hadn't been anything wrong with the sex—it was fine, just different from the previous night.

Now that I could see, everything was different.

Jacob pulled me closer, and his breath skirted across my hair. "Whether you remember it, or you've recently relearned it, tell me what Father Gabriel says about a wife's thoughts."

I exhaled. "Just like everything else, they belong to you, but," I added, "I'm not keeping anything from you. I really don't know how to say what I'm thinking. Honestly, I'm not even sure what I'm thinking." As more tears silently fell to the pillow, I tried to still my shudders, not wanting Jacob to know I was crying. When he didn't respond, I swallowed and went on. "I wanted to remember your face. Why can't I remember? Will I ever have a past?"

He kissed the top of my head. "We all have a past. This morning was your past, so was the day before and the one before that. If further back never comes, a year from now, this will be our past."

A closed-lip smile came as I nodded.

"A past is as long or as short as we want to make it. When we came here to follow Father Gabriel, we chose to leave our lives in the dark behind."

When his hold loosened, I rolled toward him. "I don't want to go back to the dark. I just want to know, to have the memories. Is it wrong to want that?"

"To want it?" he repeated. "No. To question the reason it was taken from you, yes."

I sighed. "That means that I can't ask about it."

Jacob leaned over me, his chest flattening my breasts. With our proximity in the darkened room, I could only make out his form, his shoulders, arms, and the silhouette of his hair against some distant faint light. There were no details. Hearing his familiar voice, without seeing his unfamiliar eyes, eased my anxiety. He smoothed the hair away from my face and kissed my nose. "We both follow Father Gabriel. You aren't the only one who must obey the rules. I can't question why you lost those memories any more than you can question me. All I can do is hold tight to the memories I have of us, for both of us. Even though you don't remember my face, I remember yours." He traced under my eyes, wiping away the remnants of tears. "I remember your beautiful blue eyes, the way they open with amazement at new discoveries and the way they flutter as you come apart beneath me." He was back to stroking my hair. "I remember the first time we made love and every time since.

"I remember the first time I saw you, the first time I heard your voice, and"—he brushed his lips against mine—"the first time I kissed you." He scoffed, "It wasn't supposed to happen, but I couldn't resist. I knew you were mine from the first time I saw you, even if you didn't."

His memories gave me a sliver of my past. "I didn't?"

"No, not then. You were dating someone else."

"What? That was before we were here, right?"

"Yes, it was before everything."

He sighed and laid his head back on his pillow. I was afraid he'd stop talking, yet more scared to ask him to continue. Thankfully, he didn't stop, but when he resumed speaking, his voice had a faraway tone, as if he was seeing it all again.

"You were laughing, and I thought you were one of the prettiest women I'd ever seen. You have a great laugh." He reached for my hand and intertwined our fingers. "I know this crash course in remembering how to be an Assemblyman's wife hasn't given you many opportunities for laughter. That's why I want your memories to come back. Sometimes it seems like we're back at the beginning. I want to be beyond that . . ." He was back up with his elbow beside me and his head on his hand. Looking down at me, he continued, "To where you laugh instead of cry."

"I'm sorry."

He touched my lips. "To where you're not constantly apologizing."

I kissed his finger. "I'd like that too, but you have to admit, this hasn't been easy. I mean my eyes, leg, and ribs. I've just gotten my sight back. We've been banished, and my hair is gone."

"I do." He exhaled. "I admit that it's been a rough few weeks, but we can see the light at the end of the tunnel."

"The Light?" I asked with a smirk.

"Yes. See? It's something everyone wants."

"I do see that, and I understand that we're here, on the biggest campus, as part of the chosen." I ran my palm over his handsome cheek. "And at one time, I chose to be here with you. Though I don't remember that, I wanted it, and I still do. I want The Light." I shook my head. "I'm sure that as we go forward there'll be times when I mess up and you'll correct me, but when I do, I'm asking you to understand that it's not intentional. Today, driving off the campus made me sad. I want to go back. This pole barn and the hangar might not be the dark, but for the life of me, I don't think I was driving away in your truck. I can't imagine wanting to leave you or Father Gabriel. I mean, first off, you said we're on the edge of the circumpolar north. Second, Father Gabriel travels by plane." My volume rose. "Third, there are polar bears. None of that makes it even seem possible to drive away, and if it were, it wouldn't be something I'd be willing to do alone."

"Once our banishment is over and Father Gabriel reintroduces us to followers, the accident is over. Just like any other correction, it's gone, as if it never happened."

"Reintroduces us? Do you mean like in front of everyone?"

"Yes."

I groaned and buried my head in his hard chest.

"Don't make me tell you again about your hair and how proud I am to have you at my side." His tone was somewhere between tender and stern.

"I think maybe I could wear a scarf."

"Around your neck to stay warm."

"A hat," I tried.

"Sara."

Yes, I was pushing this too far. "Fine, whatever you say. Jacob?"

"Do not suggest another head covering."

I shook my head. "I'm not. I wanted to thank you for arranging to have Raquel here today and Sister Ruth tomorrow."

"I'm confident that Brother Timothy and Sister Lilith won't try anything else, but Brother Daniel suggested that Sister Ruth come out, and I thought it would make you more comfortable."

"Why are you confident they won't do anything else?"

"Sara." His tone wasn't joking.

"I'm sorry." *Shit!* Now I'm apologizing. "I know you said Brother Daniel is our overseer, but he's on the Commission. I'm afraid that all the Commissioners are like Brother Timothy."

"They're not." He lay back and pulled me to his shoulder. As I cuddled close with the knee in the cast on his thigh, I listened as he talked about Brother Daniel and Sister Ruth. Apparently when we first arrived I hadn't been as good a cook as I was now—I didn't know I was—and Sister Ruth had spent a lot of time with me, teaching me. "It's pretty obvious she's a great cook," he added.

I laughed. "I knew it. From the way she hugged me at the hospital, I knew she was a bigger woman."

"Did you hear that?"

I lifted my head; all I'd heard was his voice reverberating from his chest with the steady beat of his heart. "No, I didn't hear anything."

"I did," he said, lifting me and pulling my cast across him. "It was your laugh."

"Jacob?"

"I believe you mentioned something—an alternative—at the clinic."

Oh, wow!

I laughed again. Holding on to his chest, I moved my knees to either side of his torso. With my breasts hanging above him, he leaned forward and captured a suddenly hardened nipple between his lips. As he sucked, noises came from my throat and my insides came back to life.

Gazing up at me, he brushed my cheek. "Sara, I'd like this to bring back your memories, but if all I get out of it is that magical laugh, I'll take it."

Placing my hands on his shoulders, I rose to my knees, and asked, "Is that all you're getting out of this?"

With my hips trapped in his strong grip, he grinned and replied, "No, I'm getting more; I also want those sexy moans of yours." A mere shift of his arms and I was up and then down.

"Oh, God," I whimpered as we came together for the second time in one night. I'd definitely be tender tomorrow; however, as his rippled torso flexed under my palms and his neck craned with pleasure, tomorrow wasn't one of my concerns.

Though I was on top, I held no illusion of control. Jacob's large hands choreographed, directing my speed and position. I was merely along for the ride, but oh, what a ride. He knew exactly how to manipulate, taking me to the brink and backing away. On and on I rode until finally my world imploded. My body, no longer mine, fell slack against his. When our foreheads came together he pulled my hips toward his, animalistic need radiating so strongly through his grasp that I wondered if I'd have marks in the morning. Before I could give it a second thought, a deep guttural growl came from his chest and his lips curled to a smile just before they captured mine. Compared to the desire he'd just shown, his kiss was tender. He released my hips and hugged my shoulders.

Once our breathing settled, still lying on top of him, I asked, "May I ask you something?"

"You may ask . . ."

"But you may not answer," I quipped, mocking his usual response. My behind stung with the swat of his hand.

"You're too smart for your own good. Ask before I use more than my hand."

"I guess it isn't really a question. It's just that I wanted to say I loved hearing your memories, like our first kiss, the first time we saw one another, and the first time we . . . did this. Thank you for sharing."

"Thank you for making those memories with me."

I COULDN'T HAVE BEEN MORE wrong, thinking Brother Daniel would be like Brother Timothy. The moment Jacob met him and Sister Ruth at the door, I knew they were different. Even when Brother Timothy had come to my room right after I woke, I'd sensed Jacob's unease. With our overseer my husband was as comfortable as he was when the two of us were alone.

After greeting Jacob, Sister Ruth came straight to me, framed my face with her cool, pudgy hands, and looked me right in the eye. The faint scent of vanilla surrounded her. "Sara, I want you to know that I've prayed every day for your sight. Thank Father Gabriel that you've been healed." Her smile stretched her cheeks. "And, my dear, Sister Raquel has done quite the job: you're absolutely lovely. I know Brother Jacob knows how blessed he is." She winked. "But I'm going to remind him, just for good measure." She whispered the last part as she surrounded me in her hug.

I looked to Brother Daniel, a tall, older man with graying hair, and said, "Thank you, Brother and Sister, for coming out. Jacob shared that it was your idea. Thank you for helping me feel better."

"Sister," Brother Daniel said in a deep, commanding voice, "on behalf of the Commission and Father Gabriel, while it will take a while for your hair to grow, once your banishment is complete, the incident will be behind both of you." He reached for my hand. "That is what Father Gabriel teaches. Never doubt his word."

My head moved from side to side. "I never would, Brother. I willingly accept his decree, and I'm anxious to return to the community."

He smiled from me to Jacob. "Sister, that's good to hear." Looking to Jacob, he said, "Call once you land. I'll come back and get Ruth."

"I will, Brother. The plane is ready. I should be able to leave soon."

Brother Daniel clapped Jacob's shoulder and turned to Sister Ruth. I had no doubt they had the same type of relationship that I shared with Jacob, yet I wondered how long they'd been married, because the adoration in both of their gazes was tangible. "Ruth, remember, if necessary, you have my permission to use the phone."

"Thank you, Daniel." She squeezed my hand. "We'll be so busy, nothing will bother us."

I liked her confidence, and wondered what she had planned.

"Brother Jacob," she said, "we had to park outside. In the back of Daniel's SUV are some bags. If you'd be so kind as to bring those in for us, I believe your lovely wife will have a dinner fit for a king when you return."

The way his eyes grew at that possibility made me smile.

"I'd be happy to get whatever you need to make that happen."

It was true that so far we'd eaten only already prepared meals. With my lack of sight, my great cooking skills had been limited to warming things and to preparing cereal, toast, coffee, and sandwiches. This morning I'd ventured to eggs and bacon.

After a few minutes the men were gone, and I was putting the contents of Sister Ruth's bags on the kitchen table. Salmon wrapped in white paper, sweet potatoes, onions, peppers, apples, the ingredients kept coming, and not one of them was from a box or packet.

"Sister," I sighed as I looked at everything, "Jacob told me that you taught me how to do this once. I admit I don't remember. I'm excited to receive a refresher course."

She patted my hand. "We made notes the first time. I believe they're in the kitchen of your apartment. Hopefully, that can help you, but you know that you can always ask me. With Daniel's permission, I'd love to spend more time with you."

I lowered my chin. "I'm sorry if I embarrassed the Assembly and Commission wives."

She lifted my chin. "Sara, I'd never be ashamed of you. I accept the Commission's decision and Father Gabriel's decree, but the strong, intelligent young woman I know would never willfully leave The Light nor her husband. I remember the first time I saw you and Brother Jacob. The love that you two shared hasn't disappeared. I know that. Brother Daniel and I've been married for over thirty years. The way you look at Brother Jacob and the way he looks at you, your love is still there. Isn't it?"

"It is," I admitted. "I don't know if it's as obvious as what I noticed between you and Brother Daniel, but it's there. I love my husband."

Her inviting smile filled me with the sense of a mother or grandmother. "Now," she said, "let's get started. You have a lot of cooking to do."

I bit my lip. "I really don't . . ."

"Stop. When I first came to your room after your accident, you didn't remember Father Gabriel. Do you know who he is now?"

I nodded. "I do."

"If I asked you to recite our declaration of faith, could you?"

I took a breath and stood tall. "I could. 'We the followers . . .'"

She winked. "I know it; you don't need to recite it. I'm proud of you. In another week you'll be making your husband's meals just like you used to."

The day flew by as we chopped, sliced, peeled, and created. The entire time we talked like old friends. When I put the apple pie in the oven, I blew out a breath. "If you hadn't told me otherwise, I'd swear I'd never done that before."

Sitting at the table with a cup of coffee, Sister Ruth said, "I'm sure you remember that not all meals will be this elaborate. When I was your age and still worked, I used my Crock-Pot much more often."

I hadn't thought about my job. Brushing the flour off the counter, I turned, and asked, "What do I do?"

"Oh, Sara, you really don't remember?"

I moved my head back and forth. "Sister, everything really is gone."

"You work in the chemistry lab with Brother Benjamin and Brother Raphael."

I widened my eyes. "I do?" Scrunching my nose, I asked, "You don't know what I do there, do you?"

"No, my dear, Assembly wives have more distinguished jobs than the average follower. Obviously most of them, men and women, work in the processing plant. It takes a lot of manpower to produce Father Gabriel's product."

I nodded. "Does his product have something to do with chemistry?"

"Yes, Brothers Raphael and Benjamin perfect the formulas. To be honest, I don't know how it all works. You probably know more than I do, since you work with them."

I moved to the table and sat. "And the followers produce the . . . ?"

She patted my hand. "Medications—pharmaceuticals. Father Gabriel delivers medication to those in need all over the world. It's a wonderful ministry that spreads The Light to those who can't afford it or areas where health care is limited."

"That's great."

"It is. We've been with Father Gabriel since The Light began. Even early on he knew this vision of his would come to fruition. It's not up to us to question how it all works. We do our part to make it happen. Truly, we're blessed to be part of this ministry. Now, of course, in case you've forgotten, the particulars of his vision can't be discussed with all the followers. There's a reason we're part of the chosen."

I nodded, thankful that she'd come and helped me remember so much. My mind wandered to my job, and I worried about Brothers Raphael and Benjamin. I hoped they'd be as patient with me as Raquel, Sister Ruth, and Jacob. "Sister? If I have difficulties at my job, would Brother Raphael or Benjamin . . . correct me?"

"Of course, they're men—it's their right." Losing her grip on the warm mug, she patted my hand. "However, only our husbands have the right to deliver the correction you're concerned about. But rest assured, if they believe it's necessary, they'll tell Brother Jacob."

I'm sure they will.

THE REMAINING days of our banishment passed without incident. Sister Ruth visited two more times, always leaving me more confident than she'd found me. I actually made edible meals and continued to study Father Gabriel's teachings. By the time Jacob came back from Assembly on the final Wednesday morning of our banishment, I thought I was ready to be back in the community. However, when he announced that Father Gabriel wanted us at service that night, my stomach knotted; I swallowed as my expression undoubtedly gave away my trepidation.

"Sara." The one word was delivered as both a warning and a reprimand, one I'd learned to discern, having heard it a thousand times in the past month.

"I want to ask about the scarf again, but I won't."

"Good."

"I just thought that our banishment didn't end until tomorrow. Today isn't two weeks. Tomorrow will be."

His brows lowered and his more familiar eyes narrowed. "You've done so well. I don't want to correct you before service or make that a Wednesday-night habit, but if you question even one more time, I will."

I shook my head. "Thank you for your reminder. I won't."

"After service we won't be coming back here. We'll be going back to our apartment. So today while I'm working, you'll need to pack our things. I'll bring the suitcases in from the garage."

"Yes, Jacob."

"Also, dinner will need to be done and cleaned up before we leave. We want to leave the living quarters as we found them."

Nodding, I slowly turned, taking in the living quarters, and sighed. I'd studied Father Gabriel's word on the comfortable sofa in the living room, gazed out the large windows at the wall of trees, and relearned how to cook in the small kitchen. I turned toward the stairs and mentally traveled upward to the room where I'd rediscovered my husband.

"Do you have any questions?"

I grinned toward my husband. "No, I was just thinking that this place will be my past."

Jacob's lips curled upward and his brown eyes sparkled. "Yes, it will."

That evening, with my hand tightly encased in Jacob's, we entered the temple. Though I saw all the people in the foyer, Jacob led me down a hallway and up a staircase. I didn't know where we were going, though I was relatively sure we hadn't gone this way two weeks before. My palms moistened with each step as we approached double wooden doors.

I bit my lip to keep from asking about our destination; however, as we neared, I had a good idea. When Jacob knocked on the large door, he whispered, "Remember what I said. Do not embarrass me. This is almost over."

I didn't have the chance to verbally answer, so I nodded. The lecture I'd received for most of the truck ride into the community suddenly made sense. Taking a deep breath, I worked to keep my chin even.

"Enter, Brother," came from the other side of the door.

When Jacob opened the door, I inhaled and began my own monologue. Instead of telling myself to keep my head up and wear my short hair proudly, as Jacob had done, my internal lecture was much simpler.

Don't faint!

The table we stood before held five men. Though I didn't

remember having seen him, I was confident the man in the middle with slicked-back blond hair and a very nice gray suit was Father Gabriel. I recognized only one of the other men, Brother Daniel. When our eyes met, he smiled and nodded. Based on expressions, I deciphered that the man on my far left was Brother Timothy.

"Father Gabriel, thank you for your correction. Sister Sara and I are ready to reenter The Light, with your blessing."

I bowed my head as Jacob spoke. Once he was done, I looked up.

"Yes, Brother Jacob and Sister Sara." I was right. I'd know his voice anywhere. "I'm pleased to have you back where you belong. Sister Sara, is there anything you'd like to say to me or the Commission?"

Oh, my!

Apparently, I didn't swear even internally in his presence.

Straightening my shoulders, I concentrated on Jacob's hand over mine, as it'd been the day I awakened. "Father Gabriel, Brothers of the Commission, I deeply apologize for my behavior, thank you for your correction, and I look forward to being back in The Light."

Father Gabriel smiled and stood. Looking from side to side, he asked, "If any on the Commission has issue with our brother or sister's return to the Assembly, speak now."

As silence fell, I held my breath, summoning all the self-control I could muster to keep my eyes on Father Gabriel and away from Brother Timothy. Just as we all grew confident in the silence, it ended.

"Father," Brother Timothy said.

Jacob tightened his grip.

"Yes, Brother."

"I don't have an issue; however, before reintroductions, I'd like to hear Sister Sara's answer to one question."

Father Gabriel sat. "Go ahead, Brother."

Brother Timothy stood. "Sister, what is the purpose of your new hairstyle?"

I tilted my head down, ever so slightly, gathered my poise, and spoke clearly. "Father Gabriel and Brothers of the Commission, my hair was cut as a reminder of my correction. As I wait for it to grow, I'll continue to remember my transgression. Thank you for my correction and my reminder."

Jacob's grip relaxed and I took a breath. He approved.

"Brother and Sister," Father Gabriel said, seemingly also content with my answer. "Please go to the vestibule. I'll be down after prayer. You'll enter the stage after the Commission. Once I reintroduce you, you may go to your usual seats."

"Thank you, Father," Jacob replied.

"Thank you," I added.

After we'd left the room, I walked silently, wondering why Jacob hadn't told me where we were going. It wasn't until we were in a small area that must have been the vestibule that Jacob brushed my cheek and whispered, "I couldn't tell you. Remember me saying that I also had requirements? You were perfect."

"Thank you," I whispered. "Although I'm still embarrassed about my hair, I promise I won't show it."

"You're the wife of an Assemblyman. Never forget that."

Moments later, following Father Gabriel and the Commissioners, we stepped onto the stage. While we waited to be reintroduced, I scanned the crowd, looking for Raquel and Sister Ruth. I found Sister Ruth first; her smile shone toward us. As my gaze went behind her, I gasped.

Though Jacob's stare silenced me, I couldn't believe my eyes. The two rows behind the Commission wives held eleven women and one empty chair. I immediately recognized Raquel on one side of the seat I knew was mine and on the other side was a beautiful redhead who I surmised was Elizabeth.

The reason I'd gasped was the Assembly wives' hair. Every one of them had a cut similar to mine.

I had indeed started a trend.

TWENTY-SIX

S tella

I SPOTTED Bernard as soon as I entered the coffee shop. This wasn't Starbucks or anything that tried to duplicate the modern-day successful chain. This restaurant had been sitting on this corner in Midtown for over fifty years, and if I were to guess, the Formica tables and plastic-covered seats had been here on opening day. That didn't stop the patrons. The place was always busy. The bar with the swivel seats bolted to the floor was filled to capacity as I made my way toward the back and eased myself into the red vinyl booth. The overpowering aroma of grease hung in the air like a cloud, and grew stronger as I neared Bernard's partially eaten plate of eggs, bacon, and potatoes. I didn't know how he could eat that every morning and stay fit.

His dark eyes lifted to me as he paused between bites, wiped his mouth on a napkin, and said, "I ordered you a coffee. Do you want food?"

"No, I've eaten."

"Do those cardboard bars count as eating?"

My stomach was in knots. "Is this my last meal?"

"I sure as hell hope not, but I need more answers than I've gotten in the last"—he dropped his fork to the plate, the clank echoing above the din of patrons—"since Mindy went missing. I think that's the problem."

I steeled my shoulders and lowered my voice. "You think it's a problem that my best friend is missing? Or you think that because my best friend has dropped off the face of the earth, I'm no longer able to do my job?"

The waitress placed a cup of coffee in front of me, but hearing my tone, backed away before asking if I wanted anything to eat. Bernard's beady eyes watched me over his coffee mug. When he didn't respond I sighed and fell back against the seat, forcing the air from the vinyl with a whoosh.

Finally he spoke. "Stella, give me something. What's going on in that pretty little head of yours?"

I pressed my lips together at his sexist comment. Did he ask Foster what was going on in that *handsome* head of his?

Instead of divulging all, I replied, "I've been following leads. It's just that they've been coming up empty."

"You told me about the women, no pattern, just women in this area turning up dead. I've done some research, and you may be onto something."

My eyes widened. "What have you learned?"

"The incidence of female homicides, as well as the potential for women to end up missing, is statistically higher per capita here, not only in Detroit, but in this general region, than in any other place in the country. Yet with all the stats that people spout, this one is rarely mentioned." He leaned forward. "My gut tells me that it's because of what you called the nonpattern. If the women were all tied together by one race or any common factor, it would send up red flags."

I nodded. "Why isn't it enough that they're all women?"

"We need more."

"I followed your informant's lead in Highland Heights. I don't know what the building is used for, the one that holds the address of the registrations for the cars that cross the border. It looks abandoned to me; however, I don't think it is."

"Why?"

"While I was watching, an SUV pulled up and some men got out. They walked between the buildings." I shook my head. "They didn't stay long. So when they pulled away, I followed them to another part of Highland Heights. They all got out at a church and went in. I've been back and I've seen the same SUV there again."

"Why haven't you told me any of this?"

"Because I don't have a connection from the church to drugs crossing the border. As a matter of fact, I think the reason they're going in and out of Canada is because of preserves." I nodded toward the little rectangular packets stacked in a silver bin at the edge of the table.

"You think they're transporting jams and jellies?"

I shrugged. "I found the church on the Internet. It doesn't have much information, but what little it does have says that they sell homemade preserves to support their ministry."

"In Highland Heights? Why would a church in that part of town be selling preserves? I wouldn't think there'd be a big market for anything homemade, other than meth."

I released my lip. "I know. I've told myself the same thing. It's kind of weird. I've been back a few times. I've seen men in cars and women walking from the church to what seems like an abandoned school. I think that they make the preserves in the school. And maybe there isn't a market here; that's why they're going to Canada."

"Who owns the old school? Does the church?"

Shit!

"I don't know. That's one way I didn't take this."

"Look that direction. Find the money trail."

I nodded. "So you're not taking me off of this?"

"Not yet, but you need to keep me informed."

"I know you believe my thinking is off because of Mindy, but I recently learned that HHPD has been trying to keep tabs—in a good way—on their transient populations, primarily females. This has been going on for a while, yet no one talks about it, maybe because they lose them. What I mean is runaways and prostitutes go missing."

"I'm not sure that's newsworthy."

I scrunched my nose. "Who knows, I could be trying to pull too many things together? I'm trying to connect all of it, and most likely none of it is connected."

"I've found that money talks," he said between bites. "I'm talking following the money trail, not paying someone off. See if you can come up with any connections under the surface since on the surface things aren't materializing."

"I will. May I ask you something?"

Bernard took a long drink of coffee. "Of course, but if it's classified, well, I may have to kill you."

I grinned. "I'll take my chances. This isn't specific, but what do you think about cults?"

"Cults?" His brows disappeared beneath his dark salt-and-pepper hair. I didn't know why he didn't wear it like this on the air. The way he greased it back for television made him look more like a used car salesman. This style was actually becoming. "I think," he said, "it's a derogatory term associated with deviant or unusual beliefs."

"What if it isn't, or they aren't? I mean, what if they aren't all like Waco or Jim Jones? What if they exist right in front of us?"

"Are we talking brainwashing, kidnapping, sexual abuse, and mass suicide?"

I shook my head. "I don't know. I don't think so. I don't have any proof of anything. Probably too many nights with wine and my computer."

Bernard grinned. "You'd better be careful. My wife killed her motherboard that way."

"That's why my glasses are stemless."

"I'm glad to know you're being cautious."

I shrugged. "They're bigger too."

"I don't know if you're barking up the wrong tree or not. It seems like you're trying to pull too many things together. Concentrate on the money trail and get back to me."

I looked at my coffee. I hadn't even touched it. "Thanks for not firing me."

"Stop worrying. I'm not firing you, but I am setting a deadline. If you don't have a story for me in by the end of the month, you're moving on to something else."

"Got it, boss."

INSTEAD OF GOING STRAIGHT to WCJB, I did what I'd led Dylan to believe I wouldn't. I drove back to Highland Heights. I didn't plan to get out of my car. I just wanted to drive around and get a feel for the property I'd be researching. In front of the old school was a large FOR SALE sign. I recognized the realty company immediately: Entermann's Realty, a client of Preston and Butler. I'd done some work on a case in which a woman sued Entermann's because she'd tripped and fallen on property owned by the company. My job was to discredit the claimant. It wasn't difficult; she was one of those litigious people with multiple cases pending. Apparently she'd been successful in more than a few of her endeavors, because without record of employment she was financially solvent. Following her from her meeting with the attorneys, I found her walking around the deck of her twenty-five-foot boat docked at the river. It was a beautiful Hydra-Sports with two motors and a lower cabin. It wasn't the boat that interested Preston and Butler—it was the lack of the walking stick or neck brace she'd sported merely an hour earlier.

As I drove back to the building I'd watched weeks before, I longed for an open-and-shut case like that one. Externally the building hadn't changed. It still appeared abandoned and the one beside it that looked like an old firehouse did too; nevertheless I wondered what the men did between the buildings. Though I drove slowly, the way the passage between the buildings was shaded meant I couldn't see anything but light at the other end. I drove around the block again and parked at the far end of the building, away from the street. I wanted to get my Nikon out of my trunk, but hearing Dylan's words, I opted for fast, and turned on the camera app on my phone. I stepped out of my car and tried to shut the door softly. Once I had, I shook my head. No one was there. I was just being ridiculous.

Birds squawked above my head as I moved toward the building. My low-heeled shoes weren't especially good for walking through the taller grass, but I chose that direction to avoid the obvious path of the sidewalk. Approaching the gap from the rear, I peered around the corner. Closer to this end were two doors directly across from one another, one to each building. Taking a deep breath, I stepped into the passage. The closer I came to the doors, the more audible voices became. I pressed my body against the rough brick and listened, trying to decide which building the sounds were coming from. Just as I determined it was the one that wasn't the old firehouse, the sound of tires on the loose gravel in front of the buildings made my heart race.

With only the nose of a black SUV visible, I hurried in the other direction, out the passage, and toward my car. Once inside, I let out the breath and hit the "Lock" button. Before I could convince myself that it was Dylan's fault I was so jumpy, a big dark hand knocked once on my window.

I recognized the man immediately: his picture was on my computer. He was the driver of the SUV I'd seen on my first stakeout.

Of course, from behind the tinted glass I hadn't gotten the full experience of his girth. His waist was higher than the bottom of my window, and he bent forward. His not-so-welcoming face was at the glass as I eased my window down a little bit.

"Yes?" I asked.

"Lady, you lost?"

"I may be," I lied. "I'm supposed to take pictures of some real estate for my company. Do you know if these buildings are for sale?"

"Not to my knowledge. I suggest you get yourself out of here, and tell your boss if he sends you here again, you better have a gun."

I nodded. "Thank you," I mumbled, rolling my window up and backing away. I may not have taken a full breath until I was back on Woodward Avenue.

I was so lost in the money trail of the buildings that until my phone buzzed, I'd forgotten about my lunch with Tracy.

Tracy Howell: CHARLOTTE, I'M SORRY. INSTEAD OF LUNCH, CAN WE DO DRINKS, SAY FIVE? I'M WORKING THROUGH LUNCH AND WILL DEFINITELY NEED ONE BY THEN.

Shit!

Stella: YES! I'M KIND OF BURIED AT WORK TOO. SEE YOU AT FIVE . . . JUMBO'S?

Tracy Howell: I'LL BE THERE.

I turned back to the computer screen and rubbed my temples. Since I'd been back to WCJB I hadn't left my cubicle or even stood up. The pages of chicken scratch I'd accumulated wouldn't make much sense to anyone but me, and even I wasn't sure what it all meant.

The school that I suspected was the preserves processing center was indeed owned by Entermann's Realty. According to everything I could find, it was officially empty, out of commission, and had been since Highland Heights Public Schools closed the doors in the midnineties due to decreased enrollment. I wondered if anyone was even aware that it was being used.

Entermann's had purchased it two years earlier from a bankrupt developer. The developer, Uriel Harris, had snatched up numerous run-down and vacant properties over a ten-year span. His plan had been renovation, all hinging on tax breaks and grants. Though the tax breaks had been approved, the revenue base continued to drop. That was when Entermann's stepped in and bought it for pennies on the dollar.

Before Harris, HBA Corporation made a bid on the property. It's one of the largest builders of hospitals in the country. I understood that the size of the building meant it would have made a good hospital, and the area needed health care; nevertheless HBA was outbid by Wilkens Industries. Fifteen years earlier, Wilkens had paid $5 million for the property, purchasing it from Highland Heights.

What I found interesting was that the old firehouse and the large building beside it had at one time also been owned by Highland Heights. The money trail for the firehouse was different, but currently it was owned by Wilkens Industries. The building housing The Light was owned by The Light, a not-for-profit, paid in full, having been given to the ministry by Marcel Clarkson, a wealthy benefactor.

I made a note to research Marcel Clarkson and tried another route. I called a friend at Preston and Butler.

"Jenn?" I asked, hearing her voice on the other end of the line. She and I'd hung out after work on more than a few occasions. Her choice in men always lent itself to some late nights filled with plenty of beer and pep talk. I hadn't seen her in a while, not since leaving the firm, but I hoped we were still close. "It's Stella Montgomery."

"Hey, Stella, what's up? How are you doing?"

"I'm good. I've been working a story, and I was wondering if you could help a friend out?"

"I'm not sure," she replied. "But I'll give it a try. What do you need?"

"I'm following a trail on some property. I keep seeing Enter-mann's Realty coming up. I remembered that the realty firm was a client of Preston and Butler. Would it be possible to send me a list of all the properties they currently own?"

"Jeez, I'm not sure."

"Jenn, I totally get it, but if you could, you'd save me a ton of time, and I can't tell you how depressing this has been. I keep coming up empty on all counts."

"Stella, for all those times you sat and listened to me bitch about Jimmy, I'll give you this. Can you give me a day or two to get it all together? Then I'll e-mail it to you."

I bit my lip. "How is that scumbag?"

She laughed. "You always did have a way with words. I actually kicked his lazy ass to the curb."

"Good for you!"

"Yeah, you convinced me I didn't need a man around. We need to hang out sometime."

"We do. I'd love to catch up. Guess what?"

"What?"

I smiled. "I'm kind of dating someone."

"No way! Single-for-life Stella . . . we do need to catch up. Just tell me he's not like Jimmy."

"So far no, and he's employed."

"Sounds like a winner. I'll get that list together as soon as I can and send it to your e-mail."

"Thank you!"

I hung up and tried a search for Wilkens Industries. Founded in the early nineties by the original CEO, Marcel Clarkson . . . *ding ding* . . . it served as an umbrella for a few defined subsidiaries. In 2000 Clarkson stepped down due to medical reasons and was replaced by Matthew Lee. He was still the CEO. Under Lee's supervision Wilkens Industries had grown exponentially. The board of directors read like a who's who of nobodies. With last names like Smith, Johnson, and Jones and first names like Robert, Steve, and John, I couldn't have found the individuals unless I'd entered a board meeting and asked for their Social Security numbers. Being as Wilkens was a privately owned company, accessing its payroll records would take some time. Though it was private, I was able to access tax information through IRS records. Currently the net worth of Wilkens Industries was listed near $55 million, with a plethora of diverse investments and subsidiaries, one of which was Entermann's Realty. *Ding.*

Interesting.

As the clock neared four fifteen, I closed my search and sent a text to Dylan.

Stella: I'M MEETING A FRIEND FOR DRINKS. I'LL CALL WHEN I GET HOME.

Dylan: IF YOUR FRIEND IS A FIREMAN, WE NEED TO TALK BEFORE THEN.

I grinned.

Stella: YOU'RE THE ONLY PUBLIC SERVANT I PLAN ON TALKING TO. MY FRIEND'S FEMALE.

Dylan: GOOD TO HEAR.

"That's the best smile I've seen on your face all day."

I looked up at Foster. "I haven't had a lot to smile about."

"Still coming up empty?"

"I just feel like I search for days and all I do is go in circles." I shook my head and stood. Oh, my back didn't appreciate sitting at a computer all day, but after my scare in Highland Heights, I wasn't in the mood for surveillance either. "Hey, I meant to tell you. I spoke to Dylan. Whatever you found isn't connected to him. His parents are deceased, and he doesn't have a rich uncle."

He nodded. "I haven't had a chance to follow up. I know you don't want me to, but I probably will anyway, just to keep Bernard happy."

I shrugged. "Fine, have at it. You're wasting your time. I'd rather have you help me figure out how Uriel Harris is connected to Wilkens Industries."

"Uriel Harris, the developer?"

"Yeah. He owned some property I'm looking into."

"He owned a lot of property, paid way too much for it, and lost his shirt."

"That's what I saw. His loss was definitely Entermann's gain."

"Are you looking into Entermann's holdings or their tax write-offs? They purchase shit property all over the city so they can take the loss. It's not uncommon, but they're one of the best."

I nodded. "That makes sense. I was wondering why they owned so many dilapidated buildings. I hope to get the full list of their holdings soon."

Foster smiled. "I'll be glad to take a look when you do. Sometimes two sets of eyes are better than one."

"Thanks," I said, grabbing my purse and phone. "I need to run."

"It was good to see the smile."

I grinned as I made my way to the elevator.

This time as I walked into Jumbo's, Tracy was waiting for me. She had a short glass of a dark drink. It looked like Coke, but judging by the way her face scrunched as she sipped, I suspected it contained something stronger. "Hi," I said, sitting down. "Bad day at the morgue?"

She huffed, blowing her bangs in the air. "Is there ever a good day at the morgue?"

TWENTY-SEVEN

S ara

DESPITE EVERYONE'S best efforts to the contrary, my past continued to begin the day I awoke in the clinic, nearly four months ago. My cast was gone and my body healed. It was my mind that couldn't remember. Over time my closest friends, Raquel and Elizabeth, shared secrets from our past, and Jacob continued to remind me of forgotten memories. Each story or statement helped me reconstruct a time I couldn't recall and gave me glimpses into my former self.

Since the end of our banishment and our return to The Light, the community, and our lives, when I was with Jacob, whether in public or in private, my movements no longer required conscious effort—they belonged to him. While my mind continued its struggle, my body willingly submitted. With a touch, a glance, or one word, his expectations were made clear. Though some small part of me resisted, the sensible part of me wanted to be the best wife an

Assemblyman could have. After all the support from the unified Assembly wives, as well as the way Father Gabriel had welcomed us back to the congregation, I understood that Jacob and I truly were part of the chosen. The idea that I'd somehow almost jeopardized it made my heart hurt.

After we first returned to the community, I had problems. Often I'd awake in the middle of the night chilled to the bone, my heart racing, engulfed in darkness. The terrors of my nightmares included dragons with foul breath and razor-sharp teeth as well as a faceless man screaming stop in the darkness. Once awake I'd fall victim to an overwhelming sense of remorse—guilt over what I'd almost taken away from not only Jacob, but myself. When I felt that way, I was careful not to wake my husband. I'd usually move from his embrace, cling to the far edge of the bed, and muffle my tears with my pillow.

I knew Father Gabriel's teachings; I studied hard. According to him, once a correction was complete, the transgressor was freed from the responsibility of the sin. It was done, as if it'd never happened. Yet I didn't feel free.

One night as I clung to the far side of the bed and my body shuddered with muffled cries, Jacob's warmth came behind me. I froze, completely unable to move and fearful that he'd be upset. Instead, his arms once again surrounded me and he asked, "What is it?"

I'd been crying too long; my words didn't form. All I could do was shake my head.

Gently he rolled me toward him, and in the darkness he asked me two things: "Who are you?" and "Who am I?"

I tilted my head to the side, pondering his unusual questions. With stuttering breaths I replied, "I'm Sara Adams and you're my husband, Jacob Adams."

He tenderly wiped my cheek with his thumb, and brought our noses together. Whispering softly, he said, "That's all that's important. Go to sleep."

Though it seemed too simplistic, he was right. Concentrating solely on us, I curled into his warmth and laid my head on his chest.

With the sound of his steady heartbeat against my ear, I drifted to sleep. When I awoke the next morning, I remembered not having been able to answer him the first time and my overwhelming sense of guilt and loneliness. I expected a reprimand, more questions about what had happened, or a lecture on how all my thoughts were his. He didn't mention it.

The next time the dragon's hiss woke me, instead of rolling away, I cuddled close and remembered his questions. As his even breaths flowed across the top of my head, I reminded myself of who I was and who he was. Before long I drifted back to sleep. In time the dragons faded away.

Although I knew I should talk to Jacob about my nightmares and guilt over the accident, my courage to do so waned with each passing day. After all, if I'd followed Father Gabriel's teachings, I would've told Jacob immediately. I knew the penalty for disobeying; I'd experienced it more than once.

It wasn't until I had multiple consecutive nights of uninterrupted sleep, while we were alone in our apartment, that Jacob asked me again about what had happened. He led me to the sofa and calmly demanded answers.

"Sara, I've been waiting for you to tell me this on your own. Obviously you haven't. I'm not sure why, but I want answers. Tell me why you were crying during the night."

I took a deep breath, wanting to be truthful, but equally fearful of his reaction. "It started as nightmares. I think." I tried to explain. "That's what woke me, but then I believe it was my guilt." My chest heaved. "I still can't believe I risked everything here, you and our friends, by taking your truck. I don't understand why I'd do that. I don't think I would, but obviously I did." A tear fell from the corner of my eye.

He lifted my chin. The way he stared stripped me bare. His soft brown eyes sought not only me, but my honesty. I didn't look away, nor did I want to. Captive in his grasp, I needed him to see my sincerity. Holding my breath, I waited for his gaze to narrow and his voice to lose emotion.

"What does Father Gabriel say about correction?" His eyes still searched, while his tone remained full of emotion.

I exhaled. "I know. I do. I know we were banished and now we're back. I know it should be gone." Unable to move my chin, I lowered my eyes and slid my lip between my teeth. I'd confessed and now all I could do was await the punishment I deserved for doubting Father Gabriel's teaching.

"Sara, it's not that it should be. It is."

I nodded, and my body trembled. "I do believe it, but I just don't know . . ."

He lifted my balled hands and opened my fists, finger by finger, until he could kiss my palms. Then, with his thumb, he gently freed my lip. "Why are you so tense?"

"Because I know Father Gabriel's word, but I must not be living it. If I were, I wouldn't have those thoughts, a-and I don't know what you're going to do."

"What do you think I should do?"

My heart sank as the dinner we'd just eaten churned in my stomach. I hated when he asked me. Those simple questions turned the responsibility back to me. I didn't want it. It was his. Again I tried to lower my chin, but to no avail. I sighed and added to my transgressions. "I've also kept something from you. I didn't tell you that this was going on for a few weeks."

His grip on my chin tensed.

"I didn't want you to worry," I added hastily.

"Have you felt this way lately? Have you awakened in the middle of the night upset without telling me?"

I shook my head. "Not since the night you asked me who we were. Well, only once, and when I did, I did what you said: I reminded myself of us and stayed close to you. Since then, nothing."

Jacob exhaled. "Sara Adams, what does that tell you?"

"That I should be punished for not telling you sooner?"

His hands slipped to my arms, moving up and down with a

ghostly soft touch. "It does say that you should have told me sooner, but no, this isn't about correction. It's about learning. Thoughts come and go; it's dwelling on them that's detrimental. The way you let them go is to release them to me. If I punished you for your thoughts, why would you share them with me?"

I hadn't thought of it that way.

"The accident," he went on, "is over, and now that you've shared your sense of guilt, it's over. I want all of you"—he caressed my cheek—"even if it's a part that hurts and makes you cry. Give it to me. Once it's mine I won't let it hurt you anymore, and no more apologizing for what's in the past. Remember, it's as if it never happened."

Nodding, I fell against his chest. Even though in my mind our history was short, as his arms wrapped around my shoulders, I knew I was where I was meant to be. My earlier feelings of doubt no longer existed.

As we made our way through the temple, when Jacob slowed or stopped to speak to other followers, I'd slow or stop with him. As we arrived at the room where the Commission and Assembly wives met for prayer, he reached for my hand, and I peered up through my lashes. When my light-blue eyes met his, my heart swelled at his silent message. I might not remember the beginning of our life together, but we'd found our way back. In the crowded hallway, his brown eyes, the slight upward turn of his lips, and the squeeze of his hand said more than words. The shimmer of suede in his eyes and partial smile told me that he loved me, while the grasp on my hand warned me to think before I spoke. I didn't need the warning because I had no intention or desire to receive his correction.

Though I'd relearned Father Gabriel's lessons well and knew my place, my continual area of downfall was my inquisitiveness. No matter how hard I tried, there were times when my mouth spoke before my brain could tell it to stop.

Eleven of the women gathering in the room I'd entered were my sisters, equal sisters under Father Gabriel. All the Assembly wives had made a significant sacrifice for me when they cut their hair. Truthfully, it had also been a show of support for Jacob. Without their husbands' consent, it never would've happened. As I glanced about, I was glad that all our hair was growing. Most of us could at least gather it at the backs of our heads, but nevertheless I'd never forget their gift. As we gathered together, we showed affection with a hug, squeeze of the hand, or warm greeting. Although the Commission wives hadn't cut their hair, they'd also welcomed me back without reservation, even Sister Lilith.

Father Gabriel taught to forgive and forget. That was what Jacob said I should do with Brother Timothy and Sister Lilith. While I'd forgiven, forgetting wasn't as easy. Not only did I remember, I also wondered why they hadn't been punished for the way they'd treated me. After all, Jacob had said it wasn't their place. The night I voiced that question aloud, to my husband, gave a prime example of my mind not controlling my tongue. As soon as I had asked my question, it hung in the air like a cloud, and I immediately knew it was wrong.

"Sara?" Jacob said, using his emotionless tone and narrowed gaze. "Who are you that you can question Father Gabriel's decisions?"

In the past he'd told me not to kneel; an Assemblyman's wife shouldn't be on the ground. The first time he'd mentioned kneeling, the idea had seemed incomprehensible. Yet four months later, when his voice and eyes reprimanded, I had an almost irresistible urge to fall to my knees. It wasn't that I wanted to beg for mercy; mercy was at his discretion. It was that his simple cues filled me with an overpowering sense of shame as I realized that I'd failed him once again. Instead of kneeling I respectfully bowed my head and, through veiled eyes, apologized: "I'm sorry. You're right; I don't have the right to question Father Gabriel's decisions."

Thankfully, that night I received only the tone and the gaze. Though Jacob was probably more lenient and patient than many of the other husbands, since I'd awoken I'd received correction by Jacob's belt a total of three times. Never, other than when I first awoke, had he struck me with his hand, and never had he willfully harmed me. He made it clear that it was as he'd explained: discipline, not abuse, and even though each time my transgressions outnumbered one, he never gave me more than five lashes. That was more than enough to help me remember to try harder.

As everyone sat for prayer, I noticed Deborah, one of the Assembly wives, wince. It wasn't obvious; however, since we'd all experienced it firsthand, we were proficient at catching the subtle signs of correction. Each time, we'd offer support, while reminding our sister, as Raquel had reminded me after my first correction—in my new memory or new past, as I liked to think of it—to thank God and Father Gabriel for a husband who loved enough to correct. Yet as Deborah settled into her chair, I knew my thinking was wrong and I needed to confess it again to Jacob. Instead of telling her to be thankful, I wanted to tell her to talk to one of the Commission wives, and I wondered why they didn't notice.

As I watched my Assembly sister, my gut told me that things were different for Deborah than for most of us. Not only had she recently given birth to a beautiful son, she'd gone back to her job and worked six hours a day at the clinic with Raquel. Sister Esther mentioned once in confidence how difficult it was to leave her baby and return to work; however, there wasn't an option to do otherwise. It was Father Gabriel's rule that all babies be under his word in day care by five weeks of age. What bothered me about Deborah was that even while she was pregnant, she was often corrected. Brother Abraham not only used his belt, but often her cheek or eye was bruised. More times than I could count there'd been visual evidence.

It wasn't up to women to question Brother Abraham's reasoning, but after the short time I remembered having known Deborah, I found it difficult to believe that she was that disobedient. Honestly, she was quiet and sweet, and now that her son Philip was here, she was tired. Once in a while in service, I'd watch Brother Abraham. Truth be told, not only was I concerned for Deborah, but he also scared me. Though I knew Jacob would never allow another man to touch me, I wasn't comfortable around Brother Abraham. If my instincts were correct, Deborah felt the same. As others comforted her and reminded her to pray, she said the right words. Still, there was something missing.

After prayer meeting Elizabeth, Raquel, and I walked down a corridor toward our husbands. As we did, I rubbed the tips of my fingers together, wondering if I'd ever get used to the strange sensation. Once a month, all followers pressed the pads of their fingers onto a special prayer sponge. Symbolically it removed our individuality, making us all equal parts of Father Gabriel's family. Though we were chosen, our behavior was an example to the other followers. It didn't hurt. It just felt odd.

As we were on our way to the Assembly room, a female follower with long blonde hair secured in a braid approached. Though something about her caught my attention, I couldn't remember having seen her before. Then again, as an Assembly wife I was rather isolated.

"Sister Elizabeth," the blonde said.

Elizabeth nodded toward Raquel and me as she greeted the woman, "Sister Mary, so nice to see you." Since Elizabeth and Brother Luke worked with new followers, she seemed to know almost everyone. It wasn't uncommon for female followers to come to her with questions. Though I wasn't a new follower, I understood the appeal of having women to help you understand.

Not wanting to intrude, Raquel and I stepped back. Elizabeth reached for Sister Mary's hand and spoke softly as Sister Mary nodded. I watched as Elizabeth's red hair fell in soft curls near her shoulders, veiling her lips and keeping their conversation private.

"She's so good at what she does," Raquel whispered

I nodded. "Have you ever seen her before—Sister Mary?"

"Yes, in the clinic."

My eyes widened. "In the clinic? Was she sick?"

"No, it was just . . . when she first arrived. You know . . . to make sure she's healthy and didn't have any illnesses from the dark."

"Oh, yes, that makes sense." I watched as Mary bit her lower lip and smiled. "I don't know why, but she looks familiar."

Raquel laughed. "I know why."

"You do?"

"Yes, don't you see it?"

I scanned Mary one last time as she wiped a tear and nodded to Elizabeth. "Not really, but I must admit, I admire her hair."

Raquel tapped my arm. "She looks like you, even her hair."

I pouted. "Was it really that long?"

"It was, and it will be again. I've enjoyed the shorter cut. It was a fun change."

Before I could respond, Elizabeth was back, and we made our way toward the Assembly room.

All the Assemblymen lived in the same building in similar apartments. The only differences were the color and placement of the furniture, not that there were many options. Space within the community was limited, but we had what we needed. No one questioned. After all, even Father Gabriel lived as we did. According to Elizabeth our apartments were bigger than those of the regular followers. Her and Brother Luke's jobs meant they often visited followers in their homes. As an Assemblyman's wife, I too was supposed to help with the wives of followers under Jacob's direction. So far I'd met with them only in the temple. But going to them and helping them understand Father Gabriel's word was a responsibility I was honored to perform again, and one of the reasons I'd studied so diligently.

When we arrived back at the apartment building, Brother Benjamin asked Brother Luke and Jacob to come to his apartment. The way they looked at one another, I assumed they wanted to discuss something from their meeting. Whatever it was, we wouldn't be told the details, especially if it was something they believed needed to be discussed in private. Before they left, Jacob said to the others, "With your permission, the ladies may wait together in our apartment."

I bit my lip and waited: there was something I wanted to discuss too. As part of the chosen, we had to be careful what we did or said in public.

Brothers Luke and Benjamin agreed.

"Come on in," I said, as my two best friends entered my apartment. "Would you like something to drink?"

Raquel chatted about something as I made coffee and contemplated bringing up the question of Deborah. If it had been only Raquel, I wouldn't have hesitated, but sometimes Elizabeth was more rigid with the rules.

"Elizabeth?"

She looked up from the sofa as I handed her a cup. "Thanks."

"What's up? You look far away." I looked to Raquel, who shrugged.

"Nothing," Elizabeth said. "I'll talk to Luke about it."

"Do you always tell him everything the women tell you? Like whatever you were talking to Sister Mary about?"

She nodded. "I have to." Her striking green eyes scanned from Raquel to me. "I mean, we work together. For example, if Sister Mary were to tell me something that her husband needs to know, then Luke would be the one to do that." She shrugged. "It's up to Luke, really."

"But if she talks to you in confidence?" I asked.

Elizabeth's head moved back and forth. "Sara, you know that there can't be any secrets or confidence or whatever you choose to call it between a wife and husband."

I nodded. "What if all marriages weren't like ours?"

"What do you mean?" Raquel asked.

I sat on the other end of the sofa from Elizabeth, pulled my knees to my chest, and tucked my skirt around my legs. "I mean, what if some husbands take the whole discipline thing too far?" I exhaled. "OK, I'm just going to say it. I'm worried about Deborah."

Raquel nodded while Elizabeth's lips formed a straight line of disapproval.

"Why," I pointedly asked my friend, "Elizabeth, is it bad for me to be concerned?"

"Concern is your right, but you need to give it to Brother Jacob and pray about it. Not gossip about it."

I blew on my coffee, helping it cool. "First, I'm not gossiping. If I were, I'd be telling you something you didn't know. You know what I'm saying. And, second, I have given it to Jacob."

"You have?" she asked, surprised.

"Yes, and it's still happening."

Raquel became uncharacteristically quiet.

"Raquel?" I asked. "Deborah works with you. Do you think my concerns are unfounded?"

She shook her head, and then, looking to Elizabeth, she said, "I've done the same as Sara."

"And what did Brother Benjamin say?"

"He said to pray and support Deborah."

I placed my cup on the table and flung my body back to the sofa. "I don't think she's happy, not like us. I mean, I get that Jacob is the head of our household. I even accept his correction, but I also know he loves me, and I love him."

Elizabeth and Raquel shared some strange secret smile.

"What?" I asked.

Raquel patted my knee. "Nothing. We're just happy to hear you say that."

I scrunched my nose. "Isn't it obvious? I mean it is with you and Brother Benjamin and you and Brother Luke." I smiled at Raquel. "Even when Brother Benjamin mentions you at the lab, his eyes go all adoring."

Raquel's cheeks blushed as she looked down.

"It is obvious," Elizabeth said with a smile. "It's also nice to hear."

"But that's just it," I pursued. "It isn't obvious between Deborah and Brother Abraham. I mean, have you watched them together? I think she's afraid of him, and I don't see the adoration or love, from either of them."

"Sara!" Elizabeth said, "You can worry and talk about Deborah, but you can't presume to talk about Brother Abraham."

I exhaled, unable or unwilling to hold my tongue, even if it meant my own correction. "We're wives of Assemblymen. Are we just going to sit back and wait until Deborah isn't at the clinic as a nurse, but as a patient?"

Raquel sighed. "It's already happened."

"What?!" I asked, while simultaneously Elizabeth exclaimed, "Raquel!"

"Elizabeth, you heard Sara. She's here, fully. She needs to know."

I tilted my head. "What do you mean, I'm here . . . fully?"

"I mean, you're back, like a hundred and ten percent. As you were recovering from your accident, we didn't want to burden you."

"I don't understand. Why can't we help her before it's too late?"

"Because," Elizabeth began, "Brother Abraham is also an Assemblyman. If he were a follower, like Brother Adam, it would be different."

"Who's Brother Adam?" Raquel and I asked in unison.

Elizabeth shook her head. "Forget I said that."

My mind spun. "Is Brother Adam the husband of the woman who spoke to you, Mary?"

"It's not something I can discuss." Her green eyes shot toward me. "Forget I mentioned it."

"Wait, so let's say hypothetically"—I paused. When she didn't respond, I went on—"a female follower comes up to you and tells you in confidence that she has a problem with her husband. I'm just going to say it. He's abusive. Then do you tell Brother Luke and let it go from there?"

"Hypothetically," Elizabeth said, "yes."

"So with Deborah, if she said something to her overseer's wife, could that Commissioner's wife tell her husband, and then could he talk to Brother Abraham?"

"Theoretically," Raquel said, "but guess who's Brother Abraham's overseer."

I had four choices: Brothers Raphael, Daniel, Noah, or Timothy. I knew Brother Daniel wouldn't turn a blind eye, and I worked with Brother Raphael. He'd always been kind to me. I didn't know much about Brother Noah, other than Jacob said he worked with the finances of The Light. When new followers came to The Light they sold all their possessions from the dark and donated the money to help buy supplies. That left me one option: Brother Timothy. "Either Brother Noah or Timothy. I'm going to guess . . ."

Raquel nodded. "Without Brother Timothy's consent, the concerns, even if they're voiced by Deborah and Sister Lilith took them to her husband, can't be taken to Father Gabriel. Nothing can be done." She looked at Elizabeth and then back to me. "It's better if you don't say any more. It was brought up about a year ago, and you probably don't remember . . ."

I shook my head.

"After that was when she was a patient. It didn't do her any good. It made it worse."

Horrified, I turned toward Elizabeth. "Is that what happens to people like Mary if you tell Luke?"

"Hypothetically?" she asked.

I nodded.

"Sometimes, but usually not. Followers respect the opinion and advice of Assemblymen. Luke carries a lot of weight. He can usually help the situation."

"But just like Jacob helps Brother Daniel with the followers he oversees, doesn't Brother Abraham help Brother Timothy?"

They both nodded.

"So if a follower is unfortunate enough to be assigned to that chain of command . . . ?"

Elizabeth nodded. "Then they still have Luke and me. We just have to be sure to follow the rules, but we still can do our best to help."

I took a drink of my coffee. "Wow, Elizabeth, I didn't realize how difficult your job was. I'm never complaining about the lab again."

Raquel laughed. "Hey, you complained about working with my husband?"

"No," I said, smiling. "I actually like working with him and Brother Raphael. They've been very patient, and so has Dinah. She's been great."

They both nodded. "She's one of us. We stick together."

I sighed. "I wish we could help Deborah. I still worry."

CHAPTER

TWENTY-EIGHT

S tella

I HANDED Foster the list of properties Jenn, from Preston and Butler, had e-mailed to my personal address last night. "I've only glanced through it, but it seems like a lot of property. I always assumed that realty firms arranged the sale of property from the owner to the new buyer. I wasn't aware that the firm would own so much itself."

Foster shrugged. "They do both. It really depends on the size of the company. While Entermann's began as a broker, looking at this list, now I'd call them an investment company."

"Did you know that Entermann's falls under a list of subsidiaries of Wilkens Industries?"

"I thought you were talking the other day about Uriel Harris and his connection with Wilkens Industries?"

"I was. Here, let me see this list." I took the list and circled the property on Glendale, the old school. "This property is currently owned by Entermann's, but before that it was owned by Harris, and before that Wilkens Industries. Since Wilkens owns Entermann's, well, I'm seeing a circle, but why?"

"It's only a complete circle if Harris is connected."

"That's what I want to know. I've been trying to find current information on Uriel Harris. In the day, he was all over, buying property, but then all his holdings were sold. He took a big loss and disappeared." I shook my head. "I don't mean literally. There's no record of his death. What I mean is that I can't find him. His last known address was 12560 Kingsway Trace, Bloomfield Hills." As soon as I said the address, my heart clenched, and I looked up at Foster. "Tell me that isn't same address as the MOA house you told me about."

"Shit, it isn't, but it's damn close."

I shook my head, my braid skimming across my back. "See, this is what I mean. Circles, that's all I'm getting is circles."

"Have you accessed Harris's taxes?"

"I did up until he sold everything. For the last two years there's nothing. No personal or corporate. Nothing."

"Stella?" Foster asked, looking at the list of properties. "Did you just say 12560 Kingsway Trace?"

I nodded, looking down at where Foster's finger was on the list. "Entermann's owns that too?" I asked in disbelief.

"According to this list."

Remembering a recent conversation with Dina Rosemont, I asked, "What do you know about a private airstrip off of Woodward Avenue and Eastways Road?"

"Not much, but that's up in Bloomfield Hills. There are lots of wealthy people, so a private airstrip wouldn't surprise me. Why?"

"I promised a friend I'd go check it out. I think while I'm up there I might check out this house on Kingsway Trace."

"Well," Foster said, "be smart and take I-75. Woodward would get you there, but I recommend you avoid Highland Heights."

Why hadn't I thought of that? Woodward goes straight from Highland Heights to Bloomfield Hills.

I rolled my eyes. "Have you been talking to Dylan?"

"Me? No. Why?"

I shook my head. "Nothing. I'll call after I have a look around. While I'm up there, do you want me to check out the MOA house?"

"No. You have enough things going on with this story. You don't need another. Besides, there's no reason to think it's connected."

"You're right. I'm overly suspicious of everything. It's the whole compilation theory."

"Compilation?" he asked.

"Like everything is a piece of something bigger. I think I'm trying to fit everything together when they don't fit."

Foster's voice softened. "I just picked up a story about a teacher at East Grove. A mother claims she saw inappropriate pictures on her daughter's phone. If you'd like to take that, I'll take this over. I can tell it's wearing on you."

"Thanks, but I don't want to give it up. I feel like I'm so close. I just need one break."

"OK, the offer stands."

I smiled at my friend as I gathered my things.

Driving on I-75 to Bloomfield Hills, I remembered my conversation with Dina Rosemont and how impressed I'd been with her strength and determination. She had said she would never give up her search, and from the sound of her voice I believed her. We both knew the statistics weren't in Mindy's favor and got worse the longer she stayed missing. I shook my head, thinking how it had been over two months. I didn't know if the story I was researching would help her or help us learn about her, but my gut told me it would. That was why I couldn't hand it over to Foster. Even so, Bernard had given me only until the end of October. That was less than three weeks. I needed to learn something, soon.

Dina told me that she'd received a phone call from a woman who had seen one of the flyers she'd hung. The woman wouldn't give her name, but said that as a mother she needed to call. Apparently the caller lived near Woodward Avenue and Eastways Road, and there was a wooded area near her home where her children liked to play. A private airstrip was located there too.

The caller admitted that a twelve- and thirteen-year-old weren't the most reliable witnesses, and though she didn't want them personally involved, she felt compelled to share what they had told her. Even before the caller heard about Mindy on the news, her children had told her a story about a man carrying a woman from a truck to a plane. The woman calling admitted that because her children had been known to be imaginative, she hadn't paid much attention to their story. She'd figured there could be any number of good reasons why they thought they'd seen what they described. However, once Mindy's picture appeared on TV, her children brought up the story again. Even then, they only told the story; they didn't mention the connection. It wasn't until they were out one day and saw one of the flyers that her thirteen-year-old daughter pointed at Mindy's picture and specifically said, "Mom, that's the lady who couldn't walk, so they carried her on the plane."

My heart stopped as I asked what they'd meant by couldn't walk. Dina said she'd asked too. The woman hadn't known. After they hung up, the woman had asked her children and called Dina back. Her children told her the woman had been sleeping.

Dina said she'd called the detective in charge of the investigation, and he'd said he'd look into it, but she wanted me to know. I'd looked up private airstrips, but the ones I'd found weren't in the area the woman had indicated. That was the main reason I was driving north on I-75.

Exiting the interstate, I made my way into Bloomfield Hills. As I drove around the beautiful area, I thought about Foster's suggestion that Dylan could afford a home here. Honestly, it was too bad that he and I together couldn't afford one. Though I wasn't ready for full-time cohabitation, as I drove the curvy roads around the majestic homes I found myself imagining the interiors with a very nice shelf for Fred's bowl.

The last known address of Uriel Harris wasn't one of the big homes lining the hilly streets. The address took me instead to a large solid gate. Shrugging, I parked my car, walked up to a box beside the gate, and pushed the button.

A man's voice came from the box. "May I help you?"

"I'm looking for Uriel Harris."

"You have the wrong address."

I knew I didn't. "Maybe I have his old address. Can you tell me how long you've lived here?"

"This is private property. I suggest you leave."

Well, that was rude.

"Thank you for your time," I said as I released the button.

Going back to my car, I grabbed my Nikon and walked the perimeter along the front wrought-iron fence. It didn't seem to matter where I tried—I couldn't see the house, or even get past the trees to take a picture. Though most leaves were gone, this property was lined with rows of pine trees, creating a living wall beyond the fence. Not only couldn't I see the house, I couldn't even get a feel for the size of the property. Still I snapped a few pictures here and there.

I hoped that once I downloaded the photographs, I would be able to enlarge them and make out more than I could see in person. When I reached the end of the front fence, I saw that the angle of the side fence indicated that the property was wider in the back. As I took a few more pictures, I decided I should get the schematic of the property from the assessor, but first I'd try Google Earth.

It wasn't until I got back into my car that I noticed the security cameras at the gate. Sighing, I fought the urge to wave. Well, I couldn't see them, but apparently they could see me.

Next I spent an hour driving in circles. If there was an airstrip off Woodward Avenue and Eastways Road, I couldn't find it. I couldn't even find the access road. Maybe I did, but instead of an accessible street it was another one of the gated private driveways like the address on Kingsway Trace. The more I drove the more frustrated I became.

Dead ends, I was so damn sick of dead ends!

While I was on my way back to WCJB, lamenting my progress, my phone rang. Dylan's name appeared on the screen in my car. I hit the green image and said, "Hello."

"Stella?"

His voice sounded different. Maybe something had happened at work. "Hey, is everything all right? You don't usually call during the day."

"Where are you?"

Shit!

I'd been so frustrated with the dead ends I'd forgotten to take the interstate and was on Woodward Avenue, approaching Highland Heights. "Why? I'm on my way back from checking out a lead."

Wanting to be able to honestly answer that I wasn't in Highland Heights, I turned east toward the interstate, just north of the city limits.

"I just had . . . never mind."

I wasn't used to hearing Dylan anything less than confident.

"Did something happen?" I asked.

"No, I was just wondering if you could do dinner tonight?" His tone lightened. "Or do you have drinks with that hot fireman again?"

I laughed. "Dinner would be great, but I need to be home tonight. I have things to do on my computer."

"You work too much."

"It doesn't have to be all work. You could stay?"

"Only if you let me take you out to eat."

"Sounds good. I'll go home after work and you can come over. We can go out after that."

"See you tonight."

AFTER DINNER, while I downloaded my pictures, Dylan sat on my sofa. His legs were up on the ottoman as he watched TV. Looking at him, I wondered if this was what it was like when two people were together long enough to be comfortable. I'd never really dated anyone long enough to move into that stage. Maybe it was finding out about his parents, but since that morning a few days ago, I'd found myself thinking about him a lot more.

Once I had my pictures from the day on my computer, I entered the address of the house I'd visited. Google Earth wouldn't show me the exact dimensions of the property, but I was curious what was beyond that gate. The house was huge—no wonder it was valued at more than $7 million. There were a pool and tennis courts. Beyond the tennis courts were multiple smaller buildings, and then behind that, away from the road, closer to Eastways, was what I'd been searching for. There was an airstrip.

"Holy shit!" I gasped.

"What?" Dylan asked, coming up behind me.

I shook my head. "I really don't know." I pointed at the screen. "See this?"

His hands tightened their grasp on my shoulders as his face came up beside mine. When I turned toward him, I saw the muscle in his jaw flex.

"It's an airstrip," I explained when he didn't speak.

"Are you looking to do some flying?" he asked, from behind clenched teeth.

"No. See, Dina Rosemont called me about a phone call she received from someone who saw her flyer. She said that the caller told her a story about seeing a woman matching Mindy's description being carried onto a plane."

Dylan spun my chair around until our noses touched. "She needs to tell that to DPD, not you. You have too much going on. I'm worried about you."

I kissed him. "I'm worried about you too. Did you ask about getting time at Christmas? And don't worry, she did call DPD. Have you heard about it?"

"No, I'm not directly involved with her case." He shrugged. "You don't want me to be."

"You're right. You're homicide. I'd rather her case not make it to you."

"So was that where you were today, following that lead?"

I nodded, though I had been there for my story too. Our agreement was to discuss only Mindy-related work information. Turning back to the screen, I answered, "Yes, I couldn't find it."

"Well, I guess that's why it's private. Did some lady really say she thought she saw Mindy getting on a plane?"

I shook my head. "She said her children saw a woman, not getting on a plane—being carried onto it. It's the first news that gives me hope. I mean it scares me, but at least maybe there's a chance that she's still alive. Now I want to learn who owns this property." I shrugged. "I know who owns it. I want to know who's living there. I guess I didn't realize the airstrip was on it."

"What do you mean you know who owns it?"

I put my finger on his lips. "We're getting into non-Mindy stuff."

"Stella, please stop. You're too smart for your own good."

I brushed his lips to mine. "I love your support, but if I'm so smart, why is none of this making sense? Foster offered to take the story and put a fresh set of eyes on it." I sighed.

"Do that!"

"You know I can't. I mean, yes, I was at this property for Mindy, but I'm so close to something—something big—that I can feel it."

"Quit WCJB. We could use you at DPD. You're really that good."

"Oh, I don't know if we should work together. I get the feeling our styles match better in private."

Dylan took my hand. "No more computer, pictures, or Google Earth searches. Let's work on that private compatibility."

CHAPTER

TWENTY-NINE

Stella

"STELLA," Dr. Howell said, "I need you to meet me at the medical center—right away."

I blinked awake at the sound of her anxious voice. "What is it?" I focused on the clock near my bed; it wasn't even three in the morning.

"I'd rather show you. Can you be here, in the ICU, in half an hour?"

This time of morning there wouldn't be much traffic, but that was still cutting it close. "I can be there in less than an hour. I'll hurry."

"OK, and please don't tell anyone where you're going."

I looked to my right, saw Dylan with a pillow pulled over his head, and replied, "If it's that important, I won't."

"Believe me, it is."

"OK. I'll see you as soon as I can. Bye."

The line went dead. Dylan rolled, his eyes blinking in the red glow from the bedside clock. "Jesus, Stella, do you ever get to sleep through the night?"

I leaned down and kissed his lips. "Go back to sleep. You can lock up before you leave. I need to run."

He huffed, rolled back under his pillow, and muttered, "Shit, I'd argue, but I've got a lot happening today. Besides, you wouldn't listen anyway."

I hurried to the bathroom and made myself presentable, as presentable as one wants to be this early in the morning. Less than ten minutes later, dressed in jeans and ready to go, I made my way back to Dylan. "I'm sorry this woke you. I'll leave a key for you on the table by the door so you can lock up." I bent down to kiss his cheek. His inviting scent combined with his radiating warmth pulled me closer. The outside temperature had dipped the last few nights, making Dylan and my bed a much more compelling option than Tracy and an ICU. Just as I was about to kiss him good-bye, he wrapped his arms around me and pulled me closer.

With a raspy morning voice, he asked, "A key? You're giving me a key?"

I shrugged in his embrace. "You have to be able to lock up."

Burying his stubbly face in the nape of my neck, he mumbled, "I'll give it back tonight."

It took every ounce of my willpower not to climb back into my bed. "Or you could hold on to it, and then if Fred ever needs something, and I can't be here, you could swing by."

"I could do that. The little guy and I really bonded. Did you see how excited he was last Sunday to watch the Lions game with me?"

I laughed. "Yes, you two were something else. Call me later?"

"Or since I have a key . . ."

"I"—I hesitated—"will see you later." I kissed his cheek and went to find my warmer coat.

Since that night over a week ago when Dylan had stayed at my place, he'd done it more. I'd thought about giving him a key before now. After all, I had one to his place, though I'd been reluctant to accept it. He'd convinced me to take it at the same time he'd convinced me to leave clothes. I guess they kind of went together; however, I'd never used his key. Maybe I hadn't felt comfortable being at his place without him. While I waited for my car to warm, my cold cheeks rose; I was comfortable leaving him alone at my place. As I exhaled, faint crystals of ice hung suspended in the cool morning air. My empty stomach clenched at the realization: as I'd said good-bye to the sexy man in my bed, I'd almost told him that I loved him.

When the hell did that happen?

Last week when I'd told my mom, on the phone, that I'd invited him to Christmas with us, you would've thought I'd told her that one of my stories was being considered for a Pulitzer. She was beyond elated that I was in a steady relationship. With two daughters, she was champing at the bit for grandchildren. Currently all she had was Fred. I'd felt bad when I let her know that he wouldn't be making it for Christmas. Fish and carsickness made for a messy bowl.

I shook my head at the possibility. Maybe at twenty-nine years old I was ready to look at a future with someone. I'd never thought it would be with someone like Dylan, a detective, and someone others considered a hard-ass. However, when we were together, I didn't see him the way others did.

The Saturday before he and Fred bonded over football, had started a little rocky. For some reason he wasn't happy about my strawberry jam. I'd walked into the kitchen and found him staring at the jar. When I asked him what was going on, he explained it was an allergy. I promised I wouldn't use it when he was near, but I would eat it. It was delicious.

Later that day we went to Dearborn for the Apple Harvest Festival. Though my research was finally falling into place and I wanted to keep working, Dylan persuaded me to take a day away from everything. I smiled at the memory; I had enjoyed the outing. The day was one of those unseasonably warm autumn days, a gift from the prewinter gods. With a warm breeze and a clear blue sky, we walked hand in hand around the festival, talking, laughing, and enjoying candied apples. As evening came, we sat on a blanket with another one wrapped about our shoulders, drinking spiked apple cider and listening to live music. While Dylan drove back to my place, I dozed off and on. For the first time ever, I experienced a complete sense of security and contentedness.

Later I told myself that it wasn't all about Dylan; it was also about the progress I'd made on the money trail surrounding the buildings around The Light. Doing as Bernard suggested, I'd finally connected some dots. Though I'd done it all without revisiting Highland Heights, I planned to go back as soon as the first snow fell. I wanted proof that the abandoned building was in use. Footprints behind the locked fence would be that evidence, and with the way my teeth currently chattered, I'd be getting those soon.

My most exciting connection I'd made, the one I'd yet to share with anyone, was about Marcel Clarkson, the benefactor who'd donated the building that currently housed The Light. Marcel was also the original CEO of Wilkens Industries. He'd begun that private company in 1972 and had one son, Garrison Clarkson. My moment of discovery came when I realized that prior to 1990 Gabriel Clark, the founder of The Light, didn't exist, and after 1990, Garrison Clarkson ceased to exist. The paper trail on Garrison's demise was fuzzy at best. There was a small hospital notice listing Garrison Clarkson as deceased; however, I couldn't verify that with state death records. The only other mention of Garrison was in a 1998 interview with Marcel in which he mentioned the loss of his son.

Though The Light's website gave little information on Gabriel Clark, other than that he claimed to have risen from the ashes of darkness, assuming I was right and he truly was Garrison Clarkson, that couldn't have been further from the truth. Garrison had grown up in a stately older mansion in Angell, one of the most expensive neighborhoods in Ann Arbor, Michigan. He came from old money, earned off the backs of autoworkers. His father, Marcel, had begun Wilkens Industries and diversified the family fortune during the stock market boom, increasing its worth exponentially. Garrison had attended the University of Michigan, followed in his father's footsteps, and climbed to the top. Then in the late 1980s the markets crashed and, according to undisclosed insiders, a family feud ensued. That was about the time Garrison disappeared and Gabriel Clark was created.

If I'd connected the right dots, Garrison Clarkson became Gabriel Clark, a divine preacher and prophet of God.

The early 1990s was the boom of self-discovery. Men and women faced with financial devastation flocked to self-help and motivational seminars. From what I'd pieced together from archived media blurbs, Father Gabriel, as he branded himself based on the archangel, rose to the top. Perhaps ordained, or perhaps recognizing the financial potential, Gabriel traveled about the country conducting free seminars for thousands of participants. Each seminar encouraged only the participants interested in personal success to purchase his materials. According to the IRS, in 1992 sales from his books, manuals, and videotapes topped $10 million.

Near the turn of the century, the same time that Marcel became ill, Gabriel stepped away from the traveling circuit and settled down with The Light. By that time he had a ring of three trusted advisors who were named as members of his advisory commission. Their names were listed on the original application for tax-exempt status: Michael Jones, Raphael Williams, and Uriel Harrison—interestingly, all archangels.

If Uriel Harrison was Uriel Harris, the developer, my circle was complete.

Without evidence, I assumed the feud between Marcel and his son had ended before Marcel Clarkson's death, because in 2001 Gabriel Clark's and Marcel Clarkston's combined net worth was transferred to The Light. On paper, Garrison Clarkson or Gabriel Clark, was penniless.

My theory was that Father Gabriel was still connected to Wilkens Industries, the entity that also owned Entermann's Realty. It was still a leap, and I was working on the particulars; however, if I was correct, Father Gabriel didn't live in a run-down church building in Highland Heights. He lived in the mansion in Bloomfield Hills, the one with the landing strip. He also wasn't penniless, but based on flight plans, flew in a multi-million-dollar plane.

His having the old school building under his control guaranteed its abandoned appearance, and he also had control of the two buildings with the passage between, and the perfect cover for production of anything he wanted.

If I took my theory to the next logical step, and the witnesses' mother was also correct, there was a connection between The Light and the missing women. I wasn't convinced it also included the dead women. Perhaps that was me trying to incorporate too much, but I knew that at the very least I had something for Bernard, and that story alone could get him entry to the old school building on Glendale. If the only thing that was being done inside its walls was the making of delicious preserves, then we had a missing-persons story, possible tax fraud of a not-for-profit, and tax evasion of Gabriel Clark/Garrison Clarkson. If instead there was a connection to the drug story I'd originally begun researching, then Bernard Cooper would hit pay dirt. With a week and a half to spare on Bernard's deadline, this story that had taken me months had the potential to give him national exposure.

Since the pieces were just now falling into place, I hadn't shared them, but I'd saved everything on my laptop. Each day I also e-mailed the zip files to myself, knowing that in the case of fire or burglary, they'd at least exist in cyberspace. As one last precaution, I backed everything up on a hard drive that stayed hidden in my underwear drawer. Though it seemed excessive, I knew this was big. For that reason I purposely didn't have any information on my work computer. I feared the server wasn't secure.

The rush of it all made me almost giddy. I made my way

through the medical center in search of Tracy. I found her sitting in the waiting area with her knee bobbing up and down. As soon as our eyes met, she got up and hurried in my direction. My elation evaporated at the lines around her eyes and her furrowed brow.

"Tracy, what is it? Is someone you know . . . ?"

That didn't make sense. She wouldn't call me.

"No," she said, taking my hand and leading me through a pair of double doors. "I have a good friend who's an emergency room doctor. We went to med school together." Her voice was a low whisper. "We were talking a few weeks ago about unusual cases; I mentioned some of the things we'd discussed. Then last night she called me." As we moved along the quiet corridor, she looked about nervously. "I promised her that you wouldn't use her name. HIPAA violations are seriously frowned upon, but when she told me about the woman's fingertips, I came to see. That's when I called you." We stopped at a private room where beeps came from behind the door. Tracy squeezed my hand and whispered excitedly, "Wait until you see this!"

My heart raced as we approached the woman in the bed. She was connected to multiple tubes and equipment. Her right cheek was swollen and purple and her eyes were closed. Tracy reached for the unconscious woman's hand and turned it palm upward. Her fingertips were white, the skin freshly burned.

I gasped. "Has she spoken? Does anyone know what happened?"

Tracy shook her head. "No, she was found near Woodward Avenue and Richton Street, running and stumbling with no coat or shoes. A motorist picked her up and brought her here. The man said that she was barely conscious when he found her, but by the time he arrived, she was passed out."

"Did she say anything to him? Have the police been called?"

"I don't know any more from the man who brought her here. Even what I've told you is classified. DPD came when she first arrived, but nothing can be done without her statement."

I scanned her from head to toe: only her upper chest, head, and arms were visible. "Other injuries?"

Tracy nodded. "Again, I haven't been told much. We need to get out of here before someone finds us. That's why I wanted you to come now, before the morning commotion."

"We passed the nurses' station," I reminded her.

"I have a few friends. Officially we've never been here."

I touched the woman's arm and thought about the victims in Tracy's morgue. Thankfully, despite what she'd been through, this woman was warm.

"Let's get out of here," Tracy said. "As long as you promise her anonymity, my friend who was the attending doctor last night said she'd talk with you."

I agreed.

A few minutes later we were seated in the hospital's cafeteria, nursing cups of hot coffee and talking with Dr. Jennings, a young woman of Asian descent, with tired eyes and pulled-back hair.

"I can't go on record," she began.

I shook my head. "You won't. I promise. Thank you for speaking to me."

She nodded toward Tracy. "She told me what you've been trying to do. As soon as I saw the fingertips, I remembered Tracy's stories. That's why I called."

"Did the patient say anything?"

"No, she's been unconscious since she arrived. Not only is she injured, but she was suffering from hypothermia. I think it was near twenty degrees last night."

I took a deep breath. "What about the Good Samaritan who brought her in? Did she say anything to him?"

Dr. Jennings shook her head. "He said she was incoherent, all she talked about was a light." Dr. Jennings rubbed her temples. "The poor man said he kept telling her not to go toward it. I think he was afraid she might die right there in his car."

My entire body trembled. I needed to speak with this woman or even the man who had saved her. A light had to be The Light, it just had to be. This would be the connection to the dead women.

Dr. Jennings agreed that I could wait for the woman to regain consciousness, and if that happened before her identity was learned and her family or the police stepped in with an order prohibiting visitors, I could talk to her.

I waited impatiently, wishing I'd brought my laptop to record my observations and nursing my third cup of coffee. Without food, my stomach continued to twist, creating knots upon knots. Perhaps that was why I startled when one of the nurses from the ICU tapped my shoulder. "Miss Montgomery?"

"Oh! Yes, is the patient awake?"

"No, ma'am, not yet; however, there's a call for you at the nurses' station."

I straightened my shoulders. "For me?"

"Yes, ma'am. He asked that I get you."

I nodded. "OK"—I stood—"thank you."

As I followed the larger woman in dark-blue scrubs, my mind searched for who could possibly be calling me at the hospital. It wasn't yet seven in the morning, and I hadn't even told Bernard or Foster where I was.

"Hello?" I asked tentatively.

"Stella Montgomery?"

My forehead furrowed. "Yes?"

"My name's Paul. I'm the man who found the woman last night on Woodward. I have a few minutes before work if you'd like to get my statement."

My tired mind came to life. "Yes, Paul. Thank you, I'd love to do that. Thank you so much for helping her and talking to me. Can I get your last name, and where I can meet you?"

"I'd rather do this off the record, so no last name. But I want to help that lady. I work at a dry cleaner on Grand Boulevard in New Center. Martin's. Can you meet me there?"

My body tingled with excitement. "Yes, I understand. I won't use your name. I'll be there in less than half an hour."

"It's kind of busy this time of day, but there's a flat lot two blocks away behind Market on State Street."

Behind Market on State, I made a mental note.

"Thank you, Paul, I'll be right there."

It was probably all the coffee and the lack of food, but my grip tightened on my steering wheel as I approached Market. It wasn't a street, but a big building filled with different establishments. It had another name, but people who were familiar with the area called it the Market. Over the years, locals shortened that to just Market. Turning off the main street, I turned onto State. In this area of town it was more of an alleyway than a street. The flat lot had an attendant.

Rolling down my window, I asked, "May I park here?"

"Five bucks for an hour, thirty for all day," the man said, handing me a ticket.

As I put the ticket on the dashboard, the screen in my car lit, indicating a new text message. Out of habit, I hit the button for my car to speak.

Text message from Tracy Howell: I SPOKE WITH PAUL SWIVEL, THE MAN WHO FOUND THE WOMAN LAST NIGHT. HE SAID HE'D THINK ABOUT GIVING YOU A STATEMENT. I'LL KEEP YOU POSTED.

As I looked back up at the attendant, the large black man suddenly seemed vaguely familiar.

There was a sharp pain in my neck and my world went black.

THIRTY

B ernard

I sent another text message to Stella; that made four. She'd never refused to answer me before. I knew I'd been a hard-ass about the deadline, but there were other stories out there that she could research. She said it wasn't because of Mindy that she continued to pursue these leads, but I knew in my gut it was. I also knew that if she could connect the dots—if there were dots to connect—it'd be one hell of a story. That's why I'd given her so much time. It wasn't as if I had to answer to anyone. She worked for me. I worked for the station, but WCJB wouldn't question my allocation of hours.

I picked up the desk phone and called Foster. "Have you heard from Stella today?"

"No, she's probably checking out one of her leads. She's been getting excited about things coming together."

"Has she told you any of it?" I asked.

"Some. I know she was checking out properties owned by Entermann's Realty. There was something about a private landing strip in Bloomfield Hills. That's all she's shared."

"I wish she'd text me back."

"Bernard, she's not Mindy. She's smart and has a good gut. Besides, she's got Richards looking out for her. Give her some space. She'll text back."

I rubbed my temples. He was probably right. Mindy's disappearance had us all on edge. "Hey, speaking of Richards, what did you learn about him?"

"Nothing that we don't already know. There was that one quirky thing about a utility bill on some mansion, but none of it checked out. Stella told me his parents were deceased. That checked out. Everything else was pretty boring."

I shook my head. "Fine. If you hear from her, let me know."

"Sure thing."

Meetings, calls, and general business ensued. It was nearing five in the evening when Foster knocked on my door.

"I'm heading out. I never heard from Stella, have you?"

Shit!

"No, hang on a second. Let me call her again." I'd already called three times and had no idea the number of text messages I'd sent. Just like the other three times, the call went straight to voice mail. I shook my head.

"What about—?" Foster asked.

"Richards? I've got his number here someplace."

Foster placed a Post-it note on my desk. "I'll admit it, the Mindy thing has me worried too. Stella's a smart girl. I'm sure everything is fine. I'd just like to know."

Nodding, I dialed the number on the Post-it note. Richards answered on the third ring.

"Richards."

"This is Bernard Cooper. I was wondering if you've spoken to Stella today."

"This morning, why?"

"When this morning?"

"Why? Where did you send her?" Richards's volume rose.

"What are you talking about? I didn't send her anywhere." My eyes met Foster's.

"Sure you did," Dylan Richards replied. "She got a call early this morning. I don't know, like three o'clock or something. Hell, I don't remember. I went back to sleep."

My heartbeat quickened. "What the hell are you talking about? I didn't call her at three in the morning."

"Well, fuck, someone did. She took off."

I shook my head. "And you have no idea where she went?"

"Listen," Richards said, modulating his voice. "Tell me she said something about wherever she went once she got to the station."

"That's just it. She never came to WCJB. I haven't been able to reach her all day."

"How about her apartment?"

I shook my head. "What about it?"

"Maybe she went back there and fell asleep. It was early when she left."

I took a deep breath, my eyes still fixed on Foster's. "Foster's with me. We'll meet you there."

"OK, shit. I have a key. I can be there in forty minutes."

"Richards, I'm calling DPD to meet us." My chest clenched at my next sentence. "In case it's a crime . . ." I couldn't say it.

"Fine, I won't go in, but I'm knocking the shit out of that damn door. This better be some big fuck-up, or else . . ."

My neck straightened. "Or else what?"

"You know where you've been sending her. Don't you give a fuck about her safety?"

"Richards, shut the hell up. We'll be there with DPD in forty minutes."

"I am DPD. I'll have someone with me."

ONE WEEK LATER—STILL nothing. The evening at Stella's apartment had come up empty. I might not have liked Dylan Richards, but the man was a basket case. Between the DPD officers who'd accompanied him and ours, we'd had a shit-ton of officers there. He kept it together better than most would in his situation with his girlfriend missing, but once the crowds thinned he did little to hide the frustration and desperation on his face. I'd talked to him almost every day since.

DPD taped off her apartment and searched it thoroughly. Her laptop was missing. I'd seen it with her sometimes while she worked. All we could assume was that she took it with her that morning. Richards said he didn't know. He'd fallen back asleep after she'd left. No flash drives or backup hard drives were found.

The DPD forensics team was able to get her MAC address from her router. With that the team searched for her computer. All it would take to find it, would be for it to be turned on and connected to Wi-Fi. It hadn't been since the night before she disappeared.

Foster gained access to her personal and work e-mails as well as her search history on her computer at WCJB. The search history confirmed her research into Entermann's Realty and Wilkens Industries. She'd searched Google Earth, but specifics couldn't be found. When Foster went back in time he found her preliminary research into the property on Glendale Avenue in Highland Heights. It was what had prompted her to dig into Entermann's Realty. Foster said he'd seen a list of their holdings, yet it wasn't in her e-mail. We could only presume she'd deleted the e-mail to protect her source. Of course her e-mail trash was empty. One of the oldest and usually most reliable ways to back up information is to e-mail it to yourself. There was no evidence that Stella had done that.

The only other source of information was her phone. A call had been placed to her at 2:48 a.m. the morning of her disappearance. It had come from the assistant forensic pathologist at the Wayne

County Medical Examiner's private cell number. Dr. Tracy Howell claimed she and Stella had become friends and admitted to calling her and asking Stella to meet her at the medical center to see a patient. Unfortunately, the patient she mentioned had never been identified and was now in the Wayne County Morgue. There was an ongoing internal investigation at the medical center, but primary information indicated the patient had suffered a severe allergic reaction to pain medication. Anaphylactic shock had occurred before treatment could commence, and resulted in death.

No calls or text messages had been sent from Stella's phone the day of her disappearance. Calls from Richards, Foster, me, and Tracy Howell had been received but never answered. Some of us had left voice mails. Text messages had been received from Dr. Howell, Richards, and me. There was absolutely nothing else.

Her car had been found the day after her disappearance in a flat lot in New Center. The crime lab dusted it—nothing. Unfortunately, Stella had chosen one of the few lots in the New Center area without video or even picture surveillance.

Each day was worse than the one before. Two women working for WCJB were officially missing. Vanished from sight. Disappeared into thin air. While speculations ran wild, for those of us who knew them, it was devastating.

THIRTY-ONE

S ara

ONE MORNING IN JUNE, Dinah and I met Raquel and Elizabeth in the coffee shop before work. Since the Assemblymen needed to be at Assembly early, the night before at prayer Raquel had mentioned that we should start our day with friends. To my delight our husbands had agreed to this unusual impromptu outing. Standing at a tall table, I stirred cream into my coffee and half listened as the other wives chatted about nothing in particular. When something was said about the dark, my ears perked up.

I leaned over the table and spoke quietly. "I know I shouldn't, but I wish I remembered. I think it's cool that you do."

"I don't remember either," Dinah said. "I think I blocked it out."

Elizabeth sighed, her green eyes moist.

I reached out and touched her hand. "What's the matter?"

She looked up. "Nothing."

Raquel hugged Elizabeth. "Maybe we should go somewhere a little more private?"

Standing taller than her already tall height, Elizabeth swallowed and nodded.

"We'll see you later," Raquel said as she led Elizabeth away.

I turned to Dinah. "What was that? I've never seen Elizabeth that way."

Dinah leaned close. "I feel so dumb. I wasn't even thinking."

My eyes silently questioned.

"She's not allowed to talk about it, but she did open up once in prayer meeting. You must not remember."

"I don't, but if she said it in front of me once, would it be wrong if you shared?"

She wrinkled her nose. "I don't think so, but not here. Let's head over to the lab. Brothers Raphael and Benjamin will be at their meeting for a while."

Scooping up our cups, we moved out of the shop and toward the lab.

Once we were there, she exhaled. "Elizabeth loves Father Gabriel, The Light, and Brother Luke. She'll be the first to tell you that she has no regrets about coming to The Light, but once a year, around the time of her birthday, she gets sad."

I shook my head. "We don't celebrate birthdays." It was something I'd learned early on with Sister Lilith.

Dinah's lips formed a straight line. "That doesn't mean they don't happen."

I nodded. "OK, but why is she sad?"

"In the dark she has a sister, a twin sister. From what she said, they decided to follow Father Gabriel together, but after they did, her sister changed her mind. Elizabeth doesn't begrudge her sister that right. After all, we're all here because we want to be, but according to her, she never got the chance to say good-bye. Being twins and all, they were very close. She said she knows that the dark isn't death, but after Brother Luke told her that her sister changed her mind,

Elizabeth felt a loss, as if her sister died. Like all of us, Elizabeth was ready to give up everyone and everything from the dark. She just didn't expect to give up her sister. It bothers her the most around her birthday." Dinah shrugged. "Their birthday."

"Wow, poor Elizabeth."

"Please don't mention it to her. Of course, we were all glad we could help, but Brother Luke didn't approve of her sharing. As you know, Elizabeth is usually the poster child of obedience. Being corrected for her plea for help reminds her not to bring it up again."

Reminders!

I nodded. "Thanks for telling me."

THERE WASN'T much extra space within the walls of the community, but on the north end there were a few acres of woods with paths. When I first awoke from my accident it was the beginning of the dark season; now we were into full light. Though it never got warm at the Northern Light, it was considerably warmer near the end of June than it had been in November.

"Hurry up," Jacob teased as he ran ahead.

"I am," I said with a laugh as my feet pounded the hard dirt and my lungs filled with fresh air.

Lately Jacob had been required to be gone more, including for overnights. However, since the weather had warmed, whenever he was home, we tried to run together, either early in the morning, before our days began, or later, before dinner. The first time he'd mentioned running was the first time I remembered the memory I'd shared with Elizabeth six months earlier. Though Jacob said we'd done it regularly before, the first run since I'd awoken had been when the frigid temperatures finally broke in April. Two months later we were still running together.

Reaching the end of the woods, we came to the small grassy area just before the innermost wall. With the sky bright above, Jacob reached for my hand, and brought us to a stop. Looking out to the wall, I thought about running a longer distance. Not leaving, just having more room.

"I'd ask if we could go to the hangar and run where we had more space, but . . ."

"You'd rather not be eaten by polar bears?" he asked with a grin.

"Yes, that's a big deterrent."

"But," he teased, "just think how fast you'd run."

Smiling, I leaned into his embrace.

Now that I was no longer in what he'd called a crash course of remembering, I loved the way he was when it was just the two of us. His wit and humor made me laugh. That didn't mean he didn't correct me; it meant it wasn't often necessary.

As chosen, we had the responsibility of setting examples for the followers; thus in public we didn't show affection. However, running, especially in the early morning, allowed us more freedom. Despite being outside, we were alone. I rose up on the tips of my running shoes and kissed his cheek. "You know, I love this."

His features softened. "I know you do. So do I."

I sighed. "It's strange, but it's one of the few things I think I remember."

He kissed the top of my head and played with my still-short ponytail. "Who knows, maybe more will come back."

With my hand still in his, we began walking and I confessed, "I'm not trying to be selfish, but I miss you when you're gone. I wish you didn't have to leave so often."

"You know that I . . ." He'd mentioned that he'd been given more responsibility but couldn't tell me more.

I nodded. "I know you can't say and I'm not asking. But I've been wondering about something else."

"You have? That inquisitive, intelligent mind of yours scares me. Sometimes you're too smart for your own good."

I didn't say more; instead I pushed my lower lip out playfully.

Jacob kissed my pout. With sparkling eyes he said, "Go on. What have you been wondering?"

"Before my accident, did we ever talk about children?"

Jacob's feet stopped. When I looked up, his face was ashen as if all the blood had drained from his cheeks. "We did," he finally admitted.

"We did?"

"We decided that we weren't ready." He began walking again.

"We did, or you did?"

"Sara, even though that is questioning, it was a decision we made together."

I sighed. "Then I'd like to ask to revisit our decision."

He kissed my cheek. Releasing my hand, with a smirk, he lengthened his stride, and called over his shoulder, "If we hurry home, we could practice." He shrugged. "I'd want to be sure we had it right first."

Though I shook my head, I couldn't stop the smile that pushed my cheeks higher. I was confident we had it right, but there was always room for practice. In no time we were running side by side, back through the woods, while long beams of light shone down, and back to the community on our way home. As our strides took us closer to our apartment, I thought about the babies at the day care. I'd been going there lately to meet with a female follower. Often I'd hold and rock one of the babies as she did the same and we talked. At first the small humans had seemed foreign, but now I found myself excited to go there. Their soft skin and sweet smell woke something inside me. Maybe it was like it was for Jacob with me. I wanted to love someone so much that I took full responsibility for them, like he had me.

As Jacob helped me out of my running clothes, I contemplated the birth control medication that I took every morning. The idea of not taking it seemed more and more appealing. I'd probably receive correction for making that decision without Jacob's permission, but I knew my husband. Once he found out we had a baby coming, he wouldn't stay upset; he couldn't.

Once we were both completely naked, Jacob captured me in his arms and pulled me close. Though our skin was warm and slick from our run and the temperature wasn't cool, as my breasts flattened against his chest, goose bumps peppered my flesh and my nipples beaded. The scent of desire mixed with his normal leather and musk created an intoxicating concoction. Inhaling, I inclined my face toward his and chuckled. "You know I need to be at the lab by nine and you need to be at Assembly."

"An advantage of living in the community is that our commute time is minimal."

I shook my head. He was right. We both could walk to our destinations in less than five minutes.

Loosening his embrace, Jacob tugged my hand. With a sly grin and his sexy, raspy voice, he said, "I think we both need to shower."

"I thought you promised me a practice session?"

"I'm all for killing two birds with one stone."

As Jacob turned on the rain of warm water, the muscles in his arms, back, and tight, bare rear flexed, causing my insides to liquefy at the magnificent man in front of me. Only fleetingly did I recall the showers after my accident. At that time my husband's touch had been gentle but aloof, and he'd obviously been fearful of hurting me. No longer was he tentative—in any way. I was his to have and claim whenever he desired. Yet when he did, it was always with complete reverence, always confirming that I was willing and ready for him. He needn't have worried; just the sound of his raspy voice and the way his eyes shimmered with lust had me ready. I couldn't recall ever having had an issue with being willing either.

That didn't mean I wanted to forgo foreplay.

Under the warm spray, I leaned my head back as moans escaped my lips. With my breasts willingly exposed to his masterful inclinations, I ran my fingers through his dark hair and pulled his mouth closer. His stubbly cheeks created the perfect abrasion as a fever burned within me, making the water sizzle as it fell upon our hot skin. The sensations he produced as his tongue and lips teased my hardened nipples sent pulsations throughout my body. In time his ministrations turned to nips as he cupped my behind and pulled me tightly against him, capturing his hardness against my stomach.

No longer just ready, my body ached with need as my insides tensed to a painful pitch. "Please," I begged.

A resonating growl filled the shower as his fingers probed, no doubt learning just how ready I was.

One finger, in and out, and then two . . .

I tasted his salty skin as my tongue and lips kissed and sucked his bristly neck. My grip on his broad shoulders tightened as my body mindlessly moved to his touch. When my breathing quickened and I was ready to quake in his grasp, his strong arms lifted me, pinning me to the wet tile. As he continued his erotic assault, eliciting my pleasure, pushing me toward the edge, my legs tightened around his waist. Just before I fell to ecstasy, his fingers disappeared, and we came together.

"O-oh, God, Jacob," I moaned. My core clenched as I adjusted to accommodate his size. The delicious stretch filled me, electrifying every nerve in my body. From my fingers to my toes, sparks ignited.

"You feel so good," Jacob said. "I'll never get enough of being inside of you."

"It's where I want you," I purred.

His lips captured mine, swallowing my words and sounds. Our tongues danced to the song our bodies sang. He created the rhythm, but the melody came from both of us. The combination of his resonating hiss, my whimpers of desire, and the slap of skin against skin filled the shower with the indistinguishable sound of two people moving in sync and lost in one another. Up and down we moved, until the sparks he'd ignited detonated.

As I teetered once again on the edge, my breath stuttered and my legs tightened.

He didn't stop. He knew my body better than I did. He knew the signs that I was close. Nipping my breast, he commanded, "Come on, Sara, come for me."

Fireworks, volcanoes, and stars falling from the sky paled in comparison to the explosion.

I cried out as every cell inside me discharged, leaving me shattered, held together only by his arms. Holding tight, I clung to his neck as wave after wave rippled through me, instigating uncontrollable spasms. Another thrust and I opened my eyes in time to watch his handsome face go from strain to utter bliss. Seconds later Jacob's eyes met mine and I smiled.

Seeing him like this let me know just how much influence I had over my husband. He was in charge of our lives, but I held power too. With a sly grin, I admitted, "I may not be able to stand."

His smile grew. "I've got you."

Exhaling, I said, "I think you'll have to let me go. I'm not exactly ready for work."

"Oh, don't worry." He kissed my forehead. "I'll help you with that too."

My kisses trailed from his shoulder to his chest as he lowered my feet to the floor. "How did I get such a helpful husband?"

"Lucky, I guess," Jacob said with a smirk as he reached for my shampoo.

I felt my cheeks rise, loving his expression and the tone of his voice. I didn't know—and couldn't ask—about things on the Assembly or with his flying, but I knew that lately he'd seemed stressed. It wasn't anything he'd said, more what he hadn't. The only thing he'd shared was that Xavier, the pilot who came to the Northern Light, had been ill and until there was a replacement, there was more work for him and Brother Micah.

Though I wanted to help, without being disobedient and questioning all I could do was help him relax. Running was one way, but I witnessed his expression of pure bliss only after we'd come together as one. Even if I hadn't loved every second of making love to my husband—and I did—I'd willingly have given myself to see that.

As he massaged shampoo into my hair, the scent of flowers replaced the musk, and the warm water continued to rain.

"Do you think I could ever go away with you? So we wouldn't need to be apart," I asked.

Behind me Jacob tensed. I spun around, putting my small hands on his chest. "I'm sorry if I shouldn't have said that."

One side of his lips turned upward. "Don't be sorry for wanting to be with me. I love having you with me."

I exhaled and turned back around. "I know I have my job, and it couldn't be done without permission, but if I could, I'd love that too."

"No matter where we are, I love you." He kissed my neck.

As I craned my neck toward his lips, my heart was full. We kissed. "I love you too."

THIRTY-TWO

J acob

THE SMALL AIRSTRIP nestled in an unassuming valley of the Rocky Mountains was near Whitefish, Montana, as the crow flies. To drive from Whitefish to the Western Light required off-road vehicles. Accessing the Western Light's campus by land was almost as difficult as driving to the Northern Light, in Alaska. That was Father Gabriel's plan—keep them remote.

Passing the challenges Father Gabriel and the Commission had put before me, I'd finally earned the right to learn the specifics regarding the unique calling and activities of the Western Light. Not its fellowship or religious activities; those mirrored ours, as did the Eastern Light's. To the unsuspecting tourist or resident of the nearby ski towns, the Western Light was nothing more than a group of religious zealots who kept to themselves. Those people had no idea of the billion-dollar operation happening in their midst.

The Light's tax-exempt status, as well as the freedoms afforded by separation of church and state, kept all of The Light's campuses a mystery to outsiders. Father Gabriel might have stated in the beginning that God had given him visions of The Light's current greatness; however, even as an Assemblyman, I wondered if he had ever fathomed its current magnitude.

The Northern Light was the brightest, the most profitable. However, this campus, the Western Light, was doing better than many Fortune 500 companies, a fact most would disbelieve based solely on its outward appearance. The Western Light's deceptive facade was even more important than ours. Though driving to the Western Light was difficult, flyovers were much more common in Montana than Alaska.

While our community concentrated on the production of product, the Western Light had a twofold goal. Primarily it packaged and distributed the pharmaceuticals. Its second goal was production of Preserve the Light preserves. Most of the females of the Western Light worked around the clock—literally, in shifts—producing and canning preserves. The jams and jellies were made from local berries, grown in the community. The Western Light followers who weren't part of the chosen worked tirelessly in the gardens, the greenhouses, and the preserve plant, producing and canning. If they weren't working there, they were in the packaging plant, preparing the pharmaceuticals for distribution.

Production of the preserves never stopped. To the outside world it was the acceptable source of income for The Light. To those who were chosen to understand, Preserve the Light was the cover for the illegal distribution of pharmaceuticals created at the Northern Light.

Members of the Western Light's Assembly and Commission organized all the logistics. Father Gabriel had chosen the location of this campus perfectly, as Canada made the perfect market for low-cost medications. With Brothers Raphael and Benjamin's research, the pills and capsules created by the followers of the Northern Light were indistinguishable from those produced by mainstream pharmaceutical giants. Since Father Gabriel's followers worked not for worldly goods or money, but to maintain their standing in the community, production costs were minimal. The followers believed they were making the medications to help others.

They were, just not the others they thought.

When I first entered The Light, it was through the smallest campus, the Eastern Light, in Detroit. At that time I was led to assume that the production and sale of illegal drugs was the focus. Over the last three years I'd learned that illegal drugs were present, but only as the smallest piece of The Light's revenue pie. The crack and meth produced and sold through the Eastern Light were more of a diversion—Father Gabriel's backup plan. If the time ever came when the operation was discovered, each campus had enough paraphernalia to give the perception of a large illegal drug network. The investigation would satisfy the FBI and ICE, Immigration and Customs Enforcement. Though they would boast the closing down of a large illegal drug organization, in reality they would have stopped only the tertiary source of income.

Even the preserves made more profit.

Until my recent promotion, I hadn't known the breadth and scope of the entire operation, governed by Father Gabriel, on three campuses, with twelve Commissioners—four at each campus—and thirty-six Assemblymen—twelve at each campus. The hundreds of non-chosen followers were completely unaware.

Being Father Gabriel's pilot offered me access that others didn't enjoy. I had the pleasure of flying to Father Gabriel's mansion outside Detroit, though I was never invited up to the big house; I'd seen the telecasts that gave the appearance of mundane surroundings while knowing they were recorded in the large luxurious mansion. Keeping those secrets had been some of my first tests. Passing those first tests undoubtedly aided my rise to the chosen.

Sharing my knowledge wouldn't benefit anyone. It would result not only in my banishment, but also in the banishment of whomever I told, including other members of the chosen. I wouldn't nor could I risk that. Micah and I were the only followers at the Northern Light who saw things away from that campus.

Each challenge presented to me was a test or a stepping stone. The only way to access the knowledge of the inner workings of The Light was to succeed. With the addition of a wife, I hadn't only passed one of the final tests, I'd become vulnerable. That vulnerability made me less of a threat, less likely to breach The Light's trust.

That vulnerability was one of the reasons Sara's desire to have children could never be fulfilled. I couldn't increase my susceptibility. There was already too much at stake.

Over the past three years, each decision I'd made and each action had worked together to gain Father Gabriel's confidence. It also helped that Xavier had recently become ill. Since his replacement wasn't trusted enough to ship product, Father Gabriel decided that I was.

Finally I'd been entrusted to deliver a full order of pharmaceuticals. While I finished the transaction, from the depths of my jean pocket, my cell phone buzzed. Though the men before me were capable of appearing as nondescript as any member of The Light, they were undoubtedly professionals. Father Gabriel didn't use run-of-the-mill traffickers in his organization. This well-oiled machine required over-the-top devotion as well as top-notch performance. Kinks in the system were eliminated with the utmost proficiency. Without a doubt my phone could wait. I'd come too far to appear as anything other than completely devoted. I couldn't risk becoming an eliminated kink.

Under the cover of the hangar, my plane sat emptied of merchandise and fully refueled.

"Brother Jacob," said Brother Michael, the leader of this small party, offering his hand.

Though I was larger physically than Brother Michael, he'd been on the Commission of The Light from the beginning, and the aura of power and control that surrounded him was equaled only by that of Father Gabriel. He was one of the four founding fathers. While everyone within The Light was given a biblical name, only the founders had been given the names of archangels. According to Father Gabriel that was because, like the archangels, these three men and he were with God, welcomed into His holy of holies and His private sanctuary. Brother Raphael at the Northern Light and Brother Uriel at the Eastern were also among the founders.

Brother Michael's power didn't come only from his aura; the two large men on either side of him helped to maintain his standing. They obviously were more than members of the unloading crew. As Brother Michael and I discussed the transaction, his bodyguards made no attempt to conceal the weapons strapped to their sides. If I were to guess, each had at least one more gun strapped to the inside of his ankle. I knew I would, if I could, but delivering the pharmaceuticals unarmed was one of Father Gabriel's requirements. He said it was a show of faith to our brothers.

Even if I could, I wouldn't have argued. This was Father Gabriel's show and they were his rules.

We shook. "Brother Michael, I'll be sure to inform Father Gabriel that you inspected the shipment personally."

"Yes, do that, and let him know I'm pleased." Michael tilted his head toward the big guy on his right. "Brother Reuben has something for Father Gabriel."

I looked in his direction, my gaze scanning his large muscular frame. Whatever he had for Father Gabriel wasn't a payment. Actual money never changed hands. Untraceable overseas accounts kept people like Brother Noah at the Northern Light extremely busy. The billion-dollar operation had the whole checks-and-balances accountability thing happening. It involved accountants from all three campuses. That was the one part of the business I'd yet to learn. As far as Father Gabriel and The Light were concerned, money handling wasn't my thing, nor was accounting. I was first and foremost a pilot.

Brother Reuben reached inside his jacket, suspiciously close to his gun, and paused. The dramatization was for effect. I was the new kid in this assignment and no doubt was being tested at every turn. I nodded with a cocky grin, letting him know I didn't fall for his ploy, all the while praying he wouldn't shoot me before I made it back to Sara. Finally he removed an envelope from his jacket and handed it to me. The outside simply read Father.

"Thank you, Brother Reuben," I said as I took the envelope and turned back to Brother Michael. "Brother, is there anything else you'd like me to pass along to Father Gabriel?"

"No, everything appears in order." He stepped forward and patted my shoulder, sharing a grin of amusement at my reaction to Brother Reuben's show. "I believe this will work well. Father Gabriel's judgment has not been proven wrong yet. I'm sure we'll be seeing more of each other."

"Thank you, Brother, I'm honored to have been chosen."

"As you should. You've reached an honorable level within The Light in a short time. Keeping our chosen with us and productive is our goal. To that end, my brother, have you seen the forecast? It's been changing by the hour. Perhaps it would be better if you chose to stay here until tomorrow. Northern Light is a far journey."

I smiled respectfully, hoping the new vibration of my phone would continue to go unnoticed. "Thank you. My flight plan has me landing at Lone Hawk for the night. I won't be heading back to the Northern Light until morning." I wasn't sure if his invitation was another test, but my flight plans were set and clear. Even with a small plane, it was best to have records of arrivals and departures. Lone Hawk was one of my favorite airports, privately owned with few questions asked. Even so, I'd never land my plane there with a full load of product. Once I landed, I planned to buy supplies. I wasn't looking for anything to draw attention, only normal living-type stuff, things to make my stop believable. Besides, it didn't make sense to fly back to the Northern Light in an empty plane.

I checked my watch.

Yes, right on schedule.

"Very well, Brother, safe travels."

Once I completed my preflight checklist and was in the air, I checked my phone. It hadn't vibrated since I'd spoken with Brother Michael, and due to the recording device in the plane, I wouldn't be able to return a call until I landed at Lone Hawk. Above all, I didn't want to risk anyone from the Western Light questioning my ethics.

When the screen came to life my pulse quickened. I'd missed one call from Brother Benjamin's phone and five from a burner phone.

Shit!

After the incident with Brother Timothy and Sister Lilith, I'd set up an emergency chain of communication. The long and short of it was that I was simply gone from the Northern Light too much. Even if Father Gabriel believed that the entire episode with Brother Timothy and Sister Lilith had added to Sara's eventual success, I refused to allow anything like that to blindside me again. While having a wife increased my risks, with this system, I increased my odds. It was a gamble, but I believed Sister Raquel would help, if necessary.

According to the screen, it was time to cash in the chips.

Once I had the Cessna secured on Lone Hawk's tarmac, I searched for the manager, Jerry. He was a quiet man, friendly in an unobtrusive sort of way. I made my way back to a small apartment area near the back of the hangar. I didn't know if he lived there all the time, or just when he was working. Either way, I was happy when he answered my knock.

"Jacob, I saw your approved arrival on the CBP e-mail. Welcome back to the big city of Whitefish."

"Thanks, Jerry. I have some business in town and was hoping you had that truck here I could borrow. I'll bring it back in the morning, promise."

"No. Sorry. That piece of shit has seen better days." His furrowed his weathered brow. "But I'll tell you what, my old lady's Chevy Tahoe is sitting out back. She ain't going nowhere tonight. Besides,

I've got my new truck if she needs a ride. You're welcome to take the Tahoe into Whitefish."

"Thanks, Jerry. I owe you."

"Next time you're here, you can bring me some of that Preserve the Light jelly. The old lady goes nuts for that stuff."

"I'll do my best," I promised, taking the keys he handed me and heading toward the beat-up Tahoe.

If Raquel had used that burner phone, it meant only one thing: trouble, serious trouble. As we'd agreed, I could answer a burner only with a burner.

Before checking into the cheap hotel, I stopped at a gas station and purchased two burners. Something in my gut told me one wouldn't be enough. Once in the hotel room, I plugged them both in and recalled the telephone number I'd hoped I'd never need to call. I waited for the ringing to stop. Once it did, I asked, "Raquel?"

"Brother Jacob, tell me she went with you."

"What are you talking about?"

Her voice changed to a low whisper. "Sara. Benjamin said you asked the Commission about her going with you on some of your flights. Please tell me that you did it, you took her without permission, and she's with you."

I had asked the Commission, but I sure as hell wouldn't bring her on one of these trips. The last thing I wanted was to have my wife around Michael's goons. I took a deep breath. "Raquel, I left her in our apartment. She was in the kitchen cleaning up after breakfast." I tried to hide the trepidation. "She couldn't have come. I didn't have the Commission's permission, and besides, she was scheduled to work in the lab today."

"I know. Benjamin was the one who contacted me and asked if I knew why she didn't show up at the lab."

No longer content to sit, I paced the confines of the ratty hotel room. "That doesn't make sense." I searched for answers. "Was she ill? Have you checked in on her?"

"I went to your apartment. When she didn't answer, I used my key. She wasn't there."

"And you're sure this doesn't have anything to do with Brother Timothy or Sister Lilith? God help me!" I wasn't even trying to hide my distress any longer.

"I really don't think it does. At least nothing approved by the Commission."

"Why?"

"Because Benjamin said it wasn't mentioned during Assembly. He didn't know until he got to the lab. Then when I couldn't find her, he took me out to the pole barn." She muffled a cry. "I prayed, but sh-she wasn't there. Oh, Brother, I'm so scared."

My left hand held a fist of hair as I tried to think. "Talk to me, Raquel. Tell me what you're thinking. Because right now, all I can think is I need to get in the damn plane and confront Timothy and Lilith, the Commission, hell, even Father Gabriel. If Timothy came up with another reason to have her banished, a reason to get at me . . ."

"Brother Jacob, what if they didn't do it? What if it had nothing to do with Brother Timothy?"

Her words reverberated in my head. "What do you mean?"

Raquel took a deep breath. "I should have said something. I just knew she wanted—"

"Tell me!" My desperation sounded foreign, even to my own ears.

"I know Benjamin will punish me when he learns I didn't say anything." She swallowed, suddenly sounding more composed. "And he'd be right too. I should have told him, but . . . Sara's my friend. I didn't say anything because I didn't want to get her in trouble with you or the Commission and because I understand her desire for children."

I couldn't make sense of her words. "What are you saying?" My voice echoed against the dingy white walls.

"A little over a week ago, she and I were talking. She told me that the two of you were discussing children."

I nodded. "We were. She said she wanted one, but I'm not ready, not with my new responsibilities." Among other things that I can't explain. "What does that have to do with anything?"

"Sara said she hoped you'd change your mind if she became pregnant." Raquel paused. "She confided in me that she stopped taking her birth control. She didn't tell you . . ."

Her words trailed away as I doubled over, holding my stomach.

I was going to fucking throw up.

"When? How long ago?" My questions were barely audible over the mayhem in my head.

She'd stopped taking her birth control. It wasn't just birth control. It was the drug that specifically suppressed her episodic memory while allowing new memories to form. It was the unique creation of The Light and the foundation of why she believed she was Sara while having no recollection of being Stella Montgomery.

"Over three weeks now."

My heart fell to my feet and tears blurred my vision. "Oh, God, do you think? Did she say anything to make you think she remembered?" I couldn't even say it: I couldn't say her life before me, before us.

I hadn't wanted a wife. I'd avoided it, but from the first time I saw her, before she was brought to the Northern Light, before Abraham and Newton hurt her, before I lied to her, I fell in love with her. I fought it with all my might. That day in the cold, her injuries were supposed to be worse, but I couldn't let him keep going. I had to stop him. And then when I arrived at the hospital and her neck was bruised, I knew that Newton had hurt her more, and I refused to leave her again. I couldn't.

Raquel was speaking. ". . . didn't, not that I picked up on at the time. Now I'm not sure. And there's one other thing."

I nodded, trying to quiet the voices in my head, trying to still the chaos. "What?"

"When we went to the hangar this afternoon, Brother Micah said that Xavier's replacement, Thomas, had recently left."

"What are you saying?"

"Well, he's been in the community, unlike Xavier. I've seen him a few times."

I couldn't speak. Sara wouldn't risk punishment by speaking to a man she didn't know. She surely wouldn't leave the community with a man. My head moved dismissively from side to side. No, she wouldn't do that. She was just talking about children, about wanting us to be a family.

God, I was really going to be sick.

Sara had said she loved me. That was the last thing I'd heard her say. "Raquel, are you saying Thomas may have taken my wife?"

"Technically, yes, but I'm wondering if it wasn't an abduction." Silence filled the room. Finally she continued, "Brother Jacob, I'm afraid Sara may have gotten her memory back, or at least some of it, enough to confirm that she wasn't Sara. Benjamin and I haven't said anything to anyone. We know what Sara's leaving will do to you with the Commission. They've already met today. Tomorrow Benjamin said he'd have to say something if Sara wasn't back. But when he does, Benjamin said he'd remind the Commission that you requested permission to take her.

"Do you think you can find her and bring her back?" Hope came back to her voice. "If you do, you can tell everyone that you took her. They won't know she left."

"Find her . . . ?"

My entire fucking world was gone, exploded, imploded. Years of work and sacrifice threatened, hell, most likely ruined. And while that should have been my focus, it wasn't, not really. All I could think about was Sara. If she'd remembered, if she'd figured it out, then she undoubtedly thought I was responsible and knew I'd lied— that we'd all lied. "Raquel, if she remembers . . . she won't want to see me."

"I remember."

I didn't know what to say.

"I've known for a long time," she continued. "When my memories returned, Benjamin told me the truth and I chose to stay. That's what I was praying would happen with Sara. Brother Jacob, Sara loves you."

"Sara, Raquel. Sara loves me. If you're right, if she remembers, then I'm not looking for Sara. I need to find Stella, and I suspect Stella hates me."

"Think about it. I remember the Eastern Light. What will happen if The Light finds her first?"

A cold chill ran through my body. "If you remember, then you know what will happen."

Raquel cleared her throat. "Brother Jacob, I'm completely out of line and I'll pray about it, I will. If you choose to tell Benjamin, I won't deny it, and I'll accept whatever punishment he deems necessary. But I'm breaking the rules by asking you to question everything, no, I'm begging you . . . please, go to Detroit and bring Sara home."

"How?" I asked. "How did you know she's from Detroit?"

"Because that's where I came from—the Eastern Light. Isn't that where we all come from?"

I took a deep breath. "If I make it back to Northern Light with Sara, we never had this conversation. If I don't, we never did. No matter what, it never occurred. You know what would happen if the Commission learned that you withheld information from them."

"I can't lie to Benjamin. I trust him."

I nodded. "That's between you and your husband. I'll pray too. Destroy the phone you used. I hope we see you again."

"Me too. Godspeed, Brother Jacob."

The line went dead, and seconds later the phone that I'd been holding in a death grip struck the wall and, leaving a dent in the plaster, shattered to pieces. Picking up the largest piece, I pulled out the battery and the small SIM card. Then I dropped the remaining parts and, using the heel of my boot, smashed them to bits. With each stomp I contemplated my next move.

I was so fucking close to finishing this, to reaching the end. Three long years. But . . . now . . .

I knew without a doubt where she'd try to go, whom she'd try to reach.

Nearly a year ago when I'd seen her in Dearborn outside Detroit, she'd been with him. She had been so happy, smiling and holding his hand. They had been walking through a sidewalk festival and laughing. I remembered the look I'd seen in her eyes. It took months before I saw a smile even close to the one she'd given to him. She'd trusted him.

Fuck!

Even if I did reach her before The Light found her, she wouldn't trust me. If The Light got to her first, there wouldn't be a question of what they'd do. My question was about Dylan Richards.

What would he do? Would he do it again? Would he do what he'd done last October? If she contacted him first, would he willingly hand over his girlfriend in exchange for his pathetic existence? Would he once again deliver Sara to The Light?

Once a dirty cop, always a dirty cop.

I knew that.

What I didn't know anymore was what kind I was.

Taking a deep breath, I recalled the number I'd memorized and stored away. I steadied my hand as I fired up the other burner phone and dialed. Running my fingers through my hair, I listened to the rings.

Special Agent Adler, my handler, answered on the fifth one. "Agent McAlister?"

"Yes, sir," I answered through gritted teeth.

"Fuck! We haven't heard from you in over two years. Tell me you're calling because you've got the evidence. Tell me to get the bureau ready, that you're ready for the raid. Tell me you've got what we need to bring Gabriel Clark down."

"Special Agent, we have a problem."

TURN THE PAGE FOR PART II
AWAY FROM THE DARK

PART TWO
AWAY FROM THE DARK

Forever is composed of Nows.
—Emily Dickinson

CHAPTER

THIRTY-THREE

S ara
More than a week earlier

THE GRANULATION WAS OFF. From what I was seeing, that had to be the answer. I wasn't sure why it had caught my attention or whether I should mention it to Brother Raphael or Brother Benjamin; however, the more I scrolled and clicked, the more apparent the problem became. From what little I'd picked up over the months I recalled working in the chemical lab, I understood the medications we created allowed Father Gabriel's vision to be shared with the world.

Due to the energy constraints at the Northern Light, most of our electricity coming from the hydropower, we were forced to use dry granulation in the manufacturing of the pharmaceuticals. If the granulation of this new medication was off, slightly larger than that of its model medication, it could affect the absorption rate. I'd overheard many of Brothers Raphael and Benjamin's formulation discussions.

The difference in the weights of the finished products was what caused me to question.

"Sara?"

Why am I questioning?

"Sara!"

Small beads of perspiration dotted my brow as my research all but drowned out the sound of Dinah's voice. I reasoned that with most patients this minor difference might not be a significant issue, but I also worried that in others it could be life-threatening.

"Sara, what are you doing?"

Dazed, I looked away from the computer screen into Dinah's concerned expression. My coworker, friend, and Assembly wife sister had an expression of sheer terror as she scanned the screen of my computer.

"I'm . . ." My words faded away as I looked from the report beside the keyboard to the screen. My mouth dried. I wasn't in the program I was supposed to be in. I wasn't adding the data and quantities I was supposed to be adding.

My pulse suddenly quickened. "Oh, Dinah, I don't know what I was doing."

She looked toward the wall and my eyes followed hers to the clock. It hung near the ceiling and was simple, plain, with a round silver frame. It reminded me of the clocks in my elementary school when I was a child.

When I was a child!

I recalled a clock in my past. It was the first thing I could recall in nearly a year.

Shutting my eyes, I tried to see beyond the twelve numbers and the hands in my memory. As if it were right in front of me, I saw it. I even saw the skinny red second hand running circles around the black minute and hour hands. I blinked twice, wishing for more of the scene to materialize and at the same time fearing that it would. Below the clock from my childhood was a large green blackboard.

Wait, that didn't make sense. Blackboards weren't green.

Besides, my elementary school would've been in the dark, a place that was gone to me forever. How then could I remember that clock?

Dinah was speaking, and finally her words broke through my thoughts. ". . . Brother Benjamin will be back from Assembly. What will he say when he sees you've not completed your assignment, but taken the liberty—"

I moved my head back and forth as I exited screen after screen that I didn't recall opening. "You're right. I don't know what I was doing. It was because something in the numbers seemed wrong, like it didn't fit. I was curious. I started looking . . ." I pulled my lip between my teeth. "I'll confess." My head hung in shame. "To Brothers Benjamin and Jacob."

Dinah's arm moved protectively around my shoulders. "We still have a few minutes. I'm not saying you shouldn't tell Brother Jacob. You should. But if I help you, maybe we can get the data entered before Brother Benjamin gets back from Assembly. Besides, Brother Raphael won't be here for another hour. He still has the Commission meeting. Depending what Brother Benjamin wants us to do, I'm sure we can get this entered before then."

I let out a long breath. "Thank you, Dinah. I'm not even sure how I knew what I was doing. I don't know. It was just—" I knew the answer. It was the same problem I continued to battle. It was my curiosity. "I didn't want anything to be wrong. Father Gabriel's mission is too important."

Its importance was real. We all believed in his mission.

Dinah pulled a high-backed stool from her workstation up next to mine. The wheels easily glided across the smooth cement floor. "Do you want to read or enter?"

I pulled the correct screen back up on the computer. "I'll enter. You read. Start with yesterday's production . . ."

It was only a few minutes past ten when Dinah stopped reading and asked, "Sara, how did you know how to get out of our program? I mean, we don't know any of the passwords."

As I tried to recall, the memory was a blur, as if someone else had taken control of my movements. My lip disappeared between my teeth. I wasn't trying to be deceitful or cunning. What I'd wanted to do was to help, to figure out why the weights weren't matching. Finally I replied, "I don't know. I don't remember."

It wasn't like me to be secretive, but as I answered, I willingly shadowed the truth in ambiguity. Brother Benjamin had created this program. I recalled entering Raquel's name and *05*. Raquel had told me once that she and Benjamin had been together here at the Northern Light for five years. It was a guess, but I'd been correct on the first attempt. From that moment on, I hadn't thought, I'd just clicked and scrolled as if propelled by a sense of inquisitiveness that felt familiar yet foreign.

I replied to Dinah the way I did because if I confessed to Brother Benjamin that I'd been outside my program and he changed the password, I'd never be able to go outside it again. And though my conscience weighed heavily upon me, the yearning to keep access and learn more was too strong to ignore. Therefore, as we worked to complete my early morning duty, I simultaneously contrived a way to confess without disclosing everything.

As the last number was entered, the door to the lab opened and Brother Benjamin came inside. The summer months at the Northern Light required less outerwear than the cold, dark months. Brother Benjamin hung his light jacket on the row of hooks near the door and ran his hand through his hair.

"Good morning, Sisters."

"Good morning, Brother Benjamin," we answered in unison.

His brow was furrowed as if he were deep in thought. I knew that things had been stressful with the Assembly lately, and Jacob had been spending more and more time away at other campuses. I didn't know the particulars, only that it had something to do with Xavier, The Light's other pilot, being ill, and a new pilot helping.

Swallowing my shame at my unusual bout of disobedience as well as an unusual, overwhelming desire to hide my behavior, I nodded to Dinah, who squeezed my hand. "Brother Benjamin," I said, "may I speak to you about something?"

The creases in his forehead deepened. "Is this a private matter? Would you like me to call Jacob?"

My natural reaction was to shake my head, yet my training was too strong. I lowered my eyes. "If it's your will. In the meantime I'd like to tell you about something that happened this morning."

With my head down, I couldn't see his expression.

"Sister Dinah, would you go to the coffee shop and get three coffees?"

My chest heaved at his calm tone. This was my chance. If I confessed outside of Dinah's hearing, I could do it without admitting to everything.

"Yes, Brother," she said, giving my hand another squeeze.

Once the door closed, Brother Benjamin asked me to continue.

I lifted my gaze. "This morning, I was entering the data like I always do. Well, the products, batch 3F789, the weight seemed wrong."

His lips formed a straight line.

"I know it isn't my place to question. I'm not questioning." Silently I said a prayer to Father Gabriel that Brother Benjamin wouldn't tell Jacob I had been questioning. "It was an observation. I went back to previous orders. The weight isn't off by much, but it's not the same. If the quantity is equal, the weight should be too."

Though I waited for his reprimand, it never came. Instead he said, "Show me."

I nodded, swallowing what little saliva I could muster, and walked back to my workstation. The report with the data we'd successfully entered was on my screen as I moved the mouse and brought my computer to life. I pointed to the numbers. Brother Benjamin stepped closer and stared at the screen. Without asking he took my mouse and began clicking and accessing past reports. The entire time I stood motionless, afraid that he would look at the search history and learn that I'd accessed information outside my scope.

It was bad enough that I'd done it, but to not confess and be caught would be worse.

"Sara, copy and send me the last three weeks of reports on 3F789. I know you have other work to do, and I don't want to take your computer."

"Brother, I'm sorry if . . ."

"Don't be sorry." He sounded genuine. "This is Father Gabriel's vision. We don't want there to be a problem."

My exhalation of relief filled the lab.

"Sara, we won't say another word about this."

I wanted to ask whether that meant he wasn't going to tell Jacob, but I stopped myself, suddenly aggravated by the whirlwind of unruly questions and thoughts infiltrating my mind.

The mental image of the clock had me confused. The simple, insignificant timepiece was burrowing into my consciousness. How did I know it was a memory? Maybe it was something I'd seen at the Northern Light. After all, there was a school here. Children went to day care at five weeks and began school at four years.

That didn't answer why the image had expanded—why I now envisioned myself sitting behind a small wooden desk with my name scrawled on colorful paper taped to the upper edge.

This line of thinking was wrong. I'd been taught that. I needed to confess to my husband and study Father Gabriel's word more diligently.

CHAPTER

THIRTY-FOUR

S ara
Two days later

EACH WEDNESDAY NIGHT, everyone on the Northern Light campus attended service, but before it began I needed to meet with a follower at the day care. She and her husband had arrived at the Northern Light at about the time of my accident, and she'd requested help with her transition. Her husband was under Jacob's supervision, which left her walk in The Light to me.

As I walked from the lab to the day care, I told myself to focus on Sister Priscilla and forget the fog of uncertainty that seemed to have settled around me. Strange visions plagued my thoughts. I planned to talk to Jacob. He could help, except he was still gone, and I hadn't had the opportunity to confess my actions at the lab or my thoughts to him.

Whatever was happening with The Light had him gone more often and for longer periods of time. I didn't even think he'd return tonight, as services on the other campus would have already started. All I could hope was that he'd be back to the Northern Light some-time tomorrow.

The reality was that Jacob's schedule—like everything else—was up to Father Gabriel.

My thoughts went back to Priscilla, the female follower I was about to meet. We'd been meeting once or twice a week for a few months. I tried to do for her what Sister Lilith had done for me after my accident, recommending lessons for her to study and talking about Father Gabriel's teachings. Part of my duty as an Assembly-man's wife was to remind her of her place and role as helpmate to her husband.

Though Dinah's and my workday was done at the lab, the non-chosen followers' workdays lasted longer. As I made my way inside the large metal structure situated near the school, the voices of young children filled my ears. As soon as the children could speak they were taught to recite Father Gabriel's word. I smiled at the sound of repeated verses and edicts. No doubt these children would grow to be strong soldiers and workers for The Light.

My boots clicked on the concrete floor as I passed partition after partition, making my way toward the youngest followers. Some classrooms were allowing free time, which I knew from my visits was precious to the young children. As little faces turned my way, "Sister Sara" echoed around me.

Even the children knew the chosen. Though perhaps it was prideful, my heart grew a fraction at each recognition. I'd spent many hours getting to know the wives and children assigned to Jacob as an Assemblyman. In my heart I hoped they saw me as a friend and confidant as well as an Assemblyman's wife.

Once I entered the infant room, Priscilla looked up and her eyes smiled. It wasn't her entire expression, but I saw a sense of relief as I approached.

"Sister Priscilla, can I help you for a little while?"

"Oh, Sister Sara, thank you. Thank Father Gabriel. I know not to complain, but today has been"—her words trailed off—"it has been a challenge, but one I'm happy to conquer."

The baby room wasn't nearly large enough for the number of occupants. Apparently the followers were taking "Be fruitful and multiply" quite literally. There were two and three babies in each crib; some had bottles propped while others cried, waiting for their afternoon meal. Thankfully, not all were anxious. Some were sleeping, somehow immune to the wails reverberating off the walls.

Taking it all in, I shook my head. How had I never before noticed how many babies there were, or how short-staffed the day care was?

I went directly to a chubby little boy I'd held many times before. His cheeks were red and his nose runny as his little chest heaved with cries. As I lifted him, the weight of his diaper caught my attention. "Priscilla, I believe he's wet."

She nodded. "Father Gabriel set a limit on the number of diaper changes per day. It's designed to teach the children control. Unfortunately, little Tobias must have had an upset stomach. He's already used his daily allotment. And while maybe I shouldn't have used them so early, he was very messy."

I shook my head in disbelief. "Tobias is an infant. He's what? Three months?"

"Four."

"When was his last diaper change?"

Tears teetered on Priscilla's lids. I wasn't sure whether they came from my questioning or her own frustration.

"About four hours ago. I-I can't..."

"How many changes per day are the children allowed?" My question came louder than I intended and more selfishly than Priscilla could possibly understand. I wanted a baby—for Jacob and me to have a family. I understood Father Gabriel's reasoning for the day care, but control? These were babies. They needed comfort, not control.

"I-I don't..."

My shoulders straightened. "I'm a member of the chosen. Answer me."

"Three. If more are needed, the family's credits are reduced and the parents must put in extra hours at the plant to make up the difference. If they don't, other credits are cut." Her explanation came quickly and quietly. "Sister, Tobias has two other siblings. His mother asked that I not exceed his limit. It's my fault, I shouldn't have changed him so many times this morning."

My lips formed a straight line and an internal battle raged. Had I never heard this before? Why did it suddenly upset me? It must be my desire for a baby. My maternal instinct was rearing its ugly head.

The stacks of cloth diapers filling the bins below the only changing table in the room caught my attention. "There are plenty of diapers." As soon as I spoke I realized my error. Priscilla might be a female, but questioning Father Gabriel's decree was unacceptable. "Perhaps"—I looked down to the calmer child in my arms. Simply the act of holding him and swaying my body back and forth had settled his cries. I lifted my cheeks in a weary smile—"perhaps Tobias will be fine until his mother arrives."

Priscilla took a deep breath and pushed strands of hair away from her face. "Thank you, Sister. Sometimes I wonder . . ."

This time tears fell from her eyes.

I reached for another baby and tucked one in the crook of each arm. Sitting on one of the two rocking chairs, I smiled as the babies' eyes closed. "You can talk to me, Priscilla. It isn't questioning to ask another woman. What do you wonder?"

For the next thirty minutes I rocked the small humans in my arms as Priscilla fluttered around the room taking care of the other babies. She spoke about her studies and answered my questions. She also confessed her uneasiness with some of the ways in which her life had changed since she and her husband joined The Light as fully committed followers.

Though I couldn't admit it, I envied her perspective. She could compare life in the dark to life in The Light. My accident nearly nine months ago had taken that from me.

Priscilla never voiced disappointment in their choice, only a sense of disillusionment. I asked all the right questions: Did she love The Light? Did she want to follow Father Gabriel? Did she believe in his word? Did she love her husband and trust him with their life decisions?

These conversations had been going on long enough in Priscilla's transition that I knew I should tell not only Jacob but also Elizabeth. As new-follower coordinators, Elizabeth and her husband, Brother Luke, knew what to do. When lingering signs of doubt occurred, there was a prescribed course of action.

The last question I voiced—Did she love her husband and trust him with their life decisions?—caused a faint flicker of shame. I hadn't trusted Jacob with the decision to stop my birth control. I'd done it on my own.

Maybe that was the cause of my new uneasiness. I felt guilty. After all, with each hour it seemed as though I continued to amass new transgressions that I would eventually need to confess to my husband.

By the time I left the day care and made my way to our apartment, my head and heart were heavy. Though I didn't want to experience correction at Jacob's hands, I longed for the peace that came with giving my concerns and infractions over to him. If only he'd come home tonight, but he wouldn't. He was with Father Gabriel at another campus. I think he'd said the Eastern Light.

Priscilla's talk of the dark had me wondering about the image of the clock. I didn't know whether the image was real or whether it was something that had been planted by a benign conversation with one of my sisters. If there were more childhood memories, I couldn't retrieve them. Only the classroom with the clock above a green chalkboard, a vision that had now expanded to include an elegantly swirled cursive alphabet separating the board from the clock. The teacher in this image was a mystery, but on the small desk before me was my name carefully scrolled. It wasn't on the desk, but on a piece of colorful paper. The S was tilted to the right and connected to the a and the r and the a.

Even though I wasn't trying to remember . . . the images continued to appear behind my eyes, creating a fog that distorted my reality. Our apartment building appeared different—the same as it had been, yet more run-down. No. More basic. Unpainted siding showed the effects of the Alaskan weather. My shoes scuffed the worn boards of the stairs as I made my way up two flights to our apartment.

I shook my head, trying to clear away the uncertainty.

Sighing, I made my way inside and collapsed upon the sofa. Rubbing my temples, I closed my eyes and wished for Jacob.

"Stop it!" I said aloud to no one.

Our empty apartment mocked me.

"I don't want these thoughts." My head ached with an uncommon pain behind my eyes. If only I could go to bed and forgo service, but that wasn't an option. I had to move forward.

My mind swirled with a whirlwind of thoughts; pieces and fragments unable to create a complete image floated about as service concluded and Father Gabriel's image faded from the screen at the front of the sanctuary.

"Sara, are you not feeling well?" Raquel asked in a whisper.

I forced a smile as I stared at my closest friend. "I think I'm tired, and I miss . . ."

Raquel's forehead came close to my own. "You miss Brother Jacob. Of course you do. I could ask Benjamin if you could come over for a little while. We could have coffee."

The mention of her husband's name reminded me of what I'd done a few days before at the lab, and that I hadn't had the chance to confess my exploration to my husband. "Thank you. I think I'd like to go home. Maybe I just need a good night's sleep. I don't sleep as well when he's gone."

"I can't imagine. From the day Benjamin and I were married, I've never had to sleep alone."

"Were you married in the dark?"

Raquel's eyes grew wide as she peered from side to side. "Sara!" Her voice was a hushed whisper. "We're in the temple, surrounded by the chosen." She lowered her tone even more. "Not the place to discuss such things."

My lips formed a straight line. "I'm sorry," I said with an edge to my voice. "I didn't realize I was speaking to Elizabeth."

The recognition in her dark eyes told me she understood my remark. Elizabeth was our friend; however, she never strayed from the straight and narrow. Besides her job with new followers, she was the poster child for obedience. She would never mention the dark, anywhere, and definitely not in the temple.

"What?" Elizabeth said as she turned toward us, her green eyes shining and her lovely red hair pulled back to the nape of her neck. "Did I hear my name?"

Raquel shot me a just stay quiet look and scoffed. "Sara and I were discussing going back to our apartment building. Will you and Luke be walking with us?"

"That's up to Luke," she answered without reservation. Then her eyes narrowed. "But Sara, you can't go alone."

I sighed. "I walk alone during the day. It's July. It's daytime all the time."

She shook her head dismissively as the other Assembly and Commission wives were claimed by their husbands one by one. Beyond our chosen seating I noticed the other followers, mostly couples leaving the benches and heading toward the doors. There were so many people I didn't know. Being chosen was a blessing and a curse. The followers I saw had the pleasure of sitting with their spouses, yet they all looked exhausted.

When I thought about the hours Priscilla and the others worked, I understood.

Elizabeth was still talking. ". . . if it's light or dark in the sky. Brother Jacob left instructions for either Luke or Brother Benjamin to accompany you. You can't argue."

The pain behind my eyes had intensified, making my response less censored. "I'm not arguing. I'm tired. That's all."

"She misses Brother Jacob," Raquel volunteered.

The judgment present only a millisecond earlier on Elizabeth's face dissolved. "Oh, dear. I'm sorry. Of course you do."

"Ladies." Brother Benjamin's deep voice interrupted our conversation. "It's time to head home."

Beyond Brother Benjamin was Brother Luke. We all nodded in agreement and followed the men from the sanctuary out to the evening sunshine. Though the two men continued to talk, I allowed myself to fall into silence. It was the obedience I'd been taught, but more than that, it was my private way to make sense of the rush of uncertainty I was now feeling. I wanted nothing more than to climb into bed and wake revived.

In the morning I'd feel like my old self.

That was my last thought as I closed my eyes with my head on Jacob's pillow. His signature leather scent surrounded me as I fell asleep.

CHAPTER

THIRTY-FIVE

S ara

SHRILL SCREAMS ECHOED throughout our dimly lit bedroom, accelerating my heartbeat and pulling me from the terrible nightmare. I waited for more, until the realization struck. The screams were my own.

"Jacob?" I called, my voice shaking with dread as I reached for my husband. Instead of reassurance, my fingers met cold empty sheets. He was gone—still away at another campus.

What just happened? Was it a dream?

I clung to the covers as I puffed my cheeks and slowly exhaled. While each breath helped to still the chaos, the exercise wasn't enough.

Who am I? Who is he?

Jacob's questions from months ago came back. They were my security. They'd worked before.

I am Sara Adams and my husband is Jacob Adams.

Pushing the images from my dream, or nightmare, away, I imagined Jacob's comforting embrace. Slowly I threw back the down comforter and willed the cool air to soothe my perspiration-drenched skin. From the way my heart galloped in my chest, I might have been running a marathon, not sleeping.

In my sleep I'd been battling to escape a vehicle, and then an explosion of heat.

It had been a dream, I reassured myself—a nightmare. The accident I'd had, nearly nine months before, had been different. I couldn't remember it, but I'd been told that I'd been injured and gone unconscious. In the nightmare I had been out and away from the wreckage.

I shook my head.

It seemed so real.

In my dream I hadn't been able to see past the darkness, yet I'd known I wasn't injured.

My arms surrounded my midsection as the memories replayed like pictures in my mind. Someone was hurting me—purposely harming me, and there was a voice—a deep voice.

Jacob's voice?

No. He wouldn't hurt me.

My entire body shuddered as goose bumps peppered my skin. Sitting upright, I reached for the bedside lamp. With trembling fingers I turned the knob and my eyes adjusted as the soft light combined with the sun's perpetual summer glow.

I closed my eyes and tried to concentrate on Jacob's questions.

Who am I? Who is he?

This time I said the words aloud, praying that if I spoke the truth, the images would disappear. "I am Sara Adams. He is my husband, Jacob Adams." I pulled myself from the bed and walked to the bathroom. Turning on the light and the faucet, I cupped the cool water and splashed my face. As I reached for the cup and began to fill it, a metaphoric dam that had been constructed to hold back my past burst.

My mind was flooded—no longer with simple images, but with scene after scene.

For the first time since I could recall, I knew the woman in the mirror. I knew me.

The colorful paper taped to my childhood desk hadn't read Sara.

The S was still there, but the rest of the name was different.

I knew my own soft blue eyes and blonde hair.

I recalled its length and the way it used to flow over my shoulders.

Though I met my own gaze for only a millisecond, I also saw my own panic—not only that, I felt it. In the pit of my stomach I knew that what I'd just experienced hadn't been a nightmare. It was my reality—my past, the one I'd thought was forever gone.

At the realization, my muscles lost their ability to grip. Water splashed about the vanity and onto the mirror as the cup I'd held fell to the base of the sink. No longer capable of supporting my weight, my knees buckled and I slid to the floor.

"Oh my God! Is this real? It can't be." I spoke to the empty bathroom. "Jacob? The accident. It didn't happen. Did it?" I longed for him to make it right, to take it all away.

Acid bubbled from the depths of my stomach. The dinner I'd eaten long ago refused to stay down. My nightgown clung to my moistened skin and I lunged for the toilet. Like an old film reel, the scenes continued to play behind my tear-dampened eyes: the accident, my awakening, my crash course as an Assemblyman's wife, our temporary banishment, my reminders . . . nearly a year of my life—of Sara's life. Everything within me ached as my body convulsed. Over and over I heaved, purging all I'd known, been told to believe, told to remember—all the lies.

When the running water finally registered, I stood, rinsed my mouth, and splashed my face again. This time, as I stared at the woman in the mirror—at myself—the terror I'd seen was gone, replaced by betrayal. Hurt and anguish washed over me, crashing down, drenching my body, soul, and mind.

I tried to fight it, to argue with myself. *If only Jacob were here to help me understand.*

Turning off the water, I slid back down the wall and settled on the cool tile. Hugging my knees to my chest, with tears coating my cheeks, I recreated the timeline that was supposed to remain forever lost.

For the first time in nearly a year, I could answer Jacob's question—I knew.

"I am Stella Montgomery!" My verbal declaration reverberated against the walls as my heart ached.

It had to be real.

Lies! I'd been fed lie after lie. And like the ice chips after my awakening, I'd accepted each and every one.

Sobs replaced my voice as I fought to make sense of what had happened. Nothing made sense. All the people I held dear—my husband, friends, sisters, and brothers—were all a sham.

Lifting my left hand, through blurry vision, I stared at the simple gold band. I wasn't Sara Adams, nor was I married. My chest ached as my heart begged me to be wrong, to believe the life I'd lived was mine, but I couldn't.

I *am Stella Montgomery, an investigative journalist for WCJB in Detroit.*

I knew that was true.

I had a career and a life, with a real family and friends. I recalled blue eyes—piercing blue eyes. I had a boyfriend named Dylan, Dylan Richards, who was a detective.

My breathing hitched at my internal monologue warning me not to question. It wasn't my place. As a woman I needed to accept. I should pray to Father Gabriel and confess to Jacob.

The hell with that!

Questioning was what I did—what I had done. It was part of my job. No wonder this had been so difficult.

Holding the walls for support, I walked back to our bedroom.

Our bedroom.

Again I hugged myself as my now-empty stomach twisted. Jacob and I weren't really married. I wasn't against premarital sex; memories of me with Dylan confirmed that. But as I stared at the bed where I'd made love with my husband, a new question surfaced.

Have I been raped?

I shook my head. No. Despite the lies at every turn, my heart confirmed that I hadn't. Never had Jacob forced himself on me, but then again, were the lies he'd fed me any better?

Had he? Did he know the truth?

I couldn't think about that . . .

Shit! The nausea. What if I'm pregnant with his child?

I didn't even know his name. Mine wasn't Sara; maybe his wasn't Jacob. I couldn't have the baby of a man whose name I didn't know. Pulling my robe tightly around me, I looked at the clock—nearly four in the morning.

With the whirlwind in my head, I knew I'd never be able to fall back to sleep. Instead I slowly walked through our quiet apartment, taking in everything anew as I passed down the short hallway, through the living room, and into the kitchen. With the drapes opened, even at this early hour, the summer's perpetual sunlight allowed me to see our world. Everything around me was my past, the only one I'd thought I'd ever have, the one Jacob and I had created together, the one that only a few hours ago had held the potential for a promising future.

No longer.

Deceit tarnished everything, everywhere I looked.

My hands trembled as I stood and turned slowly, mindlessly, around and around. Everything was wrong. I was surrounded by lies.

How had it happened? Why had it happened? Who had done this to me?

I grasped at a shred of hope.

Perhaps Jacob was disillusioned too. Maybe he believed we were truly married. Could we both be victims?

I wandered to the table and sat, not sure which of my thoughts to believe.

"Dear Father Gabriel," I said between sobs, "please take away these impure thoughts. I confess I remember my life before . . . no, I confess I have allowed evil . . ."

I took a deep breath.

The thoughts weren't evil; The Light was.

I stared at the stove where I'd cooked dinners for my husband. I was a good cook, even though I remembered that as Stella I didn't cook. As Stella I hadn't been ready to co-own a fish, yet in this life that I'd been forced to live, I'd been ready to have a baby.

Why had I been forced to become someone I wasn't?

Yet I was . . . I'd been Sara. None of it made sense.

Standing, I walked toward the cupboards and reached for a bag of decaffeinated tea. As I began to fill the teakettle with water, I decided I wanted coffee. I needed coffee. I'd gotten the decaffeinated tea in preparation for pregnancy. With the confusion and hurt filling my heart and soul, I refused to consider that pregnancy was possible. After all, I'd been without my birth control for only . . . I did the math . . . almost two weeks. People didn't usually get pregnant the first month.

How had they done it? Why had they done it? What would happen now that I knew?

While the coffeepot began to sputter, I made my way to the kitchen table and collapsed back into a chair. I needed more than coffee. I needed to get away from the Northern Light and back to my life. I needed to find a way to be free from The Light.

The Light!

The incomplete slivers of scenes were forming complete movie reels. I, Stella, had been investigating The Light. It was the last thing I could recall doing in Detroit.

Other facets of my life came back: my parents, my sister, Dylan; Bernard, my boss; Tracy, my friend; and Foster, my coworker.

Although the lies that I'd been fed and willingly consumed sickened me, to have a past—when I'd had none—excited me. My head ached as the gaping holes that I'd accepted would forever remain void were closing with record speed, filling with a real past that had been hidden away.

Or was it more lies? I couldn't be sure.

If I didn't belong here, why was I here?

And then it hit me. I wasn't the only one here.

I thought about Tobias, all the other babies, and the children who called my name from the depths of the day care. I envisioned the followers, the chosen and the ones I didn't know as well—the women, men, children. How many of them were living lies? How many were lying?

My friends . . . more heartbreak. Did they know they were lying?

My thoughts were all over as my eyes roamed our small apartment and I clenched my teeth.

Father Gabriel lives as we do—bullshit!

Bloomfield Hills. The new images clawed at my newly founded belief system: Father Gabriel had a huge, sprawling, multimillion-dollar mansion in Bloomfield Hills with a landing strip.

My heart continued to crumble.

For the past nine months I'd been conditioned to turn to Jacob, to seek not only his approval but also his guidance. Admittedly, there was still part of me that wanted that. I wanted to close my eyes in his arms and give this all to him, but the newly awakened part of me knew I couldn't.

Jacob had told me stories of our past, a past I now believed had never existed. Our entire relationship was based upon lies that he'd perpetuated over and over until I believed his every word. Had he invented those stories, or had he been told to tell them to me? He'd said more than once that he had rules to follow too.

Despite the evidence, I wanted to believe that my husband had done what he believed.

My head fell onto my folded arms as I willed my new thoughts to stop.

He wasn't my husband.

An internal battle raged between desire to know and willingness to accept. My heart told me that Jacob loved me and would always do what was best, but the images, the memories, all painted another picture.

Grudgingly I acknowledged that Jacob had to be part of this deception. After all, not only had he played into the lies about our being married and about our past together, but also he flew planes. He flew Father Gabriel. He was with him right now at the Eastern Light.

A new thought surfaced.

Could the Eastern Light be Detroit, more accurately Bloomfield Hills?

If it was, Jacob knew about the mansion. He knew about the landing strip. He knew that Father Gabriel didn't live as he professed.

My recently emptied stomach continued to twist. Not only did I need to get away, but also on the off chance I was pregnant, I needed to get my baby away from this madness.

I peered out the window at the bright, clear summer sky. I was in Alaska—Far North, Alaska. There were walls and polar bears. This wasn't only a physical prison but a mental one. I had to think. I had to plan. I had to tell my heart to forget the man who'd been my comforter, disciplinarian, and rock. For my survival, my possible child's, as well as others', I needed to think.

I poured a cup of coffee, and as the cream swirled through the darkened liquid, questions continued to swirl within my consciousness. As flickers of my former self fought through the uncertainty, I realized that I no longer needed Jacob's approval to question. I granted it to myself. My mind went to my parents, my sister, and

Dylan, and how they must be suffering with my disappearance. It had to be as it had been with Mindy's disappearance.

Shit! Mindy!

My hand fluttered over my heart. Mindy was here too, with me. I was confident. I remembered the blonde woman who'd spoken to Elizabeth a few months ago. Now it made sense that she'd looked familiar. She wasn't Mary; she was Mindy Rosemont, my best friend from the dark. However, just as I hadn't recognized her, she hadn't recognized me. More than likely her past had been erased, leaving her without memories of her true identity.

How many of us were there? How many of the women and maybe men had been programmed?

Sitting back at the table, I reached for the warm cup of coffee and timidly moved it toward my mouth. I'd learned to be careful. Since heat no longer registered with my fingertips, I'd burned my mouth before. Heeding the steam's warning, I sucked my lip between my teeth and lowered the too-hot coffee back to the table. With a sickening realization, I rolled my wrists and stared at the ashen flesh on the tips of my fingers.

Oh my God!

I was one of those women—the ones with the burned fingertips, the ones from Dr. Tracy Howell's table at the Wayne County morgue. The women who'd ended up dead.

A new chill ran through me, and I pulled my robe tighter. I wasn't investigating a life-and-death story—I was living it!

CHAPTER

THIRTY-SIX

S ara

AFTER WAKING EARLY to my revelations I spent most of the day trudging through the thick fog of confusion. Everything took effort and concentration. Tasks that had become second nature now seemed foreign. Something as simple as making my own breakfast set my mind back. As the slices of bacon fried in the iron skillet, I had flashes of smoke and firemen.

I questioned the validity of each recalled image. Were these memories, or were they thoughts that fleetingly appeared real? Without warning doubt would creep in. What could I believe? Was I recalling my life or was it my imagination? As my bacon crackled in the pan, I reasoned that since we didn't have firemen at the Northern Light, the images of men with heavy coats and helmets were real—a memory from the dark.

Here, in case of fire, there was an understanding that every male follower would do what was needed. I wouldn't know that if I hadn't overheard Jacob speak of it to one of the followers under his supervision. The threat never seemed to be a concern, but given that most of the construction—besides the wall surrounding the community—was wood, fire could be devastating.

Methodically I managed to complete each task: breakfast and work at the lab.

I was keenly aware of everything I did and said, weighing each word of my conversations, no matter with whom. As I entered the data into my computer, waves of urgency flowed through me, an undeniable desire to obtain information. Questions such as I hadn't allowed myself to ask in months bombarded my thoughts. Why had I been placed in the chemistry lab? Did anyone know what I'd done before? What was the truth behind the manufacturing of medications by the followers? Was there more to it, or was it purely philanthropic?

With my fingers hovering above the keys and Brother Benjamin's password repeating in my brain, I wasn't sure what I wanted to find or even what I was looking for. And then a moment later, I'd return to my prescribed task with guilt squelching my inquisitiveness and reminding me of my place as a woman and a member of the chosen.

The entire process—from the elation of memories to the doubt and shame of questioning—was infuriating, unsettling, and tiring.

By lunchtime I was exhausted. Needing a change of scenery, I asked Dinah to accompany me to the coffee shop for a sandwich. The new surroundings didn't help. Something about my revelations had changed everything. No longer did I see a thriving small town, but a compound or camp of sorts. I fought the need to lift my eyes and truly study the world in which I lived.

I'd been taught to keep my eyes cast downward. Yet I longed to stand and stare as I had alone in my apartment. I wanted to take in the buildings along the dirt-packed streets and paths. They now seemed solid, yet basic. While some, like the coffee shop and school, were made of sheet metal, most were made of wood like the pole barn.

The investigator in me who was trying to break free made connections I'd never before stopped to consider. Jacob had told me that near the power plant, just outside the walled community, was a small mill where followers worked to convert hundred-year-old trees into lumber. How else would they have built this place? It was in the middle of nowhere. Flying in all the construction materials would have been difficult and more expensive. From what I could remember of the planes Jacob had shown me, neither one was large enough for that.

"Do you ever think about the people Father Gabriel's medicines help?" I asked, as I nibbled on my cold turkey sandwich.

Dinah shrugged. "I guess not really. I mean it's a wonderful thing his ministry does. I can't imagine not having all of my needs met."

"Are they?"

"Are they what?"

I leaned closer. "Are all of our needs met?"

Dinah nodded. "Mine are. That's what Father Gabriel teaches. Any needs not met aren't necessities but desires."

"Yes, that's what he says. What do you think?"

"Sara! I don't know what's gotten into you, but I don't question Father Gabriel's teaching and neither should you."

"I'm not questioning it. I'm curious."

"Are you without food, a roof, or clean clothes?" she asked.

"No."

"How about your spiritual needs?"

"What about them?" I replied.

"Are they met?"

I swallowed a sip of my water. "Yes, of course."

"It isn't our place to have curiosity."

"I know." I hung my head. "I think I'm just missing Jacob." Thank God I had that excuse. Otherwise I didn't know how I'd be able to explain my odd behavior.

As we were about to exit the shop, a group of three female followers entered, their heads bowed as they scanned the room with their eyes. All of their heads were covered with scarves, something I'd seen on the women who worked in the greenhouse that grew fresh fruit and vegetables for our daily consumption. It wasn't until the pale-blue eyes of one of the women looked in my direction that I recognized her. They were eyes I'd known for years. I had no doubt. I was looking at my friend Mindy Rosemont.

Without thinking I stood and moved in her direction. The pain at her disappearance, the visits to the morgue, all came back. A lump formed in the back of my throat as my arms ached to hug her. She was alive, here, and safe. Before I could process or filter my thoughts, I reached for her hand.

"Mi—" I stopped the name from rolling from my lips as I registered the look of shock on her face.

"Sister, did I . . . is there a problem?" she asked, her voice soft and weak. The other two women stood dumbfounded, staring at me, as did Dinah.

My mind raced. I remembered seeing her before at the temple, speaking with Elizabeth. I had to think of something.

"No," I reassured her, hoping I'd see any recognition in her eyes. I didn't. "I-I—" I struggled for words. My audience listened expectantly. "Sister Mary? Correct?"

"Yes," she replied, her eyes now down to where I held her trembling hand.

"Please look up."

She did.

"Sister Elizabeth asked me to speak to you. May we talk for a moment?" The lie left a disgusting taste on my tongue, but I couldn't think of anything else.

Mary nodded, first to me and then to her friends. I looked over to Dinah, whose eyes were wide with wonder.

Shit! I needed to think of something to tell her too.

"Sister," I said toward Dinah, "I'll be back to the lab in a few minutes."

"I can wait."

"That's all right. This won't take long. Elizabeth asked me to do her a favor." My explanation seemed to satisfy Dinah, because she simply smiled and walked toward the door.

Letting go of Mary's hand, I walked back to the table where Dinah and I had eaten our lunch. "Please, have a seat."

"I-I don't have long," she said as she obediently lowered herself to the chair.

Of course she didn't. She must be on her break from her workday.

"I don't want to interrupt your lunch, and I want you to know that nothing we say will be repeated."

"What?"

"On occasion I help Sister Elizabeth and Brother Luke. You can only imagine how busy they are." With each word and sentence the lying became easier.

"Sister Elizabeth has been very helpful."

She continued to stare toward her hands, which were now on her lap. The sight of her with the two other women had brought back an image of women crossing the street in Highland Heights. I couldn't think about that now.

I lowered my voice. "Mary, please look at me. Do I look familiar?"

Mary peered upward and back down. "Yes."

My heart leaped.

She went on, "I've seen you in the temple, with the other chosen."

And it sank.

My long-ago conversation with Elizabeth about abusive husbands came back to me. I scanned Mindy's face and body. Her long-sleeved blouse covered her arms, while jeans covered her legs. But thankfully I didn't see any signs of abuse on her face. "Are you all right?"

She nodded.

"Are you sure?"

Her pale-blue eyes glistened with moisture. "Are you going to tell Sister Elizabeth something? Will it get back to Adam?"

"No!" I lowered my voice. "No, Mary. There's nothing wrong. I'm not telling Elizabeth anything. I'm sorry. I didn't mean to scare you."

"B-but I thought you were speaking to me for Sister Elizabeth?"

"I am. Just take a minute and think. Have we met before?"

"Before?" she asked. "I'm sorry. I don't remember before." She looked up. "You mean in The Light? We aren't allowed to talk about the time before that."

"Do you remember the dark?" I asked in a whisper, hopeful and suddenly curious about whether others had had their memories taken away.

"No. Adam says that we were married before we came here. I don't remember that either."

I tilted my head. "Did something happen to affect your memory?"

Her lower lip disappeared between her teeth in a familiar habit. "I don't remember. Adam said I fell. I woke in the clinic about a year ago. That's all I know."

My heart beat rapidly as I contemplated this happening to all the women of the Northern Light. "Did you hurt yourself when you fell?"

"Yes, I broke my arm and hurt my head." She fidgeted in her seat as she sought out her friends. They were seated at another table, eating. "I-I am sometimes quite clumsy. Was there anything else Sister Elizabeth wanted you to ask me?"

Guilt settled heavily in my stomach.

Lies, questions, and now I was stopping her lunch.

My eyes went to her friends' table. "I'm sorry. I didn't mean to make you miss your lunch. Did they get you food?"

Her head moved back and forth. "We only have rations for our own meal. No one can get more than one."

She and I were sharing the same life, yet it wasn't the same. Mine was chosen. Often Dinah or I would make a run for sandwiches for everyone at the lab. How had I not fully noticed or understood the hierarchy in The Light before?

"Oh. Then please go. I'm sorry, Mary. But the next time you see me, please don't be afraid of me."

"I-I'm not. You seem nice. Sister Elizabeth is nice and so is Sister Esther, our overseer's wife. I don't know any other chosen. I don't even know your name."

I tried to smile. "My name is St-Sara, Sister Sara. Please feel free to speak to me anytime."

She looked back at her hands, waiting for me to dismiss her, as my stomach twisted. "If you hurry, will you have time to eat?"

"Yes," she answered quickly.

"Then please go. Thank you for talking to me."

"Thank you."

I sat silently as she hurried from the chair to the line and then the counter. From the depth of her pocket, she removed a slip of white paper. It was her lunch ration ticket.

More questions came to my mind. Did everyone experience an "accident" upon arrival? Why? How many hours a day did she and her friends work? What did they do in the greenhouse? What did others do in the production plant?

Walking back to the lab, I contemplated the dichotomy of Mary and Mindy. No longer was she the confident woman who'd been my roommate, classmate, and best friend. Somehow The Light had turned all of us into Stepford wives.

When I entered the lab, Dinah looked up at me, silently questioning my unusual behavior. It wasn't until we were alone that she finally asked, "Elizabeth? What did she want you to do?"

I licked my lips and lifted my shoulder in a shrug. "She wanted me to ask that follower about a memory she'd had."

Dinah's nose scrunched. "A memory? Of what? And why you?"

My eyes widened. "I don't know. Elizabeth is our friend. I can't imagine her asking me to do anything that I shouldn't. Can you?"

"No. It seems odd."

"I thought so too. It doesn't matter. The follower didn't remember."

Though Dinah seemed satisfied, I silently said a prayer. *Please, Father Gabriel, don't let Dinah say anything to Elizabeth.*

Before the end of our workday, Brother Benjamin came to my work desk. "Sister, this morning at Assembly, I learned that Jacob will be returning this afternoon. He'll be home by dinner."

A smile spread over my face, before I had the chance to respond differently. "Thank you, Brother Benjamin. That's the best news I've heard in days."

He winked. "Why don't you go home early and get ready for his return. I'm sure he's missed your home cooking."

Although I was suddenly worried about facing him, the man who had worked so hard to make me believe I was his wife, my body and mind were conflicted. Truth be told: I had missed him.

THIRTY-SEVEN

J acob

I'D CALLED our apartment telephone as I passed the final gate to enter the community. It was nearly five o'clock, and I hoped that Sara would be home from work. On this trip I'd been gone for three nights. I didn't like leaving her for hours, much less days.

This trip had been spent solely at the Eastern Light. While Father Gabriel did whatever he did in his mansion, Micah and I stayed down past the pool and tennis court in the small outbuildings.

When I'd first started this assignment, I'd considered investigating the big house, until I saw the cameras. Every move Micah and I made on the property, or at least inside the outbuildings, was watched. Late at night I'd sit on the steps and watch the big house. In the darkness I was hidden, but the large mansion was visible, its windows often lit, the house looking like a Christmas tree. Even from the distance of the outbuildings, I could see the multitudes of people celebrating with our leader.

Although my job was to infiltrate The Light, my training told me that I could accomplish my goal only by following Father Gabriel's rules. He specifically forbade my or Micah's presence closer to the mansion. I wouldn't have gotten where I was today if I'd broken that simple an order.

Whenever I was at the Eastern Light, I rarely left the grounds. If I did, it was to attend temple. Usually Elijah, an Assemblyman from the Eastern Light, drove us. This past Wednesday, Brother Uriel, the senior commissioner at the Eastern Light, had been with him. During our drive to and from the estate, I'd had the distinct impression I was being interviewed. If I was right, hopefully, my duties would be increasing and so would my knowledge of The Light.

I believed that I was very close to learning more about the pharmaceutical distribution. Each new piece of information was another step closer to getting away from this assignment and resuming my real life.

While that thought of leaving The Light used to motivate me, now it also saddened and worried me. As I walked up the stairs toward our apartment, the most recent piece of my life that demonstrated my obedience and commitment to The Light—my wife—was the one piece I couldn't imagine living without.

I took a deep breath and pushed thoughts of the dark and life beyond The Light away. Reaching for the doorknob, I inserted my key, waited for the sound of the lock, and opened the door.

Standing precisely where she'd been told to stand was the most beautiful woman in the world. Though her head was bowed, with her hair pulled back to a short ponytail, I could see her raised cheeks. I reached for her chin and brought her light-blue eyes to mine.

"Mrs. Adams, I've missed you."

Her head tilted and her eyes closed as she brushed her cheek against the palm of my hand.

"I've missed you."

The stress of the assignment, the tension of the flight, everything disappeared into the melody of Sara's voice. As soon as I entered the apartment, the aroma of something cooking brought to life a different hunger from the one brought on by the sight and touch of my beautiful wife. I pulled her close and kissed her soft lips.

Almost immediately I reached for her shoulders and stepped back. With her at arm's length, my dark eyes narrowed as I searched her face. It had been only a second, but something seemed off—different.

"Sara?" I evened my tone. "Is there something you need to tell me?"

Her eyes widened and then dropped.

"I've missed you," she said. "I don't like you being gone for three nights."

There was more. I sensed it. Taking her hand, I led her to the couch. "Tell me. Do you want me to ask again?"

Her breasts heaved with deep breaths as her shoulders straightened. "Two days ago, at the lab, I found an error. It wasn't my place to find it. I wasn't looking for it, but once I noticed it, I did more research . . ."

I didn't interrupt as her confession came one word on top of the other. While she spoke I prayed to Father Gabriel that whatever she'd done didn't warrant correction. If it did, I would do it. However, after my being away from her, the last thing on my mind was punishment.

". . . Brother Benjamin said he was glad I found it. He said we wouldn't need to mention it again, but I knew you needed to know."

"Was Brother Raphael involved?"

She shook her head. "Not with me. I don't know if Brother Benjamin spoke to him. It was never mentioned again, but Dinah saw me looking into it. She had to help me catch up with my work. Well, she didn't have to—she offered."

"Was this before or after you told Brother Benjamin?"

"Before."

I reached for her hands, neatly folded on her lap, and felt the slight tremble. "Sara, look up at me." Obediently she lifted her eyes. "Tell me again what Brother Benjamin said."

"He said it would never be mentioned again."

I lifted her hands to my lips. With each kiss of her knuckles, the tension melted from her grasp, and I looked back up to her trusting gaze. "It was right of you to tell me. We won't mention it again."

The tips of her lips moved upward.

"Thank you, Jacob."

"Now, what do you have cooking? It smells wonderful."

As if I'd taken the weight of the world from her shoulders, she bounced up from the couch and headed toward the kitchen, the menu she'd prepared spewing forth from her lips. I listened to not only her words but also the sound of her voice.

Over the past nine months I'd fallen for my wife. Part of it was undoubtedly the training and manipulation of The Light. But that wasn't all. I had an overwhelming desire to protect her from the darkness that lurked within The Light.

Father Gabriel's word taught each husband to bear the weight of his family. It was my place. Yet there were times when I wondered what it would be like to be in a more equal relationship, one where I could share my burdens as she'd just done.

It wasn't that Sara didn't do everything she could to help me. She did. It was that I couldn't talk to her. I couldn't talk to anyone. That had never bothered me before. Now, each time she confessed a misdeed and gave it to me, I longed for the relief she obviously felt.

According to Father Gabriel's teachings, men received that sense of relief through confessing to the Assembly or the Commission. My case was different. Confessing my anxiety over the termination of my FBI mission could not happen. It was up to me.

THIRTY-EIGHT

S ara

MY HEART BEAT FRANTICALLY as I rambled on about our dinner, something about wanting Jacob to have a home-cooked meal. I wasn't sure of what I was even saying. I was more aware of what I wasn't saying, what I wasn't admitting. Somehow in this messed-up scenario, this pretend, ridiculous, outrageous life I'd been sentenced to live, the man listening to my ramblings knew me. He knew my thoughts without my so much as saying a word. Only seconds after he arrived, he'd known there was something, something I hadn't said.

That new realization shook me to my core.

Jacob knew me, in many ways perhaps better than I knew myself.

Yet he didn't know the real me. He knew the me he'd created.

It was such an odd thought. As I continued to talk about food, the lab, and anything else I could think of, I wouldn't allow my mind to dwell upon the ramifications of his intimate knowledge.

I fought the urge to confess my memories. As bizarre as that sounded, it was a real battle. The investigator and independent woman I'd once been knew that telling Jacob or anyone in The Light was dangerous, perhaps even a death sentence. Memories of bodies in the Wayne County morgue worked to keep my confession at bay. Yet the conditioning I'd experienced for the last nine months kept the words *I remember the dark* on the tip of my tongue.

As Jacob reached for my hand and blessed our meal, the carefully prepared food lost its appeal. A sheen of perspiration dotted my brow as I worried I wouldn't be able to stop the words.

What if I admitted to memories in my sleep?

What if he asked and I couldn't help myself?

My internal battle raged throughout dinner and as I cleaned the kitchen. I spent more time than usual assuring cleanliness, purposely avoiding what I knew was coming. Jacob had been gone for three nights. The way his warm hand encased mine even after he blessed the food and his soft lips met mine when he entered the apartment alerted me to his future intentions.

I tugged my lower lip between my teeth, contemplating our immediate future. If I confessed my newfound knowledge, or recovered knowledge, as an Assemblyman, Jacob would be bound to take my confession to the Commission.

Would he condemn my memories as lies? Would he punish me for entertaining such thoughts? Each question added fuel to my concerns.

I wanted to believe he'd listen and help. My heart wanted that. Yet my inquisitive mind feared the worst. At best he too was a pawn and wouldn't believe me. At worst he was intimately involved in the lies, and my knowledge would be a threat.

If I were to survive and find a way out of the Northern Light, I needed to continue to maintain the farce that I was Sara Adams, the content Stepford wife of Assemblyman Jacob Adams.

Wringing the excess soapy water from the dishcloth, I decided to take another swipe at the countertop. Just as I was about to turn back toward the counter, the signature leather-and-musk cloud announcing my husband's presence penetrated the scent of my dish soap. I'd been too caught up in my thoughts to hear his approach. I closed my eyes as his strong arms surrounded my waist and his lips neared my neck.

"I've missed you."

His deep voice tugged at my heart, while the warmth of his embrace tore at the flimsy walls I'd constructed in an effort to keep him away. My head fell back against his chest as my pulse raced. I'd always had the option to tell him no, yet I never had.

If I did now, would he suspect something was different?

Butterfly kisses skimmed my skin as the scruff of Jacob's tightly trimmed beard heightened my senses.

My head told me the truths. We weren't really married. He was part of the lie.

The words that hours ago had been loud and convincing grew dim as Jacob's hands began to roam.

The dishcloth dropped back into the soapy water as I ran my hands over his forearms. Jacob not only knew me, he knew my body. With the perfect combination of baritone words and ministrations, my insides began to respond.

Agreeing to him, to this, was what I needed to do to survive.

It was the mantra my consciousness tried to recite.

Convince him nothing is different. Don't hesitate. He will know. I heard the words though they weren't audible.

It was interesting the deals one made with oneself in an effort to excuse what could be perceived as unacceptable behavior. After all, I was about to sleep with a man who wasn't really my husband, a man who'd lied to me, punished me, and yet my body was willing—more than willing. As I slowly spun toward him, my arms encircling his firm torso, I pushed my new revelations out of my mind and concentrated on the man who wanted me.

As he led me down the hall, I didn't think about the deception or the lies. I thought about the excuse I'd given others for my unusual behavior—I'd missed Jacob.

Later in the night, while the heavy curtains kept the ever-shining summer sun from our room, Jacob pulled me against his chest and sighed. His breath moved across my hair as his heart beat against my back.

"Did anything else happen while I was gone?"

In the afterglow of our lovemaking, I battled against my training. In his arms I longed for the openness we'd shared and the relief that came from complete honesty. And then, just as quickly, I reminded myself that it wasn't real openness or honesty—not on his part. If it had been, he wouldn't have lied to me.

"I'm not sure why you keep asking," I replied.

His chin moved over my hair as he shook his head at my slyly worded question. I couldn't help but smile as I turned toward him.

"That wasn't a question," I confirmed.

He kissed my forehead. "No, Mrs. Adams, it wasn't. But I could infer—"

"You could," I said with a hint of laughter, trying to steer him away from his initial question. His use of my surname sounded so familiar, the falseness of it barely registered.

"If I did, after I took matters into my own hands"—he playfully cupped my behind—"I might say that you seemed different somehow when I first got home. When did the incident at the lab occur?"

I took a deep breath as I lowered my chin against my chest. "Monday."

"Hmm."

Though I wondered what that meant, I knew not to ask.

"I see," he said.

I shook my head as I closed my eyes. Maybe if I stayed awake I'd know what he meant. Yet if I stayed awake, I risked saying more than I wanted. Even though I hadn't been completely honest, in his arms my lids grew heavy and Jacob's breathing evened. In no time at all we both drifted to sleep.

As a week passed, each day was more difficult than the one before. Each day memories came mixed with emotion. I'd be working at the lab or doing a mundane task such as sorting our laundry, and something from the dark would infiltrate my thoughts. Some memories were benign: my apartment or Dylan's house. That was always the way they began, the prelude to more, my fish (his name was Fred), or Dylan's backyard and the way he grilled steaks or salmon in the warm Detroit air. Some were so intense; they were more than images, also sounds and smells. The authenticity of them made each one difficult to dismiss.

Even in the summer, the outside air at the Northern Light held a chill. I found myself longing for the oppressive Michigan humidity I used to detest.

Somehow I learned to shut off the old me when I was with Jacob. I'm not sure how I did it, but I did. I concentrated on him, on us. Whenever the old me tried to break through, I became hyperalert, fearing a change in Jacob's expression, afraid he could see my internal battle raging. Maybe it was simply paranoia, or perhaps it was real. Either way, I worried constantly that I'd give myself away.

My other battles came around female followers. As time passed I deduced that those women who recalled the dark, like Elizabeth, had come to The Light of their own volition, while others, like Dinah and Mary—Mindy—had come as I had, forced to accept a life they couldn't question.

As we all pressed our fingers into the prayer sponge and I contemplated our lack of fingerprints, the women in the morgue fueled my desire to leave The Light. The world needed to know what was happening.

I was an investigative journalist. Fate had somehow given that job to me. I had the responsibility not only to expose this travesty but also to rescue my sisters and the children of The Light.

While I used to look forward to my visits to the day care, now entering the doors and seeing the small trusting faces broke my heart. The babies and children hadn't chosen this life. They were prisoners behind the campus's walls as much as we all were. I couldn't decide about the men. I wanted to ask whether they'd all come freely, or whether any of them were here as the result of an "accident." Of course I couldn't.

As days passed, the old me found ways to glean information.

I spoke less and listened more. As Jacob spoke to other men, I bowed my head and took in as much as I could. While I sat quietly at the coffee shop, retrieved our groceries, or did laundry, I listened. Since we'd all been trained to leave the dark in the past, I learned little about that, but I did pick up other things.

At one point Raquel mentioned medications. When I first woke, I had been given many of them. I didn't want to ask in front of Elizabeth, but the simple comment that I might not have noticed before now had me wondering. Did The Light possess medication that made us more adaptable—more accepting? Obviously they had something that had taken away my memories while allowing new memories form. Since the only medication I took regularly after leaving the hospital had been birth control, I concluded that in those pills was where I'd been receiving the memory suppressant. It wasn't until I stopped taking the birth control and after the medication had time to leave my system that my memories came back. If The Light could do that, then I assumed that anything was possible.

Since the return of my memories, I was constantly on edge. Though I'd been pretty diligent, speaking about my birth control was one of the glaring mistakes I'd made. Thankfully it had occurred with Raquel. I told myself that I could chalk it up to the building stress or perhaps a sense of friendship, but whatever the cause, once the words were out of my mouth, I feared the worst and prayed for the best.

I hadn't meant to say anything.

With each such instance, my fear and paranoia grew.

I had a plan.

I would leave the Northern Light with Jacob.

Over a month ago I'd mentioned that I wanted to travel with him. That was what I'd wanted, then—to spend more time with him. Now I wanted to get away. He'd never told me that he'd petitioned the Commission; however, one day at the lab, Brother Benjamin let it slip.

My plan was to leave with Jacob. I didn't care where he took me. I didn't care whether it was to Fairbanks for supplies—he did that often—or to another campus. I'd already deduced that the Eastern Light was Highland Heights. No matter whether it was the Western or Eastern Light, wherever we went had to be less remote than the circumpolar North.

Once Jacob flew me to another destination, my plan was simple: I'd find a phone and call for help.

As days and nights passed, I contemplated whom I would call. I considered my parents, Bernard, and Dylan. No matter how I looked at it, Dylan was the best possible alternative.

I recalled an Internet thread I'd found while researching The Light. It was about a woman who claimed to have been taken by a cult.

Even today that word sent shivers down my spine.

The woman on the thread claimed that the authorities didn't believe she'd been held against her will. They claimed her story was tainted because she'd abused illegal drugs before her abduction. I hadn't. I reasoned that my story would be more believable. And even if local authorities didn't believe me, Dylan would, and he was a detective. More than that, I couldn't wait to let him know that I was alive.

The last memory I had of my old life was from late October of last year.

As I sat in service and listened to Father Gabriel preach, it took all my control to smile, nod, and bow my head. What I really wanted to do was scowl and ask how he could do this to so many people—people who not only followed but also trusted him.

With each passing minute, the truth became clearer. I needed to get out of here!

S ara/Stella

IT WAS MORNING, and Jacob had already left for the hangar. He'd told me that he was heading to the Western Light and wouldn't be back until tomorrow. The pressure to gain freedom was mounting. With our breakfast dishes clean and more than an hour before I needed to report to the lab, I decided to take a walk. Each day the weather was warmer. Though I hoped the fresh air would help clear my head, I'd also become addicted to exploring and witnessing the community through my new perspective.

Each glimpse of the world around me showed a new paradigm. No longer did I see a bustling community. Now, as an investigative journalist, I saw things as they were. Our coffee shop and stores were simply warehouses, similar to the pole barn, divided by partitions and filled with only the supplies the Commission deemed necessary. The walls surrounding the community no longer served as our protection; they were our cage, designed to keep us all peacefully within.

I wondered whether they truly were necessary. After all, it wasn't as if, on the edge of the circumpolar North, we followers had many options for leaving. Nevertheless, the walls made any notion of escape impossible.

I recalled from when Jacob and I had been sentenced to our temporary banishment at the pole barn that the only acceptable way to pass beyond the walls and the multiple gates was within a vehicle. No one walked away.

For that reason few people had access to vehicles. Primarily it was the chosen men and those followers who had clearance to work beyond the walls, those who needed to access areas such as the pole barn for supplies, the power plant, or the mill.

The world where I'd been forced to live became clearer with each passing day. Our buildings were mostly accessible by foot. Snowpack paths in the winter and hard dirt paths in the summer connected one to another. The apartments where we lived were closer to the temple and main buildings than those housing the non-chosen followers. While ours were in what looked like three-story barracks, theirs were in what resembled dorms on a run-down college campus. Each building was sufficient to protect people from the elements, not constructed for visual appeal. Since vehicles weren't needed to get from housing to work or community centers, when not in use, they were parked away from the main cluster of buildings.

As I took my morning walk, I made my way past the followers' housing and toward the outskirts, the direction in which Jacob and I often ran. Because it was at the opposite end of the community from the greenhouse and production buildings and more remote, fewer people were in this area. The solitude gave me a sense of freedom, allowing me to lift my eyes and truly see.

It wasn't until I reached the place where many vehicles were parked that I noticed what I believed to be Jacob's truck, parked along a row of vehicles. It caught my attention because Jacob was gone. He would have left it at the pole barn and hangar. Making the only logical deduction, I figured that Thomas, the new pilot, was the one who had driven it into the community.

At nearly the same moment:, my heart began to thunder in my chest: Thomas was my ticket to freedom.

I scanned the area. Seeing no prying eyes, I hurried to the truck and hid under a blanket on the floorboard in the backseat. With each passing minute, I contemplated Thomas's return. I'd seen him before within the community. I wasn't sure why he was allowed to enter. Xavier never had. However, I knew he'd done it. One time in the coffee shop with Raquel, I'd noticed him. He was a large man, about Jacob's age, with short hair in a military cut.

Raquel and I had both recognized Thomas as new. There was something about him, the way he behaved: nodding and making eye contact with females before he said hello. The men of The Light didn't do that. In general male followers didn't acknowledge female followers. As Elizabeth had once told me, they didn't owe us their words. If a man and woman crossed paths, the woman looked down and the man moved on.

That was the way it was.

I sucked in a breath as the door opened and slammed shut. From my hiding place, I caught a glimpse and knew I was right. Thomas was in the driver's seat. Slowly he backed up and turned toward the gates. I feared he could hear my racing heart as the truck slowed and he pressed the code on the first, the second, and finally the last gate.

As the truck lunged forward, a sense of freedom bubbled from deep inside. Elation at passing the final barrier fought with the fear of the unknown. I hadn't been out of the community since Jacob's and my banishment. And up until a week ago that hadn't bothered me. Given the way the tires bumped against the floorboard of the truck, the road was as uneven as it had been all that time ago.

I fought the urge to take a deep breath and fill my lungs with the air outside those walls. I couldn't. I wasn't really free, not yet. Once I made my presence known to Thomas, if he decided to take me back, I knew that I'd be punished. What I didn't know was how severely.

Would I end up dead, like the women in Tracy's morgue? Would it be Jacob's decision, the Commission's, or Father Gabriel's?

Although what I'd done was a risk, I couldn't stay at the Northern Light another day. I needed to get back to my life and do whatever I could to help my sisters and the children. I wanted to save Mindy. After all, she'd been part of the reason I'd first learned of The Light.

I silently said a quick prayer to Father Gabriel that I wouldn't fail her or everyone else.

My heartbeat echoed in my ears as the road noise faded and the truck came to a stop. Though it'd been a long time since our banishment, I was relatively certain that we hadn't driven long enough to reach the hangar. I held my breath as the driver's door opened and then the one beside me. When the blanket was ripped off me, I didn't know what I feared more, Thomas, my possible punishment, or the polar bears that could be near.

Thomas smirked as he leaned back on his heels, as if to get a better look, and shook his head. "Look what we have here."

I moved from the floor to the seat. "Please, I'm begging you to help me."

"You're begging me? I like the sound of that."

My stomach rolled. "If you'll take me wherever you're going, I can pay you."

"You can?" He touched my cheek as I resolved to remain still. "Tell me, pretty lady, why are you hiding in the back of this dirty old truck?"

Oh, shit! Maybe I should have waited for Jacob to get approval.

I willed my eyes to look at his and found it interesting how well I'd been trained. Even now, when I knew it was wrong, I had physical difficulty doing what I used to consider natural. Nodding, I swallowed and asked, "You're Thomas, Xavier's replacement, right?"

He nodded. "I didn't think they let you women know what was happening."

"They don't, not really." *Should I tell him that I'm Jacob's wife?* "I'm a good listener."

"And, Miss Good Listener, what do you expect me to do to help you?"

I had to try. "I don't belong here. I don't even know how I got here. I've been here for almost a year, but I have a life off the Northern Light." My words came fast, each one landing on the one before. I hoped he was listening well enough to understand. "I have . . . had a job, a good job. I have money and so does my family. If you can get me off this campus and away, I'll make sure you're compensated."

His golden eyes narrowed as they scanned me from head to toe and back again. The jeans and sweater I wore seemed to evaporate as his expression morphed. It was as if he could see what was underneath. Finally he said, "So you're saying The Light kidnapped you?"

I nodded.

"What would Father Gabriel say if I turned this truck around and took you back?"

Tears threatened my eyes. "P-please, you're my only hope. If you take me back, I don't know what will happen, but it won't be good."

The longer he stood with the door open, the more concerned I became about the bears. "You do know there are polar bears around, don't you?"

He laughed. "Is that what they tell you?"

I sat straighter. *Is everything Jacob told me a lie?*

He opened the door to the front passenger's seat. "Here, pretty lady, sit up here." He patted the seat. "And convince me to help you."

Convince him?

Slowly I moved from the backseat. When both of my boots stood upon the hard ground, I scanned the sparse trees at the side of the road. If there weren't really polar bears, maybe I could make a run for it. Thomas's hand grasped my arm.

"In the truck."

I swallowed and nodded as I moved to the front seat. After he'd shut both doors and as he walked around to the driver's side, I once again considered the idea of running. The opportunity was short-lived as Thomas opened the driver's door and eased himself into the truck.

"Go," he said, his cocky grin back in place. "Convince me."

"I-I'm not sure what you mean. I told you that I don't belong here. I just need someone to take me away, someone to believe me."

One of his cheeks rose as his lips thinned. "I've heard stories. You see, there are rumors. That's why I wanted to go into the community. I wanted to know if they were true."

"I'm not sure what you've heard, but please help me." The truck still wasn't moving. "I won't tell anyone that you're part of this. I promise." My breath caught in my throat as he reached out and again brushed my cheek. "Please, don't touch me," I pleaded as I backed away and my nausea returned.

Pushing my now-longer hair behind my ear, he leaned closer. "See, pretty lady, what I've heard is that you bitches in The Light like to obey. If you don't, I heard you get punished." His eyes moved up and down my frame, lingering too long at my breasts. "Is that true?"

Oh, God, what am I doing?

"I-I promise, my family will pay you."

He laughed, the stench of his stale breath filling the noncirculating air in the cab. "If you think your family will pay me better than Father Gabriel, your daddy must be Bill Gates, and I ain't heard nothing about Bill Gates's daughter gone missing. But don't worry, sweetheart, I think we can work this out." He traced a line from my ear and down my neck to my breast.

I slapped his hand. "Forget it. Take me back. I made a mistake."

Thomas started the truck and laughed a deep echoing laugh. "I like a bitch with spunk. She's all the more fun to tame."

Biting my lip, I sat in silence as he drove toward the hangar. My mind searched for possibilities. Brother Micah. If he was at the hangar, maybe I could convince him that Thomas had taken me against my will. As I contemplated my options, I didn't care what Brother Micah or anyone else thought or about my possible punishment. I just wanted to get away from Thomas.

Even though I'd lived at the hangar, in the living quarters of the pole barn, for two weeks, I'd never really seen the outside of the building, the landing strip, or the hangar. When Jacob had first driven me to it, my eyes had been covered, and when I could see, it was winter and everything was cloaked by darkness. Now, as we approached in full light, I scanned the area for vehicles and saw how truly massive the building was. Even though I didn't see any other vehicles, I didn't give up hope. Obviously the building was big enough that Brother Micah could have parked inside.

My pulse increased again when Thomas hit the button on the garage and pulled Jacob's truck into the bay near the living quarters. This was wrong. This was Jacob's truck and Jacob's parking area. It was where he'd brought me, where I'd felt like a newlywed. In reality I had been. I just hadn't known it.

Thomas hadn't said a word since he'd told me he wanted to tame me.

I didn't know who was telling the truth about the polar bears. Nevertheless, I waited for the garage door to close before I opened my door. As soon as the door stopped, I opened my door and ran toward the hangar. Opening the door on the opposite side of the garage from the living quarters, I screamed, "Micah, Brother Micah! Are you here? Help! Brother Mic—"

Thomas's hand covered my mouth and stopped my words. I closed my lips, swallowing the disgusting taste of grime and sweat.

"Shhh," he whispered menacingly in my ear as he pulled my back against his front. "You're going to be a good girl, or we'll start that punishment right now."

When he spun me around to face him, I nodded, all the while listening for the sounds I'd heard when others were at the hangar. Even though I didn't hear anything, I couldn't let Thomas take me, not if there was a chance I could save myself. His eyes narrowed in warning as he slowly removed his hand from my mouth.

As soon as I was free, I screamed, "Help! Micah! It's Sara! Please . . ."

My world spun as Thomas's hand stung my left cheek.

"Shut the fuck up!"

I swallowed, tasting the telltale copper of my own blood. As I fought the dizziness his slap induced, my feet obeyed as he pulled me toward the living quarters. As soon as Thomas opened the door my chest ached with memories of Jacob's and my past. I needed to leave The Light. I wanted to leave. But no matter the injustices I'd endured, never had Jacob treated me the way Thomas was doing right now.

Thomas shoved me forward. Awkwardly I caught myself and landed in one of the kitchen chairs.

"Sit here. Don't fucking move." He rubbed his obviously hardening erection. "I'd love to get a better look at Father Gabriel's gift, but I don't know who's coming out here." His lips separated into a broad smile, exposing his stained teeth. "And I don't plan on making this quick. I guess it'll have to wait until we get to Fairbanks. Don't you worry, pretty lady, once we're there we'll have all the time and privacy we want."

My stomach knotted. "T-Thomas, I'm going to be sick."

He pulled me up by my arm and pushed me toward the bathroom. Undoubtedly my arm as well as my face would be bruised.

"Go in there. Don't make a fucking mess. I'm not losing this job over you."

I nodded as I rushed to the bathroom and shut the door. There wasn't a lock.

Shit!

My heart sank.

"I'm getting my stuff from upstairs," he called through the door. "When you come out, sit where I put you. If you don't, I'm taking my belt to that pretty little ass." The sound of his laughter trailed away as his footsteps climbed the stairs.

Looking at the woman in the mirror, I noticed the way my left cheek was already beginning to swell. Though the tips of my fingers lacked feeling, as I pushed on the reddening and slightly purple skin, I felt the tenderness. Shaking my head, I contemplated my options. I could take off running. If I did, I'd need to run back to the community. I'd never survive in the wilderness on my own, with or without polar bears. Even if I made it back to the community and was allowed to live, I feared I'd never get away from the Northern Light.

Better sense—or was it delusional thinking?—told me that this could be my only chance.

My thoughts went to Mindy and the others. If I left with Thomas, there was a possibility of my saving not only myself but also the others. Taking a deep breath, I surrendered to my decision. I opened the bathroom door and scanned the living area.

Conceding to my choices didn't mean giving in to the man walking upstairs. With the sound of Thomas's footsteps echoing from above, I rushed to the kitchen and opened a drawer. I peered into its depths, knowing what it contained. Lying side by side were varying knives. I scanned the possibilities; I needed one big enough to do harm, but small enough to be concealed.

When the sound of footsteps stopped, I held my breath. Quickly I turned toward the stairs, but Thomas wasn't there. When the steps began again above my head, I grabbed a four-inch paring knife and concentrated on Thomas's footsteps as I quietly shut the drawer. Raising the leg on my jeans, I slipped the knife into my boot, and quickly moved to the table. Counting his steps on the stairs, I sat and tried to calm my breathing. Since I'd been unable to see when Jacob and I first moved to the pole barn, I'd memorized the number of steps. Thomas still had four more before he reached the bottom.

Only my eyes moved as I watched him enter the lower level. He glared in my direction before walking past me to the bathroom.

"Good girl," he called, just before the sound of his urinating echoed through the living quarters.

I scrunched my nose. Gross!

Clenching my teeth, I thought about how much I hated the phrase good girl. It was such a condescending form of praise.

The toilet flushed and Thomas returned. "I thought you might try to leave something in there, like a message. Either you're a fast learner and don't want your ass beat, or you're not very bright. Either way, I can't wait to get you to my place and find out." He bent down until our noses were mere millimeters apart. His breath reeked of coffee, twisting my stomach into more knots. "No matter how well you obey"—he emphasized the word—"I'm sure I'll find some reason to turn that ass red."

Though I bit my lip and told myself to remain still, I couldn't stop my flinch as he reached out to once again tuck my hair behind my ear.

"Don't look so worried, pretty lady. I'm sure I'm not as depraved as what you're used to." He shrugged. "Or maybe I am." With a smirk he added, "You'll have to let me know."

I swallowed my response: Jacob might have lied to me, but he wasn't depraved.

Why did I think this was a good idea?

When Thomas reached for my arm, I pulled away. "I can walk."

He snickered. "For now."

When I stood he told me to walk in front of him. As we made our way through the length of the pole barn, I scanned each area we passed: the garage, the long hallway, and doors to offices and work-shops. Each area confirmed my fear: we were indeed alone. In the hangar, the final, largest area, I saw Father Gabriel's stunning plane. Though months ago I'd only felt it, by all the windows, I knew it had to be the one with the soft leather seats. That meant Jacob had the smaller jet, the one that took only one pilot.

That meant Micah could still arrive any minute. I tried to think of a way to stall, but when Thomas cleared his throat and pointed to a door, I made my way in that direction.

As we stepped back outside into the late-morning sunshine, a cool breeze blew through my hair, causing it to swirl around my face. Fearful the change in temperature would be visible, I crossed my arms over my chest.

We'd exited the building all the way at the other end from the living quarters. Squinting against the brightness, I saw our destination. On the tarmac was a small white plane with a red stripe, and large letters and numbers on the tail. Unlike any of the planes Jacob flew, this one had a single propeller.

Thomas opened the plane's back door. I presumed that on his way to the Northern Light the open area of the fuselage had been filled with supplies. Now, with it empty, he unfolded a seat and tilted his head.

Come on, Sara . . . Stella . . . do this. It's your only chance to get away.

Inhaling, I climbed aboard and sat in a seat very similar to one in Jacob's truck. There weren't even any fancy straps, just normal-looking seat belts. Before I could latch mine, Thomas's large hand reached across me, pulled the belt, and buckled it tight. Once I was secure, he allowed his hand to graze my lap and smiled.

"Three and a half hours." He winked. "You might want to get your rest. You're going to need it."

Not if I put this knife in your artery first, asshole!

CHAPTER

FORTY

S ara/Stella

THOMAS HAD TOLD me to sleep, but as we flew over Alaska with the sun streaming down, my nerves were strung so tight there was no way that was possible. Besides that, each time the plane changed altitude, I was certain I'd vomit. I'd even searched for some kind of bag but found none. Fear of what Thomas would do if I threw up all over his plane was the main motivation keeping my breakfast where it belonged.

All I could think about was getting free. It didn't matter that through the windows and below was some of the most majestic scenery I'd ever seen. I'd always imagined Alaska covered in snow; however, at the Northern Light we never got much snow. It wasn't because it didn't get cold enough. It was that the latitude was so far north there was rarely enough moisture. Mindlessly I noticed that the farther south we flew, toward Fairbanks, the more the landscape below was covered with deep greens, rolling browns, and crystal-clear lakes. I debated my options as the beautiful blue sky I was used to seeing filled ominously with clouds.

The engine and propeller's loud roar made it impossible for Thomas and me to speak. Before we'd taken off, he'd placed earphones over my ears, but unlike his, mine didn't have a microphone. I wasn't sure whether he could speak to me. If he could, he hadn't. Maybe he thought I really would sleep.

As I peered up toward the front of the plane, I saw Thomas's short hair and shoulders from around the seat. I sadly remembered the first time I'd asked Jacob to take me with him on his flights. At that time I'd wanted to be with him. However, now that I was away from the Northern Light and my perspective was different, I reasoned that I neither wanted to see Jacob again nor would allow myself to think about what he would do if he ever found me. Fear turned to indignation at the thought of his possible correction.

With each mile I concentrated not on the man I'd left behind or the one flying the plane, but on the one who would help me. I thought about Dylan.

I recalled everything about him, from his vibrant blue eyes to his toned muscles—everything except his phone number. It had been programmed into my phone. I tried to envision the screen. I recalled the sound of his distinctive ring, yet I couldn't visualize the number. My only choice would be to call the Detroit Police Department. After all, I should be able to find their number with a quick online search.

All I needed to do was slip away for a few minutes and borrow someone's phone. I didn't imagine that it would be easy, since I was being flown by a madman who'd already struck me, causing my cheek to swell. But if I succeeded, the payoff would be worth it.

I would hear Dylan's voice.

He would know I was alive.

A small smile crept across my face with the knowledge that the man I'd imagined while I was without sight was real. At the same time, the realization hurt. If only I'd listened to his warnings about Highland Heights. One of the first things I'd do once we were together again would be to apologize for the heartache I'd undoubtedly put him through.

As urban sprawl began to appear below us, I assumed we were nearing our destination. In the distance were more mountains, but beneath us a flat city began to materialize. Slowly the buildings began getting closer together. Though Fairbanks was the biggest interior city in Alaska, I didn't suspect that Thomas would land his small plane at the Fairbanks International Airport. Since he was Xavier's replacement, I wondered whether he flew extensively for Father Gabriel. If he did, he probably flew out of a private airstrip. I prayed it wouldn't be like the one in Bloomfield Hills, that instead it would be more public. To have a chance to get away, I needed people around.

Thoughts of what my future held caused my hands to ball into fists and my nails to bite into my moistening palms. My investigator's mind filled with the possibilities Thomas had in store. Each scenario was worse than the last, and none of them included my ability to place that call to DPD.

Believe in yourself.

The words came back to me. I couldn't project too far ahead; instead I needed to look at my situation in steps. Getting away from Thomas had to be my first priority.

As our altitude began to decrease, I crossed my legs and slowly lifted the hem of my jeans. With my seat directly behind Thomas's, I hoped he couldn't see what I was doing. I also hoped that since he was speaking on his headset, his attention was elsewhere. Lifting the cuff, I slid my hand down inside my boot. The handle of the knife was against my ankle and the sheathed blade was near my foot, but without unzipping my boot, I couldn't quite reach the knife.

"Sara."

I jumped at the sound of Thomas's voice through the earphones and quickly lowered my boot. I lifted my eyes to the front of the plane, and our gaze met in a rearview-type mirror.

"Don't try to talk. I can't hear you, so listen."

I pressed my lips together and nodded. In front of him were windows and gadgets. Casually I lowered the leg of my jeans, thankful he hadn't seemed to notice.

"This airport is small," he said, "but I don't want you making a scene. If you do, I'll be glad to return you to Father Gabriel, but that's not happening until I'm thoroughly done with you."

Fighting the urge to vomit, I pressed my lips together and shook my head.

He turned his head toward the side window as he flipped a switch and began talking to someone else. Just like that, he'd spun my world, warning me about a future I'd already imagined.

Clenching my fists, I concentrated on my second objective. It was to get in contact with Dylan. I knew that if I could reach him, my story wouldn't end like that of MistiLace from my Internet search. Besides, it wasn't as if I could get to the Fairbanks International Airport and fly home to Detroit, even if I wanted to. I didn't have any identification. The TSA wouldn't allow me to travel. I needed the help of the police. Dylan could help me with that.

As the plane touched down, I willed my fist to open and looked at my fingers. Hell, forget about identification, I didn't even have fingerprints.

The small plane bounced as Thomas brought us to a stop near the hangar, and I glanced around. This hangar didn't even seem as big as the one at the Northern Light. This one had only two runways going in opposite directions, a large paved area, and the hangar. An old chain-link fence surrounded the entire compound. I sucked my lower lip between my teeth, waited, and contemplated my knife. It would have to wait. I feared that I couldn't reach it without bringing my movements to his attention. If there was any chance of being successful with it, it had to be a surprise.

Taking off his headphones, Thomas leaned to his side and craned his neck. With a disgusting toothy grin, he said, "Welcome to your new home."

Removing my headphones, I replied, "I know what you think about women in The Light, but you're wrong. Father Gabriel won't let this go unpunished. You stole me from the Northern Light."

I was playing with fire, but I had to try. Through the last few days I'd gotten better at lying, something Sara or any other woman of The Light would never do. Now it was time to go for broke.

"It was a test," I went on, "a test designed by Father Gabriel, and you failed. He does care about me. I'm the wife of an Assemblyman. I didn't want to leave. I said what he told me to say. It was for The Light. You're new. Father Gabriel was testing your response. You failed."

With each of my phrases, Thomas's confident grin dimmed as the color faded from his ruddy cheeks. "You're lying. You're lying to save your ass."

I crossed my arms over my chest and turned toward the window. "You can either take me back and suck up to Father Gabriel or you can let me go and I'll contact my husband."

He'd unbuckled his seat belt and was fully turned toward me in his seat. "How the fuck are you supposed to do that? You people don't have phones."

I lifted my chin confidently. "The chosen men do. I've been told how to reach my husband." This was it. It was all or nothing. "Besides, he's a pilot. He'll come get me."

Thomas's shoulders relaxed and he shook his head. "Bitch, you had me going for a minute. I'm going to enjoy tanning your—"

"What?" I asked incredulously. "My husband is a pilot."

"No way, I heard how you yelled for Micah."

I shook my head. "Not Brother Micah. I'm Jacob's wife." I fumbled for my necklace, pulling it from beneath my sweater. "See this necklace? It's only worn by the chosen. Jacob's on the Assembly and Father Gabriel's pilot!"

"Fuck!"

When he opened his door, I quickly unbuckled my seat belt and scooted toward the other side of the plane. My heart beat in double time as I fumbled with the handle. My efforts were in vain, though; it was locked. My blue eyes grew as big as saucers when Thomas peered through the window, undoubtedly knowing I'd wanted to escape. My mind was a blur. I prayed to God and Father Gabriel for a miracle I didn't deserve.

Just as Thomas began to open my door, out of nowhere two men in dark jackets with badges came running forward. The front door of the plane was still open, and through the wind I could hear raised voices. The men were yelling at Thomas, and one had a gun drawn.

I stared in disbelief as Thomas forgot about me and spun in their direction. There was a split second when his body twitched in indecision. He might have considered running, but just as fast, he lifted his hands in the air. Between the wind and my blood rushing in my ears, it was as if the rest of the world were on mute. I couldn't make out their words. Instead, it was as if I were watching a silent film and praying the good guys would win.

I sat statuesque as one of the men secured Thomas's hands behind his back and led him away. Maybe if I remained still, they wouldn't know I was here. And then the other man in a dark jacket looked through my window. When he nodded, I knew my wish wouldn't come true.

Opening the door, he asked, "Ma'am, are you all right?"

I let out the breath I'd been holding and replied, "A-are you the police?"

"No, ma'am, US Marshals." He offered me his hand.

I stepped from the plane, contemplating which story I should lead with: I was taken against my will almost a year ago, or I was taken earlier today. "Thank you," I said softly, forcing myself to look into the older gentleman's eyes.

"Ma'am, what happened to your cheek?"

I lowered my eyes. "It was him."

The marshal's jaw clenched as he reached for his phone. "Excuse me, I need to make this call."

I stared momentarily at his phone, then nodded and wrapped my arms around my body as the wind blew my hair around my face. While the marshal spoke quietly, I turned completely around and took in the small private tarmac. It wasn't the way I'd planned it, but I didn't care.

I was finally free.

Relief flooded my system and a renegade tear slid down my cheek.

It was over. It was really over.

I was no longer trapped in someone else's life in the circumpolar North. I was alive, with a US Marshal, in the city of Fairbanks.

When he finished his call, the marshal turned back my way and offered me his hand to shake. "Ma'am, my name is Deputy Hill."

Willing the inner voice, the one I'd worked hard to suppress, the one I now knew was the real me—Stella—to emerge, I trepidatiously accepted his hand. "Thank you, Deputy Hill, may I please use your phone?"

I supposed I should have introduced myself, but I wasn't thinking straight. With my first objective accomplished, I needed to call Dylan.

Deputy Hill's dark aviators reflected the afternoon sun as he glanced from his phone to my face. "Let's get you to the safety of the station first. You've had a traumatic experience." If he only knew. "We have a female marshal who can assure your well-being and then we can progress."

The cloak of freedom that I'd lost nearly a year ago weighed heavily on my shoulders. At the same time relief overwhelmed me. My tense muscles gave way, causing me to stumble.

Deputy Hill reached for my elbow. "Are you all right? Can you walk?"

Sucking my lower lip between my teeth, I nodded. "I'm just so relieved. I was frightened of what he was going to do."

"Yes, ma'am, we received a tip and have been waiting for his arrival."

"A tip?" I asked, more than slightly concerned. "From whom?"

Had it been The Light? Had they known I would be with him?

"Ma'am, the important thing is that you're safe." Deputy Hill continued to speak as he led me to a dark, unmarked SUV and helped me into the backseat.

Once he was in the driver's seat and we began to pull away, I asked, "What happened to Thomas?"

"My partner took him. We thought by that shiner you're sporting you'd prefer not to ride in the same vehicle."

My fingers fluttered near my eye as I leaned back against the seat. "Thank you. Once we get to the station, I need to make a call."

"Did Mr. Hutchinson take you against your will?"

"Mr. Hutchinson?" I asked.

The deputy's eyes met mine in the rearview mirror. "The man who was with you, Thomas Hutchinson."

"Yes, but . . ."

"But?" he repeated.

I shook my head again. "Please, once I make a call I can explain everything."

"Yes, ma'am. After we get to the station and get your statement."

I settled back and watched the city streets. There were more people out and about in the community at the Northern Light than I saw on these urban streets. As we drove I marveled at the world I used to take for granted. Stores and fast-food restaurants clustered at each intersection. I'd forgotten how normal the dark was. It wasn't scary and unknown like The Light had told me. Instead, it was comfortingly familiar.

The US Marshals' station was small, reminding me more of a house than a police station. Deputy Hill pulled onto the gravel lot, mostly filled with SUVs. As soon as he parked, he opened my door and helped me out. It wasn't until we began walking that the rubbing against the outside of my foot reminded me of my knife. I thought about confessing that I had it, until he asked whether I'd like anything to eat or drink.

Suddenly the thought of food monopolized my thoughts. I hadn't eaten since I'd cooked breakfast for Jacob. "What time is it?"

As we entered the building Deputy Hill looked up at a clock hanging above the empty front desk. "It's nearly four."

The clock was large, round and plain, like my first memory of the dark. Despite my feeling weak from hunger, it made me grin. "Thank you, I'd love something to eat."

Below the clock was a large circular sign that read "Department of Justice, United States Marshal." The US Marshals must not be very busy in Fairbanks. I remembered a Detroit police station, from the few times I'd gone there for work or to visit Dylan. It was always bustling with activity. This office seemed abandoned in comparison.

Deputy Hill walked me down a hall, opened a door, and ushered me over the threshold. "Please have a seat. I'll get you something to eat. There's a restroom across the hall, and in a few minutes Deputy Stevens, the female officer I told you about, will be in to talk with you."

"Thank you," I replied as I sat. Before the door closed, I asked, "Will Deputy Stevens be taking my statement? I'd like to make that call."

"It will be just a few minutes."

The door closed, and I sighed. I glanced around the stereotypical interrogation room, seeing the pale walls, tile floor, and metal table with four chairs. There weren't any windows to the outside, but one wall contained a large mirror I was relatively certain was actually a one-way window. From my side of the glass, I saw only my own muted reflection. Though the colors didn't seem right, I could tell that my eye was getting worse.

After a few minutes, I took Deputy Hill's offer of a restroom. When I slowly opened the door, I peered in both directions. Though I'd expected to see someone, instead there were only empty hallways. Entering the bathroom and turning on the light, I cringed at the woman in the mirror.

Damn, Thomas had done one hell of a job on my cheek. The bruising was much more visible under the incandescent lighting.

Not wanting to miss Deputy Stevens, I hurried and returned to the room.

Eating the turkey sandwich and stale chips Deputy Hill delivered, I debated my statement and decided I'd first tell the marshal that Thomas had taken me. Then, once I was granted my telephone call, I'd call Dylan and tell him I was alive and about The Light. If I told the marshals that story first and they didn't believe me, I might not get the chance to call Dylan.

I suddenly thought about the time difference between Fairbanks and Detroit. I didn't know what it was. I knew Pacific time was three hours behind Detroit. I believed that made Alaska four hours. My heart sank. Dylan wouldn't be at the station this late.

Undeterred, I decided I could persuade them to give me his number. I would do whatever I could to avoid staying in this hell, even if it were nighttime in Detroit.

Drinking from the water bottle, I continued to wait for Deputy Stevens. Maybe it was the nourishment or perhaps the rush of freedom, but with each passing minute, I started to become more anxious. Silently I watched the door.

As I waited, for the first time since the night my memories came back, I mentally returned to the accident—the supposed truck wreck that had not only taken my memory and resulted in banishment but also marked the end of my life as Stella Montgomery and the beginning of my life as Sara Adams. Even now I couldn't recall what had preceded the accident. My last memory from before that was of a parking lot in Detroit. I remembered waking in the mangled truck without sight, crawling from the wreckage, and scrambling in the darkness. My teeth clenched as I recalled the intense pain in my leg and ribs. My hand fluttered to my now-swollen cheek, the same cheek that had been swollen then.

Pacing the small room, I recounted the hard, vicious blows that had assaulted me as I lay trapped upon the cold, hard ground. Tears formed as I came to the same conclusion I'd come to the night my memories returned. I'd been kicked and purposely abused as, throughout the entire assault, the wind whipped around me, whistled in my ears, and filled my mind with white noise until . . . the voice.

In my mind I heard the deep, demanding voice ordering me to stop, even though I didn't know what I'd done. And then I was lifted into someone's arms.

My turkey sandwich rolled in my stomach as the scent of musk and leather came back. I opened my eyes and peered around the small room. The memory was so intense that it was as if I could actually smell it, but no. It wasn't real.

It was familiar—Jacob's signature scent. I knew in the depth of my soul that Jacob was the one who had lifted me. He had been at my accident. Was he the one who'd yelled, the one who'd hurt me?

I tried to devise another plausible scenario, something other than naming him as my assailant. Nothing came to my mind, no other possibilities.

Eventually Deputy Hill returned, apologized for Deputy Stevens's delay, and promised she'd be there soon.

"If I could please make a call? I just need to use your computer—"

"Ma'am, soon. I promise," Deputy Hill said, as he disappeared again behind the door.

The relief I'd experienced at the airport was beginning to fade. This didn't seem right. Someone should have taken my statement.

With each ticking minute, I remembered who I was. I was no longer compliant Sara. I was Stella, and I was alive. I had parents, a sister, and a boyfriend who deserved to know that I was no longer missing. I had friends who needed to be informed. There were people I needed to help and an organization I needed to expose.

With a huff I stood, scooting the metal chair across the hard tile, and headed for the door. Just as I did, the door opened. Deputy Hill met me and I gasped.

Deputy Hill wasn't alone.

His next sentence took everything away. My newfound freedom disappeared as he spoke. "Ma'am . . . your husband is here to take you home."

FORTY-ONE

J acob
A few hours earlier

IT WAS A GAMBLE, but it was also our only chance. If Raquel was right and Sara had not only remembered her past but also found a way to leave the Northern Light, Thomas would have been her only option. On the off chance she was with him, his plane had to be intercepted. If Raquel was wrong, then we were without options and time. As I flew toward Fairbanks, all I could think about was getting to her, Sara or Stella, I didn't know. When I left Montana, her whereabouts had still been unconfirmed.

My Citation X flew considerably faster than Thomas's Cessna 206. He might have left the Northern Light with Sara before I left Whitefish, but despite the impending weather, I was able to gain on them.

The entire flight, unsure whether I'd find Sara in Fairbanks, I contemplated Special Agent Adler's plan. It was brilliant and totally contingent upon Sara. If I found her, I would then need to convince her to help. If I accomplished both goals, then we'd be going back to the Northern Light. Going back would give the FBI more time to sync the raids at all campuses. It was the only way to reduce loss of life if, indeed, there was an extermination plan that one raid at one campus would set into motion. If I couldn't find Sara or convince her, then the operation was over.

Everything.

Three years of deep-cover operative work, embedding myself in The Light, learning the ways, proving my loyalty . . . it was all done. I had until tomorrow morning to pass Sara's answer on to Special Agent Adler.

Agent Jacoby McAlister wasn't ready to be done. I'd learned too much and was too close.

As I got closer to Fairbanks, I continued my fervent prayers that she was there. Being certain of her safety became paramount. With that in mind, if she was there Jacob Adams decided he wanted Sara to say no. That wasn't completely true. As her husband I wanted to make the choice for her. Ever since I'd taken her as my wife, I'd been worried about how to protect her when the raids finally went down —not if, but when: they were inevitable. I'd been terrified that someone would execute a possible contingency plan while I was away. That was why I'd taken her plea to travel with me to the Commission. She'd always been intelligent and inquisitive, and with her request, I'd hoped she'd provided a way for me to save her.

No matter what decision was made or whether she was found, her life as Stella Montgomery was over. If she found a way back to Detroit on her own, I knew what would happen. The Light would eliminate her as a threat. Under no circumstances could she return to her hometown. It was too dangerous.

Assuming she was found and she chose not to help, the federal agencies were ready to take her into the witness protection program and the raids would happen—tomorrow. If Sara and I didn't return to the Northern Light, the FBI feared it would raise suspicions and put more lives at stake.

On the off chance that Father Gabriel would see Sara's and my desertion as the beginning link in a chain that would bring him down, the sting operation had to be over, and the FBI had to move. The bureau wasn't willing to jeopardize the intelligence I'd discovered. Though there were still unknowns, such as the location of the money, I'd unraveled enough to stop The Light and put Father Gabriel behind bars for a very long time.

Without question, with each mile while I prayed she was in Fairbanks, I was conflicted over whether to take her back to the Northern Light and continue my mission, or to hand her over to witness protection and assure her safety.

When Hill called my burner to tell me they had Sara and what Thomas had done, I was still in the air and unable to receive calls. It wasn't until I landed that I heard the voice mail. Learning that she was safe almost took me to my knees with relief; however, as his message continued and I heard that Thomas had struck Sara, blackening her eye, my death grip on the burner phone almost crushed it.

I reminded myself that the most important thing was that we'd found Sara.

I'd devised a story to help with the cover-up of her escape. I contacted Brother Daniel and told him that Whitefish hadn't been ready for me. I hadn't been able to get the supplies I needed, so I'd flown to Fairbanks.

For that story to be believable, I had to purchase supplies. Since I wasn't leaving Sara alone once I had her, I needed to leave her at the marshals' office where I knew she was safe. Per Special Agent Adler, she'd come into contact only with two marshals, and Deputy Hill was the only one who'd spoken with her.

It hadn't taken Adler long to learn Thomas's flight plans and discover that he had been headed to Fairbanks. Unfortunately, there wasn't an FBI field office in Fairbanks. The only one in Alaska was in Anchorage. That gave the FBI the choice of the US Marshals or local police. Adler chose to contact Deputy Hill and involved the US Marshals in our operation. Without divulging too much, he explained the urgency of finding, securing, and isolating Sara, as well as taking care of Thomas.

After the message about Thomas's hitting Sara, I would've liked to have been the one who took care of him; however, undoubtedly my method wouldn't be approved and there wasn't enough time.

With a motel room set, a call in to Brother Daniel about my change in plans, and supplies purchased, I finally arrived at the marshals' office and sat behind a window watching the woman who'd been my wife for nearly a year. Though I'd wanted to go straight to her, Hill insisted that I see her first, see her injury. Even though I saw it only through the glass, my teeth and fists clenched.

"Tell me Thomas is no longer a threat," I said, though my jaw wouldn't move.

"Agent, he'll be lost in the system for more years than you'll need to complete your assignment," Deputy Hill said, shrugging confidently, as only a man with years of experience could do. "With his cocky attitude and affinity for hurting women, he might find more than he bargained for behind bars. Who knows? He may not make it long enough in general population for his messed-up papers to ever be straightened out."

I nodded, the muscles in my neck and shoulders screaming from the tension and strain. "What did she say in her statement?"

"I haven't taken a statement."

I turned toward the older man's blank expression. "What do you mean? You've had her here for hours."

"And if I'd taken a statement, I'd have had to record it. If I forgot to take a statement or record her detention, then maybe it didn't happen."

I inhaled. Puffing out my cheeks, I slowly released the air. "Did she say..."

"She hasn't said anything. She's tried, but I just kept telling her we'd be ready soon." He nodded toward the window. "Mostly she keeps asking to make a call."

"If she decides . . . they'll let her call her family." I couldn't say if she decides to go into witness protection. As much as I'd convinced myself, as I flew to Fairbanks, that having her safe was the best option, having her in the next room, I couldn't imagine letting her go.

Not that my intentions would convince her. I was probably the last person she wanted to see. Well, looking at her eye, maybe I trumped Thomas, but that wasn't saying much. I had to think of something. Everything and everyone was riding on this.

First I needed to get her away from the marshals' office. I ran my hands through my hair as Sara stood and walked.

"We'd better . . ." Hill said as he exited the room.

My steps stuttered as I watched Sara move toward the door. Immediately my temperature rose. Something was off with her stride. Hill had said that Thomas hadn't done more than strike her—as if that were OK—but by the way she was walking . . . biting my cheek, I suddenly wondered whether he had done more.

So help me God, if he had touched her sexually . . . once this was over, I'd unravel the fucking paperwork and make him pay.

I made it to the door of the interrogation room, just as Deputy Hill opened it and said, "Ma'am . . . your husband is here to take you home."

As I stepped around Hill, my gaze met Sara's. Though her eyes remained fixed, her feet backed away. In that second I didn't see the horrible purple bruise. All I saw were the most beautiful light-blue eyes staring back at me. In that gorgeous stare was a kaleidoscope of emotion: shock, fear, disbelief, and resentment. They all swirled together with hurt and disappointment. I searched for the love I swore I'd seen that morning. Fear was winning her emotional battle.

Needing to refocus her thoughts, I evened my voice. "Sara."

Her neck straightened. Despite her eye, she had strength. She was fighting not only me but also the months of training, submission, and conditioning. Stella and Sara were battling before my eyes. If only she'd listen to my true intentions. I wasn't Jacob, not completely.

Her protests started softly, and then her eyes widened, and Stella grew stronger. "No," she whispered. Then, after clearing her throat, she repeated, "No. This isn't happening." I closed the gap. "No," she said louder. Turning toward Deputy Hill, she spoke louder: "I'm not his wife. No!" Her face was suddenly tight with terror as she realized he wasn't going to help. "Deputy Hill, please! You haven't even taken my statement."

"Sara," I repeated calmly. "It's time to go home. We need to talk."

As I closed the gap, she slid against the wall, working her way toward the door, as if I'd allow her to escape. Instead of looking at me, her gaze searched for Hill, as she pleaded, "No! Don't listen to him. My name is—"

"Stop!" I yelled, my voice echoing against the walls of the small room. We hadn't told anyone from the marshals her true identity. It wasn't safe. Special Agent Adler had confidence in Hill, but we suspected The Light's power could be far-reaching. We couldn't take that chance.

I didn't mean to scare her, but when she looked back to me I swear I saw raw horror. Her expression was like none I'd ever seen on her before, even when I deserved it. This time I didn't. This time I wasn't going to correct her or punish her. I was trying my damnedest to save her.

She fell to the ground, pulling my heart out of my chest and throwing it to the floor below. Her cries and pleas replaced the reverberating sound of my one-word command. "Please . . . I'm not his wife . . . please believe me . . . I'm not Sara . . . I'm . . ."

I lowered myself before her, needing to stop her words, and keeping my tone even. I lifted her chin, forcing our eyes to meet. The purple bruise taunted me, telling me I'd already failed to keep her safe. Not wanting to hurt her, I brushed the puffiness softly with my thumb and said, "Sara, we need to go. Now," I emphasized. "Don't make me repeat myself."

My words came too easily. I'd lived the role for so long.

Sara's head moved from side to side with her chin still in my grasp, her eyes closed in submission. Her despair ripped at my chest, shredding the remaining pieces of my heart.

I reached for her hand. "Sara, it's all right. We'll get this taken care of. I promise."

With her lip between her teeth, she grudgingly stood. Defeat and apprehension rippled from her every pore. After a few steps, she stopped, and with her head still down, she looked at me with only her eyes and asked, "Will you . . . ?"

I placed my hand at the small of her back and directed her toward the door. "Shhh, not here, Sara. We'll discuss it in private."

I guided her to the truck I'd borrowed from the private hangar. Her continued battle raged: Sara versus Stella. She'd straighten her neck and purse her lips, and then just as quickly she'd bow her head. By the time we'd made it to the motel in silence, I'd had enough. No doubt the death grip on the steering wheel was evidence of my own discontent.

What the fuck did I think I was doing, trying to convince her to return? Hell, there was an excellent possibility this plan would blow up in our faces. There were too many variables.

What if Benjamin and Raquel talked to Brother Raphael? After all, Brother Raphael was Benjamin's overseer and one of the original Commissioners. He might be nice and kind, but he knew what really happened in The Light. He was the one who continued to formulate the pharmaceuticals.

I understood why Father Gabriel did what he did. I'd seen his mansion and heard the celebrations from the depth of the property.

But what was in it for Raphael, Uriel, and Michael?

They were intricate pieces of the puzzle. They worked diligently, yet to me they seemed sorely undercompensated.

During our drive Stella continually looked in my direction with a thousand questions, ready to bombard me, and just as quickly Sara would quell every one of them.

Sara knew the repercussion of questioning. She'd experienced it more times than I cared to remember.

Right now I wanted her questions. I needed them. I was a fucking chicken and needed her to begin this conversation, though I had no idea how it would go.

As I parked the truck outside the old motel, I took a deep breath and looked in her direction. When our eyes met, I wanted nothing more than to take her in my arms and make her forget the hours she'd spent with Thomas. I wanted to make her feel safe enough to tell me the truth about what he'd done. I wanted to see the love I thought I had seen nearly twenty hours earlier.

But I was a damn fool, because what I saw in those blue eyes was a whirlwind of contempt and suspicion. Despite what I'd been taught to believe, it wasn't up to me to make anything happen. It was up to her.

I exhaled. "This is where we're spending the night."

"W-we're not going back to the Northern Light tonight?"

My brow rose at her question. I was conditioned as well as her. Lesson after lesson had been recited, learned, and eventually regurgitated to other men followers. Beginning at the Eastern Light, I'd been made to believe that men were the stronger, smarter sex. We made decisions. Women didn't question. They couldn't.

"I-I'm sorry." Her chin fell and her lip quivered.

I reached for that chin and pulled the blue gaze toward me. "No, Stella, it's over. Never be sorry for your questions. I owe you a lifetime of answers, and it's going to start tonight."

FORTY-TWO

S ara/Stella

WHAT DID HE JUST SAY?

Releasing my chin, Jacob said, "Let's go into the motel?" It sounded more like a question than a command.

For the first time since Deputy Hill had handed me off to Jacob—the moment I realized my nightmare was not ending—my chest filled with air and my neck straightened. Incredulously, with my mouth agape, I turned in his direction. It was my turn to narrow my eyes.

Sighing, Jacob reached for my hands.

I pulled them away. "What the fu—? What did you just call me?" I asked, with more anger in my tone than I'd ever used with him.

Nevertheless, the expression that stared back at me didn't frighten me. I didn't understand it and didn't know what had happened, but something was different. No longer was Jacob my disciplinarian: he was my equal. Something in his dark eyes told me that he felt it too.

With only the lights from the outside of the motel, I scanned the man who claimed to be my husband. His face looked older and more tired than I'd ever recalled. Slowly he ran his hand through his dark hair as defeat filled his voice. "We've both had a long day. Let's get out of this truck and go inside where we can talk. You deserve answers."

"Answers? Answers?" My volume rose exponentially with each word. "I fucking deserve a lot more than that!"

"Sara."

"No! No! I'm not Sara!" Blood rushed to my ears and face. My body trembled as nine months of submission boiled out of me. I was losing control, and I knew it. "I'm Stella! And you knew it! You knew! Fuck you! You've known it from the very beginning!"

Unable to stay seated, I reached for the door handle and shoved the door open. Though Jacob spoke, his words didn't register. As soon as my feet hit the parking lot, I ran, the sheathed blade of the paring knife rubbing against the side of my foot. With each stride the world lost more focus. I rushed forward, each step becoming more important than the last. I didn't know where I was going, but I had to get there.

Being farther north, the Northern Light had very few hours of darkness this time of year, but thankfully, Fairbanks had some. Since I'd spent so long at the marshals' office, the sky was now black. As I ran I imagined the darkness was my cover, my invisibility cloak, allowing me an escape from my ongoing nightmare. But alas, it wasn't. Before I made it through the next parking lot, Jacob seized my shoulders.

Burrowing his lips into the nape of my neck, in a hushed whisper he said, "You can hate me for the rest of your life. Just, please, trust me for a few more hours. If you don't, I'm afraid the rest of your life won't be long."

I spun toward him. Under the lights of the street, in the eyes of the man I wanted to hate, I saw what I suspected was the most honest expression I'd ever seen. Still I asked, "Are you threatening me?"

He shook his head. "I'm trying to save you."

"I-I don't understand."

Releasing my shoulders, he reached for my hand. I didn't fight as he laced our fingers together. "I'll explain. I'll tell you everything." He lifted our joined hands and kissed my knuckles. "Then it will be your decision." Looking at my hand, he smiled. "You're still wearing your wedding band."

I looked down at our joined fingers and shrugged. He was right. I wasn't sure why I hadn't taken it off, but I hadn't.

"Please," he pleaded, "come to the room and let me try to explain."

With the warmth of his hand and the cloud of leather and musk, I nodded. I didn't understand what had happened, but somewhere between the marshals' station and the motel, my husband had changed. Maybe we'd both changed. As we silently walked, hand in hand, I didn't know.

Once we were inside the room, Jacob locked the door and turned in my direction. My heart ached as I watched the handsome man before me. From his dark wavy hair to his brown eyes, defined jaw, and broad shoulders, I saw a storm of emotions I'd never before seen. His normally confident demeanor had been replaced by one of sorrow and fear.

Holding a fistful of his dark hair, he said, "Before I start, I need to know . . ." His chest expanded and contracted. "Tell me the truth. What did Thomas do to you?"

Though his tone wasn't demanding, I had no reason to lie. Sitting on the edge of the bed, I sighed. "He scared me and slapped me, but that was all."

"He didn't . . . ?"

I couldn't help but smile at his genuine concern. I shook my head. "No. He told me he would, once we got to Fairbanks, but as soon as we landed, the marshals were there." Remembering the scene, I stood. "Were they really US Marshals or were they part of The Light? How did they know I was there? What really happened to Thomas?"

Though my questions came fast and furious, the shaking of his head was lethargic and slow. "Sara, there's so much I need to explain."

My back straightened. "Do not call me that. You know my real name. Use it!"

"Stella," he said.

My name sounded painful on his lips, as if it ripped him apart, exposing him in an unfamiliar way. The angst resonating from the one word made me want to tell him to forget it and just call me Sara, but I bit my lip, stopping the words. I was the one who'd been living a lie for the past nine months, the one who'd been ripped from her real life; he deserved to feel a fraction of the pain I felt. My eyes dropped to his hips.

Pain.

All I had to do was look at his damn belt to remind myself that this was the man who'd hurt me—controlled me—brainwashed me, not only mentally but also physically. With each second of silence, my contempt grew. Crossing my arms over my chest, I exhaled and turned away.

"Don't," he said, his warm hand reaching for my shoulder and his fingers directing my movement.

Spinning toward him, I yelled. "No! You don't. Don't you touch me. I'm not your wife. You know that. You've known that and still you . . ." My words began to fail. "You . . . made me . . ." Shaking my head within the confines of the small motel room, I walked as far away as I could, refusing to cry. "Jacob . . . I . . ."

When I turned back toward him, he was sitting on the end of the bed, his elbows on his knees and his hands holding his head. His normally proud broad shoulders slumped forward. Unable to see his face, I stared, feeling the palpable defeat wafting off him.

Finally, still looking down, he said, "My name's not Jacob, not really, but you probably figured that out."

When his dark eyes peered upward, I nodded. "I assumed. I mean what are the chances that everyone has a biblical name? I think I've figured out that most of us were given a name that starts with the same letter as our real name."

He shrugged. "You're right. It has something to do with recall. It's supposed to make accepting the new name easier. My real name is Jacoby McAlister, and what I'm about to say will be the reason Stella Montgomery will never be able to go back to her life in Detroit."

The compassion that continually licked at my heart for this man evaporated.

"Then don't say it," I said with alarm. "Whatever it is, Jacob, please don't say it. I want to go back. I need to go back."

Though he sadly shook his head, one side of his lips turned upward. "See, Stella, it isn't that easy. You just called me Jacob. Sara is who you are to me."

I nodded. I hadn't even realized I'd said his name. "Jacoby," I said, the name sounding foreign. "Please don't say whatever it is. Just let me go. I need to. I have connections. I can save Mindy. I can save others."

"Mindy?" he asked.

"She's my friend. She's part of the reason I started investigating The Light."

He sat taller. "What? You were investigating The Light? Are you with the police?"

"I'm not police. I was, or am—hell, I don't know anymore—an investigative journalist. I'd been following some leads that led me to The Light."

He stood, again fisting his hair. "Shit! I didn't know that. They didn't tell me. All they said was that you were chosen."

"What? What do you mean . . . I was part of the chosen, or I was chosen?"

"Most men don't get to see their wives until they arrive, but I was different. I'm a pilot." He grinned a real grin. "See, not everything is a lie."

"Army?" I asked.

He nodded. "That's true too, and so was Iraq. Anyway, because I travel to the different campuses, about a week before you were taken, Brother Uriel, from—"

"Eastern Light," I interrupted. "Uriel Harris or Harrison."

Jacoby's eyes grew wide, staring at me as if we'd never met. "Shit!" he exclaimed. "Yes. Well, he took me to this festival in Dearborn, Michigan."

It was my turn to collapse onto the bed. "You saw me there? You saw me with Dylan?"

"Yes, I saw you." He sat beside me. "Do you remember me telling you how the first time I ever saw you I knew you were mine?"

I nodded, trying to forget the emotion I'd felt that night, the night he'd started painting me a mental picture of our past.

"Well, it was true. I saw you with Richards . . ."

Gasping, I covered my lips with the burned tips of my fingers. "You know his name?"

He nodded. "But like I said, I did know you were mine. I wasn't being figurative. Brother Uriel told me that you were. I remember listening to you laugh, how fucking carefree you were. At the same time, I knew. I knew it was all about to end."

I didn't understand. "Why? Why? Why did you do it?"

Jacob seized my shoulders. "I didn't do it. Don't you get it? It wasn't up to me. Father Gabriel said I was to have a wife. I didn't choose you. You were chosen for me."

"So you didn't want me?"

He gently reached for my face and, so as not to hurt my eye, tenderly cupped my cheeks. "I didn't want a wife. I'd tried to avoid taking one, but from the first time I saw you, I wanted you."

He released my face and stood. As he paced the length of the room and back, the silence grew. Each step upon the carpet was a beat of a mystical drum, each one increasing the pressure until he exploded. "I know it makes me as fucking wrong as all of them! But I did! Damn it, I wanted you. And once you were there, at the Northern Light . . . once you were there and you were mine, I did everything I could to save you."

Indignation rose as I stood. "Really? Really? Lying to me, correcting . . . fuck that . . . beating me, was to save me?"

"Yes, Sara, it was."

"Stella! Use my goddamn name!"

In two strides he was before me, his large hands holding my shoulders, our noses nearly touching. The heat of our breath grew as his chest touched mine. "Stella." He'd calmed his tone, yet his words were separated, punctuated for emphasis. "Every. Goddamn. Thing. I. Did. To. You. Was. For. You." With only a whisper of distance between us, his lips crashed over mine. Their warmth was the fire that ignited my body in a way I no longer wanted to admit.

I reached for his shoulders and pushed him away. "No!"

Hurt swirled in the depths of his eyes.

"No!" I continued, "You want me to believe that you didn't get off hitting me with your belt. Well, I don't believe you."

"Think about it, Sara. Just think about the bigger damn picture."

I was too upset to correct my name again. "Bigger picture. Fuck you, Jacob, or Jacoby, or whoever the hell you are! I didn't see a bigger picture. I don't see it. Remember me? I'm the one who had the reminders on my ass!"

"We were being watched, continually. Every encounter was a test. If I failed, you failed. If you failed, I failed. The only time I corrected you was when your transgressions were witnessed. It was when it was expected of me. Only once did I do anything without someone to witness it." Remorse filled his words. "It was at the clinic when I slapped you, but even that, like the other times, was for your success."

My mind spun. I thought about all the times he'd corrected me. I tried to recall what had preceded or followed each instance. He was right. There were so many times I'd expected him to do it, and he hadn't. Yet there were other times when I'd thought my transgression was minor, but he had. I sank back to the bed. Every instance had had witnesses.

"Why?" I asked. "Why not just let me fail?"

Jacob's eyes grew as he dropped to his knees near my feet. "You said you researched The Light?" He turned my hand over and touched the tips of my fingers. "Do you know what happens when someone fails?"

I swallowed and nodded.

"From the first time I saw you at that festival, I knew failure wasn't an option. I didn't know for sure why you were chosen. Now I suspect it was because you were getting too close to them, but no matter why, I knew you needed to live. I wouldn't let them banish you."

I shook my head. "But we *were* banished."

"That wasn't real banishment. In all the time I'd been with The Light, I'd never heard of temporary banishment, not until us." He ran his hand through his hair. "The night after service when Father Gabriel said that we were to be banished, my heart stopped beating. I was so fucking scared."

I reached for his face and palmed his scruffy cheeks, seeing his pain. "That was the first night I went to service, wasn't it?"

He nodded, his face still in my grasp.

"It was the night you were so quiet. I was afraid that I . . ."

Jacob stroked my cheek. "It was the night I almost claimed you as my wife, your body. Despite all that they'd done to you and all you'd been through, you were still so beautiful, so strong, and yet so scared. I wasn't supposed to, but I wanted to make it better." He shook his head. "But I couldn't. I didn't want to hurt you."

My eyes narrowed. "They? They did to me? You did it. I remember being hurt. I remember your voice. You were the one who hurt me! There wasn't an accident. Father Gabriel banished us for something that never happened!"

"Oh, God, no! Yes, I was there, but I wasn't the one who hurt you. They made me watch. I was supposed to be quiet and let God's plan . . ." He stood again and paced. "Fuck that! It wasn't God's plan. It was Father Gabriel's. I was supposed to stay quiet, but I couldn't. I yelled at him. I told him to stop.

"If I hadn't been on the Assembly, fuck, if I'd been a mere follower, I never would've gotten away with what I did. But I couldn't watch him hurt you. When he wouldn't stop, I finally stopped him. I was the one who carried you away." He fell back to my feet and reached for my hands. "Of all the things I've done, please know, that wasn't one of them."

"Father Gabriel? He's the one who hit me and kicked me?"

Jacob's head moved back and forth. "No, hell no. He doesn't do any of his own dirty work. He's always a few steps removed."

"Then who?"

Jacob closed his eyes. When he opened them, sadness and regret flowed through the swirling brown. "You know how you said you didn't like Brother Abraham, that he made you feel uncomfortable?"

"Oh, God." My stomach twisted.

"There's a good reason for that."

"Does Father Gabriel know?"

Jacob nodded.

My eyes narrowed. "You're not defending him? I . . . I don't understand."

He leaned back on his toes, kneeling, as he'd told me not to do. With sadness in his eyes, he confessed, "Stella Montgomery, my name is Jacoby McAlister. I've been an agent with the Federal Bureau of Investigation for over seven years. The last three have been spent embedded in a deep undercover investigation of The Light."

I couldn't move or speak. The pieces of the puzzle that I'd tried to arrange over the last year all slid into place. From the first time I'd seen the white building that housed The Light in Highland Heights, I'd tried unsuccessfully to make the pieces fit. Even the pieces I'd managed to maneuver as Sara now combined, fitting into place like a key in a lock . . . a lock that I slowly realized meant the loss of my past.

"That's what you couldn't say? That's what you said would never allow me to go back to Detroit. Isn't it?"

He nodded.

"Then take it back. I don't want to know!"

Jacob reached again for my hands. "I can't take it back. Do you understand now? Do you understand how crucial your success was —is?"

"Because if I failed, you failed?"

His lips formed a straight line. "Yes."

"Jacob." I shook my head. "Jacoby, what do you mean is? How did you find me so fast? Did The Light tell you or the FBI?"

He exhaled. "There's much more to The Light than what you know. I've spent the past three years trying to get at its secrets, trying to learn what's really happening. You were my ultimate test. Although I prided myself on how fast and well I learned the ways of The Light and Father Gabriel's teachings, I think they suspected that I wasn't like them. Not until you. You convinced them that I was. I didn't want a wife"—he stood and resumed his trek—"for many reasons. The obvious one was that this was all a sham. It's my job. The other was because I don't agree with all their ways. I could preach it and teach it to new followers." He shrugged. "I thought of it like the military. I justified it as taking and giving orders, but taking a wife made it different. Taking a wife meant I had to live it. I didn't want to do that.

"Though Brother Daniel was always supportive, Brother Timothy was equally as negative. I suspect he was involved in forcing a wife on me. He wanted me to fail."

I hated that man, even the sound of his name. "Why? What is his problem with us?"

Jacob shrugged. "I suspect he doesn't like you because you're my wife. I really don't know why he doesn't like me. To be honest, I never let it bother me, until . . ."

I reached for my hair, which now fell past my shoulders. "Me?"

His cheeks rose and his brown eyes shone. "God, I hated them for what they did to you, but Sara, I loved you so much more. You were so strong. That was the night I fully believed in you. In us. If what they did to you didn't break you, I knew you'd survive, and I knew I'd stop at nothing to not only complete my assignment but get you out too."

I remembered that night. "That really was our first time?"

His Adam's apple bobbed. "I'd promised you—it was when you were still unconscious. I promised I'd give you time. I needed to make you believe you were Sara Adams to keep you alive, but what we did in private was different. I swore I'd never force myself on you." His smile disappeared. "That's not the way it is with all the men in The Light. I'm on the Assembly. I hear stories."

My skin crawled as I thought of Brother Abraham's wife. "Deborah?"

Jacob's jaw clenched. "Abraham is an ass." His eyes pleaded. "I never forced you, nor did I ever lie about my feelings." He ran his hand over his face. "You can hate me forever, and tomorrow we can part ways and never see each other again, but if that happens, I pray you'll give me the gift of letting me know that you understand why I did everything. And that you know I never meant you harm."

It was so much, too much. He'd taken too much. I wasn't ready to give him what he asked, not yet. "What do you mean that tomorrow we could part ways? What's happening tomorrow?"

"Tomorrow is up to you."

When has anything been up to me?

FORTY-THREE

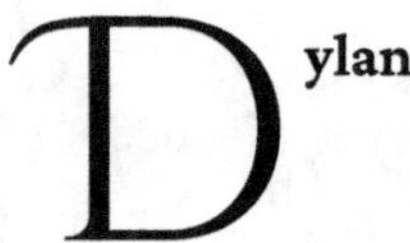

I RAN my fingers through my hair and sighed as my phone continued to ring. Each week the same call. Each week the same conversation. As I stared at my screen and read Beverly Montgomery's name I contemplated hitting ignore.

Ring four.

Ring five.

She'll just keep calling.

"Hello, Mrs. Montgomery," I said, trying for my calmest tone. If I'd let it ring one more time it would've gone to voice mail. Either she'd have called back or left a message. If she'd left a message, I'd be forced to call her back. It was easier to just talk—like ripping off a Band-Aid.

"Bev," she corrected. "How many times do I need to ask you to please call me Bev? I'm not interrupting you, am I?"

"No, Bev. I'm clocked out and on my way home."

"It's been another week since Stella . . ." Her voice momentarily trailed away. "I just can't believe it. My baby's been gone for nearly nine months. Please tell me you've learned something new, something that can help."

I shook my head as I eased my unmarked Charger into early evening Detroit traffic. "I wish I could. As you know, I'm not on the case."

"We know that, but you're on the force. You're her boyfriend—were."

I considered correcting her, telling her I wished I were still her boyfriend, but it would only take this conversation the way of many others, down an emotional path I wasn't up to navigating this evening.

She went on. "Surely they'd let you know . . ." Beverly Montgomery's words began to crack.

So much for avoiding emotion.

"The truth is that they wouldn't," I explained. "I'm not on the missing-persons task force. They can't tell me every time they learn anything new. Besides, because of Stella's and my relationship, they're less likely to tell me anything until they know for sure. They wouldn't want to get my hopes up."

"But . . . if they found something, that wouldn't get your hopes up. If they found her"—this time she couldn't disguise the audible cry before she whispered—"body."

"Nothing like that has happened. I promise you, if anything like that is found, you'll be contacted."

"It's strange how grown children live their own lives and as parents we're OK with that. Days and weeks can go by without speaking, and it's all right, because it means your children are doing what you raised them to do, to be independent, to be adults, and then in an instant it can all change . . ."

I clenched my teeth as I listened. Stella's mother had told me once that her therapist said talking to me would be helpful, therapeutic even for her loss. Sometimes the conversations were more upbeat, about Stella's sister, the one who'd been divorced. She'd recently remarried. Apparently losing a sister—well, having a sister go missing—had made her reevaluate her choices. The man she'd married had been her friend and now they had a child on the way. Beverly was elated at the prospect of being a grandparent. And then she'd think again about Stella and how much she'd enjoy being an aunt. Some conversations were too difficult to continue.

"...thank you."

I'd been listening, but also watching the moving traffic. I didn't hear why she was thanking me, but didn't want to ask.

"You're welcome. I look forward to your calls."

"I wish . . . well, a lot of things. I remember how excited Stella was that she'd asked you to our house for Christmas. I'm never giving up hope, but I want you to know, we'll always think of you as part of this family, even if you"—she took a deep breath—"find someone else."

"I'm not dating, but maybe someday. I'm not ready to give up either."

"I meant to tell you." Beverly's voice filled with a new sense of excitement.

"What?"

"Bernard Cooper called me the other day."

I felt my grip tighten around the steering wheel. "He did?"

"Yes. It wasn't much, but since both Stella and Mindy went missing, apparently there's been an internal investigation at WCJB. They hired some computer forensic guy. You know they never found either one of the girls' personal laptops, but they've been able to uncover deleted files from the television station's server."

"They have? What have they learned?"

"Nothing yet. But he was very excited about the possibility of discovering more. I am too. Anything is better than nothing."

"Please keep me up to date on Bernard's progress."

She sighed. "I will. I was afraid he hadn't told you."

"We spoke quite a bit when she first . . . but we don't exactly see eye to eye on everything."

"I get the feeling that Mr. Cooper feels responsible, like a father who didn't do all he should have for his children. Both girls' disappearances have been very difficult on him."

I was sure they were. He should feel responsible. Sending Stella to Highland Heights. I told her over and over to stay away. She wouldn't listen. It was when she went to Gabriel Clark's mansion in Bloomfield Hills that my hands were tied.

Her fate was better than it could have been.

That's what I told myself as I disconnected the call, made my way into my house in Brush Park, and checked on Fred. He was blissfully unaware of all that had occurred as he swam circles in his little bowl.

"It's OK, little guy," I said as I sprinkled betta pellets on top of the water. "The clock's reset. We won't need to have that conversation again for another week."

CHAPTER

FORTY-FOUR

J acob/Jacoby

I TOOK Stella's hand in mine, and at least this time, she didn't pull away. I couldn't ask her to go back to the Northern Light. It wasn't fair. Sitting beside her, I tried to smile. If it was our last time together, maybe, just maybe, she'd have some fond memories of me. "Before we get into tomorrow, would you please tell me about your memory?"

"My memories? Of what?"

"No, your memory. When did it come back?"

She sighed and lay back on the bed. Though her feet were still on the floor, with her head back, her yellow hair fanned around her face, reminding me of a halo. On her neck was the silver cross necklace that I'd put around her neck the night of her first service. Like the wedding ring, she'd worn it consistently since that day. I didn't deserve her, and she didn't deserve this. Scooting up on the bed, she arranged the pillows and leaned against the headboard. As she did she scanned the room.

"What?" I asked.

She shrugged. "I just realized there's only one bed."

I stood and walked to the small table near the window and sat in a chair. "You can have it. I can sleep in a chair. I did that for over two weeks."

She nodded and smiled at me. "Now that makes sense."

"I promised."

She patted the bed beside her. "I'm not having sex with you, but you can sleep here."

"Are you . . . ?"

"Jacob, I'm not sure how much sleep we'll get. We have a lot to talk about."

I moved back to the bed. "Your memory?"

"Over a week ago, when you were gone for a few nights. You went to the Eastern . . . Detroit."

I nodded. "I can't believe I didn't know."

Crossing her arms over her chest, she shook her head. "I was afraid you did. The moment I saw you again, I knew I couldn't hide it from you. So I didn't try. When I was with you, I turned Stella off. I had to."

"What do you mean, you turned her off?"

She turned to face me. "How have you done it? I mean for three years. That's a long time."

I stared up at the ceiling. It was one of those bumpy ones, painted, but the white paint had discolored to a faint yellow with time. "You know what?" I said. "I get it. When I first went to the Eastern Light, I had to think about what I said and how I acted, but then, with time, I became Jacob."

I recalled the earlier training. Women weren't the only ones to be indoctrinated. It wasn't called that with men. It was called training —making it sound military or strategic. The first few weeks at the Eastern Light were a boot camp of sorts. It was where the men deemed unfit were weeded out. It was where Father Gabriel's word became second nature, where The Light's way of thinking was either embraced or rejected.

Those who rejected it didn't succeed. They didn't go on to become Assemblymen. I studied. I listened, and I performed. I couldn't fail.

I sighed at the memories and went on with my answer. "In the back of my mind I kept my objective, but I didn't have to think anymore. I was."

"So with me . . . ?" She left the question open.

There were so many ways I could go. "With you I had time. You were unconscious for a week."

"Did you really stay with me, or did I imagine that?"

"I stayed with you." I didn't want to tell her that Dr. Newton had injured her more between the attack and when I got to her. She didn't need to know how depraved he was too. When she only nodded, I went on. "So I had time to work through my issues. I talked to you. I confessed the truth about our relationship."

"That we didn't have one?"

"No. I said it was new, but I also told you that I'd seen you, and I'd do my damnedest to make you laugh like you had."

Staring straight ahead, she wiped a tear.

"I'm so sorry."

Sara shook her head. "The thing is, you did. In that whole fucked-up world, I wasn't really unhappy. I was at first, but then it felt . . . I don't know . . . right." She turned toward me. Her cheeks were dotted with blotchy red patches, the way they were when she cried. "I want to hate you. When my memories first came back, I hoped you were a victim too. That's what I tried to convince myself. But now, knowing that you knew, that you were part of it . . . I want to hate you.

"The thing is, as Sara I'm so different than I am as Stella. Different, not better or worse. Stella had a career and a fish." She laughed. "I hope Dylan took care of Fred."

I doubted that asshole had done anything, but I wouldn't say that either. "Fred? Was that your fish?"

Her eyes sparkled with unshed tears. "Yes. I feel like I'm two different people. Stella had a fish. Sara wanted a baby."

"Do you understand why I said no?"

She nodded. "Now I do, but I . . ." She looked down.

"I know what you did. It's why your memory came back."

Her gaze snapped back to mine. "You know? How do you know?"

"The drug that kept your memory away was in your birth control medicine. And, well, Raquel told me."

She nodded with the confirmation of her theory and then huffed. "So much for friendship confidentiality."

"In all fairness, she didn't tell me until today."

"Today?"

"Well, it seems like longer ago than that. After the incident with Brother Timothy, Sister Lilith, and your hair, I worried about leaving you alone, especially since I had to be gone overnight. So one of the times I left, early on after we returned to the community, I bought a burner phone. You know, a disposable one, untraceable?"

She nodded, her eyes wide.

"I took a chance. Elizabeth is too conditioned. I knew I couldn't ask her to break rules."

"So you asked Raquel?"

I nodded. "Benjamin knew too. We all prayed that the phone would never need to be used."

Sara reached for my hand. I rolled my wrist so our palms would touch and our fingers intertwine. "See," she said, "I'm so mixed up. I hate that it was all a lie, but things like that make it seem real."

I lifted her hand and kissed her knuckles. "I told you that I didn't lie about my feelings."

Though she sighed, she didn't pull her hand away.

"So," I said, "your memories have been back for over a week, and when you were with me, you were Sara?" She nodded. "This morning, before I left, you told me you loved me." She nodded again. "And that was a lie?"

"Sara loves Jacob." She squeezed my hand. "That's all I can give you."

It was my turn to nod. "What happened with Thomas?"

She quickly turned toward me. "I told you, nothing."

"No, I believe that. I'm asking how you ended up with him. Deputy Hill said that you said he took you against your will, but . . . what did the but mean?"

She sighed. "I went for a walk before work, and I saw your truck."

"My truck?"

"I knew you hadn't driven it into the community. You were gone. I'd seen Thomas in the community before. I didn't understand how he did it. Xavier never did, but I took a chance."

My pulse quickened. "You spoke to him in the community where others may have seen you?"

She shook her head. "No, I made sure that no one was around, and I got in the truck. I hid in the backseat, on the floor under a blanket."

Though she'd totally fucked up both of our lives, my cheeks rose as I shook my head with newfound admiration. "Damn, you're brave."

"It was stupid. I took a chance and it almost cost me more than I was willing to pay."

I didn't know how to respond. It had cost both of us, it wasn't almost.

"I thought I was good until he drove through the gates and then a few minutes later stopped the truck. He knew I was there." Her eyes opened wide again. "Jacob? I mean Jacoby?"

I lifted her hand and kissed her knuckles again. "I'd be OK if we stick with Jacob and Sara. I recently heard something about Sara, and I'm confident Jacob feels the same way. "

"I can't . . ."

"I'm not asking you to," I reassured her. "What did you want to ask?"

Her baby-blue eyes held the innocent Sara gaze I'd come to adore. "Are there really polar bears?"

"Yes!" Of all the questions she could have asked, this one made me smile. "I've seen them myself, especially out by the landing strip."

"Then I hope he gets mauled."

"You don't need to worry about him."

"Will you tell me why?"

"I'll tell you anything. You never need to ask that way again."

She nodded.

"I don't know the details, but the US Marshals took care of him." When her expression blanked, I realized what that sounded like. "Not as in dead. Your confirmation that he took you against your will gave them probable cause. Deputy Hill guaranteed that Thomas would be lost in the federal system longer than I needed."

"Longer than you needed? What does that mean?"

"My assignment isn't over. The FBI needs more time to coordinate all the raids, and there's more I want to learn. Today was only the second time in nearly three years that I've spoken with my handler. Thomas is a weak link. He could have easily talked to Father Gabriel. He had to be silenced."

"Are you going back? Did I mess everything up?" She sighed, adjusted her pillow, and lay back.

"It's like I said, it depends on you." When I looked toward Sara, she was on her side with her knees drawn up. "What is it?"

In a short time, her complexion had paled. With her eyes closed, she shook her head. "I think I'm hungry."

"Damn, I'm sorry. I wasn't thinking." I stood. "When did you last eat?"

"Sometime at the marshals' office. It's probably the stress too."

Her forehead glistened with a sheen of perspiration.

"Let me go get you something to eat. It's kind of late. I can get fast food."

She nodded. "Thank you. I think that would help."

"If I leave you alone?" I looked at the phone on the stand near the bed. "I can't. I can't leave you alone."

"I'm not sure I can go with you. I'm suddenly not feeling very well."

Even if I pulled the phone cord out of the wall, she could always walk next door and borrow someone's phone. I couldn't say it, but in reality she too was a weak link.

Looking around, I found plastic cups wrapped in cellophane. Opening one, I filled it with water and brought it back to her. "Here, try drinking some water." Her beautiful eyes opened as she sat back up.

"Thank you," she said, taking the cup. Though the water sloshed in her shaky grasp, she smiled. "This reminds me of the clinic."

I watched the color return to her cheeks. Once she was done, I took the cup and brushed my thumb over her right cheek. "See, we do have a past."

I ROLLED the handle of the paring knife in my fingers as I paced the room and Sara slept. I should have been sleeping too, but I couldn't. My mind couldn't settle from the whirlwind of thoughts. Though I hated what Thomas had done to her, the knife made me smile. I hadn't been able to believe it when she removed it from her boot. It was obviously the reason I'd thought she was walking oddly, why I was worried that he'd hurt her sexually. She was so much braver than I knew.

I'd finally gotten the nerve to ask her the question that had eaten at me since my call with Raquel. I'd asked whether she was pregnant. Her answer made me feel neither better nor worse. She said she didn't know. It had been only three weeks since her last period, which she said was too early to know. I wasn't sure whether that was totally accurate. Though it'd been three years since I'd watched television—yes, even while in motels, I didn't; I wanted to stay in Jacob mode—I seemed to remember commercials that talked about home pregnancy tests that could determine results earlier than that. With her sound asleep, I considered driving to a store to buy one, but I wasn't sure I was ready to know.

We'd talked about so much, but I'd never posed the question that the morning would require. Once she ate the fast food we'd gone together to get and began yawning, I'd decided it could wait. Obviously the future was something neither one of us was ready to tackle. However, we'd done a bang-up job on our past. Maybe it was because it was relatively short, but we'd covered nearly everything, and I'd done my best to explain the whys behind each decision. The time of forbidding her questioning was over. For there to be a chance at a future, she needed to understand everything. The change in dynamic was refreshing yet unsettling. The conditioned man from The Light wanted to take control and tell her what to do. The man I had once been, and hoped to be again, appreciated a partner, not a submissive.

Sara wasn't the only one who felt like two different people. My two perspectives had me torn.

I didn't want to ask her to come back to The Light. It was too dangerous. Then again, the idea of never seeing her again created a void I couldn't imagine navigating. There was a reason agents stayed unattached. Lying in the bed, in nothing more than her bra and panties, was that reason. No, it wasn't that I'd waited for Sara. It was that I fucking hated having an Achilles' heel.

She made me more vulnerable. For that reason alone I should forgo asking and just tell Special Agent Adler that she'd said no. Then I should kiss her good-bye and let her walk away into witness protection. She'd be blissfully unaware of the repercussions, but I'd be confident of her safety.

Sitting at the table, I laid my head on my arms. With my eyes closed, I tried reassuring myself that the entire three years weren't a bust. My testimony alone could put Father Gabriel, the three Commissions, and the three Assemblies away for a long time. They all knew something. It wasn't as if each individual knew the extent of the wrongdoings. Hell, I hadn't even known about the entire pharmaceutical scheme until recently. But once this was over, deciphering the details and determining the extent of each person's involvement wouldn't be up to me. It would be up to others in the FBI and then the judicial system.

The idea of putting all those men behind bars made me think about the wives and other followers. As the fast food churned in my gut, I feared that if the timing was off—at all—if all the raids didn't happen at the exact same time, Father Gabriel had an escape plan and would use it. The only part of his plan I knew for sure was that it involved flying to an unknown destination. What concerned me was the fate of those he would leave behind. Every day, as I became closer and closer to people like Raquel and Benjamin, I feared more for their safety. I'd never been told of a mass suicide plan, but I was terrified one might be in place.

Sara's hand landed on my shoulder. I hadn't even heard her get up.

"Why aren't you asleep?" she asked.

I covered her hand with mine. "Investigative journalist, huh?"

She walked in front of me, wrapping herself in a blanket she'd found in the top of the closet. Though the lights were off, with the soft glow of a night-light from the bathroom, I watched as she covered her bra and panties. "Yes," she replied, sheepishly adding, "I'm good at asking questions."

"Too good."

"So why aren't you sleeping? You were the one who said we had a long day."

I took a deep breath. "I'm thinking about tomorrow."

"Tell me."

"I can't."

Her volume rose. "I thought you said no more secrets."

"I can't tell you, because it's not up to me, and if it were, I can't decide what I'd choose."

She sat on the edge of the bed. "You're saying that tomorrow is my decision? Then give me my options."

I sat back and ran my hands over my face. My normal scruff had grown longer and softer. "Number one, we say good-bye to each other and you're taken to someplace safe. I'm leaning toward that option, by the way." I didn't know how far I was leaning that way, but her being safe outweighed the alternative.

She nodded. "You want to say good-bye?"

"No, Sara, I want you safe."

"And option number two?" she asked.

"Number two, we go back to the Northern Light and resume our lives."

"Option two means that you get to continue your assignment and keep working to bring down Father Gabriel?"

I nodded.

"What happens to Father Gabriel if I choose option one?"

"Well, right now he's at the Eastern Light."

"In that huge-ass mansion in Bloomfield Hills?"

"Jesus, you know about that too? Don't tell me Richards took you there."

"No! He didn't even know that I knew about it." She shrugged. "I guess he did know I knew about the house. I remember him being with me when I looked it up on Google Earth, but the way I figured it out had to do with a trail of ownership. I deduced that Father Gabriel was really Gabriel Clark, son of Marcel Clarkson."

I stared in amazement as she recounted the accurate information. No doubt The Light had taken her before she could expose them. More accurately, Richards had handed her over before she could expose The Light. As she finished speaking, she asked, "So what happens to Father Gabriel?"

"If you choose option one, the FBI will move as soon as it can.

They want their raids coordinated. If neither of us returns to the Northern Light, those in control will undoubtedly get suspicious. I don't know the particulars. There's a lot I'm still learning, but I suspect the Commission on each campus has a plan in case of discovery."

"What kind of plan?"

"Like I said, I don't know."

Sara stood and paced, the blanket falling from her shoulder, revealing the satin strap of her white bra. "A plan, like Jones's Kool-Aid?"

"It's not your concern. You didn't ask for any of this."

"What about all the followers? What about our friends, the women who didn't ask to be there? What about the children?"

I shook my head. "That's not how this works. I can't pick and choose. I can hope the raids happen before the Commissions figure it out. I mean, they all have to be timed perfectly."

"But you said you don't know it all. Why can't you go back without me?"

"Because I can't explain your disappearance. If I show up without you, they'll go after you. That's why you can't go back to your life. You have to go into witness protection."

"What? Wait! That's what you mean by me being safe? No way. No fucking way."

I pinched the bridge of my nose as I fought the urge to bring attention to her insolent tone and vulgar language. "Excuse me?"

"I said no."

Standing, I towered over her petite frame. "I'm not risking your safety. Besides, what if you're . . ." I motioned toward her midsection.

"Then you're going to send me away to have a new identity, like two aren't enough? And you're never going to see me or our baby again?"

"What the hell? Ten hours ago you were trying to call Richards. Would you have let him raise my kid?"

She crossed her arms over her breasts. "Ten hours ago I thought you were some whacked-out Light fanatic who'd kidnapped and assaulted me. And with that profile, hell yes, I wanted to get away from you."

"Light fanatic?" I asked with a hint of amusement.

She snickered. "Besides, I'm not pregnant."

"What? I thought you said it was too early?"

"It is, officially. I mean I don't know. So we shouldn't base anything off the unknown. Talk to me about what we do know." Before I could answer, she continued, "Let me start. If I don't go back with you, the FBI will raid all three campuses . . . today? Father Gabriel is in the big-ass mansion, which is probably one of the worst places to catch him, and if the raids aren't perfectly timed, there's the chance of Kool-Aid?"

I shrugged. "No confirmation on Kool-Aid."

"If I go back, we continue to live as we did. We continue to gather evidence to bring down Father Gabriel, otherwise known as Garrison Clarkson, and The Light. And we give the FBI more time to coordinate the raids."

"No."

"No?"

"There's no we. There's me. The FBI can't ask a civilian to enter into an investigation."

She smiled.

At that moment, I wasn't looking at Sara but at Stella. Though her cheek was battered, the beautiful woman before me exuded confidence. With a sexy smile, she dropped the blanket and moved closer. Pushing me back to the chair, she spread my knees apart, walked directly in front of me, and bent closer, until our noses nearly touched. With the mounds of her breasts peeking from her bra and a sultry tone, she whispered, "I don't think it's the FBI who's asking me." Her finger traced my jawline, burning my skin with her touch. "I think it's me saying I want to do this." Continuing her assault, she gently teased the collar of my shirt. "It's me, volunteering to keep your mission going." Placing her petite hands on my shoulders, she moved her lips closer to mine. "Tell me, Jacoby, do you really want to send me away?"

I am so fucking screwed!

CHAPTER

FORTY-FIVE

S tella/Sara

JACOBY DIDN'T ANSWER my question, but by the expression on his face, I knew I was winning this battle of wills. It was the power I'd learned I possessed months ago. Despite his dominance, there had been times when I had control. Now I wanted to use that power to help him and his mission. I'd told him things I knew about The Light; now I wanted to know all he knew—there were still so many questions. Nevertheless, I was confident that together we could do this. We could bring Gabriel Clarkson's world crashing down, and I prayed we could do it without Kool-Aid or any other plan that would have catastrophic results.

I knew that Jacob and I could help each other. But there was something I needed to do first. "I want to call my parents and let them know I'm alive."

Jacob sighed. "If you choose witness protection, they'll help you with that."

I stood and pulled the blanket tighter. "I don't want witness protection. But I can't not tell them or"—I didn't know how Jacob would respond—"Dylan."

His stare darkened. "It's not up to me. You can't."

"It's not up to you? You're right. It's up to me. I need to call. My parents probably think I'm dead. My mom could call Dina Rosemont, my friend Mindy's mom, and then they'd have hope."

Jacob shook his head. "I don't know who you're talking about, but this is why witness protection is best."

"How long would we need to be back? Days? Weeks? Months?"

"As short as possible. Just long enough for the FBI to get organized on the raids. The best possible scenario is for all three campuses to be raided at the exact same time."

I pressed my lips together. "I don't like it—not calling—but I understand."

I did. Though Jacob had lied in the past, as we'd talked, I'd understood both his motivation and the reason I couldn't call. I even believed that he'd protected me and that our collective success had been contingent upon the success of each of us.

When I brushed my lips against his, his dark eyes widened suspiciously.

I tried for my most innocent Sara expression. "What?" I sat back on the bed and faced him. "Will you tell me a few things, a few things about The Light?"

"I told you, I'd tell you anything you want to know."

"How many of the women, wives, came to The Light like I did?"

He shrugged. "I've only been there for three years, but as a pilot I see more than most. After all, the women have to get to the Northern Light or Western Light somehow."

My stomach rolled as I scrunched my nose and lowered my chin. "Oh, God." My words sounded more like a cry. "Y-you transported them—us?"

"Micah and I." He reached for my hands. "Sara, remember why. Remember my goal. I had to gain Father Gabriel's trust. No follower has ever obtained the Assembly in as short of a time as I did. It was because, well"—he sighed—"I convinced them I had PTSD. I convinced them all that I reveled in the structure of The Light, and I thrived following and giving orders."

My eyes narrowed. "But you knew what you were doing." Suddenly cold, I released his hands and tightened the blanket around myself. "It's human trafficking."

He nodded.

No denial or even regret.

Shaking my head, I stood. "I've been struggling with what are real memories and what aren't, but one thing I remember vividly, not only from what I've lived but also from what I believe I recall from my research of The Light, was"—I walked to the bed, turned on a lamp, and returned to Jacob. Then I deliberately held out my hand, fingertips up—"this. I was looking for something to tie everything together." I rubbed the tips of my fingers against my thumb. "Women were showing up in the Wayne County Morgue, and their only connection was the burned fingertips. Actually, there were even a few men who had them."

Jacob rolled his hands. I knew his were the same as mine. It was why when my eyes were covered I'd thought his hands were callused. They weren't, not really. It was the roughness of his acid-burned fingertips. "What are you asking?"

"Were those people, those dead people, ones who were banished?"

He nodded. "Some of them. The Eastern Light is the entry point, the place for visitors' assembly. There are also informational hubs that are set up around the country. The Assembly at the Eastern Light is proficient at follower acquisition. They decide who can and can't join. Believe it or not, people are turned down."

I shook my head. "Are there really that many willing to join?"

Jacob nodded. "That was why, when I approached The Light, I

had to stand out as a good recruit. The FBI chose me for this assignment not only based on my success in other undercover missions, but also based on my history and my lack of family commitment."

I sank back to the bed.

Oh my God! I'd never considered that he might be married to someone else. Obviously my expression gave away my thoughts.

"You didn't ask," he said, "but I wanted you to know. I'm not married, as Jacoby McAlister. I never have been."

I nodded, unable to do more.

"I was also chosen for the assignment," he went on, "because of my real-life military experience. I handled my transition from military to law enforcement well, but I know of others, I have friends, or had them, that didn't. I studied what they went through and like I said, I was able to become a veteran with PTSD. As Father Gabriel's pilot, I had more access to him than others. I didn't take advantage of that—on the surface. I never questioned—"

My brows rose.

He smiled. "Yes, in case you didn't know, questioning is frowned upon in The Light."

"Really?" I said in my best sarcastic voice.

This time his brows rose. "And so is being a smart-ass to your husband."

"So I've been told."

He went on, "I did what I was told to do by Father Gabriel, my overseer, members of the Commission, everyone. Eventually, Father Gabriel began asking me questions about my past. Slowly I wove the story I'd given at the Eastern Light, and it worked. With time I was given more and more responsibilities. Each step in the hierarchy of The Light was a test. At first I only flew with Micah, and then together we flew Father Gabriel from campus to campus. Then I was trusted alone to gather supplies, often coming here to Fairbanks. The first time I was told to transport acquired members, I expected it to be like when I was taken to the Northern Light. I was among seven individuals who'd all come willingly into The Light. Initially there were more in our group; however, only seven went to the Northern Light. We were told that some didn't perform to The Light's requirements and were banished. That term has always implied the ultimate punishment.

"We were also told some went to a different campus. Followers don't know how many campuses exist, other than that the Eastern Light is the point of entry, and, of course, they learn about the campus where they're assigned. Most people who come willingly are men or couples. Rarely do women join of their own accord. Yet some do."

"Elizabeth," I said.

Jacob nodded. "Luke told me that, but she joined before me, so I don't know anything about that."

I looked down.

"What?" he asked.

"I believe I know more about that, about her twin sister, but I'd rather hear what you have to say first. Please keep going."

He took a deep breath. "The operations at the other campuses are different. Men are needed for physical labor. Women are needed for other tasks, but primarily to keep men content."

I clenched my teeth.

Jacob shook his head. "I'm not saying I agree with the philosophy. I'm telling you, honestly, that it's the mind-set of the Commission. The Light needs men. At the Northern Light they're needed to work the production of the pharmaceuticals, to load the merchandise, to work the power plant, I could go on and on—to build buildings, the exterior walls, and fences." His eyes opened wide. "It's a huge operation. Women do some of that work too, as well as female jobs like day care, laundry, cooking. Mostly they're there to provide men with what they need."

"It's so fucking sexist."

He lifted one of his eyebrows. "You're an investigative journalist, and you just now realized that?"

I pursed my lips. "No, I figured it out as Sara. What I don't understand is how I was OK with it." I shook my head. "Because as much as I hate it at this moment, two weeks ago I didn't."

"That's because we all worked to condition you. Assuming we're going back, if we were to end up there longer than a few days or weeks, the time will come when you're expected to help condition others. It's required. Refusing isn't an option, not without punishment and possible banishment. The community as a whole works to welcome new members, no matter how they're obtained. Working together is essential to keeping it all running. In some ways you've already done it. The women you meet with, you're conditioning them to accept the way of The Light and Father Gabriel's word."

I didn't want to think about that—about how I'd helped. "Tell me about the women in the morgue."

Jacob's shoulder rose and fell. "I wasn't at the Eastern Light for very long. I progressed fast and the Northern Light happened to have an opening for a pilot."

"Happened?"

"I don't know. I really don't," he reassured me. "I assume the one before me was banished, but I've never been told. The only people who know are the Commission, and I can't question them."

"Have you asked anyone on the Assembly? It seems like you're close with Brothers Benjamin and Luke."

"We are, but no. I can't let my assignment affect Jacob's behavior. If I did . . . if I became too inquisitive, it would make people leery."

"Dead women?" I asked again.

"Like I said, The Light needs women, not just for sex, but for jobs that men are too busy to do. It's the Eastern Light's responsibility to determine if the women that are chosen or who volunteer will be able to handle it. Once they're brought into The Light, if it's determined they aren't fit to be a follower, they're removed."

"Does that only happen at the Eastern Light?"

"No, but that's where most of it happens. However, every new believer has a probationary period."

"Do you dispose of bodies at the Northern Light?"

"Me personally? No."

"But it happens?"

He nodded.

"That first time you were asked to transport followers, they weren't willing participants, were they?"

"No."

"Women?"

"Yes, all five of them."

I seriously thought I might be ill. "What happened once they got to the Northern Light?"

"You know what happened. You lived through it."

"I've been asking questions, since I started having memories. It seems like many women have similar stories."

"Similar, but they vary," he admitted. "The similarities are injuries. For many they occur at the Eastern Light. It's part of the process to see how well they adapt. The main component is lack of sight. It's been determined that loss of vision is an essential psychological factor in making the new follower dependent upon her husband."

A tear slid down my cheek as I stood. "Well," I said, walking to the end of the bed. "I guess I should congratulate whoever put the plan together. It works."

Jacob came up behind me and wrapped his arms around my waist. Leather and musk fell over us as I laid my head back against his chest. "I'll tell you I'm sorry forever, but I know it'll never be enough."

I turned into his warm embrace. The steady beat of his heart comforted me, as it had over the last nine months. Keeping my cheek against his soft shirt, I asked, "Is it still my decision, if I go back?"

"Yes."

"I was all ready to say yes. I mean, I want to help. I want Father Gabriel to be brought down . . ."

"But now?" His chest vibrated with his words.

I shook my head as tears began to freely flow. "It's so wrong, so perverse. I'm not sure I can watch other women suffer, like I did, or help condition them. The fact I already have sickens me."

"People like Raquel and Deborah, at the clinic, are very good at it."

I nodded, the feeling of betrayal slicing deep inside me. "I thought Raquel was my friend."

Jacob grasped my shoulders and held me at arm's length. Looking deep into my puffy eyes, he said, "She is. Don't doubt that. She's the reason I found you. She risked punishment to save you."

"To bring me back. I'm not sure it's saving me."

His eyes narrowed. "Listen to me." His even tone held an edge of harshness. "Raquel didn't know what kind of man Thomas was, but by getting you away from him, she saved you. What she does know, what she's the most concerned about, is what would've happened if The Light found you. She risked her own well-being to save your life. Her lies were no more malicious than mine. She isn't undercover, but she believes. Like many of the others, she sincerely believes that what she's doing is for the greater good. She only wanted your success."

My chin fell to my chest. "It's just so hard to wrap my mind around." I looked back up. When his grip loosened and his arms again surrounded me, I fell back against his chest. "I have so many more questions."

He led me to the bed. "We need to leave this room in a couple of hours. One way or the other. Either we're both going with the FBI or we're both going back to The Light. No matter your decision, we should try to get some rest."

I lay back down, the blanket still wrapped around me, and Jacob covered me with the bed's cover. As I settled against the pillow, I asked, "What if I'd been given to someone like Abraham?"

Jacob's neck straightened and the vein along the side pulsated. He didn't speak, only shook his head.

"How can you watch that and transport women knowing that they could end up like that?"

He kissed my forehead. "I'll need your answer when I wake you."

I swallowed my tears. "Will you please lie here with me?"

"Sara?"

"Please, I know it isn't fair. I meant what I said about sex, but I have no idea what I'm going to do." I sniffled. "All I know is I want you near me right now."

Jacob sighed and climbed onto the other side of the bed. Scooting closer, he wrapped his arm around my shoulder, and I nuzzled against his chest.

"I had images of the two of us saving them all," I said, "but that's not what's going to happen, is it?"

His chest moved with his answer. "No. There will most likely be casualties."

"But I can't go back to my life . . . either. Can I? I mean to my life as Stella?"

"No, I'm sorry . . ."

I closed my eyes and refused to listen to the rest of his apology. He was right. He could say it a million times and it wouldn't be sufficient. Though he'd done his best for me, there were others, so many others, and he'd had a hand in their fate. For three years he'd transported unconscious women across the country to enslave them in a life they never wanted or imagined in their wildest dreams. It wasn't as if The Light were a horrific orgy. There were specific rules about the sanctity of marriage, yet it was all a farce. The marriages weren't real. Unless . . .

My head popped up. "Wait. Is Father Gabriel really a minister, like ordained?"

"Yes. He has to be, for tax purposes. He's the head of a church."

"Then . . . does he marry the women—" I jumped to my real question: "Are we really married?"

His embrace loosened as he sighed. "He does. I mean he did. There wasn't a ceremony as such, but he married Jacob Adams to

Sara, making you Sara Adams. I'm not Jacob Adams and you're not Sara."

Using my thumb, I turned my wedding band. "I'm so confused. I wish I still hated you."

"You should."

I agreed, I should, but I didn't. "Will I ever know what's real and what's been conditioned into me?"

"Take option one. There are people who help with deprogramming. They'll work with you; they'll help you."

"Will they help the others?"

"All that they can."

The motel room fell into an eerie silence; only the hum of the heating unit near the window made noise. It was our reminder that time was passing, the tick-tock telling us that our clock was running. Someone else had wound it up, and neither of us could make it stop.

As I lay in his embrace, sleep stayed out of reach. Despite his even breaths, I was certain that Jacob couldn't sleep either. My mind was in a constant battle. I didn't know if it was Sara versus Stella, or the desire to help Jacob and our friends while bringing down a tyrant versus walking away. All I knew was that I was walking a figurative fence, each thought pulling me from one side to the other. No matter where I landed, Stella was gone, and the pain of that loss was paralyzing.

There was also the man with his arm around me.

Did I love him, or was I only conditioned to love him? Did I dare think about Dylan?

Dylan and I hadn't been that serious, yet it had been more serious than I'd ever been—than Stella had ever been. A tear fell onto Jacob's chest as I remembered Dylan's warnings about Highland Heights. He'd lost his parents and now he'd lost me. The ripples continued to move further and further away.

After everything that Jacob had done, I decided I couldn't leave him without giving him the one thing he'd asked for. Wiping my tears, I sat up and said, "Are you awake?"

"Yes."

"You asked me for something earlier. You asked me to tell you that I understood why you did what you did." I lifted his hand, intertwined our fingers, and kissed his knuckles, as he'd done to me over and over. "It's totally fucked up, but I do. I don't think I could've asked for a better husband. I mean if this was my fate, predetermined for whatever reason, I'm not sorry I was assigned to you, Jacoby. I believe that you made it as good as it could be."

Jacob sighed. "Jacoby?"

"Yes, thank you. I know it could've been a lot worse." Did he understand what I wasn't saying?

His chin fell. "God, I'm going to miss you."

I swallowed the emotion forming a lump in my throat. Witness protection was best. I needed to face that. "Will the FBI . . . will I be able to contact you if I'm . . . ?"

I was so stupid. Why the hell had I risked getting pregnant?

"Not me. They won't allow it. But since it happened as part of a sting operation, I believe there's some kind of financial—"

I sat straighter. "Stop!"

His eyes opened wide. "What?"

"I'm not asking you for money! Is that what you think this is about?"

"No . . . no . . . that's not what I meant. I just mean, you'll need to be able to provide . . ."

I threw back the covers and stood. I was a fucking wreck. One minute I was sad, the next I was mad. I wanted to go back. I didn't want to go back. I loved Jacob and I'd miss him. I hated him and I never wanted to see him again.

Holding my head, I paced along the side of the bed.

"Sara, come lie down."

"No! I feel like I'm going to jump out of my skin. I don't know who the hell I am, or even what I feel." In the darkened room, Jacob sat up against the headboard, but he didn't try to speak, to tell me who I was or what I should feel.

Part of me wanted him to do that.

The Sara part.

That was the part of me that was conditioned to do exactly what my husband said, what he wanted, even before he said it.

"Damn you!" I screamed.

His shadow didn't flinch.

"Did you hear me? I hate this! It might not be your doing, and I may have forgiven you your role, but it was still you!"

"I wasn't . . ."

"I know," I interrupted, "you didn't choose me. You didn't even want a wife, but it was you who made it all right. If you were Abraham, I could easily walk away."

His head moved from side to side. "You're right," he said sadly, "I'm so fucking sorry I tried to make it the best I could for you." His tone evened as he stood from the bed. "Maybe that's all you need to push you over the edge into making the right decision." Each word came forth with less and less emotion. Walking toward me, he reached for his belt. "You've always been smart. It scared the shit out of me, but this time, I thank you. You just gave me the goddamn answer."

My breathing quickened as I backed away and he unlatched the buckle. "What the hell do you think you're doing?"

"What I fucking promised I'd never do."

"No way! Don't do this. It's not you."

He pulled his belt from the loops, one at a time, the sound echoing through the room. "Don't worry, Sara, I think you'll have your decision soon."

I swallowed and stepped backward away from the bed until my back bumped into the vanity at the end of the room. His dark form moved closer. By the light of the night-light, I watched as he ran the length of his belt through his hands.

"Jacob, don't do this."

In the semidarkness, the belt dangling from his left hand reminded me of a whip. It didn't take a stretch of my imagination to see it that way. To my left was the door to the bathroom containing the shower and toilet. I lunged for it, making it inside as Jacob's foot entered the jamb. Though I pushed with all my might, I couldn't shut the door.

"Come out here. It's time to prepare."

FORTY-SIX

J acob/Jacoby

"YOU CAN'T DO THIS," Sara yelled from the small bathroom. Her volume decreased as she surrendered the door and sank down onto the closed toilet seat.

She was wrong, I could do it. I couldn't do it out of anger. That was Father Gabriel's teaching, but I could do it, as her husband it was my right. Besides, her bravery was nothing more than stupidity. Three fucking years of work down the damn drain because she wanted a baby. She didn't have the right to make that kind of deci-sion, not in The Light. That was up to me. Punishment for that alone was justified.

Opening the door, I narrowed my gaze, and worked to speak calmly. "Don't make me repeat myself."

The blue that stared up at me, veiled by the bowed head and long lashes, would haunt me forever, but I knew what I was doing. Sara couldn't go back and neither could I. The operation was over. It was up to me to make her feel right about leaving me and about telling me to go to hell.

She didn't need to tell me, because without her and our possible child, I'd be in hell—figuratively as well as literally. As I fought my own fight against my three years of personal conditioning, I was standing at the entrance to fire and brimstone. The twisting in my stomach told me it was a one-way door.

I stood silently watching the conflict between the two women inside her as it continued to rage. With each ticking second it was as if I could see both individuals. Slowly Stella was relinquishing control to Sara. This was, after all, Sara's world; nevertheless, Stella wouldn't go away quietly. Even as Sara's shoulders rolled forward, Stella spoke.

"Fuck you," she muttered.

I shook my head. "Vulgarity was never a real problem at the Northern Light, but I've had quite enough for tonight."

"Too fucking bad!" Stella's eyes sent daggers through my heart. "I was wrong to accept your apology. You're an asshole!"

I reached for her arm. "Sara, stand." As I pulled her to her feet, she looked back down at the ground. "Tell me, how many lashes per transgression?"

Her jaw clenched as she fought with herself to answer. Finally she whispered, "Five."

"Now tell me how many times you've used vulgarities tonight."

Her body trembled in my grasp, yet when her eyes fluttered back to mine, her neck straightened with defiance. Raising her chin, she spoke clearly and resolutely. "If you fucking do this, I will press charges. I'll tell the FBI what a whack-job they have for an agent."

Undeterred by her threat, I smirked. "Remove your underwear."

"Fuck you," she whispered, lowering her chin again to her chest.

I straightened my neck and spoke as I'd been trained to do, as I'd trained others to do. "Vulgarity and disobedience are only two transgressions. I've heard you use two vulgarities in the last thirty seconds. As always, the severity of your correction is at my discretion." I grabbed the waist of her panties and pushed them down. Spinning her around, I unlatched her bra and pulled the straps from her arms. "I recommend you stop saying any more before I decide to give you the accurate number of lashes."

"Jacob, please don't do this." She spun back, her firm breasts pressing against my chest, as she appealed with her gorgeous blue eyes. The left one was a stark contrast, the color of her iris so light compared to the purpled skin surrounding it. Her cheeks were sprouting red blotches as we stood. When I narrowed my gaze, she obediently turned back around. However, her stare never left mine, now glaring at me through the reflection of the mirror. She gripped the edge of the vanity and asked, "Please . . . why?"

I ran the length of the leather through my hands, not allowing myself to sense the despair seeping from her every pore. "Enough questioning."

Her lips came together, forming a straight line. She didn't need her mouth to tell me her thoughts. I saw both the pleas and the insults shooting from her eyes.

"You know what to do."

"I hate you," she whispered.

I stood unmoved and maintained my stance. As I made Sara wait, her words gave me the strength to continue. With each second her proclamation darkened the remaining shreds of my heart. If making her hate me would save her, then I'd do it. Everything she'd said was right; though I hadn't wanted a wife, I'd taken one. I was the one who had done this to her. I was the one who had held her hand while she lived in that hell. I couldn't take her back there, not again.

As I slapped my belt against my hand, the sound echoed throughout the room. Gasping, Sara spread her legs and leaned forward. Just as her cheek contacted the cool vanity, she whispered, "I really do."

Blonde hair fell over her battered cheek as her body shuddered with tears.

In nine long months she'd awakened something inside me that had been dead for over a decade. I'd suspected what she was capable of doing to me the first time I saw her, when Brother Uriel showed her to me. Now it was time to shut it off. This was different from being in The Light. Taking her back wasn't saving her. She'd been given to me to protect. It wasn't up to her. It was my decision. Now that she had the real chance to be free and safe, I wouldn't take that away from her.

Sara's lip disappeared between her teeth as she finally shut her eyes. The way the muscles in her legs and behind tensed, I knew she was ready for the correction to commence solely for it to end. The wait was nothing more than part of the game, psychological warfare, and Father Gabriel made sure that every male follower knew how to play.

The reason she was in this position, bent over the vanity, was my fault and Father Gabriel's teachings. She'd been conditioned too well. If she hadn't been, Stella would have fought more. The FBI would help her—help Stella—deprogram her. This was for the best, no matter whether she was or wasn't carrying my child. Nothing about going back to The Light was right.

I bit my cheek, not allowing myself to smile at her latest declaration. She'd said she hated me. It was what I wanted. Lifting my belt, I said, "Good, I'm glad to hear that. Now I'll give you a reason not to forget it." I twisted the proverbial knife. "Tell me, Sara." I leaned above her beautiful body. "Tell me what helps you not forget."

She pressed her lips together defiantly.

I slowly ran the rough underside of the belt over her bottom, watching her muscles flinch, as if the leather were fire. Even so, she maintained her tight hold on the counter's edge. "I'm waiting," I whispered.

"Go to hell."

I stepped back and lifted the belt, its weight multiplying exponentially with each millisecond. "Sara."

Her eyes opened at the sound of her name. Seeing my stance in the mirror, she replied, her words drenched in tears as well as defeat, "Reminders."

"What do they do?"

"They help me to not forget."

I stepped closer and rubbed the leather over her round behind one more time. "Don't forget it's your job to count."

With her lip still between her teeth, she nodded. I stepped back. The belt cut through the still air, creating a whistling sound; however, the crack never came. I'd stepped just out of reach. The clank of the buckle as it hit the linoleum floor bounced off the walls.

Sara's eyes opened, questioning what had happened, yet she remained as statuesque as I'd taught her.

Reaching to the ground, I picked up her bra and panties. All the while her frightened eyes in the mirror watched my every move. Placing them next to her on the vanity, I said, "Get dressed, Stella. I'm calling my handler. This is over. The FBI will help you."

Her back collapsed as she exhaled in relief, her small breasts flattening against the fake marble.

I expected an expletive, something. Instead she slowly straightened herself and stood. Staring at me incredulously, still through the mirror, I found the acidic contempt I'd sought. After gathering her underwear as well as her jeans and sweater, she walked into the small bathroom containing the lavatory and shower. The click of the lock eroded any lingering pieces of my heart.

Sinking to the bed, I rubbed my hands over my face.

Fuck!

That wasn't what I'd wanted to do.

Holding her and explaining everything felt right. Risking her life didn't.

I'd told her it was her decision, and it was. Her conflict was clear. And then, the way she'd used my real name when she accepted my apology, I'd known she was leaning toward the best decision, toward taking the offer of deprogramming and witness protection. I also knew that if I was the reason she returned to The Light and anything went wrong, I'd never forgive myself. Though she might not have said her decision in words, she had in her tone and actions. I knew her well enough to hear it loud and clear.

I heard the shower through the thin walls. Reaching for my jacket, I pulled two phones from my pocket. The one that I always used, my The Light phone, blinked. I looked at the screen and my heart sank. Though it was only nearing four in the morning in Fairbanks, in Detroit it was nearing eight. That meant the Assembly and Commission would be meeting soon.

I had a voice mail from Father Gabriel.

Apprehensively I pushed the sequence of buttons that allowed the voice mail to play.

"Brother Jacob . . ."

I replayed the message again, hoping I'd imagined it. After all, I hadn't slept much in the last twenty-four hours. Maybe it was nothing more than a mirage.

Can mirages be auditory as well as visual?

Running my fingers through my hair, I turned on the burner phone. Special Agent Adler answered right away. I turned away from the bathroom and lowered my voice. "She knows a lot, not everything, but she's not going back."

"Then that's it. Stay where you are, we'll send a plane. We'll bring you both back to the Anchorage field office."

I swallowed the bile. "Yes, sir. We'll be waiting for the call."

"McAlister, you've done your best. Going back without her wouldn't work. Hell, going back with her would've been risky."

"Yes, sir. I know it's not up to me, but I need to tell you, move fast."

"You know we can't possibly get enough people to the Northern Light for at least three hours. Even then it would take most of our

Alaskan agents. One or two more days would allow us to get more agents there and be prepared."

I fisted my hair, pulling it from the roots. "Sir, I woke to a message from Father Gabriel."

"And?"

"As I told you, he's in Detroit right now, at the Eastern Light."

"Yes, and . . ." My handler was beginning to sound impatient.

"He instructed me to take my supplies back to the Northern Light and leave tonight for the Eastern Light."

"Tonight?"

"Yes, sir. It's approximately a four-and-a-half-hour flight, but with the time difference if I leave Northern Light at nine tonight, I'd arrive at Eastern Light by six in the morning, Detroit time."

"Is this an unusual request?"

"Part of it was," I said, having trouble coming up with the words to explain it.

"Agent, I'm waiting."

"A few weeks ago, I petitioned the Commission to allow me to take Sara with me when I flew. They hadn't made a decision. That's why if I tell them I took her, it'll be a punishable trans-gression."

"Yes, you mentioned that yesterday during our short debriefing."

"Sir," I said, "Father Gabriel said in his message that my petition was granted. I was told to bring Sara."

"Oh my God! What does that mean?"

I spun at the sound of Sara's voice. Her hair was wet, and her complexion matched the tips of our fingers.

"Agent, it's time to stop this," Special Agent Adler said.

I nodded, relief flooding my synapses.

"What?" Sara came to the bed and sat beside me. "What does that mean? Does Father Gabriel know what I did, that I left?"

"Yes, sir," I said into the phone, while turning toward Sara and shrugging.

"You can't just shrug. If I go back, will it give you more time?"

"Agent," Special Agent Adler said in my ear, "I'm assuming that's Miss Montgomery that I hear?"

No, it's Sara Adams.

That was what I wanted to say, but unlike Stella, I had the ability to bite my tongue. "Yes, sir, it is. I didn't know she was listening." My eyes narrowed her way, but instead of Sara's demure response, Stella gave me a close-lipped fuck you smile as she cocked her head to the side.

"Give her the phone."

"Sir?"

"I know you've been living in the dark ages when it comes to men and women, but give her the damn phone. I want to hear her response, from her."

My teeth clenched as I covered the mouthpiece and turned toward Sara. "This is my handler. You may call him Special Agent. The less you know the better. I already told him your answer. It's over. You're going into witness protection."

She reached for the phone.

"Sara," I said, in my customary warning.

Her brows rose.

"Don't—"

Taking the phone from my grasp, in a stage whisper she quipped, "Embarrass you? Oh, I wouldn't fucking dream of it." Placing the phone to her ear, Sara said, "Hello, Special Agent, this is Sara . . . I'm sorry, Stella Montgomery."

A smile crept over her lips as she stood and walked farther away. "Thank you . . . I'm all right." She looked my way. "I'd like to say it's the first time I've ever been struck, but I can't."

Holy fuck!

"Yes, he told me . . ." She went on, "Yes, I do understand . . . Sir, may I ask, if I change my mind . . ." Again she looked toward me. "If I change my mind, would that give the bureau more time to arrange the raids in a way that may eliminate the loss of life? . . . That's what Jacob/Jacoby said, sir . . . I do . . . I am . . . One more request, if I may . .

. If something were to happen to me before we get out of The Light, would the FBI please contact my parents and those of Mindy Rosemont? . . . Yes, sir, she is . . . Yes, I've seen her . . . And a Detroit detective, Dylan Richards."

She shrugged as she wrapped one arm around her midsection. "We were dating. He used to say I should join the DPD. Maybe he'd understand what happened if he knew I was working with the FBI . . . I understand." She nodded. "Nothing until . . . Yes, sir. I hope you don't either . . . Yes, I'll give the phone back to him. Thank you, I believe it's an honor . . . Good-bye."

She handed the phone back to me. "Here, he needs to work out the details with you. We're heading back immediately."

What the fuck just happened?

"Sir?" I asked.

"If this weren't so damn serious and dangerous, I'd like to hear how you managed to keep that woman oppressed in The Light. She seems very strong-willed."

"You have no idea."

CHAPTER

FORTY-SEVEN

S tella/Sara

SCENES of normal life passed by the windows of Jacob's borrowed truck. Though it was still early, not even five in the morning, this far north the sun was shining, illuminating the empty streets and giving me a glimpse of what life could be. Sighing, I took another bite of the breakfast bar Jacob had gotten for me from a convenience mart. If it weren't for the bottle of water, I wasn't sure I'd be able to swallow. I remembered Bernard saying that I ate cardboard for breakfast. I'd never thought I did, until now.

From my peripheral vision, I watched as Jacob took the last few bites of his breakfast sandwich and thought how strange it was that even my tastes were different now than they'd been as Stella. He'd offered to buy me something from the fast-food restaurant for breakfast, but after what we'd eaten late last night, I hadn't thought I could stomach more grease.

475

"How's your sandwich?" I asked, needing to hear his voice.

Swallowing a drink of his coffee, he replied, "Not as good as your cooking."

"Good."

"How's your"—he nodded toward my remaining bar—"whatever that is?"

I shrugged. "I'd rather have my cooking too. Which is hilarious, if you knew how I, or Stella, used to cook."

"Sara, no more Stella. It's too big of a risk."

I nodded, heeding his warning—more than resenting it.

"Coffee?" he asked, holding his cup for me.

I shook my head. "No, thank you." He'd offered earlier to get me my own cup, but the idea of drinking the caffeine still ate at my conscience.

But the idea of putting yourself in greater danger doesn't?

I ignored my inner monologue and turned back to the window. With each passing mile I became lost in the promise of Fairbanks. It wasn't until Jacob's voice registered that I came back to the present.

"Sara, are you listening?"

"No, sorry."

"I've decided that our story is that you never left the Northern Light."

I turned toward him. "You've decided?" Though I asked my question with a bit of resentment, the relief that came with his control surprised me.

"Yes," he simply replied.

"How? I didn't go to work yesterday. You said you spoke to Raquel, and she and Brother Benjamin looked for me."

He nodded, his profile revealing the concern his words refused to utter.

"I'm sorry, Jacob. I'm sorry that I've messed up all your hard work and that now we're in this situation."

Dark eyes overflowing with remorse settled briefly on me before turning back to the road. "Don't be."

Apparently our time for heart-to-heart talks was over. Since we'd spoken to his handler, I had been lucky to get more than a couple of words strung together. Though I wanted more, I knew the man beside me. I knew that when he was thinking and worrying, he was quiet. He was the one currently devising a plan for our future, not necessarily one where we were together, but one where we were both alive.

"Something you must remember," he began, "is that since you didn't leave the Northern Light, you can't be on the plane. All of our planes have what is essentially a black box. It records everything. Once you're on the plane you can't speak, and I can't speak to you."

"All right. Hopefully I won't snore," I said, trying to break the tension.

A corner of his lips moved upward. "If you do, I'll throw something in your direction."

"Hey, are you saying I snore?"

His shoulders moved up and down.

"If we can't talk on the plane, please, fill me in on our cover story."

"I've spoken to Benjamin and promised I'd be at Assembly this morning. Thankfully, since it's Saturday, you don't have work at the lab today. I told Benjamin that you spoke to Thomas, which you shouldn't have done, and he took you against your will. I told him that after Raquel's call, I flew to Thomas's hangar and found you before anything happened, other than your blackened eye. I also asked him to keep the truth a secret. We both know what happens to people who leave The Light."

His words sent a chill down my spine.

"He won't even tell Raquel. The fewer people who know the better. But since Raquel was so worried, I said she could come check on you later today. And you'd be back to work after our trip to the Eastern Light."

"That scares me."

He simply nodded.

Was he scared too, or simply acknowledging my concern? I didn't want to think about Jacob being scared. Instead my hand fluttered to my darkened eye. "And this?"

He shook his head. "Isn't it obvious? I did it."

"You?"

"I corrected you, probably for questioning too much." He added the last part with a smirk.

I shook my head. "I thought you said that I could now—"

"When we're alone, but the point is, correction is my right. No one will question it. I've also decided it's the reason you didn't go to work yesterday."

Yesterday? Has it only been twenty hours since I left the Northern Light?

"Sara, we can't utter one word, or even think in terms of Stella and Jacoby. No one, and I mean no one, not Benjamin, not Raquel, no one can know what we've discussed. Brother Benjamin believes what I told him. I also told him that you hadn't remembered your past. When I found you, you were mostly scared and afraid I'd be upset."

Well, some of that was accurate. "Other people have their memories," I protested. "Why can't I?"

"Because other people weren't investigating The Light when their memories were suppressed."

I turned in his direction. "Do you really believe that's why I was taken?"

"You said you Google Earthed the mansion in Bloomfield Hills?"

"Yes, but no one knew that. The thing is, I went there too."

His head snapped in my direction. "You did what?"

"I went there. I went to the front gate and pushed the button and asked for Uriel Harris."

"Jesus, Sara!"

"The voice from the box said I had the wrong address and asked me to leave."

"So you did, right?"

"No."

Jacob struck the steering wheel with the palm of his hand. "Of course fucking not. What did you do?"

I sat taller. "I'm an investigative journalist. It's what I do, did, whatever. I walked around the front fence and tried to take pictures." I shrugged and looked back out the window. "When I left I saw a surveillance camera. Unfortunately, it probably recorded everything I did." Thinking about the timeline, I added, "That was a few days before we went to that festival in Dearborn." The realization made my stomach turn. That was the day Jacob had seen me for the first time. "Oh, God, my future was already set by then. Wasn't it?"

With his jaw clenched, Jacob nodded. "Yes, do you see why you cannot get your memory back?"

"What about my medicine? Raquel and Benjamin know I'm off it."

"Medicines work differently on different people. Just because you quit taking it, doesn't guarantee that your memories will return. Beginning at the Eastern Light, acquired wives are given high doses of the medication intravenously. Brother Raphael has hypothesized that in some individuals that initial regimen is all that's needed. The idea being that the receptors become permanently blocked. He's said that the daily boosters in many women are merely an insurance policy. Not everyone's brain responds exactly the same way. As soon as you have your period, you're going back on the medicine."

"What? No, I'm not!"

"Sara."

Panic filled my chest as I tried to suck in air. Closing my eyes, I reminded myself that this was the world where husbands made the decisions, but we were still alone, and I had a chance. "No, Jacob," I implored. By the way he turned, my response obviously surprised him. I kept going. "I can't help you if I don't have memories. Think about it. What if the medicine blocks everything I learned at The Light?" I sucked my lip between my teeth and put my hands between my legs to hide their trembling. "I can't go back to that. Besides, how would we explain it if I suddenly forgot all Father Gabriel's teachings or my job or how to cook, or what if I forgot you?"

"Fuck," he said, pulling the truck into the small airport. "I guess I hadn't thought about all of that." Once Jacob had the truck inside a hangar, he turned toward me. "Give me those hands."

Though I looked down, I obeyed.

As he took my hands, it wasn't his words but his tone that pulled my gaze to his. "If we have any chance at all of getting through this alive, you and I both have to put on the best performances of our fucking lives. That's why I wanted you to resume your medicine. I thought it would make it easier for you, but"—he kissed my knuckles—"you've always been so smart, and you're right. I don't want you forgetting what you've learned in The Light. You worked too hard. Just please remember, no one is trustworthy, no one. Everyone is programmed, not just the acquired wives. Most of the men aren't on medication; their programming is more environmental, tribal mentality really. It keeps everyone content to work toward Father Gabriel's goals. If they weren't programmed, they wouldn't accept everything Father Gabriel says as gospel and they even may try to question his authority. That can't happen.

"It's literally you and me against The Light. We have to convince everyone that nothing has changed. The next eighteen hours are crucial."

I nodded, knowing I needed to put my full and unyielding trust in the man who held my hands, the one who'd kept me alive so far.

"Leaving The Light," he went on, "is a transgression punishable by banishment. No one leaves The Light and lives to talk about it. No one. You, Sara Adams, are an Assemblyman's wife. We love each other, and you're usually well behaved. Thursday night after the prayer meeting, once we were home, you weren't. I corrected you. You were embarrassed that it resulted in a blackened eye. Since I left early Friday morning, you went running on the campus, like we do. It's summer and you chose to stay out in the north acres. Being upset with me, you forgot about the lab. That's why you weren't in our apartment when Raquel came to find you."

I sighed. What he'd just done was the comfort that came with being Sara. The story, my choices, everything was up to my husband. Jacob told me who I was and what I thought. It was a realization that bothered the Stella side of me, but I knew that to survive what we were about to do, I needed to keep Stella quiet. I could use her keen thinking and survival skills, but in everything visible, I needed to be Sara.

Thankfully, last night I'd been granted something that I hadn't previously had. Last night I had been given permission to question. "I'm scared. Why can't we tell everyone that Thomas took me? I hate people thinking you did this to me."

"Because this"—he looked out through the hangar's open garage door and over the airstrip. I followed his gaze and suddenly realized we weren't at the same airport where Thomas had brought me yesterday—"is where I fly in and out of for The Light. I'm not sure how I'd be able to explain to Xavier or Father Gabriel how I knew Thomas's destination."

I swallowed. "H-how did you know?"

"My handler searched flight plans. Flight plans are supposed to be filed in advance. VFR, visual flight rules, don't require it, but for safety, especially with such large areas of unpopulated wilderness, most pilots do it. Thank Father Gabriel, Thomas had. He'd filed his plans before leaving for the Northern Light. They included his estimated time of return to Fairbanks and listed the airport. Technically, there's no way I could've made it from the Western Light to Fairbanks in time to save you, which was the story I gave Benjamin and the reason the US Marshals were there instead of me. But Benjamin has no way of knowing that. He hasn't left the Northern Light in years. Father Gabriel would know and so would Micah, if he were questioned."

I shook my head. "This is such a mess."

"Well," he said coldly, "I'm sorry you're still involved."

My neck straightened. "Now, as in because we're going back, or you're sorry I was ever assigned to you?"

Jacob's narrow gaze silenced me—Sara—the way only he could. "No more. We've been through this. Now we're going back as Sara and Jacob. Later today I'll take you to Brother Raphael and you'll need to explain and apologize for your absence. He's a Commissioner. Correction will be at his discretion."

"No, Jacob. No more, ever."

He lifted a brow. "You had that option. You chose otherwise."

I felt suddenly nauseous.

"We need to hurry," Jacob said, "so I can make it to Assembly."

"What about Thomas?"

"I told you, he's no longer a threat."

"But won't The Light question his disappearance?"

"Minimally, that's not our concern. It's his. Like I said, no one enters The Light and leaves. Theoretically he shouldn't have been in the community. Once Xavier is informed of what Thomas did— entering the community on more than one occasion—even Xavier won't question Thomas's sudden disappearance. Benjamin knows what Thomas did to you, so he won't question his disappearance. Once Father Gabriel learns Thomas entered the community, he won't question it either. He'll assume there was a problem, and it was handled."

I shrugged. "Maybe there are advantages to not questioning."

Jacob reached for my hand, and with a grin said, "It's taken you long enough to figure that out."

My cheeks flushed as I glanced toward our intertwined hands.

"This hangar doesn't have cameras or surveillance inside," Jacob explained. "That's why I didn't park outside. I'm going to help you onto the plane, and then I have some last-minute things that need to be done. Remember, do not talk."

As he helped me from the truck, I replied, "Yes, Jacob."

His lips curled upward as his gaze devoured me. "Life would be so much easier if you could remember that is always the correct response."

I was exhausted, had a battered cheek, had been gone nearly a day from a place no one leaves, and had my hand in the hand of a man whom twenty-four hours ago I'd never wanted to see again. I was out of fight.

With a shy smile, I lowered my chin, looked up through my lashes, and repeated what my husband wanted to hear. "Yes, Jacob."

Just before entering the plane, he stilled our steps. With his free hand he surrounded my waist and pulled me close. "I pray that one day I'm able to call you by another name, but in the meantime, you're my wife, my Sara Adams, and while I do and will respect the boundary you placed on sex, right now I want to kiss my wife, and I plan on doing it. Do you want to stop me?"

Before I could answer, he pulled my hips tighter against his, causing our chests to collide. Needing to see his face, I lifted my chin and looked into his dark gaze. As leather and musk enveloped us, he rephrased, "More importantly, do you think you can stop me?"

I shook my head. "No, I don't want to stop you. After all, you're my husband."

He smiled, an exhausted smile, just before our lips reunited. For a few moments, in the drafty hangar, our world was right. After all we'd said and done, the danger I'd put us in and how he'd tried to push me away...after all of it...our bodies knew their rightful place. Drawn like magnets with an irresistible pull, they carnally remembered what my mind believed it wanted to forget. As his kiss deepened, heat radiated from my head to my toes, melting everything in its wake. Simultaneously his touch made me liquid, molding me against his solid warmth.

I didn't fight as fingers twined in my hair and tugged my head backward. When Jacob's tongue slid across the seam of my lips, I willingly granted him entrance, accepting the invasion that gave our tongues license to dance. He swallowed my moans as the friction from his broad chest pebbled my nipples, and my arms wrapped around his firm torso. When our lips finally parted, I settled my cheek against his chest and held tight, listening to the steady beat of his heart.

We both knew that there was a possibility we'd never make it out of The Light, and still, when he lifted my chin and stared deeply into my eyes, I couldn't say the words my heart longed to say; instead I did the next best thing. With a soft kiss to his cheek, I whispered, "Sara loves Jacob."

He kissed my forehead. "And Jacob loves Sara. Please never forget that."

I shook my head. "Neither Sara nor Stella will."

"I never thought of myself as a bigamist," he said with a grin.

When Jacob opened the Northern Light's smaller plane, I quietly climbed aboard.

Though the fuselage was filled with boxes, Jacob pointed to one of the jump seats, and I sat. Next he strapped me in. Its seat belt was much more elaborate than the one in Thomas's plane. Briefly I wondered whether this was how the unconscious women were transported—how I'd been transported. Instead of allowing myself to dwell on that thought, I surveyed the boxes, assuming they were filled with supplies; however, as in my first few days in The Light, I couldn't ask. My speech was once again restricted.

The difference was that this time I understood why. I knew that Jacob's rules weren't to dominate me, but to save me. As we flew away from the dark and back into The Light, the weight of our mission settled over me. It was up to us. If we failed there were others who would never be saved.

CHAPTER

FORTY-EIGHT

S^{ara}

MY HEART WAS ready to beat out of my chest as the full impact of Jacob's words, "The next eighteen hours are the most crucial," settled over me and he left our apartment for Assembly. All it took was one person who saw the truth or knew what had really happened.

I should have been tired, but I was mostly scared—scared to be separated from Jacob, and of what could happen at Assembly. More than once I'd prayed that Brother Benjamin had kept our secret. After all, Jacob said that Brother Benjamin and Raquel were believers, and that what they were doing by helping us was against Father Gabriel's teachings. Just as all of my thoughts and behaviors belonged to Jacob, all of our husbands' thoughts belonged to the Commission and Father Gabriel.

What if Brother Benjamin confessed to the Commission?

I bit my lip and continued to pace.

We'd gotten into the community without anyone's seeing that I was in Jacob's truck. Riding in his truck wasn't forbidden. I did it from time to time. It was leaving the community that was forbidden. No one could know I'd been out to the pole barn, much less into the dark.

To corroborate our story, as soon as we entered the community, I stayed hidden inside the truck while Jacob drove as close as he could to our apartment, went in, and returned to the truck. As we drove to the parking area, I came out of my hiding place in the backseat. Then together we walked to the coffee shop.

Since the story was that I was upset with him about leaving the reminder on my cheek, taking me into public was his punishment for my missing work yesterday. The thing that I continued to mull over was that he hadn't explained any of this to me—any of the reasoning. Nevertheless, I understood it.

No matter how I fought it, I was conditioned. Sitting at a table at the coffee shop with my eyes down, I obediently waited for him to return with our drinks. Of course he didn't ask what I wanted, and I wouldn't have refused whatever he'd ordered; however, when I peered into the cup and found tea instead of coffee, I smiled. Though he briefly returned the smile and whispered, "It's decaffeinated," his gaze immediately narrowed, reminding me that I was supposed to be upset with him.

Jacob was right about my blackened eye. No one seemed to notice it. If I allowed myself to think like Stella, the unspoken acceptance of my husband's correction was more evidence of the perverse nature of The Light. I hoped that the unique position of having both perspectives would be an advantage as we continued the best performances of our fucking lives.

A knock on the apartment door startled me as it brought me back to the present. I took a deep breath and steadied myself to open the door. I'd known Raquel would be coming ever since Jacob told me he'd given Brother Benjamin permission for her visit. I reached for the doorknob as I prepared to see the best friend I'd had while in The Light.

In the coffee shop I'd needed only to look the part, now it was time for speaking. There was more riding on this performance than before I'd left the Northern Light. Now my success wasn't just for me, but also for Jacob and his mission. It was for everyone.

I opened the door to Raquel's questioning blue eyes.

"Come in," I said, "Jacob told me you'd be coming."

She shook her head and waited for me to close the door. Once I did she wrapped me in an embrace, her slender arms squeezing with all her might. "Oh, praise Father Gabriel. I was so worried about you." Backing away, she playfully hit my shoulder. "I should be mad at you . . ." Her words trailed away as she noticed my eye.

I wasn't sure how she hadn't seen it first thing, but then again, she'd been too busy hugging me. I reached for the puffiness and a tear fell. "I know. I'm sorry I worried you."

Raquel wrapped her arm around my shoulders and led me to the sofa. "Sara, it's all right. I'm sorry. I shouldn't have responded like that. It just surprises me." As we sat she asked, "Have you thanked Father Gabriel and God for your husband?"

I nodded as more tears flowed. I didn't know where they were coming from, exhaustion probably. I'd slept a little on the plane, but the flight was much faster in Jacob's plane than it was in Thomas's. We had been in the air for under an hour.

Raquel hugged me again. "Benjamin and I were so worried when you didn't go to work."

"I'm sorry. I was selfish." I lowered my chin. "I honestly didn't think about anyone but myself. I was embarrassed. I mean, it's the first time I ever remember this"—I tilted my head to the left—"happening, and I didn't want anyone to see it."

"We're sisters. We understand. It happens. No one will think less of either you or Brother Jacob." Raquel smiled her biggest, shiniest smile.

Gratitude for all she'd done for me from the beginning of my journey in The Light came bubbling out. "Thank you, for always being so great. I'm so glad we're friends, and sisters," I added.

"I had so many thoughts running through my head. I was afraid you were . . . were taken, that you were lost in the dark."

"Taken? Why would you think I'd been taken? By whom?"

"This is going to sound crazy, but by that pilot guy, Thomas. I don't like that he comes here into the community. I told Benjamin that I was afraid that's what had happened, and he said he'd bring up that Thomas comes into the community to the Assembly. I mean, it just isn't right."

If she only knew! "He does give me the creeps. I'm sorry I worried you. Jacob said you went looking for me."

Raquel nodded. "When I couldn't find you here, Benjamin drove me to the pole barn. Brother Micah was there. He's the one who said Thomas had recently left. I guess Brother Micah arrived just after Thomas took off. I was the one who jumped to conclusions." She squeezed my hand. "I'm sorry. I should have known you'd never willingly go back to the dark, not after the last time."

"I don't remember doing it then either."

"Sometimes," she said, seeming to weigh her words, "when people stop taking their birth control medicine, it does something to their chemical balance and they remember things. Have you had any memories?"

I shook my head. "No, not really. It's still as if the day I woke from my accident was the day my life began."

She nodded and laid her head back against the sofa. "The other day you said something in the temple about the dark. I remember the dark. I didn't at first either, but now I do. If you do, talk to Brother Jacob. Benjamin helped me more than I can say." A tear slid down her cheek. "I'd never go back. I'd never leave The Light."

"Raquel, what is it?"

She pressed her lips together and swallowed. "Nothing, I was just so scared that you were out there, and I wouldn't wish that on anyone."

"I know we're not allowed to talk about the dark, but if it would help you, I promise not to tell."

Shaking her head, she whispered, "No, I can't. I know you wouldn't tell, but I don't want to be the cause of any secrets between you and Brother Jacob." Taking a deep breath, she forced a smile. "The most important thing is that we're here now. We're in The Light and you're safe. Benjamin said that when I came looking for you, you were out running?"

"Yes, I was in the north acres, but that won't happen again, not without Jacob."

"So this"—Raquel tilted her head toward my eye—"happened before Brother Jacob left?"

"Yes, Thursday night after prayer meeting." I looked down. "He's really patient—usually. It's my fault. I need to stop questioning. I think that's why I'm so embarrassed. I don't want anyone to think of him like Brother Abraham."

Just speaking his name gave me chills.

"Oh, don't worry. That could never happen." Raquel paused. "Why won't you be running without Jacob? You like running."

I nodded. "I'm no longer allowed. Jacob wasn't happy when he arrived this morning. He knew why I didn't go to work." I sighed. "It's like he always knows everything. Instead of staying here and discussing it, he made me go out into the community with him, to the coffee shop."

Raquel's eyes widened. "Were there many people?"

I shrugged. "I kept my eyes down, but even though it was early, yes. I didn't see any chosen, but there were many followers."

"I guess that was his way of easing you out of your embarrassment."

Really?

"It was mortifying, and this afternoon after the Commission meeting concludes, he's taking me to Brother Raphael and Sister Rebecca's apartment." I lowered my voice. "I have to apologize for missing work."

She squeezed my hand. "It could be worse. You seem to be sitting fine."

"Now," I interjected. "He said my correction will be up to Brother Raphael."

Raquel shrugged. "I guess I'll know how that went tomorrow morning at service."

I sat straighter and opened my eyes wide. "Tomorrow! Oh, do you remember me telling you that Jacob petitioned the Commission for me to travel?"

"Yes."

"Apparently it was approved. Father Gabriel told Jacob to bring me with him when he comes to pick him up from the Eastern Light."

Raquel's expression clouded. "The Eastern Light? He's supposed to take you there?"

"What's the matter? Do you know where that is?"

"Do you?"

I feigned a smile. "I'm assuming east of here."

She nodded. "I guess, since it's not the dark, I can say. I remember the Eastern Light. I was there for a little while before I was brought here."

Oh. My stomach sank. What happened to her?

I couldn't stop my inquisitive mind. "You say that like it's a bad thing."

"It was just different, harder. If you're allowed to see other campuses, Father Gabriel must really trust you."

"I don't understand. Isn't the Eastern Light like here?" Though I was doing my best to keep her suppressed, the Stella part of me was dying to ask more probing questions.

"Not really. You can tell me what you think when you get back."

I couldn't push too much, or she might become suspicious. As I sat there with Raquel, I understood what Jacob had meant last night when he'd said he couldn't allow his assignment to affect his behavior. Though it was tempting, I wouldn't either.

"Thank you for coming to see me. Again, I'm sorry I scared you." I admired her clear, bruise-free olive complexion as her round cheeks rose.

"Hey, now that you're all right, let's talk about something more exciting."

I genuinely smiled. I was doing it, being Sara, and if my best friend since I'd awoken in The Light wasn't suspicious, I must be doing a good job. Settling against the sofa, I stifled a yawn and listened as she chatted away.

MY SLEEP-DEPRIVED NERVES were stretched to the point of breaking as we walked silently to Brother Raphael and Sister Rebecca's apartment building near the temple. Though Jacob hadn't told me, I assumed he'd spoken to Brother Raphael at Assembly, because when we arrived, they seemed to be expecting us. The only other Commissioner's apartment I'd visited was that of our overseer, Brother Daniel, and his wife Sister Ruth. The Commissioners' apartments were bigger than the Assemblymen's, but not by much. Since all of the Assemblymen's apartments were similar, I wasn't surprised that Brother Raphael and Sister Rebecca's was similar to Brother Daniel and Sister Ruth's. What made theirs bigger than ours was that it contained an office, which was where Sister Rebecca led us as soon as we arrived.

Brother Raphael greeted us as he stayed seated behind his desk. Sister Rebecca moved a chair next to her husband and sat, leaving Jacob and me standing. It was probably their way of making our visit about the matter at hand and not a friendly visit.

Though Brother Raphael had always been nice to me in the lab, as we stood before him and Sister Rebecca, I remembered his position. Not only was he a Commissioner, he was second in command at the Northern Light, second only to Father Gabriel. With Father Gabriel gone, he was in charge. Nothing, not even banishment, was outside the scope of his power. That knowledge, plus Jacob's warning about the next eighteen hours, weighed heavily on my mind as I waited to speak. If our story was to be disputed, it would probably be here and now.

"Sister Sara, I'm glad you're not ill. Go ahead. Brother Jacob said you wanted to say something to me."

Though I didn't remember having said I wanted to do this, I nodded and began, "Brother Raphael and Sister Rebecca, I'm here today..."

I attributed my emotional outbursts to my lack of sleep. Just as had happened when I talked with Raquel, as I apologized to Brother Raphael, tears coated my cheeks. It wasn't an ugly cry, but it was enough that Sister Rebecca stood, even as I spoke, handed me a tissue, and gave me a hug.

I didn't tell them why I didn't go to work, only that I was upset and selfish, thinking only of myself. When I was done, Brother Raphael asked me whether I enjoyed my job at the Northern Light. I assured him—I did. Then he asked me a similar question about my husband, did I love him and accept his decisions? When I turned toward Jacob and saw the pride in his eyes, more tears flowed. "I do. I really do," I answered.

I didn't think about Stella or how wrong this was. I didn't think about how I was essentially telling the person in charge that I was all right with my husband blackening my eye, which he hadn't. In that moment all I thought about was what Jacob had told me to remember when I had the nightmares: I was Sara and he was Jacob.

Sara loves Jacob, and Jacob loves Sara.

Brother Raphael didn't respond; instead he looked at his wife. "Rebecca, please take Sister Sara into the kitchen. I need to speak with Brother Jacob privately for a few minutes."

As far as Commissioners' wives went, Sister Rebecca was more like Sister Ruth than like Sister Lilith. Though she was thin and always well dressed like Sister Lilith, she was also sweet, with the maternal quality of Sister Ruth. Whenever I'd spoken with her, she'd been kind, and her lessons during Tuesday and Thursday prayer meetings were thought provoking and often emotional. We Assembly wives didn't know which Commission wife would lead the meetings until we arrived. Whenever I learned it was Sister Rebecca, I knew I wouldn't be disappointed.

Once we were in the kitchen, Sister Rebecca gave me a new tissue and smiled. "My dear, I'm glad you're all right. When you weren't at work, Brother Raphael was concerned that you may've been ill. I heard Brother Benjamin was concerned too." She patted my hand. "It'll be all right. My husband's a fair man."

My head began to ache as I hiccupped and nodded. After the way Jacob had scared me the night before, I knew I didn't want correction or reminders. I also knew that it wasn't up to me.

Setting the teakettle on the stove, Sister Rebecca said, "Let me make you some decaffeinated tea. That always helped me relax. Though I did miss coffee while I was pregnant."

My eyes opened wide. "W-what did you just say?"

Her soft hazel eyes sparkled. "Come now, you heard me."

"I-I'm not . . ." I shook my head. "I don't know if I am."

"But you want to be, don't you, Sister?"

"I'm really not sure anymore."

"Is that why Brother Jacob corrected you? Did you not tell him?"

Oh, shit! Where is this going?

I swallowed. "Sister, I have a problem with questioning. I try, I really do, but sometimes I think all I do is try his patience."

"Brother Jacob seems to be a patient man."

"He is. That's why I'm so embarrassed. I don't want people to think less of him."

"You do love him," she asked, "don't you?"

I smiled a closed-lipped smile. "I do. I know that God had a reason for bringing us here. I'm so thankful I've had Jacob to help me, and"—I lowered my eyes—"to correct me." Though the words once again hurt my pride, they flowed easily from my lips.

Again she patted my hand. "Let me get you that tea." Once she set the cup in front of me, she whispered, "I doubt Brother Raphael picked up your signals. You know how men are."

"My signals?"

"Your hand protectively covered your stomach the entire time you were apologizing, you're emotional, and the way you looked at your husband . . . goodness, if you're not sure yet if you're expecting a child, you certainly think it's a possibility."

I shrugged as my cheeks blushed. "I mean, I know how it works. There's a chance."

"When I was pregnant, I had all sorts of strange cravings." Her eyes lit up. "Oh, and odd memories. I'm not even sure they were real. They seemed real. Have you had any of that?"

I bit the inside of my cheek. She was good, and she was sneaky. I shook my head. "No, I haven't. Do you think that means that I'm not pregnant?"

"No. Everyone is different. Besides, this is early, if you aren't sure."

I nodded. "Very early, I haven't even missed a period."

"Well, when you know something, do tell. I just love babies. Sometimes I go to the day care just to be around them."

"Sister?" I asked, "Your child, or children, are they here, in The Light?"

"One, our son. He was raised under Father Gabriel's teachings, even before The Light. He's not at this campus, but he's an Assemblyman."

I smiled. "I'm sure you're proud. You only have one child?" As soon as the question left my lips, I regretted it. A shadow of sadness fell over her expression, returning the tears to my eyes. "I'm sorry. Please don't answer."

Her neck straightened. "Not all stories have happy endings. I'll always remember my beautiful daughter; however, Father Gabriel knows best. I trust in him and Raphael in all things."

The opening of a door and footsteps alerted us that our husbands were coming down the hallway. When Sister Rebecca pressed her lips together and patted my hand again, I knew she was silently telling me not to say anything about their daughter. I nodded my understanding as the men entered.

As we were about to leave, Brother Raphael said with his still-thick Boston accent, "Sister Sara, we'll welcome you back to the lab as soon as Father Gabriel sees fit to return from the Eastern Light. I trust your husband to do what is best."

It took all my willpower not to look toward Jacob; instead I lowered my eyes. "Thank you, Brother Raphael."

A few minutes later, as Jacob and I walked along the sidewalk with my hand in his, I whispered, "What does that mean? What Brother Raphael said."

Though Jacob didn't turn, his grip tightened, and he simply replied, "Sara."

"You said I could—"

"When we're alone. Does this look like we're alone?"

No. We weren't alone. We were walking among followers who were going from here to there. However, in my opinion, they all seemed preoccupied, all heading to their own destinations. No one was paying attention to us, except the occasional male follower who'd address Jacob with a nod and a "Brother Jacob." I assumed that most of those were the followers he counseled. I should know their names and for a few I did, but mostly I didn't. I probably knew their wives' names. I rarely saw couples together. Whenever I counseled the wives they were alone.

"No. I'm sorry," I said softly, pressing my lips together.

CHAPTER

FORTY-NINE

S ara

ASCENDING the stairs into Father Gabriel's private plane, I was in awe of the splendor. Taking a deep breath, I immediately remembered the rich aroma of leather. Of course my husband wore it like cologne, but it was different as I stepped across the cabin's threshold. It was the new-car smell that everyone loved, only amplified. The only other time I'd been inside this jet had been when I was without sight, during Jacob's and my temporary banishment, when he'd given me a tour of the planes. Now my vision was overloaded and my eyes darted about. From the shiny wooden facade of the cabinets that greeted me as I stepped inside, to the beautiful cream-colored leather chairs up and down the aisle, everything was over-the-top luxury.

It was definitely nothing like the plane I'd flown in this morning or Thomas's plane. The cabinet near the door held a sink, refrigerator, and coffeemaker. Wineglasses hung upside down from a rack. For only a moment, I wondered whether there could be wine. No one in The Light drank alcohol, but the Stella part of me questioned whether Father Gabriel did when he was flying or in Bloomfield Hills.

"Sara," Jacob instructed, "go sit near the back. You won't have to listen to Brother Micah and me in the cockpit."

I nodded and obediently walked toward the rear of the plane. With each step down the aisle, the backs of my fingers brushed the soft leather. Closing my eyes, I remembered the first time Jacob had brought me onto this plane—I remembered our past.

There were eight seats. Consecutive rows faced in opposite directions, creating clusters. I chose a seat all the way in the back. From it I could see up to the cockpit, but I was far enough away that their talking wouldn't bother me. Scanning the seat belts, I smiled. They were normal, not the jump seat kind like in the other plane.

Having difficulty suppressing my curiosity at Father Gabriel's extravagance, I opened the bathroom door and peered inside. With my mouth agape, I covered my lips, physically stopping myself from making an audible gasp. Even the bathroom was over the top. The cabinetry matched the stunning, shiny cabinets in the cabin, and the fixtures glistened. Lowering my hand and closing the door, I was glad I'd remembered to stay quiet. During the drive out to the hangar, I had been reminded more than once that everything within the plane was recorded.

Since we weren't sure when we'd have privacy, and couldn't be assured that we weren't being recorded, Jacob had spent most of the truck ride preparing me for what I might see. While he did, he admitted he was nervous about this trip. When he'd asked permission for me to go with him, he'd assumed that meant going to Fairbanks for supplies. He'd never expected permission to take me to another campus, especially back to the Eastern Light. The fact that he'd been specifically told to bring me only added to his concern.

When I asked about the mansion, he said he'd never been invited up to the house. There were small buildings closer to the landing strip. I remembered seeing those on Google Earth. Apparently they were similar to the living quarters in the pole barn. When he was required to spend the night at the Eastern Light, that was where he and Micah stayed. When Father Gabriel came to the airplane, he was driven through a side gate. He didn't walk through the yards to the back of the property. The only people from the mansion who ventured close to the outbuildings were those who played on the tennis courts or swam in the pool. Jacob said it wasn't uncommon for there to be many people around and it often sounded as if parties were being thrown. Father Gabriel referred to them as *celebrations*.

Jacob also told me that sometimes, if he was at the Eastern Light for any length of time, he could leave the property, as he had when he was taken to see me in Dearborn or when he went to service at the Eastern Light's temple. Since we'd be arriving early Sunday morning, more than likely we wouldn't just pick up Father Gabriel and return to the Northern Light. Father Gabriel always broadcast his Sunday and Wednesday sermons live. That meant he actually did each sermon three times, one for each time zone. The first in Detroit—in Highland Heights—was at nine Eastern time. Since we had been told to be there before then, there was a good probability that we'd be told to attend.

All I could do as he spoke was stare. There'd been a time when I'd longed to see inside the white building in Highland Heights. I reminded myself that now was my opportunity to do as Sara what I hadn't been able to do as Stella.

The Western Light was on Mountain time, which meant the next sermon would be two hours after the first, and the final sermon would be four hours from the first and broadcast to the Northern Light. With that schedule, we couldn't possibly be ready to fly back to the Northern Light until three or four in the afternoon at the earliest. Since everything was contingent upon Father Gabriel, Jacob wanted me to be prepared to spend the night in Bloomfield Hills.

He'd reminded me several times that Sara had never seen the

mansion before. She'd never Google Earthed it nor stood outside its gate. I needed to act as if everything was new, while at the same time turning a blind eye. Jacob credited his quick rise to the Assembly to his ability to ignore the wealth and exuberance that occurred behind the scenes.

That begs the question, Why is Father Gabriel willing to expose his secrets to me?

We'd both napped after our visit with Brother Raphael. Nevertheless, I was still worried about Jacob's lack of sleep over the last twenty-four hours. He'd promised it would be all right, that the Cessna Citation X used instruments for navigation and Brother Micah was there. They were both confident in each other's abilities as a pilot and alternated as copilot. Jacob had volunteered to be the copilot on the way to Eastern Light, claiming that he wanted to be able to check on me. Personally I wanted to sleep. Making it through our return to the Northern Light undetected had left me more exhausted than relieved.

If I was supposed to be corrected after I apologized to Brother Raphael, Jacob had never done it. Though I'd tried to ask about it while we walked home, I hadn't tried since. Even though he'd given me permission to ask questions, my correction was a subject I preferred to avoid, mostly because it made me mad.

Why hadn't I restricted corporal correction before I agreed to return?

Instead I'd restricted sex. I liked sex, being struck with a belt— not so much.

As I settled into the soft leather seat, I looked around and realized that even seeing what was before me was a privilege. I doubted any of the regular followers, or even most of the chosen, knew how extravagantly Father Gabriel traveled.

Once we were in the air at the right altitude, Jacob came back and showed me how to swivel and recline my chair. It didn't just recline, it lay flat, creating an incredibly comfortable bed. The last thing I remembered was being covered with a blanket and Jacob's kissing my forehead, before he kissed me again, letting me know we were almost to the Eastern Light.

Maybe it was all the flying and lack of sleep, or maybe it was the idea of being back at the campus where I had originally been taken after my abduction and where they'd begun suppressing my memories, I wasn't sure of the reason, but as I moved my seat from reclined to upright, my stomach violently twisted. Shaking my head, I shoved Jacob out of the way and ran toward the bathroom. Once I'd successfully emptied all the contents of my stomach, I turned and saw Jacob's stare.

Be careful what you say. We're being recorded.

The warning was loud and clear in his dark eyes. Shaking my head, I moved to the sink and rinsed my mouth. Under the cabinet I found mouthwash and swooshed away the terrible taste. Though I'd have liked a toothbrush, I was probably already overstepping my bounds by using the mouthwash. When I looked up, in the mirror I noticed how the bruise around my eye was less swollen but darker than it had been. As I splashed water on my face, Jacob entered the small bathroom and shut the door. While the bathroom was lavish, it was also small. His presence backed me up against the wall. In a hushed whisper, he demanded, "Tell me."

My eyes opened wide. "Tell you what?"

"You know, don't you? You're pregnant."

"I don't know, but seriously, there's a lot happening right now, a lot to make me nauseous. I'm scared."

He wrapped his arms around me, and kissed the top of my head. "So am I, but no matter what, you're my first priority."

I shook my head. Still whispering, I replied, "No, you have a first priority, and I'm here to help you with that, not mess it up any more than I already have."

"We're about ready to land. Once we're at the Eastern Light, stay close to me at all times and keep your eyes down."

"I know you don't want me to, but I can help. I'll have access to women followers, unlike you. I can learn things too, things to help your case. This is what I do—what I did. I want to help gather evidence."

Jacob's expression hardened as a tendon in his neck pulsated. "No." He laced our fingers together. "I'm not letting this go on much longer. It's not worth the risk."

"Don't worry about me. I'm in a much better place than I was. At least now I know what's happening."

He closed his eyes and exhaled. The hardness from before morphed to a look of pain. "It's not better. You were perfect at Brother Raphael's. You have to keep that up. Sara must always be in control."

I nodded. "I promise, I understand. But think about it. I'll act the part of Sara and help you at the same time."

He took a deep breath as the plane began to descend, and continued our whispered conversation. "I said no."

The words were definitive, as though any argument I made would be wasted breath.

He continued, "I'll do my best not to leave you alone. If I'm not with you, Brother Micah will try to be. Remember what I said about each move being a test?"

I nodded.

"I don't know why or what it's about, but I know that somehow bringing you here is a test. I just don't know which one of us is being tested. I honestly believe it's me. Somehow you're involved."

A chill ran through me. Jacob must have felt me begin to tremble, because he released my hand and hugged me again. His signature leather and musk filled my senses.

In the middle of our storm, I relished the peace. "I trust you," I whispered with my cheek against his shirt.

With his chin on the top of my head, his words skirted warm breaths across my hair. "Thank you, I didn't know if you'd ever be able to say that again, after everything."

"Everything is why I do." I craned my neck upward, searching for the honesty in his stare. "I can see now that everything you did was done for a reason. Besides, I wouldn't be back here if I didn't trust you."

As the urgency of what we were about to do threatened, our lips collided and a new fire replaced my earlier chill. Though I wasn't ready to forget the restriction I'd placed on our relationship, the hunger in Jacob's kiss drew me closer, filling me with desire. Without a word he claimed my body, allowing my tense muscles to relax in his embrace. Our lips remained firm, giving and taking with an unquenchable need to be nearer. Without provocation, I willingly surrendered to his craving. As I did I realized what I'd probably already known—I'd already trusted Jacob with everything: my mind, body, and life. Even now, with Stella awake inside me, I knew—both parts of me knew—the trust wasn't misplaced. We also knew we'd never trusted anyone else so completely, ever—not even Dylan.

After all, I'd only shared the key to my apartment with Dylan the day . . . the last day . . .

My entire body shivered. I couldn't let my mind go there, not now.

When our fervent kiss ended, Jacob smoothed my hair and reached for my hand. "Let's get you seated before we land."

I nodded and smiled at his choice of words. For once it wasn't an order.

As I flipped off the light switch, I caught a glimpse of my reflection. I didn't notice only the blackened eye, but from our kiss, my lips were red and slightly swollen. Grinning as I buckled my seat belt, I realized how our brief passionate kiss had provided us with an alibi. Obviously we'd been together in the bathroom to make out.

"Keep your eyes down," Jacob reminded me after we'd landed, as he opened the door and lowered the steps.

With my hand in his, we took the steps down. A light breeze blew, sending strands of blonde fluttering about my face as my long skirt billowed. As I inhaled the familiar scent of Michigan summer, humidity and heat filled my lungs. Even in the still of the morning, the promise of the sun's rays taunted, creating an ache that I could satisfy only by raising my chin and exposing my cheeks to the radiating light. It'd been too long since I'd truly felt the sun's warmth. As I fought the building desire and maintained Jacob's demanded pose, my heartbeat echoed in my ears.

Keeping my eyes veiled, I took in the open area of the landing strip, seeing only the edge of the surrounding trees. This was the wooded area where Dina Rosemont's witness had said her children saw the abduction. It was where they'd seen Mindy carried to a plane . . . a plane possibly piloted by the man beside me—my husband. I couldn't think about that, not when I needed to trust him.

Placing his hand on the small of my back, Jacob directed me to turn. Lifting only my eyes, I saw that beyond the outbuildings, upon a hill, was the mansion. I sucked in my breath as Jacob frantically whispered, "Eyes down! Don't look up there."

It was too late. I couldn't unsee.

I reached for Jacob's arm, my knees no longer able to support me. "How? Why?"

"Sara, not now." His words were harsh, coming from between clenched teeth.

From the distance the man on the balcony couldn't hear us or maybe even recognize me, but I knew. I knew in the depth of my heart that the man standing and watching the plane land and the passengers disembark was the man I'd imagined while I was without sight. Perhaps if I hadn't known every inch of him intimately, I wouldn't have been able to identify him from so far away, but I did.

By the time Jacob got me into the first building, my cheeks were covered with tears, and words were difficult to form. It was all right. From Jacob's expression I could tell he didn't want me to speak. Instead he casually walked the perimeter of the room before disappearing behind a door and, moments later, returning. Taking my hand, he silently led me to another bathroom.

Closing the door, he grabbed a towel and rolled it before placing it near the bottom of the door. Then, once again speaking in a whisper, he said, "I saw two cameras out there. There's nothing visual or audible in here."

I nodded, hearing but not comprehending. My mind swirled with too many thoughts and memories.

Uncharacteristically, Jacob violently seized my shoulders. Instead of his normal calm, anger exuded from his touch. Through clenched jaws, he said, "Hold it together. Don't you see? That's it. That's the fucking test. You had to know, in your heart. Think about it. How did Brother Uriel know you were at that festival?"

My head moved from side to side.

No. There is some mistake. I didn't. I never even suspected the blue-eyed man I'd trusted.

"I don't know what Father Gabriel knows," Jacob said, "or why he'd even suspect that you remembered your past, but what bigger test could he present than to make you face Dylan Richards?"

FIFTY

J acob

"Maybe not. Maybe he's been kidnapped too?" Sara questioned, her blue eyes begging me to make this right, but I couldn't.

I should've told her about Dylan Richards when we were at the motel; however, at the time, I was afraid she wouldn't believe me. There was too much she was trying to comprehend. It wasn't that she wasn't intelligent enough to do it. It was me. I'd seen the distrust in her eyes at the marshals' station. I was afraid that if I told her about Richards, she'd think I was lying, and I'd promised no more lies.

Taking a deep breath, I loosened my grip on her shoulders. "Sara." My tone was low and hushed. "I need you to trust me. Look at me. Do you trust me?"

Her dampened cheeks, combined with the pain in her expression, made me hate that bastard more than I already did.

"Do you?" I asked again.

Her shoulders drooped. "I told you I wouldn't be here if I didn't."

"Then believe me, Richards knew your fate. I remember being shocked when Brother Uriel took me to Dearborn, and while we were watching the two of you Brother Uriel let it slip that Richards was a cop. I didn't know then what his connection was with The Light. Now, I've come to the possible conclusion that as a cop, he helps with acquiring women. I don't know, but Sara, not only did he know your fate, he delivered you on a platter."

"Why?" she cried more than spoke, as her chin fell to her chest.

Gently lifting her chin, I bent down until our noses touched. "So that I could meet the most intelligent, beautiful, amazing woman, and she could royally fuck up my life."

She didn't speak as her eyes searched mine. Just before I released her chin, I gently kissed her lips, and she melted against my chest. I wrapped her in my arms as her body shuddered with silent sobs. Time stood still as I rubbed her back. Finally I looked at my watch. It was after three in the morning at the Northern Light, but that meant it was after seven here. We'd been here for nearly an hour and I'd done nothing to help Micah.

"I don't know what's going to be expected of us. Why don't you lie down and rest while I help Micah?"

She nodded against my chest. "I'm sorry."

"Why?" I asked, once again pulling her eyes up to mine.

"For messing up your life."

"Don't be. It wasn't your doing." I kissed her. "I'm sorry I didn't tell you or warn you. I didn't think they'd be that cruel."

"I wouldn't have believed you." Her red-blotched neck straightened as she took a deep breath. "I've been thinking about it as we stood here. I think there were clues, but I missed every one. So much for being a kick-ass investigative journalist."

"Shhh. Don't even talk about it. I'd suspect the exact opposite. Not only do I believe you were very good at your job, but I believe that's the main reason you're here."

"It just doesn't make sense."

I wanted to fix it, to make everything make sense for her. After all, that had always been my role. She was to give her sadness to me and I was to take it. That was Father Gabriel's teaching. But I couldn't make this better. Stella needed to deal with it. I just wanted her to do it without bringing attention to her or us. Instead of telling her it was done, as The Light proclaimed, I changed the subject. "I'll show you where the bed is, and I want you to rest." When she looked as if she were about to argue, I stood straighter. "Sara?"

Lowering her eyes, she said, "Yes, Jacob."

"Look at me." When she did, I continued, "We didn't talk about your friend Rose?"

Sara's forehead furrowed as she shook her head. "Rose? No, not Rose. Her name is Mindy, Mindy Rosemont. She goes by Mary at the Northern Light, and all I know is she's married to a man named Adam."

"Do you remember when you saw her?"

She nodded.

"What did you do or say?"

"The first time, I don't remember . . . oh, yes, I told Raquel she looked familiar, but I didn't know why until—"

Though she was whispering, I touched her lips with my finger. "That's what you need to do, exactly like that. Please tell me you can do it."

"I'll try."

Holding her hands, I found my even, demanding tone. "No, Sara, you must not try. Tell me you will."

Through her lashes, she obediently replied, "Yes, Jacob. I will."

∽

It wasn't unusual for Micah and me not to hear from anyone up at the mansion when we arrived. Since this was only a landing strip and not a functional hangar, our job had always been to call for the refueling truck and wait. It'd never bothered me before, nor had the cameras I knew were in the outbuildings, but today everything bothered me. My nerves were frayed.

With Micah next door and Sara sleeping, I paced the living room and waited for my phone to ring. A little after eight, Detroit time, it did.

"Hello?"

"Brother Jacob?"

"Yes," I replied, not recognizing the number or the voice.

"Father Gabriel expects you and your wife at service in less than an hour. A car will arrive to transport the two of you and Brother Micah. It'll be there in ten minutes. Be ready."

"We will."

The line went dead.

My mind filled with thoughts; most weren't good or even promising. Surely Father Gabriel wouldn't do this little reunion of Richards and Sara in front of the entire church, not that there were that many people at the Eastern Light—but still.

As I went to wake Sara, I thought about breakfast. There was no way we'd have time to eat much of anything. When I entered the bedroom, she was under the covers, curled on her side. Her light-blonde hair covered part of her cheek. The side with Thomas's bruise was against the pillow. She looked more peaceful than I'd seen her in what seemed like forever—since before she left.

Part of me wanted to keep her that way, allow her to sleep, and let her remain in whatever dream world she was visiting. Wherever it was, it had to be better than here.

When I sat on the edge of the bed, she turned toward me with her knees still pulled up and reached out for my leg. For only a second, her sleepy eyes opened and a smile graced her lips. And then it was gone. For only a second, she'd felt safe, knowing I was here, but then just as fast the memories and reality had come back. The sleepy blue of her eyes had clouded with doubt and fear.

I smoothed her hair away from her face, revealing her bruise. "It's time. I just received a call. There's a car coming to take us to service."

She nodded.

"Are you feeling all right? Can you get up?"

Slowly she sat, assessing. "I do feel all right, as good as I can, I guess. I'm a little hungry."

I shook my head. "If you get yourself ready, I'll check the kitchen and see if there's anything to eat."

We'd already determined that even the bedroom had a camera. When I pulled back the covers, she was still fully dressed. Her skirt was some kind of gauzy material that didn't wrinkle, and other than shoes and whatever she needed to do privately, she was ready.

In the kitchen I found bread and hurriedly put it in the toaster. In the refrigerator I found her favorite flavor of Preserve the Light preserves—strawberry. I looked up as she walked toward the small galley kitchen. She looked so pretty. I was glad she'd rested, if only for a little while. Despite the ugly bruise, her coloring had improved, bringing back the pink to her cheeks and lips.

When she reached for the plate with the toast, she gasped, "Oh!"

I narrowed my gaze.

"I just remembered," she said, recovering quickly, "how much I love the strawberry preserves. We've been out of it at the Northern Light for a while."

I suspected that she had remembered something other than that, but I could play along. "I knew it was your favorite. It always has been."

She shrugged as she chewed. Once she swallowed, she said, "Sometimes I forget that you remember further back than I do. All I remember is liking it." She wrinkled her nose. "It's much better than the blueberry."

I exhaled and prayed. Just maybe we could pull this off.

As I handed her a glass of water, we both turned toward the sound of knocking.

Taking a quick drink, she asked, "Is this like our service? I'm nervous."

"It is, only smaller."

I opened the door to Micah. Beyond him, on the driveway that passed the buildings and ran out to the landing strip in one direction and to the road in the other, was a black SUV. Under the warm Michigan sun stood a driver, waiting ominously by the car door. Sunglasses covered his eyes, and a white button-down shirt stretched over his large arms, a stark contrast to his dark skin. I immediately recognized him. Although Brother Elijah was on the Assembly, from my experience at the Eastern Light and the way he resembled a professional football player, I believed he also acted as a bodyguard whenever Father Gabriel was present.

"Hello, Brother Elijah," I said.

He nodded. "Brother Jacob. Brother Micah."

Although Sara followed closely behind, with her eyes down, Elijah didn't acknowledge her. He wasn't expected to, nor was I expected to introduce her. When she glanced up and saw Brother Elijah, her lip disappeared between her teeth and she reached for my hand. Damn, I wanted to know what she was thinking. Instead I searched her expression as I helped her into the backseat. She was true to our plan, and other than the fact that the pink had left her cheeks, her expression revealed nothing.

Though Brother Elijah often accompanied Father Gabriel, thankfully, Father Gabriel wasn't in the SUV. I sat next to Sara in the backseat and tried to silently reassure her as I squeezed her hand. With Micah in the front seat, we rode in silence as Elijah turned the SUV around, headed into the trees, and drove toward the gate. After he entered an access code, the solid, wide gate moved, allowing us to leave the mansion's compound. It wasn't until we entered Highland Heights that Elijah spoke.

"Brother Jacob, as an Assemblyman, you'll sit with the Assembly-men, and Sister Sara, you're expected to sit with the Assembly wives."

Her hand flinched within mine, but her head never moved. "Of course," I replied. "I'll show Sara where that is. When we were here before, I wasn't on the Assembly."

Shit! Now it was me who was rambling.

Elijah's head turned slightly toward the rearview mirror. I nodded, doing my best to keep my tone and facial expression neutral. Fuck, it wasn't going to be Sara who messed this up, it was going to be me, if I didn't calm down.

"My wife," Elijah went on, "is Sister Teresa. I told her to tell the other Assembly wives to expect a guest. They'll be ready."

I hoped that was a good thing, because given the way Sara was clinging to my hand, I didn't want to be separated from her, not even in a church filled with followers, and I was certain that she felt the same. So much for keeping promises. Not only couldn't I be with her, but also neither could Micah. The two of them knew each other only from services, but each had heard the other's name often.

Micah was also married. His wife and their young son were back at the Northern Light. He and I both knew this entire situation of taking Sara to the Eastern Light was highly unusual. When we were getting the Cessna ready for the trip, he had reached for my arm and whispered, "I don't understand this. I piloted Father Gabriel for years before you came. I've never transported a woman back to the Eastern Light."

I nodded, my concern obviously visible.

"Brother, I'll do all I can to help," he reassured me.

"We just have to bring her back."

Micah nodded. "I hear you. I mean, we don't choose them, but once they're ours . . ." His words trailed away. Micah was a good man, a good pilot, and a good husband. There weren't a lot of men who treated women the way Abraham did, at least not at the

Northern Light. I mostly credited Luke with that. He worked hard, monitoring and doing what he could to keep the wives safe. If someone else had his job, the outcome could have been much different. I didn't know how it was at other campuses.

We pulled up to the back of the large white building housing The Light, located on the corner of Second and Glendale Avenues. When I turned, Sara's eyes were closed. She was concealing her fear visually, but damn, from her pulse and grip I felt it. Hell, I even smelled it, if that was possible. It emanated from her, creating a cloud.

The Northern Light had grown to nearly five hundred followers, and yet the Eastern Light had stayed relatively stable, its population hovering around one hundred. With that number, its temple was much smaller than ours, composing only a small part of the total building. Taking Sara's hand, I led her through the doors. Each step was smaller than the one before, the old tile floor became figurative quicksand, sucking my shoes into the muck, slowing our steps as dread glued our hands together. Even the thought of letting go of her seemed impossible.

Perhaps I was paranoid, but as the followers made their way to their seats I sensed a different atmosphere from the one at the Northern Light. Everyone here seemed more tired and reserved. It made sense. The only male followers who remained at the Eastern Light were the ones who worked on either recruitment or logistics. Most of the female followers worked in the building across the street. While they had a small Preserve the Light operation, mostly they made illegal substances. It was Father Gabriel's backup plan, his way to deflect law enforcement from the bigger illegal operations, if operations behind The Light were ever questioned. These followers were more aware of the dangerous side of The Light because they lived it.

Using the seating at the Northern Light as my guide, I took Sara to where I assumed the Assembly wives sat. I must have been right, because a woman stood.

Bowing her head, she said, "I'm Sister Teresa, my husband said to expect a new sister."

New? What? Not new, just visiting.

"Sister Teresa," I said, "this is my wife, Sister Sara. We're visiting from another campus. I'll return for her after service."

She looked to the empty seat beside her and then reached for Sara's hand. "Welcome, Sister."

I made my way to the front, where Elijah too had an empty seat beside him.

"Brother," Elijah said, "before service begins, I believe you're wanted for a few minutes in the offices, on the second floor. Do you remember where you're going?"

I swallowed my concern. I didn't want to leave this room, not with Sara out there alone. "Yes, I remember."

He nodded. "I'd try to be back before Father Gabriel gets here."

My gaze narrowed. "Father Gabriel isn't the one who wants to see me?"

Elijah shrugged.

I took a deep breath and looked out toward the congregation and sighed. I felt a little better seeing Teresa and Sara speaking.

The Eastern Light's temple was on the first floor. This building was quite large and used for many purposes. When I'd first entered The Light, like most voluntary followers I'd spent most of my time in this building. The second floor held offices as well as classrooms for new-follower training. Part of the introductory process was learning and retaining Father Gabriel's teachings. The third floor had testing centers—individual cubicles where daily examinations were performed. There was constant analysis of a follower's dedication to The Light before that follower could be assigned to one of the other campuses. The fourth floor had dormitories for new followers and apartments for permanent residents. The Assemblymen and Commissioners' apartments were in the far end of the building across the street, giving them some privacy.

As I rounded the corner at the top of the stairs for only a brief second, I saw Richards as he stepped in front of me.

What the fuck?

"Let's see how you like it, asshole."

I didn't have time to process his words before his fist contacted my jaw, catching me off guard and sending my face flying to the left. Instinctively I reached to the wall. Before I steadied myself enough to retaliate, my arms were seized from behind.

FIFTY-ONE

S ara

I couldn't believe I was in the building I'd watched. Memories of my investigation came back, reviving my curiosity. As I looked around, I contemplated the size of the temple. There had to be more in this building. I wondered what that included. And then I remembered the abandoned school building across the street—the one I'd seen women walk to. For only a moment, I considered asking the other wives what they knew, but then I reminded myself that Sara wouldn't question.

When I first sat, I had a strange sense about the other Assembly wives making me wonder how we at the Northern Light would react if a new wife came to us. Almost immediately my unwelcome feeling faded as Sister Teresa and the woman on my other side, Sister Martha, seemed to relax and greeted me. Soon the other Assembly and Commission wives were shaking my hand and telling me their names.

Since they were all part of the chosen, I could tell them that I was from the Northern Light. While the followers weren't as informed, the chosen knew about the other campuses. It was as Sister Teresa spoke that I realized what had facilitated their acceptance.

"Sister Sara, have you thanked God and Father Gabriel for your husband?"

Lowering my eyes, I nodded. "Yes, Sister, I have. I'm thankful he loves me enough to correct me."

It was a bond—a sick, twisted bond, but somehow, in this fucked-up world, it gave the women of The Light a connection. For only a moment, I thanked Thomas for the bruise that had opened these women's hearts. I didn't want to be here among them, but if I had to be, I was glad we could find a common denominator to keep me from being the outsider.

"How long have you been in The Light?" Sister Martha asked.

"My husband said we've been at Northern Light for over three years."

"Your husband?"

I nodded. "Yes, about a year ago I had an accident. I don't like to talk about it, but I must have hit my head. I don't remember anything before that."

"Oh," Sister Teresa said, "that must be terrible."

I sighed. "It was, but everyone's been so helpful." I shrugged. "I think I've just accepted that my earlier memories weren't important. If they were, and if remembering them was God and Father Gabriel's will, I'd get them back."

"It's good to have you with us, Sister," Sister Martha said.

From time to time, I'd try to look about. I searched for the piercing blue eyes in my memory. However, Dylan's being at service didn't make sense. He'd never left on Sunday mornings or Wednesday nights when we dated. Not that I'd spent every Sunday and Wednesday with him, but I had spent some.

I watched the room as men and women of all ethnicities continued to enter. The sanctuary wasn't only smaller than ours, it was much older. The walls were painted cinder block, and everything was clean, but obviously worn. The threadbare carpet was in need of replacement. From what little I'd seen and learned, I believed The Light's money went other places.

Polished wooden beams peaked at the center of the ceiling, and long cylindrical lights hung from cables. Toward the front was a raised stage. Where some churches might have had a choir was the seating area for Commissioners and Assemblymen. I held back my panic as I realized that Jacob wasn't there. I'd watched him walk in that direction, but as I took in the surroundings, I realized something must have happened. The chair next to Brother Elijah was empty.

I turned, searching for Brother Micah. He wasn't too far behind me. When our eyes met, he opened his wide and slightly shook his head.

What does this mean? Where is he? Where did he go?

Biting my lip, I debated my options. I knew that Jacob wouldn't leave me. Besides, Micah was still here. If I had been the one to go missing, he would have searched for me. I owed him the same.

"Sister Teresa," I asked, "is there a restroom that I could use before service?"

"It's about to start."

I wrinkled my nose. "I haven't told anyone," I whispered, "but I think I could be pregnant."

"Oh, I understand. Yes, let me show you . . ."

Just as we were about ready to stand, the room quieted, and Father Gabriel entered the stage from a door on the right, and walking behind him was Jacob. Sister Teresa shook her head as I nodded my understanding. We wouldn't be leaving our seats until the service was done.

I narrowed my eyes, trying to see my husband more clearly. Though he appeared fine to all the followers as he took his seat by Brother Elijah, I could tell something was off. Continuing to stare, I waited until his dark eyes met mine. When they did, his jaw clenched, and even from far away, I saw the anger in his eyes and the tension in his shoulders just before his expression changed.

Something had happened, and he was trying to shield me. I just didn't know what.

Throughout the entire service I waited for something, for anything from Jacob or Father Gabriel. I didn't know whether he would make a big deal about our visitor status or whether he'd make some kind of announcement. Instead the service progressed as it would have at the Northern Light. I stood and sat at all the right times, recited the responses and verses as well as anyone.

I'd learned my lessons well.

As I began to relax, I noticed Sister Teresa's hands upon her lap. With her dark skin, the burned tips of her fingers were even more pronounced. Rolling my wrist and seeing my own fingertips fueled my need to help end this travesty. And then everything changed.

FIFTY-TWO

Jacob
Minutes earlier

"WHAT THE HELL?" I said, as my arms were pinned behind me. I couldn't see the person holding me back, but I sure as hell could see the asshole in front of me.

"I saw her face," Richards said, his jaw clenched.

Heat boiled in my chest as I worked to relax my arms. Apparently he was done with his little right-hook demonstration.

"What are you talking about?" I asked.

"Stella! That's her fucking name."

"Stella?" I did my best to sound confused. Moving my shoulders, I said, "Let go of my damn arms. I'm not going to hit this asshole."

"No, of course not," Dylan replied. "You only hit women."

Whoever was behind me released my arms, and I took a step

toward Richards. "You're talking about my wife. And what happens between me and my wife is none of your damn business."

He ran his hand through his hair. "It is my damn business, more than you fucking know."

I took a deep breath and spoke louder than I should. "Father Gabriel gave Sara to me." I emphasized her name. "If I choose to correct her, it's my decision. Not yours."

When I turned I saw a large man I didn't recognize. Though he'd taken a step back, I had no doubt that if I went for Richards, he'd go for me.

"She's . . ." Richards turned away before spinning to face me again. "She's walking around like the zombie women around here. What did you do to her?"

"What did I do?" Fuck you. "Go to hell! I remember you. You were with her in Dearborn. You had her and you turned her over. She's mine now, and I'm keeping her."

"You're keeping her? Like she's a fucking possession? This is insane."

"No, not a possession, my wife."

"Gentlemen."

A chill went through me, silencing us all, as Father Gabriel emerged from a doorway farther down the hall. The man behind me and I immediately shifted our stances, standing taller and bowing our heads, to reflect the reverence we felt for Father Gabriel. Conversely Richards casually leaned against the wall and shoved his hands in the pockets of his jeans.

Patting Richards's shoulder, Father Gabriel said, "This is The Light, we don't argue, we don't fight, and"—he leaned toward Richards, his voice low and methodical—"We. Don't. Drop. Fucking. F. Bombs. Am I clear?"

"Yes, Uncle," Richards said, though it appeared it pained him to do so.

"Brother Jacob," he said, looking in my direction.

"Yes, Father."

"We have much to discuss." He pulled up the sleeve of his silk suit, revealing a watch, as well as cuff links that I would guess could have been sold to pay off the debt of a few small nations. "However, now is not the time. Service is about to begin." His brow rose. "I assume Sister Sara is seated with the other Assembly wives?"

"Yes, Father."

"Very well." He turned back to Richards. "Won't you join us? It'd be good for you."

Pulling himself away from the wall, Richards again ran his hand through his hair. Although he was answering Father Gabriel, his stare never left me. "No, I need to get the hell out of here."

I'd never in three years heard anyone tell Father Gabriel no, but from the way Richards walked away without waiting for Father Gabriel's response, I got the distinct impression that neither of them found it unusual.

"Children can be so disrespectful," Father Gabriel said, looking at me.

Child? Richards had said *Uncle*. They were related?

I wanted to ask what all of this meant, for me, for Sara, but of course I couldn't.

"Brother," he said, laying his hand on my shoulder. "I see you have questions and admire your restraint. I always have admired that about you. The thing is that I have questions too." He patted my shoulder. "The difference is that I can ask mine. Before I return to the Northern Light, we will talk."

What the fuck does that mean?

"Yes, Father."

As he walked past me and the other man, he casually asked, "How is Fairbanks this time of year?"

Thoughts bombarded my mind. "Fairbanks? It's fine. Whitefish was out of some of our supplies. I called Brother Daniel—"

He waved his hand. "Never mind that right now. Do you have my envelope from Brother Reuben?"

Envelope. What envelope? I had a faint recollection of Brother

Reuben's handing me something at the Western Light. I couldn't recall anything after that.

"I do. It's at the Northern Light." I hoped it was. Was this the test?

He nodded. "I see." Walking away, he said, "Come, it's time for service."

I followed him down the hall and down the stairs. The other man followed closely behind, as if he needed to be sure I wouldn't make a run for it. There was no way I'd do that, not with Sara in the congregation.

As I sat, Brother Elijah nodded.

Had he been doing Father Gabriel's work or Richards's by telling me to go to the offices? Did Richards possess the power to direct Assemblymen? With each minute, the questions multiplied.

Looking out to the congregation, I found Sara and exhaled—she was all right. When her eyes met mine, I tried to relay calm, to let her know that it would be OK. At least I knew Dylan Richards wouldn't be surprising her here during service.

I responded correctly as Father Gabriel preached. I stood and sat, and even recited. However, what I didn't do was listen. My mind was too aghast at the turn of events. I tried to remember what I'd even done with the envelope from Brother Reuben. I'd taken it right before all hell broke loose. At the time I hadn't thought it was important. I also tried to decipher Richards's connection to The Light. Whoever he was, he had the most casual relationship with Father Gabriel that I'd ever seen.

My thoughts continued to swirl from subject to subject with no answer in sight, until Father Gabriel's words cut through my confusion.

"Therefore, do you not agree with our Lord, that we would rather be away from these earthly bodies, for then we will be at home in The Light?"

Away? Was this the Kool-Aid?

"Yes, Father," came the congregation's response.

"Are you certain, my children?"

"Yes, Father."

"Remember the Lord detests lying lips, but he delights in men who are truthful. People in the dark lie, but you are in The Light. You've taken off your old self and become new. Who among you would like to go back to the dark?"

No one replied, and heads shook.

"It is taught that outside are the dogs, those who practice magic arts, the sexually immoral, the murderers, the idolaters, and everyone who loves and practices falsehood. Is that where you want to be?"

"No, Father."

"Where do you want to be?"

"In The Light."

"But can everyone stay in The Light?"

"No, Father."

"What have we been told to do with our eye if it causes us to stumble?" He didn't wait for the response as his voice rose in volume. "We've been taught to gouge it out. For it is better to go through life with one eye than to have two and be thrown into the dark!"

"Yes, Father."

"Brother Abel, you and Sister Salome may come to the front of the congregation. Brother Uriel, please also come forward."

I sat in awe and horror. My gaze searched for Sara's, but she wasn't looking at me. She was looking down, as were many of the women. No doubt they all suspected what was about to happen. I'd heard of services with banishments, but I'd never witnessed one. At the Northern Light the only banishments I'd known about had been done privately. When they were made public, it was more of a production for the other followers than for the ones who were to be banished—their fate was set.

A solemn hush fell over the temple as a young couple, probably in their late teens or early twenties, made their way to the front. She was crying and holding on to his arm. Apparently they'd needed encouragement to come forward, because the man who'd been behind me in the upstairs hallway was walking behind them. Brother Uriel stood from the row of Commissioners and moved to the center of the stage.

"Followers of The Light," Brother Uriel said. "Do you trust your lives and souls to Father Gabriel?"

"Yes, Brother," was said by all. The volume was considerably lower than it had been, the sense of impending correction falling like a damp blanket.

"What have we learned about disobedience?"

"It deserves correction."

"Brother Abel, tell us what happened in production distribution."

The young man bowed his head and began to tremble. "I'm sorry. It won't happen again."

"Brother?" Father Gabriel asked.

"I-I didn't take . . . it wasn't much . . . I just needed . . ."

"Brothers and Sisters, the product you toil to make is for what?" Brother Uriel asked.

"The Light."

"Apparently Brother Abel forgot that as he was working to package product for shipment." The followers inhaled collectively. "Not caring about The Light, he chose to keep some for himself." Brother Uriel turned toward Sister Salome. "Sister, is Brother Abel your husband?"

"Y-yes."

"And as such he's caused you to stumble. Isn't that correct?"

"F-Father, p-please, we won't—"

"Congregation, is it better to gouge out these followers or allow them to drag us all into the dark?"

My empty stomach churned. When I looked for Sara, she was bent forward with her blonde hair falling down. However, as I stared, she momentarily sat up. Though her eyes were closed, I saw the telltale red blotches covering her cheeks and knew she was crying. I balled my fists, willing myself with every bit of self-control I possessed to remain seated.

I couldn't comprehend.

Father Gabriel had invited Richards to this service. Surely Richards knew what was going to happen. Could he really have watched this and turned a blind eye? He was a fucking cop, but then again, I was a federal agent and I was watching.

"Yes, Father." The response to Father Gabriel's last question was the softest yet.

"Children, do you follow me?"

"Yes, Father." It was a little louder.

"Do you believe in me?"

"Yes, Father."

"Do you trust in me?"

"Yes, Father." It was getting louder each time.

"Brother Uriel, the decree."

Brother Uriel pulled two syringes from his jacket and handed them to Brother Abel and Sister Salome. Though they hesitated to take them, they did.

"Father Gabriel's word tells us that all are to follow the rules of The Light. Correction is to be quick and appropriate. Brother Abel, you chose to take merchandise from the production center for your own use. You put yourself above The Light. As your punishment, Father Gabriel's decree is to grant your desire and give you more."

"Roll up your sleeves and show everyone your punishment."

"P-please," Sister Salome cried.

The big guy from the hall held her arm while another follower came forward and injected the contents of the syringe.

"N-no, she didn't do anything," Brother Abel cried, as his wife fell to the floor.

I wondered what the drug was and how much they were being given.

Was the intent to kill them?

"Brother Abel, your turn."

Slowly, he did as he was instructed. Immediately after the contents of the syringe were injected he fell to the ground. Their mouths began to foam and their bodies twitched. Without being asked, the big guy and three others came forward, lifted the bodies, and carried them out.

"Children," Father Gabriel said, bringing everyone's attention back to him. "Correction isn't pleasant. It's not meant to be pleasant. It's meant to keep everyone within The Light safe. When we have malfeasance among us, no one is safe. What do you say for the privilege of knowing that you are now safe?"

"Thank you, Father."

Blood seeped from my cheek as I bit the soft flesh, controlling my protests.

For the next fifteen minutes, Father Gabriel continued to preach his sermon, talking about the beauty of correction and the importance of obedience.

CHAPTER

FIFTY-THREE

S ara

Oh my God.

I couldn't watch and I couldn't run, but I wasn't alone. The other wives around me were responding the same way. Women I'd met only an hour ago held my hands. The toast Jacob had made me for breakfast threatened to return. Closing my eyes, I concentrated on keeping it down and not vomiting all over the worn carpet or my new sisters. It was a welcome distraction, because I couldn't concentrate on what was happening in front of me. I'd seen dead bodies; however, I'd never watched someone die, or, more accurately, be murdered.

This had to stop. The evidence was mounting and both Jacoby and I were witnesses. With each passing second, I wanted nothing more than for the FBI to come running through the doors and stop this horror show. I wanted to look Father Gabriel in the face and tell him who I was and that I was helping to bring him down.

I took deep breaths, concentrating on my role. Although I recognized Brother Uriel as Uriel Harris, the developer, I couldn't dwell on it. When the scene finally ended, the other wives and I released hands and fell into our own thoughts as Father Gabriel continued to preach.

I wasn't listening to what he said, nor did I care. With my eyes down, I waited. Eventually people began to move around me, but I remained still, paralyzed by the correction I'd witnessed. And then I heard the one voice that could free me. With the one word, Sara, in his deep tone, the tone that had praised me as well as corrected me, I was able to move.

Looking up with just my eyes, in the midst of this chaos, I was safe again, because Jacob was beside me, offering me his hand. It was another realization, one that the old me would never have admitted or probably experienced. Even with the mental checklist of laws I'd witnessed broken, I wanted the relief that came with giving my cares over to Jacob.

As I placed my hand in his, his warmth washed through me, alerting me to how cool I'd become. As I stood I wanted to fall into him and be surrounded by his strong arms. I wanted the only sound to be that of his steady heartbeat as my ear lay against his broad chest. I wanted him to protect me and to take me away from all this madness.

When our gazes met, his told me that he knew my every thought. Surrounded by the Eastern Light's followers, without words, we spoke not only words but also an oration to each other. We both wanted out. This had to end. Coming back had been a mistake, but we would survive.

I couldn't process what had happened, how it had happened, or why no one had tried to stop it. Biting my lip, I trapped the protests and declarations of indecency that had surfaced in my thoughts.

How could everyone just sit and watch two young people

murdered—people who'd end up on Tracy's tables at the Wayne County Morgue—people whose fingerprints were gone?

I knew the reality. No one would question their deaths. A young couple dying of a drug overdose, their bodies found in Highland Heights, wouldn't even make WCJB's news. No one in the dark would question. Why should they? No one in The Light had.

Silently we walked to the black SUV, my hand tightly encased in Jacob's grip. Across Second Avenue from the parking lot was the old school building I'd watched. The curiosity I'd possessed even at the beginning of service no longer existed. Like my fingerprints, it was gone. I didn't care what they did over there. Maybe I should restart my medicine after my period. Maybe then I could forget what had happened. As the tragedy of what we had witnessed consumed me, my only desire was to know that Jacob and I were safe and away from The Light.

Jacob, Brother Micah, and Brother Elijah spoke during the drive back to the compound, but I didn't listen. Only the final words of the young couple, Sister Salome begging and Brother Abel pleading for her life, replayed in my mind.

Did things like that happen at the Northern Light? I'd never seen it or even heard of it. If leaving The Light wasn't possible, at the very least, I wanted to go back to Alaska.

As we drove north on Highway 1, sitting straight took every muscle I possessed. The urge to melt into Jacob's warmth was stronger than it had ever been. I knew it wasn't an option. We were chosen. Public displays of affection weren't permitted. When we arrived back on the compound, I dutifully followed Jacob into the outbuilding's living quarters. Though the Michigan sun was shining and warm, I was chilled to the bone as I collapsed on the sofa.

Before I could speak, Jacob did. "Sara, cook Brother Micah's and our dinner."

I gazed up at him in disbelief. He wanted to eat after that?

He reached for my hand as his tone softened. "There's food in the refrigerator. It only needs to be warmed." As I stood he continued, "It'll give you something else to think about."

I nodded as I walked to the small kitchen. Jacob was right. I needed a distraction, but it wasn't enough. I could have cooked a five-course meal and it wouldn't have erased the images of what I'd seen. Besides, what I warmed wasn't a five-course meal. Quite honestly, I would've rather cooked, but there weren't ingredients. Pilots usually occupied these quarters, and they wouldn't be expected to do more than warm their food.

After I cleaned up the dishes and the kitchen, Jacob took my hand. "Let's go for a walk."

"All right." I didn't care what we did. We knew Father Gabriel had two more sermons to preach before he'd be ready to fly back to the Northern Light. Besides, I wanted to talk to Jacob, and since the only place that was possible was in the bathroom, we couldn't. Surely if we spent too much time in there together it would be questioned.

As we stepped outside, the sun and breeze warmed my skin. Lifting my face without sunglasses, I squinted. I didn't care that I was supposed to keep my eyes down. Allowing the summer sun to kiss my cheeks reminded me of how much I loved fresh air. "I wish we had running shoes."

Jacob smiled. "We have to walk toward the rear of the property. We aren't allowed up near the mansion." He took my hand and led me toward the landing strip.

As we walked past the Cessna, I said, "I want to leave."

"I should have forced you to," he replied sadly as we made our way farther and farther away from the cameras.

"I don't mean that," I corrected him. "Although yes, I want away from The Light. I meant I want to go back to the Northern Light." I took a deep breath. "Tell me the truth. Does anything like what we saw today happen there?"

"I promised you no more lies. I'll always tell you the truth. You don't have to ask for it. And no, at least not that I've ever seen.

There've been a few banishments since I've been on the Assembly, but they've been done privately.

"The Eastern Light is different than any of the other campuses. It's in the middle of the dark. No one can walk away from the Northern or Western Light, not easily. They're too isolated. So dealing with disputes or corrections doesn't need to be as public or as severe. Here, obedience on every level is mandatory."

"Are you defending what happened?" I asked, staring up at him.

"Hell no. There's no defense. I'm justifying it, to you and to me."

"I don't want it justified. I want it stopped. Those kids will be left in some abandoned house in Highland Heights, and no one will question their death, just another drug casualty."

"If you were a follower here, after what you just witnessed, would you steal drugs or even a paper clip?"

I shook my head.

"Would you disobey any directive?"

"No."

"Those kids served as reminders for the entire Eastern Light."

I shook my head. "I've always hated reminders."

Jacob squeezed my hand. "By the way, Brother Raphael left your correction up to me."

"And?" I asked, with my eyes open wide.

"And I took you to the coffeehouse. It's done. As if it never happened."

"Thank you."

Jacob led me past the open space near the landing strip and into the woods at the perimeter. Looking up, I saw the tall trees and the way the leaves rustled in the breeze. Now that we were away, not only from cameras and microphones, but also from eyes that could peer from the mansion's balcony or windows, the tension surrounding us lessened, and I leaned against his arm.

"Jacob, where were you right before service?"

"Oh, shit. With all that happened, I actually forgot."

"What?"

"I received an invitation to go up to the offices on the second floor."

"Father Gabriel?"

"No. Although he was there, eventually," Jacob said, rubbing his chin. "It was from your . . . well, I don't like to think of him as your anything. Ex, maybe?"

I stopped walking. "Dylan? You saw Dylan?"

Jacob nodded. "He punched me."

My eyes opened wide. I couldn't imagine it. I remembered how people had told me that Dylan was a hothead, but Jacob was bigger, much taller than Dylan. "Why?"

"He said he'd seen your face. It must have been on the cameras. I doubt he'd have been able to see it from the balcony, especially with your eyes down."

"That doesn't make sense. He turned me over to The Light, and then punched you because he assumed you're the one who did this to me?"

Jacob shrugged. "I don't get it either. Did you know he's related to Father Gabriel? Probably he's related to Garrison Clarkson."

My brow furrowed. "No, no, he's not. His parents died when he was eighteen. He said his grandparents were dead, and he didn't have any siblings."

"I promised you honesty. I'm telling you what I heard. After he punched me, we exchanged a few words, and Father Gabriel came out of an office. Richards called Father Gabriel Uncle."

I stopped walking and sat on the ground with my back against a tree. Pulling my knees up to my chest, I searched my memory. "No, I'm not doubting you," I said quietly. When Jacob sat beside me, I reached for his cheek. Running my fingers along his jaw, I pouted. "I'm sorry he punched you. You didn't do this. You didn't deserve it."

He inclined his face to my touch. "I don't deserve it for that, but I'm sure I deserve it."

"Well . . . that could probably be true," I admitted with a grin.

Glancing over his shoulder, I nodded in that direction. "What's that over there?"

Jacob turned. In the distance was a concrete wall. With the trees I couldn't see how high it was, or see the rest of the building. I didn't remember seeing other buildings at the rear of the property when I'd looked on Google Earth.

"It's a wall, like we have at the Northern Light. Although I'd guess polar bears aren't too much of a problem around here. When I first started flying here it wasn't here. I assumed they thought the woods would keep them safe, but a little under a year ago"—he reached for my hand and smiled—"about the time my life became fucked up, I saw the construction as I'd fly in. It took them a few months, but it completely encases the rear of the property."

Even if I hadn't seen Dylan on the balcony, what Jacob had just said confirmed that Dylan was involved, and that he'd lied to me. "You may think I'm crazy, but I think I'm the reason they built the wall."

"You. Why?"

"My friend, Mindy Rosemont—Mary at the Northern Light," I added to help him remember. "Besides researching The Light for a drug story and missing persons and fingertips . . . I was trying to find Mindy."

"So how does that connect you to that wall?"

"I wasn't finding anything. It was like Mindy had disappeared into thin air. Anyway, her parents live in California, and they wanted to do something to help find her. About a month after Mindy went missing, her parents came back here and posted a bunch of fliers all over the city and suburbs. I thought it was a waste of time. I mean, this is the digital age, what good would paper fliers do?

"I was wrong. A while after they were posted, Dina, Mindy's mom, received a call from a woman who said her young kids liked to play in the woods behind their house. She said they played near a landing strip, and one day they said they saw a woman being carried onto a plane. Dina called and asked me to look for the landing strip. She was told it was near Highway 1 and Eastways Road. That was the day I drove up here. I had the address of the mansion, but after I couldn't get in or even get any good pictures, I drove around for over an hour trying to find the landing strip. I couldn't find it. After today, I know why. It was because of all the gates.

"At the time I assumed if there were a landing strip, there'd be an access road. I never imagined it would be gated."

Jacob scooted against the tree. When I looked up, he was staring at me. In his eyes I saw something I didn't recall having seen before.

"Why are you looking at me funny?" I asked.

He lifted my hand and kissed my knuckles. "I'm not looking at you funny. I'm looking at you with utter amazement. You are a kick-ass investigative journalist. I can't believe they assigned me—an FBI agent—a wife with so much knowledge on The Light."

I grinned. "I'm pretty sure they don't know about you."

He shook his head. "No. If they did, that would've been me in the front of the temple."

I closed my eyes. "Please don't say that. Don't even joke about that." A tear ran down my cheek, and Jacob gently wiped it away with his thumb.

"I'm not joking. We're getting out. I just need a burner phone so I don't alert The Light by using my phone. It's been more than twenty-four hours. They should have enough manpower in Anchorage very soon."

"What happened to the phone you had in Fairbanks?"

"I had to destroy it. I couldn't risk having it on me when we went back. I wasn't sure we'd get away with what we did, getting you back into the Northern Light." With our hands still united, he laid his head against the tree and sighed.

"What now?" I asked.

"I remembered something else. Before service, Father Gabriel asked me about Fairbanks. Before I went there, I called Brother Daniel and told him that Whitefish was low on supplies so I was going to Fairbanks. There would be record of me being there, and I needed to justify it."

"What did Father Gabriel ask?"

"Just how the weather was in Fairbanks this time of year."

My pulse increased. "That's weird. Don't you think?"

"Yes, but then he asked me for an envelope someone gave me after my delivery. For the life of me, I don't remember what I did with it."

I didn't ask about the envelope. If I did, I knew Jacob would tell me—he'd promised. I also knew there was still so much about The Light I didn't know, but at this moment my curiosity was waning. I knew too much. That's why I was here, with my make-believe husband, sitting on the cool ground in the shadows of tall trees, within the compound of a man I believed to be mad, one who'd authorized the killing of two people in front of more than a hundred witnesses.

When I turned toward my make-believe husband, his eyes were closed, and his breathing steady.

How much sleep had he gotten in the past seventy-two hours?

It was hard to comprehend that I'd only left the Northern Light on Friday morning, and now it was Sunday. So much had happened.

Releasing his hand, I gently traced his jaw with my knuckles and enjoyed the abrasion of the stubble against my skin. My cheeks rose as I remembered how I'd traced his face before the bandages were removed from my eyes. When I'd done that, I'd been trying to see him, to envision the man in my bed. He wasn't the man I'd envisioned.

Now I knew he was so much more.

As I began to stand, Jacob reached for my hand and pulled me back.

"No," he said, as I landed on his lap.

"I thought you were asleep. I was going to look around." Not that I could be looking around now, not with the vise grip he had on me.

"You're not allowed out of my sight."

"Allowed?" I asked with more than a bit of rebellion.

"We're still in The Light, so yes, allowed."

I shook my head and kissed his cheek. "You were sleeping. I wasn't in your sight."

The light brown staring intently back at me sparkled with the flickers of sunlight raining through the leaves.

"Yes, you were. You're always there." He kissed my nose. "I even see you in my dreams."

Framing his face, I puckered my lips. Our kiss was soft and understanding. Loosening his embrace, Jacob reached for the back of my neck and pulled me closer. As the fervency of our connection grew, our kiss and need deepened. When his tongue teased my lips, I willingly parted them, releasing a moan as our tongues danced.

When Jacob's hand sought the hem of my shirt, I remembered the boundary I'd placed, but instead of reminding him, I pulled my blouse from the confines of my skirt. His touch was warm as he unfastened the clasp of my bra and released my breasts. Sighing, I closed my eyes and enjoyed the sensations as the scarred tips of his fingers heightened my desire, caressing and taunting my beaded nipples. I pushed my chest toward him, wanting more of what he could do to my sensitive skin. Bowing his head, he delivered, sucking and nipping and sending pulsations elsewhere.

"Oh, Jacob," I purred, weaving my fingers through his dark wavy hair.

The ground where we sat was hard and dry, hardly the place to make love. It was also private and isolated. Moving from his lap, I lifted my shirt over my head and laid it on the ground. Discarding my bra, I reached for Jacob's hand and tugged him over me as I lay back with my head on my shirt.

"You said . . . ," he reminded me.

"Please, I want you."

Jacob's eyes never left mine as he bunched my skirt to my waist and removed my panties and shoes. "I," he said between kisses, "will always want you."

Reaching for his belt, I smiled as I rubbed the erection straining against his jeans. His groan rumbled through the trees. Ever since the first time—that I now knew had been our first time—when I'd asked to be the one to unbuckle his belt, he'd always left it for me. As I pulled it from its loops, I realized it was one of the ways he'd never forced me. I'd always wanted to make love with him. It'd always felt right.

Leather and musk replaced the scent of dry leaves, and my back arched upon the solid ground as he slid inside me. Humming, I adjusted to the delicious fullness as we moved in sync. Leaving a trail of fire, Jacob peppered my skin with kisses as he teased my neck and breasts and everything in between.

Unbuttoning his shirt, I ran my fingers along his chest and reveled in the way his muscles hardened and flexed beneath my palms. When I opened my eyes, the brown I sought was staring down at me.

"I love you," I said, choking on the emotion in my own voice. It was true. It wasn't Sara or Stella who loved Jacob; it was me, the new combination of each individual I'd once been.

Jacob reached behind my head and removed the tie securing my ponytail. Fanning my hair over the shirt, he grinned. "I've loved you since the first time I saw you, and now, the more I learn about you, the more I love."

He continued his slow sweet torture as he moved in and out, building the tempo, without rushing. During this brief reprieve, it was as if we didn't have the fate of nearly a thousand people in our hands. It was just us, husband and wife, making love on a warm summer day. I lifted my hips, wanting to be closer, needing him deeper.

"God, Sara, you feel so damn good."

I smiled. "I do." It wasn't a question. I felt good—stretched, filled, and good. Pressure began to build as my back again arched and my toes curled. Jacob knew exactly what I wanted, exactly what I needed. He didn't back away, but pushed me higher until the trees and the beams of sunlight disappeared, and my body convulsed around his. Whimpers replaced the rustling of the leaves as I clung to his shoulders while wave after wave of pleasure momentarily washed reality away. I opened my eyes in time to see the expression that I loved, strain morphing to bliss and a contented smile.

When our breaths began to even, Jacob collapsed, his chest flattening my breasts, and he brushed my hair away from my face. I was home in the arms of a man whom, if life hadn't been so cruel, I'd never have met. Despite it all, I'd found the place I wanted to be. In that moment I knew we'd make it. I did love Jacob.

FIFTY-FOUR

S ara

IT WAS MORE than a little disconcerting to sleep in a room that we knew had cameras, but we didn't have any choice. Father Gabriel had messaged both Brother Micah and Jacob in the evening to inform them that we wouldn't leave for the Northern Light until the next afternoon. Apparently it was because he had plans. Last night the music and voices could be heard as the celebration ensued up at the mansion. I really didn't care what Father Gabriel did in his free time. I was just happy to know he wouldn't be doing it much longer. Today he had three Assembly and Commission meetings to attend before we could leave.

Thinking about the flight back to the Northern Light made me uncomfortable. I would need to ride in the cabin of the plane with him and didn't know whether he'd expect me to talk. My plan was to busy myself with reading his word and pray that he ignored me.

A little after three, Jacob looked up from his phone as the color drained from his cheeks. "Sara, finish getting ready. A car is coming to pick us up in fifteen minutes."

"A car . . ." I began to question, but his narrowing gaze reminded me of the cameras. "Yes, Jacob."

The timing was right. The last Commission meeting would have recently ended.

To finish getting ready, I just needed to gather our things and touch up my hair. I was thankful Jacob had told me to prepare for the possibility of spending the night. If he hadn't, I wouldn't have had clean clothes. Not only had yesterday been long, beginning at the Northern Light, but also our walk in the woods had covered my shirt and skirt in twigs and dirt. From the way my cheeks blushed at the memory, I wasn't complaining.

I was standing in front of the mirror when Jacob entered the bathroom. I knew the routine and waited for him to roll the towel blocking sound from escaping at the bottom of the door. He spoke first, his volume low.

"I don't like any of this. My gut tells me we need to run. I just don't know how."

"Where are we going in the car?"

He shook his head. "I'm not sure. I just spoke to Micah. He didn't receive the same invitation."

I took Jacob's hands. "It's probably that test. I mean, other than when we first arrived, I haven't seen Dylan. Why bring me all this way, if that's the test, to let me leave without seeing him?"

The muscles in Jacob's neck tensed as he inhaled and exhaled. "I'm going to have a fucking heart attack before this is over."

Smiling sweetly, I said, "I told you yesterday—I can do this. I can do it because of you." I shook my head. "It's more than me not wanting to mess this all up for you or me wanting to help bring this travesty down. I meant what I said. I really do love you. I won't be lying when or if I have to speak to Dylan. The only part I'll be lying about is not remembering him, but I'm a woman of The

Light. I shouldn't be talking to him anyway, not without your permission."

"I thought of that. Father Gabriel supersedes your husband."

How had I forgotten that?

I did my best to sound confident. "Don't worry. I can do this."

Jacob stood behind me and moved us in front of the mirror. For a split second, I had visions of seeing us for the first time in the bathroom of the pole barn. Now our faces were familiar.

With his arms around my waist and his chin on top of my head, he said, "Your bruise is getting lighter."

Nodding, I grinned.

"You're still beautiful."

I lowered my eyes as my cheeks flushed.

"Sara, look up. I want you to know, I'm getting us out—away from The Light and away from the dark."

Spinning in his arms, I brushed my lips over his. "Where does that leave?"

"The real world."

"I trust you with my life. I have and I'll continue to do it. I also want Father Gabriel stopped. If I didn't before, after yesterday, I want him locked away forever. So, as much as I'd love to run, you've put too much time and energy into this. We'll make it a few more days." I had a thought and scrunched my forehead. "Do you think that's the Kool-Aid plan—drugs?"

He nodded. "I do. Some kind of drug, more than likely ingestible. I don't think even Father Gabriel could expect a thousand people to inject themselves."

His lips met mine.

"I never planned on falling in love," he confessed. "But I did. Do you know what I want, someday?"

I shook my head.

"To call you Stella McAlister."

My cheeks rose. "Was that a proposal?"

"No." His eyes sparkled. "You're already my wife."

The knock at the outer door shattered the warmth of his embrace as his arms stiffened. My heartbeat quickened as he whispered, "Only a few more days."

I inhaled his cool aroma of shower gel and replied, "Yes, Jacob."

Once again Brother Elijah was the one who came to get us. I'd forgotten to tell Jacob that I'd remembered Brother Elijah from before. I was certain he was the man who'd knocked on my car window when I'd been at the other buildings in the other neighborhood in Highland Heights. He had also been the parking lot attendant—my last memory.

This time I sat alone in the backseat, as Jacob sat in the front. Our ride didn't last long, and I wondered why Father Gabriel had sent a car at all, because once the SUV left the gate, it was barely a minute before it entered another gate, the one for the main house. My stomach twisted as the gate I'd tried to see past nearly a year ago opened, revealing a tree-lined cobblestone driveway.

Bloomfield Hills was an older, prestigious neighborhood, and many of the mansions had been built by the auto-industry moguls of the past. As we approached the stately home, its exterior a combination of red brick and limestone, I got the sense of American nobility.

Once Brother Elijah parked, I waited until Jacob opened my door. As soon as he did, I read the panic in his eyes. He'd told me more than once that he'd never been invited to the house, and here we were, about to enter. I'd seen the back of the house and the limestone balcony from the outbuilding, but up close it was even more stunning, showcased by the landscaping and the fountain in the center of the driveway.

As we walked up the steps, the door opened. At first I wondered whether it was on a sensor, but then I saw the woman who had opened it. She stood silently beside the door, and though she was never acknowledged, the blue scarf around her neck caught my attention. Other than that small bit of color, her plainness made her invisible. She never looked up, but in a few seconds I took in her fair complexion and the way her dark hair was secured in a low bun. The way she stood statuesque wearing a knee-length white shapeless dress and soft flat slippers facilitated the illusion that she didn't really exist.

As I entered the mansion, my senses on high alert, as if I were preparing for a story, I took in everything from the high two-story foyer with the domed ceiling and large chandelier to the mirrored set of curved staircases. With each step our shoes echoed against the opulent marble tile as Brother Elijah led us down a hallway. We came to a stop outside a set of French doors, their windows filled with thick ornate beveled glass, making it impossible to see inside.

As we stood, I tried to swallow, but couldn't. My mouth was suddenly dry, a contrast to my palm in Jacob's grasp, which slid against his, clammy with perspiration. Brother Elijah's knock shattered the reverberating silence as the recurring rap of his knuckles ricocheted off the intricate woodwork and marble floors.

Without lifting my eyes, I knew who'd opened the door. The faded jeans and boots were my first clues; the way Jacob's hand flinched, tightening his grip, was another.

"So nice of you to join us," Dylan said condescendingly as he opened the door.

Together we stepped over the threshold onto incredibly soft carpet. It was deep red, the color of blood. I tried to push that thought away. Brother Elijah entered last and shut the door. When I glanced in his direction he was standing with his arms crossed over his large chest, blocking our only means of escape.

What the hell? Did he think we'd try to run away?

I turned away from the door in time to see Dylan sit in a chair beside Father Gabriel. They were both on the other side of Father Gabriel's desk. From the way Dylan leaned back with his ankle resting on the opposite knee, I knew Jacob was right. Dylan and Father Gabriel were somehow connected. I'd never seen anyone appear as casual around the leader of The Light.

I waited to be told where to go before I looked up; however, we weren't directed to do anything. Instead we were left standing while

Father Gabriel remained silent. When I gazed upward and my eyes met the piercing blue of my memory, my head tilted questioningly to the side, and then I shook my head, so fast it would be almost imperceptible, and lowered my gaze.

"Brother Jacob and Sister Sara," Father Gabriel began, "is there anything you'd like to say?"

"No, Father," Jacob replied.

"Sister?"

My breaths became shallow, and the room spun. "No, Father."

Dylan stood and stepped toward us. Just as quickly Jacob pulled my hand, moving me behind him as he stepped in front of me, blocking Dylan's path. Though Jacob didn't speak, from the way his body tensed and the closeness of their shoes, I envisioned the two men standing chest to chest. I was sure Jacob was taller than Dylan, but after what had happened yesterday, I feared that wouldn't stop Dylan from being the aggressor. As the silence grew, I closed my eyes and bit my lip.

"Gentlemen," Father Gabriel said, breaking the quiet. "That is not why I asked Brother Jacob and his wife here this morning."

At the phrase his wife, Jacob's grip loosened.

"Dylan, you'll have plenty of time to speak with Sister Sara. First we have business."

"Father, I'd prefer for Sara—"

"Brother Jacob," Father Gabriel interrupted, "I told you yesterday that I had questions. Dylan"—his tone became impatient—"sit down or leave."

I swallowed.

Why am I here? Why am I involved in this?

When Dylan sat, Jacob stepped to the side and pulled me forward. Once again we were standing side by side. Raising my eyes, I kept them locked on Father Gabriel.

"Brother Jacob," Father Gabriel continued, "since your entry into The Light, I've been impressed with you and your ability to learn quickly. You've known that, though, haven't you?"

"I've done my best to please you, Father."

"I spoke to Brother Michael."

Who is Brother Michael?

"He said he was pleased with the delivery," Jacob replied.

"Yes, he did. He told me the same. He also said that you refused the offer to stay the night at the Western Light."

"Yes, I had flight plans to fly into Lone Hawk."

"Did you fly into Lone Hawk?"

"Yes, I did. I borrowed the airport manager's truck and drove to Whitefish, and although I'd alerted them that I was coming, their inventory of supplies was shamefully low."

"Therefore, after completing one of the biggest shipments you've ever been entrusted with delivering, you took it upon yourself to change your prescribed flight plans, the same flight plans you weren't willing to alter for a Commissioner to stay at the Western Light."

I didn't understand what was happening or what they were saying. Maybe I should've asked more about his delivery and the envelope. Then again, my not knowing was the way it should be.

Jacob shifted, standing taller. "Yes, as an Assemblyman, I took it upon myself to decide that securing supplies for the nearly five hundred people at the Northern Light was most vital."

"And yet you called Brother Daniel."

"Yes, he's my overseer. I call him often."

"And Brother Benjamin?"

Shit!

"Father, if you're asking if I spoke with Brother Benjamin, I did, and Brother Luke, and Brother Abraham, and others on the Assembly. I wasn't aware that was a problem. If it is, I can certainly discontinue."

"It's no longer an issue."

What the hell does that mean?

My hand flinched, but Jacob secured his grip.

"Brother," Father Gabriel continued, "tell me where the envelope is that Brother Reuben gave to you."

"I'm most certain it's at the Northern Light. I apologize. I was distracted once I returned to the Northern Light."

"Distracted?" Dylan asked.

When Jacob didn't respond to Dylan, Father Gabriel told him to explain. Now Jacob was going to have to relay our cover story, in front of Dylan.

Jacob turned to me and let out a deep breath. "As you can see, Sara's been corrected."

"Yes," Father Gabriel replied.

"It happened Thursday night. Brother Benjamin called me on Friday after I'd left the Western Light to inform me that Sara had not been to work. When I arrived back to the Northern Light, as a husband, I needed to concentrate on my wife and why she'd missed work."

"Sister . . ."

My heartbeat raced. It wasn't Father Gabriel speaking to me. It was Dylan. When I didn't respond, he repeated himself.

Finally Father Gabriel said, "Since your husband obviously isn't going to give you permission to reply, I do. Answer my nephew."

Nephew, there it was.

I lifted my gaze to Dylan. "Yes, Brother."

"No . . . I'm not . . . never mind. Why didn't you go to work on Friday?"

"I was embarrassed that I had a visible reminder. I didn't want people to think poorly of my husband." I looked up at Jacob. "He's a good man."

"This is bullshit," Dylan mumbled under his breath. Louder he said, "So what happened once he came back?" His jaw clenched. "Did he correct you again?"

"Yes."

Dylan's hand slapped Father Gabriel's desk.

"Dylan, it's the way of The Light. You knew that," Father Gabriel replied. Then he asked me, "What did Brother Jacob do?"

"Because I was ashamed and didn't want to face people, my husband took me to the coffee shop, and later, after the Commission meeting, he took me to Brother Raphael's. I apologized to him for being selfish. I should've gone to work; instead I ran in the north acres and stayed there."

Father Gabriel stood. "I've heard enough. Brother Jacob, the envelope you received was not meant for you. I need it, and I need it now. I believe you need fewer distractions. Obviously you've been privy to an extraordinary amount of private information, even being here, in this house. I've been content, even pleased with your confidentiality in the past. The change of plans to Fairbanks bothers me. I assure you, if I had evidence of wrongdoing we wouldn't be having this conversation. You've been trusted with a great deal. I want to believe that The Light is your first priority, and that you're as dedicated to The Light as The Light has been to you. I've decided that we will be going back to the Northern Light as soon as possible."

Thank God!

I exhaled.

"To facilitate your ability to not only remain focused and find the envelope Brother Reuben wrongfully gave to you, but to also continue the duties you've been given, Sister Sara will remain here at the Eastern . . ."

No!

Jacob caught me as my knees buckled.

"Please, no," I begged, new tears blurring my vision and ability to witness the horror on Jacob's face.

"Sister!" Father Gabriel said. "Questioning me was one thing, arguing with my decision is quite another."

"B-but"—I said a silent prayer that this wouldn't make it worse—"I'm pregnant."

Jacob's eyes closed as both Father Gabriel and Dylan asked, "What?"

I collapsed in Jacob's arms.

CHAPTER

FIFTY-FIVE

J acob

What the fuck is happening?

I scooped Sara's limp body into my arms, her cheek against my chest. With everything in me I wanted to run out of this house, into the street, and beyond, yet I knew with Father Gabriel and Richards demanding answers, we'd never make it. Sara and I would be dead before we escaped this room.

"What the fuck? She's pregnant?" Richards asked, his volume louder than necessary.

"Dylan! Brother Jacob, Brother Elijah will take her," Father Gabriel offered, nodding toward Sara.

I readjusted Sara in my arms. "She's fine. I have her."

"For God's sake," Father Gabriel said, "at least put her on the sofa."

I turned to the wall behind me and saw a sofa I hadn't noticed when we arrived. Nodding, I gently laid her on the soft leather and smoothed her hair away from her face. For only a millisecond her eyes opened and I knew the truth—she was awake. I feigned a smile at her, wanting her to know how proud I was of her, and what a great job I thought she'd done. Damn, I'd wanted to pick her up and swing her in my arms when she'd called Richards Brother, but now . . . now . . . it didn't fucking matter. Now it was all falling apart around us.

"Brother Jacob." Father Gabriel demanded my attention.

I turned and straightened my stance, my leg against the sofa, not willing to leave Sara.

"Did you authorize your wife to stop taking her medicine? As an Assemblyman, you should know this is too early. She's only been on it for less than a year."

I exhaled. "No, I didn't. She's been counseling a female follower who works at the day care. After visiting the day care a couple of times, she began talking about children."

Richards shook his head in disbelief.

I went on, "I told her we'd decided to wait." I shifted my stance and exhaled. "I didn't know she'd stopped taking her birth control until Thursday night, after prayer meeting."

Father Gabriel's dark eyes opened in understanding as his brow disappeared behind his un-slicked-back hair. "I see."

Richards glared in my direction, sending more daggers with each second. If his uncle weren't right next to him, I suspected he'd try to give his right hook another workout. "You fucking beat her because she's pregnant?"

"No," I replied matter-of-factly. "I didn't beat her. I corrected her, and not because she's pregnant, but because in The Light, it's not her place to make such decisions. It's mine. She was willful. Her thoughts are my thoughts. She was disobedient not to share her plans for a child and make an unauthorized decision . . ." The entire time I spoke, regurgitating Father Gabriel's rules, Father Gabriel pressed his lips together and nodded, while the vein in Richards's neck pulsated and his nostrils flared.

Richards stood and walked around his chair to the window. The large pane looked out over the backyards, pool, and tennis courts, and beyond, to the outbuildings and landing strip.

"Dylan," Father Gabriel said, "do you have anything to say?"

He quickly turned. "Oh, yes, I have a shit-ton of things to say."

"Father," I began, trying to stop Richards's speech. With the pounding of my heart, the heart attack I'd mentioned to Sara earlier this morning seemed as if it was about to happen. "I'm not questioning your decision. I agree that I momentarily put my wife and her behavior above my duties. I assure you, I bought supplies in Fairbanks. Brother Noah can verify the purchases. Brother Micah can verify the supplies from the manifest, as the plane was unloaded. However, if I may, I beseech you to reconsider Sara's fate. You gave me a wife and instructed me to bring her into The Light. As you can see, I did that. Even without her medication, Sara is a woman of The Light—part of the chosen. If you find fault in my behavior, correct me. Sara hasn't been well. The morning sickness has been severe. Please let me take her back to the Northern Light, to our home, to Dr. Newton."

Richards's hands came together, the clap echoing as another one filled the air, their recurrence coming faster and faster. "Bravo, Brother, for an abuser you almost sound sincere."

"Shut the hell up!" My nerves were fried. "You want her back. Why? You don't care about her. If you did, she'd still be with you. If you did, she wouldn't be with me!"

"You don't know what the hell you're talking about!"

Father Gabriel's hand went in the air. "Enough. I've had enough of this pissing contest. Sara is staying here."

I clenched my teeth at the pain as he ripped my heart from my chest. After closing my eyes, I opened them in time to see Father Gabriel nod. I turned as Brother Uriel lifted a syringe from the bookcase.

"No! Wait! What the hell is that?" I asked as I moved between him and Sara.

"Step back, Brother," Brother Elijah warned.

"Father? What is that?"

"It's a syringe of the high-dose memory suppressor," Father Gabriel said, as if he were discussing a glass of water.

"Why?" Panic infiltrated my words as I remembered Sara's reasoning for not resuming her medications. "She hasn't gotten her memory back!" I took a deep breath, still keeping Elijah at bay. "Father, she knows your word. If you allow this, she'll have to relearn it all. She studied hard, well enough that she counsels other females. She's been doing your work. Why take that all away from her?"

"Don't you see?" Father Gabriel asked. "With no memory of the Northern Light or what she's seen here, she can be reassigned. I can't allow her to go back and tell others of what she's seen."

Reassigned?

"She won't! I haven't. You know I haven't. Sara may be strong-willed, but she's obedient. She won't disappoint you or me. And what will that drug do to our baby?"

"Brother, you said she stopped the medication of her own voli-tion. You said you didn't authorize a child. Besides, she can't be reas-signed if she's pregnant."

"I said I didn't authorize it, not that I didn't want it. Father"—my voice held more emotion than I wanted—"don't punish Sara and our child for my indiscretions. I'll do whatever you want. Please let my wife go back with us to the Northern Light."

Father Gabriel waved Elijah away and looked at Richards.

"No medicine, not yet," Richards said, looking directly at his uncle. "Obviously she doesn't have her memory. Fuck! She called me Brother." He turned back toward the window. "I don't understand how the hell it all works. Will I ever get Stella back?"

"You gave her away," I repeated for the millionth time.

He spun toward me and through clenched jaws sneered, "I saved her fucking life!"

"Enough!" Father Gabriel commanded. "I will not tolerate any more of this debate." He waved his hand toward Elijah. "Take her."

"Father—" I said, once again blocking Elijah's way.

"Brother Jacob, if you do not step aside at this moment, I'll be in need of a new pilot, and my nephew's efforts will have been for naught. I'm tired of this. A female is not worth this much trouble."

Yes, Sara is.

"You gave her to me. May I say good-bye?" I couldn't stop the tears now descending my cheeks.

He nodded. "Be quick about it. You may carry her to where she'll stay. Dylan will show you the way."

Richards's shoulders drooped, but he didn't argue or turn back around.

My body trembled as I turned and looked down at Sara. Her cheeks were coated in tears, though she'd managed to keep her emotions unheard. Hell, I didn't know whether she had or not. If she'd made noise, we'd made more. However, even Elijah seemed unaware that Sara had been listening. Once I had her in my arms, I turned back to Father Gabriel. "I promise I'll do all you ask. I've devoted myself to The Light and you. Father, I'm asking you to please keep her alive and safe. Please, after I've given you the envelope and earned back your trust, let me have her back. I'll be the perfect follower, Assemblyman, and pilot. I'll do anything you ask."

Father Gabriel stood, put his hands on the desk, and leaned forward. "Brother, because of your past performance and not based on anything you've said today, I'll reconsider my decision after I see results. In the meantime she'll stay alive."

I exhaled.

"However," he continued, "this female has caused me more problems than any who've been granted the same privilege. If the time comes to grant you your plea, be warned, you may not like what you find."

What the fuck?

"Me," I tried one more time. "Me, correct me. None of this is her fault."

I couldn't see Richards's face, as he was still peering out the window. Though his voice was low, I heard every word. "It's all her fault. If she'd only listened."

I wasn't supposed to understand, yet I did, and the clarity his words provided sent a chill down my spine.

"Dylan," Father Gabriel demanded, "show Brother Jacob to Sara's new room. Hurry, I have a plane to catch and I need a pilot."

I turned away, unable to look at Father Gabriel a second longer. I'd crash the damn plane if I thought it would save her.

As Elijah opened the door, I looked directly into his dark eyes. Instead of meeting mine, his gaze dropped to the floor. We were Assemblymen. It was a fucking brotherhood, and yet here he was, holding the damn knife as Father Gabriel twisted. Richards remained quiet as I followed him down the hallway past an archway that led to a large kitchen. I didn't pay any attention, but noticed women in the kitchen, all wearing the same white dress as the woman I'd seen by the door. Finally we came to another door.

When Richards opened it, he hit a light switch and said, "Watch your step."

Really? Like he gives a shit.

My entire body chilled as I stepped out of the opulence and into a cold, dreary world. As if she could sense my apprehension, Sara's body shivered in my grasp, and her sad blue eyes peered up toward mine. I didn't want Richards to see, but in our brief gaze I tried to convey as much as I could. I tried to tell her I loved her, I'd move heaven and hell to get back to her, and I didn't want to do this.

Step by step, down into the underbelly of the mansion we went. The length of the staircase told me that this was more than the lower level—it was a subbasement. Even the temperature dropped as we continued down. When we neared the bottom, the wall to my right ended, and I stood in disgust at where we were, at what I saw. Unpainted concrete blocks created thick walls, while instead of crystal lighting fixtures, as I'd seen upstairs, naked lightbulbs hung from the ceiling. The room was nothing more than an unfinished cement box—even the floor was smooth, cold cement.

The permeating odor of disinfectant stung my lungs and reminded me of the clinic at the Northern Light. When I looked up to the ceiling there were exposed wooden beams with thick insulation stapled in between.

I didn't want to think about its purpose. Was it to keep the cold from the floor above or sound?

The only furniture in the room was four worn couches, appearing as if they belonged in a fraternity house or a garage sale, not a multi-million-dollar mansion. Four doors interrupted the concrete block. The first one was open, and I stopped, glancing inside. The room reminded me of barracks I'd inhabited, but more cramped. In a space I doubted was bigger than ten feet by ten feet were three sets of bunk beds with thin mattresses. As in an army barracks, each bed was made, the sheets perfectly folded and tucked in place, and like the larger room with the couches, this one was without color. Gray walls, gray metal bed frames, and gray blankets. Only the pillows were different. Still void of color, they were white.

"Over here," Richards said, reminding my feet to move.

Each step physically hurt; the pain inside me was excruciating. I couldn't leave her here. I'd promised her I'd stay with her. The sound of an opening door caused me to look up, away from Sara's face, which was burrowed into me, as it had been when I first lifted her after her accident.

Suddenly the smell made sense. The door Richards opened revealed a room that looked like our clinic, or more accurately one room of our clinic. This room had two hospital beds. I swallowed, knowing that the newly acquired wives were kept in a clinic in the building across from the church.

Why was there one here, in Father Gabriel's house?

My feet forgot to step as I saw the occupant of one of the beds. Her face was black and blue, as Sara's had been when I found her at the clinic. Her eyes were covered in bandages, and around her neck was a thick, leatherlike collar. Though I was sickened by the woman's injuries—or more accurately the girl's—it was her identity that shocked me. Attached to an IV was Sister Salome from yesterday's service.

When I turned to the other bed, I saw the IV pole with the clear bag of solution. I recognized it from Sara's accident.

"You said no medicine," I said, more as a question. I didn't want to trust this asshole, but I was out of options.

Richards nodded. "I meant it." He shrugged. "I just can't promise for how long."

He pulled back the sheet and blanket of the unoccupied bed. At least it all appeared clean. When I laid her upon the mattress, the déjà vu almost knocked me off my feet. It was as if I were back nine months in the past. I wished with everything in me that I were. If this were nine months ago, I would call my mission complete before Sara ever stopped taking her medicine. I would take her away, make her safe, and call for reinforcements.

Sniffling like a child with a cold, I gently smoothed her beautiful blonde hair away from her face, and turned to Richards. "Please?" I was too devastated to fight.

After he nodded and stepped from the room, I collapsed upon Sara's chest. "I'm so sorry. I'm so sorry." My words were indistinguishable as they ran together and overlapped one another. "I love you, Sara. I won't let this be the end. Stay strong. I know you can do this. Believe in yourself. Give this to me. I'll take it. I'll make sure you're safe any way I can. Never forget me or how much I love you."

The eyes that stared up from her bruised face shredded me. If I stared at them much longer there wouldn't be anything left. I reached for her hand and whispered, "Like before. Remember? Do you trust me?"

She squeezed my hand once, and despite the hell we were in, I smiled.

"I will get you out. I promise."

She squeezed again.

"I love you and our baby."

She squeezed again.

"Only a few days," I said, softer than everything else.

As she squeezed my hand she tugged me closer.

With my ear near her lips, she whispered, her words barely audible, "Bring him down. Don't think about me. I'll figure a way. You worry about your mission. I know after everything we've been through, we won't fail."

I started to shake my head. It wasn't her place to be the strong one.

She tugged me closer.

"We won't. Because one day I'm going to take you up on that promise of a new name."

I took a deep breath and closed my eyes. As much as I wanted to be the one to save her, I knew I had to have faith in her. I had no idea what was in store for her, but I believed that while Sara knew how to survive The Light, Stella would be the one to figure out how to escape.

Covering her with the blanket, I kissed her forehead.

"Jacob," Richards called from the other room. "You'd better hurry. My uncle's already pretty pissed."

I swallowed my emotion and whispered, "It will happen"—I lowered my voice more—"Mrs. McAlister."

And then I did the hardest thing I'd ever done in my life. I walked away.

FIFTY-SIX

I PULLED THE DOOR CLOSED, but not before taking one more look at Stella. She had to be unconscious. She hadn't moved since she'd collapsed in Gabriel's office. Maybe if she could stay out cold for a little longer I'd be able to get back to her. Once I was sure Gabriel was in the air then I'd be in charge.

The tumblers echoed against the cement block walls as I locked the door.

"Tell me you're the only one who has a key to that door."

My teeth clenched at the sound of Jacob's voice.

I wished I were the only one with a key. I really did. If he hadn't fucked up and gone to Fairbanks, she'd still be at the Northern Light. It wasn't as if I wanted her there, but it was a hell of a lot better than what Gabriel had planned.

I found my cockiest tone. "Are you now saying you'd be OK with that?"

His hands balled into fists, but at least he was keeping them at his sides. "No. I'm not OK with any of this. You're pissed because she had a blackened eye. Have you looked around this place? Did you see the woman in the other bed?"

I put my hand up to make him stop. "I'm serious. My uncle will be more upset than he is, if he has to wait for you."

"That's it? You're going to leave her here. What do you think will happen to her?"

I knew damn well what would happen. Did he think I was a fucking moron? But this place did have one advantage. I took a step toward him as my answer came out staccato. "I. Think. She'll. Be. Away. From. You."

Hatred glowed in his eyes. I'd seen it before, but not in a follower. Most of these Light psychos had the intellectual fortitude to be frightened or at least respectful of me. That wasn't the vibe this guy was giving. His expression wasn't like that of a normal follower. It reminded me of the look I'd seen on more than one asshole's face as I was about to arrest him. They were the ones breaking the law, but they blamed me for locking them up. It was the same thing. This guy had been the one to screw up, to cause my uncle to question his loyalty. He'd been the one who blackened Stella's eye, yet from the way his nostrils flared, he was blaming me because she was here.

Before I registered his movement, he was on me. His words spewing with spittle through clenched teeth. "You asshole! You think what you just did is better?"

He was the asshole. One word from Gabriel and me would turn him into polar bear food.

Before I could tell him, his forearm came against my throat, pinning me to the wall and momentarily halting my breathing.

"I could kill you right now," he threatened. "No one would hear or find your body until your uncle's forty-three thousand feet in the air, flying across this goddamn country at nearly seven hundred miles an hour."

I pushed toward him and backed away, giving myself much-needed air. "Asshole!" I seethed. I was a fucking cop. I dealt with lunatics like this before breakfast. I didn't care how fucking big or strong he was, I knew what I was doing.

My hands came up, and as they did so did my leg. My boot planted to his torso. As soon as my leg straightened, he was the one gasping for air, his body tumbling backward against one of the filthy old couches before he regained his balance.

If I told my uncle now, Stella wouldn't have a chance. "You're really losing it," I said. "If I fucking tell Gabriel any of this, you're the one who's dead."

"I don't give a damn about myself. You think I give a shit about me when my wife and child are locked in there? If I can't help Sara, I don't—"

Wife and child? As if any of this shit was real.

I ran my hand through my hair and slowed my words. "That's not her name."

"I know that. I was told the name she used in the dark, but now she's in The Light—where you put her."

"She'd be dead if I hadn't, and you were wrong earlier. It is all her fault. I tried to stop her. Hell, Mindy hadn't gotten as deep into it, and they took her. I did everything I could to stop both The Light and Stella. She's stubborn as hell, and too damn good at what she did. By the time she was too deep, Gabriel wanted her dead. I convinced him to take her as far away as possible, and do the memory thing. I didn't know how it all worked. Fuck, I can't be seen around the temple or any of the buildings in Highland Heights. I'm mostly only here. I don't want to know what happens here, much less over there."

Jacob stilled before tilting his head to the side. "Wait, who's Mindy, and are you saying Sara's a cop? Or she was?"

This guy really was clueless, and the last thing I needed to do was be the one who filled him in. I shook my head. "No, and fuck, I shouldn't be saying any of this, but I did try to save her. Now, Gabriel's pissed at you. I overheard the conversation. You did something that's made him suspicious. That never ends well. I know enough about how this works to know that if you don't get your shit together, your days are numbered, and if you're banished, so is she."

I went on, "I had to think of something, so I asked Gabriel for confirmation that she was alive. For some reason he agreed. There were never any plans for her to go back to Alaska. Reassignment was, is, her only hope." I shrugged toward the locked door. "I even tried to have her given back to me, but he was adamant that wasn't an option. They're too concerned that allowing her back to her real life would result in the return of her memories."

I refused to think about my uncle's plans—the brides. I had a plan too. It was to get Stella assigned to the Western Light. It was better than here. I respected my uncle and all he'd built, but he was a sick twisted bastard when it came to women.

The shrill ring of Jacob's phone filled the basement, echoing off the walls. From the look on his face, the way the color drained from his cheeks, I had a pretty good idea of who was calling. Father Gabriel didn't like to wait.

I shook my head. This guy was doing everything he could to be polar bear food. Pressing my lips together, I leaned against the wall and watched as he pulled the phone from the pocket of his jeans.

He took a deep breath, and his chest inflated and deflated before he answered. "Brother Jacob . . . I'm on my way . . . Yes, I understand . . . I'll go through the yards."

I gave the guy credit. He held it together on the call.

His eyes met mine. "They've already driven to the landing strip. I'll get your uncle everything he needs. I'll find that damn envelope, and get my shit together." He emphasized my words. "Please, watch out for her."

I nodded. "It's safer here right now, with him at the Northern Light."

That was the truth. Part of me actually felt sorry for this guy. No matter what he did, he wasn't coming back. Once he found the information that Gabriel needed, he was as good as dead. I'd even heard they had a new pilot set up to take his place.

Gabriel didn't put up with shit from anyone. Half of this fuckup had started at the Western Light. The envelope Reuben was supposed to give to this idiot had been simply a test. Somehow either Michael or Reuben had given him the wrong one—the one with the pass-phrase needed to access overseas accounts. Michael might be one of the original three, but I'd bet he'd received an earful from my uncle on that move.

Personally I would have laid Michael out too. Then again, if he hadn't given Jacob that envelope, even by mistake, Jacob probably wouldn't have made it back to the Eastern Light, and then neither would Stella. If he had made it here with the envelope, tomorrow on the police scanner I'd be hearing about some tall white dude with no fingerprints dead in an abandoned building in Highland Heights.

They really needed to spread out the bodies better. I'd told them more than once.

"If you ever cared about her—"

I lowered my voice. "Haven't you listened to a goddamn word I've said? I cared. I still do."

"Then watch out for her, and try to hold off on that medicine."

I nodded, though the medicine was exactly what she'd get. It was the only way to reassign her to the Western Light.

I glanced at my watch. Right now he needed to get out of here, so Gabriel would be gone. That would give me at least a few days to figure out my plan. I tilted my head toward the steps. "Let me show you the best way to the backyards."

I hesitated on the second step while Jacob stared at the door to the room where we'd left Stella. When I cleared my throat, he squared his shoulders and turned toward me. I didn't turn back around. I didn't need to. The heavy sound of his boots stayed close behind as I walked back up the stairs and closed the door to the basement. We walked silently through hallways and rooms, down another set of stairs, and finally out to the back lawns.

There were things I could say, things to hurt him. Part of me wanted to. By all rights I should do more than that. I imagined pulling my gun from the holster and planting a bullet in his forehead. After what he'd done to Stella, not just the eye, but changing her, turning her into one of the zombie wives, he deserved it.

I didn't need to be the one to dirty my hands. As soon as the envelope was found, his fate was sealed. The way I saw it, he'd never see Stella or even Bloomfield Hills again. Jacob was yesterday's news.

As he passed me he didn't turn in my direction. That was all right. As I watched him start running through the grass toward the landing strip, an appropriate movie quote came to mind.

Under my breath I muttered, "Dead man walking. No"—I smirked—"running."

FIFTY-SEVEN

J acob

SARA'S WORDS HAUNTED ME, while at the same time they reinforced my resolve.

"Bring him down." Her determination and faith in me repeated over and over as I ran down the hill and through the yard.

It took everything I had to walk away. I wasn't sure I could have done that without knowing that Stella was awake inside her. Sara's conditioning could have left her vulnerable, and I'd have been responsible for that. But Stella, she was the backbone behind Sara, and I had to have faith that she'd make it.

If it weren't that the Cessna Citation required two pilots, I'm certain Father Gabriel would have had Micah leave without me. As I passed the pool and tennis courts, I recalled the other reason that he wanted me to return to the Northern Light. It was that damn envelope.

I forced my mind to do what Sara had said and think about the future—the mission. Why would Brother Reuben give me something so important that Father Gabriel was asking for it? Had he? Or was this some mind trick—some dumb test—some move to get me back to the Northern Light where my banishment would be more easily hidden?

I tried to remember what I'd done with it. At the time I'd concentrated more on the way Reuben removed it from his jacket, purposely exposing his firearm. I'd never suspected that it contained something important.

Richards's words came back, blaming Stella for all of this, and indignation rose up. He was wrong. The Light was to blame, and so was Father Gabriel. It wasn't her. Being good at her job was why she'd decided to come back to The Light. She wanted them to go down as much as I did. I said a prayer that the stubbornness he'd mentioned would keep her alive.

Though she'd sworn to save herself, I couldn't stop the weight of responsibility that bogged down my steps as I neared the outbuildings. Regardless of what Richards said, Stella Montgomery was in this compound, in that basement, for one reason. Because of me. If she hadn't agreed to help my mission, she'd be safe in witness protection. Barring some miracle that would allow her to escape, the only way to save her, once I left for the Northern Light, was to authorize the raids.

In the chaos a small smile graced my lips. Damn, he was right about her stubbornness, and I loved it. I wanted it.

Sara and I ran farther than the distance from the mansion to the landing strip all the time, but today was different. Today I was running for my life, for her life, and consequently, by the time I reached the outbuildings, my breathing was heavy and labored. As I opened the door of the building Sara and I'd shared, the scent of floral shampoo caused my chest to clench.

Instead of my giving in to the overwhelming urge to crumble, the aroma gave me strength. I needed to be strong too. I couldn't let leaving her here at the Eastern Light ruin me. If I did, all that I'd accomplished over the past three years would be for nothing. For her future as well as my operation, I needed to face Father Gabriel and convince him that I was a changed man. I wasn't the man who had stood in front of him and pleaded for his wife. I'd learned my lesson, and was now the best damn follower he'd ever had. It was the only way—our only chance.

As I'd said—the best performances of our fucking lives!

Taking a deep breath, I remembered that today was Monday, only three days since Sara had left the Northern Light. A glance at my watch told me it was just after four in the afternoon here in Michigan. With the time difference and the time it took to fly to the Northern Light, we'd land about half an hour after we left Bloomfield Hills. Taking a deep breath of the floral-scented room, I turned, straightened my shoulders, and walked back out into the Michigan sunshine.

My goal was that both Sara and I would make it until Wednesday. Just two more days.

Micah and I were scheduled to fly to Fairbanks on Wednesday for supplies. There was a special distributor that provided the ingredients for the pharmaceuticals. We made the exchange only once a month. I'd been included on those runs since I first came to the Northern Light. Since it was only raw materials, this exchange didn't require the higher clearance I'd needed to deliver the actual pharmaceuticals. However, due to the sensitivity, it had always been done with two pilots. It was one of the reasons Father Gabriel had insisted I return to work after Sara awoke. When we made it to Fairbanks, I'd buy a burner phone and authorize the raids. It wouldn't happen immediately, but it would happen.

Sara and I both had to make it a couple of days.

As I walked toward the Cessna, my eyes met Micah's. He didn't need to speak. I saw the combination of question and devastation in his expression. Ten minutes ago that look would've crushed me, but not now. Pressing my lips into a straight line, I nodded. "I'm sorry I made you wait," I said, looking around for Father Gabriel.

Micah grabbed my arm and whispered, "Jacob, I-I'm . . ." He didn't finish. There were no words.

I stood taller. "I'm getting her back. Let's go, so I can come back. Where is he?"

"In the plane, with Brother Elijah."

My eyes opened wide. "Is Elijah going to the Northern Light too?"

Micah shrugged. "I don't know what's happening, with anything, and I hope you're right."

I nodded. His expression told me that he didn't believe my declaration that I would get Sara back. If I were only Jacob Adams, I wouldn't believe me either; however, I wasn't Jacob Adams. I was Agent Jacoby McAlister, and I was fucking doing this.

Step by step I climbed the stairs, ready to get this show started. Standing at the top of the stairs, with the glare of the sunshine behind me, I was waiting for my eyes to adjust when Father Gabriel spoke.

"We're not off to a good start."

It wasn't enough information. Micah wouldn't know what he meant, but Elijah, sitting across from Father Gabriel, did, and so did I. I saw Elijah's dark eyes staring in my direction. No longer did they convey the pity I'd seen at the mansion. Father Gabriel was referring to the promise I'd made standing in front of his desk, the promise to be the best pilot and follower he'd ever had. And instead of doing that, I'd made him wait—something I'd never done before.

Of course I'd never been forced to leave my wife locked in a dungeon either.

Exhaling, I held my hands behind my back and spread my stance. "I apologize, Father. As you've assured, I no longer have distractions. My devotion is fully with you and The Light."

He nodded to me and turned to Elijah. "It seems things are under control. I'll contact you once we're at the Northern Light. For every minute my call's delayed, you know what to do."

I clenched my teeth, but refrained from speaking.

Elijah looked at his watch. "Father, what time did you plan on making that call?"

A smirk came to Father Gabriel's lips. "I'd planned on leaving here no later than three-thirty. With that schedule I'd be calling by eight."

Fucking asshole!

"Then we'll stick with the original plan. It'll be my pleasure," Elijah replied.

Yeah, so much for the brotherhood of the Assembly.

The next time I saw Elijah, I hoped it would be in a holding cell. Kool-Aid was too damn good for him. Our eyes connected as he stood, and this time he didn't look away. Once he made his way down the steps, Micah came aboard, lifted the stairs, and locked the cabin door.

The sound reminded me of the lock Richards had secured and momentarily opened a floodgate of thoughts. As I worked to corral them, Micah spoke.

"Father, is there anything you need before we take off?"

"No," Father Gabriel said, looking at me. "However, I don't want the curtain closed to the cockpit."

What the hell did he think I'd do? He'd just threatened my wife in my presence. My main goal was to fly this $30,000,000 tin can as fast as it could go. He'd be back to the Northern Light in time to make that damn call. As Micah and I entered the cockpit, I went for the pilot's seat, but Micah blocked me. We'd always agreed to switch off responsibilities with each flight. We'd been doing that for years, and he'd piloted us to the Eastern Light, which meant it was now my turn. However, instead of arguing, I nodded, thankful, as Micah spoke wordlessly. His eyes told me that he was upset too, but he'd be able to concentrate, better than I. My mind would be somewhere else.

"As fast as possible," I whispered.

He nodded.

Once we were airborne and had given our coordinates and plans to the Detroit airport, I settled back. With the open sky and setting sun ahead of us, continually out of reach, I let my mind go somewhere else. It was as Micah had predicted, but it was different. I wasn't allowing my thoughts to linger in the mansion in Bloomfield Hills. I let them go there only long enough to say a prayer that Sara would make it two more days. Then I switched gears and allowed my mind to focus on the future, one different from the one the man sitting in the cabin of this plane predicted, a future I planned on delivering—sooner rather than later.

With each mile I formulated my plan. Wednesday's shipment couldn't be canceled or changed. It had to happen. Too many alarms would sound if everything didn't go as scheduled. The Light was a too-well-oiled machine. I didn't mean the religious organization. I meant the large moneymaking enterprise.

That was when I remembered Thomas. I wondered when he was next scheduled to fly to the Northern Light and if anyone had figured out that he was missing. If someone had, would that lead to unwanted attention on the Northern Light? The flight plans I'd been happy he'd made last Friday now had me worried. If Father Gabriel had been notified of his disappearance, I hadn't been informed, and I doubted Thomas was scheduled to return on the weekend. It would be today or later this week.

I didn't know whether Father Gabriel's concern over the stupid envelope was real or not, but either way it needed to be found.

I worked to mentally retrace my steps. The obvious conclusion was that I'd put it in the pocket of my coat; however, Montana wasn't Alaska. I didn't remember whether I'd worn a jacket at the Western Light. If I had, that was probably where it was. If I hadn't and I'd had it in my hand when I boarded the plane, maybe I'd left it in the cockpit. Or I could have taken it with me into the airport in

Lone Hawk. Hell, I couldn't remember. Maybe I'd taken it in the truck I borrowed or left it in the motel room . . .

Perspiration dotted my brow. The possibilities were multiplying, and each one added to my apprehension.

As soon as we arrived, I planned to check the cockpit of the smaller plane, after I made damn sure Father Gabriel got to his apartment or the temple, or wherever he wanted to be to make that damn phone call to Elijah.

Delivering that envelope was the first step toward buying me the time I needed—just a couple of days.

CHAPTER
FIFTY-EIGHT

S ara

Though my eyes ached to open, I stayed still, contemplating my next move as questions bombarded my mind, momentarily quelling the fear I should have been feeling at my new circumstance.

Was I being watched? How would I escape? How, in this day and age, could this be happening? How did one man have so much power?

The answer to the final question was simple. We, Father Gabriel's followers, had given it to him. With each follower—chosen or otherwise—we'd given him our minds and our bodies. We'd willingly done his bidding, physical or psychological, without considering the consequences or the human toll.

Each day without my medicine made the world clearer. I could look upon The Light with a new perspective. The daily psychological warfare was fierce and perfectly executed. If it were only a religious cult, it would be well planned, but now, considering the numbers I'd seen at the lab combined with the small bit of information Jacob had shared during our late-night talk about the pharmaceutical enterprise, the operation as a whole was flawless.

Each and every person in The Light fortified Father Gabriel's strength. He couldn't do what he did alone, but with nearly a thousand people, he moved mountains and ruined lives. He did it in the name of God, but he was the only one profiting. Each of us was made to believe that without him we'd be no one. The reality was the opposite.

Without us, he'd be nothing.

I recalled the young couple at the temple yesterday. In front of more than a hundred followers, Father Gabriel had ordered their deaths. Then today he'd ordered mine. Not literal death, but the death of Sara Adams. He'd said the loss of my memories of the last nine months was necessary for reassignment.

Were women so worthless in his mind that he could manipulate their lives as if they were toys he could take from one man and give to another?

As my memories of life in the dark and in The Light continued to blend, I recalled a prayer Jacob had said on one of my first days as Sara. At the time I hadn't understood the full impact. I hadn't been able to comprehend. Now I did. Jacob had said the prayer as I was about to eat for the first time. He'd said, "Let this food be a reminder that privileges given can be taken away." That's what Father Gabriel had done today. The life Jacob and I'd built, no matter how perverse our circumstances, had been a privilege, and in a simple declaration Father Gabriel had taken it away.

Perhaps I was suffering from dissociative identity disorder. As I lay motionless, I had the unreal ability to see everything from two different perspectives—Sara's and Stella's. I recognized how well The Light had conditioned me. If it hadn't, I would have fought the descent into this cold dungeon. Most normal people would. However, from this dual perspective I could assess that as Sara I was no longer normal. I'd been conditioned to accept that the men knew best and to never question.

Though there was a sense of peace in that mentality. I would fight heaven and hell to stop them from doing it to me again. I wasn't in the circumpolar North. I was in an upscale community in Michigan. All I had to do was get out of this compound and get to the FBI. Though that seemed a difficult goal, considering the obstacles I'd already survived, it wasn't impossible.

As both mind-sets settled into my psyche, I took Sara's peace and put my trust in the man who'd kept me safe for the last nine months. I also took Stella's fear and let it come to life. Fear had a purpose. It kept people safe. It was that little voice that said not to go down the dark alleyway, or the rapid pulse that occurred when things weren't as they appeared. Fear happened for a reason, and I needed to embrace it.

To survive this, I needed both, the peace and the panic. I needed out of this basement.

Muffled voices continued to waft from the other side of my locked door. Though some were louder than others, I couldn't make out the words; however, I recognized both voices. I also heard the emotion in both. I had difficulty comprehending that Jacob and Dylan were even talking to each other, but recognized that the absurdity was more than coincidence.

I tried to recall all I'd heard in Father Gabriel's office. I didn't have enough understanding for any of it to make sense. We had been prepared for the test. When I'd called Dylan Brother, it hadn't been a Herculean effort. Though I'd known him in what seemed like another life, he hadn't been introduced to me. Until Father Gabriel gave his permission, I hadn't been told I could even speak to him. Therefore, once I was granted permission, the title came without thought. After all, as Sara, I knew that all men deserved a title.

Definitely dissociative identity disorder.

I'd hoped that after announcing my pregnancy I'd be allowed to stay with my husband. Since that'd been my goal, I'd failed.

However, the announcement may have helped me avoid the drug Brother Elijah had planned to inject. Though Jacob was the one who initially stopped Brother Elijah, we both knew Jacob's power was limited. He and Brother Elijah were both Assemblymen. Father Gabriel's decrees were the final word. Then again, it wasn't any of them who'd stopped the injection. It was Dylan.

How did Dylan have that much power? Had he always, even when we'd been dating? How could I have dated someone involved in The Light and not known?

I remembered my boss, Bernard Cooper, his concern about Dylan, and how he'd had Foster, my coinvestigator, look into his private life. I'd been the one to tell him to stop. I also realized that I'd discovered all the information I had about The Light while Dylan was right there. He'd gone with me to the morgue. He'd seen my pictures of the white building in Highland Heights. I'd given him a key to my apartment. Suddenly I wondered if my research had ever been found. I wondered if Bernard or Foster had gone through all I'd uncovered.

Of course they hadn't.

My inner turmoil turned to anger as I thought that like my memory, more than likely, my research had been cleared away. Then again, Dylan had been the one to stop the medicine—the medicine that would allow my reassignment. What Brother Elijah had been about to inject wasn't like the pills that Jacob had wanted me to restart. Father Gabriel had called it the high-dose memory suppressor.

I didn't want to think about it. Instead I held tightly to a sliver of hope that maybe together Jacob and Dylan could buy me some time, time I needed to save myself. I continued to believe until the voices stopped.

A muffled sob erupted from my chest and my breath stuttered. The voices were gone. They'd left me and soon Jacob would fly back to Alaska. I was truly alone.

The new silence came like a thick cloud settling in the chilled basement. In some ways it reminded me of my psyche after my accident. Time lost meaning as only my breaths moved me, and then slowly I became aware of the world beyond my closed eyes. I fought the cloud and pushed it away. The fine hairs on my arms stood to attention as Stella's fear was realized. I wasn't alone.

Slowly I opened my eyes and turned my head. On one side of my bed, radiating coolness, was a gray wall. In the dim light I made out the rectangles and knew it was made of cement blocks. The far wall was also made of cement blocks. There was the one door, the one Jacob had walked through, and the one I'd heard lock. A dim light came from a lightbulb hanging from the ceiling. Unlike the grand ceilings upstairs, this ceiling was nothing more than insulation and boards.

As I turned to my right my breathing hitched. There was another bed in the room and someone was in it—a woman. Opening my eyes wide, I quickly sat and backed away, scooting myself to the top of the bed. Backed against the cold cement wall, I pulled my knees against my chest, while my heart beat erratically and I stared at the silhouette of a body. Memories of bodies on Tracy's table in the morgue prickled my skin with goose bumps as I tried to determine whether the woman was alive.

I released a breath as recognition propelled me from the remnants of my fog. Despite the bruises, contusions, and bandages around her eyes, I recognized the girl in the bed. Moving as quietly as I could, I eased myself to the cold hard floor. With my gaze narrowed to the other woman, I gasped as I nearly toppled an IV pole holding a bag of clear liquid near my bed.

Shit! Have they medicated me?

Quickly I scanned my arms. For only a moment, I feared that somehow I'd lost time, but my arms were clear of IV marks. Step by step I moved closer. Standing at her bedside, I saw the thick leather collar around her neck. Only a few inches wide, it wasn't a brace, and seeing it, I was once again reminded of the bodies in the morgue. The one I recalled seeing with Dylan had had a thick bruise around its neck. Taking a deep breath, I reached for the woman's hand. In the dim light, the tips of her fingers had the same ghostly hue as mine, and even in the coolness, her hand had warmth.

Thank God!

She was alive.

She might have been alive, but the swelling and black-and-blue contusions of her face peering out from the bandages over her eyes, as well as the ones on her exposed arms, told me she'd lived through hell. Attached to her other arm was the IV, with two bags hanging from the pole. One was the same as the one near my bed. I hoped the other was pain medicine. I eased her blankets down and found a cast on her right leg. I knew where I'd seen her before. She was the girl from the service.

"Sister Sara, leave her alone."

I turned at the voice. I'd been too interested in the unconscious woman to hear the opening of my cell. In the doorway was the figure of a woman. By her attire, I wondered whether she was the same one who'd opened the door when we first entered the mansion.

"Come with me," she said.

Nervously I tugged the silver cross on my necklace and ran it up and down the chain. This was my means of escape. It couldn't happen from within this cell. I needed to comply, no matter where she led. As I followed, I squinted—not that the outer room had natural light, but it was brighter than the room where I'd been held. I quickly scanned the new room. It was depressingly like the one I'd just left, unpainted cement block and cement floor, with only old couches as furniture.

"In here," the woman called from another room.

As I followed her voice, my steps slowed at the threshold of the room where she'd led me. It was a bathroom.

"You have three minutes, strip and shower."

"Excuse me?" I asked, my knees once again feeling too weak to hold me.

Up close I saw that she wasn't the same woman who'd opened

the front door. This one had dark-blonde hair in a bun at the back of her head and was wearing the same shapeless white dress and soft shoes, but her scarf was a darker shade of blue. Her lips pursed and her eyes narrowed. Stepping closer, she lifted my silver cross and pulled. I gasped as the fine chain snapped.

"Strip and shower. That means your jewelry. You're no longer chosen nor are you married. I personally don't care if you succeed or fail. However, I'll give you a bit of advice—follow directions the first time."

When I didn't reply she went on, "We all know the chosen think they're so much better than the rest of us."

Defensive at her tone and words, I stood taller.

She closed the distance between us until we were nose to nose. "Do you have a problem with following directions from followers?"

"No, I don't know what you think about the chosen, but I assure you we follow directions. We are also used to sisters being helpful, not cruel. Give me back my necklace." I wasn't sure where my strength came from, but I'd spent nine months subservient to men. I didn't plan on adding women to that equation.

She smirked. "Well, like I said, your success or failure is no skin off my back." She laughed. "It will be off yours. And I am being helpful. Strip, shower, you'll not need the necklace. Here we wear something else, something that defines us as Father Gabriel's personal followers, the brides of The Light. So do as you're told and shut up. You may live long enough to understand the honor of being here."

Brides of The Light?

I couldn't process. All I knew was that I needed to play this damn game long enough to get out. What I didn't know was what that would entail.

"Please," I tried, hoping for compassion. "I don't know what's happening. Give me back my necklace. I'll keep it and my ring hidden."

She stepped past me. "You now have two minutes."

Biting my lip, I began to shut the door when she stopped me.

"You're on constant surveillance. I'm not getting punished because of you. Hurry."

I turned toward the shower and began to take off my clothes. Once I was down to my underwear, I turned on the water. The trickling stream was freezing cold. I tried to adjust the warmth, but my clock was ticking and the temperature wasn't changing. When I looked back over my shoulder, my new sister shrugged.

"You don't have time to wait for it to warm. Besides, down here, it doesn't."

"Why do I need to shower?"

"You have a lot to learn. Did your husband allow you to question?"

"No, but you're a female. I can question females."

She pointed at her scarf. "Only if you've earned a darker color. Today you'll receive your white scarf. You may only question females with the same color or lighter. To everyone else you don't exist. Now get in."

Removing my underwear, I stepped under the ice-cold shower. My teeth chattered and my skin prickled as I wet my hair and body. The entire time I avoided turning toward the woman who watched my every move.

"Time's up," she announced, turning off the water. "Follow me."

Soaked and without a towel, I shivered as I wrapped my arms around myself in an attempt to shield my body. Next she opened a door to a new room. My eyes opened wide as I took in another concrete cell. This one was empty of furniture. On the cement floor was a white dress similar to the one she wore, a pair of underwear, and shoes.

"Sister?" I tried asking. "Could I go back into the bathroom? I didn't get a chance to use the toilet."

She rolled her eyes. "Hurry."

Thankfully no one else was around as I walked nude back to the bathroom, leaving a wet trail. On the floor, where I'd seen it earlier, was the silver cross that had come loose from my necklace. She'd put the chain in her pocket. As I sat on the toilet, I covered the cross with my bare foot. Seconds later she was watching me again. I kept it hidden as I washed my hands.

When she stepped away, telling me to hurry and dress, I reached for the cross. With no other alternative, I ran it under the water and placed it on my tongue. Swallowing, I vowed they weren't taking everything from me. Once back in the other room, I dressed, the material of the white shift clinging to my wet skin. Just as I was beginning to feel better about being covered, I held my breath at the sound of heavy footsteps crossing the outer room. They were getting closer.

Instinctively my chin dropped and my head bowed. With no bra, the cold temperature, and the light weight of my dress, I was keenly aware of my hardened nipples. Turning my shoulders forward, I tried to hide my breasts, which rubbed against the shift.

"Sister Mariam, will Father Gabriel be pleased?"

Mariam must be the name of the woman who'd been directing me. Through veiled eyes I watched the large man I'd never seen before talk with her, while at the same time scanning me up and down. When his gaze lingered on my breasts it added to my unease.

"No, Brother."

What were they talking about?

"That's too bad. We can't disappoint Father Gabriel."

"No, Brother. She'll learn this is an honor."

The man brushed Mariam's cheek. Though the action could have seemed affectionate, in reality it twisted my stomach.

"Leave us."

"Yes, Brother Mark."

Still barefoot, I backed away as Brother Mark stepped closer. When my back hit the far wall I gasped, causing him to laugh.

"Sister, Father Gabriel is particularly interested in your lessons and your correction. He's put a strict zero-tolerance policy on you. Assuming you're allowed to continue your lessons, we'll get well acquainted."

I flinched as he brushed my cheek.

"Please."

"Sister, I'll tell you when it's time to beg. Now it's time for your first lesson."

The bile from my stomach surged upward as Brother Mark reached for the buckle of his belt.

FIFTY-NINE

J acob

WITH THE WINDS in our favor and more acceleration than we usually needed, we landed with time to spare for Father Gabriel and Elijah's timetable. As we unbuckled our seat belts Micah nodded in my direction. Taking a deep breath, I reined in my nerves and walked to the cabin of the plane. It was time to make the same speech I'd made numerous times. "Father Gabriel, would you like either Brother Micah or me to drive you to the community or would you like one of us to call for another member of the chosen?"

Leaning back against the soft leather, he casually looked up at me. "It does seem we've made excellent time."

"Yes, the winds helped to keep you on schedule."

Father Gabriel stood. "I need that envelope now, yesterday even. I'll contact Brother Raphael, you two do what you need to do for the plane, and you find me what I need. I expect to hear from you this evening. I don't think you want to disappoint me."

"No, I don't. The call to Brother Elij—"

He lifted his hand, stopping my words.

"Is no longer your concern. Remember, we've eliminated your distractions. Finding the envelope is your only concern."

Eliminated? I swallowed my retort as cool Alaskan summer air filled the plane and we turned toward Micah and the open door. "Father, I will get the cart," Micah offered as he lowered the steps.

Ever since we'd seen polar bears on and near the landing strip, Father Gabriel had decided he needed a ride to and from the hangar. While that normally didn't bother me, right now I secretly thought how fortuitous a bear mauling would be.

"Go, Jacob," Father Gabriel said, "you have things to do."

I nodded, following Micah from the cabin and down the stairs. A quick scan of the trees and open space revealed nothing out of the ordinary. As we walked toward the hangar, Micah was a few steps ahead of me.

"I'll get the cart. You get the tug," he called.

That was fine by me. I'd much rather secure the Cessna than transport Father Gabriel. Quite frankly, if it had been up to me, I'd have tied fresh meat around his neck and left him for the bears.

Getting the tractor and the tug, I thought about the parts of this mission I'd miss. The flying and even ground crew duties were at the top of my list. I purposely didn't put Sara on that list, because after this was over, I wasn't losing her.

I had the Cessna pushed back and inside the hangar by the time Micah made it back inside. I'd just started the post-flight checklist when he said, "Go. Do whatever he keeps telling you to do."

I nodded, but the idea of setting foot back in our apartment without Sara had me trembling with both anger and fear. Though I kept trying to think of other things, I couldn't stop the thoughts of what she was enduring at the mansion in Bloomfield Hills. No matter what it was, as long as she was alive, we'd survive.

"Did someone come get him?" I asked.

"Yes, Brother Raphael. I'm probably paranoid, but I get the feeling there's something up. As soon as I'm done with this checklist, I'm heading back to the community. I want to get to Joanna . . ." His expression saddened. "I'm sorry, Brother."

"Don't be sorry. Take care of her and little Isaiah." I tried to not think about the man who'd become my friend and his small family. The human side of The Light was the reason we were back here, why we'd risked everything to give the FBI a few more days.

"I'll do my best. You know I've been praying for Sara."

"Thank you." It was all I could say. My first job was to focus and try to remember what I'd done with the envelope. Walking toward the small plane, I imagined the cockpit and where I could have stashed it. If I hadn't been looking at the floor, I wouldn't have seen them, but I was and I did. On the concrete floor, every few steps were small drops of something.

Anger swelled inside me, causing my pulse to race as the thudding of my heart filled my own ears. Was it blood? Was it Sara's? Had Thomas done this?

I scuffed one drop with the toe of my boot, and the dot smeared. It couldn't be from Sara. If it were, it would have happened last Friday. It wouldn't still be moist enough to spread. Why was there fresh blood in our hangar?

Just as I was about to open the door and enter the small plane, my phone rang. Father Gabriel's tone echoed throughout the large space. Micah's eyes flew to me, filled with both question and trepidation.

I answered before the third ring. "Father, I just started to—"

"Come into the community immediately. We're convening an emergency Assembly."

Shit! What does that mean?

"Father, the envelope?"

"At the moment, you're still an Assemblyman. You need to be here."

The line went dead.

I took a deep breath and contemplated my options. Without a phone to call the FBI, I had none. "I'm headed into the community," I said to Micah. "Forget that checklist. Go to Joanna."

~

Parking my truck as near our apartment as possible, I went directly to the temple. The sense of impending doom lurked around every corner. As I neared the Assembly room, I saw Luke and grabbed his arm. "What's happening?"

He shook his head. "I'm not sure, but it's not good. Not good at all."

When we entered, a sea of eyes turned in my direction, and for the first time I could remember, Brother Timothy's expression wasn't contemptuous; instead I'd describe it as smug.

"Now that we're all here, have a seat, Brothers," Brother Raphael said, standing to the right of Father Gabriel.

I peered around the table at the sixteen men. With Father Gabriel present, there should be seventeen. "Where's Brother Benjamin?" I asked.

"Apparently, much has happened while we were away," Father Gabriel said.

Yes, a lot had happened. My wife had been left at the Eastern Light.

"Brother Timothy," Father Gabriel began, "please tell the entire Assembly what you just relayed to me."

Timothy stood. "It's possible that not all of you are aware of the lengths we go to, to supervise our campus. We monitor the use of cell phones and the activity of the cell tower very closely. The Light can never be too careful or too trusting." He looked directly at me.

Shit! The cell tower. My pulse quickened.

"Other than an occasional hunter or pipeline worker, our cell tower is monopolized by us, the chosen, the only ones who have cell phones in this community."

Suddenly Father Gabriel's comments about whom I'd called came back to mind.

Fuck!

"You can imagine our confusion when last Friday an unknown number called from our tower. Incoming calls do happen with wrong numbers. This call originated from our campus."

From the sober expressions of the Commission, I gathered they'd already met and discussed this; however, most in the Assembly appeared shocked.

Brother Timothy went on, "That unknown number made five outgoing calls and received one call."

"Brother, does this have anything to do with Brother Benjamin?"

The table murmured at Brother Peter's question.

"Brothers," Father Gabriel commanded. "Let Brother Timothy continue."

"This could be attributed again to a hunter or pipeline worker except that the five outgoing calls all went to a familiar number, one that received the calls from a tower near the Western Light."

Perspiration dotted my upper lip.

Where were Benjamin and Raquel? How long had Father Gabriel known this? Maybe I'd been right and the envelope had been only a pretense to lure me back to the Northern Light.

"That doesn't make sense," Luke interjected. "Who'd even know to call anyone at another campus?"

"That's a good question," Brother Timothy replied. "It was something we would've questioned if it were not for the one familiar number the unknown number called initially—five times."

I took a deep breath. "Father, Brothers, did the unfamiliar number spend enough time on the call to speak to the familiar number?"

"No," Brother Timothy replied. "The only call that was answered resulting in a discussion was the one received by the unfamiliar number."

"Father, Brothers," Luke implored, "could the five calls to a familiar number have been made erroneously, a wrong number?"

Father Gabriel nodded. "That could be possible, unlikely, but possible." He stood and nodded to Brother Timothy. "This meeting is to inform you, members of the chosen, that the guilty parties have been punished. While Brother Benjamin will be missed, The Light will not tolerate deception of any kind on any level. We've unfortunately lost members of the Assembly in the past. It's never an easy decision, but I support the stance taken by Brother Raphael and the Commission in my absence."

My heart clenched as I peered toward Luke. His eyes now glistened with unshed tears as the muscles in his jaw clenched.

"While I've decided to not publicly call out the coconspirator in this travesty, rest assured, he too is undergoing correction."

The room stilled as everyone but me nodded. I couldn't move.

How had I not thought that they'd monitor the tower? Was Sara currently paying the price for my mistake?

"Nominations for the open position on the Assembly," Father Gabriel continued, "will be heard at tomorrow's meeting. Brother Luke, you have a wide knowledge of the followers here at the Northern Light. Bring a list of possible candidates. We may be in need of more than one nomination, depending on the near future."

My lungs forgot how to breathe at his last statement. I couldn't move, much less speak, as everyone but me responded.

"Yes, Father."

"Brother Noah, please pray for our Assembly, and we'll adjourn this meeting."

Fuck!

I needed to get to Fairbanks. Two more days.

Lost in my own thoughts during the prayer, I didn't realize it was over until Father Gabriel said my name.

"Brother Jacob, were you listening?"

All of the other Assemblymen were standing and moving toward the door.

"I'm sorry, Father. I admit I wasn't."

"I thought we'd eliminated your distractions."

Why does he keep using that word?

"Father, you said you'd keep her alive."

Brother Abraham nodded and closed the door, leaving me alone with Father Gabriel and the Commission.

"And she is. Your job is too valuable right now for you to meet the same fate as Brother Benjamin. Sister Sara's current position is your warning."

I looked to Brother Daniel, but his jaw was set and his eyes were on Father Gabriel.

"Father, I won't fail you. I promised that."

He narrowed his dark gaze. "You already did. Tell us what was said during your discussion and why it couldn't be done on your real phones. Explain to us why you needed deception."

The obvious answer: because that our real phones were monitored wasn't acceptable. I fought to make sense of the lies we'd told while I simultaneously wondered what Benjamin and Raquel had said. With my elbows on the table, I held my head. Three years of hard work and this was going to end over a damn phone call.

"Brother, speak now or I will make a call to the Eastern Light."

The room blurred as I summoned my Light persona and ignored his blatant threat. "Father, I'm sure Brother Benjamin explained."

"No, he didn't. As a matter of fact, you can cut to the chase. We know it was Sister Raquel whom you spoke with, not Brother Benjamin."

Brother Timothy replied, "We have the technology to triangulate the location of the phone. The call came from the Assemblymen's apartment building. That was the best we could isolate it. Everyone was accounted for, except Raquel and Sara. When Raquel was questioned, she finally admitted to having the phone, and swore

Benjamin didn't know anything about it. She said she called about Sara and used the phone to not get Sara in trouble."

"Brother Raphael, remember Sara's confession?" I asked.

"Yes."

I ran my hands through my hair. "Ever since the time Sara was corrected by Brother Timothy and Sister Lilith, I've been worried about her when I'm gone." Timothy sat back and crossed his arms over his chest. "I asked Sister Raquel to alert me if anything unusual happened while I was away. This is my fault. I should be banished, not Benjamin or Raquel and not Sara."

"Brother Jacob, decisions made by this Commission can't be unmade. Go on."

"Sister Raquel was worried when Sara didn't go to work, especially when she couldn't find her. That was why she called me using the phone I'd given her."

"I'm going to ask this one more time," Father Gabriel said. "Why did you go to Fairbanks?"

"Because Raquel was afraid that Thomas took Sara. She said she'd seen him in the community."

"You lied, to me and to Brother Daniel."

"Yes, I did."

"Why?"

"Because I found Thomas and eliminated him as a problem."

Father Gabriel leaned back as the rest of the council shifted in their chairs. "You killed him?" he asked.

"He was a threat to The Light. I didn't want anyone to know what I'd done. After I did it, I worried that it could somehow come back on The Light."

"Why did you kill him?"

"He'd been in the community. Xavier never comes into the community. Thomas threatened to expose things he'd seen as well as our location."

"His body?"

I shook my head. "I brought him back here. That was my true

distraction, not Sara. I brought him back here, and left him for the wildlife."

Father Gabriel nodded. "I believe that in light of this new information, we'll need to reconsider our safety measures. You're correct that he should never have been given access to the community. How did he learn the codes?"

"I don't know the answer to that," I answered honestly.

"Each Assemblyman and Commissioner has his own code for the gates. We could go back through and assess the surveillance . . . ," Brother Timothy offered.

"The video's on a loop. It erases every third day," Brother Daniel replied, finally meeting my eyes. "Besides, there's also the code used by followers who work at locations outside the walls."

"Change everyone's codes," Father Gabriel said as he turned to me. "Thank you, Brother Jacob. It seems as though we may have rushed to assume the worst. Pilots are in precarious positions. I'll take this new information into consideration regarding our situation at the Eastern Light."

"Thank you. I was only thinking of The Light."

"What you did was acceptable; however, it was outside of your scope of decision making. The proper way to have handled it would have been to tell Brother Daniel the truth, and then follow the guidance of the Commission."

"I apologize. I was afraid that he had Sara," I admitted.

"Well, as we've stated, that's no longer an issue. Now produce that envelope, and I'll reconsider your current correction."

"Yes, Father."

I stood and nodded toward Brother Daniel.

"Brother Jacob," Father Gabriel said, "call me as soon as you have it."

Benjamin and Raquel's fate hit me as I closed the meeting room door. The weight of my knowledge staggered my steps as I contemplated their consequence for helping me.

CHAPTER

SIXTY

S ara

VOMITING on Brother Mark's shoes wasn't intentional, but that didn't stop me from receiving additional correction. Never had Jacob whipped me like what I'd just experienced. Though Brother Mark hadn't told me to count, I had. I couldn't ask, but eventually I suspected he wasn't going for a particular number. His belt continued to strike my cold skin until it opened and blood ran from his lash.

"So dark," he said, assessing my blood, as he roughly spun me around to face him. He said my correction was to remind me to listen to directions the first time. From the bulge in his jeans, I believed it was also about his pleasure. The sickening thought came accompanied by a shiver of fear. In my current position, I was powerless to stop any other type of pleasure he might choose to require of me.

Before he'd started my correction, he'd made me remove my

dress. I'd wanted to remind him that only husbands were supposed to be able to do this, but I knew it wouldn't help. Crying and wearing only my panties, I covered my heaving breasts with my arms and studied his vomit-splashed shoes. While I was afraid to ask whether I could get dressed, the longer he stood there staring at me, the more afraid I was to remain exposed.

Finally he simply turned and walked away, leaving me alone with blood dripping from my back and tears coating my face. The cool temperature of the basement added to my trembling. Biting my lower lip, I stood still, watching the door, unsure what I was expected to do. My dress lay near my feet, while my shoes were still where I'd found them. And near the back wall was the puddle of my vomit.

Though I knew my back was bleeding, I wanted to be covered. When I reached for my dress, I noticed the naked ring finger on my left hand. My thumb reached for the missing wedding band as my trembling, as well as tears, increased. I would survive this, not only for me but also for him, for Jacob, for his mission.

With my hair still damp, I pulled the dress over my head. The material irritated my fresh wounds, while the cold water and blood glued the fabric to my skin. I slid my feet into the soft formless slippers.

The next time the door opened, it was Sister Mariam. She didn't speak; instead she scrunched her nose, shook her head, and disappeared. When she returned she had a bucket of antiseptic-scented water. Placing it on the floor, she handed me a scrub brush.

"Clean your mess," she commanded, and walked away.

I tried to do as she said, but too soon the water was filled with pieces of my long-ago-eaten lunch. All I was doing was spreading it around. When the door opened again, I lowered my head, knowing Sister Mariam would reprimand me. It wasn't her. Another woman wearing a white dress, this one with a white scarf, entered. It was the color of the one I'd been told to expect. Remembering Sister Mariam's words, I knew this was one of the women I could question, but with my back sore from my latest reminders, I didn't want to risk it. She didn't speak either. Silently she took the bucket I'd been using and replaced it with one containing fresh antiseptic water.

The scent of the cleaner combined with the pain of my back had me on the verge of vomiting again, but I continued swallowing, scared of what would happen if I didn't do as Mariam had said. Tears mixed with the water as I scrubbed the concrete floor for the second time. Each time I moved my arm, the material of the dress tugged and rubbed my back, intensifying the sting of Brother Mark's reminders.

I would have done a better job on the floor with better tools. The scrub brush she'd given me was as dilapidated as the old couches in the main room. The bristles were short and worn. Though I didn't notice it at first, the tip of one of the fingers on my right hand was raw and bleeding from scraping across the floor. As I was almost finished, footsteps and voices came from the main room. I wasn't sure how many people were out there, but I knew it was more than Sister Mariam. As I waited for the door to open, I wondered whether it would be better in here with the wet strong-smelling floor or out there with them.

"Sister Sara," Sister Mariam said, as she unlocked the door. "Come out. It's time you understand the honor you've been given."

Honor?

As I stood, my muscles and wounds cried out. My legs ached from washing the floor on my hands and knees. And the white dress I'd been told to wear was damp and dirty from being on the floor. Without bandages over my back, surely I'd bled onto the white material.

Five women, all wearing similar shifts, stood in the main room forming a semicircle. Four of them wore blue scarves in varying shades. The one who'd brought me the fresh bucket of water was the only one wearing a white scarf. I recognized the one with the lightest shade of blue as the woman who had opened the front door.

I never had time for a sorority in college. I was too focused on my grades. But as I stepped in front of them, I had the strange sensation of some sick college movie. What I feared was that I was about to be the unsuspecting participant in the deranged hazing scene.

"Kneel, Sister Sara," Mariam demanded.

Willing to do almost anything to avoid Brother Mark's return, I did as she said. The weight on my tender knees caused me to grimace. Apparently Sister Mariam was the designated speaker, because everyone else remained silent, watching my every move.

"Father Gabriel has chosen you to be one of his personal followers, a bride of The Light. You used to call yourself chosen, but you weren't. We, the brides of The Light, are the true chosen, the only ones privileged to care for his needs."

My thoughts moved from my physical discomfort to her words as I struggled to understand their meaning.

"It's a calling," she went on. "Now you've been called to share that privilege."

With my stomach twisting, I lowered my chin, trying to hide my disgust—the privilege of caring for Father Gabriel's needs? I didn't want this honor or privilege. I didn't even want to know that any of this existed.

Mariam continued, "We care for the house and for him. Sara, look up."

When I did, my eyes widened. In her hand was a leather collar like the one Salome wore, in the hospital bed in the other room.

My hand went to my throat. "No, please."

"Sister Leah, take off your scarf."

The woman with the white scarf untied the soft material and revealed the collar beneath. Seeing the purple bruising around the edges, I was reminded of the body I'd seen in the morgue. At the time I'd thought that whatever had left the bruise around the victim's neck had been in place for a period of time. When I turned back to Mariam, she'd removed her scarf to show the same collar, and then they all did.

"Sister Leah was our most recent sister given the honor to

perform the duties of brides, or she was until you. She's a fast learner." Mariam turned toward Leah. "Take off your dress."

A tear slid down Leah's cheek, but she didn't hesitate to carry out the command. As she lifted the white material, I covered my mouth to keep from speaking. Dropping her dress to the ground, she slowly turned around. On both her back and front were various shades of lash marks, some newer than others. Bruises prevailed, but silvery-white scars as well as crusted scabs indicated the places her skin had been sliced. The markings extended beneath her panties and onto her thighs. When she made the full turn, I winced, seeing the lashes on her stomach and breasts. Thinking how badly my back hurt, I couldn't imagine a belt striking my tender breasts.

"Leah," Sister Mariam continued, "had the honor of spending the most time with Father Gabriel the last time he was home."

"Did he do that to you?" I asked.

Lightning-fast, Mariam stepped forward and slapped my cheek. "You don't ask questions. You listen. Apparently you're not as fast of a learner as Leah. Our leader is more than a man. He's The Light, and The Light needs fulfillment to be its brightest. We, the brides, are fortunate to be chosen for that duty. Everyone within The Light has their job to do.

"Being as close as we are with Father Gabriel, giving ourselves in all ways to The Light, we must willingly allow all darkness to be removed from us. Father Gabriel's pleased when he sees the stripes we gladly bear to exorcise the darkness from our bodies. After all, he wouldn't be able to enter us if we harbored darkness."

My stomach rolled.

"This"—she held up the collar—"also pleases Father Gabriel. As we wear it, it's a constant reminder that our lives are in his hands, and we have no choice but to trust him in all ways. He knows what's best for us."

My body trembled at the realization of what she was saying. These women served as Father Gabriel's brides, his wives, his harem. I had no doubt that when he tired of one, she ended up on the table in the morgue. The collar served as a reminder that these women belonged to Father Gabriel. If they didn't do as they were told and willingly accept their calling, if they didn't meet his needs, they would meet the ultimate punishment, banishment into the dark.

"There have always been seven brides, since the beginning of The Light. The collar you're about to wear was worn by brides who failed to fulfill The Light. We all wear the collars of brides who've failed. It's another reminder to do our best to please Father Gabriel, to do our best to keep The Light bright."

Do these women actually believe this is an honor?

"Sister Sara, do you accept this honor?" Mariam asked.

"I want to go back to my husband."

My cheek stung as she slapped me again. "You're really not very smart. I don't know why Father Gabriel would want you to be part of us." Grabbing hold of my hair, she lifted my face upward. "Let's try this again. Do. You. Accept. This. Honor?"

Though I kept my lips together, my scalp screamed as she moved my head up and down.

"That looked like a yes to me." She turned to the others and asked, "Do you think it looked like a yes?"

The other women agreed.

"Lift your hair or it'll be taking space you may want for breathing or eating."

With trembling hands I gathered my still-damp hair and lifted it while Mariam secured the leather collar that had been worn by other women, women who were now dead. I worked to be sure I could swallow as the heavy collar applied pressure to my throat.

"It must be tight enough," she explained, "so that Father Gabriel can see the darkness leaching from your skin. Until our skin no longer bruises, there's darkness within us that must be removed.

"Beginning tomorrow, you will be given responsibilities within the household. Can you cook?"

"No, she can't."

All six of us gasped at the deep voice, as our eyes immediately dropped to the floor. That wasn't all. Suddenly the other five brides fell to their knees. I didn't need to see the man with the deep voice to know who'd spoken. In one sentence I recognized Dylan.

My eyes darted to Leah, who was still wearing only her panties. She'd never been told to dress. Even with her face down, I saw her cheeks glisten as new tears descended and her body trembled. However, instead of covering herself, she had her hands at her sides, like everyone else.

"Stand," he commanded.

We all simultaneously did as Dylan said.

"Sister, put your dress back on."

Through veiled lids I peered in Dylan's direction. Unlike Brother Mark, who'd scanned me up and down when I was in front of him in only my panties, Dylan had his back to us. I quickly moved my eyes back to the floor as he turned back toward us.

"Sister Sara, come with me."

I swallowed and, while keeping my eyes down, I walked toward him. With each step my heart beat faster than it had before. My palms moistened, and I fought the sense that the world would tilt.

Silently he motioned for me to go up the stairs first. Nodding, I stepped past him. As I did, he touched the small of my back.

Wincing, I flinched. Though I bit my lip before I said anything, undoubtedly he was able to see the blood that had seeped through my dress.

"Fuck," he murmured, removing his hand.

CHAPTER
SIXTY-ONE

S ara

STEP BY STEP, as I ascended the stairs in front of Dylan, I contemplated what I'd say, what I'd do. Standing before him with Jacob at my side had been difficult enough. Doing this alone would be nearly impossible. I tried to think rationally; however, the more absurd the situation became, the more determined the Stella part of me was to come forward.

The echo of Dylan's hard-soled shoes alerted me that he was only a few steps behind me. I had no idea what the back of the dress looked like, but he was getting a good view. For some reason that made part of me happy. I was here because of him and he'd had the audacity to be upset with Jacob over a blackened eye that Jacob hadn't even caused. Besides, the way the women downstairs reacted to him, they knew him. They feared him—I'd sensed it and wondered whether I should too.

I rationalized that it wasn't so much that I should fear Dylan, but any man in this depraved house. This place was worse than the Northern Light, by far. My stomach twisted at the thought of the duties of the brides. Sister Leah was so young, as was Sister Salome. Not only would I call Father Gabriel crazy, but also he was practically a pedophile.

Each new bit of information about Father Gabriel made me more disgusted.

With each step I clung to the promise of the FBI. Surely enough time had passed. All that needed to happen was for Jacob to get a phone or for me to get free. Though I wondered what was going on at the Northern Light, I tried not to worry about Jacob. I reminded myself that he was an agent and had been doing this for a long time. I had to believe he'd survive—that we both would.

Passing through the door at the top of the stairs gave me the sensation of coming out of a black-and-white photo. Once again the world had color. The marble floor below my soft shoes glistened with golden flecks, while the walls glowed with a rich beige hue and shiny white ornate trim. Even the door was different, gray on the side of the basement, but pristine and white on the side in the house. I stepped to the side and waited, eyes down, for Dylan to emerge from behind me.

Except for the echo of Dylan's footsteps, the mansion was silent as we made our way down the long hallway. Every few feet we passed white pillars supporting arches, and between the arches crystal light fixtures sparkled, sending prisms of color reflecting rainbows that danced upon the floor. When he stopped, I recognized the French doors with the beveled glass and bit my lip, praying that Father Gabriel wasn't in here.

Opening one of the doors, Dylan gestured for me to enter.

Through the window the sky had darkened since the last time I'd been in the office. I wasn't sure of the time, and while I was certain I'd missed a meal, Brother Mark's whipping and Mariam's speech had taken away my appetite. The pool in the distance caught my eye.

In the middle of the darkness, its illuminated beauty reminded me of a tropical resort. Underwater lights changed its color, while around it the landscaping sparkled with tiny white lights. The mini-paradise appeared to be surrounded by nothingness. The tennis courts, outbuildings, and landing strip that I knew were there were all cloaked in darkness.

When my eyes settled on Father Gabriel's desk, my heart fluttered. In an ordinary plastic container—the type to store leftover food—was Fred, swimming in circles, unsure of his new bowl. Lowering my chin, I sucked my lip between my teeth and worked to contain my smile. A simple blue betta fish should mean nothing to Sara.

Oh my God! This is hard!

I hated Dylan and, at the same time, remembered thinking I could love him. Even with all that had happened, he'd kept Fred. Refusing to look up, I stayed rooted to the soft red carpet as Dylan walked to the front edge of the desk. Crossing his arms, he casually leaned back and studied me. It was his detective look, the one where he assessed, analyzed, and silently stared. Finally his broad shoulders sagged as he sighed and ran his hands through his dark-blond hair.

"I brought you in here," he began, "because it's one of the few places in the house that isn't under constant surveillance. There're no cameras or microphones . . ."

My pulse raced.

". . . Stel—Sara, will you please talk to me?"

Not lifting my eyes, I hid behind The Light's expectations of a female. I couldn't look directly into his piercing blue eyes. "Yes, Brother, Father Gabriel gave me permission to speak to you."

"My name is Dylan, not Brother."

I shook my head. "All men deserve a title."

"No, they don't. Fuck. Most don't deserve anything." He uncrossed his arms and they fell to his sides. "I know that I sure as hell don't."

I closed my eyes, and a tear escaped my lids. "I'm sorry. I don't understand."

"Will you fucking look at me?"

He reached for my chin, but I backed away. Too many thoughts were swirling about.

"Jesus, I'm not going to hurt you."

Maybe not physically, but he had hurt me, and now hearing the emotion in his voice was hurting me more. I wrapped my arms around myself, as my cold hands gripped my own elbows and hugged. The dirty white dress pulled against my new reminders as I gave in to the emotion. Tears burned my cheeks as my shoulders shuddered, and I gasped for air.

"I'm sorry," I mumbled, thinking that I would never have reacted this way before, but now I was. My off-the-chart emotions were real. "Why do you want to be away from cameras?" I hiccupped a cry. "I shouldn't ask. Questioning is my greatest weakness."

Dylan reached for my arms, and I froze, paralyzed by the thought of anyone but Jacob touching me—first Brother Mark and now Dylan. It was wrong.

If he sensed my discomfort, he didn't say anything. Instead he sighed and led me to the sofa, the soft leather one where Jacob had laid me earlier.

Dylan's tone overflowed with compassion. "Why don't you just sit for a minute? I wasn't trying to upset you. I'm not going to do anything away from cameras. I wanted to talk to you."

I shook my head. "Please, may I stand?"

"Oh, shit. I wasn't thinking. Yeah, sure, stand." Releasing my arms, he paced a trek around the office, stopping again at the desk. Picking up the plastic container, he said, "I brought you something. I know you don't understand why, but, well, I was hoping maybe you would." He put Fred back down and shook his head. "It's dumb. I shouldn't have done it. If I hadn't taken the time to go get it . . . if I hadn't, maybe I could've stopped whomever . . . goddamn it! I can't do this again."

Handing me a tissue, he collapsed in the same chair where he'd sat earlier. "Are you really pregnant?"

"I think I am. I haven't taken a test."

Dylan nodded. "Yeah, you're kind of emotional."

Really? I wonder why.

"I'm scared," I confessed truthfully. "And I miss my husband." It pained me to say that to Dylan, but, like my first statement, it wasn't a lie.

"I don't get it. How can you miss a guy who does that to you?"

I swallowed. "I'm not certain I'm allowed to speak so freely to you."

Though my Sara answers were saving me, the Stella side of me made the mistake of looking up. For only a moment, our eyes met. In his stunning blue orbs surrounded by lush lashes, I saw what I'd been hearing: remorse swirling with regret. It was the storm from my dream, clouds covering the clear sky. The ache in my chest grew.

"What?" he asked, as I broke our momentary connection and bit my lip.

"Nothing," I replied softly.

"Nothing?"

"I was in an accident almost a year ago. I drove my husband's truck and crashed. During the time of my recovery, I kept seeing— not really seeing, imagining—blue eyes." I shook my head, unsure which part of me was speaking. "I'm sorry. It's not appropriate, but, Brother, your eyes remind me of my dreams. I really don't think I should say more."

"Dylan, not Brother, and I give you permission," he offered.

I smiled and lowered my chin. Damn, if only it were that easy. "Bro . . . Dylan, only my husband or Father Gabriel has that author-ity. But I will say my husband has never done what Brother Mark just did to me. He's never harmed me."

"Mark?" he questioned, and then went on, "You don't think what he did to your eye was harming you?"

I forgot about my eye.

"It was the first time he'd done that, and it was my fault. I shouldn't have made the decision to start a family without his permission."

"What if he'd decided to start a family, and you weren't ready?"

"I'd trust his decision."

"What if he told you not to go somewhere, like Highland Heights? Would you go?"

I shook my head. "No. Obeying isn't optional." It was one of the first things I remembered Jacob telling me.

Dylan stood and walked toward me. "Turn around."

Though his proximity caused my trembling to resume, my conditioning wouldn't allow me to refuse a man's command. Slowly I did as he said, but when he touched my hair, I sucked in my breath.

"Don't worry. I'm not going to do anything," he explained, "except take this damn collar off you."

I nodded as he gathered my now-dry hair to one shoulder and fumbled with the buckle. Once it was off, I sighed and massaged my tender neck. "Thank you."

"Why are you shaking?"

"I'm scared. I don't know what's going to happen to me or to Jacob. And I'm . . ."

"Yes, you're pregnant," he said, with palpable defeat evident in his voice.

"No, well, yes, but that's not what I was going to say. I know I can't question, but I'm hungry. I was downstairs. No one brought me anything to eat."

For the first time, I saw Dylan's smile, the one I remembered. "Of course you are, it's after ten o'clock, and this is something that I can do something about. Let me get you some food."

My skin prickled with alarm. "I don't know."

"What?"

"You're being nice, but so far, you're the only one. What if someone sees me, and I'm not allowed to eat? Withholding nutrients is an acceptable decree."

Dylan's eyes closed as his jaw clenched. "I hate hearing you spout doctrine."

Bowing my head, I whispered, "We all study Father Gabriel's word."

He touched my chin, and this time I didn't flinch. "I don't need to hear it. And don't," he said, lifting my face to his, "be sorry. I'm sorry." He reached in his pocket and pulled out his phone. "I'll go get you something from the kitchen. No one will say anything to me. You can stay in here. Lock the door and don't let anyone but me back inside. Here"—he swiped the screen of his phone—"I have two phones. One's for MOA . . . never mind . . . anyway, I just put the number of my other phone in this one. If anyone tries to get in here before I get back, call me." He put the phone in my hand. "Can you do that?"

"I don't know."

The warmth of his grasp encased mine as he closed my fingers around the phone. "You can. I give you permission."

I shook my head. "That's not how it works."

"Here it does."

The sound of my own heartbeat echoed in my ears as I stared down at the phone in my hand. By the time I turned, Dylan was opening the door, and before he walked away, he turned the small latch on the inside doorknob. With only a nod and a half smile, he closed the door, locking me in and him out.

This was my chance, my chance to escape this hell.

Careful not to drop his phone with my shaking hands, I stepped cautiously to the door and jiggled the handle. It was locked. Really lifting my eyes for the first time, I scanned the office and searched for cameras. I couldn't be sure whether Dylan had been truthful when he'd said this room wasn't under surveillance, nor was I adept at recognizing secret cameras. My only experience was with the ones Jacob had pointed out in the outbuilding's living quarters. From what I could assess in the nice office, there weren't any.

That would make sense. Father Gabriel probably did a lot of business from inside this room that he didn't want recorded.

Hurry! Call someone! How much time do I have?

My list of candidates came fast and furious—my parents, my sister, Bernard, Foster, or Tracy. If only I could call the FBI. Calling the police was out of the question. Dylan was police—not Bloomfield Hills, but he was a detective. I zeroed in on Bernard. My old boss could help me. He was the only one with the connections to help. As I searched my memory, I had the strangest sensation of knowledge so close, yet out of reach. And then I remembered.

I remember Bernard's cell number!

I swiped the phone and backspaced through Dylan's number. The trembling in my hands increased, not out of fear, but out of excitement and relief. This was really almost over. Holy shit! This would be the biggest news story of Bernard Cooper's career, of my career. I'd be just like Jacob, going undercover and infiltrating The Light.

My heart clenched. Just like Jacob . . .

Jacob . . . all his work. The FBI. Kool-Aid. My friends.

Oh my God! If I do this, I may save myself, but at what cost?

CHAPTER

SIXTY-TWO

J acob

THE DOOR to our empty apartment weighed hundreds—no, thousands—of pounds. The simple act of opening it was almost more than I could bear. Since I was back in the community, checking our apartment first for the envelope made the most sense.

Once inside, I stood, slowly turning and taking everything in. It was all her. Yes, the other sisters had decorated so Sara would think we'd lived here, but over the last nine months, she'd added her own touch. I stared at the throw pillows she'd been so excited to find at the store. Knowing she couldn't do it without my permission, she hadn't purchased them on her own. But I remembered the night, at dinner, when her eyes sparkled as she told me about them. A splash of color was what she'd called them. Though I was tired, and it was one of our few nontemple nights, we hurried to the store before it closed. If it were possible, I'd never tell her no.

The deafening silence tore at my insides. Not only was our apartment silent, but so was the one next door, Benjamin and Raquel's. I palmed my temples and squeezed. This was so hard. Maybe I wasn't cut out for this. School, training, academy . . . fuck! None of it was like real life. With every fiber of my being, I wanted Father Gabriel to go down. Hell, after what he'd just pulled, as well as three years' worth of offenses, I wanted him to suffer, but he wouldn't be the only one.

The Light offered its followers enlightenment—knowledge of God's purpose without the darkness of everyday life. The entire organization was a well-oiled machine. Each voluntary follower sold their earthly possessions and abandoned the dark, willingly entering a world of slave labor. While the chosen had the elite jobs, the average follower worked in more physically demanding jobs like those in the production plants. Whether producing the pharmaceuticals at the Northern Light, the Preserve the Light preserves at the Western Light, or the illegal drugs, mostly meth and crack, at the Eastern Light, or working at the packaging and distribution sites, followers eagerly devoted ten or more hours a day to be enlightened.

Father Gabriel's teachings preached the promise of clarification by devoting one's life to others, being part of the body, and fulfilling Father Gabriel's missions. In the process the followers were relieved of the burden of pressures and decisions that plagued their lives in the dark. Hours worked in their assigned jobs earned followers credit in the commissary as well as the clothing and furnishing stores. The more hours worked above the required sixty-five a week, the more credits they earned. As long as followers worked their prescribed jobs, every need had the potential to be met. The Light provided anything they needed. If it wasn't available or within their reach, then it wasn't necessary.

One of the most frequently mentioned reasons for entering The Light that I'd heard since I began counseling followers was that The

Light offered the ability to walk away from the stress and struggles they faced in the dark. In The Light they were free to devote their lives and be enlightened. Working as part of the body gave them purpose.

Before Sara I saw The Light for the sham it was. After Sara I admit that I fell into the rhythm. That may have been part of the reason the Commission had insisted I take a wife. When Sara and I were in Fairbanks and she'd confessed to not hating the life she was now able to look back on and see as depraved, I hadn't told her that I understood exactly what she meant, but I did. The months following her initial indoctrination could be labeled pleasant. Without meaning to I'd fallen under The Light's spell.

As I brushed the burned tips of my fingers over the cover of our bed, memories of our short time together ran like a highlight reel through my head. I remembered the way her lower lip disappeared when she was nervous or excited and the way she looked first thing in the morning. My skin chilled as I thought about her warmth as I'd wrapped my arms around her and spooned her soft yet firm body. Those terms seemed contradictory, but they weren't. Her skin was as soft as velvet and so was her body, in all the right places. At the same time, running and genetics had blessed her with firm muscles and a flat stomach.

I sank to the bed, my knees suddenly weak.

Will her stomach change? Is she really carrying my child, our child?

I looked at the clock on the bedside stand. It was after six in the evening here, which meant it was after ten at the Eastern Light. I'd left Sara over six hours ago. Six hours, and I was losing it.

How am I supposed to make it until Wednesday?

I refused to believe she'd meet the same fate as Benjamin and Raquel. I refused. If she didn't survive until Micah and I made it to Fairbanks on Wednesday, when I would contact the FBI, there would be only one person to blame, and it would be me.

I could try to point the finger at Richards or even Father Gabriel, and my accusations wouldn't be unfounded; however, three nights ago she and I had been in a cheap motel in Fairbanks. As the continued silence echoed throughout the apartment, I knew I wasn't her savior or anyone else's. Despite all my grand proclamations, I had a good chance of experiencing the same fate as Benjamin. If I did, at least I had Sara to thank that the FBI now had a case against The Light. I hadn't given them everything in our short debriefing, but they'd gotten enough. Even if I were banished, I'd die knowing Father Gabriel would soon be going down.

Fuck! I needed to snap out of this.

I walked to our closet. As I opened the door, the fresh scent of fabric softener knocked me backward. Before Sara, my laundry had been done by female followers whose job it was to do the unmarried men's laundry. Though they were efficient, it wasn't the same. Then I'd find my clothes packaged outside on the stoop of my apartment. Now I never saw laundry done, or rarely, but the clean clothes appeared, hanging perfectly straight, ready for me whenever I wanted them.

I fought the onslaught of emotions brought on by something as stupid as fabric softener as I searched for my jacket. It was my lightweight one, the only one I could've possibly worn at the Western Light. It was hanging exactly where Sara would've hung it, on my side of the closet. I anxiously ripped it from the hanger and fumbled through the pockets, coming up empty except for a wadded-up tissue and a piece of gum.

No envelope.

Dropping the jacket on the bed, my hands went to my hair. I once again held my head and pushed, forcing myself to think. I could envision Brother Reuben handing the white envelope to me as Brother Michael and I laughed about the production. I recalled my phone vibrating again as we laughed.

I rushed to the clothes hamper and searched for the jeans I'd been wearing. My phone had been in my front pocket.

Did I stuff the envelope in there after I got my phone out?

There was nothing in the pockets of my jeans.

I knew I hadn't taken my phone out of my pocket until I was in the air. I hadn't wanted Brother Michael, or anyone at the Western Light, to misinterpret my talking on my phone. The damn envelope had to be in the plane. I considered calling Micah to check, but then I remembered that he'd left the hangar right after I had.

That meant that at this moment he was where he should be, at home in his cramped apartment with Joanna and Isaiah. Clenching my jaws tightly together, I prayed that nothing would alert Father Gabriel and the Commission before the FBI arrived. The loss of Benjamin and Raquel hurt too much. I'd need more than deprogramming if anything happened to the followers I oversaw and those I considered friends.

Quickly I searched the top drawer of our dresser—nothing. One last look and I grabbed the jacket and walked out of Sara's and my private world. I needed to go back to the hangar and search the plane.

It was still bright outside as I drove toward the gates. This time of year, on the edge of the circumpolar North, the skies were never fully dark. Twilight extended from one day to the next. For some reason the northern lights came to mind. They were something I'd add to my list of things I'd miss about this mission. During the winter months they were spectacular.

DENIED.

What the fuck?

I entered my code again into the inner gate—the same message flashed across the screen—*DENIED*. I pounded my palm against the steering wheel and took out my phone. Brother Timothy oversaw security. He was undoubtedly the one who'd figured out the cell tower.

I had to get back out to the hangar if Father Gabriel wanted that envelope.

I dialed Brother Daniel.

"Hello, Jacob."

"Brother Daniel, my code won't work at the gate. Have they all been changed?"

"Yes," he replied drily.

"Father Gabriel asked me to find something for him. I didn't have time when we first landed due to the emergency meeting. I need to get back to the hangar."

"I'm on the Commission, but this is beyond me. You can understand your actions regarding Fairbanks and, well, the call. I'm sorry, I am. Only Father Gabriel can authorize your new code."

Fuck!

"I understand. Thank you, Brother Daniel. I regret not being straightforward about Thomas."

Brother Daniel sighed. "In the end you did what was best for The Light. That's what matters."

"Sara?" I couldn't say her name aloud without its overflowing with emotion.

"Jacob." Brother Daniel paused. "It's beyond me."

Swallowing, I nodded. "Thank you, Brother Daniel. Whom should I call?" I wasn't thinking straight. Following his orders seemed like the best course of action.

"I'll call Father Gabriel. Stay at the gate. No one else will be leaving the community today. I'll call you back."

"Thank you. I'll be waiting," I said, ending the call. A few more pounds on my steering wheel and I ran the palms of my hands over my growing beard. Nothing helped to calm my nerves. I couldn't sit in the truck. I had to move. Keeping my phone in hand, I got out of the truck and paced, back and forth, back and forth. The hard cracked ground beneath my boots reminded me that it hadn't rained in weeks. The climate at the Northern Light was a far cry from the humidity in Michigan.

My palm struck the side of the truck, once, twice, three times, each strike sending shock waves up my arm, pain from each impact. It wasn't enough. The pressure was mounting, and I was about to explode.

The sound of tires against the gravel made me turn, back toward the community.

Brother Daniel had said no one else would be leaving the community. Only the chosen had their own vehicles. There were also panel trucks used by followers to transport supplies and product to and from the hangar. This was a car, and the closer it got the more my chest clenched. I recognized it—Brother Timothy's.

Widening my stance, I stood, waiting beside my truck, as both doors opened. Brother Timothy came from the driver's side and Brother Abraham from the passenger's door. My chest inflated as I stood taller. There was no love lost between me and either one of these men.

Not knowing what they wanted or intended, I sized them both up. Brother Timothy had to be in his early sixties, and though he could be intimidating in voice and with the power he wielded on the Commission, physically he wasn't. Abraham, on the other hand, was in his early thirties, a little younger than I and maybe an inch or two taller. I was bigger, wider, and undoubtedly stronger. Doing my share of ground crew duties as well as running had kept me fit.

I took a step toward them as they approached.

"Brother Jacob," Brother Timothy said.

"To what do I owe this pleasure? After all, we just saw each other at the Assembly meeting. Did you miss me?"

Not amused by my greeting, Brother Timothy formed a straight line with his lips. "Brother," he continued. "Due to the recent events, as we said in the meeting, all codes have been changed."

"I understand not wanting Thomas or other unauthorized individuals entering the community. However, I'm hardly an unauthorized individual. The last I heard, I'm still an Assemblyman."

Brother Timothy shrugged and tilted his head toward Abraham. "Brother Abraham, also on the Assembly, is here to escort you to the hangar and back. We want to be sure there are no unforeseen changes in your flight plans."

My chest inflated and my fingers balled to fists as I suppressed the first response that came to mind. Instead I swallowed my retort and replied, "I don't anticipate any, unless I am forced to once again protect The Light."

"Father Gabriel wants the letter you need to find. Brother Abraham is merely joining you to help. Once you retrieve what you've lost, then the future is up to Father Gabriel."

I knew he was baiting me about Sara, but I couldn't let him know how close to losing it I was. I stepped closer. "Father Gabriel will see that I'm devoted."

As the two men exchanged glances, it took every ounce of self-control I possessed not to knock the smirks off their damn faces. "Of course he will, Brother," Brother Timothy said, still using his overly placating tone. "I spoke with Brother Mark from the Eastern Light. Your devotion has been noted."

I audibly exhaled.

"Now," Brother Timothy continued, "Father Gabriel wants the message in the envelope from Brother Reuben. Go out to the hangar and find it. Brother Abraham has a new code. He'll help you." He turned toward Abraham. "Won't you?"

"It'll be my pleasure." Abraham turned my way. "I'm always willing to do what the Commission and Father Gabriel ask of me."

This wasn't good.

"Fine, get in the truck," I said, turning around. "I have an envelope to find."

"Give him your keys, Jacob."

What the hell?

My expression, as I spun, must have spoken for me, because Brother Timothy continued, "The security codes are entered from the driver's side."

"They're in the ignition," I replied through clenched teeth as I walked past both men to reach the passenger's side. Slamming the door, I waited. In the side mirror, I watched as they conversed about something. Finally Abraham walked to the driver's door. Before getting in, he smiled through the window.

I hated that man, well, both of them, with a passion. Every time I looked at Abraham I remembered what he'd done to Sara, and how he'd planned to do more. Out of the corner of my eye I watched as he consulted his phone before entering his new pass-code. By the third gate he had it memorized.

What a genius!

The truck jiggled over the rough terrain of the road as we traveled toward the hangar in relative silence. Only road noise and the occasional screech of a hawk flying low could be heard until we neared the pole barn.

Turning toward me, Abraham asked, "Thomas? You said you dumped his body out here?"

SIXTY-THREE

Sara

I STARED at the phone's screen, representative of a number pad but devoid of numbers Dylan had programmed. And then it changed. The keypad vanished and the time—10:36 p.m.—appeared. Biting my lip, I sighed.

A few more days!

That was what Jacob had said. I was numb. The hunger that had rumbled earlier in my stomach was gone, and so was the excitement. In the middle of Father Gabriel's office, I was without direction. With the solution in my hand, literally at my fingertips, I couldn't proceed.

Calling Bernard would risk the entire FBI mission. It risked everything and everyone.

Bernard may have had contacts, but would he be able to get to the right people? Involving my old boss risked too many lives—the lives of all my friends at the Northern Light, the lives of terrible people I didn't honestly give a damn about at the Eastern Light, including those in this mansion, and even the lives of people I'd never met at the Western Light. Involving Bernard could put his life at risk, yet as I stood motionless, staring at a now-dark screen, the only life that I honestly cared about was that of the man I'd called my husband. If I called Bernard, I would jeopardize not only Jacob's mission but also his life.

I couldn't do it.

With my freedom a phone call away, I couldn't dial the numbers. It was clear that I loved Jacob more than I craved the biggest story of my career, and somehow even more than I feared this terrible house.

A lump formed in my throat as I imagined explaining to my dark-haired, dark-eyed son or daughter that it was I, the child's mother, who'd made the call that had cost my child his or her father.

Turning slowly, I laid the phone on the desk near Fred and walked toward the large window.

As time passed and the scene through the window went unchanged, I concentrated on what I could do. I made a mental note of each person, each name I'd encountered at the Eastern Light. I'd recall their names and faces as I testified to whoever would listen. This might be Jacob's case, but I was a witness and I wanted a part in bringing down The Light.

It wasn't until the doorknob rattled that my attention came back to the present. Through the beveled glass, all I could make out was that the figure was a man. With trembling hands I reached for Dylan's phone. Swiping the screen, I realized my mistake as my stomach dropped. The numbers he'd programmed into it were gone. I'd erased them when I contemplated calling Bernard. The door once again rattled, this time with a knock, and my eyes darted around the office as I searched for a place to hide. For a moment I considered locking myself in the attached bathroom.

"Sister Sara, it's me," Dylan called in a stage whisper. "I'm alone. Please open the door."

Relief momentarily flooded me as I grabbed the desk for support and stared at his figure. Slowly I stepped toward the door, listening for any sound to indicate that he'd lied and wasn't alone, but there was nothing except another faint knock and request for me to open the door.

"Brother Dylan, is it really you?" I asked, pretending not to recognize his voice.

"Shit, yes, it's me."

My cheeks rose as a small smile crept across my lips. I'd never before noticed how much he cussed. Living in The Light, where vulgarities were frowned upon, made each one he uttered sound foreign. I marveled at how, in the Northern Light, even my thoughts had been without vulgarities—well, until my memories returned. Using vulgarities was the transgression Jacob had chosen as being in need of correction in Fairbanks.

Turning the small latch within the doorknob, I opened one of the doors. Keeping my eyes down, I watched as Dylan's boots crossed the threshold onto the red carpet, then quickly shut the door, mindful to again turn the latch. The tray he'd been carrying clattered as he placed it on Father Gabriel's desk near Fred and his phone.

"I made you a sandwich and brought you some water," he offered, as if a sandwich could make up for what I'd been through. "I almost got you a beer, but then I remembered the pregnant thing. I didn't know if you should have tea. So, well, I settled for water. I hope that's all right."

Beer. I hadn't even thought of beer in months. Suddenly memories of the two of us came to mind. I recalled evenings on his back deck with beers while he grilled, but just as quickly I remembered that he was the one who'd handed me over to his uncle. Taking a deep breath was all I needed to solidify my more recent memories, those of hours ago in the basement of this horrible place at the mercy of Brother Mark. When I inhaled, the white dress tugged and pulled against the new lashes, pushing any pleasant thoughts away and doing what they were intended to do: remind me.

"Thank you," I said quietly. "It's very kind of you."

He motioned toward the food. "Do you want a chair, or would you rather—?"

"Standing is fine," I replied, hoping that my pain inflicted guilt.

When I didn't move closer, he asked, "Are you going to eat?"

"I'm waiting, for you."

"Me? I ate earlier." The confusion in his voice was audible.

"Brother Dylan, I'm waiting for you to bless the food so I may eat."

"Shit, yeah, well, I did that already. So go ahead and eat."

When he reached for the phone I'd left on the desk, my heart skipped a beat. I was grateful I hadn't made a call.

"You erased the number I put in here? What if someone had come?"

"I'm sorry. I didn't know what to do. I was holding it. I think I touched something, and it went dark." I smiled at my own creativity as I took a long drink of water. My amusement quickly faded as I noticed my empty ring finger and my thoughts went to Jacob.

"It's all right. I'm back."

"Why?" I asked, taking a bite of the turkey sandwich. As my teeth sank into the soft bread I realized how hungry I'd become and almost hummed at the taste of mayonnaise. I hadn't eaten that since before The Light, and the unique gooiness was like heaven on my tongue.

"What?" Dylan asked.

I put the sandwich down and lowered my chin. "I'm sorry. I know better than to question a man. It is my biggest struggle. I just don't understand why you're being nice to me. No one else is."

"I had a talk with Mariam. Things will be different."

I nodded, again reaching for my sandwich. When I did, my breathing hitched as Dylan covered my hand with his. "I know it doesn't make sense to you, but if it did, I'd tell you that I didn't have a choice."

Bullshit! We all have choices.

I bit my lip, doing my best to keep my Sara persona intact. The part of me that was Stella was no longer reliving pleasant memories. She was ready to take Dylan out for the hell he'd put her through.

"My uncle won't be back here for at least a few days. I'm trying to come up with something."

"Brother," I said, conscious that the title made him uncomfortable, "I don't want to stay here. I want to go back to my husband." A real tear crept down my cheek. "I don't want to be a bride of The Light. I know by not accepting this honor that Sister Mariam spoke of, I deserve to be punished, but I don't want the honor."

With each word I spoke about brides of The Light and honor, Dylan's hand upon mine tensed.

"Here," he said, scooting the phone closer to me. "Take this again. I put my number back in it. Don't touch anything unless you need me. I have a few more people I need to talk to before I can leave you alone. Just stay quiet and finish your dinner."

"Yes, Brother."

He huffed and pointed toward a door I'd explored earlier. "There's a bathroom, if you need it. Remember, don't let anyone in but me."

"Yes, Broth . . . Dylan."

And just like that, he left me alone for the second time. I wasn't sure whom he was going to speak to or whether it would help. No matter how convenient it would be, I wasn't willing to put my faith in him. It was already taken by Jacob's promise.

After I finished the sandwich and water, I looked out the window at the colorful pool. No matter what I did, my mind drifted to the Northern Light. I worried about Jacob and the envelope Father Gabriel had mentioned. I worried about Benjamin and Raquel. Father Gabriel had said something about speaking with them. He'd said it was no longer an issue. I didn't want to even consider what that meant.

I eyed the computer at Father Gabriel's desk. Could there be something, anything, there that I could access? Could it help Jacob's case?

Carefully I sat in Father Gabriel's large chair, but as my fingers hovered over the keyboard, I feared that trying to access information would set off an alarm. Instead I opened drawers and peered inside for anything.

Certainly, once the raids occurred, the FBI would thoroughly search the entire mansion. Maybe it would be better if I didn't disturb anything.

Sometime around midnight, my tired muscles cried for rest. It might have been only after eight at the Northern Light, but unfortunately I'd awakened at the Eastern Light, and was still here. Not only were my muscles tired of standing and walking, but also exhaustion tugged at my eyelids. Over the last hour I'd formed a fleeting sense of security locked away in Father Gabriel's office. I didn't know where I would be told to sleep, but since I was here and so was the sofa, I decided to see whether I could sit. Though the leather was incredibly soft, sitting was too painful to allow me to rest; however, after maneuvering around, I found that if I lay on my side, I could get comfortable.

With Dylan's phone tightly in my grasp and his number still available, I sighed and my tight muscles eased a bit. I closed my eyes. Lost in the familiar leather scent, in no time at all I drifted to sleep.

In my dream I was no longer a hostage in Father Gabriel's mansion, and the talk of brides of The Light was forgotten. I wasn't holding Dylan's phone; instead my palm was warmly and safely encased in Jacob's. In a gentle breeze, we were walking through the north acres at the Northern Light.

The warm kiss of the sun touched my hair and our arms brushed each other's as we walked. When I looked up, I squinted. The bright sky behind him created a glow, but it was Jacob's gaze that brought a rush of blood to my cheeks. I quickly looked down. I didn't need to ask why he was looking at me or what he saw. It wasn't because I wasn't allowed to question. It was because I knew. I knew the swirl of emotions behind his soft brown eyes. I knew his consuming thoughts that words could never fully describe. I knew where we'd gone and what we'd done when merely his expression had the ability to accelerate my heart and twist my insides.

Leaning closer to my husband, I melted against his strong arm, closed my eyes, and drank in his intoxicating scent of leather and musk. While tall grass rustled all around us, Jacob pulled us to a stop, removed his jacket, and laid it upon the cool ground. In the middle of the circumpolar North he'd provided us with the perfect place to sit. When I did, he laid his head in my lap, and I ran my fingers through his dark, wavy hair. His deep voice and soft laugh were but drugs to my already-inebriated system, electrifying my senses as they reverberated from him to me.

As we spoke, the gentle breeze tousled my blonde hair, fluttering pieces around my face. Jacob's large hand gently tucked a renegade strand behind my ear. Eager for more of his touch, I inclined my cheek toward his palm. His warmth combined with the rough tips of his fingers lingered, cupping my cheek as he wordlessly encouraged me forward until our lips were but a whisper apart.

Their contact overloaded my body—soft yet firm, demanding yet giving. My chest heaved as a moan escaped. With the increase in my pulse, my nerves came to life, and impulses sparked synapses that only he could ignite.

Noise.

Commotion.

Startled.

The office door opened, rattling the beveled glass with excessive force. Lost in my dream, I couldn't make out the words or accusations hurtling from his lips, though my skin prickled with goose bumps at the tone and volume. Blinking away the haze of sleep, I momentarily focused on Brother Elijah, our eyes meeting, mine scared and confused while his burned with hatred and vengeance. Lowering my eyes, I searched for Dylan's phone, but before I could find it, my scalp cried out in pain.

Grabbing a fistful of my hair, Brother Elijah threw me from the sofa to the floor. Dazed and sore, I tried to make out the words as his threatening voice boomed through the office, echoing in my ears.

". . . playing us for a fool. No one leaves The Light! Your zero-tolerance policy has expired."

"I don't understand," I managed as he pulled me to my feet. However, as I stood I saw his fist, not even an open hand as Thomas had hit me with, and I turned, shielding my face. Unfortunately, my cheek hadn't been his intended target.

I coughed and spit as my lungs tried to inflate. The second blow to my stomach sent me back to the floor.

"No!" I screamed, covering my face and pulling my knees to my stomach.

This couldn't be happening.

Who would do this, knowing I could be pregnant?

As Brother Elijah's large foot reared back to kick where he'd punched, I closed my eyes and prayed for a miracle.

Sound.

Loud.

Deafening.

The room exploded. A flash through my closed lids sent shock waves that accelerated my already too-fast heartbeat. The vociferous bang echoed endlessly against the walls, submerging and drowning out everything else. The kick never came, as I floated in the waves of the explosion, and my heart ached at the loss I feared I'd already suffered.

A few days, that was what Jacob had said.

I didn't want to open my eyes. I wanted to go back to the north acres. Maybe if I gave in to the waves . . .

"Sara," the deep voice coaxed, as a warm hand smoothed my hair away from my face. "Sara, we have to get out of here."

I shook my head. No! This wasn't Jacob. It was Dylan. I needed Jacob.

"Sara," he said more emphatically, pulling on my hand. "Can you stand? Oh my God! I heard him. Get up. I need to get you out of here."

My eyes, filled with questions, opened.

Before I could process the idea that Dylan was taking me away, I gasped. Inches from where I lay, right in front of me, were the dark eyes that had looked at me with intense hatred. No longer did they send fear through my body. They were open and lifeless while around them Brother Elijah's black skin sagged and spit dripped from his partially open mouth.

Painfully I jumped to my feet.

"Oh! He's . . . he's . . ."

"He's dead," Dylan confirmed, tucking his gun back into a holster I remembered he occasionally wore beneath a sports jacket. "And we need to get out of here."

"B-but." I couldn't articulate as my stomach cramped, doubling me over and bending my knees.

"No, Sara. No fainting. We need to leave now."

I nodded, petrified to leave but terrified to stay.

Dylan seized my hand and pulled me toward the door. Just as my slippers hit the marble and I left behind the carpet that was now literally red with blood, I stopped. When Dylan's panicked blue eyes met mine, I said, "Fred! We can't forget Fred."

Immediately, I knew my mistake.

"Brother Dylan," I said, trying to recover, "wasn't that what you called the fish?"

For a millisecond his panicked expression changed and his eyes narrowed. And then, instead of speaking, he rushed past me, into the office, and grabbed Fred's container. Securing it in one hand and my hand in his other, he led me through unfamiliar hallways, pulling me until we emerged into the backyard.

"We need to get down to the outbuildings. There's a car down there. There's no way we can leave from the front of the house."

I gasped at the darkness. With the only indication of light coming from the pool, the expanse before the outbuildings seemed insurmountable. I stood unmoving, my midsection cramping and the reminders on my back still sore.

"I don't know," I said, "I'm not sure if I can make it."

He gripped my shoulders and spoke slowly. "Listen, Stella, I know you fucking remember. I also know I need to get you out of this house. We don't have any choice. I'm sorry that I'm not as big as your damn husband, and I can't carry you all the way, but if we don't move now, there won't be a later."

I didn't understand what Dylan was saying, but the urgency in his voice was loud and clear. Even though I'd blown my charade with Fred's name, it seemed like with whatever was happening at this mansion, leaving with Dylan was my best option. I nodded, bit my lip, and ran through the pain. I concentrated on my footing, careful of the wet, slippery grass, made that way from sprinklers. By the time we reached the outbuildings I was clammy with perspiration and my slippers were soaked.

I waited as Dylan disappeared into the building where Micah had stayed. The still night hung heavy with a feeling I couldn't identify as I searched the sky for stars that were more visible during the dark season at the Northern Light. Looking up to the heavens, I knew the feeling I was having. It was an impending sense of doom, and it was getting closer with each passing minute. The opening of a garage door caused me to turn and face the far end of the building.

"Get down here!" Dylan yelled.

Standing still after running had intensified the cramps, yet I pushed past the pain and made my way to the SUV that he'd pulled out of the small garage. It was older than the one Brother Elijah drove and reminded me of one of the vehicles I'd seen nearly a year ago in Highland Heights.

Dylan opened the back door. "Get down on the floor. If the cameras at the gate are still working, they won't be able to see you."

Loud, angry voices cut through the thick, humid air, coming from Father Gabriel's mansion. Momentarily I turned back, peering through the darkness toward the mansion.

"Get in, now!"

Dylan didn't need to tell me again.

CHAPTER

SIXTY-FOUR

J acob

"YOU WERE TOLD what I'd said to the Commission?" I asked Abraham. My fried brain couldn't remember who'd been present when I'd told my story, but I thought it was only the Commission.

Abraham smugly turned in my direction. "I've been told lots of things—things about here, Fairbanks, phone calls, and the Eastern Light."

I turned away, watching rows of small trees clear to large areas of open land to be swallowed up again by trees. As the landscape passed by the windows, I tried to assess what he was saying. "Congratulations," I finally replied. "You're apparently in the know."

"You'd better hope whatever it is Father Gabriel wants you to find is out here."

Abraham stopped the truck and pushed the button for the garage

623

door. After he pulled inside the pole barn and as the door was going down, I turned in his direction. "Wait a minute."

Abraham's eyes widened as his brow furrowed.

"He has it, doesn't he?" I asked. "Father Gabriel already has it. Someone went through our apartment while I was at the Eastern Light and found it, or came out here. What the hell am I doing out here if he already has it?"

Abraham shook his head. "That's not what I was told. I was told that I'm supposed to be here until you find something that Brother Noah needs . . . something Brother Michael from the Western Light never intended for Brother Reuben to give to you. I heard you screwed up and if you don't find this thing, you're not the only one who'll suffer."

Veiled threats against Sara were becoming less veiled.

I opened the truck's door and started walking in the direction of the hangar. Pointing behind me, I called over my shoulder, "There's the living quarters. I don't need a damn babysitter." Without turning, I knew Abraham hadn't listened and was following in my direction. As I opened the door to the middle part of the pole barn, the area before the hangar, his footsteps got closer.

"I was told to not to let you out of my sight. I follow Father Gabriel's orders."

Asshole.

The hallway veered to the left and ran through the center of the building, allowing space for the offices on the right and workshops on the left. If I wanted to be nice, I could have flipped the switch and turned on the lights, but I wasn't being nice. Besides, the hangar had windows, and the beams from the perpetual sunshine created a literal light at the end of the tunnel.

"Fine, whatever," I offered sarcastically. "Knock yourself out."

Only our boots echoed against the concrete floor as we made our way down the hall. When I reached for the handle of the door at the end of the hallway, the one leading to the hangar, my steps stopped. I spun backward, my movement precipitated by a loud thud followed by another odd noise that had come from behind me. I watched, in shock, as Abraham fell to the floor, his knees buckling before he fell backward. A sickening *squish*—like the sound of a dropped watermelon—filled the hallway as his skull made contact with the concrete. Within seconds a dark pool of liquid began to form around his head.

When I dragged my gaze away from Abraham, my eyes met Benjamin's. In his shaking hand was a large wrench, now dripping with the blood of our Assembly brother. I rushed toward Benjamin and, before he could say a word, wrapped my arms around his shoulders.

"You're alive! I'm so sorry." My emotions were jacked. Guilt flooded through me, guilt at what had happened to him and to Raquel because of me. "I'm sorry about you and Raquel. I never thought about the cell towers."

Benjamin's shoulders hunched forward as his head moved from side to side. Very quietly, he whispered, "Microphones? Out here?"

"Didn't used to be," I answered softly, flipping the switch to acknowledge his concern. The bright light brought crimson to the dark pool around Abraham's head. I looked away, focusing on the ceiling and seams in the tiles. I scanned the floorboards and door frames. "No, there're none in here. There are some out in the hangar, but we usually only turn them on during loading and unloading of merchandise and supplies." I shrugged. "That doesn't mean they're not on now. I don't know what the hell's happening."

"Sara?" he asked.

Pressing my lips together, I slowly shook my head. "She's still at the Eastern Light. Father Gabriel's holding her there until I get him some envelope I was given at the Western Light." I ran my hands through my hair. "I just can't remember what I did with it. It was when Sara . . ." I let my words trail away. We both knew what'd happened. We were both living with the consequences.

I took a step back as the loud clank of the wrench hitting the floor reverberated through the air, and scanned Benjamin up and down. Normally, he was well dressed, always neat and clean. Not now. Today his pants were torn and the knees were covered with dirt and grass stains. His shirt hung loose and was equally filthy. On his shirt were smears of blood, and, judging by the color, it was dry and hadn't come from Abraham.

"What happened? I thought they said . . ." I didn't want to say the word banished.

It was as if someone had deflated Benjamin, as if he were a balloon losing air. His entire body shrank and lines covered his face as he cleared his throat to speak. "Him," he said. "Him!" He spoke louder, kicking Abraham's side. The man didn't move. With the way his skull was opened, with some sort of gray matter visible, I was pretty sure he never would.

"He what?"

Benjamin took a step back, avoiding the growing pool of blood. "While I was at the lab, he went to our apartment, to the place we lived, our home! He questioned Raquel."

My already knotted stomach convulsed. "Questioned?"

In Benjamin's dark eyes, which usually held compassion and understanding, I saw an unfamiliar glare of hatred.

"Questioned," he repeated through locked jaws. "I had no idea it was happening. It wasn't until I was called to the temple to the Assembly room that I knew anything about it. Something to do with isolating the location of the phone and only two possibilities."

I nodded. "The Commission told me, Raquel or Sara."

"I told them I'd talked to you, on our regular phones. I had no idea where it was leading, but with all four of them sitting there he" —Benjamin nodded his head toward Abraham—"brought her to me." Tears descended his cheeks, clearing paths through the dirt, grime, and blood. "She was crying, and bruised, and upset, and apologizing. I wanted to kill Abraham. I wanted to kill them all."

I looked down and lifted my brow. "Looks like you accomplished part of your goal."

Benjamin shook his head. "I know it upset him."

I doubted it had upset Abraham at all.

Benjamin went on, "He was my overseer, *our* overseer. I worked with him every day, but Brother Raphael said he didn't have a choice."

"But you're not..."

"Dead," he said, finishing my sentence. "Not yet, but I will be. Brother Raphael told us to run, to go into the dark and see how long we'd last."

The flicker of hope that was born when I saw Benjamin grew to a flame, fearful of being snuffed out. "Raquel?"

He nodded toward the hanger. "She's in there, but Abraham beat her pretty bad. I've never been so scared. Even if we had a place to go, she can't walk. I carried her here."

"Wait," I said, lifting my finger to my lips. Opening the door to one of the offices, I went to the computer and prayed they hadn't changed the password. A sigh left my lips as the screen came to life. A few clicks of the mouse and pass-phrases later and I was into the hangar's security feed. With Benjamin over my shoulder, I nodded. "The cameras are off. The last recording was the day I came back from Fairbanks."

"Does it have Sara? Had they seen her?"

I shook my head. "No, I knew it'd be running and got her out of the plane before I tugged it into the hangar."

"I'm getting back out to Raquel."

"Take her to the living quarters. This computer oversees all the security. Nothing's being recorded in there either."

As we stepped back into the hallway, I kicked Abraham's side. "We need to get him outside."

"I'm moving Raquel first."

Nodding, I reached for Abraham's jacket and took out his phone. Holding it in my hands, I suddenly wondered whether I could use it to call the FBI. But first I needed the envelope, praying it would buy me time.

"I need to check the plane in the hangar for something Father

Gabriel wants," I explained as we started to walk away from Abraham's body. "How did you know he'd be here?"

"I didn't."

I turned toward Benjamin with my eyes wide. "So the wrench was for me?"

The very corners of my friend's mouth moved upward. "I heard the garage door and was on my way to see if it was you when I heard your voice and his. The wrench was just handy, and someone should have done that a long time ago."

I patted his shoulder. "No argument from me, Brother. Take me to Raquel."

As we walked toward the far end of the hangar, I saw the drops of blood I'd seen earlier on the floor and tried to scuff one. This time it didn't budge.

"You were here when we first got back from the Eastern Light, weren't you?"

Benjamin nodded. "We'd just gotten here. The door on the far end by the landing strip was unlocked. I'd just gotten her inside. That's how I knew about Sara. I overheard you and Micah talking when you arrived from the Eastern Light."

"I'm getting her back."

He didn't respond. No one believed me, except me.

Benjamin led me to the far corner of the hangar, behind a row of skids and shelves filled with boxes of supplies. I stopped walking as the bile rose from my stomach. Raquel's normally pretty face was red, with areas of darker blue. One cheek and eye were swollen so badly that it didn't appear as though her eye would open. She was lying unmoving on her side.

As I stared at my friend, I felt no remorse about Abraham. I was glad he was dead and hoped he rotted in hell. How he could continue to do this to women was beyond me. The man was a psychopath who'd found an acceptable outlet for his desires. I hadn't thought of his wife until this moment, but I doubted that Deborah would mourn her husband's loss.

"Raquel," Benjamin said softly, kneeling by his wife's side. "Brother Jacob's here. He said for a little while we can move you to the living quarters. It'll be better than having you lie on this hard floor."

She nodded and her face contorted as Benjamin helped her sit.

"B-Brother Jacob . . . I'm sorry . . ." Her voice was weak.

I knelt beside her. "No, Raquel. You have nothing to be sorry about. It's my fault. All of this."

"But Sara . . ."

"Raquel, don't worry about her. I'm going to get her back. I just need to find something first."

We all jumped as the phone in my pocket buzzed. Benjamin's eyes met mine. "Yours?" he asked.

Pressing my lips together, I shook my head. After a deep breath, I swiped the screen of Abraham's phone and read his new text.

Father Gabriel: HAS HE FOUND IT?

I looked up to Benjamin. "Well, that blows my theory that Abraham brought me out here for something else."

"You'd better answer him."

I hit reply and held the phone so we could both read.

Abraham: NOT YET. STILL LOOKING.

Father Gabriel: DON'T LET HIM OUT OF YOUR SIGHT AND GET ME THAT ENVELOPE.

Benjamin's and my eyes locked. "What about you?" he asked. "Is he supposed to take you back to the community?"

Fuck!

My heart raced as I hit the buttons.

Abraham: JACOB?

We waited.

Father Gabriel: AS WE DISCUSSED.

I blew out a puff of air as Benjamin shook his head. Well, that wasn't informative. I slid his phone back into the pocket of my jacket.

Raquel winced as Benjamin lifted her from the ground. As he did, her blouse rode up, revealing a large purple bruise. I opened my eyes wider. Her side wasn't only black and blue as Sara's had been, the skin was distended. I'd seen it before, not at The Light, but in Iraq. I swallowed.

"Is that hard to the touch?"

Benjamin nodded.

"Brother, I think she has internal bleeding."

His eyes glazed over as his chin fell to his chest.

If she didn't get medical treatment soon, she wasn't going to make it. I wasn't a medic, but I transported enough injured soldiers in that C-12A and heard enough discussions. Images I'd hoped would remain buried came to the forefront of my mind.

I closed my eyes and whispered, "I'm so sorry." I was. My heart was breaking as my friend held his dying wife.

Raquel turned toward me, her one blue eye staring directly at me. "It was me. My doing," she said. "I agreed to help Sara. Don't ever be sorry." She looked up to Benjamin, whose cheeks now contained multiple tear paths through the grime, descending to his chin. "What happened to me," she went on, "would've happened a lot sooner in my old life. I know that. I was destined to die this way." She smiled. "I'm just thankful that before I did, I got to know love. I know there's a lot of things wrong with The Light, but I don't regret a day I spent as your wife."

I was suddenly an intruder in their private conversation, a voyeur watching as Raquel's eyes closed and she leaned her good cheek against her husband's chest.

My temples throbbed as I contemplated Abraham's phone. This had to end.

"Oh," Benjamin said, stopping and turning around. "My wife didn't do as you told her." He peered down at the crumpled woman in his arms. "However, as it's at my discretion, I've chosen not to correct her."

What the hell is he talking about?

Benjamin walked back to me and stopped. "In the inside pocket of my jacket. Can you reach it?"

I carefully pulled at his jacket, trying not to disturb Raquel.

"There's the phone. She didn't destroy it as you'd told her to do. She turned it off and hid it."

My heart raced. This was it. I needed to call. I couldn't wait for two more days.

I spoke with new purpose. "Benjamin, I was never told the plan, if there is one. What would happen if Father Gabriel believed his dreams were threatened. Is there a plan, a Kool-Aid plan?" I added the last part to emphasize my meaning.

"There isn't one for here. No one can find us up here, and there's no place to run."

I inhaled. "OK, what about at the Eastern Light?"

He shrugged. "Mandatory service. The followers know too much. If The Light is threatened, it would be time for communion."

Please, God, I prayed, *don't let Sara take communion.*

I flipped open the cheap burner phone and brought it to life. Undoubtedly the call would show up on the cell tower. I just didn't know how long it would take for it to be discovered. After all, Abraham, who worked under Timothy, wasn't exactly on the job right now. I dialed the number I'd memorized.

Special Agent Adler answered after the first ring. "McAlister, where are you?"

"Northern Light, sir." I held Benjamin's stare, and briefly wondered what he was thinking.

"We're forty minutes out, on all campuses."

My mind spun. "What? I didn't authorize . . ."

"That boy the marshals took?"

"Thomas," I said. "What about him?"

"Someone fucked up. Over an hour ago he was allowed to make a phone call."

The world dropped out from under me and I fell to my knees.

"Bloomfield Hills, sir. Eastern Light, they have Sara . . . Stella there. Go now, don't wait. Please go get her. Please."

"She's not with you?"

My vision blurred. "No, you have to get her. Do it now! There's no Kool-Aid here, but there is there."

"Agent, if you have any way to get out, do it. They don't know everything, but I listened to the recording of Thomas Hutchinson speaking with someone named Xavier. Hutchinson told him about Sara and the marshals. We were able to trace Xavier's next call to the cell tower up there at the Northern Light." My thoughts overlapped while Agent Adler was still speaking, ". . . don't know who he spoke to, but someone knows why you were really in Fairbanks."

"Shit!" Now Abraham's question about Thomas's body made sense. From the time I'd been speaking to the Commission to the time I made it to the gate, they all knew I never killed him or dumped his body.

"Agent, get out of The Light now. That's an order."

"Sara?"

"We'll move."

SIXTY-FIVE

J acob

"Benjamin, don't take Raquel to the living quarters. Come with me."

His quizzical expression asked more than his words. Still Benjamin tried, his voice unsure: "What's happening? Who did you just call?"

"We need to move." I pulled out Abraham's phone. "Let's pray this buys us some time."

Benjamin didn't speak as I began to text.

Abraham: HE JUST FOUND IT IN THE PLANE. I'LL BRING IT TO YOU, AFTER I TAKE CARE OF THINGS.

"What if we were wrong and there wasn't a plan to do anything to you?"

I gritted my teeth. "If there wasn't, after what they just learned, there is now. I'm sure of it."

"Are you sure enough to bet our lives?"

I nodded and then inclined my head toward Raquel. "Benjamin, what you do is up to you. Take your chances with the dark up here, or come with me. I'm tugging the smaller plane out to the strip. It's fueled and I'm getting out of here. Come with me and I'll explain everything. First we can get Raquel in the plane, and then you can help me get the plane out."

Confusion came and went in Benjamin's eyes. "I don't know. We . . . I thought . . . weren't we friends? I don't know what's happening."

I grabbed his arm. "Listen to me. Do. You. Want. To. Save. Her?" Before he could answer, I continued, "Because I sure as hell plan on saving Sara. I'm leaving now. Come with me or don't. It's up to you."

His chest inflated and deflated. "Let's go."

Normal procedure was to return the tractor and tug to the hangar before taking off. I wasn't worried about following normal procedure. Benjamin sat in the cargo section of the plane, strapped into one of the jump seats beside Raquel. She was now unconscious. It wasn't the first time I'd transported an unconscious woman, but it was the first time I'd felt good about it. This was her only chance. Besides, Raquel's state of unawareness was probably better. At least now she wasn't in pain.

Just before takeoff, I looked back and he was holding her hand.

Benjamin and I had talked the entire time we strapped her in as well as while we got the plane ready. Our freedom of speech was no longer restricted. The black box that recorded all our words was within the plane. It didn't broadcast. The physical box had to be removed to be analyzed. We'd be away from The Light before anyone learned what we'd said, and then it wouldn't be The Light that learned it. It would be the FBI.

As we spoke I told Benjamin everything. I told him the truth of who I was and what I was. I told him about Stella, that Sara had gotten her memory back, and that she had agreed to play along until the FBI could organize enough force to raid all three campuses simultaneously.

Just as we were about to take off, Abraham's phone buzzed. I looked back at Benjamin, our eyes met, and I tossed him the phone. It was my gesture of faith. He was letting me take Raquel and him out of The Light. With Abraham's phone he could alert Father Gabriel, the Commission, and the Assembly to everything.

Catching it, he swiped the screen. As I flipped switches on the panel before me, he spoke through our headphones: "Father Gabriel told Abraham to wait at the hanger. He said Xavier's on his way and should be here in less than ten minutes. He wants Abraham to drive him into the community."

"It's going to be a crowded airspace and landing strip," I said.

If Agent Adler's timeline was accurate, the FBI was twenty to twenty-three minutes out. I'd texted my handler the new code to the gates to enter the community, the one I'd gotten from Abraham's phone.

"What should I text back?" Benjamin asked.

"That's up to you."

The roar of the engine grew louder as we rolled forward. I didn't concentrate on Benjamin's movements. I couldn't be sure how long it took him to text back or what he texted. It wasn't until we'd reached about twelve hundred feet that I had visual confirmation of Xavier's descent. If we'd been in the dark season, I might not have seen his white plane with the blue letters and numbers, but it was the light season and I did.

For only a second, I thought I saw the nose of Xavier's plane move upward, changing course toward me, but it was too late. In order to crash into me or send me off course, he'd need to be proficient in maneuvers most often seen at air shows. I was above and passed him. At that realization I closed my eyes and let out a long breath.

The Northern Light was behind me. With Xavier there, Father Gabriel would have two pilots; he could get away. Hell, he could get away in Xavier's plane and leave Micah behind. I couldn't worry about it. The drive to the hangar was over twenty minutes from the community. By my calculations the FBI would land before Xavier's plane could be refueled and back in the air. My cheeks rose as I realized that with the emergency meeting and everything that had happened, we hadn't refueled the Cessna Citation X. Assuming Father Gabriel would want to leave The Light and go into seclusion somewhere unknown via the luxury of the Cessna Citation X, the FBI had more than enough time to arrive first.

Now my only concern was Sara. I prayed that the FBI had already conducted the raid on the Eastern Light, and that agents had found her. With the increased altitude my phone was useless. I wouldn't learn anything until we landed.

I rolled my neck, trying to relieve the tension that wouldn't lessen. As I did, my eyes veiled and I looked down. Beside my seat, wedged next to the controls, was something white. Fumbling for the corner, I squeezed my fingers into the tight space and pulled.

Whatever Father Gabriel had been so desperate to find was in my hand. I read the front of the plain white envelope: Father. Instead of opening it, I folded it in half and slid it into the inside pocket of my jacket.

Father Gabriel's teachings came back to me with new understanding. I suspected that after three years, it would be a long time before all the doctrine I'd learned didn't come to mind. However, the one I was thinking about wasn't necessarily perverse. It was one of the ones I'd recited to Sara and made her recite to me. It was about a wife giving everything to her husband, releasing it and being free. I'd seen the relief in her beautiful face more times than I could count—times when she was upset or sad, times when she was scared or guilty. Even when she knew that sharing her concerns or confessing her transgressions would result in correction, the process of giving it over to me had given her peace. Whatever was bothering her was no longer her concern, but had become mine.

That same overwhelming rush of relief that I'd seen on her face filled me as I pocketed Brother Reuben's envelope. I was no longer responsible for deciding whether its contents were important. I was no longer alone in this fight. As soon as we landed in Anchorage, I'd pass the envelope and all my information on to my team at the bureau. What they did with it was at their discretion and no longer my concern.

I planned to leave Benjamin and Raquel in Anchorage. I'd gladly debrief for the entire flight to Detroit, but getting to Sara was now my main concern. The FBI could handle The Light. I now fully understood the gift that lesson had been to Sara. For a moment, as I flew above the white rolling clouds, my neck lost its tension.

"How long until we get to Anchorage?" Benjamin's voice reminded me where we were. In my mind I was already beyond Anchorage and on my way to Sara.

"It's about an hour and a half. Agent Adler will have teams waiting for us. They'll have an ambulance ready for Raquel. How's she doing?"

"I'm scared. She's cold, but I feel a pulse."

"I'm praying for her, and doing my best."

"Are you?" Benjamin asked.

"Am I what?"

"I'm just confused. What was real?"

"I don't know," I answered honestly. "I know I had a mission. I know there were parts of The Light I recognized as wrong. I also know there were parts that I understood and made sense. I know what I feel for Sara, or Stella, isn't fake. We spent a lot of time talking after I confessed who I was and knowing who she was. I don't know if she's pregnant or not, but either way, just because this is over, I don't want to give her up."

"Pregnant? Really?" he asked.

Shit!

He and Raquel had been trying for a few years to get pregnant.

"We don't know. She's been sick and, as you know, she quit taking her birth control, but we don't know if she's pregnant. There's been a lot happening. She might just be ill and throwing up because of nerves."

"Yeah, I remember when Raquel got her memory back. It was a rough time, but at the same time, it was good. It felt liberating to finally be honest with her."

I sighed. "It did, but we haven't had much of a chance to discuss it." I looked at my watch; it was only ten after nine. "She left Friday morning. Monday isn't even done. Our whole damn lives have changed in less than four days."

"Tell me about it."

I looked back. He was still holding Raquel's hand with his head back against the seat, and his eyes were closed.

"Tell me about Raquel. What did she mean when she said she was destined to die that way?"

"I don't like to think about it, but"—his voice hitched—"I suppose it's easier than seeing how she is now."

"Hey, you don't need to say—"

He interrupted me. "No, talking keeps my mind off the future." He paused. "Before she was brought to The Light she was a prostitute in Highland Heights, a runaway. Her parents died and she ended up in the foster care system. When she was seventeen she hitched a ride with a trucker. It was her first time, and she said he wasn't terrible. Afterward he gave her cash, and she'd found her new profession. She doesn't exactly remember how she ended up in Highland Heights, but if you were to ask her, she'd tell you it was divine intervention. She'd also tell you that despite the indoctrination, she was thankful she did.

"I can't imagine her living that life. Even the thought of it breaks my heart. When Brother Raphael released us, I knew we'd die out there, in the dark. I just wasn't willing to let her die alone. That's why I took her to the hangar. I honestly thought someone would find us and just kill us. It would've been easier than starvation, exposure, or animal attack. I knew about banishments, but I'd always suspected that we would . . . I really didn't even consider."

"I'm sorry . . ."

"Don't be. You heard Raquel. She wanted to help Sara. I should have figured. I mean, I guess banishment is a very viable option when you accept a seat on the Assembly. It's not like seats become vacant because the previous Assemblyman resigns. The thing was, I was proud to be part of the chosen, and after the life Raquel had suffered when she was younger, I was proud that through me she could be part of the chosen too."

The airwaves fell silent as I thought about his honesty. No doubt the stress and turmoil, as well as holding his dying wife's hand, had fueled his words.

"Who else?" I asked.

"What?"

"I know about some of the followers, but I wasn't privy to any of the chosen who were banished. Who else on the Assembly or Commission has been banished?"

"Well," he said, "I've never known of anyone on the Commission. The first Assemblyman I know of, after I was on the Assembly, was Brother Joel and his wife, Sister Chloe. You can imagine how difficult that was."

I shook my head. "Was I there? When did that happen? I don't recognize their names."

"Oh, you're right. It was right before you came, and you probably don't recognize their names because no one is supposed to talk about it. Probably your coming was one of the reasons it was able to happen."

"I don't understand. Who were they?"

"Brother Joel was a pilot. It's a job with a lot of scrutiny, as you know. The thing was, no one ever suspected Joel of anything. After all, he'd been raised in The Light, not actually in The Light itself. Before The Light even existed, he followed Father Gabriel as he preached around the country. Timothy and Lilith were some of his first devoted followers. They took Joel everywhere with them. He'd known Father Gabriel most of his life."

"Wait a minute," I said. "Joel was Timothy and Lilith's son? He was the pilot who was banished just before my arrival?"

No wonder they hate me.

"Yes, and Chloe was the daughter of Brother Raphael and Sister Rebecca."

"Holy shit! What happened?"

"The Commission was given evidence that Joel was in contact with people outside The Light. I never heard the particulars. It went over the Assembly straight to the Commission—"

"Which contained two of their fathers," I added in amazement.

"Yes."

"And Timothy and Raphael went along with it?"

"They believe that Father Gabriel's word is divine."

This news definitely shed new light. Timothy and Lilith disliked me because I'd replaced their banished son. If I hadn't been available, Joel might have been forgiven or found innocent.

"We're making our approach in Anchorage," I said. "I need to talk to the tower. Soon we'll learn more."

"Thank Father Gabriel," Benjamin said under his breath.

I looked back. His eyes were closed and he was clutching Raquel's hand. I doubted he even realized what he'd just said.

CHAPTER

SIXTY-SIX

S ara/Stella

FROM MY VANTAGE point on the floor in the back of the SUV, I couldn't tell where we were going. When the SUV finally stopped, I tried to see where we were. It was the rumble of the garage door that let me know we were inside a new building.

When the back door opened, I looked up at the blue eyes of my dreams. He offered me his hand; however, in those piercing eyes, I didn't see the Dylan I'd known. It seemed as though his learning my deception had changed something. What I witnessed was a growing harshness I didn't recognize.

Was this the hard-ass Dr. Tracy Howell had warned me about?

"Dylan," I began, meeting his gaze. "What happened? Where are we?"

As he helped me from the SUV, his head tilted and his lips formed an unnatural grin. "I thought you weren't supposed to question.

641

Maybe I should correct you. That's what happens according to the doctrine you've been spouting all night, isn't it?"

"That's not you," I pleaded. "Tell me the truth, and I'll tell you the truth."

Grasping my upper arm, he forcefully ushered me up some steps and through a door into a very nice house. Judging from the amount of time we'd been in the SUV, we were still in Bloomfield Hills. With each light switch that he pushed, the beautiful interior came to life.

Once we were in the designer kitchen, he led me to the table and motioned for me to sit in one of the chairs. For a brief moment, I considered refusing, but the Sara side of me obeyed. The lashes on my backside were no longer as big a concern as the man who had now taken me somewhere that I wondered whether Jacob would be able to find.

In a matter of minutes, Dylan's demeanor had morphed into something neither part of me recognized, but he seemed to be the kind of person the Sara part had more experience dealing with, someone who expected obedience.

Pacing near my chair, Dylan appeared to collect his thoughts and rein in his words.

"Truth," he began. "You want the fucking truth? Well, so do I."

My ability to keep my chin down was waning by the second, as were my eyes' ability to maintain the conditioned submissive pose. This wasn't a man of The Light. This man had at one time been my boyfriend. And never in our relationship had I allowed him to speak to me with that tone.

Slapping my hands on the granite tabletop, I glared. "OK, truth. Let's start with the fact you fucking gave me to The Light. Do you have any idea what kind of hell I've lived through?"

He reached for my chin. Clenching his jaws, he spoke slowly and deliberately. "No. Stella. Do. Not. Talk. To. Me. Like. That . . . I. Saved. Your. Goddamn. Ass . . . Show. Me. Some. Fucking. Respect . . . For. Once. In. Your. Damn. Life . . . If. You. Can. Give. It. To. Him . . . Then. I. Fucking. Deserve. It. More."

I searched behind the manic blue for the man whom, at one time, I'd thought I loved. "Explain it to me, Dylan. Tell me what's happening, what happened. I thought we . . . I thought we were going someplace. I didn't lie earlier. After my accident, which wasn't real, but some drummed-up scenario that The Light put me through. A scenario that harmed me—like broken leg, concussion, injured me— I did dream of you, of your eyes. When I was finally able to see, Jacob's brown eyes upset me. I couldn't remember you, because of the medicine they gave to me, but I wanted to remember. Please tell me why you did it."

"How can I trust you?" he asked, taking a breath and sitting in the chair to my left.

Trust me? *Is he serious?*

"You lied about remembering," he went on. "You acted like you didn't know me."

"I was afraid, and I didn't lie about that. I'm still afraid." I met his gaze. For the first time with any man other than Jacob, I felt empowered, back on an even keel. I wanted information. I just needed to figure out the best way to get it. "If I ever meant anything to you, tell me what's happening. What was Brother Elijah saying? Why was he so mad?"

Dylan shook his head. "It's you. It's fucking been you. You have that effect on people."

I waited as he ran his hand through his hair and leaned back with a look of utter exhaustion.

Reaching out, I covered his hand lying on the table. "I don't understand."

"I fought to keep you alive and now, this is what happens. Gabriel must be . . . shit . . . I can't imagine." He removed his hand from mine and pinched the bridge of his nose. Suddenly his eyes widened. "Where's my phone?"

I looked from side to side. "I-I don't know. I reached for it, but Elijah threw me to the ground. I think I left it on the sofa."

"Fuck! I won't know what Gabriel is thinking, unless he calls this one. I need to get my phone out of his office."

"What? Why? And what is Gabriel Clark or Garrison Clarkson to you? How are you connected to all of this? I mean, you didn't seem like"—I looked down and took a deep breath—"with me, you were never like them."

Emotions flooded his expression, creating a spinning kaleidoscope. Happiness and sadness battled, and at the same time, I saw loss and duty as well as pride and shame.

"You may think you know The Light," he said with an eerie calmness. "But you don't. You only know what you've been allowed to see, and," he added exasperatedly, "what you learned in your fucking research."

I knew more than he thought because of Jacob, but I wasn't going to correct him.

"Then tell me," I said, adjusting in my seat as the cramps continued to ache. "Help me understand."

"It's bigger, so much bigger than you know. I'm not part of this fucked-up religious sect. I don't beat or use women. The man you knew, that's who I really am. And believe it or not, Stella, I tried to save you. If you would've had a damn ounce of the obedience you appeared to have with that asshole, you could be living your own life right now."

My back straightened, rebelling at Dylan's description of Jacob, but I decided that learning more about The Light was more important. "What do you mean, it's bigger? And what did I do that caused Brother Elijah to be so upset?"

"You left. Nobody leaves and talks about it! Did you think you'd get away with it?"

Shit!

"I left the Northern Light and came here, because Father Gabriel ordered it. I didn't, no, I don't, want to be here. I'd rather be there."

His gaze narrowed. "Truth? Really? Stop the fucking lies! You left the Northern Light four days ago with some douche bag named

Thomas. I don't fucking know if he took you willingly or unwillingly, but I know he said that you begged him to help you get away. He said you claimed you'd been kidnapped."

It wasn't only the cramping from before that caused my discomfort, but also nausea, bubbling, no, gushing and churning the sandwich in my stomach. If Dylan knew this, then so did Father Gabriel, so did the Commission at the Northern Light.

Where is Jacob? What have they done to him?

Perspiration dotted my brow and lip as the blood drained from my face. "Dylan, I-I . . ." I looked down, unsure what to say.

He reached for my chin. "What's the matter?" he asked in a tone I didn't recognize. "Cat got your tongue? I don't think I've ever seen Stella Montgomery speechless. Is that who I'm talking to now, or is this Sister Sara?"

"How? How do you know that?"

His palm slapped the table. "I told you, The Light is bigger than you think. What The Light doesn't know is how the US Marshals became involved. Why would they be there when you landed and how did Jacob find you?" His expression softened and his tone morphed to that of the man with whom, at one time, I'd considered sharing a life. "That's what I need you to tell me." He reached for my hand. "Come on, sweetheart, I'll show you mine, you show me yours. We used to be good at that."

I pulled my hand away. "Stop it, your bipolarness is scaring me."

"Really?" His chair scooted across the expensive flooring as he stood and began pacing. "I scare you? I never gave you a damn black eye."

"Neither has Jacob!" I retaliated. "This came from Thomas. The man you're willing to believe. He's the one who did this, and I didn't want to go with him. He not only took me against my will but threatened to rape me once we got to Fairbanks. I don't know why the marshals were there when we landed, but I'm sure as hell happy they were. They left me alone in an interrogation room for hours. They fed me, but kept promising I'd see another marshal and get to make a call.

"Guess who I wanted to call? Guess who I thought would be my knight in shining armor. You! I was going to call you! But the female marshal never came. Instead the first marshal walked in and told me my husband was there to get me. It was Jacob. I don't know how it all went down, but I was fucking terrified."

"Of?"

"Of everything! I was scared to go back with Jacob and scared not to. These last nine months have screwed with my mind. I didn't know who to believe or what. I mean, I was with the US Marshals for Christ's sake, and I thought my nightmare was over, but it wasn't." A tear slid down my cheek. "It still isn't, and I'm with the person who I thought would save me."

"You lied to me!"

I couldn't reply; instead I crossed my arms over my chest and pressed my lips together. For the first time, I looked at the room around me and saw the tall, dark cabinets, high ceiling, and designer lighting.

Where are we?

"So," Dylan said, "you and dear old hubby concocted this lie about you missing work . . ."

I nodded. "Yes, he was afraid of what could happen to me if The Light knew I was off one of their campuses. I was afraid to tell him I'd gotten my memory back. So I told him Thomas took me."

"How did he know where you where?"

I shook my head. "I really don't know. Don't you get it? I'm not allowed to question."

Dylan smirked. "Stella Montgomery couldn't question. How did you function?"

I slapped the stone table. The sting in my palm took a bite out of my response. "Not well, not at first. It wasn't easy. It was my biggest difficulty."

"I can see that."

"Dylan, you said The Light is bigger than the three campuses. What do you mean?"

"How do you know there are three?"

"My husband, I mean Jacob, is a pilot. He'd tell me when he'd fly to the Eastern Light or Western Light. He never told me where they were, but he'd use those names. I also knew we were at the Northern Light."

We both stopped talking as the earth shook. Wineglasses hanging upside down from racks clinked against one another as the table trembled under my grasp. My eyes opened wide as we waited for it to stop.

Did we have an earthquake?

Dylan hurried to a wall of windows and then rushed to another room. The next thing I heard was a long tirade of curse words. Scooting my chair, I quietly made my way toward his voice. The house wasn't nearly as large as Father Gabriel's. From the front window of the living room, I could see other homes. From their size I presumed we were still in Bloomfield Hills. It wasn't the neighbors' homes Dylan was watching, but a glow in the distance. Above the glow, suspended in the night air, was a plume of smoke.

He reached for his other phone and dialed a number. Though I could barely make out what he was saying and my conditioning told me not to intrude, the Stella part of me wanted to listen to every word. Quietly I inched closer. I heard the name Joel and more curse words. He asked something about all of them, but he was speaking too low for me to make out anything more.

Once he put the phone back in his pocket, I asked, "What happened?"

Dylan spun toward me. "You, and I don't know what fucking else. I won't. I don't have my damn phone!"

"I don't understand," I said to his back and broad shoulders as he turned again toward the window. On the wall I saw a clock, a quarter past one.

Pulling his other phone back out, Dylan swiped some numbers and turned toward me with disgust. "Damn circuits are overloaded."

"Dylan, what happened?"

As I asked, the air filled with the shrill wails of sirens; though muffled by the walls and windows, they seemed to be coming from all directions. For a moment I prayed they'd be coming to us, and I might be saved, but that didn't happen. Just as fast as they'd come, the sirens faded away, growing fainter with distance. I stepped toward the large window and watched as the dark Michigan sky filled with red and blue lights speeding toward the glow.

"I guess I won't get my phone back or my car," Dylan stated matter-of-factly.

"W-what?" I asked in disbelief. "That's Father Gabriel's—"

I couldn't finish before Dylan turned back to me. "Go back to the kitchen. You wanted answers? Well, Stella Montgomery, you're going to get them. Go sit the fuck down and listen."

More sirens roared, only to fade into the general chaos occurring in the distance. Unsure what I had to do with any of this and why Dylan blamed me, I did as he said and went to the kitchen. He followed close behind.

After pulling a beer from the refrigerator, he turned a chair backward, sat, and stared. Once I sat, he took a long swig of his beer and began, "As I was saying, The Light is bigger than you think. The three campuses your husband"—each time he said *husband* he made a point of exaggerating the word—"told you about, that's only a portion. The Light is everywhere. It's not just about the followers on the main campuses. The Light needs followers in the field, in the Shadows, willing to do what it takes to bring light to the dark. Those followers are in law enforcement, like me. They're in the medical field. They're in every profession throughout the United States and Canada. The Light reaches beyond those borders, because only The Light can stop the dark."

My heartbeat raced. I'd never seen Dylan like this. His blue eyes glowed with conviction, yet he wasn't looking at me, but seeing things I couldn't. In that moment I had no doubt he was part of it. "Why? Why you? How long?"

He shook his head and took another long drink from the brown bottle. Grinning, he said, "I bet good old hubby had a field day with your questioning. Did he get off beating your ass? I remember you having a mighty fine ass."

I gritted my teeth. "Is Father Gabriel really your uncle?"

He nodded. "My mother's half brother."

"And when your parents died?"

"They were part of it. They died doing work in the Shadows for The Light."

"So he took you in?"

"I lived with my grandparents, like I told you. But Gabriel and I had always been close. He never had any children." Dylan shrugged and lifted a brow. "None that he let be born. He always wanted me to work with him, but I refused to be involved in the shit like you've been doing. I prefer the Shadows."

"So those brides, have you ever . . . ?" I wasn't sure I wanted him to answer.

"Hell no! They are, or were, his. They just know I'm a man with high ranking. That gives me unlimited power. I told you, I've never been into that shit. But, up until now, I never stopped it."

"Until now?"

"Elijah. Shooting him. I'd given orders to keep you untouched." Dylan lifted his shoulders and cocked his head dismissively to the side. "He disobeyed. When it comes to the Eastern Light, being Gabriel's nephew, I hold my share of power. You said it yourself, earlier tonight, disobeying isn't an option."

"Those women . . . you said . . . were . . ." I swallowed the churning bile. "Are they dead?"

"Didn't you see the fire? Did you feel the explosion?" he asked. "No one in that house survived."

"Why?"

"Damn, Stella, have you lost your ability to comprehend? I told you. This all started because of you and the fact that Thomas Hutchinson was in the dark, making threats. There's always been a contingency plan. Witnesses are too dangerous."

Oh, God!

Because of me?

"Kool-Aid?" I whispered.

"Only at the Eastern Light. Uncle was confident the other campuses are too well hidden."

Thank God!

No Kool-Aid at the Northern Light.

"What did you mean that Thomas was making threats?"

"He was part of the outside Light, a follower in the Shadows. But when he called his connection, he told him that he wanted out of prison, where the marshals had taken him. He knows The Light is capable of getting him out."

"Will it?"

"The Light can do anything. Will it? No, and it's his fault."

"The threats?"

He smirked. "Maybe you are listening. Yes, he didn't just ask to be released. He said that if it didn't happen soon, he'd start talking to anyone who'd listen." An amused grin graced Dylan's lips and his eyes narrowed. "The Light is everywhere. I'm sure that if it hasn't already happened, very soon, the asshole who threatened to rape you will no longer exist. Who knows, if it's another inmate, Hutchinson may get to know your fear of rape before he leaves this world. If I have anything to say about it, and now that I know what he did to you, I'll suggest it."

Part of me cringed at the idea that Dylan had that much power. The other part of me liked the idea of Thomas suffering for what he'd done to me. The evidence was mounting supporting my diagnosis of dissociative identify disorder.

"But you're a policeman, a detective. You help people."

"I do. I just helped you, for a second time."

I looked down at my hands and lifted my fingers for him to see.

When I did he closed his eyes and took another drink. I waited for him to finish before I said, "You knew. When we were at the morgue and the woman, the one who we were afraid was Mindy, you knew she was part of The Light?"

He nodded. "What do you want me to say, that I'm sorry? Because I'm not. It's the way it is. You work the game in your favor or you lose. I'm not a loser, neither is Gabriel."

I took a deep breath, my cramping nearly gone. "Mindy?"

"Last I heard, she made it to a campus. I'm not sure which one, and I honestly didn't want to know."

"But she wasn't investigating The Light. Why did they take her?"

"She was investigating a business from outside The Light, Motorists of America, MOA. It's a shell corporation. She stumbled across too many things, like you."

I recognized that name. It was the company Foster had told me about—the one I had been too impatient to listen to him discuss. Oh, shit, it was the one that Foster had found when he was investigating Dylan. Dylan's name was on a utility bill for a house in Bloomfield Hills that was owned by MOA.

Could that be where we were? Was this the house Foster had found by researching Dylan's name?

Dylan ran his hands along the dark-blond scruff lining his defined jaw. "I fucking warned you. I told you to leave it alone, but you were too stubborn."

I closed my eyes. "Did Bernard or Foster ever see my research?"

"Come on, you're smarter than that."

A tear trickled from my eye. "So they never knew what I'd learned?"

"No."

"My parents?"

"Your mom still calls me."

My chest clenched as I laid my head on my arms. "How could you do this and talk to her like you didn't know?"

"I didn't see any other options. Do you?"

"Yes," I whispered. "Yes." My words gained strength as I lifted my head. "I see many other options. Tell the truth. Tell law enforcement. Do something. Stop this travesty. What The Light is doing is human trafficking and drugs. Oh, God . . ." My volume decreased. "Do you know what happens? Last Sunday, here at the Eastern Light, I witnessed a man and woman—"

Dylan raised his hand. "I don't want to know."

"What? That doesn't make sense. You're supporting this, condoning this, and you don't want to know?"

"We are all part of a greater good, part of the body. I have my responsibilities. I don't need to know about the others and what they do unless it interferes with what I do."

It was time for my eyes to narrow. "I don't know what your responsibilities entail, but let me tell you, I watched a man be murdered. The woman, she survived to end up in the basement . . ." My stomach knotted again. "Now she's dead."

"If you're talking about the woman in the bed, in the room where you were left, she was unconscious. The explosion was probably easier on her than the others."

"How can you be so callous? How can you talk about life like it doesn't matter?" Suddenly a thought occurred to me. "How? Wait a minute. Why are you being this open with me? Why are you telling me all of this?" My hands began trembling. "Are you going to kill me?"

Dylan stood and his footsteps moved about the kitchen. "Glass of water, Stella?"

What?

"No." The hairs on the back of my neck rose to attention and my skin prickled with goose bumps. "Tell me." My volume rose and I stood to face him. "Dylan, tell me." I stared into his piercing blue eyes and tried again. "For old times, for what I've been through, please tell me what is going to happen to me." My volume rose. "If you're going to kill me, be man enough to own it."

He reached out and caressed my cheek. I sucked my lip between my teeth and forced myself to remain still as his words rolled forth and his warm beer-scented breath skirted my cheeks. Though his tone was soft like an apology, his words were sharp in their meaning. "Stella, I know you may hate me, but you should know, at one time, I thought I could love you. The you I loved was strong and sure. I've been around subservient women all my life. My mother was one. I loved her but hated the way she acted around my father and the other men." He looked deep into my eyes, his finger tracing my cheek and lips. "I loved your fight, sharp tongue, and stubbornness. I loved all of that, but it wasn't worth the cost. The price was too high—not only to you, but to me and The Light."

His tone softened as his touch dipped to my collarbone and his gaze lingered at the neckline of the dress. "Besides, they took those parts of you away. That asshole you call your husband did that."

I wanted to tell him it hadn't been Jacob, it had been his uncle. It was Father Gabriel who was responsible, but I kept my lips closed and let him continue.

Dylan took a deep breath. Bringing his eyes back to mine, he tucked a piece of my hair behind my ear. "Even so, for all the reasons I said, I wanted you to know the whole truth. I wanted you to understand that I tried. I really did."

I took a step back. "Please . . . you're scaring me."

"Don't you understand? Don't you see it now? The Light can't be stopped."

I nodded, again pulling my lip between my teeth.

"That explosion changes everything," he explained. "I'm trying to make you understand. No matter what happens to me or to you, The Light is here and there and everywhere. There's no escaping it. My uncle was right. Allowing you to go back to Stella's world would be impossible."

I shook my head. "No, it's not! I won't tell. I promise. I'll pretend, like I was doing earlier. I can do that."

He took a deep breath. "Believe me when I tell you this hasn't been an easy decision."

"What hasn't been easy?"

He leaned closer, once again cupping my cheek. "Do you remember how good we were together? Do you remember how easy it was?"

I nodded, tears raining down my cheeks.

He cooed, "It was easier with you than anyone. I wanted . . ." He touched his lips to mine, the cold contact feeling more like a good-bye than a hello. "But," he went on, "we don't always get what we want. I've known it all my life. The Light is bigger than me, than you, than both of us.

"I told you everything, because things changed tonight—because of you. I wanted to be honest, for old times' sake . . ."

I saw the syringe from the corner of my eye. It was like the one Elijah had tried to use on me earlier.

". . . even though I know that when you wake up, you won't remember a word of it."

"No!"

The sharp pain in my neck transported me back to the parking lot in Detroit, just before my world went black.

SIXTY-SEVEN

J acoby

I LANDED the small plane in Anchorage a little ahead of schedule; however, as we rolled to a stop along the runway, my mind wasn't thinking about the time or even about the blur of commotion on the tarmac. My mind was in Bloomfield Hills. The raids should all have been started if not carried out, and I wanted details. I needed to know Sara was safe.

"Thank you." Benjamin's voice came through the earphones, reminding me that I wasn't the only one worried about a wife. "Jacob, I mean Jacoby, Raquel's pulse is weak, but she still has one. Thanks to you. I know if you hadn't . . . she wouldn't . . ." His voice trailed away.

I turned and, with a strained smile, nodded in his direction. "They're waiting on us. They'll have her in surgery soon."

Though it was after ten at night, the airport where I'd been told to land was alive with activity. Just as Special Agent Adler had promised, there was an ambulance, and as I unbuckled my seat belt, it was moving slowly toward the plane. I opened the hatch door and lowered the steps before going back to help Benjamin.

As I reached for Raquel's seat belt, Benjamin grabbed my hand. "I don't know if she'll make it, but I know she wouldn't have made it up there. I owe you. Anything. You've got it. You can count on me."

"Right now, concentrate on Raquel. Until we know how the raids went and what's ahead for us, listen to the FBI. They'll keep her safe. They know what we're dealing with better than we do. I'll do my best to convince them to let you stay with her, but . . ." I shrugged. "Honestly, you were on the Assembly. There's a case against you. You knew things. You worked in the lab, but really your future is up to you."

Benjamin took a deep breath. "It's up to me, like we told followers. Nothing was up to them, and I have the feeling that nothing's really up to me now either."

"It is. I'll talk to my handler. I'll do all I can to persuade them to allow you to stay with Raquel until she's no longer critical. If you want more time than that—"

Benjamin looked away, his red-rimmed eyes downcast. "I want forever. Is that too much to ask?"

"No. I want the same thing. You just need to talk to the agents—be one hundred percent honest with them, be willing to turn state's evidence and testify. That's what you can do to get back to Raquel." I patted his shoulder. "I'm behind you. I hope you know that you've got my support."

We turned as paramedics made their way into the fuselage.

"What about Abraham?" Benjamin asked in a hushed tone.

I shook my head. "You should get a damn medal. You also saved my life. I'll tell them what happened."

"What about her?" he asked, looking at Raquel as the paramedics lifted their gurney. "Legally, I mean. Is there a case against her too?"

"It's not up to me. It's all up to the FBI, but I'll tell them what I know, which is, as far as the Assembly wives are concerned, from my knowledge they were all blissfully unaware. They were never informed of the workings of the Assembly or Commission. I'll be truthful in everything."

"Sir, is this your wife?" the young female paramedic asked, looking to Benjamin.

Benjamin looked at the paramedic and again at me.

"We," I said to Benjamin, "were married under The Light. I plan on using that legality to find Sara. Until it's disproved, your answer is yes."

Benjamin nodded and turned toward the young woman. "Yes, she is."

The woman's eyes widened as she scanned Raquel's injuries and looked back to Benjamin, seeing his bloodstained shirt.

"Miss," I said, attempting to derail her obvious train of thought. "I'm Agent McAlister of the FBI. This woman was attacked and beaten by someone who has been dealt with, not by her husband. I'll testify to that."

"Yes, Agent. Sir," she said to Benjamin, "please come with us. They're waiting for us at the medical center."

"Miss"—I read her name tag—"Kellogg, this woman's husband and another agent need to stay by her side."

"Agent, they can follow—"

"No, they will be with you."

"Yes, sir," she said, tightening the restraint and securing Raquel on the gurney. Without another word she and the other paramedic wheeled Raquel down the stairs toward the ambulance.

I handed Benjamin the burner phone. "I'll get one from the bureau and call you. I plan on heading east immediately."

He nodded and tucked the phone in his pocket. "You know, the last time I accepted this phone . . ."

I shook my head. "I know. I'm sorry."

"No, Raquel was right. She wanted to help. Just find Sara."

I took a deep breath as Benjamin stepped through the doorway and followed his wife.

As I descended the steps, the weight of three years lifted from my shoulders. I'd done my part. The Light was behind me. Looking out at the sea of faces, I searched for ones I recognized. When my eyes met one man's, that of an agent probably fifteen to twenty years my senior, a weary smile graced my lips. I'd spoken to him, but I hadn't seen him in over three years.

When he nodded in my direction, my grin broadened toward Special Agent William Adler. While he'd grown a few more gray hairs and even gained a few pounds, I recognized my handler immediately. When I reached the bottom of the stairs, he met me and patted my shoulder.

"Agent McAlister, you're a sight for sore eyes." He scanned me up and down. "It doesn't appear that you're too much the worse for wear. Maybe you'd like to do another three years in The Light?"

"No, sir. Let's flip that switch and move on."

Adler's welcoming expression faded. "Come with me, Jacoby. We need to talk."

The four words we need to talk splintered my already frayed nerves, leaving them in shreds. Before I could speak and ask him what we needed to talk about, he ushered me away to a waiting vehicle. I tried to protest, letting him know I didn't want to go to the field office. I couldn't go to the field office. I needed to get on a plane to Detroit. Instead of listening or even acknowledging my protests, he and two other agents flanked me and herded me into the large black SUV.

Once we were safely away from listening ears, Special Agent Alder turned toward me. "Listen, Jacoby, you're not authorized to leave, not yet."

"What do you mean? I told you on the phone that Sara's at the Eastern Light. I told you that you needed to get to her . . ." My shoulders drooped and words failed to form as the weight I thought I'd shed fell heavily back upon me.

"Listen to me," Adler said. "Can you do that?"

I nodded. I could listen, but first I needed to quiet the mayhem alienating the words and phrases coming from his mouth. Though his lips were moving, I wasn't seeing him. All I saw and heard was her. I was back in that damn bathroom in the outbuilding at the mansion with Sara in my arms. Her sweet trusting voice filling my ears while her beautiful blue eyes dominated my vision. With her hand reassuringly upon my chest, she said, "I trust you with my life. I have and I'll continue to do it."

Her confidence was steadfast, and I'd left her, walked away and abandoned her.

"Agent, did you hear a word I just said?"

The vehicle had pulled away from the small airport, taking me farther away from Sara, not closer, not where I'd promised to stay. I looked beyond my visions and searched for the ambulance. It must have already left. If I strained I could hear its sirens wailing in the distance.

"I'm sorry," I replied. "What? You completed the raid at the Eastern Light?"

Agent Adler nodded. "When's the last time you slept?"

"That's not relevant."

"I'm sensing you're in shock or going into shock. That's understandable. You deserve to rest. Without you this would never have been as successful—"

"Special Agent, you were telling me about the Eastern Light—about Sara."

He nodded. "After I spoke to you, we moved on the Eastern Light first. That raid begin earlier than the rest. Once you told us there was no mass suicide or homicide plan at the other campuses the timeline seemed safe. Being that we struck after one in the morning, we believe that helped decrease the number of casualties. We found everything you promised on the campus and hidden in what appeared to be abandoned buildings, including four women who were in a room resembling a clinic."

My heart clenched.

"Sara?" I asked.

"We don't believe so. Due to their injuries, it's difficult to be sure. Once we get to the field office we have pictures you can check for visual confirmation. There were only eighteen casualties on the campus in Highland Heights. They appeared to be the crew of followers working within the production plant. Identification is underway, but given the lack of fingerprints, we have our work cut out for us."

"The rest?"

"Taken into custody."

I nodded. "Sara wasn't on the campus."

"No one came forth with that name, or Stella Montgomery, under questioning. Of course, few are talking, especially the women. According to the agents at the scene, they believe the women were too afraid to speak, even with female agents and interrogators. However, after my brief conversation with Miss Montgomery on your phone, I'd assume that she would talk and give her true identity."

I nodded. She would. "Bloomfield Hills, sir?"

"Agent, the raids were planned simultaneously. The timing was close."

Oh, fuck! I was going to be ill.

"Close? What does that mean?"

"The subdivision that housed Gabriel Clark's home in Bloomfield Hills is gated. The mansion on Kingsway Trace is also gated. By the time we gained access, there was a five-minute discrepancy."

Though the vehicle was moving, I couldn't feel it. I couldn't focus. The weight was crushing, suffocating. My body fought to complete involuntary tasks. Expanding my lungs and contracting my heart required thought. The life-sustaining processes were chaotic at best. I worked to speak. "What happened in five minutes?"

I waited, wondering whether I'd actually spoken.

He reached for my arm. "They must have known we were

coming. The entire mansion blew. The way it exploded, it was a planned defensive measure. The home must have been sitting on a powder keg of explosives or maybe it was an intentional natural gas explosion. ATF is working on it. It's still burning. The investigators can't get close enough to even start looking for bodies."

"Bodies? What about survivors?"

"Jacoby, no one survived that blast."

"Maybe they got out first," I tried. "There are other exits, down by the airstrip?"

"Our agents had the property surrounded. We had aerial confirmation of the property and all the possible ways on and off. Every gate was blocked at least ten minutes before we tried to enter, even before the initiation of the raid on the campus. No one tried. Whoever was there is gone."

"Ten minutes? Then why weren't they up to the house five minutes earlier?"

"Agent." Adler's voice was calm, as if it would make what he was saying any easier to comprehend. "The bureau did the best they could. We only had eighteen casualties, forty-six overall. If we'd made it into the mansion five minutes earlier, we would have lost agents in the explosion."

"Forty-six? Does that include victims in the mansion?"

"No, but it includes all the campuses. Over one thousand people are in custody. Those outcomes are very good."

Incredulously I sought the right words, yet none came forth. "Outcomes, numbers? Shit! This isn't about numbers. I need to see the pictures of every woman you found, alive and dead, at the Eastern Light. And once they get in that mansion, I need to see that too." I turned my blurry vision out the window, before I turned back. "Special Agent, I request permission to go to Detroit. I need to see for myself."

"Agent, we understand that you became close—"

"She was assigned to me as a wife—nine months ago!" He didn't seem to understand. "She's pregnant with my child."

The interior of the SUV went silent. Not even road noise registered any longer.

"She's not dead," I said.

"Agent, we don't—"

"No. I know. I don't know if I ever believed in this shit before, but I would know. I would feel it if she were dead. She's not, and I'm going to find her."

He didn't respond as we continued to drive. Finally I managed to pull my thoughts from Sara and broaden my scope to the entire mission. "What about Gabriel Clark?"

"We have him. We have them all—him, the members of the Commission and Assembly. Well, unfortunately, we're missing one member of the Assembly at the Eastern Light. He could have been at the mansion. Also, one of our forty-six casualties is a member of the Assembly at the Northern Light. I don't know if you know anything about that. He was found in a hallway of the pole barn near the offices attached to the hangar."

"I know he was sent to accompany me to the hangar"—it was then I remembered the envelope—"to recover"—I reached into my jacket and pulled out the envelope and handed it to Special Agent Adler—"this. I have no idea what's inside, but whatever it is, my gut tells me that I owe my life to it. Father Gabriel was suspicious of me since Fairbanks, four days ago. I'd received this letter from a brother at the Western Light. I'd forgotten all about it, with everything that happened with Sara." Saying her name caused my heart to clench. "I have the feeling if he didn't need me to fly him back to the Northern Light or need whatever this contains, I wouldn't be sitting here right now."

My handler looked closely at the innocuous-looking envelope. "We'll take it in to the field house and have it analyzed." He turned toward me. "Jacoby, you have hours, days, and maybe even weeks of debriefing ahead. You have more knowledge of The Light than you're even aware. As you know, we have people who can help you recover that information. I'm deeply sorry about Stella Montgomery. Maybe in all that information floating around in your head you'll see how what you did, what she was willing to do, was beneficial to the success of this mission. Agent, because of you and her, we've opened a Pandora's box of illegal activities. You're right. We don't have a body count at the mansion, but there have been hundreds lost to this organization, even one more is one too many. Your sacrifice will not go unnoted—and neither will hers."

I did my best to hold it together, to be the agent I'd been trained to be, but I couldn't. "I promised her I'd keep her safe. I promised her a few more days. I even pleaded . . ." My teeth ground together. "Where is he?"

"Who?"

"Where is Gabriel Clark?"

"He's still at the Northern Light. We're arranging transport here to Anchorage."

"I need to see him as soon as he's here."

Special Agent Adler's head moved slowly back and forth. "You know we have protocol."

Anger and hatred seethed from my every pore.

"I want to look the motherfucker in the eye and tell him that I was the one who brought him down."

"Agent, one thing at a time."

SIXTY-EIGHT

"Good-bye, Stella Montgomery," I whispered as her body fell limp against mine.

Damn her! This was all her fault. She could fucking listen to her husband, but she wouldn't listen to me. I didn't want the submissive shell he'd created. But how hard would it have been for her to keep her damn nose out of The Light?

None of that mattered anymore. I wasn't sure what exactly had happened in the last hour. On the phone, Joel had said all the campuses had been raided. I mean, what the fuck? How all? My mind was a cyclone. This was never supposed to happen. The Eastern Light, sure. There was always that possibility. That was why I hated going over to that place. But all of them?

I tried to rein in my nerves as I laid Stella on the couch. Somehow she had something to do with this. US Marshals? I needed information and I needed it yesterday. Someone in the Shadows will know something. *If I only had my real damn phone! It was cleared to access the network on the dark web.*

The medicine I'd given Stella wasn't the memory suppressant, not yet. What I'd injected was only something to knock her out. The other shit was touchy, and I didn't know enough about it to risk administering it. If I gave her too much, too quickly, all of her memories could be lost—everything including things like eating and speaking. I'd heard stories from when they'd first started using it. On more than one occasion they'd been left with an infant in a woman's body. Then again, if not enough was given, there was that chance it wouldn't work.

She'd already had the medication in her system once. Did that mean she'd built immunity and she needed more, or that only a little would work?

I ran my hand through my hair and exhaled. I wanted to know what the fuck was happening. Where the hell were Joel and Chloe? I needed to prioritize. I also knew that if Gabriel were here, he'd never think a woman was worth this much trouble.

The way I planned it, once Joel and Chloe arrived, Joel could help me carry Stella to one of the bedrooms. Before they were banished, Chloe had worked with her father in the lab at the Northern Light. She understood all the science stuff and how the medication worked. She could administer the memory suppressant while Joel and I figured out what the hell was happening with The Light and the Shadows.

Once Chloe erased Stella's memories, Sara Adams would be gone forever. If she really did have feelings for that guy, this would be easier anyway. More than likely, Jacob was already gone—polar bear food. Gabriel had forbidden me from keeping Stella, but as I grabbed another beer from the refrigerator, I reasoned that if he was now in FBI custody it was no longer his decision. It was mine. And once Chloe was done, the woman with me wouldn't be Sara or Stella. We'd find her a new name.

I paced from the kitchen to the couch and back, fisting my hair. Too fucking much!

All of this was on me. I tried again to call Joel, but the circuits were all still busy.

I flipped on the television. The first thing that came on was an interruption of normal programming. On the screen in front of me was aerial coverage of the Bloomfield mansion explosion. The caption read, "Gas leak suspected as the cause of an explosion in Bloomfield Hills. House is believed to be the part-time residence of accused cult leader Gabriel Clark." As I was about to change the station, a reporter appeared, broadcasting live from Whitefish, Montana. Behind her were buses filling with followers.

Clenching my teeth, I didn't listen to what she had to say. Instead, I shut the damn thing off.

Taking deep breaths, I reassured myself that I'd learned how to do this. Most of my life had been spent in preparation for my role in assuming power. I needed to take the lessons I'd learned from Gabriel and put them to use. First and foremost, no one would or could argue with my decisions. As long as Gabriel was out of commission, I was in charge. Second, as leader, I could authorize and/or witness activity, but I was always to stay at least one step removed.

Keeping his hands clean was what Gabriel had done. It was how he would survive whatever was about to happen. No matter how far and wide the Shadows were scattered, we all knew Gabriel Clark would survive. Like a phoenix he'd rise again.

When I finally got a hold of Joel, he was both shocked and elated to hear from me. He'd tried my other phone and I hadn't answered. He said the chatter among the Shadows was that I'd been in the mansion.

Maybe I was the phoenix, rising from the ashes of the explosion.

My plan was to lie low for a few days and let the dust settle. This house was a great place to do that. It didn't have any connections to me or to The Light. It was connected to MOA. After a couple of days of organizing our strategy, we'd be ready. And after a few days of pumping the drug into Stella, she'd be ready. When we woke her, she'd be whomever we wanted. I would convince her that she was part of the Shadows.

In our brief conversation Joel told me that Gabriel had passed the mantle. He'd told the Shadows I was in charge. I just hadn't known it, or seen it. I looked over at Stella.

"Because I don't have my fucking phone!" She couldn't hear me, but saying it out loud made me feel better.

While my temples throbbed with the task ahead and the responsibilities Gabriel had bestowed upon me, I still managed to grin, knowing I wouldn't be doing this alone. Shit, in The Light Stella had been chosen. In the Shadows she'd believe she was married to the leader—to me. It didn't get much fucking higher than that.

I wasn't interested in a harem or brides of the Shadows. There was one woman I wanted. And now that I was the leader, my every desire was obtainable. I wanted the old Stella, but I'd take an improved version. She really was smarter than shit. I liked her quick tongue and questions. In the new version, I'd encourage her strengths, as long as she knew that when it came to my word, it was indisputable. I smoothed her hair away from her face and tried to ignore the blackened eye. With her beside me, and the Shadow resources, we would be unstoppable.

My first official proclamation after Joel arrived with a new phone would be to assure Thomas Hutchinson's fate. My neck straightened as I brushed my thumb over her swollen eye. Before he died, that fucker would know the fear Stella had experienced when he threatened to rape her.

I paced by the large window, the glow of Gabriel's house still lightening the horizon. Shaking my head, I tried again to log my MOA phone onto the private network, but it didn't have authorization. Fuck! I'd missed so much by not having my real phone. At least now I didn't need to worry about anyone finding it and connecting it to me. With that explosion, they might not even be able to identify my car, and they definitely wouldn't find Elijah.

That stupid asshole.

Under my regime things would change. Then again, I wasn't as narcissistic as my uncle. I understood that not everything had to be my way. He believed he was invincible. I'd warned him to have contingency plans at all the campuses. He wouldn't listen. He was so damn sure that the isolation would be enough.

I didn't need to worry about that with the Shadows. Our growth over the last few years had knocked the number of followers on the campuses out of the damn water. We'd also known that what had happened tonight was always a possibility.

My phone buzzed. Finally. Maybe the damn circuits were catching up.

Joel: WE'RE HERE. LET US IN.

I glanced at Stella, still sleeping like a baby, before I walked through the house and opened the front door.

"Shit, D. This is worse than we imagined," Joel said, shaking his head as they entered. By their expressions they both looked as if they'd just suffered through an FBI raid, not heard about it.

"Get your head in this," I said as I patted Joel on the shoulder.

Chloe buried her tearstained face in my chest as she wrapped her arms around my waist. "Dylan, I never thought . . . do we know yet? They have Gabriel. Don't they?"

I shook my head and gently rubbed her back. The three of us had been friends for most of our lives. Their parents and mine had been some of the first followers. While their parents had gone to the campuses, mine had gone to work in the Shadows. Gabriel had known he needed reinforcements scattered about. "I don't know," I replied. "I don't have my real phone, only the MOA one, and it's not authorized for the network. Besides, the damn circuits have been swamped. If Gabriel did try to reach me, well, he couldn't."

"The last communication didn't sound good," Joel said.

Slowly Chloe released her hug, and I led them back to the kitchen.

"We can't reach anyone at the Northern Light," she stammered. "M-my mom. My dad . . ." She walked toward the back living room.

As Joel reached into the refrigerator and pulled out a beer, he asked, "Where's your phone? Why don't you have it?"

"Dylan!"

Joel and I turned toward Chloe's scream. Her lips were pressed together and her arms crossed over her chest as she stared at Stella's sleeping body.

"This! She? Are you crazy?" She didn't wait for my answer as her earlier sadness morphed to indignation. "This is that woman, the one you were dating, the one that was sent away. Isn't it?"

I pulled my shoulders back. "Yes."

"Gabriel told you—"

I took a step forward. "Gabriel isn't in charge anymore, at least not currently."

"But he said—"

"Chloe," Joel warned. "D's right."

"Either you're with me on all decisions or on none," I declared.

Fuck! I sounded just like my uncle, but at the moment I didn't care.

Chloe took a deep breath. "Fine. Is this why you wanted me to bring the drug?"

"Yes. She's spent the last nine months at the northern campus. When she first disappeared there was a lot of press and police activity. It's safer now. She's old news."

"D, man, I'm not questioning you, but are you sure?"

I nodded. "Yeah, I'm sure. When I first brought her here, I was thinking I could get her to the Western Light." I ran my hand through my hair. "She's a pain in the ass, but I'm not ready to let her be banished." I scrunched my nose. "I also wasn't going to leave her at the mansion."

Chloe's lips moved upward. "So instead you're decreeing that she's banished like us."

I scoffed. "I guess I am. I didn't think of it like that, but yes. Your exit from the Northern Light was a little more voluntary, but the end result is the same. She knows too much to be released, and while carrying out ultimate banishments doesn't bother me, like I said, not with her." I stood and watched as my childhood friends stared, first at Stella and then at each other. When they didn't respond, I said, "Help me carry her upstairs."

I got my arms under hers and lifted her shoulders while Joel lifted her feet. I continued talking as we walked. "I figured we could lay low for a couple of days. Gabriel's directions were for radio silence. We'll do what he said. It'll be easier on the Shadows if things progress the way they expect. Then, once we wake her up, we can move. She's smart. She'll adapt. Fuck, she adapted to the Northern Light. This time she'll have her real life back, well, kind of."

Chloe wrinkled her nose as she watched us lay her on the bed. "She's going to need to be cleaned up. Who the hell did that to her back? And why is she dressed like a bride?"

"Mark," I replied. "We had words. There was only so much I could do." I clenched my teeth together. "Fucking Gabriel told me I couldn't have her, and then I found out he planned on making her one of them—one of his brides."

"Jesus!" Chloe said, shaking her head, "I'm not questioning Father Gabriel, but I just don't get it."

Joel looked to his wife and narrowed his gaze. "Just because we're in the Shadows . . ."

Chloe continued to move her head slowly from side to side, her brown hair falling over her shoulders as she tended to Stella. The Shadows didn't follow all the doctrine of The Light. That was part of the reason Joel and Chloe had asked to move into the Shadows. The extent to which each Shadow followed varied, but Father Gabriel's teachings were still the cement, the binding that held the Shadows to The Light.

"You need to keep the messages going, for those who want it, who need it," Joel said, talking to me.

I nodded as I watched Chloe set up the medication. "I've been thinking about that. Man, you're my first Commissioner. I was wondering if you . . ." My words trailed away. The Light doctrines and preaching weren't my thing. I'd spent most of my life avoiding them. Joel knew the lessons backward and forward. He and Chloe had lived it before they were married, and after at the Northern Light.

"If I wanted to preach, I'd have stayed in Alaska."

I stood taller. "As my first Commissioner, I'm not asking you." Joel's lips thinned, but he didn't respond. "The way I see it," I went on, "you two know that side better than I do. I can oversee the operations and the money. You're right. There are Shadows who'll need to hear Gabriel's word. I figure you two can give them what they need until the dust settles. We have Shadows everywhere: police, judicial, fuck, even federal: FBI, CIA, Homeland Security. I could keep going.

"What happened tonight will be big news. I was just watching some coverage on TV. It'll be like Stella's disappearance was. Give it some time and then it'll die down. When that happens we'll do what we do. It just takes one—Raphael, Michael, Uriel, one of them. Once we get one of them out of custody, the Shadows will eat it up. It'll be like he was raised from the fucking dead, and then he can do the preaching."

Joel nodded. "Fine. We'll do it. But I don't know why we should stop there."

Chloe began putting bandages around Stella's head.

"What are you doing?"

"The loss of vision," Chloe answered, "is vital. I remember reading my father's research. If you want her to believe she's someone else, it takes time."

"Father Gabriel," Joel continued. "He needs to rise again. The Shadows have the power. If they think getting one of the originals out of prison is a miracle, getting Father Gabriel out will be better than walking on water."

I nodded and smiled as I watched Chloe cover Stella with a blanket.

When she turned my way, she said, "I'll need to get some more medical supplies if she's going to be unconscious for a few days."

"Thank you, Chloe. We all need to bide our time." I slapped Joel on the back. "But I agree, man. We can't let Gabriel rot behind bars any longer than necessary. In the meantime—"

"You're the boss, man," Joel said, finishing my sentence. "Father Dylan?" he asked with a smirk.

"I'd rather not."

"You know what you need to do," Joel said.

Chloe put her arm around my shoulders. "It'll be like when we were kids."

I hadn't used my The Light name since my parents died. At first Gabriel had tried to get me to go by it, but my stubbornness won. "Not Father, though. Gabriel's coming back. We just don't know when."

"Brother David," Chloe said.

Though my gut twisted with the title, I couldn't be the leader of the Shadows as just Dylan. I nodded.

Joel shook his head. "All right, Brother David, we need to stop playing nursemaid and get down to business. If you're sure we're safe here, this is a great place to get our plan in gear. The computer system in the lower level is stellar. I know how to use it and backdoor us into some sites. It won't be long until I've got us not only on the dark web but authorized to broadcast. I'd say by tomorrow morning, we will be able to get a message out, something short to the Shadows. Not enough to sever Father Gabriel's orders of radio silence, just enough to let everyone know that you didn't die in that explosion— that Brother David is alive and ready to keep this going, to move the Shadows to the next level."

"It's nearly four in the morning. Do you think that this could wait until morning?" Chloe asked.

They both looked at me.

"I'd say it already did. Let's keep going and see what we can learn. We can't call the campuses, but shit, let's start contacting individual Shadows."

"From what I've learned," Joel said, "This was an FBI operation. Somehow they coordinated it with all three campuses."

"Our fucking Shadows in the FBI have some explaining to do. How the hell did it get this far?"

"I don't know, but I'd suspect that just like we have people inside the FBI, they had people or a person inside The Light."

"How in the hell didn't we know that?" I asked.

"That's what we need to find out. What are you going to name her?" Joel asked as we walked down the stairs.

I'd already thought about this. I knew the name she deserved. Yes, she'd been a pain in the ass, but in a few days, she'd be awakening with a new life for the third time. "Stacy," I replied. "It means 'resurrection.'"

Chloe nodded as both of their phones buzzed.

"Hello," Joel answered. "Yes, all three of us are here." His eyes opened wide as he disconnected his phone and turned to me. "That was a Shadow on the inside of the FBI. We need to get out now! I'm sorry about Stacy, D. But the FBI is only minutes away. Shadows first, we need to flee."

SIXTY-NINE

J acoby

FOR THE MIDDLE of the night, the Anchorage field office was a hive of activity. Each new agent who came up to me slapped me on the back, congratulating me on a good run. They were all proud of the end results: no fires on the campuses, no mass suicide. Special Agent Adler said that the president had even called the director, pleased that he didn't have a PR nightmare on his hands.

After a few more congratulatory pats and affectionate ribbing as a few of my old colleagues called me Brother Jacoby, I made my way back to the evidence room. Standing at the doorway, with my mouth agape, I took in the other side of my mission. I'd lived it, been in the trenches, but this, the boxes of evidence, as well as board after board of pictures, creating theories and trails, was the end result of years of research.

"Jacoby, come in," Special Agent Adler called from his temporary office. I wasn't sure how long the operations would be located in Anchorage. Usually Adler and all the unit's operations were housed in Virginia.

I followed him into the small private room and shut the door.

"I wanted to let you see these pictures in private."

"Thank you." No one other than Adler and the other two agents in the SUV knew about my relationship with Sara.

Opening the folder, I pulled each glossy photo out and studied the faces. Every one of the women had bandaged eyes. It was standard protocol; however, that wouldn't impair me from being able to tell whether one of them was Sara. I'd spent three weeks looking at her with her eyes bandaged. I'd still recognize her nose, cheeks, hair, and lips.

Even those features weren't easily distinguishable on some of these women. Their injuries were extensive, yet the bruises and fractured bones barely registered. I'd flown women in similar condition more times than I cared to admit. I'd helped to carry their unconscious bodies onto my plane and taken them across the country. The only thing that mattered to me as I stared at the pictures was identifying Sara. I hated the thought of her being in that bad a shape in less than twenty-four hours, but if it meant she was alive, I'd nurse her back to health. I'd done it once before.

Sighing, I shook my head and placed the folder back on Adler's desk. "None of them are Sara."

"Every other agent who's looked at those photos has commented on the extent of the injuries. You didn't say a word."

I met his gaze. "I've seen it, firsthand. There's nothing new to me in those photos."

Special Agent Adler whistled as he blew a gust of air between his teeth. "We need to get you some rest and start debriefing. There's so much I want to know."

"Not yet. I want to meet Father . . . Gabriel Clark when that plane lands." I ran my fingers over my face, and as I did, I recognized the familiar disconnect with the tips of my fingers. Lowering my hands, I turned them over, showing them to Special Agent Adler. "See my fingers?"

"Yes, we've been seeing a lot of that."

"No, don't you get it?"

"What?"

"I want an alert sent out to all the area hospitals, homeless shelters, airports, police, everywhere."

"Jacoby, I don't understand. We have all the followers corralled from the campuses."

"We don't have Sara. I refuse to believe she's dead. Have the FBI tell all the places I just mentioned that we're looking for women who have no fingerprints."

"As soon as they get the fire extinguished—"

"No, let's say she escaped. If she did, she could be wandering about. If she is, she could be picked up and that is the way to identify her."

"I'm not sure that's a good idea. There's more you need to know. Let me show you something that we're only beginning to understand."

I nodded, and waited for Adler to make his way around his desk and back out into the evidence room.

An hour later, as I drained my second cup of coffee, I continued to read and follow the magnitude of evidence compiled within this room. The caffeine was essential. I was currently going on twenty-four hours without sleep and the adrenaline from Benjamin's and my escape was quickly dissipating. Undoubtedly the emotional roller coaster of the last four days was taking its toll.

I'd lived in The Light for three years, and Special Agent Adler was right. My work had paid off. Because of me nearly a thousand people would now be free to live real lives, no longer manipulated by a narcissistic psychopath. However, as I followed the leads and information accumulated on the large boards, I was flabbergasted by what I hadn't known.

"So what the hell are the Shadows?" I asked, my brow furrowed in confusion.

"The Light outside of The Light," Agent Brady explained. He was a young man, part of the small obscure team at Quantico on the special task force that investigated The Light. His knowledge was as profound as mine. Instead of living it, he'd infiltrated The Light through cyberspace, through the dark web. Admittedly I felt a pang of jealousy when I learned that he'd discovered so much without putting himself or those he cared about at risk.

"It's an interesting phenomenon," Brady went on. "When you were first sent in, we had no idea that there were even three campuses. We'd identified the Western Light, but not the Northern. Your final correspondence nearly two years ago confirmed its existence."

I remembered making that call. I'd been living at the Northern Light for a time and felt the need to at least notify the FBI that the campus existed. I'd made that call from Bloomfield Hills on a burner. Thankfully, those cell towers weren't monitored like the ones at the Northern Light or even the Western; there was too much cell activity to identify unknown users.

"It wasn't until we started following the cyberactivity from the Northern Light that we were able to identify a connection out in the real world."

"The dark," I said mindlessly.

"Excuse me?" another young agent asked.

I looked up from the aerial photograph of the Bloomfield Hills mansion. "The real world, in The Light it's referred to as the dark, the area beyond The Light."

Adler had been right. It would take me weeks of debriefing to give up all the information I'd obtained, because some things, like the term *the dark*, seemed like common knowledge to me. The FBI had people to help scour my thoughts and memories. I was more concerned about the deprogramming. Obviously I was in need of that too.

"Yeah, we've heard that term. Well, the cybertrail led me to the dark . . ." Brady's voice trailed away as he hit keys on a keyboard and a large screen came to life.

I pinched my brow and stifled a yawn. "Yes, I understand the term the Shadows, but who or what are they?"

The screen became a map of North America. The three campuses were identified.

Brady went on, "The cyberactivity has been the strongest and the easiest to identify from your campus. It's the isolation. A lot of the activity was intercampus communication. At first that was difficult to intercept. The firewalls were commendable, hell, better than some used by our government. They were layered, even triple encrypted. We'd make it through one only to be stopped by another."

"You're saying The Light's security was good."

"I'm saying it was excellent. Only recently did we penetrate it enough to see the broadcasts of the meetings and sermons. By doing that we could pinpoint Gabriel's location. We could tell if he was at Bloomfield Hills, which is where the majority of the broadcasts originated, the Western Light, or the Northern Light. We thought that most of the activity was intercampus, until we discovered this." He hit a button and suddenly the United States and Canada lit up like a virtual Christmas tree. He zoomed out and lights lit all over the world.

"What is that?"

"Hits on the latest broadcast."

"How?" I asked. "If the communication was solely between campuses?"

"Agent, welcome to the Shadows. There's a highly encrypted website on the dark web that allows followers outside of the campuses to obtain access to the broadcasts. The last broadcast was short, sent fifteen minutes before the FBI touched down at the Northern Light, moments before the explosion in Bloomfield Heights."

I couldn't think about the explosion and concentrate. I had to be

Agent Jacoby for a little while. "Do you have the broadcast? Did you see it?"

I gripped the table in front of me as Father Gabriel's face covered the large screen and his voice filled the room. How many times had I watched his broadcasts? He looked exactly as he did when he delivered a sermon, not a hair out of place.

"Children of The Light, a very unfortunate chain of events has occurred. You will hear things and see images. Remember, my children, the dark is everywhere. While The Light may be temporarily dimmed, we know it cannot be extinguished. You, my children of the Shadows, must stay vigilant and keep the vision alive. You've been given enlightenment to discern the truths. Those who wish us harm are our enemies. You are the soldiers in this war. Though I may be unavailable for a time, know that time is irrelevant to our cause and mission. My power will be held by the one who would inherit the legacy, until it is mine again. I entrust it thereupon, but never give up, never accept the lies told in the dark. Know that The Light will forever shine."

My knuckles blanched and the blood drained from my cheeks as the screen went black. "What the fuck does that mean?"

Special Agent Adler had entered the room during the broadcast. "Jacoby," he said, "there are a few bunks here. I suggest you get some sleep. We have a lot to discuss."

I spun toward him. "It's not gone? Three years, lives, Sara . . . all for nothing!"

"No," he replied calmly. "It wasn't all for nothing. The campuses were the main source of The Light's revenue. They were a hotbed of illegal activities hiding behind the separation of church and state. You brought that down. You did it! Over a thousand people freed. That wasn't for nothing."

"But"—I pointed toward the now-blank screen—"that earlier graphic, there are ten or fifty times as many Shadows." I used the new term. "Not everyone you're taking into custody was brought to The Light unwillingly. Their campus is gone, but with the right connections they'll be able to rejoin the force. What will stop them?"

Agent Adler shook his head. "The mission was successful. You do realize how unusual it is to be able to infiltrate three separate locations with the exercised precision and such a low number of casualties."

"Sara," I whispered.

"Going back last Friday made the difference in our success. We didn't have the manpower ready."

I nodded. "Have you issued the APB for Dylan Richards?"

"Not yet. The charred remains of his car were found on the grounds in Bloomfield Hills. Right now we're assuming he was in the mansion when it blew."

My knees gave way as I collapsed in a nearby chair. "No. No." My volume increased. "I don't care if it was five minutes or one, there was a plan to save Richards and I know it. Besides, did you hear what Gabriel said? He said something about his power going to someone who would *inherit*."

Brady nodded. "We've been searching, but we're coming up blank. He must mean it as a transfer of power. Gabriel Clark or Garrison Clarkson never had children."

"Not a child, Richards is Clark's nephew. He's alive, I know it. Even that asshole wouldn't allow his nephew to be blown up. I saw the two of them interact just the other day—fuck, I don't even know what day it is."

"Tuesday," Brady offered.

"Yesterday. There's no way Clark allowed that."

Agent Adler shook his head. "I don't see how—"

"Did you have constant aerial surveillance?" I asked.

Brady tapped his keyboard again; however, before he hit the key to play the time-lapsed video, he asked, "Are you sure you want to see this?"

My fight was gone. "I'm sure. Go back ten minutes before the blast."

He did. Ten minutes played in less than thirty seconds. The explosion made me gasp. Adler's hand came down on my shoulder as I wiped a tear from my tired eyes. There was nothing preceding it, just a catastrophic eruption. Obviously the means to produce such an explosion had been in place for an event such as this.

I agreed that on the video there was no activity on the grounds. If Richards had received a warning call, he hadn't heeded it.

"Is there any way he could have known earlier?" I asked out of desperation.

"It's doubtful. The timeline is tight."

While Adler answered, Brady brought up the video again and rewound to sixty minutes before the explosion. Moments after he put the time-lapsed footage in motion, I saw a blur of white in the darkness near the pool. The lights around the pool were the only illumination on the rear grounds.

"Wait," I said. "Go back and run it in real time."

Both men stilled as Brady did as I asked. Thankfully, the government had sophisticated cameras with immense zooming capabilities. Though it was grainy, there were definitely two figures who appeared to have run the length of the yard, the exact trek I'd run the day before.

"Was she wearing white?" Brady asked, interest as well as concern in his voice.

"No, not when I left, but, shit, I remember there were other women there in white. It could be one of them, or it could be that they made her change clothes." The possible reasons for the change of clothes turned my stomach. I wouldn't allow myself to let my thoughts linger there as I stared at the screen.

"It's difficult to see the other figure. I'd assume it's a man."

"Have they thoroughly checked the outbuildings?"

"Yes, and the wooded area. No one's there."

"There's a back gate. Can you access the video of that gate?"

Brady shook his head. "No, the main center for the surveillance was in the house. When it blew, we lost our connection."

"That neighborhood is within Bloomfield Hills and is gated," Adler said.

"Yes?" I asked, wondering where he was going with that.

"The neighborhood has cameras!" Brady said.

My exhaustion gave way to one last surge of adrenaline. "Can you . . .?"

I didn't even need to finish my question before the screen came alive with nearly twenty feeds time-stamped at 00:00:00 Tuesday morning. The house wouldn't blow for over an hour, but in general the streets and intersections were quiet, except for a late-model black SUV. It stopped at one stop sign long enough for us to see the driver.

"Shit! It's him!" I said, the hairs on the back of my neck standing to attention as Dylan Richards's image came into view.

"I don't see anyone else in the vehicle," Adler said.

"But we saw the woman in white near the pools. If the bureau has thoroughly investigated the rear grounds and there's no one, or no body, down there, she has to be in the vehicle. I can't imagine him taking any of the other women from that house. It has to be Sara. I told you, she's not dead."

Brady isolated the SUV and followed it to another home within the neighborhood. Once he zeroed in on the home, a smaller screen emerged and we were shown the owner of the home: Motorists of America.

I turned with my brow furrowed. "What the hell is that?"

"It's a shell corporation. One that's been on our radar as part of the Shadows. It's worth millions, probably more."

"So even stopping the production at the Northern Light won't stop the money?"

"It will stop the influx of new money. There's already a good amount out there. We just need to prove that it was obtained illegally. Hell, it could make a small dent in the national debt."

"Send agents to that house now."

While Agent Adler dialed, Brady switched to a time-lapsed feed of the house. With the time stamp reading 03:04:50, another SUV pulled up to the house. A man and woman got out and went into the house. I looked at my watch. That had been about an hour ago. By the time Special Agent Adler had given the order to go to the house, Brady had the screen on the live feed.

Less than two minutes after the order was given, three people came out of the house and got into the new SUV. It was the new man and woman plus Richards.

"Shit! What the fuck just happened?"

Special Agent Adler's eyes narrowed. "Shit!"

"There must be agents at the mansion. Get someone there now! Catch him!" I was screaming orders at men, one of whom was my superior.

Brady followed the SUV through the streets of the neighborhood; however, once the SUV left the gates of the subdivision, we lost the feed.

"I gave them the license number. We need to sit tight," Brady said.

"Please." I turned to Agent Adler. "I need to be on a plane to Detroit."

Special Agent Adler nodded. "I'm going with you."

CHAPTER

SEVENTY

S tella

THICK FOG PENETRATED MY THOUGHTS, its tentacles clawing at my memories. It wasn't new, my mind knew its tricks. I'd played this game before. Steel shutters of internal defenses snapped shut and barricades went up. From somewhere deep I knew to stop the invasion. Its deception was difficult to fight. There was a tunnel and a light. The brightness enticed, pulled me closer, and my battered, exhausted body longed to surrender.

The promise of reprieve it offered was real. All I needed to do was lift the shutters and allow the fog to infiltrate. My reward would be rest and time to heal. The appeal grew as pain from my back and cramping from my midsection remained on my side of the barricades. If only I could open them a little, enough to allow the fog to enter, it would save me from the pain.

My desire grew . . . maybe I could allow just a little . . .

CHAPTER

SEVENTY-ONE

J acoby

PICTURES from the home in Bloomfield Hills came via the agents' cell phones as Adler and I were driven back to the airport. I lost any semblance of professionalism as Sara's picture materialized.

She was there and she was alive, unconscious and alone in the house.

I didn't know why Richards had left her, but at that moment I didn't care. My cheeks dampened as tears of relief freely flowed. I wiped them away, watching as Agent Adler's iPad continued the slide show of images. As they materialized, I saw her bandaged eyes and my gut twisted. Thankfully, even though her eyes were once again bandaged, I didn't see injuries like those of the other women at the Eastern Light. What I did see, what made my heart skip a beat, was the bag of clear liquid hanging from the pole near her bed.

"Tell them to disconnect the medicine, immediately," I said, my body shaking with fear. That motherfucker had told me he'd try to keep her off the medicine. Now there it was.

"But Jacoby, you don't know what it is—"

"I do." My volume grew. "I don't know the name of it, but it's a memory suppressant. I've seen it attached to more women than I want to admit. Tell them to disconnect it immediately."

Agent Adler handed me the phone. "Here, you're not only an agent, you're her husband. You tell them."

"Agent?" I said, speaking to someone in Bloomfield Hills.

"Yes, sir, this is Agent Billings."

"Billings, disconnect the medicine immediately."

"Sir, by what authority..."

"I'm Agent Jacoby McAlister." My name had made the rounds. They all knew I was the one who'd been inside The Light.

"Sir, it's an honor—"

"Disconnect the medicine. As soon as the paramedics get there, have them start her on IV fluids. We need to dilute the medication in her system. Make certain that they only give her clear fluids. How is she?"

"She's unconscious and, well..."

"Tell me, Agent."

"Sir, her eyes are covered, but there appears to be bruising around one eye that has drifted down her cheek. I'd assume it's not new."

I shook my head. "It's not. She was struck on Friday. Is there anything else?"

"We haven't tried to move her, but there's blood on her dress." He gasped.

"What?"

"I haven't removed her dress."

"Don't!"

"Sir, her back is bloody. I'd wager to guess she's been whipped."

My teeth clenched together as rage surged through my veins. I was going to kill Richards when I saw him. The asshole got all up in arms over a blackened eye and he whipped her! "Get her to the hospital. I want an agent beside her every minute. Do not let anyone prescribe any medication. There's a possibility that she's pregnant."

"Yes, sir, but . . ."

"What is it?"

"I'm not a doctor, but she's bleeding, and not just from her back."

My chest became tight. "Get her to the hospital. Make sure she's safe. That's all that matters."

When the line was disconnected I handed the phone back to Adler and turned toward the window. The sun was rising in Anchorage, creating long shadows over the streets as we neared the airport.

As I fought the overwhelming sadness of the loss of something I hadn't realized I wanted, I tried to concentrate on the positive. Sara was alive. I cleared my throat. "What about Richards?" I asked.

"We lost them," Adler replied. "We found the SUV abandoned on Highway 1, but they're gone. We're staking out his house in Brush Park as well as the one in Bloomfield Hills. He hasn't reported in with the DPD either. We're still looking. His cell phone has been silent. We identified the other people through facial recognition. They go by Joel and Chloe Beechen."

"Joel and Chloe? I believe they're banished members of the Northern Light. I don't understand how they're still alive." I turned toward my handler. "If they were informed of our impending raid on that house, it means that someone from The Light or the Shadows somehow tipped them off. It means there's someone or multiple people within the FBI."

Special Agent Adler's lips pressed together. "Up until the raids, this task force was very small. I know it was secure. If it hadn't been . . . well, you would have been discovered. But with the raids, all the acquisitions, and then the explosion in Bloomfield Heights, the number of agents has increased dramatically. We'll begin an internal investigation, but first we need to be sure all of our witnesses are secure."

I ran my hand through my hair.

Shit, I need a shower.

As we pulled up to the airport, my eyes widened. Being ushered from an airplane to a waiting van was a line of men, all ones I recognized, all with their hands cuffed behind their backs. I reached for the door handle and Adler reached for my arm.

"Protocol. You don't want to ruin three years of work by saying the wrong thing. Let it go until you have Sara back."

My neck stiffened and my eyes narrowed. Getting out of the SUV, I moved so that I'd be in plain view of each Commissioner and Assemblyman, and especially in view of Father Gabriel.

I waited as each person passed, each member of the chosen.

Perhaps the Commission and Father Gabriel thought Abraham had killed me; maybe they hadn't given it much thought. When I saw the suit and the silk shirt, I knew.

I couldn't speak. Nevertheless I took another step forward.

My movement must have caught his attention. When our eyes met, the look Gabriel Clark gave me was classic and unforgettable. At first it was as if he couldn't believe what he was seeing. His dark eyes widened in question. It was as his gaze scanned my body and lingered on the badge hanging from a lanyard around my neck that I smiled. In his glare I witnessed unadulterated hatred. I knew the look, because if I hadn't known that Sara was safe, I would have been giving him the same expression. The next second an officer pulled Clark's elbow and he looked away.

My smile had been more of a Cheshire grin, and I didn't shine it just on Gabriel Clark. No, I maintained it with my cheeks high as Timothy passed by, his beady eyes narrowing in disbelief. It was only with Daniel and Luke that I found myself wanting to offer to help. I told myself I would, but first I wanted to get to Sara.

~

MY SLEEP-DEPRIVED MIND was a blur as I pushed my way through Henry Ford Hospital. As soon as we landed, I received an update. Stella Montgomery was in stable condition. After we left Anchorage she had undergone a minor medical procedure commonly referred to as a D & C.

I told myself to concentrate on the first sentence. She was safe and in stable condition. That didn't mean that I could ignore the rest of the update. I was an FBI agent. My job was dangerous. Hell, I'd almost been killed in the past twenty-four hours, and because of me, so had Stella. I'd never considered children, never wanted them. Until now.

There was a special security detail outside Stella's room. With the news of the Shadows, the FBI was taking every precaution. Although my face-off with Gabriel Clark had been gratifying, it was also stupid. Now I was a target. And if I was, so was Stella.

As I approached Stella's room, I struggled with what I'd find. Mostly I worried about how she'd take the news about the baby. That was, if she remembered—if they'd disconnected the memory suppressant before it had time to do its job. No one, except Brother Raphael, knew exactly how it worked or how much of the drug it would take to destroy her memory. She'd already had it in her system. Would even a small amount take her back to a blank canvas? The last messages had said she hadn't awakened, though the anesthesia from the procedure was wearing off.

"You're her husband?" the doctor asked, just outside her door.

"Yes," I said. Despite everything we'd been through, seeing her, even from a distance, made me smile. That was, until I noticed the bandages. "Why are her eyes still covered?"

"We thought maybe you could tell us. We didn't want to remove the bandages if there was a previous trauma."

I shook my weary head. "No, there's no trauma. The D & C?"

"Agent McAlister, from Stella's HCG levels, it's difficult to say if she was ever pregnant. However, due to the trauma she endured to her torso and the heaviness of her menstrual bleeding, the D & C was completed as a safety precaution."

"Trauma? What happened?"

"It appears as though blunt force was delivered directly to her uterus."

My fists balled. I'll kill him. So help me God. I was going to kill Richards.

The doctor placed a hand on my shoulder. "There's no permanent damage, if that's what you're concerned about. Your wife will be fine. Future children are possible."

I nodded. "How much longer until she wakes?"

"It could be any time."

As we turned I saw Stella's hands move shakily to the bandages.

"No! Not again! Please no!"

Her pleas were music to my ears. She remembers! I rushed to her side, pushing the nurse out of the way.

"Sara, I'm here. We're getting these off. You don't need them."

She blindly reached in my direction. "Jacob? Is that you? Are you here? Oh, God. Where am I?"

I fumbled with the bandages until they fell away. The small dark domes landed upon the covers, and from beneath them the most beautiful blue eyes blinked and focused on me.

"It's me. I'm here and you're safe."

Her shoulders shuddered as I wrapped her in my arms.

"I tried to help," she said. "I kept asking him questions, trying to get him to tell me information. But then he said I was going to forget everything, and then he stuck something in my neck." She pulled back. "Why? Why didn't it work?" Then her face dropped, her mouth slightly open. "Our baby? Did I . . . ?"

I shook my head and pulled her close. "You didn't do anything but survive. I'm so sorry I left you. I swear to God I'm going to kill him. I can't believe he did this to you."

Her face burrowed into the nape of my neck. "I'm so sorry."

"Stop it," I whispered as I rubbed small circles on her back. "You have nothing to be sorry about. The doctor said that they couldn't confirm you were pregnant. They said the hormone level was low. They also said they did a procedure for precaution, but if you ever decide to have children in the future, it's still an option."

Stella stilled in my arms. When she finally looked up to me she asked, "Me? If I ever decide?" She pulled her left hand away from the grip she'd had on me. "They took my wedding ring."

I lifted her hand to my lips and kissed her left fourth finger. "I'd be happy to put another one on that finger."

She sat taller and wiped the tears from her cheeks. "I'm done being Mrs. Adams."

"That's good." My cheeks rose as my first real grin surfaced. "I don't know anyone named Adams anyway." I brushed my thumb over her bruised eye. The color had lightened to a sickening green. "I was wondering how you feel about the name McAlister?"

The tips of her lips moved upward. "I think I like it. Sara"—her grin grew—"Stella McAlister." Burying her face in my chest, she looked up again, with her nose wrinkled. "Stella and Jacoby. That's going to take some time getting used to." She brushed my cheek. "You know, I don't care what your name is, as long as we're both safe. I love you."

"I love you too." I smoothed her blonde hair away from her face. "They told me I'd lost you. When I landed in Anchorage, they told me about the mansion."

She covered her face with her hands. "Jacob, there were women there. They called themselves the brides of The Light. They . . . belong . . ." Her hand fluttered around her neck, and I saw the faint bruise. "They said I would be . . ." Red blotches began to surface as her eyes filled with tears.

"Shhh . . . it's over." I pulled her close. "It's over for them too, I'd suspect. The authorities are waiting for the house to cool enough to check for remains."

She shook her head. "Dylan told me things, things I need to tell you."

"You never need to tell me anything. Your thoughts are yours. I'll take whatever you want to share."

Her lids fluttered with the ongoing battle Stella and Sara had been having since she'd left the Northern Light. And then her stare met mine. "I don't think that's what I meant. I meant, you're FBI. The FBI needs to know all the things he said. He told me that The Light is bigger than we know. He called it the Shadows."

I took a deep breath and exhaled. "You and I both need to spend time with agents who'll help us debrief and deprogram. I only hope that after our time in Virginia is complete, you still like the idea of Stella McAlister."

She reached for my hand and, as they'd done a thousand times, our fingers intertwined. "I can't make any promises, because I know from experience that life has a way of throwing curveballs, but if I were to guess, I will always like that name, and maybe one day when we're both ready, I'd like to verify the doctor's prognosis and create some little McAlisters."

"I can't tell you enough how sorry I am. I'll spend the rest of our lives trying to make up for leaving you. I shouldn't have done that."

"And what?" She brushed her lips against mine. "Father Gabriel would have killed you." Her light-blue eyes opened wide. "Wait! How did the raids go? What about all the others? What about our friends? Do they have Mindy? What about Brother Benjamin and Raquel?"

I laughed. For the first time in over a week, my chest rumbled, and I wrapped my wife in my arms, sending the vibrations from me to her. "I don't think I'll ever tire of your questions."

She shook her head. "That's good, because I can't seem to stop asking them."

"I've noticed." I took a deep breath. "The raids went well. Father Gabriel's in custody. I don't know anything about your friend Mindy. I saw Luke and the rest of the chosen men in Anchorage. The other followers were being transported from the Northern Light. I'm sure Mindy is among them, but there are over five hundred. It'll take a while to get them all to Anchorage and identified. As for Raquel and Benjamin, they'll be OK, but that's another story."

Her lip slipped between her teeth before she asked, "I remember Father Gabriel saying something?"

"Raquel was pretty badly injured, by Abraham, but we got her to Anchorage. I spoke with Benjamin on the way here from the airport. She's still critical, but the doctors are encouraged. They believe she made it to surgery in time. The FBI's allowing Benjamin to stay with her until she's better. All in all, there were few casualties—forty-six, not including the bodies yet to be discovered in the mansion."

"So we did it?" she asked. "Going back made a difference?"

"Yes, it made all the difference. There was a Kool-Aid plan for the Eastern Light. Lives were definitely saved there. Also, like you'd said, if Gabriel Clark had been in Bloomfield Hills, he probably would be gone with Richards."

Stella's eyes opened wide. "He's free? Dylan is still out there?"

"He's a fugitive now. Everyone is looking for him." I reached for her cheek. "I can't believe he hurt you after his show of pretending to be upset about your eye. I swear, when we find him, I'm going to—"

"Dylan? He didn't do it."

"He didn't?"

"He's the one who gave me the medicine, but he didn't hurt me. Brother Mark, who I got the feeling was on the Assembly at the Eastern Light, was the one who whipped me. It was Brother Elijah who hit me. Sister Mariam was the one who put the collar on me."

"What the hell? Whip? Hit? Collar? What?"

Stella reached out and covered my hand with hers. "We both have long stories. Let's find out about everyone first. I want to call my parents and let them know I'm all right. And Dina Rosemont and Bernard . . ."

I stilled her list with another kiss. "I know I haven't said it enough, but Stella Montgomery—"

"I definitely like McAlister better," she interrupted.

"Stella M.," I corrected myself. "You're an amazing woman." I ran my fingers through her hair. "So strong and brave. As we go through the next few months and try to undo what was done, I want to be the one there for you, the one to make your dreams come true."

She cupped my cheeks and her eyes glistened. "Waking up and having your brown eyes in front of me was my dream. You've already made it come true." She leaned forward and our lips united. "I'm all yours, Jacoby McAlister. I don't care what we need to go through to debrief or deprogram. What I feel for you isn't programmed, it's real, and I don't want you to ever question that."

I grinned. "So now I'm the one who can't question?"

"I believe that was a question," she said with a sparkle in her gorgeous eyes. "And as much as I want what you said, I want to be there for you too. It wasn't fair to give you all the burdens. I want to be a team."

"I think I'd like that."

As I stood I thought of something else. "Did Richards get a warning call telling him about the mansion?"

Her forehead furrowed. "No. I know he didn't, because I had one of his phones. The other one didn't ring until later."

"You had his phone? Did you try to call?"

She shook her head. "I thought about it, but I didn't want to jeopardize the FBI's mission and mostly I couldn't risk your life."

I was momentarily mute, imagining the hell she had been going through, and yet, with freedom in her grasp, her thoughts had been about me and the mission.

"You never cease to amaze me. But if he didn't get a call, why did he take you out of the mansion?"

Stella shrugged. "It was after Brother Elijah attacked me. Dylan shot him."

What the hell?

"And then he pulled me out of Father Gabriel's office and said we had to get away. In all the commotion I must have dropped his phone. If someone called him, he never got it."

There were too many things in her last statement for me to even articulate a question.

After a minute she added, "He did make a call, after the mansion blew. I tried to listen, but I couldn't hear him very well. I think he spoke to someone named Joel or Noel . . . something like that."

Joel? The one on facial recognition. I had to wonder if he was Brother Timothy and Sister Lilith's son. Were the Shadows made up of supposedly banished members of The Light? Ones Father Gabriel entrusted to hold important positions in the dark, supporting The Light's activities?

As I contemplated, I walked to the door and motioned for Special Agent Adler to come in. Turning toward Stella, I smiled. "Special Agent Adler, I'd like you to meet—"

"Agent McAlister's wife," Stella interrupted. "I'm Stella Montgomery McAlister."

Agent Adler was shaking her hand. "Ma'am, it's nice to meet you. You had us all very worried." He tilted his head toward me. "This one in particular. I don't think he's slept in nearly two days."

"I don't think he's showered either," she said with a grin.

"I just spoke with the doctor," Special Agent Adler said. "Now that they know your eyes are all right, you can be released. The FBI would like to put you both up with your own security detail for a few days. We can assure you each a secured hotel room with room service. Once you've rested, we'll send you to Virginia. You both have a long debriefing ahead."

"Agent," Stella said, "please tell the FBI thank you. If it's all right with Agent McAlister, I'd just as soon save our government the additional charge. I believe one room is sufficient."

"You heard my wife," I said with a grin.

"Then it's settled," Adler said. "Oh, and another thing, that friend you mentioned on the phone, Mindy Rosemont, we've confirmed her identity as one of the women still on the Northern Light. It will take some time to get everyone to Anchorage.”

Stella looked from Special Agent Adler back to me. “I want to see her. I want to help her. I tried talking to her after my memory came back, but she didn’t know me. Once her medication is gone, I want her to know we were looking for her.”

Was she asking? For once I didn’t have the answer. Instead I looked back to my handler.

“It’ll take some time,” Agent Adler said, “but I’m sure we can get that worked out. Also, we’ve contacted your parents. They’re on their way to Detroit as we speak.”

Stella’s face suddenly paled.

“What is it?” I asked.

“I wanted to speak to my mom. It’s Dylan”—her eyes filled with panic—“he mentioned that she’s been calling him every week. If she knows I’m all right, she might try to call him. Then he’ll know the medicine didn’t work.”

“I’ll call your mother’s cell phone right away,” Adler said. “Don’t worry. No one will know your location.”

“The Shadows?” I asked, not wanting to know the answer.

“I’ll personally screen the agents protecting the two of you.”

I reached for Stella’s hand and nodded. “We’ll be all right.”

She nodded. “Since I dropped Dylan’s phone at the mansion and it likely blew up, I doubt my mother could reach him. Dylan said the Shadows are everywhere. Does that mean they’re in the FBI?”

I took a deep breath. I’d promised her truth, but at this moment I didn’t want to be truthful. I wanted to make her feel safe. Nevertheless, she deserved honesty. “We believe that it was a member of the Shadows who tipped off Richards. If that’s the case, the call came from within the FBI.”

Agent Adler shook his head. “That hasn’t been confirmed. We’re investigating. But like I said, we’ll keep your location undisclosed.”

“My parents?”

I squeezed Stella's hand. "Sorry, Agent. I can testify that she never stops asking questions."

Agent Adler grinned. "We're happy you're both safe. Let me get you a phone."

"Thank you," Stella said, her cheeks pink and her eyes down.

I reached for her chin. When our eyes met, I said, "I'm looking forward to a lifetime of them."

CHAPTER

SEVENTY-TWO

Jacoby McAlister
Agent, Federal Bureau of Investigation
Two months post-raid:

CONFIDENTIAL FINAL REPORT: THE LIGHT

Following Agent Jacoby McAlister's final debriefing, his forty-one-month-long infiltration of The Light officially concluded. The results of his investigation include:

The Light, a religious, tax-exempt organization, has allegedly been discovered to be a front for illegal activities. The activities identified by A-Jacoby McAlister were divided among three campuses. On the three campuses a total of 1,070 followers were identified. These followers include men, women, and children. At the Northern Light, located in northern Alaska, was a fully functional pharmaceutical production plant, capable of creating various knock-off drugs. These medications were transported to the Western Light, located in northern Montana, where they were packaged and then transported to Canada under the cover of Preserve the Light preserves. Once out of the United States, distribution and logistics occurred via unidentified members of the extension of The Light known as the Shadows.

The Eastern Light, located in Highland Heights, Michigan, served primarily as the point of entry for new followers, both voluntary and involuntary. Women abducted for The Light were brought through this campus and transported to the other campuses. Along with the acquisition of new followers, a small production plant was also located on the Eastern Light. This plant produced illegal substances that were then transported out of the United States via the cover of Preserve the Light preserves.

Alleged charges uncovered during this mission into The Light include: multiple counts of first-degree murder, felony murder, human trafficking, kidnapping, sexual assault, physical and psychological assault, drug manufacturing, drug possession, drug trafficking, and labor code violations.

Gabriel Clark, aka Father Gabriel and Garrison Clarkson, as well as the twelve members of his Commission, are being held without bond in various high-security facilities throughout the United States. Due to his association with the current threat of the organization referring to itself as the Shadows, Gabriel Clark is currently incarcerated at ADX Florence, near Florence, Colorado. This facility is a supermax prison for male inmates with extreme limitations on communication with outside sources.

Thirty-three members of The Light's Assembly were interrogated individually by the FBI. Through hours of questioning, the level of knowledge into the illegal activity of The Light was determined. The level of knowledge and roles in activities varied. Twenty-two members were determined to have extensive knowledge and were unwilling to testify on behalf of the state. Those members are currently incarcerated awaiting trial. The remaining eleven Assembly members are undergoing voluntary debriefing and deprogramming as state's witnesses. Due to the alleged danger posed by the Shadows, the eleven members will enter witness protection until time of trials.

Wives: Of the eleven Assemblymen to cooperate, ten of their wives under The Light have volunteered to accompany their husbands into witness protection. It has been determined that none of the Assemblymen's wives held a significant level of knowledge regarding the inner workings and operations. The wives of the unco-operative or deceased Assemblymen agreed to undergo deprogram-ming. Those whose true identities could be determined have been reunited with family outside The Light, if family could be found. Even after discontinuing the memory-suppressing medication, three Assembly wives have yet to know their true identities. The FBI is still working with the Kidnappings and Missing Persons department in this endeavor.

Nine of the twelve Commissioners' wives have been determined to have knowledge of illegal activity and to have participated in various illegal activities. These nine women have been charged with crimes, resulting in their incarceration. The other three Commission wives have undergone deprogramming and have voluntarily been reunited with their families outside of The Light.

The three physicians, one at each campus, are also incarcerated and awaiting trial for various felony charges.

The envelope Agent McAlister had been given from a Commis-sioner (Brother Michael) at the Western Light contained a sequence of numbers as well as a pass-phrase. After diligent work by the FBI cyber division, overseas accounts were discovered and accessed. Until the information in the envelope was decoded, the financial side of The Light had been the missing link in McAlister's investigation. The contents of the accounts uncovered a large portion of The Light's allegedly illegally obtained wealth.

Dylan Richards is still at large. Cybertracking has identified him as the heir apparent to the operation of the Shadows, now referred to in their communications as the leader, Brother David. It is currently believed that Richards is outside the United States.

After tedious searches, most of the followers on all three campuses have been identified. While it is impossible to account for all followers, one female follower from the Northern Light is currently misplaced. Mary, aka Mindy Rosemont, was identified while on the Northern Light campus. However, when the followers were later cataloged at the Anchorage FBI field office it was discovered that she was not among the female followers. This turn of events is currently under review by an internal subcommittee.

As the bureau's key witness, A-McAlister will enter the witness protection program until the time of Gabriel Clark's trial, as will his wife Stella McAlister.

EPILOGUE

avid

"I WANT confirmation as soon as you have it," I said, my grip on the phone growing tighter by the second. From the way Agent Fisher was stumbling over his words, he knew from my tone that I wasn't playing around. "He needs to pay the ultimate price for his deceit."

My blood boiled.

Agent Jacoby McAlister, fucking Jacob Adams.

I'd had that motherfucker in my grasp. I should have killed him in the basement of the mansion. If I had, The Light would still be making the money we needed for operations. Hell, if I'd killed him then, Gabriel would still be free. I gritted my teeth. If I'd killed him, he wouldn't be at Quantico, married to Stella.

Damn her. Damn him.

At least I had a connection—a Shadow—at Quantico. Now if he'd stop stuttering and do his damn duty.

"Brother David, I-I have the necessary clearance. I'll learn where Agent and Mrs. McAlister are assigned."

Mrs. McAlister. The name made the hairs on my arm bristle .

"When you do, tell me. Don't, I repeat, do not, proceed on your own. I want the last thing that asshole remembers is that he fucked with the wrong organization. And I want him to know he didn't stop us or any of our plans. He may have slowed us down a little, but The Light is everywhere."

"Yes, Brother."

I didn't wait for the phone to disconnect before I hit the red button and sent it flying across the room. As it collided with the wall, Stacy jumped. She shook her head, and with a sassy grin looked in my direction.

"I'm going to guess that wasn't the news you wanted?"

I ran my hand along the scuff of my jaw before extending it in her direction. Without hesitation she stood from the couch where she'd been reading and came to me. I pulled her onto my lap and cupped her chin. "You don't need to worry. I've got you now. I don't want her."

Stacy smiled. "I'm not worried. But it is strange how this all worked out. Who would've thought me and you and the Shadows? I mean I'd never even heard of them and I remember when you were my best friend's boyfriend."

I wrapped my arms around her waist. If I didn't think about it too much, I could imagine she was Stella. They looked that similar. That was the reason she'd been brought to me. It was a peace offering from the idiot who'd let the FBI task force exist without his knowledge. He'd heard about Stella and for some reason thought Mindy was her.

Too bad for him it wasn't enough to stop his banishment.

"Your best friend?" I asked with a smirk.

She shook her head, her long, blonde hair moving slowly over her slender shoulders. "Not anymore. Now that I remember, I remember how she didn't help me, how she was part of the chosen—"

I touched her lips. "Baby, that's the past. Look at you now. Fuck the chosen. Most of them are in prison. You're the wife of the leader of the Shadows. And soon, very soon, she and that agent will pay."

"If you say so, David."

"I do. No one stops The Light."

Until . . . OUT OF THE SHADOWS

LEND IT: Did you enjoy LIGHT DARK? Do you have a friend who'd enjoy LIGHT DARK? LIGHT DARK may be lent one time. Sharing is caring!

RECOMMEND IT: Do you have multiple friends who'd enjoy my dark romance with twists and turns and an all new sexy and infuriating anti-hero? Tell them about it! Call, text, post, tweet...your recommendation is the nicest gift you can give to an author!

REVIEW IT: Tell the world. Please go to the retailer where you purchased this book, as well as Goodreads, and write a review. Please share your thoughts about LIGHT DARK:

*Amazon, LIGHT DARK, Customer Reviews

*Barnes & Noble, LIGHT DARK, Customer Reviews

*Apple Books, LIGHT DARK Customer Reviews

* BookBub, LIGHT DARK Customer Reviews

*Goodreads.com/Aleatha Romig

Books by ALEATHA

BRUTAL VOWS:

NOW AND FOREVER

TILL DEATH DO US PART

BOUND BY A PROMISE

READY TO BINGE

SINCLAIR DUET:

REMEMBERING PASSION

September 2023

REKINDLING DESIRE

October 2023

ROYAL REFLECTIONS SERIES:

RUTHLESS REIGN

November 2022

RESILIENT REIGN

January 2023

RAVISHING REIGN

April 2023

RELEVANT REIGN

June 2023

SIN SERIES:

RED SIN

October 2021

GREEN ENVY

January 2022

GOLD LUST

April 2022

BLACK KNIGHT

June 2022

STAND-ALONE ROMANTIC SUSPENSE:

SILVER LINING

October 2022

KINGDOM COME

November 2021

DEVIL'S SERIES (Duet):

DEVIL'S DEAL

May 2021

ANGEL'S PROMISE

June 2021

WEB OF SIN:

SECRETS

October 2018

LIES

December 2018

PROMISES

January 2019

TANGLED WEB:

TWISTED

May 2019

OBSESSED

July 2019

BOUND

August 2019

WEB OF DESIRE:

SPARK

Jan. 14, 2020

FLAME

February 25, 2020

ASHES

April 7, 2020

DANGEROUS WEB:

Prequel: "Danger's First Kiss"

DUSK

November 2020

DARK

January 2021

DAWN

February 2021

THE INFIDELITY SERIES:

BETRAYAL

Book #1

October 2015

CUNNING

Book #2

January 2016

DECEPTION

Book #3

May 2016

ENTRAPMENT

Book #4

September 2016

FIDELITY

Book #5

January 2017

THE CONSEQUENCES SERIES:

CONSEQUENCES

(Book #1)

August 2011

TRUTH

(Book #2)

October 2012

CONVICTED

(Book #3)

October 2013

REVEALED

(Book #4)

Previously titled: Behind His Eyes Convicted: The Missing Years

June 2014

BEYOND THE CONSEQUENCES

(Book #5)

January 2015

RIPPLES (Consequences stand-alone)

October 2017

CONSEQUENCES COMPANION READS:

BEHIND HIS EYES-CONSEQUENCES

January 2014

BEHIND HIS EYES-TRUTH

March 2014

STAND ALONE MAFIA THRILLER:

PRICE OF HONOR

Available Now

STAND-ALONE ROMANTIC THRILLER:

ON THE EDGE

May 2022

***

017//7081004157807

TALES FROM THE DARK SIDE SERIES:

INSIDIOUS

(All books in this series are stand-alone erotic thrillers)
Released October 2014

ALEATHA'S LIGHTER ONES:

PLUS ONE

Stand-alone fun, sexy romance

May 2017

ANOTHER ONE

Stand-alone fun, sexy romance

May 2018

ONE NIGHT

Stand-alone, sexy contemporary romance

September 2017

A SECRET ONE

April 2018

MY ALWAYS ONE

Stand-Alone, sexy friends to lovers contemporary romance

July 2021

QUINTESSENTIALLY THE ONE

Stand-alone, small-town, second-chance, secret baby contemporary
romance

July 2022

ONE KISS

Stand-alone, small-town, best friend's sister, grump/sunshine
contemporary romance.

July 2023

INDULGENCE SERIES:

UNEXPECTED

August 2018

UNCONVENTIONAL

January 2018

UNFORGETTABLE

October 2019

UNDENIABLE

August 2020

ABOUT THE AUTHOR

Aleatha Romig is a New York Times, Wall Street Journal, and USA Today bestselling author who lives in Indiana, USA. She has raised three children with her high school sweetheart and husband of over thirty years. Before she became a full-time author, she worked days as a dental hygienist and spent her nights writing. Now, when she's not imagining mind-blowing twists and turns, she likes to spend her time with her family and friends. Her other pastimes include reading and creating heroes/anti-heroes who haunt your dreams!

Aleatha impresses with her versatility in writing. She released her first novel, CONSEQUENCES, in August of 2011. CONSEQUENCES, a dark romance, became a bestselling series with five novels and two companions released from 2011 through 2015. The compelling and epic story of Anthony and Claire Rawlings has graced more than half a million e-readers. Her first stand-alone smart, sexy thriller INSID-IOUS was next. Then Aleatha released the five-novel INFIDELITY series, a romantic suspense saga, that took the reading world by storm, the final book landing on three of the top bestseller lists. She ventured into traditional publishing with Thomas and Mercer. Her books INTO THE LIGHT and AWAY FROM THE DARK were published through this mystery/thriller publisher in 2016.

In the spring of 2017, Aleatha again ventured into a different genre with her first fun and sexy stand-alone romantic comedy with the USA Today bestseller PLUS ONE. She continued the "Ones" series with additional standalones, ONE NIGHT, ANOTHER ONE, MY ALWAYS ONE, and QUINTESSENTIALLY THE ONE. If you like fun, sexy, novellas that make your heart pound, try her "Indulgence series" with UNCONVENTIONAL. UNEXPECTED, UNFORGET-TABLE, and UNDENIABLE.

In 2018 Aleatha returned to her dark romance roots with SPARROW WEBS. And continued with the mafia romance DEVIL'S DUET, and most recently her SINCLAIR DUET.

You may find all Aleatha's titles on her website.

Aleatha is a "Published Author's Network" member of the Romance Writers of America and PEN America. She is represented by SBR Media and Dani Sanchez with Wildfire Marketing.

facebook.com/aleatharomig

x.com/aleatharomig

instagram.com/aleatharomig

www.ingramcontent.com/pod-product-compliance
Lightning Source LLC
Chambersburg PA
CBHW071954190726
48293CB00001B/23